Never Look Back

A Novel

By: Ann Hope

I want to dedicate this book to my four beautiful daughters who have been blessed with the strength of character and passion of heart to persevere through life's challenges. I am amazed by the women you are and continue to become. Thank you from the bottom of my heart for the opportunity to share life's journey with you.

To all the women who have touched my life by allowing me a glimpse into their hearts and sharing the stories that shaped their lives. Thanks to Shelley and Val who not only taught me how to understand and love the person I am but also understand, accept and appreciate what others have to offer.

A Special Thank You to Emily Hood for allowing me to use her beautiful picture for my cover.

References:

Wild at Heart by John Eldredge

Ann Hope

Prologue

There were no bruises. Nothing to show for the pain and humiliation she endured almost daily. Of course he'd never hit her, he was too much of a coward. Cammi imagined he wanted to and oh, how many nights has she lain awake in bed wishing he would? Then she'd have a reason, an excuse to leave. Just one, one hard enough to leave a hand print. Then no one would question or wonder how she could have walked away from such a handsome, charming, successful husband.

It was subtle at first.....his complaints, his put downs, his anger. A contemptuous glare when she voiced an opinion different than his, an embarrassing shake of his head when she did not wear something he deemed appropriate, then a snide comment when she tried to stand up for herself. His passive-aggressive behavior when she had been too busy to make dinner, put laundry away or even if she stopped after work to meet a girlfriend for tea was shocking to say the least. Eventually, withholding love and affection became his pattern to punish her. Calling her a bitch, worthless and ugly was typical vocabulary in every fight they had. In the beginning she stood up for herself, tried to defend her honor, but eventually, Cammi learned it was better not to fight. She was beginning to see herself through the eyes of her husband. Nothing was good enough, nothing was right and nothing could compare to the perfect persona he portrayed. Since the beginning Marcus controlled the money, made all the important decisions, chose her friends and wound up alienating her family with his overbearing personality. When she found out about his habitual drug use, she chose to look the other way. When it was brought to her attention they were twenty-two thousand dollars in debt because of his gambling addiction, she knew it was best to keep her mouth shut. Then when she heard about his extramarital activities, she maintained her dignity and continued to hold her head high despite the fact that she was the target of social gossip.

No one knew the extent of her pain, the humiliation, the shame. No one knew how much she loathed herself. This wasn't who she was. She was not weak, submissive nor a victim. Not once had she shed a tear. He disgusted her. She hated him. He was not worth the tears or emotion. Cammi was completely unaware how she wound up in this marriage……or how to get out, until now.

This wasn't the first time Cammi heard the little voice in the back of her head urging her, guiding her. It was there her senior year of high school when she was tempted to sneak out her bedroom window, but didn't. It was there when she chose not to get into the car with her college roommate, Christina, after a night of binge drinking. Then again on her wedding day, she heard it loud and clear. Unfortunately, she didn't listen. But today.....today the voice was strong.

To some, the voice was intuition, for others, some sort of sixth sense. Cammi's best friend Jamie simply referred to it as "wisdom with age", but Cammi knew differently. This voice she heard, the voice that seemed to be with her at different points of her life, regardless of age, was more than gut instinct.

This time, she was going to listen.

Forcing down the oversized bulge and zipping shut her suitcase Cammi shuddered at the stillness surrounding her. Taking a deep, trembling breath, she hoisted the duffle bag along with her purse over her shoulder and reluctantly reached down to grab the rest of her luggage. This was going to be her last trip down. She'd already made eight, or was it nine? She'd lost count after three. Everything she wanted to take, the little she still owned and hadn't sold off after she moved in with Marcus was now shoved into her SUV. Once she got settled in her new apartment back in her hometown of Madison, the small mountain community two hours west of Denver, she promised herself she was going to trade in the overpriced Lexus for something more practical. She wanted something Marcus would hate, something he would've never allowed her to buy in a million years.

Feeling a slight flutter, Cammi placed her hand gently on her stomach and thought for a brief moment that she really should be more careful considering her condition.

Impossible, she thought. She'd barely just found out. Her imagination was playing tricks on her. Besides, she'd already made up her mind but the weight of the decision hit her like a ton of bricks causing an intense pain to ripple through her heart.

Briefly, she glanced around the small two bedroom loft she shared with Marcus in case she missed something of importance. Forcing herself to blink back threatening tears she stared aimlessly at the door to their bedroom. Slowly she pushed it open until her eyes came to rest on the bed. She didn't sleep in it last night. She couldn't since Rebecca carelessly disregarded their friendship and decided to share the bed with her husband.

They hadn't been married long when the rumors started, almost a year to be exact. Then it was the little whispers behind her back or a room full of people staring at her with pity that began to unnerve her. Of course, catching Marcus time and time again with his hand caressing a woman's backside or nuzzling another's neck should have been unacceptable, but she knew when they first became involved that he was a little flirtatious. It was part of his charisma; she convinced herself and an endearing quality she delighted in during their brief courtship. He was going to be a lawyer, she'd always thought proudly. He talked the talk, walked the walk. He could charm the pants off of strangers and that....she would soon learn, was his area of expertise.

As was the venomous side he saved only for her.

Cammi knew she was no longer in love with her husband. At times, she wondered if she ever really was. However, leaving was easier said than done. She was not the confident, young, free spirited lady she had been when they met. Only a few years of his despicable treatment were enough to beat her down. She barely had any money, no job since Marcus convinced her she didn't need to work and her friends were few and far in between, except for Jamie. Thank God for Jamie.

Overcome with a sudden wave of sadness, Cammi sighed. "Focus," scolded herself out loud. She wasn't going to talk herself out of leaving. Feeling was not an option if she wanted to get through this, at least for the moment. In fact, she hoped she'd never have to feel again when it came to her soon to be ex-husband.

Taking another deep breath to steady her trembling hands, Cammi removed the key from her key ring and placed it on the small glass end table that was home to their wedding album. Without the slightest moment's hesitation, she placed the quickly scribbled "Dear John" letter and gold band on top of it.

The entire week had been a whirlwind of events that finally helped her find the courage to go. Her whole marriage had been a mountain of lies, flashing signs that were indicators of a relationship gone seriously wrong and she refused to ignore it any longer.

Aside from the obvious betrayals, it was the faint pink plus sign on the pregnancy test that stirred her into action. Under normal circumstances a pregnancy would have filled her with excitement beyond her wildest dreams, but the symbol starring back at her only intensified feelings of dread. That and the humiliation upon learning not only was she pregnant, but that she also needed to be treated for an STD.

Cammi didn't want to believe any of this was happening. It had been close to four months since she and Marcus had sex. It was impossible. But not completely impossible, she reminded herself. The memory of the night he forced himself upon her made her throat constrict and her stomach turn.

The hand of fate was finally forced when she arrived home early from work the day before to hear laughter emerging from her bedroom, unmistakable male and female voices. It was definitely her husband but the second it took a moment to recognize. When she did, she felt as if she'd been struck in the head with a sledgehammer and the treachery was more devastating than she ever imagined possible.

Rebecca was her first and only friend when Cammi moved to Denver after college. As a well known and respected photographer, Rebecca happened to be the one who got Cammi hired on at the newspaper. She was also the one woman besides Jamie she trusted with her life and the secrets about her husband.

Cammi slipped out quietly and undetected, staggering along Sixteenth Street Mall, reeling with confusion, scared and definitely alone. In stunned silence, she'd sat on a park bench for hours, watching the traffic pass her by as the events of her life twisted around in her mind, slowly and painfully turning her heart to stone.

Then she called Jamie and put her plan into action.

When she returned home that fateful evening, it was well past midnight. Marcus had left a message that he was out with friends. Of course that friend was Rebecca. Neither of them knew that she knew and she intended to keep it that way. Within twenty-four hours he would no longer be a part of her life and in time, she wouldn't have any reminders of the life she shared with him. She wanted a clean-cut break, a chance to start over fresh and not look back. It would only be a matter of time before she was back to her old self, at least a part of her old self. A person could not go through what she had and not come out the other side a changed woman, hopefully more mature and making better choices, but definitely a changed woman.

Cammi looked forward to blindsiding him. The same way he blindsided her with his extra-curricular activities. But as much as she hated to admit it, she hadn't been that ignorant. The signs were all there so she had to take some responsibility for her own naiveté.

The drugs, the gambling, the womanizing, the abusive behaviors....how had she convinced herself it was all okay?

Cammi turned her attention back to the task at hand and scooped up her two beloved cats Dooney and Burk. She bought them just over a year ago as a way to make Marcus angry when in reality she was just lonely and missed the companionship of a pet. Marcus hated animals. He had been more than a little angry and she paid for it for weeks after with his subtle little comments but she was a bit surprised the cats hadn't mysteriously disappeared somehow. Rubbing her cheek against the soft fur of the friends she'd come to love, she promised them things were going to get better. Hopefully before the day was up, she would have the keys in hand to the apartment and could begin again.

Out of habit, she checked the answering machine once more in case he had called. Maybe it was some sort of desperate attempt to pretend none of this was really happening, that it was all a bad dream and she actually was married to a loving, faithful and respectful man who had immaturely and thoughtlessly behaved badly. That there was some far-fetched explanation for the STD, all the late night excuses of work, clients and meetings along with all the disappearing money. Maybe he would have a "light bulb moment" and show some remorse, be willing to get some help for the way he treated her, and life as she knew it would not turn upside down.

But there were no messages. Numbness replaced what she had expected to be a sinking sensation in her heart. It all made sense now....the lies, the far-fetched stories and his controlling behavior. This is where he wanted her to be, ignorant, dumb and naïve to what he was doing. Well, now it was his turn to be ignorant, dumb and naïve to what she was doing.

Instead of the fear she anticipated, Cammi was inspired with determination to move ahead and as she stepped out of the elevator into the mid morning sun, a hint of a smile formed around her lips. Consumed with relief, she felt a sense of peace she'd been missing for years. The life she had in Denver was over. She would never have to see Marcus again but most importantly, she'd never have to face those who knew about his secrets.

Stopping in front of her vehicle, Cammi stared up at the brick structure she had called home. Bitterness ripped through her as thoughts of the life she was determined to forget threatened to resurface. But Cammi was stronger than her thoughts. She pushed them away, buried them deep down, down where she hoped they would never find her again. And as she revved up her car engine and drove off to start a new life, she was certain it would be the last time she ever looked back.

Chapter One
Five Years Later

Cammi impatiently tapped her foot on the side of the chair. With her chin resting on her fist, her eyes adrift toward the ceiling, she attempted to tune Carissa out. This wasn't the first nor would it be the last time, Cammi had to listen to her sister drone on and on about Cammi's lacking social life.

"Cammi, he's beautiful. Just meet him. Promise me you'll say yes," Carissa begged. Though her sister's touch was supposed to be a gentle display of affection as Carissa's fingers swept lightly over Cammi's arm, it made her tense. It wasn't that she didn't love her sister and Cammi knew Carissa loved her in return she just had a way of irritating Cammi more than most people.

Aside from their looks, she and her younger sister Carissa were as different as night and day. Carissa was a free spirit, flirtatious and always on the hunt for the next best thrill. She was warm, animated and a highly successful masseuse, having managed her own business twenty miles away in Boulder for the past four years. She was a workaholic, never married, had no kids and figured she made enough money she deserved to spend most of it on the person she loved the most….herself. Therefore, she spent a lot of time traveling the world.

If Carissa had been born a decade earlier, she would have made the perfect hippie except for the fact that she was anti-drug and anti-free love. She was a Vegan through and through and though no one would guess, especially with how she came across, she had very high standards when it came to dating and love which is probably the reason Cammi trusted her. Still, she wasn't in the mood to discuss her love life, or lack there-of, with her sister.

"No! Not just no, but hell NO! I don't want you fixing me up," Cammi demanded.

They'd gone out for burgers after Cammi bribed her sister into giving her a free massage. She'd said she would do her laundry for a week, but the truth was she knew Carissa would have done it regardless. Cammi could not recall how many times Carissa commented on her need to relax, release some toxic energy, or convince her she was just the person to work on Cammi's tense, tight muscles. Yet once again, here they were, having the same conversation they'd had many times before. She didn't know what Carissa was trying to accomplish, telling her she needed to stop carrying her stress around in her body, lecturing her on meditation and relaxation techniques then not even a half- hour later *Wham!* Carissa started in on her with her dating analogies.

"That's not true. You told me yourself last week at Rosarita's you wanted to get married again."

"Uh, two margaritas and a smothered burrito later, remember? I was full, happy, and slightly tipsy. You had no right to take advantage of my state of mind."

"I didn't take advantage," Carissa replied. "You have us worried sick. Mom and Dad begged me to take you out and pick your brain. They even gave me the money for dinner. Not that I couldn't afford it, but what the heck….." she laughed. "Hey, we had a great time, didn't we? And what about those two professors from Denver University who just happened to stop there for dinner? They thought we were pretty smoking hot, *remember*? Did the dark haired one….. I can't remember his name. Oh well! Did he ever call you?"

"Yes, thank you very much. He asked me to dinner and I turned him down."

"Are you crazy? He was *gorgeous*! Jump back in, Cammi, really. Your divorce was years ago. If you don't get on with it you're going to become an old spinster. I can just see it…. my kids will be saying, 'here are Aunt Cammi and her cats coming over for *another* visit'."

Cammi laughed. "What kids? Besides, you're one to talk. You haven't been on a date in over a year, remember? Don't worry little sister. I won't become a spinster. I know what I'm doing. Trust me. But you have to stop setting me up on blind dates. I told you, I won't go."

Carissa narrowed her eyes suspiciously. "What do you have planned? Have you met someone?" Suddenly, Carissa sat up straight in her chair, gasped and pointed an index finger at her sister. "You have haven't you? What's his name? Where'd you meet him? And why do you have to be so damned private about it?"

"No, no, and no! Stop it," she said slapping Carissa's shoulder. "I haven't met anyone, not yet. But I know what I'm looking for, and I won't settle. Not again. Don't get me wrong, *gorgeous* helps, but it's not going to make me run around and rip my clothes off. Marcus was hot, remember?" She laughed when she saw the roll of her sister's eyes. "Look where that got me? I won't waste my time on a bunch of schmucks. I'm listening to my gut and will know when the right one comes along. *Trust me!"*

Yet as she said it, Cammi wondered how on earth she expected her sister to trust her when trusting her own decisions was hard enough as it was.

Carissa leaned in so their faces were only inches apart. "Are you having sex?" she asked dropping her voice to a whisper.

Cammi laughed loudly. "Are *you* having sex?" she shot back at her.

"This is getting real irritating. Why don't you just tell me what's going on?"

"Please, let it go and if something happens or *if* I decide to have sex, I promise, you will be the first person I call."

"Just be careful, okay, sis? I worry about you."

Cammi sighed. She hadn't really lied to Carissa. She just wasn't ready to lay her heart and soul on the table, let alone discuss her plans with anyone. The idea of it was still foreign to her. After her whirlwind mistake of a marriage, her whole family worried themselves sick, and they only knew *half* of the story. Hopefully someday she could forgive herself for not telling them the whole truth, but it was too big, even for her to comprehend.

Two days later, drops of rain pelted the windshield while Cammi steered her little black Toyota Camry around the bend of the mountain. She loved this car, the sleek, smooth way it took corners, the adrenaline rush that shot through her each time her foot pressed on the gas. She felt free. Of course she bought it for two reasons and two reasons only; the name was so closely linked to hers and it was the type of car that would have annoyed the hell out of Marcus.

Driving was her outlet, her sanity, her freedom. She was ecstatic about getting her license at sixteen, eventually making a habit of taking off for hours in the evening to drive around the small mountain town of Colorado. Her parents learned not to worry. She wasn't a rule breaker and always showed by curfew. Now as an adult, when she found herself overly anxious, she would grab her favorite CD's and take off for a little road trip just to clear her mind.

It thrilled Cammi to call Madison home once again. The mountains were full of tranquil beauty and she found herself relaxing a little as she hummed along to the new Matchbox Twenty song on the radio. Here, on the road with her music, Cammi could pretend problems were millions of miles away, and she was in control of her destiny.

But the reality was it couldn't be further from the truth.

And today.....well, today was different. This time she wasn't on a road trip and as she neared the coffee shop, the turn of events bringing her to this point jam-packed her thoughts, reminding her once again she'd *never* been in control. The carefree childhood Cammi remembered so dearly always lingered close to her heart and as an adult, she longed to find that peacefulness once again. The peaceful innocence she lost at too early of an age leaving her bitter and jaded.

Fortunately, divine guidance interfered and began to lead her in a direction where she was hopeful to find it. Regardless of her past, Cammi tried to remain grateful for the opportunities that presented themselves and hopefully would learn from her mistakes. Lord knows there were plenty.

Waiting impatiently for a red light to turn, Cammi began to replay the conversation she had with her sister over again in her mind. Maybe Carissa had a valid point. Maybe Cammi was too picky and *would* wind up an old spinster. Maybe she had no idea what she was doing. Just thinking about it was maddening, so in an attempt to shut out her sister's annoying voice, Cammi swerved her car around various puddles to avoid the onslaught of mud surely to drench her windshield.

Ten minutes later Cammi raced into the coffee shop as the rain came down in sheets. Shaking off her jacket, she kept her eyes glued to the floor completely aware of the fear that over powdered her conscious. This was a huge first step. What did the future have in store for her? Could she hold up her end of the bargain?

Shoving her trembling hands into her pockets, she apprehensively looked around to see if there was anyone who closely fit the description of the man she was about to meet. Within a few moments though, Cammi began to panic. She should have stayed in the car, lost in quiet thought, content with her music. There, within her safe haven, she wouldn't have to contemplate the decision she was about to make.

Friends, mostly her sister, tried time and time again to set her up on dates but she always refused. Why she changed her mind with this particular guy, she didn't know. She was definitely intrigued, but initially it wasn't enough. In fact, it took months after Jamie first mentioned him before Cammi finally gave in and exchanged her e-mail address. Then it had taken many, many months of e-mails before she finally agreed to meet for coffee.

Keeping herself in check, Cammi tried to analyze her feelings, which completely defeated the purpose of letting things go, but at least it was a good distraction from the uneasy sensation crawling into the pit of her stomach. Hopefully this time she would find the right approach and come across friendly and open instead of guarded and standoffish. Or uptight, as so many people from her past had tactlessly described her.

Not that she cared. Cammi didn't want to "loosen up". She liked being unapproachable. It made her feel strong, in control. Her male friends called her intimidating. She was confident enough to strike up a conversation with anyone, knew who she was and what she brought to the table, was attractive enough to draw attention, but also didn't want anyone to get the wrong idea or expect anything she wasn't capable of giving, not only sex, but love. She was waiting for the right one to come along, and she wasn't going to give her heart until she found him. Then she would give it completely.

Cammi's ex-husband was the first serious relationship she really had. It was a short marriage, she was young and he loved women, lots of them along with a few other vices she tried unsuccessfully to forget. In the beginning their connection had been purely physical, so like almost everything she did in her life, getting involved with him felt safe. Unfortunately, she did not escape unscathed. Heart still intact, yes, but there were deep, penetrating wounds underneath invisible scars, and afterwards, dating wasn't a priority.

Taking a shallow, shaky breath, faking confidence that wasn't there, Cammi looked around nervously. There was no sign of him, so ideally it would be the perfect moment to run to her car and go home. How could she have been silly enough to think she could actually go through with this? But determination and faith made her stay. She had to follow through. She made a deal and wasn't about to back out. But what if *he* didn't show?

Raised with a sister and brother who were born a decade after her, Cammi had grown up independent, self-sufficient and probably more mature than most of her peers. Her parent's set a wonderful example when it came to marriage, dedication and compromise. They were deeply in love after thirty-two years, but for her, becoming a wife and a mother had never been on the top of her priority list, until recently.

Ever since she was a little girl, Cammi wanted to be a writer. Night after night as she lay awake in bed, she'd make up characters and stories to help her doze off while listening to the crickets chirp out her window. Then during the day, her nose was constantly stuck in a book, usually one of the Laura Ingalls Wilder novels. She was editor of her school newspaper and wrote short stories in her spare time. Then in college, her Composition courses gave her the confidence to pursue it as her major. After graduation, the dedication to her career and other goals consumed all of her time. Cammi wanted to publish a book, travel to Greece, run a half marathon, and get a tattoo all by the age of thirty. Boy chasing wasn't on the agenda. Plus she never wanted to be one of those women who depended on a man to fill her needs. Nor did she want to be desperate enough to sacrifice what she knew to be in her best interest just to land a husband. She had her writing, her job and handful of friends. What more could there be at this stage in her life?

Though she looked and acted like a lady, there was still a hint of the fiery tomboy from her youth within her veins. Those who didn't know her considered her a snob, unapproachable and guarded, but she knew she was also kind and tactful, careful not to hurt others. The "Beaver Cleaver" home she grew up in gave her no excuses to keep a lock around her heart. Regardless, she kept the male and at times female species a safe distance away.

And frankly, she had been happy that way.

Then, at the age of twenty-two, came the marriage from hell which ended in divorce. Although she tried to deny it as much as she could, when it was all said and done, Cammi found herself alone and more fragile than she'd ever been in her life. She had friends she socialized with occasionally but even played it safe with them. Emotional connections to people took more time and energy than she could commit to. Plus, any trust she held onto before her marriage had slowly disappeared.

And then there was the baby. She detested Marcus. The idea of raising his child, still having a connection to him repulsed her, not to mention the violent way the baby was conceived. Yet, regardless of what she felt for her ex, she loved the baby. It was a part of her and even though she was only four weeks along when she left him, it was as if she could feel the life growing and fluttering within her.

Jamie was the only person she confided in, the only person who knew the whole ugly truth and the only one who knew that Cammi was still haunted by memories.

That entire month was a turning point in her life. The aftermath of heartache was indescribable and Cammi was an emotional wreck for a very long time. Feeling as if she had lost too much, she was scared to ever love again. Desperation had her searching for help, but she didn't trust enough to allow anyone in. Having had a strong religious upbringing, Cammi had been taught the one constant love in life was God, so through the pain, she sought him out.

Even as a kid, she'd always enjoyed going to church. Of course that was another aspect of her life that Marcus put the" kibosh" on. Spirituality fascinated her more than religion. She didn't necessarily understand nor have any desire to read the bible, but she craved the relationship. Believing true happiness was found through a personal relationship with the Lord, she learned to turn her life over to him. It was small ways at first, prayer, attending church services, changing the way she looked at and treated others. Living by faith and nurturing a relationship with herself was something she had to work at daily and found, at times, she fell back into her old controlling habits, but soon, she finally felt as if her life had new meaning. Just like most things, she was private about her faith, believing each individual had their own connection with God based on experiences. It wasn't her job to tell anyone else what to do, likewise, she did not want anyone telling her either. Spiritual growth was a huge, personal transformation taking time and perseverance, and she wanted to do it her own way, on her own time.

Cammi spent hours praying and talking. And then praying some more. She felt she had no other choice. Sharing all of her deepest secrets, her fears, her longings and regrets were scary, but that was the nice thing about God. He was her best friend when no one else was. It became easy and he listened. Eventually her heart opened and she was able to hear the plan he had intended for her. It was a huge relief knowing there actually was a plan and she was here for a purpose. It made getting up each morning more exciting.

Cammi could honestly say the void created after so many losses in her life was beginning to fill. She felt as if she radiated more energy and had an underlying passion in all she did. She was making friends again, socializing, and enjoying life at its fullest. Cammi realized it was nice to have human emotions, want human things regardless if it made her selfish, and admit she wasn't perfect. With God, there was a peaceful reassurance she wasn't a sinner who would be struck down by lightening with each mistake she made. She felt loved and accepted unconditionally for who she was, regardless of her vices. Knowing that alone strengthened her spiritual bond and allowed her to open her heart more freely.

Still, something was missing. Cammi was anxious to share her new found happiness with a man. But not just any man. She believed she had to follow God's plan and although she didn't feel it was her place to ask for something in particular, she wanted him to know her deepest heart's desire.

Cammi had strong convictions. She was raised with good morals and values, was ready to become a wife as well as a mother and wasn't willing to settle for the first guy who showed interest. If that had been the case, she'd be married and divorced three times over by now. No…. this was different. No more screwing around. She wanted the real thing. A real man, not some glossed over version of Marcus.

Regardless of the faith she found, a deep seated fear still held her back. There was more to love than what society demonstrated in this superficial, materialistic, world of instant gratification. Love was more than just a feeling it was a journey. Had she come far enough in her own personal journey to handle it? Was she capable of giving and receiving the love she truly believed existed between two human beings without running away? She had been burned once. Was she strong enough to handle disappointment when it came along, which was bound to happen in any relationship in which she became involved?

It seemed almost impossible for two people to fulfill the obligation. Did she really believe she was so special and unique she would find a partner who was willing to go the distance, too? Were there even men out there who wanted to go the distance? In her eyes, this was more than emotion. It was a way of life, a choice, the depth and commitment of one's soul. Love was to be nurtured and tended to, something that took discipline and hours, weeks, years of hard work. But it was also unselfish. The outcome and the rewards on the journey of love were unknown to her, but also worth the risk.

Now all she needed was to find a man who believed it was worth the risk, too and she wasn't willing to settle for some simple minded male. She manifested her dream, put it out there for the Lord to hear, and waited. But she also made a promise. If God brought the soul mate he created for her into her life, she would do whatever it took, *anything* to make the marriage and commitment work.

So here in this moment, standing in the coffee shop, following God's plan, Cammi set into motion the chain of events that would become her life.

Chapter Two

At thirty-two, three years older than Cammi, Bryce was single with a six-year-old daughter from a previous relationship. A relationship that from the sounds of it, was better off having ended. "Mental health issues" was how he tactfully addressed it in his e-mail. He moved to Madison when he was fourteen and after high school, attended CU in Boulder. He met Allie's mother right after getting his masters degree in business management. Her pregnancy and the birth of Allie kept him in town and he was now the human resource director at the hospital as well as a volunteer firefighter. Bryce was primarily raising Allie himself with the support and help of his parents who lived just an hour away in Beaver Creek.

Jamie had been dropping Bryce's name here and there for weeks before she actually suggested Cammi meet him. On first instinct, Cammi was horrified her best friend would even suggest such a thing but as much as she hated to admit it, Jamie was right, he sounded wonderful. Could this Bryce guy really be the answer to her prayers? Not wanting to jinx herself, Cammi tried hard not to allow her usual pessimism to take over. But after just a few weeks of e-mails, Cammi was impressed. He sounded stable, grounded, and articulate, which from a writer's point of view was incredibly sexy.

Basketball was his passion in high school and he still played once a week on a city league. He also enjoyed golfing and hunting, though he was humble enough to admit he was horrible at both and just liked the outdoor activity.

Obtaining custody of his daughter hadn't been a difficult process since there wasn't a court battle, but he was very evasive about the details. In Cammi's eyes it took a heck of a guy to take on that sort of responsibility, especially right after college.

His family sounded amazing, very similar to hers, in fact and she assumed his outlook on marriage was a positive one considering his parents had been married over forty years. It seemed to be blessing in disguise they were so close to help him with Allie. Bryce adored his mother, but he admitted there was a little animosity with his father due to how overbearing and critical he had been to Bryce as a child. But he still loved the man and had close relationships with his two brothers and sister.

Bryce confessed he dabbled in dating, but said it wasn't something he put much effort into, being a full-time father and all. He didn't enjoy the meat market of the club scene, was a bit picky about women after his experience with Allie's mother, and straight out told Cammi he was ready to settle down to have a real family.

"And you found all this out from e-mail?" Autumn asked suspiciously the previous week.

Autumn was Cammi's neighbor in the apartment complex in which they lived. She happened to be moving in the same time as Cammi five years ago and even though she was hesitant at first, Cammi couldn't help being drawn to her boisterous, outgoing personality and spontaneous behavior.

Cammi called earlier to see if she would like to come over for a movie while indulging in a gallon of ice cream. They were upright on the couch, feet sprawled out on the coffee table in front of them, taking turns dipping their spoons into the carton when Cammi decided to spill her guts. With time, Cammi learned Autumn was a sincere friend who was trustworthy and loyal. It was nice to have someone besides Jamie to talk to about the crazy decision she was about to make.

"Well, duh! Haven't met him yet, remember? It's refreshing to hear he is past playing games and ready to jump in with complete honesty."

"What kind of guy says he wants to get married? He sounds too sensitive, if you ask me," her friend commented licking the back of her spoon. "I thought you wanted a man's man."

"He's not twenty one, Autumn. He is in his thirties and the single dad of a little girl. Life's a bit different for him. It has to be."

"I don't know Cammi.....maybe he's just looking for a mom for his daughter."

Cammi shot her a dirty look.

"Well, do you want me to be honest or do you want me to tell you what you want to hear?" Autumn asked defensively turning the volume down on the television.

"I would imagine he's looking for a little of both. Someone he can share his life with and be a good example to his daughter. What's wrong with that?"

"Nothing. If that's what you're looking for."

"Maybe it is," Cammi replied.

"Are you sure, Cammi? Do you really know what you want?"

"Of course I do," she said slightly offended by Autumn's remark.

"I know how you feel about Internet dating…do you think this is smart?"

"This isn't Internet dating. Shawn knows him from the hospital and Jamie's met him personally. God, do you think I am stupid enough to meet a guy on line?"

"No, I'm just saying, be careful. Go slow."

"I haven't even met him yet. Can't say I even will, it's just…, you know, he seems alright. Different than other men I've met."

"What other men?" Autumn reminded her.

Cammi had been hurt and disappointed by Autumn's reaction. She thought for sure Autumn would be the one person who would encourage her instead of bring her down. In fact, her negative comments made Cammi shy away from anything more than e-mails for another month, but eventually, she got up the nerve to send him her cell phone number. Bryce's phone calls left Cammi delighted and looking forward to more. It was as if they'd been friends forever, so suggesting they meet for coffee shouldn't have seemed too forward. Or had it?

Cammi had waited this long to meet Bryce for a multitude of reasons. First, she needed to prepare herself emotionally for what might happen. She had a habit of analyzing too much and had gone over this scenario in her head many, many times. Her friends always told her she 'what- ifed' everything to death. What if everything he told her was complete bullshit just to lead her on? What if he was attracted to her and she wasn't to him or vice versa? What if he was some sort of psychotic crazy stalker?

Even worse, what if she really, truly wasn't as ready for a relationship?

Second, the idea of his daughter thrilled her, but Autumn was right, it scared her too. It wasn't that she wasn't good with kids, in fact, she loved them and was dying to become a mother. However, dating a man with a child was something completely different and something she didn't know if she was capable of handling.

They decided to meet in the coffee shop down in the town square around one-ish. She couldn't help wonder whether he was as nervous as she? He *did* sound like a sensitive guy, which she imagined was more than likely because he was a single dad raising a girl. Should it have turned her off? Compared to Marcus's insensitivity, it seemed like a nice change of pace.

But now, standing by herself gawking around the small room, breathing the fragrance of freshly brewed coffee into her lungs, she felt a little foolish. He gave her a description of what to look for but she was far too tense to remember the details. The line at the counter was at least twenty people deep and it was difficult to spot a blue, chambray, button down shirt.

"Great", she thought aloud, "how hard can this be?" By now she felt like an idiot standing by herself and her lack of confidence was beginning to alarm her.

Suddenly she felt a tap on her shoulder.

"Cammi?" She recognized the deep voice instantly. With a slight thrill shooting up her spine, she turned around to find herself staring into the most beautiful blue eyes she'd ever seen and felt an unusually unfamiliar tug on her heart.

Bryce was stunned. The face staring back at him was more beautiful than he ever imagined it would be, not to mention sexy, feminine with its own type of rare beauty. Graceful was the word he would use to describe her. Nothing you would see in a fashion magazine, but a confidence and style that she owned. Her big green eyes seemed to melt into the depths of his heart when she looked at him in sudden panic. It only took a moment, a brief second in time and he was hooked, filled with urge to take her into his arms and pull her close.

Of course he had been apprehensive about meeting today. Who wouldn't after all this time? It has been close to three months since they exchanged their first e-mail. He'd basically come to accept it wasn't going to happen and decided to make a date with the sister of a colleague for that exact evening. He didn't particularly like dating, but knew if he ever wanted to find the woman he was going to spend his life with, he wasn't going to meet her sitting at home watching episode after episode of Dora the Explorer with his six year old daughter.

Imagine how badly he wanted to kick himself in the ass now that Cammi finally reached out to him. It been a year and still Jason hadn't let up. He was adamant about setting Bryce up with his sister Lacy and any man with a penis in his pants would have been crazy not to go out with her. Not only was she gorgeous, she was brainy too with a PH.D in chemical engineering. But when he began to receive e-mails from Cammi, he put the idea of Lacy out of his head. Cammi sparked an interest and he was eager to get to know her better even though she made it perfectly clear that she had very tight boundaries. Promising himself he would not cross them until she gave him permission, he resisted many urges to ask her out.

Jamie was the wife of his golf partner Shawn Tomlin, one of the most respected surgeons at the hospital. He'd met her socially at hospital functions and liked her immediately. She was bubbly and entertaining, the life of the party although he'd never actually seen her drink. She also had a reputation for throwing great social gatherings with the best spread in town. It was at their annual St. Patrick's Day celebration earlier in the year when she pulled Bryce onto the couch next to her planting a bug in his ear about Cammi. Over time when they ran into one another she made a point to remind him about her best friend.

Of course the more he heard, the more interested he was. Jamie's was a very convincing woman and her exuberance was contagious. When she finally called him a few months later with Cammi's e-mail address, he had to admit, he was intrigued. Madison was a small town and good women…. morally good women were hard to come by. The e-mails he exchanged with her slowly turned into phone calls and he got the vibe Cammi was enjoying them as much as he was, but still, they never met.

It was killing him not being able to put a face with the voice, and God it was such a sexy voice. His curiosity got the best of him so he finally asked Shawn what she looked like. He wasn't going to ask Jamie. Her opinion, he was sure, was probably biased. In his experience, women had a habit of stretching the truth about their friends, getting the guys all hyped up and excited only to find out that they were fifty pounds overweight with major hygiene issues. But he knew Shawn would be honest.

"Oh, buddy, yeah, she's hot. And all right too. Easy to hang out with, one of those sexy, tom-boy types," he said giving him the thumbs up sign. It wasn't hard to read from Shawn's wide-eyed expression that he genuinely liked her, and Bryce was bowled over by his own sudden possessiveness over a woman he hadn't even met.

That is why when he hadn't heard from her in three whole weeks, continuing to check his e-mails daily looking for a sign of hope and anxiously picking up his phone each time it rang, he decided to give up. She had obviously lost interest somehow and he was getting himself too worked up over something that might never happen.

Jamie felt bad and could sense his disappointment, but also knew Cammi could be as stubborn as a mule when fear took hold.

As discreetly as she could, without making her best friend sound like a reject or letting him think she wasn't interested, she explained about Cammi's divorce. Bryce felt bad for her, he really did, but instinct told him she wasn't going to step out of her comfort zone anytime soon, so he reluctantly agreed to the date with Lacy. At least it would give him something to look forward to and hopefully, get Jason off his back.

He'd met her only once at last year's New Years Eve party, so it wasn't going to be an actual blind date. She was beautiful; no doubt about it, but her personality was dry. She was incredibly intelligent, but conversing with her was about as exciting as watching paint dry. And he had to admit, after a painfully dull discussion to plan the date he wasn't exactly thrilled to be taking her out. He just couldn't get his mind off Cammi and their interesting and easy banter.

It was a good thing he was on a business call when he received Cammi's invite for coffee the previous afternoon, otherwise, the shock would have blown him over in his chair. The e-mail burned into the pupils of his eyes as a grin slowly crept across his face. He couldn't help but laugh. If memory served him correctly, she told him she hated coffee. But he loved it.

Only after sending his reply did he remember his date with Lacy. His first thought was to break the date, but eventually decided to keep it. It felt deceitful, but it was probably better in the long run if he had a backup plan, especially if Cammi was as inconsistent as she seemed the past few weeks. But here, sitting across from her, listening to her stories of work, friends, and family, he was mesmerized. Lacy was the furthest thought from his mind.

The way she talked fascinated him. The way her lips curved into a shy grin before it curled up into a full smile, the way her eyes lit up, but most of all, he was enthralled by what she had to say. She was so wise. At twenty-nine she seemed to possess wisdom about life that was way beyond her years. Jamie had already told him most of what he needed to know and of course their many conversations helped him make up his mind, but listening to her now made him realize exactly how decent of a human being she truly was. The spirit and enthusiasm she radiated was infectious. He'd never met anyone like her and frankly, didn't want the afternoon to end. If he could stay in the comfort of her voice forever, he couldn't imagine anything sweeter. The thought excited and terrified him at the same time.

The hours flew by. People came and went. Time didn't matter and it didn't take long for Cammi to relax. Bryce had a calming effect on her. She felt more comfortable than she had in years. Once in a while, she had to remind herself to slow down and stop rambling but she felt she could talk to him about anything. This was strange. She didn't typically express herself so freely.

Surly she must be boring him. As much as she *wanted* to tell him everything, she cautioned herself that this *was* a first date. She didn't want to scare him off.

"Tell me about your daughter, do you have a picture of her?" Cammi inquired in an attempt to take the focus off of her.

His face lit up at the mention of his Allie. He obliged by taking out his wallet and handing over her kindergarten picture. Cammi thought the girl was breathtaking. With her olive skin and blue eyes, she was the spitting image of her father, except for her long blonde hair, which he said was the one redeeming quality she got from her mother.

Cammi noticed on previous occasions that Bryce's voice held a hint of contempt at the mention of his ex, and again today he had did not have a good comment to say about her. She couldn't help but wonder what this woman had done to cause so many negative emotions within him.

"That girl doesn't know a stranger, she'll befriend anyone. Tell them her whole life story in a matter of minutes, if they'll listen," he chuckled affectionately. "She tries to take in every stray animal on the street but I'm not much of an animal lover myself. I did break down and get a dog six months ago. A German Short Hair, Diesel. He's good, can't complain, and Allie is very responsible. She'll be a nurse or caretaker of some sort, I can see it already… but she does have her boundaries," he said his voice filled with sadness.

Cammi could definitely relate.

"She's been through a lot," he informed her. "Her mother hasn't been in her life since she was three. Believe me, she is better off, but as she gets older, I notice the impact from not having her around. At this age, she doesn't understand her mom's emotional issues, but instead, thinks she has done something wrong. I don't tell her much. She's still too young to understand. Besides, I don't want to bash her mom."

"How would it be bashing to tell her the truth?"

"Oh boy," Bryce said looking at his watch. "How much time do you have?"

Cammi laughed. "Now you've got me curious."

With her chin resting in the palm of her hand, mesmerized by the deep pool of his blue eyes, Cammi listened intently as Bryce told his story.

Chapter Three

Right after his college graduation, Bryce decided to spend two months in Madison weighing his options between jobs. He'd been offered the general manager position of a posh, five star ski resort in Steamboat Springs, Colorado as well as the head sales representative for a top sports drink company in West Palm Beach, Florida. Bryce figured some leisure time would help him gain a little perspective about the direction he wanted his life to take although most of it was spent at the lake water skiing, jet skiing and camping with his buddies from high school.

Though he didn't know it at the time, his fate rested in someone else's hands entirely.

Late one evening, after a day of hiking and drinking beer in the mountains, he and his friends all agreed to head out to the bars. Bryce had finally accepted the job offer in Florida and planned on celebrating heavily.

The White Stallion was a local hangout for the twenty-something Madison crowd and he'd seen Cynthia Rhodes in there a few times. She was a striking, voluptuous blonde and hard not to notice but he tried not to give her a second glance. He typically preferred brunettes…. quiet brunettes. This girl was rowdy, obnoxious and constantly drawing attention to herself. Yet the way she went about it, a man couldn't keep his mind from wandering. Sexual desire and femininity dripped from her every pore. Needless to say, it was obvious she spelled trouble. It wasn't long before she noticed him too, and whenever the chance presented itself, she would shoot him one of her fabulous, entrancing smiles.

That night, he had been pleasantly surprised to see her working behind the bar instead of hanging out partying. When it was his turn to buy another round, he sauntered up to the her and waited a good five minutes watching with delight while she served other patrons, lit cigarettes and bustled from here to there. He overheard her tell someone she was working her way through law school, and in those few minutes, he felt bad for the instant judgment call he'd made about her.

For the rest of the evening, he watched her silently from afar while taking long pulls of his beer. Once in a while, she would glance over in his direction and narrow her seductive eyes in acknowledgement. It wasn't long after her shift ended Cynthia and a girlfriend made themselves at home at his table, with her sitting next to Bryce, her hand immediately stroking his thigh.

One thing led to another and he took her home.

"I was young and having a good time. I certainly wasn't dating her for her mind. I worked hard in college and didn't have much time to screw off, so after graduation, I went wild. It was nice to have a warm body in my bed every now and again, but I was leaving in less than two months," he confessed. "Not thinking with the head on my shoulders was the biggest mistake I ever made. Having Allie made the hell I went through worth it, but it's definitely not the proudest moment of my life."

Pausing, he hoped to gain a sense of her reaction to his confession. In her eyes, he saw only compassion and understanding.

Cammi wasn't naive enough to think Bryce didn't have a man's needs or desires. Anymore it was hard to find a guy who didn't play around when he was younger. But she could tell he was embarrassed by his past, and oddly enough, the idea of him in bed with another woman made her incredibly uncomfortable.

Bryce and Cynthia dated casually. He found her sweet and delightful and though he wasn't looking for a serious relationship, he enjoyed their time together. Four days before he was to leave for Florida, Cynthia told him she was pregnant. He had no doubts the baby was his. She'd been on her own since high school. She told him her parents expected her to settle down and get married right away to her high school sweetheart like all the women in their family had. She was raised with old fashioned values and her parents believed a woman's place was in the home with the children. When she told them about her plans for law school, they disowned her. When Cynthia wasn't with him, she was working her tail off at two jobs trying to make ends meet and when she wasn't working; she was taking college courses at the local library. So even if she wanted to date anyone else, she didn't have the time. Allie's paternity was something he never questioned.

Turning down the job in Florida, he accepted his role as a father to his child but marrying Cynthia hadn't crossed his mind. His intention was to be close and help her raise the baby, but what they shared wasn't love. He had very strong family values and was willing to take on his responsibility as a parent but knew he could not spend the rest of his life with a woman he did not love passionately. So Bryce took a job working construction. After the baby was born he would start applying for jobs again and make more permanent arrangements.

Cynthia seemed to accept this at first, admitting she didn't love him either, but as time went on she decided her future with him was more important than the future of her child.

At first her tactics were subtle. She became needy, claiming the morning sickness kept her down all day so it was hard for her to get to work and classes. Then she started dropping hints about the two of them having a future together. Bryce ignored them. Into her second trimester, she was sleeping all the time and refused to eat properly using her nausea as an excuse. Bryce was as attentive and encouraging as he could be, spending more time at her place than he did his own just to make sure she was taken care of. They got along fine, but what she hoped would turn into love, didn't on his part.

Towards the end of her sixth month, Cynthia suggested they move in together saying it would be easier during her "delicate time". When Bryce asked what she meant by that, she told him the doctor suggested bed rest for her "high risk pregnancy." Because of work, he had been unable to attend the last few appointments with her but she had been hysterical when she told him how scared she was of losing the baby because of her high stress level with work and night classes. Bryce became very concerned. She *had* been losing more weight than she gained and when she was home, she was sleeping on the couch.

Bryce was torn. He couldn't have her homeless and not taking care of herself. He felt it was his obligation. She *was,* after all, the mother of his child. He wanted his baby safe and secure and besides, he didn't want Cynthia giving up her chance for a stable future by quitting college. Nevertheless, Bryce also knew he wasn't ready to take the next step, so instead Cynthia cut back on work. In the meantime, he paid his rent plus hers hoping to pacify her until he could figure out other options.

Yet there were details of her story that didn't make sense to him though he could never pinpoint why. Suspicion had settled somewhere deep down in his gut so before making any more decisions he took her, kicking and screaming, back to the doctor. If for nothing else, at least he would have peace of mind the baby was healthy. She came up with every excuse in the book to get out of the appointment but to Bryce, it was all the more reason to push the issue.

If Cynthia had confessed her deceitfulness before hand, it may have been the slightest bit easier for him to take, but the humiliation he felt when the doctor contradicted everything Cynthia had told him, took any prior suggestions of living together off the table. After the examination, the doctor told them he was happy to see the morning sickness had subsided, scolded her for missing three appointments and besides needing to change her eating habits to make sure she was giving herself and the baby enough nutrition, Cynthia was progressing along wonderfully. Everything was normal. The ultrasound showed a perfect, healthy twenty-eight week baby girl.

"What about the bed rest?" Bryce asked out of confusion, watching the doctor throw his surgical gloves into the nearby trashcan.

"Bed rest is only necessary in high risk pregnancies, Mr. Sheppard. Unless something changes, I don't see a need for that. Don't overdo it, of course, but small bouts of activity are good for the baby."

Bryce was enraged. His anger and distrust of her made Cynthia just that more unstable. What time they did spend together consisted of her crying and screaming, blaming him for not giving her and the baby what they both needed and deserved. When that didn't work, she threatened him, herself and the life of the baby. She became the hook, while he was the bait. But her scare tactics only succeeded in pushing him further away. By now he could hardly stand to look at her, let alone care about her. She disgusted him. He stuck around for one reason and one reason only… to ensure the safety of his child. It was the longest months of his life and as time passed, he felt trapped by her actions.

Despite Cynthia's behavior, over the course of time, Bryce fell in love with the idea of being a father. Once he saw the ultrasound, the dark silhouetted shape of a tiny nose, chin and fingers, he fell deeply in love with his baby girl and wondered how the stress of the world outside the womb was affecting the child growing inside. He couldn't just walk away, but he wasn't willing to continue a dysfunctional relationship with a woman he didn't love, let alone like.

Thank God Bryce had the support of his parents and sister. His brothers thought he was crazy, but that is what made Bryce different from them. He took his responsibilities seriously. They on the other hand were still too young to know better. Everyone had tons of advice to give, especially his father, but when it came down to it, it was his mom and sister, who guided him through it.

Bryce lived the next few months like a zombie, faking politeness and doing what he had to do to keep the peace, but according to Cynthia, nothing was good enough unless he was willing to make a commitment to her. Finally towards the beginning of her ninth month, he figured out her motive. She wanted money, financial stability and saw him as her meal ticket. When his monthly bills arrived, he was astounded by the amount he owed on his credit cards. Not only were they maxed out on clothing and furniture for the baby's nursery and layette, she had also taken it upon herself to spend *his* money on postnatal clothes she thought she deserved, lunches with friends, gas for her car and who knew what else. The worst part of it was he hadn't given her the credit cards. She had stolen them out of his wallet.

He fought an internal battle on whether or not to confront her, but with her fragile state of mind, he opted not to out of fear she might act on her threats of suicide or run away, and then he would never see his child.

Her fits of rage continued as he became more emotionally unavailable. Dishes were shattered, doors were slammed, and holes were punched through walls during her outbursts. He continued to ignore her tantrums focusing instead on the days until the baby was born. But it only intensified her instability.

Two weeks before the birth of their daughter, Bryce got some news that rocked his world. Cynthia's father called his place to check on her. When Bryce mentioned his surprise to hear from him, Mr. Rhodes said she had been calling their house leaving unsettling messages for three days and her mother was deeply disturbed. When they couldn't reach Cynthia at her apartment, they called information for Bryce's phone number.

"How did you know to look me up?" Bryce asked confused.

"She told us about you. And of course the baby," her father spoke defensively. "Please forgive us, we were just in a panic about the last few messages we got. You see we were out of town this weekend visiting Ruth's Aunt Rose in Sabetha and when we got home and had a chance to play the answering machine, all we could make out was Cynthia crying hysterically asking for help."

"Her mother was just so glad to hear from her, especially around the holidays," he rambled. "And to find out we were going to be grandparents, well that tickled us pink. It had been two years. Can you imagine, two years without even knowing if your little girl is alive or dead. Of course, she must have told you everything. We were so glad she met you. We believed she was back on track and going to do the right thing for her baby. She's been calling once a week since then to keep us posted, and of course, we agreed to send her some money to help out until you all got married, I hope that's okay," he said nervously.

"I don't understand. When did she first call you?" Bryce asked unsure he had heard correctly.

"Seven months ago. Right before Christmas."

"And you say you have been sending money?"

"Yep. Three hundred a month. She said you have a September wedding planned. Wanted to wait until after the baby was born so she could actually fit into the wedding dress, I imagine," he chuckled.

Bryce was stunned. A September wedding? When hell froze over.

Playing dumb, Bryce began to ask questions and over the next hour he was able to fit the pieces of the puzzle together and her dad, thinking Bryce already knew about her sordid past had no problem spilling the beans.

According to Mr. Rhodes, Cynthia had been a reckless teenager who hated to follow the rules, had a bad attitude, and was proud of her promiscuity. No matter what they tried, they had no control over her. Apparently she flunked out of high school her junior year. Out of desperation for money to move away and start a new life, she turned her attentions on her older sister's fiancée who came from a prominent family in Sabetha, Kansas.

One night she threw herself at him in attempts to blackmail him for money to skip town. When he refused her advances, she became physically violent towards him. He had to restrain her but the next day she showed the family the bruises on her arms and claimed he tried to rape her.

Unfortunately for Cynthia, her twelve-year-old brother witnessed the whole thing and ratted her out. Instead of taking responsibility for her actions, Cynthia blamed her family for loving her sister more than they did her, stole as much as she could right from under their noses and took off for Colorado. There were phone calls asking for more money, and she had a PO Box set up so no one could find out where she was living. Of course, there were always rumors she was dealing drugs using the bartending job as a cover up. Then one day the calls stopped, and they hadn't heard from her in over two years.

"But you already know all this, don't yeah son. Cynthia was proud as punch to find a man who was willing to forgive her past mistakes. A bit surprised she owned up to them, we were. But when she showed up out here over Christmas and gave us the low down on you, well, we couldn't deny that she lucked out. And it's about damn time. Scared shitless, that's what we were. With the way she was behaving, I was just waiting for a phone call saying she'd been found dead in a ditch."

Uneasiness filled Bryce's heart. What sort of game was this woman playing? He could not stop her from telling lies or manipulating others for her own gain, obviously it had become a way of life at that point, but he wasn't going to allow himself or his daughter to be the guinea pig for future manipulations. Bryce didn't feel the need to explain himself to Mr. Rhodes when he made an excuse to get off the phone.

The keys jiggled in his hand as he slammed the door behind him and hopped down the stairs two at a time. He didn't know where to go. All he knew was he was pissed. Angier than he'd ever been in his entire life and he'd finally had his fill. He knew it would probably be smarter to take some time to cool off, but instead he headed to Cynthia's place, his hands clenching the steering wheel. It was time she started following *his* rules and the first thing he was going to do was take her ass to court to get custody of his child, and if it meant he had to have her arrested or make a report to child services to ensure she didn't hurt herself or the baby, that is what he would do.

As he rounded the corner to her apartment building, that's when he saw them. They were standing in front of a grey Mustang convertible, arms entangled in an embrace, kissing passionately. Immediately, Bryce pulled over and parked directly in front of the couple. He could see the sinister look Cynthia's eyes when she spotted him and in that moment, he knew the lengths she would go to get exactly what she wanted and what she wanted was to trap him.

But the good actress that she was feigned shock and fright.

Bryce knew by now the tears streaming down her face as she began to chatter mindlessly were forced. And the poor sap next to her wasn't quite sure what hit him. He looked from Bryce to Cynthia and back to Bryce again, his jaw hanging open, his hand gripping her arm. Sobbing, she informed Bryce she started dating him....Ben was his name.... around the same time she became pregnant and didn't know for sure who the baby's father was.

Bryce couldn't help feeling sorry for the guy. He was clueless to the fact he was being conned even as she admitted Ben had been driving down from Denver every two weeks to give Cynthia money since he couldn't be hands on for her there. The affair continued without Ben knowing about Bryce or Bryce knowing about Ben and Ben not knowing where his money was going.

"Where did you meet him? *School?*" Bryce sneered.

Again Ben looked dumbfounded and spineless. "Uh..... at The Rodeo," he stammered.

Cynthia smacked him in the arm.

Bryce laughed. "The Rodeo, Cynthia? Really? A strip joint? Guess that explains where you were all those late nights you were out *studying*. You really are a classy lady, you know that?"

The reality of how twisted she was started to sink in. Regardless of Ben, Bryce's gut instinct told him he was the baby's father, though he would demand a paternity test just to be sure, and the money she was getting from Ben was to tide her over temporarily until she was safe and sound playing house with him. The public display of affection he'd just witnessed was just another ploy to make him jealous.

It made Bryce sick enough to throw up. Not because she betrayed him, he could care less about that, but because his precious daughter was going to have to deal with *this* lunatic for a mother the rest of her life unless he did something about it.

Not wanting to give more energy to Cynthia than he already had, Bryce calmly returned to his car. Panic stricken, she ran after him and tried to grab for the door before he slammed it, but she was too late. He drove off without another glance in her direction.

It was about five hours later, during the middle of the night, when he received the phone call informing him that Cynthia was in the ICU for an attempted suicide. Gripped with terror, he drove to the hospital berating himself for thinking that because Ben was with her, she wouldn't try something this stupid. The trip was the longest, most heart wrenching drive he ever had to endure, and he made a promise that if his baby survived, he was going to hire a lawyer and make sure his daughter had a stable upbringing. He swore he would never let her suffer at the hands of her mother again.

The suicide attempt was minor. She'd slit her wrists with a dull steak knife, barely deep enough to cause damage but enough to land her three days on the behavioral health unit of the hospital. It was just another ploy to get his attention, but it was a very dumb move on her part. It was a relief to know that his child's health was not affected and when he became rational and calm enough, he walked stone faced into Cynthia's room.

His explanation was simple. From this point forward, there would be no relationship between the two of them except for sharing the responsibility of raising their daughter. There was going to be no family, no marriage and no future. Ever.

He gave her two options. She could do this the easy way or the hard way. He would have legal and physical custody of the baby, she would be allowed proper visitation *or* she could take him to court. If she took him to court, he would do whatever it took to make sure she was seen as an unfit, unstable provider for the child which wouldn't be hard since child protective services were now involved and digging into her past as well as the allegations of drug dealing. Since she tried committing suicide while pregnant, she could potentially be brought up on charges of neglect, not to mention concerns she may have been doing drugs during her pregnancy.

Cynthia was defeated. She knew she had no choice but to agree. Two days after she was released, he didn't give a damn how unstable she was, he showed up at her house with his lawyer Ron and a social worker demanding she sign the court documents to give him full custody of their baby once she was born. Cynthia did as asked without an argument and she was granted standardized visitation; every other weekend, holiday's and one month during the summer after the baby turns two.

Allie was born completely healthy a week later and despite the standardized visitation order, Bryce allowed Cynthia to care for her three days a week, at first under his supervision. He had no intentions of keeping Cynthia from her, it was too important for a child to have a mother and a father so he put his own resentment aside to make sure his child was taken care of emotionally.

His family was a big help while he attempted to get his life in order. During that time, he found out the credit card debt totaled over twenty thousand dollars and only two thousand of it was for the baby. The tornado in his life called Cynthia had hit hard, and Bryce could do nothing but clean up the disaster.

So life in Madison was here to stay. He couldn't afford to move even if he wanted to. Luckily a job at the hospital as an accounting assistant opened up and he took it in the hopes eventually there would be room for advancement.

It didn't take long for Bryce to realize he was going to be a single parent. Cynthia's social life and drugs took precedence over their daughter. Before Allie was even a year old, Cynthia was bailing out on her time with the child. Three days slowly turned into two. And once she decided to move back to the Denver, two days turned into every other weekend. Every other weekend turned into a few times a month. By the time Allie was three, she was lucky to see her mom one day every couple months and eventually Cynthia stopped coming around at all. Bryce had no idea where she disappeared to and as his anger toward her festered he silently hoped she would rot in hell for what she was doing to his daughter.

All in all, it was as if Cynthia didn't exist. Allie was young enough she could have easily forgotten about her but once she heard her mother's voice again, she was filled with the hope and security that came along with a mother's love. The phone calls usually came on holidays, birthdays or sometimes out of the blue. Along with the calls came promises of time together, gifts, and a billion excuses. It wasn't until Allie was four that she began to react to it negatively. Bryce could feel her excitement, see in her the longing and then mentally prepare himself to deal with the disappointment and tears that were shed when Cynthia never followed through.

It would take weeks of questions, nights of crying herself to sleep and begging for her mom until Allie was back to her old self. Bryce felt helpless. He wanted to strangle Cynthia for not understanding the emotional trauma she was putting their daughter through with her actions. Her only concern was of herself. He willed the phone calls to stop in the hopes Allie could move on with her life and let go of the hurt, praying she was young enough not to be permanently scarred.

On the outside Allie appeared to be a healthy, loving, normal child with a bright imagination. At bedtime, they would read two books together, and then lie, staring at the moon and stars out her window as silhouettes danced across the ceiling from her night light. With blankets wrapped tightly up to their chins they allowed their thoughts to run free as they made up stories. But on the inside…something was missing. Something Bryce, no matter how hard he tried to replace, couldn't give Allie. Normally life was carefree and joyful but in the weeks after one of Cynthia's calls, Allie's dreams paralleled the fantasy of her mother returning home to be a part of their family.

The calls finally stopped and when six months went by without another one, Bryce put them both into therapy. It was his mom's suggestion. He had no clue what he was doing and to try to help Allie cope with the complete loss of her mother…… a professional seemed to know way more than he did.

It took a long time for Bryce to get his life back on track, financially and emotionally, but he was proud at how far he and Allie had come. They relied on one another and though sometimes he was an overly strict father and didn't always know what a little girl needed, he felt confident in the bond they shared.

Cammi, though obviously stunned by his story, could hear the love and affection in his voice as he spoke. She couldn't even begin to imagine what it must have been like to endure something so absolutely insane. Her life growing up had been normal. In fact, because of it she found herself naïve and a bit judgmental about the behaviors of others in the world. She could not fathom the idea of abandoning your own child, a child that was part of you, heart and soul.

Unforgotten guilt seemed to come out of nowhere knocking the wind out of her, a dreadful reminder that five years ago *she* was the one who made a similar decision, the one who's life was just as screwed up and dysfunctional. But it wasn't the same. *She'd* spent years trying to make it right, she convinced herself.

Pushing those ugly thoughts out of her head, she turned her attention back to Bryce. He looked so sad, sitting there, waiting for her to say something. But she didn't know what to say.

He could only imagine it was more than likely the most ridiculous story she'd ever heard. Cammi looked like a deer in headlights as she stared at him, her hands clasped around her coffee cup.

"I'm sorry," he started. "I didn't intend for this to turn into a pity party. I sometimes get carried away when I talk about Allie. Part of trying to protect her, I find myself trying to explain or make others understand why I made the choices I did. I usually end up sounding like a real bad reality show, but believe me, those are issues I put behind me years ago."

"No, no, I am glad you told me. I would be lying if I said I wasn't shocked. But at least it explains why you have such hard feelings towards her, and I can't say I blame you," Cammi reassured him. She shook her head, "I just can't understand how someone could do the things she did. It is beyond me. But it makes me feel good you trust me enough to talk about it," she said reaching her hand out to cover his.

Although it was an innocent gesture, her eyes grew wide with surprise when he looked up at her and smiled. Quickly, she pulled her hand away.

"Guess its better I found out in the beginning. I can't imagine where I'd be now if I married the lunatic," Bryce continued, breaking an awkward moment.

Cammi felt her throat tighten as tears threatened to break through her tough exterior. She was amazed with how emotionally raw the story left her. She barely knew him and had never met Allie, yet her heart ached. She wanted to know more. A man who would sacrifice everything he had to protect the one love in his life, his baby girl, had to be worth more than what she'd ever imagined.

"And Cynthia's parents? Have they ever been a part of Allie's life?" Cammi asked.

Bryce snorted. "The first year they sent gift cards, some clothes and just like Cynthia, promises to come visit that were never acted upon. Then we never heard from them again. Guess the apple does not fall far from the tree. My guess is Cynthia either convinced them of something.....who knows what or they are just as crazy and dysfunctional as she is. I can't imagine my parents not wanting to know or love one of their grandchildren. It sickens me but obviously Allie is better off without people like that in her life."

The subject was easily changed after that. In the next hour of conversation, they found out they had similar interests in music and movies and Cammi learned more about hunting and golf than she had ever cared to know before, but somehow with him, it seemed fascinating. It was a little intimidating, all these activities he did. There were house projects, it sounded like he was a real handy man, ski trips, basketball tournaments and softball during the summer.

"What do you do with Allie when you are doing all of this?" she asked.

Bryce shrugged. "I take her with me. Sometimes my parents are around. They'll come to the games and watch. At softball she sits in the dugout with me or plays with her friends. Most of the guys on the team have families. I taught her how to ski when she was three. I haven't taken her hunting yet, though. Don't know if I will. As much as I would love to, I don't think it's her thing. When I golf, she stays with Ms. Newcomb."

Cammi's head was spinning just listening to him. He was so busy, did he really have time for a girlfriend, she wondered. Despite her better judgment, she desperately hoped so. Aside from the butterflies in the pit of her stomach and the lightheadedness she felt just being near him Cammi had never felt more comfortable in her life. He was warm and animated and his sense of humor delighted her.

Bryce on the other hand could feel a layer of sweat form under his collar. His carefree charisma and fun loving spirit gained him more attention than he normally cared for and prepared him to handle almost any situation with confidence and ease. However, he could honestly say Cammi had him tied up in knots. He was nervous as hell. She intrigued him in a way he could not explain and would do whatever it took to make sure he didn't screw this up. He came with a lot of baggage but knew he could offer her the world, if she let him.

Bryce was ready to find a companion, not to have someone help him raise Allie, but for himself, although he was definitely looking for a woman who could be a positive role model for his daughter. From what he had seen of his dating options lately, they were hard to come by. More than that, what he really wanted was a best friend. Someone he could laugh with. Someone he never tired of talking to or spending time with. Someone interested in being a family and hopefully having more children. Someone he could love and cherish the rest of his life and give him the same in return. He wanted the dream.....the dream of love, real love, not superficial love.

Everywhere Bryce looked dreams were shattered, replaced with contentment, casual conversation and people who were just getting by. It seemed no one, especially his buddies, held any belief in it. But he had faith it truly existed. He convinced himself the right girl was out there, experiencing life and becoming prepared and then when the time was right, they would find each other.

Not that he would openly admit that to anyone. What guy would? But he was not like most guys. Though he'd had his share of blunders while raising a girl on his own, he thought he was doing a pretty good job considering he was thrown into the role of being not only a single dad, but the mother too. He made sure Allie's hair was done for school, her clothes washed, and that she had a bath every other day. The house wasn't always clean to his mother's standards or the beds made, and there wasn't a fridge full of healthy food all the time, but Allie was well taken care of. It took him a few years, but now instead of buying her a basketball or matchbox cars for Christmas, he was taking hints from the list she wrote which mainly consisted of Barbie's, Disney Princess movies and stuffed animals. He didn't know many men that could do as good of a job as he was, but thankfully he had his mother and sister who helped him get in touch with what it was a girl needed.

This was why he was able to get in touch with what it was he truly wanted in life. After his experience with Cynthia, Bryce knew exactly what he wanted. He was already doing the family thing, so the idea of finding *the one* to mesh into it wasn't hard to envision. Sitting there listening to Cammi chat up the latest book she was reading, he couldn't help but let his mind wander. She had these full sexy lips. He wondered if they tasted as good as they looked.....wondered if the rest of her body was as soft as he imagined it was.

"How about dinner tomorrow night?" he said stopping her mid sentence. He loved the smooth gentleness of her voice and hated to cut her off but he couldn't stand to beat around the bush anymore.

Holding his breath in anticipation of her answer, the idea of her rejection crashed down on him like at two ton weight so he casually leaned back in his chair as if he didn't have a care in the world while inside his stomach was twisting in knots.

Cammi couldn't help but smile. She could see the tension in his neck as he tried to hide his anxiety. In a strange way, it made her feel special.

"I would like that," she said timidly, surprised by herself. Though she was shy by nature, as a journalist, she'd learned to think and respond quickly. But that was for professional situations, not personal. Yet she could not help her own enthusiasm at the prospect of seeing him again.

"My sister lives in Beaver, just around the canyon, so she can come to stay with Allie. They have a great time together. Can I pick you up around 5?" he asked trying to mask the anticipation in his voice. This was the first time in a long time he had felt this eager to make a date.

Being cautious as usual, Cammi asked if they could meet somewhere instead. There were a few things she needed to take slow, and this was one of them. He seemed surprised and slightly disappointed by her request, but agreed. He also made a mental note to break his date with Lacy.

Chapter Four

They decided to meet at the new Italian Bistro downtown in the Square. Cammi loved the Square, especially on a warm summer evening. It was cool enough for a sweater in case they were outside, but warm enough to enjoy the outdoors. This time of year was her favorite. Being born and bred in Colorado, Cammi was a nature freak and hated being cooped up inside when God intended for people to enjoy the beauty of all he created. And there was more beauty in these mountains than most could imagine.

Madison was one of the oldest historic towns in Colorado. Tucked away neatly in the Rocky Mountains, twenty thousand people occupied the quaint little community that was small and cozy enough to feel welcome as well maintain some sense of privacy.

Different from other posh ski resorts scattered around them, Madison was home to only seven runs, one lift and a bunny hill, a great place for beginners to learn the sport. Most of the locals appreciated that the town didn't draw the massive numbers of tourists, but enjoyed the appeal of outdoor activities that could be enjoyed all year round by family and friends.

Cammi tried her hand at skiing several years before, her freshman year of college in fact, but was unable to catch on, figuring if she had started at an earlier age when she had no fear she probably would have loved it. As it was, the older she got, the less brave she became. But growing up here, her father instilled in her a love for fishing, hiking and wildlife. She spent hours as a child behind her house by the creek with a rod in hand, feet dangling in the water or keeping an eye out for small animals and birds.

It was from these experiences that Cammi developed a love for reading and writing. She delighted in picture books of animals at an early age. The desire to learn and read about them never went away. As she grew it was easier for her to pour her emotions and love into animals than it was people, and she was lucky enough to have parents who understood her desire to care for and rescue strays. Yes, she was heartbroken when they died or had to be given away, but it was much easier to depend on their unconditional love than risk the rejection or judgments that came with humans. When Bryce mentioned Allies common interest for all animals, Cammi's heart swelled.

She couldn't deny she was anxious to see him again. The smile hadn't left her face since their meeting the day before. If she were to be honest with herself, she couldn't remember feeling quite this wound up over a guy.

Romance had filled her heart when she returned to her apartment the night before. She'd poured herself a glass of wine and pushed play on her CD player listening to the soothing melody of classical music before calling Jamie.

"I did it!" she squealed while pirouetting around the room with the phone cradled in her ear.

"Did what?"

"Met Bryce for coffee, and he was everything you said, plus more. He's taking me to dinner tonight," she shrieked with the exhilaration of a young schoolgirl.

"I want details! Did he kiss you? Were you attracted to him?" Jamie couldn't contain her own excitement.

Jamie and Cammi met in college. Initially, they had a strong dislike toward one another. Jamie was strong willed, hardworking and stunningly beautiful but her "in your face" personality had a way of offending those who didn't know her. She excelled at everything she did, thrived on being the center of attention and was obnoxious to a fault. The exact things Cammi strove not to be.

She, on the other hand, was the pearl next to Jamie's diamond. She was down to earth and in complete control of her life and emotions. Opinionated in a dignified, rational way, she liked to make others feel important while maintaining strict boundaries. Where Jamie was the life of the party, Cammi was a loner. She enjoyed social gatherings as long as she didn't have to entertain anyone and could sit in a corner amused by the actions of those she watched. In Jamie eyes, she was a self-righteous snob.

What they hated in each other was the very thing drawing them together; their strength, perseverance and honest, loving hearts. Jamie wore hers on her sleeve, willing to open up to anyone who would accept her for who she was, where Cammi, whose heart was overflowing and ready to burst at the seams, chose to remain hidden from the world. She was an outsider who only allowed a certain lucky few to find the key to her amazing soul. Trust was not her strong suit but eventually, Cammi was drawn to Jamie's self-assured mannerism where Jamie loved Cammi's stability and calming influence.

Ten years later, they were as tight as they had been the drunken night at the Sigma Chi house when they confessed their envy for one another. With marriage and kids, Jamie became more responsible and content with the love of a good man, but never gave up her day job as her best friend's confidant and source of energy. And she watched in amusement as Cammi evolved from a wallflower into a free, confident woman who learned to have fun and not take life so seriously. That was until she met Marcus.

Jamie despised him from the start and the feeling was mutual. It had been hard for her to sit back and watch Marcus control every aspect of Cammi's life, and try as she might she failed at disguising her true feelings. She saw what Cammi was unable to and voiced her opinions, but out of respect for her friend, decided to wait patiently until the marriage unraveled on its own. Their decision to get married hadn't been thought through and Jamie was convinced it was only a matter of time until Cammi came to her senses.

Cammi, on the other hand, adored Jamie's husband Shawn and was the proud Godmother of her twin boys Chase and Cedric. It wasn't the first time Jamie tried to convince a very unhappy Cammi to leave her husband, but when Shawn took a job in Madison, knowing how much Cammi loved the town where she'd grown up, Jamie couldn't resist planting another seed.

Cammi's parents moved to Salt Lake soon after she left for college. Her Brother Kurt's family lived south towards Pueblo on some land they bought, but her sister was only a stone's throw away as well as a few girlfriends from high school who were still living in town. She'd been back five years now and had yet to regret her decision.

Jamie knew better than anyone what a hard step it was for Cammi to meet Bryce. Her divorce wasn't the only thing holding her back from love. Cammi and Jamie both had to deal with the heartache of losing a close friend in a car accident when they were sophomores in college. The loss had proved even more difficult for Cammi since Christina had been her roommate. Close relationships with women were rare for her, and what the three of them shared had been more of a sisterhood. Between her ex husband, the baby and the traumatic death of Christina, Cammi struggled allowing others close and it broke Jamie's heart watching her lonely existence.

Jamie considered herself a good judge of character and liked Bryce the instant she met him. If she wasn't so crazy in love with her own husband, she might have been a bit interested in him herself. Not only was he adorable, but Bryce was a charmer. In a sincere way though, not like the hypocrisy Cammi got from Marcus. Anyone who met Bryce could see he was filled with honest integrity.

He knew how to read people and give them exactly what they needed without asking for anything in return. That impressed her. Without thinking twice, Jamie started asking questions. He was open about his family circumstances and even though she knew Cammi would probably kill her, she couldn't help going with her gut.

Cammi *did* want to kill her at first, but now she wanted to cover her with kisses.

"No, he was a complete gentleman and *so* handsome. I loved spending time with him, but....well, I can't say I am extremely, what's the word, enamored yet. I mean, don't get me wrong, I think he is attractive, but I am not ready to jump into bed with him. The thought hadn't even crossed my mind. I just really want to get to know him better. I think with my trust issues, it is going to be awhile before I allow myself to feel that sort of passion. I also think there will have to be an emotional connection before I let myself go down that road again. Sex without intimacy isn't what I want in my life, right? I lived that with my ex and don't want to experience it again. What's the saying? If something doesn't work… change it? Do the opposite, right? Well, I am going to do what I have never done before and see what happens," she gushed as she flopped on the couch.

"Whatever!" Jamie chided. "You want to get laid so bad, you can't even see straight. You have passed the peak of born again virgin, girl. You might as well admit you want it hot, and you want it now! " Jamie laughed.

"Five years, Jamie! And I don't need you to rub it in my face," Cammi shot back running her fingers through Dooney's fur. "I'd like to see how long you last under the same circumstances."

"No friggin way! I couldn't last a week, you know that." It was no secret between the friends that Jamie and Shawn had what could be called an incredible sex life. "Seriously, though, you know I admire you for it. Most women would have used what you went through as an excuse to sleep with the first, second and probably third guy who showed interest just to make herself feel better. But you went about it all differently. Just promise you will tell me everything so I can live vicariously through you for a change," Jamie demanded.

"Not for a while. I can't deal with that yet. Plus I just met the guy. Doing things different here, remember?"

It was obvious to everyone but herself, Cammi still had a lot of walls built around her heart, and it worried Jamie she was blind to the fact she was already *enamored.* It was going to scare the hell out of her when she finally realized it.

"Stop analyzing what is or isn't happening. You've spent the past few years getting to know yourself again and making the changes you wanted to make, now go with it. I know the control freak part of you wants it all to be a certain way, but leave it up to God. He's gotten you this far, hasn't he? Trust it."

"And you think God wants me to jump in bed with Bryce? Is that what you are suggesting?" she teased.

"You know what I mean."

"I know, I know. Just promise to remind me of that every so often, K?" She begged. "A good kick in the head so I don't make the same mistakes."

"Anytime, just let me know," Jamie laughed again.

Cammi was grateful for the few friends she had. Not only were they inspiring and fun-loving, their belief in her when she struggled to find it helped guide her in the right direction when she hit rock bottom. Once again, the Lord was watching out for her when he led Jamie into her life.

Always prompt, like he warned her, Bryce was waiting on a bench under an aspen tree just outside the entrance. He watched as she walked towards him and enjoyed the sway of her hips. She was stylishly dressed in a white, lace tank top which accentuated her athletic arms, a blue, silk skirt, and white sandals with a slight heel adding to her already lengthy legs. Tonight, her brown wavy hair hung over her shoulders. It was up the day before and elegance had radiated from her, but Bryce found her relaxed look tonight extremely appealing. He had a feeling it wouldn't matter how she wore her hair, or what she had on….. he would be drawn to her. She was gorgeous.

He was relived he had broken his date with Lacy the previous evening. She seemed a bit perturbed and probably expected him to reschedule, but he didn't have the heart to fill her head with a promise he knew he wouldn't keep. He could care less if he ever saw her again and he would never pursue Cammi with another woman in the picture. He already cared too much.

They followed the host to the back patio where they were sat at a private table close to the acoustic guitar player. A gentle breeze swept the aroma of roasted garlic and basil through the room. After they ordered, they sat back, Cammi sipping on a glass of Merlot, Bryce on a beer. It was very intimate.

Bryce was full of questions. He had divulged so much of himself the day before, now he was ready to find out more about her.

"What happened in your marriage?" he asked his hand gripping the frosty mug.

She laughed, twirling the stem of her wine glass between her fingers.

"You don't waste any time do you?" she teased. "There isn't much to tell. Not as exciting as your story, I am afraid."

"Good, it will be a refreshing change then." A chill stole through her as the sound of his deep laugh vibrated around them.

"I met Marcus two months into my senior year of college. He was handsome, charming and loads of fun. We spent most of our time, when we weren't working or in class, out at the clubs. We had a fabulous social life. At the time, I wasn't looking for much more but I was instantly attracted to him. The passion was intense and that was it," she said with a shrug. "I was too naïve to know the difference between love and lust. Ironically, I think most women are."

"I am not sure why he asked me to marry him," she continued. "I don't think he was really in love with me either. He was finishing law school. I guess I was the ideal wife, and the lucky guy figured he could still have his girlfriends on the side. He also had a bit of a coke and gambling habit he kept well hidden. Once I found out about it, along with the affairs, I was halfway out the door."

Cammi intended for that to be the end of the conversation. She wasn't ready to reveal the rest….not yet. There was still too much shame.

As he looked across the table to catch her eye, he could sense her hesitation. There was more to the story, but instinct told him pressuring her wasn't a good idea.

"Do you ever see him?" He wondered aloud.

"Nope. Not since the day I left. When we were finalizing the divorce there were a couple phone conversations. He was such a snake," she seethed. "Didn't try to convince me to come home, but made a couple lewd sexual suggestions. Don't think he liked the idea he didn't have a convenient piece of ass anymore," she said. *Or complete control over me*, she thought to herself.

Unexpected anger seared through him at the thought of Cammi with another man. He closed his eyes in an attempt to remove the visual from his mind but the emotion caught him off guard.

"You said 'halfway out the door," he repeated. Bryce was treading lightly, not wanting her to close off. Jamie hadn't told him the entire story only that she'd been through hell, had walls as high as Hoover Dam, and it was going to take some effort to convince her to trust him. "Was his turning into a jerk, what made you decide to take the final step?"

"Yeah, you could say that, but my heart just wasn't into him. Something I finally admitted to myself when I found out about his affair with a close friend. My self-esteem was shot. I obviously didn't trust many people after, but my heart wasn't broken. When I took my blinders off, I realized his womanizing had gone on our entire relationship. He married me because I made it easy for him."

"So, why did *you* marry him?" He asked.

"You know, everyone asks me that, and I still don't have an answer," she smiled shyly. "I think I was in love with the idea of knowing what direction my life was going. It felt stable, but it was anything but. Like I said, I wasn't looking for more but it seemed everyone else almost expected it. I felt like a freak because love wasn't a priority of mine though it seemed to be everyone else's."

"Other times, I think I convinced myself he was everything I wanted, when in reality, I didn't know what the hell I wanted. It was something I never thought about until after the divorce. But I don't dwell on it as a mistake. I take comfort in the fact it was suppose to happen to help me get to where I am today. There is too much guilt in hanging onto regrets. I don't think I was a person of substance before I had that experience. Since then, I've had to grow up and admit a lot of uncomfortable things to myself."

Bryce couldn't believe the woman he was sitting across from wasn't always a woman of substance but he agreed with her philosophy on life experiences. It was as if someone had been preparing this moment for years. Waiting, watching as they each grew individually so when they did meet, they would be able to give and provide what the other needed.

"How long were you with him?"

"Only three years, thank God," she sighed taking a sip of her wine.

The rest of the conversation was light as they ate their meal, then after dinner they took a walk around the square. The night was clear and peaceful. A small jazz band was situated underneath a gazebo drawing attention from the many passerby's who stopped to listen as well as locals who brought out lawn chairs to sit and enjoy the music.

Bryce could smell her shampoo as it mixed with the pine and evergreen when her hair blew in the breeze. Within him the desire to reach out and take her hand stirred but he didn't dare. Cammi had been full of life and conversation at dinner. He enjoyed the simplicity of their time together, but her body language spoke volumes. Glancing sideways, he noticed she walked with her arms crossed protectively in front of her and instinct told him to take things slow.

But God knows he didn't want to.

It had been almost a year since he had been with a woman. After Cynthia, he had a couple casual relationships, if a person could even call any of them a relationship. He enjoyed their company, and they enjoyed his, but there was no future with any of them except for one.

Beth was in his life only a few months when he thought he was head over heels in love with her. It was a strict rule of his not to introduce women to Allie, but he was considering it and even looked at buying an engagement ring. It wasn't long before she skipped town, leaving a note on his door saying she was in love with an oil field worker who lived in western Wyoming.

Bryce had no warning. Even though his initial reaction was shock, after a few weeks, he was thankful. With her gone, he was able to see she didn't posses any of the qualities he wanted in a woman and was angry with himself that he'd been so desperate not to fail again. He'd been blind to who she really was and considering he'd been on the verge of proposing horrified him. Over a year had passed and she was a distant memory he tried not to dig up, but Bryce made a promise that next time around he would look before he leaped.

His past experiences were enough to make any man cautious but after only a few moments with Cammi, he knew she was the one. He couldn't explain the feeling, only that it was the strongest emotion ever to consume him. When he thought of her, he saw the future. He couldn't wait to introduce her to Allie, but that was another step he would take slowly. If he wasn't careful, he may scare her away.

Still she was hard for him to read. At different times during the night he felt extremely confident with the way she treated him, others, he was at a loss with the mixed signals she sent off. He didn't get the vibe she was playing games, only that she was hesitant. He could tell she liked him, but sensed her apprehension for trust.

"Do you hike?" he asked deciding to take another chance.

"Are you kidding? I love to hike. Have you heard of Carnegie Trail, over by Roosevelt Lake?"

Bryce laughed. "It's my favorite. Want to go Saturday afternoon? Allie has a birthday party. It's supposed to last from noon to four."

There was a hint of flirtation in her eyes as she looked at him. "You better be careful, two dates in one week, and I might think you are getting clingy," she teased.

Her casualness made him smile. "I'll pack lunches," he suggested.

She raised her eyebrows seductively and grinned. Flirting had never been something she was comfortable with, and the attempt surprised her. She enjoyed the attention he gave her, and it felt safe. It had been a long time since feelings of femininity aroused within her. During the course of the meal, she would look up to find his penetrating gaze on her, and it made her weak in the knees. The thought of spending an entire afternoon with him excited her.

Cammi was raised with old-fashioned values, and she wasn't the type you would call aggressive, but every nerve in her body begged for him to take her hand. The physical tension between them was fierce as they walked to her car. Both were nervous and disappointed to see the date end. He leaned in for a quick hug, and fire burned through him as he brushed her cheek with his lips. He wondered if he would ever close his eyes again without seeing her lovely face or the outline of her sexy body.

"Is it okay if I call you tomorrow?" he asked.

"I'd like that." Blushing, she looked down at her feet. She sounded like an idiot and hoped he didn't think she was too corny. But his gentle eyes and sexy smile gave her the all encouragement she needed. With trembling hands, she unlocked her car door, slid behind the wheel and sighed. Then with admiration and regret, she watched as he walked away.

Chapter Five

They continued to see each other twice a week over the next few months. If an evening didn't work because of his schedule with Allie, they would meet for a long lunch. When they weren't able to see each other, they made up for it with phone calls late into the night after Allie went to bed. There wasn't anything they didn't talk about and it was close to impossible for either to hang up when the time came.

"I'm starting to lose sleep over the man," Cammi giggled as she and Jamie started off on one of their early morning walks. The bags under Cammi's eyes surprised Jamie, but the exhilaration in her voice told her there was nothing to worry about.

Their long walks became a habit during Jamie's pregnancy with the twins. As hard as Marcus tried when Cammi was married to him, he was unable to keep the two apart. Jamie was the one thing in Cammi's life she refused to relinquish.

Once Cammi relocated to Madison, they started up again. Because of their work schedules, she and Jamie choose to walk three miles in the morning, four times a week. Not only was it good exercise but what it did for them mentally and emotionally was a worthwhile investment. They saw their time together as free therapy.

"You're in love with him, aren't you?"

"What? Don't be silly." she said giving Jamie an astonished look.

Jamie kept walking, pumping her hands by her side but didn't respond.

"Okay, I like. Are you satisfied?" she snapped with an annoyed look in Jamie's direction. "I'm not even close to calling this love. But God, if he doesn't kiss me or touch me soon, I think I'll go insane. I have never wanted a man this much in my life."

Jamie roared with delight as Cammi picked up the pace. Talking about him got her adrenaline pumping.

"He comes in when he drops me off, and we talk until all hours of the night. I keep thinking he is stalling, planning a way to make his move. But he doesn't! He gives me a hug or a quick peck on the cheek and leaves. I go to bed frustrated and wanting him even more than I did two seconds before. I stay awake fantasizing about him for hours and have even contemplated driving over to his house and sneaking up to his room. God, I'm such a slut," she giggled.

"Cammi, you haven't had sex for half a decade. I hardly think that makes you anywhere close to a slut."

Cammi's previous sexual experiences were nice, but nothing she looked back on with longing. With Marcus, there was passion, lots of it, but no intimacy. And then they stopped having sex at all. She had no desire to have him touch her. He had others for that. At least that is what Cammi had come to think until that one horrific night he returned home drunk and forced himself on her over and over again. It had been violent and humiliating. Very rarely did she allow herself to think about it. Now though, what she longed for and believed possible was still to come. That's probably why she hadn't slept with anyone else since. She didn't want to be disappointed or sacrifice herself for less than the real thing.

Cammi grew up with the belief sex was supposed to be a beautiful experience shared between two people who cared about each other deeply, though as a teenager no one in her school took it seriously. Most of the girls didn't have enough self-respect or pride to make sure the person they shared it with was going to respect them the way they deserved. Her mother instilled those values in her, so Cammi was nineteen before she lost her virginity. She felt very lucky the boy was truly genuine, and she cared just as much for him.

It had been a special experience, but it was just puppy love. Not what she fantasized about….. two people lost in the touch that would send a lasting tremble down her spine. She wanted a man who would look at her with such hunger, such passion she wouldn't be able to resist. She wanted to remember the taste of his kiss on her lips forever and feel his caress when she closed her eyes. She wanted a man who indulged and ravished every inch of her body, and a man who couldn't get enough. She wanted to feel like a woman in love, to be treated like a woman who was cherished, and when she reminisced, she wanted to feel the warmth of desire in her stomach. She wanted someone who would make her forget the selfish way Marcus had loved her, the forceful manner he took her for the last time, the way his breath reeked of whiskey and the way his sinister eyes filled her with fear.

Now when she envisioned love and intimacy, it was Bryce's face she saw. And to her that felt safe.

What would it take for her to admit she was falling for him? He had told her he would not cross any lines she didn't want him to cross. The nervousness she felt six weeks ago had vanished, and she was *dying* for the line to be crossed. But she would rather swim with sharks than admit that to anyone but her best friend.

It wasn't any easier for Bryce. He stared at the screen of the computer day in and day out thinking of her. What he felt reminded him of a sappy love song. Something about the best disease he ever caught and one he didn't want to cure. Besides Allie, nothing in his life felt so right.

Whether it was money, possessions or women, Bryce normally didn't get attached. Except for his minor mishap with Beth, the only thing in his life he allowed himself to miss was Allie. He loved his parents, and they shared a special bond, but he could go weeks without contact. They would call twice a week to talk to Allie without him feeling the need to catch up and vice versa. They knew where they stood with each other.

But he would be damned if this woman wasn't getting under his skin.

He ached to touch her and thought of making love to her on a constant basis. The anticipation of each date thrilled him but at the same time he was frustrated. She was beautiful and incredibly sexy. He wanted to taste her warmth, her heat, but once wouldn't be enough; he wanted to experience her love and tenderness the rest of his life. It would be pure torture to have it, then, God forbid, give it up again.

He had to be confident in her feelings for him before he took a risk that great. They had a strong foundation for a future together and he didn't want to screw it up by allowing his hormones to take over. It pleased him the way his body and his heart reacted when she was near, yet terrified him at the same time.

He wanted this, he reminded himself. It was time to settle down and have a real family. Before her, he spent nights wondering about the woman he was meant to spend his life with. Where she was, what she was doing, if she was safe, or if someone had broken her heart. Once he met Cammi, it all fell into place. He stopped wondering. From the first moment, he wanted to protect her and as time went on, the more powerful the feeling became.

Little by little she was opening up about her ex-husband. It was hard for Bryce to hear. Cammi was such a good person…. a sincere, genuine, honest to God woman, and she had not deserved to be treated the way she had. Marcus was a prick. In Bryce's eyes, men like that had no character, no balls.

If Bryce ever had the desire to beat the living hell out of someone, other than Cynthia, it would be Marcus. Not only had he cheated on Cammi, he'd emotionally beat her down for the entire three years they were together. Cammi dismissed it, and Bryce was sure there were things she was still not ready to admit, but he was definitely aware of the impact it had on her. The more he knew, the more he understood who she was. And he loved her in spite of it, wanted to love her more because of it.

Yes, he was definitely attached.

The ringing of his office phone jolted him out of his thoughts. As he checked the caller ID, he saw the call was from Wyoming. He wondered for a moment who would call his work line from Wyoming. If it was a work related call, the name usually showed up on caller ID, but this looked like a private cell number. Lost in his daydream, he opted to ignore it.

He promised to take Allie to the park for a picnic that evening. It was time to tell her about Cammi. He had plans, big plans, and it was time to start putting them into action.

The backpack of food weighed him down as they rode their bikes through the piles of burnt orange and yellow Aspen leaves. Allie had insisted on bringing the entire kitchen in case she changed her mind or wasn't in the mood for the sandwiches he made. *Such a typical woman,* he thought. Fall was his favorite time of year. It meant football, hunting and cooler weather. The aspen and maple trees were changing color as hints of red, orange, yellow and purple melted into the scenery. He couldn't think of anything more perfect than spending this time with his daughter. Well, okay, maybe one other thing, but he quickly refocused his attention.

Bryce hopped off his bike thinking he needed to get back into shape as beads of sweat trickled down his face. Allie laid her bike down next to the picnic table and sat cross-legged on the blanket her dad had spread out, elbows on her knees. Placing her hands under her chin she looked up at him adoringly while he pulled the sandwiches and chips out of the bag.

"How was school?" he asked making small talk.

"MMMM. Good," she mumbled with her mouth full.

"What did you have for lunch?" he teased.

"Dad!" Allie sang. "You *know*. You made it! Ham and cheese, a fruit roll up, Cheetos and that gross apple you cut up yesterday that I didn't eat."

Bryce laughed.

"Allie, can I ask you something?"

"I guess so. Is it serious? You look serious." Even though she was only six, she was very perceptive for her age.

He didn't want to worry her, but he also wanted her full attention.

"Sort of, but not in a bad way," he reassured her handing back the soda pop she gave him to open.

He hesitated, troubleshooting the best direction to take. "Look, we have always talked that someday I might find someone and get married. You know that has always been a possibility, right?"

Bryce was completely open with Allie about what the future might hold for them as a family. He wanted her to be confident she was the most important person in his life, but he also needed a best friend, a companion to grow old with. If he demanded her respect on the subject, he owed her that in return. He explained no one would take her place in his life. His love for her, time and attention would always be his focus, but he wanted to share his life with someone special. Discussing Cammi with Allie might be a bit premature, but he wanted to prepare her if something did happen.

"Sure," she replied. "Why?"

God, why was he so nervous? He cleared his throat. "I have been seeing someone, her name is Cammi. And I like her a lot. So much, that maybe in a few months, I would like you to meet her, if you want."

With lips pursed together, eyes squinted as if in hard thought, Allie looked up at him. He could see the dimple in her cheek that was just like his. Finally she asked, "Why do you like her?" The sunlight hit her eyes perfectly and the color of blue reminded him of a tropical ocean.

"I guess for lots of reasons, honey. She's smart, she's very nice, and she's pretty. She makes me laugh, I can tell her anything but mostly because she is proud of me for being your dad. I talk about you all the time and she really wants to get to know you. You are the most important thing in the world to me, and if a woman didn't want to hear about you, I couldn't be with her."

Cammi was selfless when it came to his time with Allie; in fact, she encouraged it, which pleased him. She agreed his daughter always came first, no matter what.

Allie smiled warmly at her dad. "Do you think she will like me?" she asked before taking another big bite of sandwich.

"I know she will. She is very loving. It will be a while before you meet her, though. She and I are still getting to know one another. She is not my girlfriend or anything, but she is pretty special," he reassured her. "If you get worried about it, or have any questions, you ask me, K?"

"K!" she shrugged taking a bit of her sandwich.

"Promise?" he asked holding out his fist.

"I promise, Daddy," she giggled touching her own curled up fist to his.

After they ate and Allie told him about Sam, the class clown getting in trouble in music today, she took off towards the slide, leaving him sitting there in awe. At six, he didn't want to confuse Allie with details of a relationship she wouldn't understand. All that mattered was she knew there was a chance someone important might come into their life and all she cared about was whether or not Cammi was going to like her. That was something Bryce could guarantee.

He shook his head watching as she landed on both feet at the bottom of the slide and giggled. Bryce truly loved being a dad and found more delight in his time with her than he thought possible. Luckily, he'd found a woman who could appreciate that, too.

Cammi was running behind. Bryce told her he would be there by seven, and of course, he was never late. She hadn't taken him seriously when he told her that, but learned early on that he was serious. Actually, he was never early either. *Always right on time*, she chuckled to herself.

Cammi decided tonight was going to be the night. Not knowing where she stood with him was driving her crazy. No matter how scared or how hard she wanted to protect herself, she needed to take a chance. They'd been tap dancing around this for eight weeks now. She was falling in love and ready to give him her heart. It was either move forward or allow her life to go in a different direction. Moving forward with him felt right and once she made up her mind, she very rarely backed out.

Bryce's mind, on the other hand, was preoccupied as he drove to pick her up. He was trying to find a way out of the inevitable.

There had been more phone calls that week from the Wyoming number. Figuring if it was important enough, the caller would leave a message so he hadn't answered but no voice mail was left. He assumed someone dialed the wrong number.

Out of curiosity, he picked it up when he saw the number displayed again the following day. It was a decision he wished he hadn't made. Bryce always considered himself to be an honest person, but cursed under his breath for the dilemma he was in. It wasn't as if he had intentionally hid Beth from Cammi, but because he moved past her long ago, it was something he would have eventually told her in time. But now he had to come clean with her. And he needed to do it tonight.

When Cammi opened the door, she immediately sensed something was off. He seemed tense, more quiet than normal. She had gotten used to seeing the appreciation on his face each time they met and disappointment settled inside her as she took note of his strained smile.

"You look beautiful," he said, his lips quickly brushing her cheek.

This was a side of him she hadn't seen before and because she wasn't sure how to react, she began to question herself. Could she have done something wrong? Had she misread his signals these past few months? Was he not interested? Flooded with insecurities, she tossed around the idea she might need to put off her conversation.

Bryce could tell his foul mood was affecting her. He didn't want her to think this was her fault. He worked so hard on earning her trust, and he knew this could blow it completely. That wasn't what he wanted. The knots in his stomach began to constrict his breathing.

An uncomfortable silence hung over them while they drove to the restaurant. With his mind muddled, it was hard to keep up with normal conversation so he was relieved when the waiter came to take their order. It gave him a minute to relax and compose himself. Figure out how he was going to say what he had to say.

He was so tense and worked up he opted not to order any alcohol and instead asked for iced tea. He needed to have all of his senses about him. Trying to ease the strain, he asked her about work but Cammi knew he wasn't really listening. He was somewhere else.

When the waiter placed their plates in front of them, Bryce was grateful for the distraction but the longer he put this off, the worse he felt.

Cammi's was slowly losing her appetite. She looked into Bryce blank face willing him to catch her eye as he toyed with his uneaten food. Each nerve-racking moment connected to the next until finally she shoved her plate away and ordered a glass of cognac. Maybe a couple sips of that would relax her enough so she could have a good time. Surely this was all in her head.

"Cammi, we need to talk," he said seriously learning forward in his chair.

His sudden announcement alarmed her. Cammi braced herself for the worst as her chest tightened.

"I haven't been completely honest with you about my past. I want you to know I wasn't trying to keep it from you, but just hadn't found the right time to tell you. I know that sounds like a lame excuse, but it's the truth. I don't ever want to hurt you, but I know if you are ever going to trust me, I need to be honest about everything," he began, his eyes pleading with hers.

As reassuring as his words were, they still made Cammi cringe. She felt like such a hypocrite knowing there were things she hadn't been entirely honest about either.

"About a year and a half ago, I dated a girl named Beth. To make a long story short, she broke up with me after a few months to move to Jackson with some oilfield worker boyfriend," he explained looking at his plate instead of her.

Cammi waited silently for him to continue.

"At the time I thought I was in love with her and even thought about proposing. What I took as serious; she thought of as a fling and when talk of the future was brought up, she got fidgety. A few days later there was a 'Dear John' note on my door. She was in love with someone else. Long story short…. I never heard from her again."

"Ironically, she did me a favor. A week later I pulled my head out of my ass and realized she was someone I *didn't* want to spend my life with. She was fun and attentive, made me feel like the sun rose and set with me, but she lacked compassion, sensitivity and morals. Besides, she had no interest in Allie. Thank God I never introduced them. And to be honest, we never had much to talk about. We were either out having a good time or having sex."

Cammi winced but caught herself before he saw how uncomfortable his statement made her.

"Once she was gone, I realized she was not what I wanted. I needed someone I could share stories with, share my daughter with, someone I could depend on and who could depend on me. Someone I could talk to forever…. about anything. And if we didn't talk, it wouldn't be awkward, we would be content silently. Do you know what I mean?" He asked staring across the table at her.

Holding her breath, Cammi nodded.

"Basically, I didn't miss her. I moved forward. I have no feelings for her one way or another. It is almost like she never existed."

"And you're telling me this because……?" Cammi didn't know what to say. "Please don't think I am rude, but I don't understand what you are getting at."

He sat up straight.

"She called me. It was a number I didn't recognize, so I never answered. Finally, I got curious. It was her," he blurted.

Cammi shifted her eyes awkwardly towards the floor.

"What did she want?" she asked quietly.

"I am not sure. She made small talk. Asked how I was. What I was doing with my life and filled me in on hers. She's planning to move back to town, says she thinks about me often, felt bad for the way things ended and wanted to apologize. That was it."

Cammi couldn't ignore the feeling of panic creeping up inside her as the picture of another woman wrapped in Bryce's arms tortured her.

"I figured I wouldn't hear from her again, but she called two more times in the past couple days."

"Of course she did," Cammi replied sarcastically. Bryce could sense she was putting the bricks, piece by piece, back around her heart.

Cammi hated this. She felt threatened, desperate and torn. Her mind and heart were locked in a power struggle, and it felt as if the two were going to suffocate her. The need to protect herself was more important right now than giving him the key. On the other hand, she had come this far, she didn't want to give up her dream or the promise she made to God.

"Did you tell her about us?" she asked simply, surprising herself.

Bryce looked straight into the eyes of the woman he'd been falling in love with the past few months. She'd become his best friend. The desire to tell her how he felt empowered him. But even more, he wanted… no, needed to know what she felt in return.

"Yes."

She felt the tension in her stomach loosen as the intensity of his answer brought tears to her eyes.

"Let's get out of here. We need to be alone," he suggested throwing some money on the table. He grabbed her hand pulling her quickly out of the restaurant behind him. They were out of breath and laughing by the time they reached the park, both anxious to say what was on their mind.

Cammi couldn't wait. She wasn't fearless, in fact she felt unsure since his story about Beth but the desire to take this leap of faith, to put all caution aside and jump in head first tugged at her mind, body and soul.

Side by side, they strolled silently in the moonlight, the stars above twinkling in approval.

"What is it you are trying to tell me, with Beth calling and all, what does this mean?"

"Beth calling means absolutely nothing. You are the only person who means anything." He interlaced his warm, strong fingers in hers as they walked. The gesture took her breath away, and she couldn't remember ever feeling this safe.

"I love being with you," he continued. "If I could...... I'd be with you all the time. When anything happens, you are the one I want to share it with. My biggest fear is scaring you away. I feel so much for you, but.....I don't know. I just don't want to make anything unpleasant." He stopped walking, turned to face her and put his hand gently on her cheek.

Leaning into his warm touch, Cammi smiled. She'd learned in this short time Bryce was private about matters of the heart but believed in only speaking the truth. This wasn't easy for him, and she admired and respected him for trying.

"You have no idea how grateful I am for that. You make me nervous, but in a good way. In fact," she laughed, blushing, "you have me.... I don't know how to explain it, but it's driving me crazy! I don't remember feeling this way, even in high school. At first I hated it because I had no control, but now I can't live without it."

They were both stepping out of their comfort zone and there was so much more to say when his cell phone unexpectedly interrupted them. Not wanting to be rude, Cammi stepped away to give him privacy while he talked to his mother. His parents were in town picking up supplies and agreed to sit with Allie while they went to dinner

"Allie's sick. Threw up all over the couch," he explained flipping closed his phone.

She understood his need to go but disappointment lingered over them on the drive to her apartment. The moment between them had disappeared and even though he still wanted to tell her, he needed to wait until he could make it special, not over the stress of a sick child.

After putting the car into park, he shifted in his seat to face her. Instinct told him to lean in and give her a kiss, but caution held him back. He didn't want their first initial physical contact to be under these circumstances. Nor did he want it to end. So once again, he gave her an awkward hug before she shut the door behind her.

It would be a few more days before he was able to see her again, and he felt cheated. They had gotten this far only to find they were shoved back to square one. He couldn't help but worry what might happen if he didn't explain himself soon, especially now with his past hanging over them.

Bryce stayed up to read Allie a couple books, but the events of the evening left him inattentive. Once her fever broke and she drifted off to sleep, he tucked her in and collapsed into his own bed. Reaching for the phone, he stopped himself short. He couldn't call. What he had to say wasn't going to be done over the phone.

How ignorant could he have been? To verbally share intimate details of his relationship with Beth. He could kick himself. Cammi tried to cover, but he could see the hurt in her eyes. What the hell was he thinking, especially knowing full well her ex had been unfaithful? He must look like a schmuck.

But regardless, she had said, "did you tell her about us?" That was enough proof she was ready and willing for more and with that idea alone, he allowed himself to drift into a peaceful sleep with visions of touching her occupying his mind.

Chapter Six

In her haste to get to the office before eight am, Cammi didn't have a chance to answer her landline as it rang. She had a vague memory of it ringing an hour earlier as she forced herself out of her slumber and into the shower. Whoever it was would surely call her cell phone if they were that desperate to get in touch with her.

Removing the key from the lock she hoisted her bag over her shoulder. Turning to the stairs she glanced briefly at her watch hoping she would have enough time to stop and fill her car with gas before the meeting she had so foolishly scheduled with Lamont.

Though Marcus had convinced her to quit her job the last year of their marriage, it was sheer luck and probably divine intervention the Denver Daily respected her work. Enough so that right before she moved to Madison, she'd begged Lamont for her job back and they agreed to staff her as a freelance journalist. Her reputation and writing skills over the last five years gained her access to stories that took most journalists months to obtain. Cammi was easily distracted at home and worked better in an office environment. Fortunately, the Madison Herald had an extra office they were able to rent out for her use. She kept her hours from ten to four unless she was traveling for a story. In that time, she was able to make necessary phone calls, write without interruptions and because her office was isolated from others, she was able to conduct normally difficult phone interviews.

Essentially she was her own boss and loved the freedom and flexibility it offered so she didn't mind when Lamont, the Denver Daily editor scheduled meetings with her twice a month. Lamont was boisterous and demanding, but Cammi had come to respect his efficient mind, dedication to his job and learned the rest was more for show.

Cammi cursed herself this morning for scheduling the appointment at eight instead of the usual ten o'clock. Sleep was hard to come by the night before. After Bryce dropped her off, she took her time getting ready for bed in the hopes he might call. She kept both phones by the bed waiting to hear them ring. But the call never came.

Neither did sleep. Just as she began to drift off, her mind would start to spin out of control. Thoughts of Bryce's lips touching hers, his hands passionately roaming and exploring her body as he removed her clothes sent a chill through her. But then her attention would shift to his past and with it anxiety filled her heart. She couldn't help thinking of him with Beth. He'd had sex with her. She didn't understand why it bothered her so much. He'd had sex with Allie's mother, but that hadn't made her uncomfortable. Maybe because she wasn't a possible threat and right now, she felt as if Beth was. She'd moved back to town after all.

The nightmares came and went as the night wore on and each time Cammi stole a look at the clock, the minutes passed excruciatingly slow. Finally around four, she was able to sleep soundly. When her alarm went off again at six-thirty she was comatose and it was seven-ten before the buzzing revived her.

Cammi rubbed her tired eyes. Running late irritated her, her dreams last night concerned her and she definitely wasn't in the mood for Lamont's chiding at her appearance. She knew she looked like hell. If she stopped to get gas, which she desperately needed to do since she had been running on fumes yesterday, it would put her at the office no earlier than at eight-fifteen. She'd better call Lamont. He didn't like to be kept waiting.

A nervous cough came from behind just as she reached into her bag for her cell. Jumping, her heart began to pound loudly against her chest, but when she turned, she was staring into a deep set of mischievous blue eyes.

"God, Bryce. You scared me to death."

"I'm sorry. I didn't mean to." Suddenly he felt awkward. "I…uh…I tried calling earlier. I wanted to see you." Eagerness filled his voice.

She looked deeper into his face and her heart fluttered at his appearance. On their dates, he was always casually dressed and she'd seen him in his suit and tie when they'd meet for lunch during the week, but still, her heart raced each time she laid eyes on him. He was so handsome….absolute man from head to toe.

"You okay?" he asked concern creasing his brow.

Distracted by the sight of him, she'd forgotten where she was for a moment and was filled with regret when she realized she wouldn't be able to stay.

"It's been a rough morning. I missed my alarm and I have a meeting with Lamont at eight. I'm running a bit behind."

"Oh." When Bryce woke, his first thought was of her. Every part of him ached to reach out to her. Allie was still sick and unable to go to school, so after dropping her off at Mrs. Newcombs, the babysitter, he headed over to Cammi's, calling the office to tell them he was going to be a few hours late. Usually Cammi's schedule was flexible so he had hoped he could talk her into breakfast. And maybe breakfast would turn into more.

She saw disappointment linger in his eyes and for a brief moment, she thought of calling off her meeting. She wanted nothing more than to continue where they had left off the evening before but knew it was impossible. Lamont drove from the city and it was close to the holiday season. They had tons of things to iron out.

Resting her hand on his arm she apologized. "I'm so sorry, I can't stay. Will you walk me to my car?"

She allowed her fingers to interlace with his strong, firm hand as they descended the stairs together in silence, neither knowing what to say, both in agreement that small talk wasn't going to suffice. He opened her car door for her. She threw her bag over the driver's seat into the passenger's side and she was about to crawl in behind the steering wheel when he grabbed her arm and pulled her against him in a tight embrace, his finger tips tickling the base of her neck.

Trembling with fear and exhilaration, he held her for several moments. Her body was warm and conformed to his perfectly. Instantly he could feel the rhythm of her heart speed up as he buried his head into her hair.

Cammi held her breath as her body weakened against the strength of his. In his arms she felt safe and couldn't help reacting to his touch. It was with great reluctance she detangled her arms from around him. She had to get to work. Never before had she hated her job as much as she did at this moment but when he gently moved his fingers to the back of her head where he brought her face up to meet his, she momentarily forgot about her job and Lamont. His eyes were filled with fiery passion, and she was sure he was going to kiss her. She wanted him to kiss her. Every part of her body ached for him to act.

His embrace softened and she held her breath as his thumb caressed her cheek. In his eyes was a plea for her to understand what his heart was saying. But he didn't kiss her. Instead he lowered his forehead to hers and sighed deeply.

He'd never wanted a woman more in his life than he did Cammi, and it took all the self control he had not to pick her up, throw her over his shoulder, and carry her back to the apartment into her bed.

"I better let you go," he grumbled.

Speechless, Cammi could only nod as she turned to stumble into her car.

Regretfully she drove away, stealing a glance into her rearview mirror. Watching as he sauntered to his truck, his hands shoved into his pockets, her heart was filled with a love she'd never quite experienced before.

It was a week before they saw each other again. Bryce was confined to working from home since Allie still had a sour stomach and ran a fever for three days. He was unable to escape even for lunch, so their relationship was limited to phone calls. Then on Wednesday Cammi had to leave for Chicago for an interview assignment.

They spoke whenever they had the chance, and he was constantly leaving voice mails to let her know he was thinking about her but both avoided the subject of their relationship.

Each time Cammi heard his voice, a shiver stole through her. The want and need for him shocked and delighted her, but alone in Chicago, she had time to think. Too much time maybe. And she didn't know if she was comfortable with the situation she found herself in.

As hard as she tried not to doubt herself or him, a little voice in the back of her head questioned whether Beth was still calling and wondered how Bryce felt about it. Cammi knew how women were, and Beth's intentions weren't just to apologize or set the record straight. Bryce may be unaware of it, but it wasn't going to be the last time he heard from Beth. She was slowly worming her way back into his life. And Cammi couldn't help but wonder what it was he felt.

Feelings of jealousy were a new experience for Cammi. Even when she found out Marcus had cheated, she was humiliated and outraged, but never jealous. By giving herself permission to fall in love with Bryce, she was going to experience a whole new set of emotions. Emotions she wasn't sure she knew how to handle. But she had to give him credit. It meant a great deal to her that he was honest about Beth. Most men would have thought it unimportant, but he continued to win her trust. His calls throughout the week reassured her, and she decided she needed to be honest too and tell him about the baby. It was only fair he know about her past.

Three hours before she boarded her plane to Denver, Bryce left her a message asking her to call the minute she got home. Her pulse quickened at the idea of seeing him.

Time was on her side. The plane landed thirty minutes ahead of schedule. She anxiously shoved the car into park before leaping out then bounced up the stairs to her apartment. As quickly as she could, she undressed and hopped into the shower, hoping with fingers crossed she would get to see him sooner than later.

Twenty minutes later, she stood in the tub, dripping wet when she heard a loud, persistent knocking at her door.

"Just a sec," she yelled wrapping a towel around her head.

It was probably Autumn. The two women had become close, as close as Cammi allowed anyone other than Jamie. Her quirky personality and artistic style intrigued her along with the onslaught of different guys she dated. Autumn's heart was as big as the smile on her face, but she didn't take crap from anyone, so when a potential boyfriend showed any signs of dysfunctional behavior, Autumn dumped him. Cammi envied her level head in a crisis and ability to stand up for herself. Something she was still working on and not completely at ease with. In an attempt to domesticate herself, Autumn convinced Cammi to take a cooking class at the city library early last spring. She was probably desperate to borrow a cup of sugar or an egg in an attempt to show off her culinary skills for one of her dates.

Cammi cinched the baby blue bathrobe around her waist and was towel drying her hair when she opened the door to find Bryce standing there with a sheepish grin on his face, two take out bags of Chinese food in one hand and a bouquet of wildflowers in the other.

"I was supposed to call you first, remember?" she scolded him teasingly. With the excitement of seeing him she forgot she was half naked with no make-up on.

It felt like years since he had last seen her. His heart took a giant leap in his chest when she opened the door and what a welcome sight she was! Trying to keep himself under control, he walked past her and set the bags on the kitchen table.

"You got a vase?" he asked rummaging through her cupboards. "I was bored. I worked half a day, so I picked up dinner and decided to come over and wait for you. I saw your car outside, so I didn't wait long," he explained finding it hard not to picture what was waiting for him underneath her robe.

He glanced over his shoulder at the food. "Is that okay?" he asked grinning, though food was the last thing on his mind.

She smiled back. “It’s a great idea. I’m starving, but I need to go get dressed first. Give me a quick minute.” She walked towards her bedroom.

The golden-orange hue of the sunset was shining through her living room window. It set the mood. Bryce struck a match to a couple candles she kept on her bookstand and turned the volume up on her stereo. The sweet melody of Josh Groban filled the air. It definitely wouldn’t have been his choice, but it would have to do. He found her in the bathroom still dressed in her robe, fingering gel into her hair when he slid his hand around her waist startling her.

“You dance?” he asked pulling her into his arms. His face was only inches away from hers as he looked deeply into her eyes and felt the warmth of her breath entwine with his. The curve of her body pressed tightly against his as he pulled her close. Back and forth they swayed in silence to the music. When the disc changed, she expected him to let her go, but was pleasantly surprised when he continued moving.

“Aerosmith, eh?” he chuckled. “A classic rock girl. Nice. I would have never guessed after that crap you just made me listen to. *You’re my Aa eh a eh angel*,” he crooned along with the music.

Resting her head against his shoulder, she enjoyed the soft, soothing sound of his voice and felt completely, totally content, though her heart was beating out of control being so close to him. “I love the serenade, but you better be careful. How do you ever expect to top that?”

“Like this,” he said sweeping her up into her arms and carrying her over to the bed.

“I want you,” he whispered into her ear. “I have from the first moment I saw you. I can barely stand it anymore. Tell me it’s okay, that you want me too,” he pleaded.

His lips brushed the side of her neck. Cammi felt a tingle rush up and down her spine as she tried to nod, but it was nearly impossible to breathe.

Gently he set her on the bed and hovered over her bringing his hand to her cheek. Transfixed, she stared into the depth of his blue eyes while his thumb caressed her soft skin. Using his other hand to steady himself, he leaned down bringing his body close to hers.

Cammi inched her face toward his, willing to accept what he was offering. When his lips finally came to hers, she melted into his arms returning the soft, slow kiss with great passion. The flavor of her lips was sweeter than anything Bryce ever tasted. The satisfaction to please her was astonishing.

She wrapped her arms around his neck. Slowly, he untied her robe watching as it slipped off her shoulders and was awestruck by her beauty. Her body was firm in all the right places. She was more enticing than he envisioned. Bending to kiss her shoulder, he shivered at the touch of her fingers sliding up the nape of his neck where they nestled in his hair.

Reluctantly, he released her but only for a moment to pull his shirt off. Cammi had imagined a million times how he looked underneath his clothes, but had no idea she would be this turned on. He was tall and lean, but athletic. Her hands stroked his back and her lips tickled his chest until she felt his muscles tighten.

His response to her was intense. The throbbing between his legs made him want to burst. As he unbuttoned his pants, his eyes never left hers. He wanted her body etched into his mind forever.

She clung to him while his hands explored every inch of her body. Cammi's fantasies of Bryce didn't even compare to the desire and passion she felt at this moment. He was giving her everything. She felt sexy, alive and wanted to give just as much. She didn't know a lover could be this unselfish.

A rush of emotion awakened her senses when he began to move inside her and she prayed she didn't do anything to end this magical moment. When they finally came together as one, Bryce made sure she came, not once, but twice, before he climaxed. Cammi had the overwhelming urge to cry. Never in her life had she felt such an intimate connection with another human being yet at the same time, an instant fear that she'd allowed someone this close consumed her.

Caught up in her emotion, Cammi kissed his cheek over and over, studying his profile as they lay together, his arm draped casually over her side. He was such a beautiful creature. Cammi was afraid to say anything for fear the flood gates to her soul would open, leaving her exposed and vulnerable, so instead she bit her lip to control the overpowering urge.

Exhausted, they finally dozed off. He woke her by caressing her stomach with his finger tips. Turning over to look at the clock, she realized it was almost eight. She couldn't believe they slept so long.

"I haven't told you my surprise yet," he said, pulling her back towards him as she tried to reach for her robe.

"Oh, yeah, I forgot. I figured *this* was my surprise. And the Chinese food of course," she replied planting several kisses up and down his jaw.

He rolled on top of her pinning her down, demanding her full attention. "Allie went with my parents for the weekend. I want to take you someplace special."

He wouldn't tell her what he had planned and while they ate, she questioned him, begging for a hint but he would not relent.

The bed and breakfast was sixty miles away. The aspens were beginning to lose their color and signs of the upcoming winter were starting to present themselves as the evening temperature dropped, and the days grew shorter.

Bryce and Cammi didn't care. They were satisfied spending their time in bed. When they weren't making love, they watched movies, went for hikes, ate and lay in each other's arms talking for hours, sharing their dreams. It was as if they were separated for too long by unseen forces and now, finally, their life together could begin.

But neither one was willing to confess their love. At moments Cammi wanted to tell him how she felt, but held back. She knew there was something else she needed to get off her chest first.

The following evening after a luxurious bubble bath, they sat on the bed wrapped in soft, flannel bathrobes eating the pizza that had been delivered. It was the right time; she knew it, but what if her confession was enough to send him running? She didn't want to lose him, but this was not something she could keep secret either. It had been years since she talked about it. The only person in her life who knew the truth was Jamie. That particular scar still festered at times and the idea of opening it up terrified her. Just thinking about it made her nauseous. But they could not have a future without him knowing the truth.

Bryce set his food down on the cardboard box and looked at her intently. "Why aren't you eating?"

"I have something to tell you," she began nervously.

In detail, she explained the story of her marriage to Marcus. The drugs, the gambling debts, and the affairs Bryce already knew about but he was shocked when she told him about the verbal attacks, the names he called her and the intimidation he used to control her every move.

Tears began to form in her eyes. "We hardly had sex any more. I was repulsed by him, kept my distance. It wasn't that he didn't try. I just knew how to avoid it. This infuriated him all the more. He made me pay in little subtle ways, such as belittling me in front of friends by calling me a prude. There was even one time he told a few of his buddies right in front of me that I was horrible in bed. He would interrogate me about everyone in my life because he was suspicious *I* was the one having an affair, and then sabotage the things important to me." Cammi shook her head. "There was this one time I was planning a surprise birthday party for Jamie. Well, just like everyone I loved, he hated Jamie the most because she took my time and energy away from him. It was the evening before her party, we only had one vehicle since I wasn't working and he informed me all of a sudden that he had to go to Colorado Springs for the weekend to prepare for an upcoming trial. He knew I had to use the vehicle to get all the food, decorations and the gifts over to Jamie's house by noon the following day. Shawn would have helped but with his job, it's not like I can just call him out of work and I could not tell Jamie, it was suppose to be a surprise. Marcus had access to a company vehicle, but refused to use it. We got into a huge fight which continued the following morning before he left. I spent the entire night in tears….. not over him…. never over him…. but because I was desperate not to have the party ruined. So I decided I was going to rent an SUV. Once he caught wind of that, he screamed at me for spending his hard earned money on my piece of shit friend and refused to let me use his card to rent the vehicle. You see, my name wasn't on the account and I didn't have much money of my own, only about twenty dollars in cash. I finally had to call Jamie, tell her what my plans had been and have her help me with her own party. I wanted to kill him. That's just one example. He played those sick, twisted mind games all the time. He would do anything to make me feel worthless."

"Anyway," Cammi continued. "He'd learned over time I didn't want him to touch me in anyway shape or form. And he didn't until one night a month before I left. We had gotten into a huge fight about my parents coming for a visit. He left the house after dinner all ticked off and when he came home around two in the morning, he was drunk, really drunk or high. Probably both. Anyways, he woke me up, yanked me out of bed yelling, pushing me around, calling me a whore and demanding to know who my boyfriend was. I grabbed a pillow and blanket so I could go sleep in the guest bedroom but before I could lock the door, he shoved it open and threw me back on the bed." Cammi looked down at her trembling hands. "He….um, he……" Cammi could not get the words out, but Bryce knew what happened next.

Shoving the pizza box out of the way, he inched closer and embraced her. Cammi's whole body trembled, though she refused to cry.

"There's more, Bryce," Cammi said pulling back. Images of the past threatened to make their way to the surface but she shook them away the way she had trained herself to do.

"Did he hit you?"

Cammi shook her head. "No. I had bruises on my arms and inner thighs where he pinned me down, but no, he didn't hit me. I bit him and drew blood. But he never hit me. I fought as much as I could, but Marcus is a really big guy."

"Did you report it?"

Dropping her head into her hands, she shook her head again. "I didn't know what to do. I called Jamie. She tried to get me to call the cops but I just couldn't. I was his wife you know. They wouldn't have believed me."

"But you had bruises!"Bryce exclaimed.

"I know, but I couldn't wrap my head around it. I'm sorry. I….I….I should have, I know I should have, but I didn't," she stammered.

"I'm sorry," Bryce said pulling her to him again. "I'm not mad at you. I want to kill *him*. I want to make *him* pay for what he did to you."

Cammi looked into his eyes. "Bryce, there was a baby," she whispered.

He looked as if she slapped him in the face.

"I was making plans to leave, and then *WHAM*! A baby. I also found out he gave me an STD and caught him having sex with my best friend all in a matter of two days," she hurried to explain. "The idea of having his child was horrific. I didn't want any ties or memories of that life. I was going to start over, but I didn't have any money either. It was too much. I couldn't handle it all," she cried. "I knew I could not be a mother. Not then. I could hardly take care of myself. Not only was I an emotional mess, I had an STD and Lord knows what else. I was only four weeks along." Cammi could not look at him. "I had an abortion," she whispered.

She began to sob harder now. "You must think I am a monster."

Bryce wasn't sure what to think. The story hadn't quite sunk in, but he knew he was angry, that was for sure. But was he angry with her? He didn't think so. Marcus? Definitely. Letting go of her, he stood up and went to the window to look out across the view of the Rocky Mountains. He loved her. That is all he could think about. He loved her, and he wanted to show her, give her a life different than the one she had before. That was five years ago. He didn't know her then. He could not imagine what it was like for her. But he knew her now. And what he knew…. he loved.

"I don't think you're a monster," he said quietly, his back still to her. "I think you went through hell and made the best choice you could in a very bad situation."

She sat quietly watching him, wondering what was going on in his head, wondering if she'd just made the worst mistake of her life. But she had to tell him the truth, he deserved to know who she was, what she'd been…. if they intended to move forward.

"What about your family?" his voice broke the silence.

"I didn't tell them. Not the entire truth. It was too humiliating. They knew about his affairs and I left it at that. You need to understand Bryce, I am an incredibly private person, and airing this….people would talk. I couldn't handle that. Not after everything else. I don't know if I will ever tell them."

Thinking about the embarrassment he felt when it came to Cynthia, he could sympathize with her.

"Eventually I got over the guilt and figured it is what it is. I wasn't supposed to have children with Marcus…. he didn't want them anyway. And I wasn't supposed to have a child then. For years I wondered if I made the right decision. I may never know, but I can't change it. Without this experience I wouldn't be me. It gave me the desire to heal. To grow, mature. I had to, I couldn't stay where I was, it was miserable and lonely, and I wasn't going to let Marcus win."

Bryce grew silent again. She was waiting for him to tell her he'd made a mistake, and she wasn't the person he thought, but he didn't. Instead, he made his way back to where she sat curled up in a ball on the floor and scooped her into his arms. Pressing his lips to her forehead he carried her to the bed.

"I'm glad you told me. Why did you wait?"

She shrugged. "Pride, fear, hell…. just about everything. It's not exactly the story you tell on a first date. I'd expect you to run," she said with a slight laugh.

"You didn't run and look at the crazy shit I told you," he reminded her. "You were between a rock and a hard place without many choices. We don't always make the most rational decisions, we just try to survive. He put you through hell, and you were what…..twenty-three, maybe four? That's awful young to deal with that sort of trauma all on your own."

She pulled him close, allowing herself to feel the comfort of his warm embrace. There was something to be said about having the support of a handsome, strong man. Something she definitely could get used to, she thought. It was such a relief, getting it off her chest. *And* she let him in. She didn't know how, but she did it. She opened her heart and let him crawl right in and settle down. Hopefully, he would never want to leave.

He was hovering over her, his face only inches from her own, caressing her brow with his fingertips. "What about now. Do you want more children?" he asked.

His question stunned her. "Yeah, I do. I think about it quite a bit actually," she admitted. "I don't deny the fact it may be difficult, but I will not punish myself by not embracing the joy of being a mother."

Bryce was relieved to know where she stood on the subject. Not only because of the daughter he had now, but for the future. He wanted to kill her ex husband. What sort of sorry excuse for a man treated a beautiful woman that way? Not just any beautiful woman. This was Cammi, the most sensual, incredible female he'd ever laid eyes on. Marcus's loss was his gain. Fate had dealt her a horrible blow, but he was convinced they were brought together because of it. No wonder she was so damn scared.

The rest of the evening was more incredible than the one before and when it was time for them to get some sleep, Cammi slowly closed her eyes as she relaxed to the rhythm of his breathing. She was grateful for the direction her life was going and she was sure Bryce was the man God intended her to share it with. Her dreams were coming true. The past was behind her. She was proud of whom she had become, not only for her sake, but for Bryce's, and as she curled up in his arms, content for the first time in years, she willingly indulged in the unspoken love they shared.

Chapter Seven

Monday morning after their weekend away, Cammi was greeted with an e-mail from Bryce first thing when she turned on her laptop.

Hey Baby,

I miss you so much already. I can't stand to be apart from you. I truly enjoyed leaving our worries behind and spending some fun, quality time with one another. I really do enjoy being with you, Cammi. I woke up this morning.....only to find that you weren't by my side, and it made me sad. I want you to know how truly glad I am you came into my life, and how thankful I am to be a part of yours. I will think of you often today and each time I do, it will bring a smile to my face.

Bryce

They had both been miserable when he dropped her off the evening before. Not knowing when she would see him again tore at her heart.

She read and reread the e-mail until the she'd memorized each and every word. Then she printed it off and took it home so she could read it as she fell asleep. His words were something she would cherish forever.

With a six year old daughter, overnights were near to impossible, so Bryce and Cammi spent the next few weeks sneaking in lunches at her apartment, his office, where ever they could find a secluded, private spot. Cammi felt like a rebellious teenager teetering on the brink of something dangerous. And she loved it. She felt alive for the first time in years.

A change had come over Bryce, also. Over the years family and friends had gotten used to the happy front he kept up in public, but at home, alone with Allie, sadness hovered over him. Bryce knew he was an involved and attentive parent, but he was often forlorn. The sadness was gone now, replaced by something else.

Bryce continued to tell Allie more and more about Cammi in hopes one day soon they would meet, but he was waiting for the perfect moment.

Allie also noticed the change in her father and told him so at dinner a week later. She was sitting at the small kitchen table working on writing her letters while he stood over the stove frying pieces of chicken. He had his music turned up loud and was singing along to it, a quirky smile on his face.

"You smile more," she told him. "You're sillier too."

"Is sillier even a word?" he asked in a teasing tone.

Allie shrugged her shoulders. "How would I know? I'm only in first grade."

Bryce laughed.

Allie could not wait to have another girl around. Her dad was fun for fishing, tackle football and shooting hoops in the driveway, but she wanted someone to do girl things with. Grandma was great and Allie loved her but she was old. And Mrs. Newcomb…..well, Allie could only win at Go-Fish and Slap Jack so many times.

In her first grade class at Emerson Elementary, she had a new teacher's aide, and she was super nice. But Ms. Nelson wasn't her dad's girlfriend and Allie wanted more than anything to have Cammi come to the house. She wanted to show off her bedroom and have a tea party with the set she got for her birthday. Maybe if Cammi was around, her stomachaches would stop. Grandma said she had them because she was stressed. Maybe Cammi would help her build a tent and they could play house or maybe if she liked to ride bikes they could go to the park and swing on the swings really, really high. Allie envisioned her dad's girlfriend sitting with her under the trees at the park, the ones with the really big trunks, reading Junie B Jones or Magic Tree House books. Allie loved to read. Then when they came home, they could play with her princess dress-up clothes and pretend they were the two princesses who escape from the evil troll.

Allie liked being a princess. That is what her dad called her. She used to pretend that the Queen would come home after a long trip with her other Queen friends to be with them. She would bring them jewelry from other lands, food she bought off peasants, and the royal subjects would throw a huge feast. The King and Queen would dance for hours while, she, the princess, would meet a handsome prince, and they would run off to the forest to play with all the animals.

But now she imagined Cammi as the Queen, and of course, her dad was the King. But she didn't want a handsome prince to take her to the forest to play. Not yet. She wanted it to be the three of them for a long, long time so they could live happily ever after.

Her dad told her she had a very vivid imagination. She liked to make up stories with him before bed time. But more than that, she loved her animals. She had a Siamese cat, Tiffany and a German Short Hair dog, Diesel (her dad picked that name) as well as two goldfish, Nemo and Dori. If it were up to her she would have two more small dogs, a pet garble, and a rabbit she would call Hoppity.

Life was perfect. Except she wanted a mom. Dad said her real mom had *issues*, whatever those were and was not a good role model. Allie sort of remembered her. She had a picture of her on her nightstand, next to her bed. She was real pretty with long curly blonde hair and big eyes. Everyone said Allie looked like her, but she overheard her dad tell her grandma one time he hoped she didn't grow up to act like her.

Maybe Cammi would want to be her mom, Allie thought stealing a sideways glance at her dad who was back to singing out loud. Allie could not help but laugh at him. He threw a cut up potato her way. She picked it up and threw it back then went back tracing the letter B on her paper.

Yes, Allie thought, it would be really nice to have another girl around. Maybe one who would want to cuddle while watching movies and even come to her class to help with projects like Heather's mom.

Call waiting beeped while Bryce was telling Cammi about Allie's traumatic day. Apparently Allie came home from school all worked up because her best friend Heather's mom was going to have a baby after the first of the year.

"You said a stork dropped them off on the porch," she had accused Bryce. Cammi was laughing uncontrollably as he explained Allie's reaction to Heather's version of where babies came from. "And she wasn't too far from the truth," he chuckled. "Hold on," he said before clicking over.

Cammi was still giggling when he returned. "I can't believe she actually told you word for word what Heather said," she chuckled.

"Yeah," he said dully.

"What's wrong?" she asked apprehensively, noticing the change in his voice.

"Nothing."

"Don't screw with a woman's intuition," she teased lightly. "I know you and can tell when you're upset."

Cammi's stomach tightened at his continued silence. She learned not to ignore her gut reaction and this time it was telling her something was off.

"That was Beth," he announced. It had been almost two months since he heard from her and Bryce honestly believed he wouldn't again.

Cammi's heart caught in her throat. "What did she want?" Curiosity overwhelmed any desire she had not to know the answer. "And how did she get your cell number to begin with anyway."

"I don't know," he said honestly. "She asked me to go to lunch."

"You're kidding right?" Any confidence she had in her relationship with Bryce was slowly deteriorating, bit by bit. "What did you tell her?"

"I said I would have to check with you before *we* set a date to meet her."

Cammi understood he was trying to put her mind at ease, but the mere fact he was even considering it put her in a panic. She had no desire to meet the woman, let alone have lunch with her. It was bad enough she moved back to town and *now* she was meddling in his life. And why would he even want to see her?

It made her sick to know another woman, besides herself had shared not only his life but his bed, too. Not to mention he'd actually considered proposing. It all made Cammi very concerned. Of course he had a past just as she did, and eventually she would have to get used to it, but she couldn't shake the uncomfortable insecurity washing over her.

Bryce felt the tension through the phone. She had every right to be upset. If her ex came to town wanting to see her, he certainly wouldn't like it. Granted her ex was a little worse than his, but still.

"Look Bryce, I am not telling you what to do, but personally, I don't want to have lunch with her. If you feel the need to, it is entirely up to you, but I don't want to go!"

"Hell, I don't want to see her, and I definitely won't go if you aren't with me. End of conversation, okay?"

Cammi was reassured for the moment, but over the course of a few days, she began to feel unsettled as fear consumed her thoughts. *What did Beth want? There must be a part of Bryce that is curious about seeing her otherwise he would have just told Beth 'no' without consulting me. Maybe he wants to make her jealous. Or maybe he wants to make me jealous.*

There were women who would stop at nothing to get what they wanted. They didn't care who they hurt or what family they broke apart when it came to love. Could Beth be one of them or was she sincerely trying to make amends? Cammi seriously doubted it. She'd spent years breaking down her defenses in order to trust others, especially women and now she felt her old self taking control to protect her heart.

Bryce noticed the change, too. She was less affectionate and emotionally distant. He refused all of Beth's invitations to see him. Maybe it was a mistake to be so honest with Cammi each time Beth called, and now Beth was calling every day, but he didn't see any other way around it. Nevertheless, the uncertainty continued to loom around his relationship with Cammi. Hopefully with time, she would see he didn't care about Beth and would let this nonsense go.

A distraction is what they needed. A step in a better direction, so Bryce finally set up a special dinner at his house to introduce Cammi to Allie, hoping the action would reassure her where his commitments lay.

But Cammi was hesitant. It was a huge step. As much as she wanted it, she couldn't help but wonder what the outcome would be. What if Allie didn't like her? What if she didn't want a woman in her dad's life? Or her life, for that matter. Maybe she was happy with the way things were. And what about Beth? Was she to blind to see what was really going on? As much as she wanted to trust Bryce, she was beginning to panic.

The evening was fantastic. Better than they all imagined. Allie was everything Bryce said plus more. She was respectful, funny, incredibly intelligent and wise for her age, but the one thing that struck Cammi the most was she was happy. It amazed her how a single man could raise such a prize.

It was the first time Cammi had been to his house and once again, she was delightfully impressed. It was an old two story Colonial home with a wraparound porch and a spacious lawn about five blocks from the house where she'd been raised. Aspen and lodgepole pine trees along with one weeping willow surrounded his yard. Just out the back door through the kitchen, Cammi could hear the bubbling water of the river she'd spent years playing in as a child.

He bought the house when Allie was two and spent each year making a different room his special project until he'd finally felt it was good enough to call home. At the present moment, he was building a tree house in the backyard.

Bryce had grilled steaks while Allie helped mix the salad. After an enjoyable dinner listening to Allie talk about the upcoming Thanksgiving program and dance classes, they played a game of Candyland and then UNO. Cammi and Allie took turns winning while a competitive Bryce pouted over his losses. Cammi hadn't expected to have so much fun and found she was disappointed when it was time for Allie to go to bed and her to go home.

Bryce didn't want her to leave either. Saying good-bye at the end of a date was the hardest part of their relationship, especially after their weekend together in the mountains. He wanted her to be a part of their family, and it killed him not knowing when he was going to see her again. Things were close to perfect, but he needed more of her. His patience was beginning to wear thin.

"Can you come over tomorrow?" Allie asked as they cleaned up the games. "So we can play again?"

"If you want me to, I had a blast," Cammi said handing Bryce the deck of cards. "Maybe you can give your dad a bit of that luck you seemed to have tonight."

They giggled at Bryce's frown. "Oh, it's not luck. Really, you just have to know how to play the game," she said proudly. "You're pretty. Just like Daddy said." She walked over to Cammi, stood on her tiptoes, and gave her a quick peck on the cheek. "See you tomorrow." And off she bounced up the stairs without a care in the world, leaving Cammi with tears in her eyes.

In that moment, Cammi fell in love for a second time.

Allie's school was having their annual sock hop and she begged her dad to bring Cammi along. But regretfully, she had to decline. She had a deadline she had to meet before eight PM, but promised to meet them for ice cream after. Bryce didn't know who was more bummed, he or Allie. This would have been their first chance to go out in public like a real family. Their time together at his house over the last few weeks didn't compare to the life he had mapped out for them.

The sock hop was a chance for the parents to interact with the teachers, and he would have loved for Cammi to be involved in something so important to Allie. Instead of being disappointed though, he focused on having a great night with his daughter.

Bryce was especially interested in meeting Ms. Nelson. She was making quite an impression on Allie, and he wanted to thank her for the influence she'd been having on her. Allie was now taking her time to sound out the words as she read instead of trying to rush through them and though she still hated math, she was working diligently on it every night.

"Dad, she is nice and spends more time with me than the other kids. She loves to read and taught me this really cool trick to subtract." Allie's favorite thing in the whole world was reading. Bryce was glad to know she enjoyed school and was getting such positive encouragement from the teachers.

The sixties music blared from speakers around the school gym. Allie scanned the crowd looking for her friends Heather and Brandi, while adults and children of all ages gathered around various games in hopes of taking home a prize. She grabbed her dad's hand pulling him across the room with her.

"Dad, Dad," she said excitedly, "you have to come meet Ms. Nelson. Look, there she is!"

Bryce, distracted by the noise, turned to stare in the direction his daughter was pointing. It was hard to see exactly who she was pointing out in the crowd, but as the people dispersed, he squinted to get a closer look at someone he found vaguely familiar.

To his dismay, found himself looking directly at Beth.

Bryce's heart sank. He had no idea what was going on but had a feeling he wasn't going to like it.

Beth looked exactly as she did a year earlier. She was tall and thin, almost too thin with sharp boyish features which stood out more prominently since she had cut her blonde hair short. As he looked at her, he wondered what it was he ever found attractive about her.

Her face lit up the instant she caught his eye, and Bryce wished he could hide.

"I wondered if you would be here," she said once she reached them. Taking him in from head to toe she squealed then threw her arms around his neck. "It's good to see you."

"I'm surprised to see you," he replied dryly untangling himself from her embrace. He was relieved Cammi opted not to come. This was the last thing he wanted her to witness.

Allie looked up at them both very confused. "Do you know my daddy?" she asked Ms. Nelson.

Beth bent down to look Allie in the eye. "Your daddy and I were friends a long time ago," she answered sweetly. "Weren't we, Bryce?"

This was a side of Beth he had never seen, this nurturing, caring adult talking to his daughter like she was the most important thing in the world. And it was a side he didn't trust.

"That's great!" she exclaimed jumping up and down. "Cause then you can be my friend *and* daddy's too. Isn't that right?" she asked with wide, innocent eyes.

Bryce wanted to knock the sly grin right off Beth's face.

He may be a day late, but it didn't take him long to figure out what was going on. How dare she use his daughter to get close to him? How dare she put him in a position to disappoint or hurt Allie because of her scheming?

Beth stepped away. When they were dating, she had never seen him angry, but she was able to tell from the frigid look on Bryce's face that he was more than just a little upset.

Getting a job in the same school Allie went to was the first step in her plan to win Bryce back. She knew he was head over heels in love with her when she left, even talking about marriage, so it would only be a matter of time before those buried emotions came back. She was sure of it. At the time, she hadn't felt the same way about him, in fact she thought she was in love with someone else. Bryce's plans for the future freaked her out, so she took off to Wyoming as fast as she could. It was the biggest mistake she ever made. Her so-called boyfriend was thrilled about her move but not so thrilled when she demanded he change his lifestyle. He laughed at her expense and ever so graciously offered her a job as a stripper at the club in which he was part owner. Beth was hard up, but not that hard up. She refused to strip, but he kept her around, using her for money and sex. When the money ran out, he just used her for sex. She stayed with him for a year until she realized that he didn't love her the way she loved him. Eventually she moved in with her brother and had been trying to get back on her feet since.

Bryce was the best thing that happened to her, and she had screwed it up. Her friends said she was crazy to let a good catch get away. He was handsome, smart, and financially stable. He would give her the life she wanted. She wasn't crazy about becoming an instant mother, but would do what she had to, to get the life, and the man she deserved.

Bryce took Allie by the hand and walked away, leaving Beth stunned and staring after them. It had been so sudden when she left town last year, she was sure he had been hurt and angry. Of course it would take time for him to come around, but she was a determined woman who wasn't going to give up.

Chapter Eight

Bryce usually considered himself easy going, but knew he could be quick to anger when pushed too far. And now he'd been pushed *way* too far. Inside he was fuming, but remained calm enough to ensure he didn't ruin Allie's night. She was puzzled but all was forgotten after she found Heather and Brandi by the bean bag toss. He would figure out something to tell her so she didn't wind up in the middle of conflict, but how in the world was he going to explain this to Cammi?

Thankfully, Beth kept her distance from him the rest of the evening but on more than one occasion, he could feel her intent stare as he moved around the gymnasium.

On the way home, Allie's curiosity got the best of her.

"You don't like Ms. Nelson," she commented.

Bryce sighed. "Look… she is a teacher's aide in your class and very helpful to you. I understand that. I am sure she is great at it, but I don't think she is a very good friend. She made some not so nice choices, and I don't want to be friends with her anymore. I hope you can respect my decision."

"Oh…okay," she agreed, but he could hear the disappointment in her voice.

Thankfully the subject was dropped the minute she saw Cammi waiting for them on the porch with a gallon of ice cream, Allie's favorite…cookie dough. He waited until she was tucked into bed and fast asleep before he dropped the bomb. The calm, coldness of Cammi's voice caught him off guard. He expected her to be mad, even yell or scream, but her nonchalant attitude was something he didn't know how to handle.

"What do what you want me to say," Cammi asked. "That I'm surprised? I told you she had ulterior motives."

Cammi was not ignorant to the fact Bryce still had feelings for Beth when she left town a year ago, and she was certain Beth was hoping her reappearance would make those feelings resurface. Maybe he hadn't fallen out of love with her but instead buried what he wasn't able to act on.

The thought of it hurt, but Cammi wasn't going to allow him see her weak or lead him to believe she cared enough to let this bother her. Nor was she going to fight a losing battle. He was an amazing man, and she wanted to spend the rest of her life with him, but if letting him go to find true happiness was something she needed to do, than she wanted to prepare before she ended up with a broken heart. She had enough dignity and self-respect to do what was right and convincing someone to love her wasn't the type of love she wanted.

"Tell me what you're thinking," he asked taking her hand and linking their fingers together.

"What I think doesn't matter in this situation, what matters is what is going to make you happy. I can't make a decision for you," she said standing up and removing her hand from his.

"Exactly what sort of decision do you think I need to make here?" he demanded, his voice growing dark. Her insinuation mystified him.

"Look, I'm fine. I don't see why we need to talk about this anymore," she snapped. "You were honest with me, I appreciate that. Can we just drop it?"

She wanted out of there fast. A lump was forming at the base of her throat and if she didn't get away soon to be by herself, she was going to burst into tears, something else she refused to do in front of him. It was bad enough she'd let him see her cry like a baby the night she told him about her past. She'd felt like an idiot for it and promised herself never to do it again, especially under circumstances like this.

Bryce knew pushing her wasn't going to help, so he did as she asked and dropped it. He wrapped his arms around her, but her stiffness frightened him. Something he had no control over was coming between them. It was obvious she was pushing him away to protect herself. He was supposed to be the one to protect her, not the guy who was responsible for the pain. If he could turn the clock back a month, he would see to it that this turned out differently. But as it was, he felt helpless.

*****

Unfortunately, it was turning out exactly as planned. Beth's plan that is and Cammi and Bryce were falling into her trap without even knowing it.

What little time they did spend together was tense. Cammi was withdrawn and moody. Bryce tried everything he could to reach her, but Beth was using every tactic she could to form this invisible wedge between the two.

At least now, Bryce could figure out how she found his number. It was in the school records. And Beth used it to her advantage, calling two or three times a day at the most inopportune moments, usually when he was alone with Cammi. She sent home notes for Allie to give to her dad, and furthermore, Allie was becoming more attached to her as the weeks went by. It wasn't unusual for Ms. Nelson's name to be brought up continuously during their time together. But Allie was too young to understand, let alone realize Cammi's feelings were hurt.

Then, as luck would have it, Beth began to stop by the house on her 'evening walks'. Last week it was three times and this week twice. Conveniently, it was always after Allie was in bed, though she tried to use the little girl as an excuse a few times.

Bryce tried to be polite, but found he was making up excuses to get rid of her. The good and bad of it was Cammi was usually there, so Beth left of her own free will but her persistence was driving him crazy. Cammi never asked questions and when he did attempt to explain, she blew it off, but slowly the trust he had earned was beginning to disappear.

The final straw was the night she showed up as Bryce and Cammi were standing on his front porch saying their good-byes. It made Bryce sick to his stomach wondering what Cammi must be thinking. Seeing the anguish on her face when she saw Beth walk up the porch steps made him ache. Hastily, she dropped his hand and shoved past Beth to her car without saying another word.

"What the hell do you think you are doing?" Bryce growled. Taking a step towards Beth, anger seeped out his every pore while he watched his girlfriend speed away. If Allie weren't already in bed, he would have put her in his car and gone after Cammi. As it was, he would just have to call later.

She put her hand up to stop him. "Truce, okay? It's obvious to me you have a girlfriend, but I don't understand what's wrong with her. She is obviously threatened by something. Good grief…. I'm only an old friend. It's harmless." Though his rage was frightening, she dared to step a few inches closer. "I'm sorry I make her so jealous," she pointed out looking at him with a bright, flirtatious smile.

Her devious tactic didn't work. With a grunt, he turned away and stormed into the house. But she was right behind him. When he tried to shut the door, she quickly inched her way through it.

"Bryce, I hardly know anyone here. Come on. Is it really so wrong of me to want you as a friend?" she pouted glancing around curiously.

Bryce stood in front of her, his arms crossed, legs spread wide to keep her from moving past him further into the house. Beth shuddered. With the combination of his height and strong physique along with the obvious irritation in his face, Bryce truly could be a frightening man. One most people probably would not cross.

"Yes, especially when you have no respect for my girlfriend, my daughter or me. My life's changed and you are not a part of it. If you truly want to be my friend, you will respect what I want, which is to have you stay the hell away."

Beth decided she was not going to be intimidated so easily. She knew from experience Bryce had a gentle side, and she was determined to bring out the best in him once again. "Bryce, we were good together, and you know it. There was so much physical chemistry between us," she said resting her hand on his chest. "The best I ever had."

It disgusted him to even think about it. There was only one woman he ever wanted to remember being intimate with, and it wasn't her.

"We could be good together again, if you would give it a chance," she added when he didn't respond. Sliding her hand down his torso, she reached for his fingers, while her other hand moved up, seductively caressing the stubble on his cheek. Standing on her tip toes, she brought her lip inches from his.

Bryce had enough. He grabbed both her arms and using as much power as he was willing to allow without hurting her, he pushed her away.

"I will tell you this once and you better listen good. You pull a stunt like this again and I will make sure you lose your job. The only reason I haven't called the school yet to report your harassment is because I am a decent human being. Get your life together. It was never my problem, and it isn't now. Don't call me. Don't stop by here, and if I find out you have anything to do with my daughter more than your assigned duties at school, there will be hell to pay. Do you understand?"

The look is his eyes warned Beth he was serious. But as they stood there staring at one another, he could tell she was too. It worried him she wasn't going to take defeat lightly.

Bryce was still shaking with anger when he dialed Cammi's number. She didn't answer her cell or the home phone so he left a message on both.

Damn, he would give anything to see her and explain this nonsense. He couldn't let another day go by allowing her to believe whatever crazy thoughts were swimming around in her head.

The circumstances with Beth were pouring salt on wounds that hadn't entirely healed. It couldn't have been easy for Cammi to find out the truth about her ex's infidelity. Love or no love, that's a betrayal hard to recover from and now Beth was here arousing her demons.

It scared him to death to watch her slipping out of his grasp. Aside from the demands he's already made, he truly felt helpless about getting Beth out of his life. He could not make it clearer he despised her and his threat about calling the school was serious, but he hoped he wouldn't have to take such drastic measures. Hopefully, she would just disappear.

The red light blinked announcing she had a message but Cammi couldn't bring herself to listen to it. She needed more time to sort out her feelings before she reacted.

Why was this happening? She finally trusted herself to open her heart, finally allowed love in her life. It wasn't supposed to happen this way and she certainly didn't expect it to hurt so badly. She needed to forget him and move on. No way was she going to be second in a man's life….not again…..not ever. She deserved better than that.

Only it wasn't that easy. She had said she would work through anything but was *this*….. was *Beth* really part of the deal?

What the hell was he doing? She knew he felt something for her, so why was he allowing Beth to play games? Granted, they hadn't made any sort of commitment. They were only dating. But he told her he wasn't interested in Beth, so why was she still showing up at his house? Was he being honest with her or was he leading them both on? Did he really know what it was he wanted?

These were the questions Cammi refused to ask him. For one thing, she didn't want to come across as possessive, but she also didn't know if she was ready to hear the answers. He seemed more involved in their relationship than ever, but what did that really mean? She knew many men who wanted the best of both worlds and knew how to play it to their advantage. Why should Bryce be any different?

Because! Because he *was* different. He's the one, the one God brought to her, the one she was praying for. The most genuine, considerate, loving man she'd ever met. Or was it truly possible for such a being to exist. When it came down to it, maybe all men really were the same.

No, Bryce had had plenty of opportunity in the past to deceive her. But he hadn't. He was honest to a fault. Could she have been wrong?

Cammi felt the insight, faith and trust she worked so hard to find were slipping away. She prayed constantly but felt disconnected. She didn't like to be afraid or helplessly out of control. It was much easier to look at his faults and convince herself she needed to get him out of her life by keeping her distance. That was the only way she could stop this horrible pain threatening to rip her world apart.

But no matter how she looked at it, the one she was the angriest with, was herself. She'd come so far, was it possible she had made another stupid mistake like she had with Marcus?

Chapter Nine

She looked left, then right and behind her shoulder, turning in circles, past the doors and windows of her old loft, the one she shared with Marcus. She ran from room to room, but she still couldn't find him. It was Bryce she was looking for. Bryce she felt in her heart. She called, left messages, sent e-mails. But he never responded. It seemed like days had passed, then months. Maybe even a year. Yet, out of desperation she continued to search. Where was he? He was supposed to be with her, love her. She was frantic, she had to find him. Only he could fill her needs, love her the way she wanted to be loved.

She ran. Ran all the way across town. In a daze, she walked up the steps until she opened the door to his house. Finally she was able to breathe a sigh of relief. He was there. Taking her into his arms, he pressed his lips against hers but it didn't feel right. He was kissing her too roughly, not the gentle way she was used to. His lips felt huge, swollen, like sandpaper, and seemed to engulf her face. Repulsed, she pushed away and saw Marcus standing in front of her. No! No! Where was Bryce? She shook her head trying to dismiss the image and touch of the man who betrayed her, the man who did not respect her, and the man who hurt her. Loneliness seeped through the core of her being. She ran down the basement steps in search of Bryce and waiting for her again was Marcus. She cried out and turned to run upstairs, anywhere to get away from him. She didn't want him, she wanted Bryce.

Bryce! She called out. Please, where are you? I need you!

Chilled by a cold sweat, Cammi at up in bed and looked at the clock. It was too early, still dark. The sun was not even touching the horizon. Lying back down, Cammi tried to bring her herself back to the present but she could not shake the images from her mind. After another hour of restlessness, she'd finally dozed off and now the alarm startled her into a state of confusion. The emptiness she felt in her dream clung to her as she drug herself out of bed and There was no good reason to get out of bed, so she fell back against the pillow, tried to clear her head, but the loneliness was haunting, her mind was racing. By seven thirty, she decided to give up the fight and pulled on her sweat suit.

A good walk would help. It was Friday morning, she didn't have too much work to do, so maybe she would be calm and relaxed enough later to take an afternoon nap. She certainly wasn't ready to face Bryce anytime soon. It was best if she kept occupied with other things like Thanksgiving which was only two weeks away.

Thinking of her favorite holiday lifted her spirits until she remembered she planned to spend it with Bryce which in turn led to the fact they had been dating for over four months now. Time had flown by.

It snowed earlier in the week, but hadn't amounted to much, just enough to cover the ground with a soft, white fluff. She was sure they would get more accumulation any day now which wouldn't melt for at least another five months. The weather was beautiful in the Colorado Rockies, but the winters could be hell for people who liked to travel into the city.

Normally, Cammi didn't get restless, but as she walked around the base of the mountain and breathed in the crisp morning air, she decided a little trip was exactly what she needed. She would call Jamie to see if she was up for taking off to Denver for a few days. They could stay with Lesley, an old friend from college, that way they could bring Jamie's boys and drive home later in the week. It was early enough in the season, the roads would be fine, and she could take her work with her. The idea cheered her up immensely.

But as she rounded the corner to her apartment her mood turned foul again. There was Beth, in an oversized green sweater, long legs clad in black spandex, looking cool as a cat, sitting on the stoop of the apartment building. Cammi couldn't help rolling her eyes in annoyance and utter disbelief. She looked around to see if there was any place to disappear to or at least hide until Beth got tired of waiting and eventually left. She would do anything to avoid this confrontation.

But it was too late. Beth spotted her and quickly stood up. Realizing her fate, Cammi pulled back her shoulders and took a deep breath to regain her composure and dignity. Coming face to face with this woman didn't appeal to her, but there was no way to avoid it and she wasn't going to let Beth think she was a coward.

Beth was attractive, Cammi couldn't deny it. But she was too skinny and the sharp appearance of cheek bones beneath her sunken eyes gave her a rather ghostly look. Her blonde hair was obviously bleached and not by a professional, and the cut and style wasn't becoming of her long angular features. If Cammi calculated right she would be close to her age, but with her small frame, radiant, supple skin, and large wide eyes, Beth looked no older than twenty.

"Hi, I hope I am not bothering you." Beth said sweetly. "I rang the bell but no one answered. I figured I would wait."

"Just getting back from a walk," Cammi said dryly, avoiding eye contact. The tone Beth used made her sick. "Can I help you with something?"

"I figured we should talk, get to know one another a little better. I know you and Bryce are close friends. And as you are aware, Bryce and I have a history, too. You know Allie is such a sweet girl who obviously adores us both, so really for everyone involved it would be better if we all got along, for Allie's sake. Try at least to be friends."

She had some nerve and the sugary sweet sincerity in her voice made Cammi chuckle with appreciation. Beth was good but not good enough that Cammi couldn't see right through.

With a suspicious grin, Cammi put her hands on her hips. "Look Beth, we're both adults here, and I am not that naïve. Why don't you get to the point?"

Cammi had a meek and mild presence so Beth hadn't expected her to be as direct as she was. It caught her off guard so she stumbled around with her words, attempting to find a different tactic.

"The point? I.....uh, I guess I don't see....."

Cammi held up her hand to stop Beth from talking.

"It is obvious to all of us you want Bryce back for yourself. You have no respect for his relationship with me, so quit pretending like you care. I've dealt with women like you my whole life so don't think I can't read between the lines. I will tell you this. Bryce is a grown man and is going to make whatever decision he wants to make regardless of what I say or don't say. The fact you think you can influence him is hilarious. You don't know him at all." Despite her shaking voice, Cammi hoped she sounded somewhat intimidating.

In spite of her surprise by Cammi's accusation, Beth immediately responded. "Look, I know how close you and Bryce have gotten. Believe me, I don't want to interfere, but due to our history, I hope you respect we have some unresolved issues needing taken care of before either of us can move on with our lives," she said sympathetically. "I just think we need to be honest with each other."

"*If* he decides he needs to take care of his "unresolved issues", it's his choice to make, not mine. This is not a competition, and Bryce is not a prize to be won. He is a person with feelings and deserves to be respected, so that is what he is going to get from me. What you choose to do is your decision. I am not going to beg you to leave him alone or try to convince you he wants nothing to do with you. It seems you are accomplishing that on your own. But I will tell you to stay the hell away from me."

As Cammi started up the stairs to her apartment, Beth reached out, grabbed her arm, stopping Cammi before she made it far. Even though her manicured nails were digging into her flesh, Cammi refused to back down. She looked Beth squarely in the eyes watching resentment sear through them while Beth sized up her competition.

"Watch your back, Cammi," she hissed. "You are not the type to play dirty, and this is way above your head. Bryce needs a woman with a spine, one who will fight for him. You're too sweet to even fake that. What kind of life is he going to have with some goody-goody like you? Once he remembers the type of lover I was, he will be back with me. Just keep your heart intact, because it *will* get broken, and you'll be all alone, picking up the pieces," she said snidely.

"Do you really believe that, Beth?" Cammi asked calmly. "That you can use sex as a weapon. Are you really that shallow?"

Women become desperate when they feel powerless and it was becoming apparent to Cammi just how threatened Beth felt because of her.

"Sounds like you're trying to convince yourself more than you are me," Cammi continued. "If sex is the only thing you have to offer him, then you should be worried. Bryce is a man of substance and character. He is looking for more. But this is between you two, like I said, not my problem. But I promise you, if his little girl ends up hurt by the games you are playing, then it will become my problem and I will make you pay."

Cammi yanked her arm free of Beth's grasp and stormed up the stairs, leaving her enemy standing alone in astonishment.

Cammi may not know how to play dirty, but damn, it felt good to finally stand up for herself. It wasn't until she leaned against the closed door of her apartment that she noticed how badly she was shaking.

Hey, this is Cammi! I am out of the office until Monday. If this is an emergency, you can leave a voicemail on my cell phone 555-8979, and I will return your call as soon as I can.

Bryce was pissed. It was Wednesday, a week before Thanksgiving and four days since he had any contact with her. He was tired of having a relationship with her answering machine. They were supposed to spend the holiday together at his parents. He didn't want to assume their plans were a bust, but with her behavior what else was he supposed to think? What was he going to tell Allie? She was counting on it. A part of him was irritated Cammi would not even have the decency or maturity to break their plans in person. Instead, she kept him waiting and wondering in misery. This was childish, but he knew he didn't have any choice but to give her time.

He hadn't heard a word from Beth either, so hopefully she took his threat seriously. It was only a matter of time now before he talked to Cammi about their future together and he didn't want anyone or anything standing in their way……*especially* Beth.

He loved Cammi and couldn't wait to spend the rest of his life with her. No matter how mad he was at this moment, his love for her continued to grow with each passing day and that was never going to change.

Over the weekend he took Allie up to the ski slopes. It was only her second time on ski's but so far he was impressed with how easily she took to it. As they rode the chair lift he told her he wanted to marry Cammi. She was overjoyed, but he had to get her to calm down and promise to keep it a secret. No one else could know, not just yet. He wanted to include Allie as much as possible in what he was doing. This wasn't just a marriage between him and Cammi, but between the three of them. She was going to be Allie's mother.

Maybe it was premature to tell Allie especially now since Cammi seemed to be giving him the cold shoulder. He understood she was upset. She had a right to be, but what else could he do? Wasn't what they shared worth working through? Shouldn't she give him the benefit of the doubt? It's not like he cheated. What was going on was nowhere near as bad as her ex had treated her. So he didn't understand why her reaction was this extreme or why she was so defensive.

Either way she could not avoid him forever. She was eventually going to have to face the truth. He loved her and she loved him. Despite the circumstances with Beth, they belonged together and no matter what her fears, she was just going to have to take a leap of faith.

Checking her e-mails for the first time since the previous week, Cammi noticed there were five from Bryce….the first four were simple apologies, but the last one nearly broke her heart.

Hi Baby,

I miss you so much and wish things didn't have to be like this. I understand if you need some space and time apart from me. Not that I want to be apart from you because I don't...you're all I think about. The last thought I have before I fall asleep is of you and you're my first thought when I wake up. Do you realize how many times you cross my mind during the day???? I will be consumed with details of my work and a thought of you will drift into my head.....your smile, your laugh, the way you look at me, the way you touch me, the way you make me feel, the way we blend as one....and for that brief moment, I'm filled with complete happiness. I consider myself the luckiest man in the world for having found you.

I'm sorry for the pain you are going through. I hope you will come to me again soon so we can talk about it.

Bryce

What the hell was she supposed to do with that? Words….they were just words, she convinced herself and none of them meant anything. If they did, they would not be in this stupid mess.

While in the city, her phone had died, and she hadn't brought along the charger, therefore, she hadn't checked her voicemail until earlier that morning. He had called fifteen times.

She admitted it was inconsiderate and a little manipulative on her part. It would have been easy enough to let him know she was leaving town, but her pride wouldn't allow it. She didn't want to answer to anyone or explain the decisions she was making. All she wanted to do was run away, as far away as she could get, from these emotions that seemed to want to drag her back into the pit of isolation she had tried so hard to escape.

Hey, went to Denver with Jamie for a few days. Needed to get away and think some things over. Sorry I didn't let you know. I will give you a call this weekend.

Cammi

Her reply was short. Though she was evasive, she hoped to pacify him with the promise that she would call. Even though she *had* figured things out, she wasn't ready to face him, not just yet, especially after his e-mail. It was easier to be in denial. But his actions and Beth's continued persistence were wearing on her. She couldn't be with a man who was confused about whom *or* what he wanted. She had more self-worth than to wait around while he figured it out.

Cammi could not remember feeling so much pain. She made a choice to fall in love with Bryce, and now she was making a choice to move on without him. Falling out of love with him was going to be the hardest thing she ever had to do because as much as she tried, her heart didn't want to stop beating for him.

He waited as patiently as he could, but the call she promised never came. The agony was more than he could bear. The need to see and hold her overwhelmed him, while his body craved her touch. Nights were the worst. He didn't get an ounce of sleep wondering what she was doing, what she was thinking and if she felt the loss as much as he was. Many times he reached for the phone but settled on waiting for her. She said she would call.

He was able to gather from her e-mail Thanksgiving together was not an option. He was able to pacify Allie by saying something came up for her with work. Allie knew enough about Cammi's job to understand sometimes she had to travel so this did not seem like too much of an impossible excuse.

Monday morning, Bryce drug himself into work after two sleepless nights of worry, hoping and praying there was an e-mail from her. His excitement at seeing her name in the inbox was immediately replaced with dread.

Sorry I didn't call. It was a hectic weekend catching up from my little get away.

Look, I've done some serious thinking and believe it would be best if you and I didn't see one another for a while. Things are getting complicated and I think you need to work through your unresolved issues before you move on with your life or before I get more involved than I already am. You and I have a great friendship, which I am forever grateful for...that won't change. But I don't need to be stuck in the middle of this triangle. I deserve more. I will be here for you and Allie if you ever need me, but until you decide whether or not Beth is going to be a part of your life, I can't be. I'm sorry. I care about you so much and don't want to hurt you, but I have to look out for my own best interests.

I hope you understand.

Cammi

He wrote back.

What do you mean until I decide? I've already made my decision. She is NOT NOW and NEVER will be a part of my life. Why don't you trust me?

Bryce

She replied.

I know you've told me that but it's been ages since you have spent any time with her. Like I said, there are unresolved issues and before I get involved, you need to make sure. Please take some time to explore what you really want and please, respect what I want. Don't e-mail me anymore.

Cammi

Damn it! He slammed his fist on the desk, sending papers flying. He needed to see her before she was lost to him completely.

She was being stubborn and a little unreasonable, but he could be just as stubborn. He spent the entire day leaving message after message, informing her he wasn't going to give up until she talked to him face to face. Still, he got no response.

Bryce was running his fingers through his hair in frustration later that day when Shawn poked his head into his office.

"You up for ball Saturday morning?"

"Can't. Going to mom and dad's for Thanksgiving."

"Oh crap, is that this week? Must explain why our kitchen looks like a typhoon hit it. I would imagine Jamie is having her usual over. That woman makes a feast. Too bad you aren't sticking around. You and Cammi could come, too. I would imagine since Jamie hasn't said anything, she will be going with you?"

Bryce's face dropped.

"Everything okay, buddy?"

"I'm in trouble, man. My ex, Beth, remember her? She showed up and is causing all sorts of problems. Cammi won't see me. Shit, she won't even talk to me. She thinks I need to 'explore my feelings.' I'll explore my feelings when I shove a brick down Beth's throat."

"Jamie did mention something about it. They went to the city last week and took the kids. I should have had you come over for a beer, but I was really enjoying being alone in my house for the first time in four years. Sounds like Jamie has your back with this thing with Cammi and is trying to talk some sense into her."

Bryce gave a strained smile. "Tell her thanks. I appreciate it."

"So…..I take it she's *not* going with you on Thursday?"

"We were planning on it before this blew up in my face. She wrote me today saying we shouldn't see each other anymore, so I'm going to say that's a big fat NO."

Watching Bryce's face turn from anger to sorrow, Shawn felt sorry for his friend. He and Jamie had some rough patches the first two years of their marriage, and he remembered how unbearable it could be. Amazing how the love of a woman could turn a poor fellow into a blubbering idiot.

Shawn glanced at his watch. "Sorry Buddy. I got to head to surgery. Let me know if you need anything, a beer or a good game of ball, oh and happy Thanksgiving, for what it's worth."

Bryce hated this. He could hardly focus on anything at work. It was pointless even being there so after Shawn left he packed up his briefcase and went home.

The next two days were pretty much the same. He went into work hopes high then had them instantly deflated when he turned on his computer. Throughout the day, he thought of nothing but her and wished there was some other way to reach her. Maybe if he gave her some space, she would come to her senses and realize she needed him as much as he needed her.

Later that evening when he was in the middle of checking the alternator on his truck, the door bell rang. He rushed to it, hoping to find Cammi, but instead was annoyed to find Beth standing on his front porch.

"I thought I had finally gotten rid of you," he grumbled leaning against the door jam, a socket wrench still in his hand.

"It's cold out here, can't you let me in?"

"Wear more clothes, and it won't be a problem." He shook his head at the ridiculous sight of her standing there in a mini-skirt, tank top and black leather boots. She looked like she came straight out of a Van Halen video from nineteen eighty-five.

"Now Brycey, that's not anyway to treat a lady," she scolded pushing her way past him hoping to find Cammi there. Beth was ready for a cat-fight. It would give her a chance to prove to Bryce who the real woman in his life was.

He was alone, which was okay too. She'd have him all to herself. Walking to the fireplace, she studied the pictures on the mantel, taking in anything that would prove he was still a bachelor and his affair with Cammi was just that….an affair.

The smell of alcohol penetrated his nose as she moved past him. She was a drinker when they dated, but never to the extreme. He wondered if the hardships she endured over the past year had her drinking more.

"Where's Allie?" she slurred.

Thanksgiving Break started that day, and Allie was spending the night at his parents. His sister was there along with her kids, and Allie had been excited to have a huge slumber party. He was looking forward to this time alone to wallow in self-pity or else maybe go over to Cammi's to try to talk some sense into her. He'd be going over to his parents tomorrow to share in the holiday feast, but he didn't feel like he had much to celebrate unless Cammi was with him.

"At my parents," he replied sourly.

"Good, then you and I can talk." She settled herself onto his couch revealing the length of her scrawny legs as the skirt she wore rode up her thighs.

This irritated Bryce even more. If she thought he was going to be swayed by her sexuality, then she was wrong. He had more depth of character than that and now that he was raising a little girl, he was repulsed by the behavior of aggressive women. Between Cynthia and now Beth, he'd had enough of them to last a lifetime. He wanted a lady in his life and he had one until Beth meddled.

"We don't need to talk. I want you out of my house."

"Allie told me you were going to ask Cammi to marry you, is that true?" she blurted out, narrowing her eyes at him.

Shit. Shit…Shit…Shit.

"It's none of your business."

Beth got up from the couch and walked over to where he was standing, swaying her hips from side to side. Bryce wondered if she had any concept she was making a fool of herself. He sincerely doubted it.

"Oh you are so wrong, Bryce. I'm making it my business. You want to know why? Because I love you and you love me. I screwed up. I never should have left you, and it didn't take me long to see the error of my ways. It just took me a long time to get my life in order before I could get back here to show you how much you mean to me."

"And you're doing such a good job of it," he commented sarcastically. "Beth, you never loved me. You only know how to love yourself. You just want me because I can provide you with the life you want. You're a selfish, spoiled brat."

"Once upon a time, you wanted to marry *me*, Bryce, not Cammi," she said trying to ignore the anger boiling inside her. She knew it could be dangerous.

"And it only took me about a week to see the error of *my* ways," he stated using her own words. "You aren't worth marrying," he added.

No sooner had the words left his mouth when her hand reached up and slapped the side of his cheek. "You're an asshole, Bryce. You owe me an apology!" she demanded, her eyes narrowing into slits.

For a brief moment, his face flushed with color, but quickly he recovered from the sting of her hand and let out the dam of laughter he was holding in. This had become ridiculous. Beth, shocked by his reaction but still fuming, took a step back.

"The only apology you're getting out of me is to say I am sorry I ever got involved with you in the first place. Get out Beth and if you ever come back, I will make your life here in Madison pure hell! Trust me, you don't want to test it," Bryce snarled.

Bryce had learned to control his hot temper but if someone was to mess with his simple way of life and those he loved, there was no telling what direction his anger would go. He didn't believe in violence against women, but Beth might force him to change his mind.

As she lunged to hit him again, Bryce grabbed her arms to restrain her. Even though she struggled, she was weak, clumsy, and drunk so it didn't take much to overpower her and shove her out the front door. Her screams penetrated his ears as he turned the lock behind him.

"If you marry her, you will regret it!" Beth shrieked banging and kicking at the door. Bryce could hear her sobs as they continued so he turned up the volume on the television to drown her out. Eventually she grew tired and left, but not before shattering his window with a rock and making a hole in the garage door with the snow shovel. Just as he began to dial 911, he heard her car drive away.

Good, he thought. *Maybe her drunken ass will drive off the road.*

Chapter Ten

Worried about her, Autumn invited Cammi to have Thanksgiving dinner at her place. It was just going to be her and her latest boyfriend, they could use an extra mouth to feed otherwise she'd have turkey leftovers for the next month, Autumn insisted. Cammi knew she was always welcome at Jamie and Shawn's too, but she couldn't make herself go, instead she stared at the blank screen of her laptop trying her best to put what she felt in her heart together into words, but she was numb.

Just when she thought she was being too stubborn and maybe, just maybe she needed to reach out and give Bryce another chance, he stomped on her heart all over again. She was tired of hurting. *It was better to be angry*, she decided, as her fingers tapped across the keyboard.

You know, Bryce, you amaze me. You tell me you don't want anything to do with Beth and ask me to trust you. No, you begged me to trust you. You were smooth, I will give you that. You knew exactly what to say, didn't you? Even gave me time to think, knowing it wouldn't take long before I realized I was being too hard on you. I played right into your hands and was stupid enough to show up at your house to hear what you actually might have to say. Guess whose car I saw parked in your drive? And she wasn't sitting in it so I guess she must have been in the house. What sort of game are you playing? I am so grateful I figured you out before I invested more of my time and energy into you.

Don't call, don't e-mail, just leave me the hell alone.
Cammi

Enraged, she hit the send button. The pain in her chest as she recalled finding Beth at his house the evening before brought tears to her eyes. A small, teensy part of her was tempted to look through the window or even knock on the door. But she resisted, knowing seeing them together was more than she could bear.

All the signs were there, it was time to let him go, and stop this unhealthy cycle she was putting herself through. But she loved him…..and that was stupid. How could she have allowed herself to believe he might be different than any other man she had met? He was just like Marcus. Out to see how far he could push her and what he could get away with.

The humiliation was too much. If she pretended she didn't care, then maybe it would go away, and she could move on, start over and forget he existed. That is what she'd been doing her whole life, though, running from her emotions. If she didn't deal with them now, she was going to spend the rest of her life running, hiding and shutting herself off to happiness. It was easier to live that way, but was it worth missing out on what life had to offer because she couldn't deal with the disappointment that came along with living?

Wasn't there anything in life that fell into place? It was unfair. It happened to others, why not her? Why did she have to be the one trying to make sense of it all only to hit a brick wall every time she thought she had it right? Why was it a daily chore to keep her head above water?

She scooped Dooney up with one arm, Burke in the other and somberly marched herself into her bedroom to crawl under the covers where she felt it might be safe. But she carried the sorrow with her, crying until she couldn't cry anymore. Her mind was spinning and no matter how hard she tried, it wouldn't stop. Just when she thought she was going to go crazy, Cammi drifted off to sleep.

Bryce's sister and brother-in-law were taking all the kids to the Christmas parade in Denver that afternoon. After a sleepless night, he woke before dawn to make the short drive back to Madison from his parent's early Friday morning. Even though he didn't actually have to work, he chanced going into the office with the hope he might have an e-mail from her. At times like this he wished he had internet on his computer at home. He felt like he was dying inside and was desperate for any contact. It thrilled him to see Cammi's name pop up under his 'you've got mail file'. But as he read, his anticipation soon changed from confusion to irritation, then finally heartache.

Tension squeezed what breath he had left out of his stomach. What sort of dumb luck did he have that kept digging him deeper into a hole he couldn't get out of? Damn Beth for interfering in his life. Damn him for not telling Cammi how he really felt. *Damn, damn, damn*! Bryce sat at his desk with his head buried in his hands. How did this all get out of control?

A thought suddenly occurred to him.

Bryce looked around in embarrassment. It was almost as if someone was there, next to him, planting the seed with a soft whisper, but that was impossible. He didn't share his office with anyone, and the door was closed. Besides, the only prayer Bryce knew was the Lord's Prayer and he hadn't said it since he was a kid. Bryce believed in a higher power. Something out there created this amazing thing called life, something much bigger that no one actually understood and Cammi believed that this thing or person actually answered prayers. But did he have it in him to say a prayer? He felt a little stupid.

Still, he had an overwhelming urge to do so. It was as if something was urging him, telling him exactly what to say. It was a strange sensation, but one too powerful to ignore. Deciding he might as well try but looking like an idiot, Bryce closed his eyes and folded his hands together. Aside from Allie's birth, Bryce had never wanted or been so willing to beg for something this much in his life.

Lord.....I don't quite know what you want me to say. I'm not good at this shit. Oops, sorry. I should not have said that. Look, Cammi says prayer works. I trust her with everything I have, and she knows more about this than I do. Um, I just want you to know I love her, and I don't intentionally want to hurt her. I have faith, and think you want us to be together. She says there is a reason for everything and that I need to listen, to trust you. She told me we are a part of you. I'm not so sure I understand. But she reassures me you have a plan far bigger than I could imagine, and it is easier to give up control, to go with your plan and purpose for us. So I'm going to try.

Please know I want to take care of her for the rest of my life. I have never wanted anything more. I don't know much about eternity or heaven, but if I can be with her no matter where she goes, then, I will do anything and everything I have to, to make sure we are together forever. Um, I guess that is it. Is there something else you want me to say? If not then...I guess I'll say Amen.

He whispered the words quietly then waited for something to happen. Five minutes passed. Staring out the window at the mountain peak just over the valley, he grew frustrated with each passing second. This was ridiculous and definitely out of his comfort zone. What did he think was going to happen, that his phone would ring and it would be Cammi or that she would come bursting through is office door and into his arms?

Shutting down his computer, he locked his office door and took the six flights of stairs instead of the elevator out to his truck. Starting the engine, Bryce decided when he got home he would go for a long bike ride and then call Shawn. Take him up on his offer for a game of ball in the morning. Both would be a good stress release for him. With his mind focused on the game he didn't pay attention to where he was going and before he knew what he had done, he pulled his truck into the first open parking space in front of Cammi's apartment. Instantly, he knew exactly what he wanted to do and say.

Standing in front of her apartment building, pulling the collar of his coat up to his chin to keep the cold draft from chilling him, Bryce waited. If he tried knocking, he knew she wouldn't answer. She had no clue he was watching her from his truck when she trotted down the stairs and around the corner so he was hoping to catch her off guard, when she was on her way back from her walk.

An hour passed before she appeared around the corner again, but to him it felt like forever. The temperature had dropped the night before, and he could still see hints of frost on the trees sparkling in the glare of the sun.

Cammi was bundled from head to toe, but her eyes and rosy red cheeks peeked out from under the scarf wrapped around her head. The walk left her feeling invigorated. She was breathing hard, thankful for the cold air penetrating her lungs. All she wanted to do now was lock her door, light some candles, put on a little mood music, and take a long hot bubble bath. Then she saw him. He stepped out of his car and stood staring at her, not moving.

Seeing him stirred up every emotion she'd been trying to ignore. He looked as awful as she felt. She missed him so much, but her blood boiled with anger when she thought of Beth and him together. Did he sleep with her the other night? Did he look into her eyes with the same love and devotion he had hers? Unable to shake the horrific images out of her head was driving her to the brink of insanity.

Now here he was, as if nothing happened, ready to say the words to bring her back to his bed, just like he had Beth. She'd learned a lot from her ex and this time she wouldn't fall for the same trick twice. But the sadness in his eyes made her knees buckle.

Finding her senses, she was determined to stay strong. She couldn't let him to push her buttons when she was at her most vulnerable.

"I have plans, if you don't mind," she said coldly walking past him up the stairs towards the security of the building. She wanted to get away before he had a chance to say something, but he followed her.

"Cammi, please! Stop! I want to talk to you. Let me explain things," he implored grabbing onto her arm.

"What else do you need to explain? I feel a little foolish having trusted you, but I can see clearly now what's going on. I care about you, Bryce, and want you to be happy. So please, if you care about me at all, quit leading me on!"

"Dammit woman! Stop being stubborn for five minutes and listen to me!" Cammi was shocked by the tone of his voice. He sounded irritated, demanding and surprisingly desperate.

"Only because I don't want you to make a scene," she surrendered sitting down on the stoop. Cautiously, he sat next to her, willing her to look at him, but she refused to make eye contact as she stared at her toes tapping the step impatiently.

"Bryce, you really are wasting my time. I have things I need to do," she stated, eager to find a way out of an uncomfortable situation before she lost all control.

He put his gloved finger over her mouth to quiet her while he explained everything that had transpired with Beth over the past few weeks. The only part he left out was his plan to ask her to marry him.

Cammi's heart was desperate to believe him, but her head told her to stand her ground.

"What goes on with you and Beth is none of my business." Her whole body shook as she spoke. "You are a grown man who can make your own decisions. I am going to make mine and right now I want you to leave. I can't deal with this, I'm sorry," she shook her head. She knew she was being difficult but didn't see any other way to protect herself.

"Did you not hear anything I said?" he pleaded.

"I will not come second, third or fourth to other women you want to spend time with. If you need other women as friends, that is your business, but when it comes to an ex-almost-fiancée, someone you slept with........ I won't hang around to see how the fairytale ends." She stood up.

"Do you think I need this drama either?" he yelled grabbing her by the shoulder forcing her to look at him.

The touch of his hand burned like fire. "Bryce, please! Leave me alone," her voice trembled. She had to get away...her self-control was beginning to crumble. Looking for an escape, she whipped open the door and ran up the stairs two at a time hoping she would reach her apartment before he reached her.

But before she had a chance to find sanctuary behind locked doors, he grabbed her by the waist and pushed her back against the door, his arms securing her on each side. She could feel the heat of his body, only inches away and her chest heaved as she tried to catch her breath.

"I have busted my ass trying to win your trust. I don't deserve to have you treat me this way. It's starting to piss me off and if I didn't love you so much, I would walk away right now. But you are *it* for me, and I am not going to give up. So stop jumping to conclusions and talk to me, okay?"

Silence eluded her. Cammi couldn't believe what she heard. *He loved her*?

Seeing he had her full attention, he dropped his arms to his side, and took a step back. He didn't want to frighten her. This time as he began to speak, his words were less aggressive.

"I have been miserable without you these past few weeks. But it's been okay. I mean it's been worth it." When he saw the confusion set in, he rushed to explain. "I thought I knew what I wanted, but until I met you, I only had an idea. We have too much good…. it would be a waste to walk away from it. I need and count on you. You are my very best friend. I trust you to take care of me when I am down and teach me how to do the right things. I cherish every moment we spend together and feel empty when we're apart. I hate wondering when I get to see and enjoy being with you again."

He dared to take a step closer, his hand reaching out to caress her arm. "I'm not real good at this and because I have waited so long to tell you….well, now all this shit has happened and Cammi, I'm scared. Scared I might lose the woman I waited to find. You are the very core of who I am. I want YOU in my future, no one else. It is YOU… I want to grow old with. YOU… I want to have children with. YOU… I want to share my life with. I think about it all the time and have never believed in anything more."

Bringing his lips to touch hers he felt a tear slide down her cheek.

"I fell in love with you from the beginning, but you scare pretty damn easy. I didn't want you to run. I'm serious now Cammi, you need to believe me. I can't lose you. I don't want to be friends with Beth, I don't even want to see her, or know she is in the same town as us. You are the part of my heart that has been missing, please don't throw it away."

His passion left her breathless. Bryce wasn't great with expressing heartfelt emotion smoothly so she could guarantee she would never hear these words out of his mouth unless he truly meant them. She didn't know if it was desperation or stupidity forcing her to believe him. Regardless, she threw herself into his arms.

"Come on," he tugged on her hand. She went willingly as he guided her into her apartment and easily, comfortably fell back into his embrace, praying she wouldn't ever have to let go. The tears would not stop and he held her while she sobbed. With her eyes closed, he kissed each one slowly allowing his lips to linger for a moment. Then he gently moved to the tip of her nose as his hand began to drift down her back. She sighed when his lips finally found hers.

They became one as Bryce continued to confess his love, satisfying her again and again. Cammi returned his love passionately, but was reluctant to speak the words he was desperate to hear.

They lay together the rest of the morning entangled in the other's arms.

"Come spend the rest of the weekend with us." Bryce's obligations to his family had him torn as he didn't want to leave her behind anymore. "Allie's told everyone about you. They are anxious to meet you, and I'm tired of hearing every one complain about how bad my attitude has been the last few days," he laughed.

Cammi hesitated, and he knew what that meant. She wanted him in her life, but was cautious about taking another risk so soon. The pain she had to bear was visible, and she needed time to heal.

But the emotional roller coaster she'd been on the past month was beginning to take a toll. She couldn't make a rational decision and began to sob again, all of the anguish trapped inside bubbling to the surface. He wrapped his arms around her.

"It's going to be okay, baby, I promise. I'm so sorry I hurt you."

Could she really trust him or even herself for that matter? Look what she let happen today.

"I'm scared I love you too much," she confessed. He kissed and held her as she let it all out. "You're the only man I've let in," she sobbed.

"I know," he whispered in her ear.

And he did know. She wasn't an open book, but with time, she'd become easier for him to read. The tough exterior was only an act to keep people away from the vulnerable, sensitive spirit he wanted to love forever.

Just as in previous moments of Cammi's life, her heart and head were in conflict. Why couldn't she see through the pain like she had after her divorce? The bigger picture was obvious to her then. Why not now?

When all else failed and the answers weren't there, Cammi forced herself to remember the path…her purpose. She made a promise, and that promise was to work through any obstacle that came her way with unconditional love. Not to run away and hide. And this time, no matter how much she wanted to, Bryce wasn't going to let her. This is what she prayed for, and now she had it.

Filled with peace, Cammi threw her arms around Bryce's neck and planted kisses all over his face reacting to the desire within. Encouraged by her enthusiasm, he couldn't help but make love to her again. After reaching a final climax, they were too exhausted to move. Cammi rolled over onto her side and clasped onto the hand of her lover looking directly into his eyes.

"I do love you, with all my heart."

He smiled and lightly kissed her lips.

"I know," he whispered.

Chapter Eleven

The next month flew by and suddenly there were only ten days until Christmas. A thick layer of snow covered the ground but the warmth of the sun in the azure blue sky made the winter chill tolerable. This year, Cammi felt incredibly thankful, and the excitement of having a family of her own to spend the holidays with filled her with a sense of belonging she hadn't felt since leaving home at eighteen.

She spent most of her evenings with Allie and Bryce as the bond between the three grew stronger with each passing day. She loved watching the anticipation of the holiday through Allie's eyes, but also for the first time, realized she was a little bit envious as she watched father and daughter interact together. The jealously hadn't been there before and disturbed her so much, at times she opted to head home early. It wasn't their fault and she grew angrier towards herself that she could possess such a selfish emotion towards a seven year old that she adored and did absolutely nothing wrong.

Regardless, she wanted more one on one time with Allie without Bryce. She felt it was important to let Allie know they had a special relationship that didn't involve her dad and vice versa. It was also important for the little girl to have time with her dad that didn't always involve *the girlfriend* hanging around. She needed to feel loved individually for who she was not because she was Bryce's daughter.

After school let out for the holiday vacation, Cammi took an entire day off work to spend with Allie. After a light lunch of salad and sandwiches, they headed to a Disney Matinee at the downtown theatre. Bryce wouldn't be home from work for a few more hours. They could take in their movie and have dinner ready to surprise him when he got home.

The movie was a classic and one of Cammi's favorites when she was growing up but Allie had never seen it. Later that evening in

Bryce's kitchen, the girls laughed and quoted the funny parts while they put together hamburger patties.

"Daddy doesn't cook much. We eat macaroni. He doesn't like chick flicks either. That's what he calls them," Allie said while she squished hamburger meat between her fingers.

Cammi was amused. "What sort of movies do you and your dad watch together?

"He likes scary movies, stuff with fast cars or big trucks and Star Wars. Yuck. I hate Star Wars. He will take me to kids' movies as long as it isn't too girly. He liked Iron Man and Transformers. He did sort of like the Little Mermaid. He thought Ariel was hot!" she said rolling her eyes.

Cammi laughed. "Boys are that way. It's okay though. They are made different than girls. If you want to see princess movies, I will take you to all of them." Cammi gave her a tight squeeze. "You are becoming quite a good cook, there Miss Allie," she commented as Allie finished whipping up the mashed potatoes.

Allie grinned from ear to ear. It made her feel grown up when Cammi called her Miss Allie. Her dad treated her like a kid. Cammi treated her like a friend.

Her dad had her seeing a counselor. Someone she could talk to about everything going on, all the changes. She didn't mind it but liked her time with Cammi better. When she was with her, she didn't want her real mom around anymore. In fact, she hadn't thought about her for a long time. Cammi made her feel special. As long as she was there, she didn't need anyone else.

Tomorrow night Cammi promised to drive them around town to look at Christmas lights while drinking hot chocolate. She talked her dad into letting her wear her reindeer outfit, the one she wore in the Christmas program last week, and asked him and Cammi to wear a Santa hat. Cammi was all excited, but her dad wasn't. Sometimes he could be a real party pooper. *But that was okay*, Allie thought sneaking a side glance at Cammi, then bursting into giggles.

Cammi hugged her. "What's so funny, silly girl?" she asked.

Allie hugged her back. "This is going to be the best Christmas ever!" she squealed.

Cammi couldn't agree more.

Bryce and Allie snuck off to the mall a week before Christmas Eve to pick out the most special present of all, an engagement ring for

Cammi. They were going to be at his house Christmas Eve, just the three of them, then split Christmas Day with her family for brunch at Carissa's and then dinner at his sister's.

For the most part, Beth left them alone. Occasionally she would leave a nasty message on Bryce's cell phone which he always made sure Cammi heard just so she didn't start having doubts again. The insecurities were still there, but if she wanted to be with him, she needed to work on trusting him. The last note Beth sent home with Allie from school told him she was hurt by his behavior towards her, but she was dignified enough to stay out of his life if it is what he truly wanted. She also told him that when Cammi broke his heart, she would be willing to help him mend, just to give her a call when it happened. It gave them both a good laugh, but deep down Cammi resented her continued presence in Allie's life.

It was a tradition in Bryce's family to put the tree up exactly two weeks before Christmas. Then later that evening, with all the decorating done, each person would bring out the presents they had bought, already wrapped and place them under the tree.

Bryce's mother always made sure he had a gift from Allie, but Cammi took her shopping anyway. She didn't want to step on any toes, but had been looking forward to their time, doing what she felt was her motherly duty. With Cammi's help, Allie picked out a new pair of basketball shoes and a tie. She anxiously wrapped them and slid them under the tree with the other gifts.

Enjoying the holidays with Allie and Bryce made everything brighter, the music more festive, the food tastier and filled Cammi's heart with a spirit of the season she almost couldn't comprehend. Despite little nagging moments of negativity, Cammi couldn't remember ever being happier, though she also found herself a little restless at times, as if she were looking for something more.

"Life should always be this good," she commented to Bryce a few days before Christmas as they cuddled on the couch watching the red-orange flames dance around in the fireplace.

"It is only going to get better," he promised as he drew her down on the couch in a passionate kiss. "The house looks great. Did Allie have fun?"

"You should have seen her. She said aside from a tree, you guys didn't really decorate much." Cammi had opted not to put any decorations up in her apartment and instead hauled the boxes over to his house. She and Allie spent the entire day Sunday hanging lights on the porch, above the fireplace and around the windows. Not only was it festive, she had to admit, it was a bit romantic too. They also spent almost every evening after Allie's homework was done baking cookies, pies and other assorted goodies to give to friends and neighbors. Bryce even joined in to help. They felt like a real family.

He couldn't wait to propose. Of course, Cammi was clueless. They talked hypothetically about their future, but he never approached the subject of marriage. He did ask her once how she felt about moving in. She said because of Allie and the example she wanted to set, it was something she wouldn't do unless they were married. Her ideals and morals impressed him. More than anything in the world, he wanted her to be his wife and Allie's mother.

She loved him.....he had no doubt about it, but she still wasn't as carefree and confident with him as she had been the months before Beth showed up in their lives. Obviously she was still mending from the damage placed on her heart and he couldn't help but worry what transpired might have caused permanent damage.

His chest heaved with emotion watching the faint smile on her lips. He loved to see her in deep thought and refused to disturb her in case those thoughts were about a future with him. There was nothing else in the world he would rather be doing than this. She was his dream, his fantasy, and he couldn't wait to spend the rest of his life proving his love to her.

Cammi stole a glance at him and smiled then placed her hands behind his neck and brought his lips down to meet hers for more kisses. She loved kissing him. His lips were warm, gentle and each time they met hers, she could feel herself relax. His kisses, his touch, the way he looked at her meant more to her than he probably realized. She knew this is what it felt like to truly be loved.

On Christmas Eve, Cammi was in a crunch to finish the four-piece interview she had been working on. She planned on taking the next five days off, so she needed to wrap it up that day. It would be an all day project, and Cammi had told Bryce she wouldn't be back to his house until four, so it gave him and Allie plenty of time to prepare.

While he was busy making Cammi's favorite meal of lobster, baked potato and crème' Brule, Allie set up the candles around the living room. Once dinner was going, she helped her dad light a fire in the fireplace "to add to the romance of the evening", he said with a wink.

At the store it was Allie who picked out a special teddy bear to hold the box with the ring. His mother hot glued the box to the bear's hands so it looked as if the bear was presenting a gift. Christmas carols played in the background, and Allie couldn't help but giggle in anticipation. Once everything was in place and they had Cammi's present wrapped under the tree, they took off their separate ways to shower, bathe and dress before she arrived.

Unlike Bryce's family, it was Cammi's tradition to attend church on Christmas Eve. As she explained to Bryce, it wouldn't be Christmas without celebrating the birth of Christ. He never looked at it that way and agreed they would go with her. He wasn't particularly comfortable in church, but wanted to make her happy, especially tonight. The service started at eight which allowed plenty of time for his surprise.

Dinner took Cammi's breath away. She hadn't expected anything so extravagant. The few romantic attempts Bryce had made in the past were wonderful, but she was learning, it didn't come naturally to him so she was very impressed with what he'd done. The atmosphere plus the glass of wine at dinner made her feel giddy.

"I didn't think you could cook," she commented winking at Allie which made the girl laugh nervously.

"In actuality, I can cook very well, I just don't enjoy it. There's a difference, my darling," he teased. "This is our first Christmas together, and I want to make it a memorable one."

The sheepish grin on his face gave Cammi a suspicious feeling. But she ignored it and drank more wine. Her day had been hectic and rushed, so it was nice to have a chance to sit back and relax. After dinner, when she tried to help clean up, Allie took the dish out of her hand, placed it back on the table and led her into the living room.

"Sit here," she demanded pointing to the couch. "I want to give you something."

Allie knelt down beside the tree and returned with a small gift obviously wrapped by a child. Cammi's name was printed in big block letters on the top of the package.

"This is from me," she explained cuddling up next to her. Bryce handed Cammi another glass of wine before sitting next to his daughter.

"Careful, I can't be walking into church drunk," she teased.

Being ever so careful not to rip the paper, Cammi opened the package. Lying beneath a cardboard lid was a clay picture frame painted in blue with tiny white snowflakes around the trim. Inside the frame was a picture of Allie and her dad. At the bottom of the frame in her own handwriting, Allie had written, 'To the woman we love. From Allie and Daddy.'

Cammi looked down at the picture as tears threatened to escape out of the corner of her eyes. She quickly wiped them away and wrapped her arms around Allie in an attempt to conceal her emotions.

Once she found her voice, she pulled back. "This is the best gift I ever received. I will keep it forever, I promise."

Bryce looked at Allie. "My turn?" he asked. Allie nodded, but Cammi noticed his voice quivered.

He walked to the tree and taking a deep breath, reached down to pick up a package. This was a huge leap of faith but Bryce was confident in what they had and knew she felt the same, not having said it in so many words, but instead by her actions.

When he turned around, Cammi noticed beads of sweat forming above his brow. *For crying out loud,* she thought, *I hope he isn't always like this when he gives gifts.*

His hands trembled as he handed her the small wrapped box. Cammi opened her mouth to say something reassuring, but he put his hand up to stop her.

"Please, don't say anything, just open it."

When he sat down next to her on the couch Allie crawled onto his lap, and they sat in silence watching her open the tiny gift.

A look of delight crossed her face when she pulled the soft, teddy bear out of the box. She didn't notice the smaller box between the bear's hands which gave Bryce an opportunity to speak.

Anxiously, he took the bear from her and set it aside taking her hands in his.

"What's wrong, baby?" she asked out of concern and confusion. His pale face was wet with sweat. She thought he might be getting sick but didn't understand why he took her gift away. She barely had a chance to look at it. "I want to look…."

He placed his finger over her lips and looked into her eyes. "Cammi, you have made me a believer in many things. Since you have come into my life, my perspective, my attitude, everything has changed. You make me believe in myself, you help give me hope for the future. You have faith in all I do and are teaching me to have the same. I want to spend the rest of my life giving all of these gifts back to you."

Bryce slowly slipped Allie off his lap so he could get down onto one knee. As Cammi's eyes widened to the reality of what was taking place, he squeezed her hands. Allie picked up the bear and opened the box to show her the ring inside. They practiced this all afternoon and she hoped she got it right.

Cammi looked from one face to the other then at the bear, finally resting her eyes on the beautiful diamond solitaire.

"Oh!" she gasped.

"Allie and I don't want you to leave here anymore, not ever. We want this to be your home. We want you to be part of our family forever."

"Bryce, I," she tried to interrupt him but wasn't able to finish. Once again, she had to choke back her emotions while her hands began to tremble.

"Cammi, will you marry me? No, I correct myself. Will you marry us?" he smiled as he put his arm around his daughter.

Unable to stop the tears as they ran down her face, Cammi looked at Bryce and could sense his fear, his anticipation, but his eyes, which were brimming with tears also, were the key to his soul, and they were filled with love.

She jumped off the couch and wrapped her arms around the both of them tightly, never wanting to let go.

"I can't believe you are doing this," she choked. "You are crazy, but I'm crazy in love with you."

Her face beamed with joy as Bryce placed the ring on her finger. Without giving her a chance to accept, he pressed his lips to hers. When he pulled away, she looked from her hand to his face and over to Allie.

"You were so nervous, did you doubt for a second I would say 'no'?" she teased, but the look on his face let her know he wanted her acceptance and commitment as much as she wanted his. She put her hand on his cheek and gently placed her lips on his.

"I never wanted anything more," she assured him in a whisper.

Allie was so excited she didn't leave Cammi's side the entire evening and was pleasantly surprised to see some of her friends from school at church. The best part of the night for her was showing off her new mom and the shiny ring. Cammi's family, knowing about Bryce's plan, was invited over after the service to celebrate with champagne.

Though he'd met Carissa plenty of times by now, he'd only been around her parents on a few occasions. He like them, they reminded him of his own, a caring, fun-loving and self-sufficient family. Not the type whose life revolved around their adult children. Since her father took early retirement, they loved to travel and just spent two months traveling Italy, Germany and France. Her brother, Kurt would be up the next day with his family so Bryce would have a chance to get to know him then. And Carissa, well, he still wasn't quite sure what to make of her, but Cammi loved her. That's all that mattered to him.

As much as he was enjoying himself, Bryce couldn't wait for everyone to leave so he and Cammi could enjoy their own private celebration. Around ten-thirty, the crowd finally dispersed. They didn't have to worry about bribing Allie to go to bed as she was anxious to see what would be waiting from Santa the next morning.

He had one more surprise left. With her eyes closed, Bryce guided Cammi up the staircase one at a time.

"Open," he said shoving the door ajar with his foot. Glancing around the dim lit room, she could make out six vases each holding a dozen long stemmed, pink roses along with individual petals he had spread over the bed. Candles illuminated the entire room and a bubble bath complete with a bottle of champagne and two glasses awaited them.

"When did you do this?" she asked suspiciously. "For not being a romantic, you are sure doing a good job."

"I snuck in while you were reading to Allie. And I had a little help. I have a sister and a mother, remember?"

To show her appreciation for the gesture, she seductively wrapped her arms around his neck, pressing her body into his.

While they laid together in bed a few hours later, Cammi radiated in the beauty of what they shared. This was a dream come true, and she couldn't believe her luck. Could he be anymore perfect? The little voice inside her head reminded her not to question it, but instead enjoy it, accept it, and be grateful for all she now had.

"How soon can you get out of your lease?" Bryce asked interrupting her thoughts as he nibbled on her neck.

"How soon can you make room for me?"

With a boyish grin, he pulled her on top of him obviously aroused again.

"I've had enough of watching you walk away from here. As far as I am concerned, you are moved in…. as of now." He pulled her head towards his demanding more of her luxurious kisses as he promised to fill her with more pleasure and love than she could ever hope for.

Part Two

Thank God he'd remembered to buckle Bailey into his car seat, Bryce thought. He wasn't in the right state of mind. Hadn't been for a while, but God forbid he do something stupid like not buckle in his kid. Bryce knew if he got pulled over they would for sure throw him in jail. He was driving like a manic. It was a wonder Bailey didn't fly out one of the side windows and land on the street.

He had to get a grip, get his head on straight. All that mattered right now was getting to the hospital.

Jumping out of the car the moment he put it into park, Bryce ran around to open the back door, his hands fumbling as he tried to unfasten Bailey's safety restraints.

"Damn it," he shouted getting angrier by the minute.

"Daddy, I stuck?" Bailey, at two, loved to throw out as many words as he could to impress whoever might be listening.

"You aren't stuck, baby, Daddy's just having a hard time getting your belt undone," he said with a forced smile in an attempt to reassure his son.

"Alright, I got it." Yanking him out of the seat and into his arms, he rushed through the corridor of the emergency room. Bryce found himself trapped in the middle of a horror movie, enclosed within stark white walls and the rapid beeping of instruments.

"I am looking for Cammi Shepard. She was brought here about a half hour ago," he told the receptionist, a woman named Nancy if he remembered correctly. She looked at him suspiciously, thumbing through the paperwork on the desk in front of her.

Bryce needed Nancy to hurry. He needed to see his wife. If it didn't happen soon, he felt as if he may snap in two.

"Okay, sir, she's in the ER right now. Are you her husband?"

"Yes, Bryce Shepard," he said as if she should know.

"If you will have a seat, there will be a doctor out here to talk to you in a few minutes." She pointed to a row of chairs by the coffee pots where he was to sit and wait. Defeated and realizing he didn't have much of a choice, Bryce sat down, balancing Bailey on his lap.

Bryce ruffled the auburn hair of his youngest child. He couldn't believe he was already two. The years had flown by. A lump formed in Bryce's throat just thinking about it. They had been so excited about another baby. A third child completed their family. If only it hadn't come on the heels of such a significant change in their life, a change which was already causing enough stress.

Jamie burst through the front doors of the lobby, carrying with her two cups of espresso, one for her and one for him.

"Bryce," she said trying to catch her breath. "What have you found out? Allie called. I came as soon as I could. Here," she said shoving the coffee into his hands. "We both could use this."

Bryce was having a hard time putting two thoughts together. He just wanted to know his wife was all right. That she was alive. That he would get another chance. He couldn't lose her now, not after everything that happened.

"Bryce?" Jamie put one hand on his shoulder while balancing Bailey on her lap with the other. He was staring at the blank wall behind the chairs looking lost and alone. "What do you need?"

He turned to find warmth and concern in her eyes. With his elbows on his knees, he bent forward and collapsed into sobs. Jamie wrapped her arm around his shoulders and for the first time in months Bryce allowed himself to accept the comfort of another human being.

"I need my wife. How have we gotten here? Where did it go wrong?" he sobbed.

Setting Bailey in the chair next to her with a sippy cup, Jamie cradled Bryce as the damn of emotions he had been holding in burst out like a raging river.

"Ahem, I'm sorry to interrupt. Hello Bryce."

Embarrassed by his display of public emotion, Bryce stood up quickly to shake the doctor's hand thinking he looked vaguely familiar, but was unable to place a name. He reminded him more of an artist than a physician. His long grey hair which was neatly tied back in a ponytail, hung out of the bottom of a surgical cap covering his receding hairline. He had a friendly smile and despite the grey hair, looked about ten years younger than he probably was.

"Dr. Brayhill," he reminded a confused Bryce.

"Oh, yes. I'm sorry....I'm not myself tonight."

"Understandable. Your wife is doing fine. A few cracked ribs, bumps and bruises, but other than that, she is very lucky. She should not have come out of the accident alive, so if you don't believe in miracles, I think you should start now," he said boldly shifting his gaze towards Jamie.

The comment took Bryce back to the first moment he met Cammi. He'd believed she was his miracle. So why, after all they had been through did he doubt the possibility a miracle might bring his wife back home?

"We want her to stay for a few more days so we can run other tests. Right now she doesn't appear to have a concussion, but it is something we would like to monitor. I will be here early in the

morning. Let me know if you have any questions. They are moving her to a room right now. The receptionist can give you directions."

"Thank you," was all Bryce could mutter. The doctor nodded and left.

His body began to shake as his mind registered the scene around him. Jamie rubbed his back some more. He was grateful to have her there.

"How about I take Bailey, pick up the other two and take them to my house? You can call me later with the details. I'll have Shawn bring you a bag," she suggested.

Bryce could only stare.

Taking his keys, Jamie left to transfer Bailey's infant seat into her car. By the time she came back, the nurse was having him fill out insurance paperwork and gave him Cammi's room number. Jamie reached up to give him a quick peck on the cheek before taking Bailey by the hand.

"We go?" Bailey asked looking from Jamie to his dad.

His soft, small voice shook Bryce out of his daze, and he reached down to give his son a hug. "Yeah buddy, go with Jamie to get your sisters. I will stay here with mommy and we'll call you later. I love you."

"Bailey, how about we stop by the store and pick up some ice cream to take to the girls?" Jamie suggested as they left the hospital corridor.

"Yeah, we get nilla?" he smiled skipping along next to her.

"Yep, we'll get you some 'nilla'," Jamie repeated with a chuckle.

He took the elevator to the seventh floor. It seemed like a lifetime before the doors finally opened. He walked into the hallway. It was surprisingly quiet at the nurse's station for seven in the evening. If the staff was doing a shift change right about now it would give him some alone time with his wife before they started invading their privacy.

A statuesque brunette dressed in a nurse's uniform was slowly closing the door as he approached Cammi's room. Her name tag said Amy. Her face did not look familiar, but she recognized him.

"Hi Bryce," she said with a bright smile holding out her hand. "She was asking for you earlier. She was in a lot of pain, so we gave her something.... she will be out of it for a few hours at

least. It might last all night. Depends on how tired she is," Amy shrugged following him as he walked past her into the room. The lifeless body asleep in the bed reminded him how close he came to losing Cammi, not once, but twice now.

"Don't try to wake her up, okay? With those broken ribs, she needs to rest and heal properly. Let me know if you need anything. The chair folds out into a bed if you want to spend the night."

Bryce watched numbly as she checked Cammi's vitals again then handed him the remote to the television and closed the door behind her.

He was scared....scared and lonely. It felt like forever since he received the phone call telling him about the accident. He and Bailey had run to the store for groceries when his cell phone rang. The man was hysterical and from what Bryce could gather, it was his semi-truck that hit the minivan, knocking it off the road. He was with Cammi, relaying to Bryce as much information as he could. She was in and out of consciousness...the paramedics were on their way...he didn't see the van...it was on the wrong side of the highway...he slammed on his brakes...hit black ice. The man was sobbing, rambling on, telling Bryce how sorry he was. Bryce remembered asking him to tell her he loved her then drove like a mad man to meet the ambulance at the hospital.

Bryce looked around, taking in the dull grey walls and the cold, blue ceramic tiled floor. It wasn't as nice as the birthing rooms two floors up. Those had been comfortable and warm, inviting. But this room was gloomy and sent a chill through his bones. Maybe it was the circumstances. Clenching his hands in anger, he swore. He would give anything to turn back the hands of time and be up on the ninth floor waiting, watching, and loving his wife while she gave birth first to Faith and then to Bailey.

Careful not to make too much noise walking towards her bed, Bryce couldn't take his eyes off his wife. She looked so peaceful lying there with her brown hair flowing all around her. She was the most exquisite creature he'd ever laid eyes on. No one would have guessed the turmoil she'd been through not only that day but for the past few weeks.

He sat on the cushioned chair that folded out to a bed and took her hand slowly bringing it to his lips while tears fell from his eyes. It had been four weeks now. Four weeks since he touched her soft, delicate skin and kissed her full, sensuous lips. Four weeks since she moved out taking Faith and Bailey with her telling him their marriage was over.

"I'm staying at Jamie's until we can find something permanent," had been her words. "I'm not going to live like this anymore, nor am I going to allow my children to be raised with all this crap you've brought into our lives."

He couldn't contain his anguish. How did it become such a mess? Why hadn't he been strong enough to put his foot down and make her come home instead of telling her he didn't want her anymore? Because he was too damn stubborn and wanted her to pay for leaving him. God, he was such an idiot.

It was all Cynthia's fault. If she hadn't come back to wreck havoc on their lives, he would still have his family intact. The nightmare they lived... well, he wouldn't wish on his worst enemy. He regretted not listening to his gut and instead, taking the easy route, being the nice guy, not wanting anyone to get hurt. But the chaos of it all hurt the ones he loved the most.

Lying in the hospital bed, Cammi looked as stunning as she had the day she walked down the aisle to become his wife. He loved her from the moment he saw her. Actually from the moment he read her first e-mail, he knew she was everything he wanted. The first four months were torture for him spending each and every night without her by his side. All he wanted was to wake up to her face every day, to keep her forever in his embrace.

It was perfect... their wedding...simple, because that was how Cammi was, simple but elegant. She didn't need to impress anyone or have the best of everything. She just wanted to live her life to the fullest and bring others happiness. She brought him more happiness than he even thought possible.

He hoped she knew that. There were many, many things he hoped she knew. Things he would regret not telling her. Things he would regret not doing.

Remembering how he felt as her father walked her down the aisle to join him made his heart leap, just as it had that day. Lord, he had begged watching her eyes melt into his, help me be man enough to meet her needs and bring a smile to her lips. She makes me want to be a better person. Thank you from the bottom of my heart for the love she gives me. I will spend a lifetime, many lifetimes, if I have to, giving it back.

The day was a whirlwind, but only they existed, lost in each other, praying for time to stand still. At that moment, every breath they shared connected their souls. Every glance they stole, cemented their future. No one on this earth could possibly break their bond.

Bryce laid his head next to Cammi on the bed whispering in her ear, urging her to wake up. He wasn't ready to let go.

"I couldn't stop loving you if I tried," he confessed, hoping the words would reach her.

If he had made different choices, then maybe she wouldn't have turned into the angry, cynical version of the woman he'd fallen in love with. And maybe if he looked beyond himself and understood the pain and denial she'd been holding onto all these years, he could have been the man he promised to be. And maybe if she hadn't been so irresponsible the past few months, he would have had a shred of hope their future still lied together, and his rejection of her wouldn't have put her in this hospital bed.

Chapter Twelve
Four Years Earlier

Cammi stared out the kitchen window into the back yard. Allie and Heather were in the tree house, heads close together, lost in their own world. Cammi watched their lips move and wondered what they could be talking about so seriously at their age.

Faith was down for a nap, so Cammi had a good hour or so to get the house straightened up. She was grateful the girls were outside. Quiet time was a rarity and Cammi needed it desperately today. There was something emerging in the depth of her hidden fears, and she was unable to shake the uneasiness. Though she continued to fight the raging battle within, it was as if the years of hard work and the emotional stability she was so desperate to find was about to come crumbling around her.

She couldn't put her finger on what it was, but she was dipping in and out of the darkness. It couldn't be her life. This was what she'd always wanted. If Cammi could describe her wedding day in one word, it would have been magnificent. She could not have wished for a more perfect day. The Colorado weather cooperated with them, there was not a cloud in the clear blue sky, the temperature was in the mid seventies and a slight breeze tickled their faces while Bryce and Cammi recited their vows, almost as if God was whispering his approval at their union. The seventy-five invited guests sat under a white canopy watching, as two people they loved, dedicated their lives not only to each other, but to Allie.

She loved Bryce with every part of her being. Even the bond between Cammi and Allie appeared unbreakable. Cammi missed out on the first six years of Allie's life, but from the moment she became her mother, every milestone in Allie's life affected her as if she were her own child. She only wished she could have been there when Allie took her first steps, said her first words, lost her first tooth. As it was, she would have to settle for the rest. She couldn't believe how open her heart was to accept all the love Bryce and this little girl wanted to give to her. But most of all, she couldn't get over the huge amount of love she wanted to give back. They both touched places in her she didn't know existed, and she truly felt blessed to be the woman who would help Bryce raise this beautiful child. But the idea of disappointing him and Allie or not being everything they expected filled her with doubt and questions continued to linger in her mind no matter how far back she tried to push them.

Their first year together was definitely a change and she and Bryce had their fair share of problems. No one said they wouldn't, but looking back, her expectations of their life together were probably a little unrealistic. Most women Cammi knew liked to delve in one activity after the other, never taking the time to actually enjoy them. Not Cammi, she was slower paced, tackling one thing at a time, taking it slow and never allowing herself to get overwhelmed or feel like she didn't have enough time in her day for other priorities. But she was unprepared for the transformation of her life and the whirlwind of events left her exhausted. Not only was she becoming a wife and a mother, she was also juggling her career. It was difficult to keep her head above water.

Cammi tried to maintain her independence as she adjusted but everything important to her before she was married began to fall to the wayside. Along with being emotionally exhausted, she was physically drained. She began to wonder who was capable of juggling this balancing act. As time went on, she felt less and less competent.

Cammi couldn't help but smile as she watched Allie and Heather swing from the branch of the tree and land in a pile of leaves, but the smile quickly disappeared. It had been years, but Cammi couldn't help feeling unsure of herself and wondered often if they rushed into things. It wasn't that she didn't love Bryce, she did with all her heart, and she loved her life, she loved her kids, but it had only been a month after they made their commitment to each other he asked her to marry him. She had no doubts he was the man she wanted to spend her life with and after four years of marriage and two kids, she was still sure he was the one. But at times, this was *so* hard.

Balancing a marriage had not been as easy as she expected. As a single woman, God was her partner in life. With him, she felt safe, loved, special and strong. In his love, she was secure. In him, her faith was constant and her joy for life, passionate. But over time, her relationship with Bryce and Allie was put to the forefront, distracting her from her convictions. She'd put everything but God at the center of her heart. Instead of having faith, she had fear, instead of having forgiveness, she held onto resentment, instead of trusting what the Lord wanted for her, she tried to control the outcome of her life and everyone around her. She'd become stressed and frustrated. The negativity brought about uncertainty.

It was infuriating for Cammi to know she had not been as self aware when she met Bryce as she thought she'd been. Hind sight is always twenty-twenty and she knew now she was nowhere near as emotionally healthy as she tried to portray.

After the first year of adjustments and trying unsuccessfully for a baby, she and Bryce agreed she should cut back on her stress load and work three days a week instead of five. As much as she loved her job, the idea of being a wife and mother excited her more, besides it would save money on daycare. Lamont wasn't thrilled to say the least and took any opportunity he could to make a snide comment, but regardless, he gave her what she needed. Cammi wasn't willing to give up her career entirely, but wanted to prioritize her responsibilities so she was available for Allie whenever possible.

In the back of her mind, Cammi tried to remain consciously aware of the damage already inflicted on Allie by Cynthia. She wanted to make sure she was never a source of pain for the child. There were times it was difficult to find a balance between giving all of her love and not allowing herself to be taken for granted or disrespected. A part of her felt selfish for trying to set tight boundaries with Bryce and Allie because she wanted to give Allie what she never had before… a mother, a friend, and someone who would love and accept her unconditionally. But in the meantime, she wasn't able to put her own feelings of inadequacy aside. She wanted Allie's acceptance also. From what Bryce told her and her own observations, Cammi knew Allie had a big heart and lots of love. Yet it seemed things were almost too good to be true, something had to give eventually, and Cammi wanted to be prepared when the walls came crumbling down.

Then Cammi found out she was pregnant. While everyone else was preoccupied with the upcoming birth of the baby, Cammi and Bryce spent a great deal of their time together, trying to make the necessary changes in their own relationship.

There had been problems.

Regardless, they were strong and dedicated to one another, wanting nothing more than to make their marriage work, though at times, the resentment would sneak up and bite her, a reminder of things he had done to hurt her. But the pregnancy was an awakening, an awakening of pain and fear from her past, which eventually filled her with a sense of love, she'd forgotten existed. Cammi hadn't lost herself, but instead allowed dark, dingy cobwebs of fear to cover a light that used to shine brightly. Slowly, she began to strip them away, one by one, once again, making God her focus for living and loving. If she wanted a strong relationship with her husband and children, she was going to first and foremost have a strong relationship with the Lord. The miracle growing inside her was a good reminder of the second chance she'd been given.

Never one to be ashamed of the things she held dear, Cammi was honest with Bryce about her faith. Even though he wasn't raised as a believer, she was careful not to put too much pressure on him to live or believe the way she did, but in the back of her mind, she always hoped he would see her way of life and want to make spiritual changes within himself, too.

Throughout her pregnancy, she could see he was intrigued. He was slightly envious of her new positive attitude but wasn't ready to believe a higher power was the cause of it. Over the years, he'd go to church with her on occasion and was definitely inspired by all he heard, but when the reality of life set in, so did his skepticism, though he was willing to admit, it was a good influence on Allie. Church, religion, and faith wasn't something he felt confident enough to contribute to, he'd told her, but agreed to Cammi's request to raise the new baby with her spiritual beliefs.

As her body began to swell with the growth of a new life, so did her heart and ironically she didn't care about the past anymore. She felt the passion she once feared she would never experience again. It was a magnificent feeling, an experience she wished everyone could appreciate. If they could, she had no doubt their faith would never be an uncertainty.

When Faith came along, something in the dynamics of their family changed. For her and Bryce, the change was for the better, for Allie...... Cammi was concerned.

Allie was getting ready to have her eleventh birthday and was blossoming into a beautiful young girl when Cammi found out she was pregnant. She'd grown out her silky blonde hair and wore it a more mature style. Cammi, despite her own lack of ability, was teaching her how to curl it, instead of keeping it braided or in a ponytail. Allie no longer spent forever in the bathtub, preferring a quick shower instead, put deodorant on every morning and asked for her first bra. Always the curious child, she asked Cammi endless questions about the changes that would take place with her body in the next few years.

"Is there anything you want to tell me?" Cammi finally asked one night after a round of questions about periods, boobs, and body hair. Allie shrugged her shoulders. "The girls at school talk about stuff like that all the time and I just wanted to know what you thought."

Relived she hadn't already gotten her period; Cammi made a trip to the bookstore and found the perfect source for her and Allie to read together. It answered all her questions and seemed to satisfy most of her curiosity. As involved as Bryce was in his daughter's life, he was grateful Cammi took over in that department. He was not ready to deal with puberty just yet and always found a reason to leave the room when they started having one of their girl talks.

Allie was the first person Cammi told she was pregnant. They laughed, jumped and squealed with delight at the prospect of a new baby as well as telling Bryce. But soon after, Cammi noticed Allie became a little withdrawn. Her attempts to draw Allie back in by involving her in decorating of the nursery and purchasing baby supplies was met with quiet cooperation. Allie even graciously donated some of her precious childhood stuffed animals to her new brother or sister, but still, the girl remained distant.

It was a cold weekend not long after Halloween and Cammi was in the middle of her seventh month when the two of them holed up in the baby's room to decorate. Bryce was in the city for a conference and wouldn't be back until late Saturday evening. Cammi missed him terribly, but thought it would be fun for her and Allie to tackle the project. The mural of balloons and baby animals Carissa painted had been finished for a while and Cammi stood admiring it with one foot on the bottom of the ladder as Allie climbed up. Once she reached the top, Cammi handed her the last piece of pastel balloon border.

"So….did you and dad decide on a name yet?" Allie asked lowering herself down.

Cammi busted up laughing. "You got some stuck to your hair," she said as she reached to pull it out. "It must have come off the piece we cut to fit into the corner."

Quickly, Allie jerked her head away. Though she was hurt, Cammi chalked it up to age. It was shocking to her how much Allie had grown over the past few years. She was almost a head taller than a year ago and her facial features were more mature the closer she got to a pre-teen.

Pre-teen. Cammi hated the word but it sounded much better than *Tween*. It was how all the mother's of Allie's friends referred to their daughters and it disgusted Cammi how fast some parent's wanted their little girls to grow up. Even Brandi's mother Rachel, whose company Cammi had enjoyed while the girls were in grade school, had succumbed to the strange behavior. Last she heard, Allie told her Brandi's parents allowed her 'boyfriend' to go on a camping weekend with them. Then she heard through the grapevine the mother of another girl in Allie's class was intercepting text messages to a boy on her daughter's cell phone. Supposedly they were talking about their first kiss. This mother then proceeded to teach her daughter about the art of kissing, professing 'they are going to do it either way, so we may as well teach them how to do it right.' Cammi was outraged!

"Kissing. *French kissing*. Call me silly, but I don't think eleven year old girls need to know what a tongue is for other than licking an ice cream cone. When I was in line at the grocery store last week, I picked up a *Cosmo Girl!* Magazine. Flipping through it, I found an article that said, 'The top ten reasons a girl should wait to have sex.' I thought….okay, maybe this magazine isn't so bad, but you know what number one was? Don't have sex because he may be having sex with someone else. The next article was on sexually transmitted diseases and then there was 'Dress for Sexess'. This is what the girls in Allie's class are reading. They don't need to know about that! I didn't figure out the whole sexy thing until I was in my early twenties! I was still playing with my Barbie until the beginning of sixth grade. Being an adult is stressful enough, why in God's name would they want their kids to have to deal with that sort of crap earlier than they need to?"

"Allie isn't growing up too fast Cammi," Bryce reassured her. "She still sleeps with her blanket, watches Disney movies and doesn't even talk about boys. No matter what the other girls are doing, she is watching you. You are her best influence right now, so telling her the right things, like I know you always do, is going to make more of an impact than anything else. You are deeply involved in her life, and for that reason, I know she is going to make good decisions. And if she doesn't, we will deal with it when it happens."

Cammi knew he was right and tried not to worry, but her opinion on the subject wasn't going to change. Mother's were more interested in being their daughter's best friend than being their mother or setting an example. And from the statistical rise in sex and teen pregnancies, she didn't think being their friend wasn't working so well.

"We don't know yet," Cammi said shifting her attention back to Allie. "Of course it will depend on what we have. Any ideas?" Cammi asked cleaning up their mess.

"You know I want it to be a girl, of course. Boys are a pain, they are too hyper and crazy, like Heather's little brother."

Cammi laughed. Robby was definitely a handful. Very rarely did a week go by that something drastic didn't occur at their household. Last week he was caught by the neighbor peeing on the tree in the front year. The week before, he broke his arm falling out of the exact same tree.

"I like the name Faith. I heard it in Sunday school a few months ago and thought it was nice. It reminded me of you."
A slow smile spread across Cammi's face as she reached for her daughter, giving her the biggest hug she possibly could considering how large her stomach was. Allie reluctantly returned it before pulling away to pick up the rest of the mess.

"I love it. It's perfect. How about Faith Hope, if it's a girl, of course. With a name like that she's sure to be something special."

Before Cammi, Allie had been the woman of the house and the only child. She had gracefully given up her role, but Cammi wondered how easy it would be to share her parents, especially Bryce, with another child. Cammi knew a new baby would be an adjustment for Allie and they wanted her involved as much as possible. She was pretty content in the relationship she and Allie shared but the older Allie got, the more possessive Allie became of her time with her dad. Cammi explained to him it was normal for girls to want the attention of their fathers, and it was vital when she entered her teenage years that he is more available to her. If she felt she didn't have his attention, she might look for it elsewhere.

Faith Hope was born two weeks early on December eighth. Everyone, especially Allie, was grateful she was a girl considering they were set on the name and completely avoided picking one for a boy.

It was an easy delivery. Cammi was in labor for only five hours before little Faith decided she wanted to take a look at the world. Everything went as planned, and Cammi was grateful to share the moment with her husband. Instead of taking Lamaze classes to prepare for the birth, she opted on a prenatal yoga class at the local Recreation Center, and Bryce who was against it at first, arguing only sissy men did yoga, attended with her. After only two classes, he felt the benefits and was slowly learning how to combat his stress and anxiety at work. Aside from helping during the hard labor pains, the yoga also helped Cammi prepare for the emotional consequences she was sure she would experience after the birth due to the abortion she had had years ago.

Cammi and Bryce decided the four of them would spend the first week together without any visitors, adjusting to the change, especially since Cammi would not only be experiencing the joy of becoming a first time mother, she also needed to give herself patience and understanding as she grieved what might have been. Eventually they would have family and friends share in their happiness, but Bryce, trying to be considerate, wanted to be prepared. Cammi would be forever grateful for the phone call Jamie made to Bryce half way through Cammi's pregnancy putting this little bug in his ear.

Faith was a wonderful baby, and Allie shined in her role as big sister. Never once did she complain nor was she jealous. Loving generosity seemed to come naturally to her, and Cammi couldn't imagine a better big sister in the whole world for little Faithy.

Cammi and Bryce also adjusted better than expected to their newest addition. He saved up a few weeks' vacation time, and they both agreed Cammi wouldn't go back to work after her three months maternity leave. She felt her place was at home, raising her children. That job belonged to her and no one else. Lamont called her day in and day out begging her to change her mind, but Cammi wouldn't budge. She spent the first month on an emotional rollercoaster filled with crying, laughing, anxiety and fear. But she was compassionate with herself, and eventually things evened out to where Cammi didn't feel she was going to fall apart at any given moment.

As he had been with Allie, Bryce was a hands on father. He was awake during the night as Cammi breast-fed the baby, helped change diapers, and would spend hours after work talking to and cooing at his new daughter as he held her.

Before the pregnancy, Cammi had been worried about their future as husband and wife. There were weeks, even months where she was content, happy and enjoying life. Then something would set her off, trigger the onslaught of issues she thought she'd pushed passed once and for all. And poor Bryce, he usually got the raw end of the deal though he wasn't immune to his own bad behaviors either.

Bryce had a different way of dealing with stress than she did, and it was hard for her to understand. When she was upset, she wanted to talk, vent. Bryce on the other hand, shut down, emotionally and physically. Even though his stress was usually work related, she felt like an emotional punching bag until he pulled out of it. At those times, it was as if she didn't exist.

Even after their lives had blended together, he was still a doting, affectionate husband, but when he was under pressure, she was lucky to get a hug or a kiss. He ignored her needs and it affected how she felt about herself. She had thought if she pleased him more, he would give her the attention she needed. At other times, she scolded herself for depending on him to make her feel worthy.

But they'd moved past that.....grown.....became stronger and ironed out their issues. For months now, life was as it should be.

But lately, Cammi found herself slipping into a dark hole of disappointment. Her life was exactly as she wanted it, and she was desperate to find fulfillment in all she did, but the stormy cloud of resentment was beginning to build again.

There were so many women who balanced full time careers, a few kids, *and* a husband. So why couldn't she do it? Not only that, but they also found time to socialize and bake cookies for the school bake sale, make Halloween costumes, and volunteer in the classroom. At Allie's last bake sale, Cammi was up until one in the morning wanting to make sure everything was perfect, only to wind up burning half the batch and crying the rest of night before she finally broke down and snuck to the store to buy cookies.

What sort of mother took store bought cookies? And in the classroom…..she was bored to death. Though she still went twice a week an hour at a time to help with reading groups, she could think of a million things she would rather be doing.

In the evenings, she was completely exhausted. All she wanted to do was lay her head on the pillow and fall into a peaceful sleep. But this was the only time she and Bryce were alone to talk. Over the years, their communication wavered. Sometimes it was good. Other times they needed to take a step back and remind themselves why they fell and love and got married.

Then there were Bryce's friends. She liked them, she really did. They were respectful and protective of her, the guys on the softball team and the volunteer fire department had good morals and family values, the same as him, but she was jealous of his "guy time". He played on a basketball league every Wednesday night and went out for beers afterwards. He'd been doing it for years and was always home by ten. During the summer, almost every Saturday, he, Shawn and Eddie golfed as long as the weather permitted. Cammi hadn't minded before, but now that they had Faith, she thought things needed to change. She wasn't going to be left at home alone while he was out having a good time. She wanted to be the center of his world, wanted him to be happy and content at home with her and the kids. Not only that, she wanted to be included in all he did. When it boiled down to it, she felt threatened, not to mention a little nagging voice in the back of her head that made her wonder if he only wanted a mother for his kids while he lived a bachelor's life.

Of course when she mentioned it, he blew up.

"Cammi, I don't understand why it's such a big deal. It's part of me. It has nothing to do with you. It's my release, like you going for your morning walk."

"I get that, Bryce, but my morning walk doesn't take time away from you or my family. What happens when the kids have an activity on Saturday or Allie needs help with homework, and I'm occupied with Faith? You won't be around to help. Or what if we want to go out of town? It is the only day we can sleep in and curl up together. I mean, really, you are with the guys at the fire department Thursday evenings and half a day on Sunday. When do I get a whole weekend with you?"

"Jesus Cammi, I'm only at the fire department one weekend a month and golf is only during the summer. Stop exaggerating."

"Until winter rolls around, and you find something else to do."

He reluctantly agreed to give up golf. Though he still played ball, he stopped going out for beers, but Cammi knew it was only a matter of time before he became restless again. A small part of her did feel guilty and could sense his unhappiness, but as time went on she only became more anxious each time he left the house. Instead of encouraging his hobbies, she made him feel awful when he was doing something he enjoyed that didn't include her.

But those were just symptoms, symptoms of something much deeper. It was as if something was brewing. Her intuition was troubled.

Shaking her head, Cammi began to unload the dishwasher. Her inner critic made her her own worst enemy. But here she was, once again, caught in the trap. At times like this all she could do was pray. Pray that God would remind her of all the good she had and help her force the negative out of her head. The mind was a very powerful tool, and she needed to get a grip before she sabotaged the things in her life she cherished the most.

Chapter Thirteen

It became an evening ritual around eight o'clock for Cammi to sing Faith lullabies as they rocked together in the nursery. Mesmerized, Allie would eavesdrop in the doorway, her heart full of love not only for her new sister but Cammi, too.

"Do you know how much you are loved?" She heard Cammi whisper. "I love you, your daddy loves you, and you have the best big sister in the whole world. She takes good care of you. You need to watch and learn from her. She is kind, unselfish and knows how to care for people. She is very special Faith and you are *so* lucky to have her."

The tears rolled down Allie's cheeks as Cammi continued to sing. Allie loved her so much, but lately she felt empty, lonely and her stomachaches were coming back. Had her own mother rocked her and talked to her the way Cammi did Faith? Was her mother willing to give up her job, her time with friends, even sleep at night to make sure she had everything she needed? Allie's only memories were of living with her dad, and she couldn't help but wonder why her mother *really* wasn't around.

She hadn't bothered to think much about Cynthia before now. Cammi'd been around forever. Allie only had a few memories of life before her, but since the birth of her sister, the questions were there, in her head, all the time. Did her mom miss her? Did she even love her? Would Cammi treat her differently now that she had Faith? If her mother *did* love her and was in her life, then it wouldn't matter about Cammi, because she would have her real mom's love all to herself. She wouldn't have to share that with anyone.

Before she started kindergarten, Allie used to get lonely and wish for someone to play with, like a twin sister who could sleep in the same bed as her. That way when the scary noises woke her up, she and her sister could hold hands, tell stories, and laugh. Allie had only one picture of her mom she kept in her nightstand. Before she fell asleep, she would stare at it, willing herself to remember a touch, a kind word, her voice, anything to make the loneliness disappear. As she stared at it, her stomach would cramp up. She hated the stomach aches. She'd had them for as long as she could remember and wished they would go away. It surprised her how quickly and strong they came on. She would take deep breaths like her grandma taught her to relax and eventually the tightness eased. Her counselor told her dad that a hole had been left when her mom disappeared, but Allie didn't feel the hole. She wondered if it was in her stomach.

Then when Cammi and her dad got married, she wasn't as lonely anymore. Cammi read her stories, would sing her songs, run her fingers through her hair and the next thing she knew, it was morning. The noises hadn't bothered her anymore. She even told her dad she didn't want her old mommy anymore, just Cammi.

Allie started calling Cammi Mom in second grade. Her dad said the last phone call she had from her birth mother had been when she was about four. She didn't remember much other than a voice on the phone, but sometimes Allie would daydream in the hopes that if they ever met again, she wanted her to be just like Cammi. At the time Allie thought of Cammi as her mom. She was a mom in all the ways her friend's moms were, the only difference was she didn't give birth to her. Cammi braided her hair, made her breakfast, helped with homework, walked her to school and once a week, they went swimming together, just the two of them. Allie had looked forward to those days. Cammi taught her how to dive, how to kick her feet in the water and after, she would take her to get a strawberry shake. If her birth mom came back, Allie knew she would still want Cammi to be her mom forever. Cynthia could just be her friend.

Allie didn't know much about why her mom left, only that her dad said she wasn't ready or grown up enough to be a mom, so he thought it was better for everyone involved if Allie lived with him. He said she had bad habits she wasn't willing to give up and those habits could hurt Allie. When she was younger, she didn't fully understand, but she was eleven now and guessed her dad meant drugs.

Allie tucked her knees under her as her thoughts drifted to her sister. Faith was only five months old and already, Allie felt protective of her, she would never do anything that would harm her, and she was only her sister. It was upsetting her own mother would choose to do something that could be dangerous instead of being a responsible parent.

Bryce never talked bad about Cynthia but it intimidated Allie to ask questions. For some reason, her dad hated her mom.

Her name seldom came up, but when it did, his eyes turned black, and he always told Allie the same thing, "You are better off without her."

Allie's eyes were beginning to burn so when Cammi stood to lay a sleeping Faith into the crib she quietly snuck back into her room. There was a soft knock on the door a few minutes later. Allie quickly wiped at her tears.

Her dad was the one who usually tucked her in now that Cammi was preoccupied with Faith at bedtime and the older Allie got, the more she liked to read by herself, but tonight she longed to have Cammi's attention. She smiled when her mom poked her head around the corner. "Can I read with you tonight?"

As Cammi crawled under the covers, Allie rested her head against the security of her shoulder and read the next few pages of the chapter book she brought home from school. After they were done, Allie rolled over and pretended to fall asleep while Cammi rubbed her back. Eventually Cammi kissed her forehead and pulled the covers up around her.

When Allie knew Cammi was safely gone, she began to weep silently. She remembered when her teacher's aide in fourth grade told her Cammi would treat her differently when she and her dad had another baby. Allie came home from school crying, but didn't tell either of her parents why. But Miss Nelson was wrong, Cammi didn't really treat her different, but lately, she did notice she was more crabby than normal. Allie wondered if it had something to do with her. Usually it was her dad's fault, but they seemed to be getting along well, better than before Faith was born. So it *had* to be her. That was the only explanation.

Cammi missed cozying up next to Allie, listening to her gentle voice sound out the more difficult words now that she was reading more advanced books. It was nice to have this time with her, just the two of them. It was rare.

It wasn't long until Allie was asleep, but Cammi stayed, gently rubbing her back, not only for Allie's comfort, but her own, too. She studied the soft features of her face, wondering what it would have been like to hold her as an infant, to sing her songs of love and promise, filling her with the security of a mother's love, to look into her face and see a part of herself. What she felt watching her was no different than with her own child, but she was filled with regret for what she wasn't….Allie's birth mother. So much heartache could have been prevented if only it was she who met Bryce earlier in life, if it was she who gave birth to Allie eleven years ago.

Sad and full of longing, Cammi pulled the covers up over Allie's shoulders, turned off the light, and shut the door before searching for her husband.

Bryce was busy balancing the checkbook in bed when Cammi slid in next to him. She needed him in a way she needed no one else. To be close to him, to love him, to have him love her, made her feel complete, whole.

And right now she didn't feel whole, she was in pain. There was a wedge between her and Allie. It was unintentional, but nevertheless, there. And if she was honest with herself, it always had been. As difficult as it was to bridge the barrier, it was even more difficult to crave a relationship that might be near to impossible to have.

She knew she shouldn't complain. Allie was the perfect stepdaughter and their connection was amazing, but Cammi wanted more. She wanted it all. She didn't want there to ever be a Cynthia. She wanted the memories, all the credit and all the love. No one else deserved it because no one else loved Allie the way she did. In all senses of the term, *she* was her mother. She knew Allie like no one else would.

The sentiment had intensified since Faith's birth. Instead of wrestling with the turmoil building inside, she threw herself into her new baby, hoping to make up for what she hadn't been around to give Allie or for that fact, her other baby.

With tears streaming down her cheeks, she turned her back to Bryce, ashamed he might see her cry. As much as she needed the intimacy right then, she first needed to compose herself.

Occupied with the money at the moment, he didn't notice her stifled sobs.

She was becoming drowsy when she heard him put the stack of papers on the bedside table and reach for her. With his arm securely around her waist, she pressed her body into the curve of his sighing as his warmth comforted her.

Bryce found her post-pregnancy body tremendously appealing. Knowing she carried and had given birth to his child was such a turn-on he couldn't get enough of her. She was an amazing mother to both his children. Treasuring each moment they shared as a family, he fell in love with her all over again.

He turned her body towards him in search of her lips. As his hands pulled her satin nightgown up over her body and he reacted instantaneously to her full, round breasts. The natural process of a woman's body fascinated him, and he found it strange a man would be turned off by the most beautiful gift a woman could give.... the life of his child.

He ravished her body and could feel her response as he caressed the softness of her skin. There wasn't any place he didn't explore. It amazed him every time felt like the first time, only without the inhibitions when they were first dating.

He slowly and carefully rolled on top of her, plunging himself inside while kissing her with so much passion, he thought his mind would explode.

Faith was starting to sleep in longer increments now, and so was Cammi. Her exhaustion usually put her to sleep before her head hit the pillow but tonight, she just wanted to curl up in the comfort of her husband's arms. She couldn't shake an underlying fear..... of what she didn't know...... but she was in desperate need of his reassurance. Cammi always loved what he did to her, but his enthusiasm since the baby was born, had her soaring above the clouds. She'd never felt so loved and desired. It was enchanting and mesmerizing all at once.

"I love you so much, baby," she whispered into his ear.

"I love you, too."

"You give me so much. I only hope I can give it back. I can be a pain....I know, but you complete my life. You filled a space that was empty for a very long time," she said her eyes searching his in the dark.

It was nice to be at a place where their love wasn't strained, so why was she allowing her fears to complicate everything? Would her doubts of the unknown push him away again? Cammi hated the vicious cycle within herself that always seemed to be in constant conflict. She worked and tried so hard to find inner peace..... .consistent happiness would be better than this wave of turmoil she seemed to always live in. When would it all come together?

"I know it's not easy, our life is a little chaotic," he whispered making circular motions on her back with his fingertips. "Two kids are a lot different than one."

Her mouth quivered as the corner of her eyes moistened. "I want you to know I am still focused on us. The love and acceptance you and Allie give has taught me how important it is to connect with people. I spent too many years pushing others away and made myself miserable. I missed out on so much. With love there's pain, but I'm actually living life and not worrying about it. Thanks for being patient with me."

She said the words he wanted to hear, the words she believed were possible, and hopefully saying them out loud would help to convince her, but she couldn't shake the uneasy feeling things were about to change, once again. The guilt threatening to resurface was uncomfortable so she pushed away the thoughts as she rolled over to straddle him. Bending her head to meet his lips, she prayed that he would never give up on her and as she drifted off to sleep a while later, she prayed she had the strength to endure whatever obstacles came their way.

Chapter Fourteen

Since the day they were married, Bryce woke up each morning more and more in love with his wife. Going home to her after work still excited him. Holding her close at night and waking up next to her in the morning was a comfort. She would always be exactly what he wanted.

At first, he was nervous about living together, the stero-typical horror stories of how life would change once the ring was on, but with them, at first, things just clicked. She was more laid back than he imagined. The only issue she complained about was he did not clean up the dishes after dinner and had a habit of leaving his shoes wherever he took them off. But other than that, they both pitched in. Being a bachelor for so long he enjoyed helping around the house. Plus he knew it made Cammi feel loved when they did the household chores together.

The adjustment of allowing her to parent Allie came easy for him, too. They had the same expectations and ideas when it came to raising kids so he trusted her completely and backed up any decision she made. He set the ground rules right away with Allie so she knew to respect and listen to Cammi.

And when he came home one night to find Allie calling Cammi 'Mom', he thought his heart would explode. He could see in the time they spent together a special bond was forming between the two. Compared to Cynthia, Cammi was such a good influence. With her love for life and positive attitude, he'd seen Allie grow and thrive in a way he couldn't show her. Having such a healthy, stable woman as a mother figure for his daughter made the fears he had in raising her disappear.

Of course their life had eventually settled down and their relationship changed as it grew. The love didn't change, but as with everything, the newness soon wore off and they began to push one another's buttons. Not that he wanted it that way. It was just how life happened. They argued more often than not, and the stress of trying to get pregnant hung like a grey cloud over all of them, while Cammi became moody, clingy and at times insecure. No matter how much she dismissed the pain inflicted by her divorce, it was obvious to him in her behavior there was definite damage by her ex-husband. What he did to her….. well, something like that does a number on someone, and Bryce could see through her tough exterior. Though she did a decent job of hiding it, she was scared to have someone she truly *did* love hurt her the same way.

Bryce knew that like most men, he wasn't great at expressing his emotions. They were there. He just hadn't become comfortable with the expression part of it. But he knew it was important in a relationship, especially for women to hear. Cammi didn't understand why he could express himself so freely when they were first together, but now he didn't even attempt. He wished he could explain to her none of those words came easy for him. In his mind, if he said it once, what was the point in repeating it? She said he had become too comfortable and was taking her for granted. It wasn't as if his feelings had changed. He just didn't see the point in having an hour-long conversation about it day in and day out.

But he tried and unlike other men, Bryce *was* aware of his faults. He knew he was critical at times and could be a complete jerk to those he loved the most while people on the outside saw him as charming, personable and easy going. He worked hard on himself over the years to ensure Allie didn't suffer from his lack of sensitivity. His own father had been extremely critical of everything he did, and he didn't want his child, especially a girl, to bear the scars of the same insults. It was ironic to him how he could be so suave, pleasant and sincere when it was work related, but in his personal relationships, Bryce was a complete buffoon. He had many regrets of how he handled things in the past, but felt he had grown, learned from his mistakes. There were times when he had not come across in the most positive light to his wife, and he didn't know the reasoning behind it. All he knew is there was a seething bitterness underlying the exterior of his love.

If he were to guess, it probably had to do with her possessiveness. The one thing he fell in love with was she didn't want to change him. Being active and independent herself, he thought she would appreciate his interests too. It drove him mad that she didn't want him doing the things he loved because they didn't include her. Of course, he understood her trust issues and hoped with time he could get back into his routine, but it had yet to happen. He did everything within his power to earn her trust. But he was beginning to resent her. Basketball and golf were a part of who he was. He played those sports as a kid, and it was his stress release. Now he didn't have one at all.

And to top it off, there was work. It had been a long two years of adjustments at work with Freddie Allen as the new Chief of Staff at Madison General Hospital. It didn't take Bryce long to realize how incredibly incompetent the man was. Freddie lacked people skills, an area where Bryce excelled. Employees were constantly offended by his brash behavior and threats to quit were heard on a daily basis. Bryce spent more time doing damage control than actual work.

Freddie also liked to micromanage his employees and coworkers. He wanted to be in control at all times and didn't appreciate others showing him up. He would take credit for a job well done and did not delegate tasks for fear someone might be more competent than he was, which, of course everyone was. He also came in with a 'holier than thou' attitude of how things were run and planned on changing hospital policies that had been in place for years.

Bryce used to come home night after night emotionally drained from a job he once loved and it was greatly affecting his home life. He was quiet, moody and withdrawn while his criticism hurt both Cammi and the kids. He tried to escape, but without his hobbies, he didn't have anywhere to turn for a release.

It was obvious Cammi hadn't known how to react. She'd never seen his anger before. Along with trying to fix it, she took everything he said and did personally, when all he wanted was to be left alone to mull over it. Even though he explained it had nothing to do with her, she still didn't get it. When he was in a bad mood, everyone paid, sometimes for days because he couldn't seem to get a handle on it. His intention wasn't to be mean. He just needed time to himself, doing the things he loved. They had no idea how degrading it was to be miserable in his job. That was his livelihood, his future, how he provided for his family.

Bryce wasn't typically a pessimist by nature, but with the circumstances eating away at him, pessimism won over. If one thing was wrong, everything was wrong. If something didn't go his way, everybody was out to get him. In his eyes this was just another in a long line of things gone wrong in his life, and he was tired of the pressure.

At home, his life with Cammi needed to be about compromise, though meeting her halfway became a struggle. They'd come to a crossroads in their relationship and changes needed to be made on both parts. Unfortunately, he didn't know what else to do.

He loved his family more than anything and didn't want to stop trying, but he subconsciously pulled away. They used to argue like adults, agreeing to disagree and respecting the others opinion even if they did not like it. Afterwards, they would come together and talk it out, but those little arguments became more heated and the behavior on both parts, less rational.

Bryce thought back to the time before he found out Cammi was pregnant with Faith. They were supposed to go to a big hospital promotion party. The Chief of Staff at the hospital was retiring and at dinner Freddie would be named as his successor. He had told Cammi three days previously he was expected to be there and now she claimed she wasn't going.

"I don't really want to go, Bryce, I'm sorry. I just don't have the energy."

"What's going on with you? You don't have the energy for anything anymore," he commented thinking about their sex life.

What he didn't know was Cammi was six weeks pregnant and they would have Faith right around Christmas time. She'd been too scared to tell him. It had taken them a long time to get pregnant, though they started trying immediately after the wedding. Cammi believed in Karma and thought it was her fault, that somehow she deserved to be punished for the choice she made all those years ago, maybe she didn't deserve to have children. She wanted to protect Bryce from the pain that might be inevitable, if for some reason she miscarried. So she decided to keep the news to herself until she was sure the pregnancy was here to stay, until she was sure all was stable and safe. The emotional guilt she felt consumed her. She wasn't sleeping well, she was waking up in cold sweats, and the headaches were frequent. She tried her best to hide the morning sickness from him, but it too was added stress. As thrilled a she was about having a baby with Bryce, she couldn't deny the news was bittersweet. Cammi could not help thinking about her first pregnancy, how it came to be but mostly, how it ended. The images of that time haunted her, though she tried to ignore them.

"They will understand," she said looking up from the magazine she was flipping through.

"They might, but I won't. I go to these work events by myself all the time and I am sick of it, Cammi. When are you going to start including yourself in my life? There is always an excuse to stay home. Really…what's the problem?"

He saw her roll her eyes and knew she thought he was being ridiculous and overly dramatic. She'd told him so many times. She felt she *had* integrated every part of his life into hers except for his work. He could see her point. All he did was complain so why should she fake politeness for three hours with people she could care less to know, then come home to hear him bitch about them for two more? But still, he wanted her there by his side and he resented going to work functions alone.

"You know how I am. I don't feel very social right now and things like that make me uncomfortable."

Frowning, he adjusted his tie in the mirror over the fireplace.

"Maybe you need to step out of your comfort zone once in a while. It helps build self-esteem, you know," he repeated the words he'd heard her say so many times.

He saw her glare at his reflection.

"Fine, I'll go. But don't you dare leave me alone with anyone that I might have to make conversation with. If the food's good, maybe the evening won't be a complete waste of time," she complained storming up the stairs to change her clothes.

If she'd just been honest with him about all of it, the evening may have turned out differently. As it was, they were both irritated and on edge.

They dropped Allie off at a slumber party on the way and Cammi graciously told her to have fun, but the instant Allie was out of the car her attitude towards Bryce turned sour. He, on the other hand, just chose to ignore her and drummed his fingers on the steering wheel to the music while she stared out the window pouting.

A private room was reserved at the Marriot, which was located on the Interstate, only ten miles from Madison. Knowing how much Cammi hated social events, he took her hand. He'd gotten used to this part of her personality. She was more content with a few close friends than she was big crowds. These types of social gatherings, where all eyes were on her because she was Bryce's wife, having to rub elbows with high-class professionals, sent her over the edge.

One would think after years in the journalism world, interviewing highly affluent people, she would be used to it. But that was just it, she was interviewing them. She didn't have to socialize with them, pretend they were her friends and they certainly didn't give a damn about her, who she was or what her life was like. She could remain private, hidden behind the questions while they talked about their favorite subject, themselves. But this left her out in the open for scrutiny and judgment. The one thing she hated most in the world.

Bryce held true to his word and didn't leave her side once. In the time they'd been together, she hadn't seen him at work with his employees. Because Madison was a small community, it was typical for them to run into co-workers when they were out and about, but still, Bryce wasn't at work, and she wasn't a wife who made a point of dropping into the office for a quick "hello". She respected his privacy.

After dinner, Bryce returned from the bar with two beers in hand, one for him and one for her. He was so preoccupied carrying on a variety of conversation with the others at their table he didn't even notice she wasn't drinking it.

"Bryce, honey, do you know that woman?" she whispered in his ear during one of the speeches.

"What? Huh?"

"The lady over there in the corner, the redhead. Do you know her?" she asked again sounding irritated. "She keeps looking over here."

"Oh yeah! That's "what's his name's" sister. You know her. Remember? The one I had a date with the night I met you?"

"What?" she shrieked standing up quickly, knocking a chair over in the process. "Um, sorry," she mumbled in embarrassment as the people around her stared.

Taking her seat, she looked somberly into her husband's eyes. Immediately, he was filled with guilt. He covered her hand with his, while silently pleading with her to understand. Never taking her eyes off his face, she pulled her hand away, reached for her purse and left the room.

Hoping to give her time to cool off, he waited to follow. Five minutes passed before he couldn't stand it any longer.

Bryce found her sitting on a lounge chair next to the ladies rest room, her face cold and dark.

"I'm sorry," he apologized. "I never told you."

"So tell me now."

"I never thought I was going to meet you. You were being as stubborn as a mule and I figured I should count my losses."

"Don't you dare blame this on me," she gasped.

"I'm…I'm not. It's just that, crap," he mumbled shoving a hand through his hair. "Nothing I say is going to make this better. You won't believe me anyway."

"Try me."

"Look, it was years ago. We are together, so what does it matter?"

"What matters is you made me trust you, but you still kept something from me."

"It wasn't even important. I broke the date with her the day I met you at the coffee shop," he admitted. "I wanted to be with you, not her."

"You said her brother set you up. Did you know what she looked like?"

"Yes. I met her at a New Year's party months before. She bored me to death and it was even worse when I called to plan the date. All I could think about was she wasn't you, but you weren't having anything to do with me. I hadn't even met you yet, what did you expect me to do?" he argued.

"I expected you not to play games. You were talking to me, getting to know me, calling me. That should have been enough for you to say, 'Sorry, but I am currently involved with someone.'"

"Christ, Cammi, I hadn't even met you, and I honestly didn't know if I was ever going to."

"But you were interested in me right? We were talking on the phone, remember?"

"You know I was."

"That right there should have been enough. It's called integrity, Bryce. I use to think you had it. But instead you were willing to take a date with the first bimbo who comes along just because I wasn't fitting into your timeframe. Where is the integrity behind that?"

"That's not fair."

"No, what's not fair is that you kept it from me. Why?"

"I didn't think about it. Honestly, it didn't matter."

"Like Beth? That didn't matter either and look at the chaos she caused in our life. Great, now there's another one. How many others are there you haven't told me about? Do I get to spend my life running into your ex-girlfriends everywhere we go?"

"She was never my girlfriend, Cammi."

"You know what? I can't look at you right now. I'm walking home. Go ahead and stay here, drink a few beers with 'what's his name's sister'. I hope you have a great time."

She bolted for the front entrance with Bryce a step behind her.

"What are you doing?" she yelled, startling him as she turned her face only inches from his. Her eyes blazed with fury.

He stepped away. "I'm going with you." He'd never seen her this upset.

"What part of 'I don't want to see you right now' don't you get?" she seethed.

"Cammi, I'm not going to stay here. If you want to walk……"

"Excuse me, Bryce isn't it?" the curvaceous woman interrupted as she glided into the hallway. She reminded Cammi of classy version of Anna-Nicole Smith only with red hair. "How are you? I haven't seen you for years. I wondered what happened to you."

"Why don't you introduce me to your friend, Bryce," Cammi smirked.

Turning his back to Cammi, he smiled uncomfortably at the woman. "Lacy right? This is my wife, Cammi," he said introducing the two women. Cammi firmly gripped the other woman's delicate hand when she held it out.

"We were just leaving, excuse us." He started for the door his hand gently guiding Cammi's arm when Lacy blocked their way.

"I didn't realize you got married."

"Four years ago," Cammi muttered.

"Hm….that's interesting. Wasn't it about four and a half years ago you broke a date with me?"

Cammi moved toward her. "Yeah, for a date with me."

"Let's go," he said taking his wife's hand, leading her through the open door.

"You certainly have interesting taste," was the response they heard from Lacy before the door closed.

For Bryce, the ride home was like a prison, nowhere to go and no escaping the punishment to come.

But to his surprise, Cammi didn't say a word. In fact, she didn't say anything to him for two days. He hated it when she gave him the cold shoulder but what worried him more was instead of dealing with the problem, she buried it. Still, he wasn't stupid enough to bring the subject up. He explained himself and figured there were some things better left in the past.

They spent more time walking on egg shells with each other than anything else. Less than a month later, they'd had another fight.

"It would be nice to come home after a shitty day of work to a clean house," Bryce commented irritably as he pulled his shirt over his head, throwing it into a heap on the floor. It had been a rough day for him at work and since he'd come home, he'd been taking his frustration out on her. Cammi had been fighting morning sickness and had looked forward to nothing more than curling up in bed with a good book. Now as she pulled the covers up around her and opened to her page, he decided to start in on her again. It was as if he were purposely picking a fight.

"What exactly is it you have been doing all day?" he demanded grabbing his toothbrush.

She gave him a dirty look slamming the book shut. "What exactly do you mean by that?" Cammi asked defensively. "If you are insinuating I don't do a good enough job taking care of the house or

Allie I suggest you think twice before those words come out of your mouth."

He rolled his eyes in disgust. "Why are you so damn sensitive? All I was saying is I am tired of the house looking like a typhoon hit it. There are things we need to do to fix it up. It's starting to look like a dump."

Cammi was irate. This wasn't the first time she'd heard the line of insults.

"I have every right to be sensitive. The house is a woman's domain and when you criticize it, I am going to be insulted. Maybe, just maybe when you come home from work, instead of sulking and spending hours on the computer looking at vacation packages to take you away from the nightmare you consider your life, you could spend some time fixing the stuff that pisses you off so much! Then maybe, just maybe…. you might be happy!"

Fire raged in Bryce's eyes. He had loved her feistiness when they first met, but now it infuriated him.

"Oh that's what I need….. to leave a miserable job and come home to more work you should be doing during the day!" he shouted.

"I have a job too, you know," she snapped.

"Not much of one. You sit around on the computer for a few hours here and there typing. How hard can that be?"

Cammi stared at him in complete disbelief. "What the hell would even possess you to say such hateful things to me?" she asked. "Who are you?"

"Jesus Cammi! Stop being so touchy," Bryce scowled.

"We could just hire someone to do everything *you* don't want to do," Cammi commented under her breath. "Like fix the leaky faucet in the kitchen or replace the warped wood on the front porch."

"The hell we will! This is my house. I am not going to pay good money for someone else to come in and do a job we are capable of doing ourselves."

"Huh? According to you, I'm *not* capable. Last time I tried to paint the bedroom you barely talked to me for a week because it wasn't the right color," she muttered flipping the pages of her book again. "Don't need that again," she replied sarcastically.

"Can't you see I am drained? Can't you see I am unfulfilled with what I am doing and when I get home, the last thing I want to do is think about something else that needs done?"

Sitting up in bed, Cammi put her book down. "Besides the job you obviously have no respect for, I take care of our daughter, make your dinner, do the shopping, do the laundry and the ironing and even mowed the lawn the last two times because you were working late and guess what? Even after all the complaints and put downs I get on a daily basis I still find time to have sex with you so we can start our own family."

"What is this.... a competition?" he growled.

"You're the one who brought it up," she reminded him. Defeated, she paused briefly before continuing. "You know what I see? I see an unhappy man. You are a miserable person who chooses to stay that way. You are allowing the issues with your job to control your life. I am sick of it. You are making me miserable and you are making your daughter miserable. Neither of us can stand to be around you. You may not see it, but you are turning into your father. You complain just to complain regardless if it is constructive or not. And it's not, it's damaging to the well-being of this family."

"Gee, I wonder why I'm unhappy. Maybe because I don't get to do anything that would make me happy," he snarled. "Thanks for the all the support you give me when things are bad. Isn't that part of our vows? For better and for worse? Or have you already forgotten what that means?"

He had remarkable way of belittling her which she tried without success to ignore. The words stung creating an infusion of rage inside her.

"Don't talk to me like I am a child," she screamed jumping out of bed. "I deserve to have you treat me with respect and if you can't, then don't expect the same in return. Just because your life sucks, doesn't mean you have to point out everything that is wrong with me. Is it your goal to make everyone in this house as miserable as you are? Because you are doing a real good job of it!"

Turning to storm out of the room, she couldn't help picking up a water glass from the bedside table. In the heat of anger, she lost control over her actions and as her arm came over her head she released the glass from her fingers, watching as it shattered against the hardwood floor.

They avoided one another as best they could, careful not to set the other one off. It was easier for them to behave this way than to swallow their pride and admit their wrongs. To Cammi, everything he said or did was an insult and to Bryce, it didn't matter how he treated her, she would still be mad so why bother.

At times like this and they happened often, Bryce felt their future was doomed and he was very unhappy. He didn't understand how two people who loved each other so much could behave so badly. They were the best of friends and when things were good, they were fabulous. But changes needed to be made on both parts if they wanted it to stay that way.

Ironically, Cammi's announcement she was pregnant a month later was just the change they needed.

Once again, Bryce walked in the door after work irritated and distracted so he hadn't even noticed the congratulations sign Allie was hanging up over the fireplace or the wrapped gifts on the dining room table. He was hungry, but it didn't seem Cammi had made dinner since he didn't smell any aroma coming from the kitchen.

Making an effort, he walked over and gave Cammi a quick kiss on the check and tousled Allie's hair before going upstairs to change.

"Hey, baby," she said rubbing his shoulders. He was standing at the door of the closet looking for a shirt to wear. "Rough day?"

"Ahhh, now that feels good," he grunted, dropping his chin to his chest so she could rub deeper. When she finished, he whipped around and wrapped his arms around her body. Silence filled the room as he buried his head in her neck.

"Things were getting better," he finally whispered. "But this week's been hell. I don't know how much more of him I can take. I was so ready to walk out of there today, let him do half the job I do. I bet fifty people or more would quit if that was the case."

He pulled away for a moment to remove his shirt, and then bare-chested he took her back into his embrace. He felt Cammi quiver under his touch.

"Have I told you lately how much I love you and how grateful I am you are in my life?" He could tell he surprised her with his praise.

Gently guiding her down on the bed, he hovered over her looking into the deep pool of her green eyes. Lowering his head, he let his lips softly brush hers before it erupted into a deeper kiss. For a reason he couldn't explain, she felt fragile and vulnerable in his arms, like he needed to be careful. His fingers combed through her soft brown curls. God, he loved her hair. It was silky, like satin and smelled of vanilla. When he wasn't with her, he could still close his eyes and breathe in her scent, one he would remember until the day he died. He often wondered how he got so lucky.

One thing he loved about Cammi was despite her other insecurities; she was incredibly comfortable with her own sexuality. Since the first time they made love, there wasn't ever a time she wasn't willing or ready. He had buddies at work who often complained their wives were never in the mood or felt like it was their 'wifely' obligation. But with Cammi, that was never the case.

In fact, he remembered how turned on he'd been to learn how open and uninhibited she was when it came to making love with him.

But Bryce had noticed changes in her, some good, some not so good. She was still radiant and full of life, and he was more attracted to her with each passing day. She made him laugh and just being with her made him feel good. In her he found an inner peace that had eluded him for a long time. Despite their rocky patches, he loved that they could always come back to this. It only proved to him how strong their relationship was. But she was preoccupied and anymore it seemed she would recoil at his touch. They hadn't had sex forever.

"Honey, I have a surprise for you downstairs," she interrupted turning her head away. "Are you in the mood for some good news?" He wasn't surprised to find her persuading him to go downstairs instead of staying up there to fool around but it discouraged him all the same.

Reluctantly, he pulled on a t-shirt and followed her down the stairs.

He couldn't help but think she wasn't interested in him anymore. With the stress he was dealing with at work, he hadn't been exercising the way he should and the extra weight was beginning to show around his stomach. He hoped she wasn't turned off by it. If he were still playing basketball, it wouldn't be an issue. He'd be a little more motivated to exercise.

"What is this all about?" he asked as Allie came down from her room to sit with them. "Are you in on this little surprise?" he teased enclosing her in a big bear hug.

"Mom has a gift for you," she told him excitedly.

They both watched in anticipation as he tore open the wrapping. First he read the title of the book and appeared stumped, but his confusion was soon replaced by understanding when he lifted the booties out of the box.

"Are you serious?" he asked half laughing, half in shock. "Are you serious?" he said again looking back and forth from his wife to his daughter with tears in his eyes.

Cammi nodded enthusiastically.

"Are you happy, Daddy?" Allie asked anxiously.

He picked Cammi up and swung her around. After a deeply passionate kiss, he placed his hand on her stomach to convince himself it was real.

"I am *so* happy! We need to celebrate. Let's go out for dinner! Oh, but wait. How do you feel? Are you sick? How far along are you?" He fired question after question, his voice wavering with concern.

"I'm fine. I've had some morning sickness, but it's almost over," she reassured him hoisting her purse over her shoulder. "Where do you want to eat, Allie?"

"What do you mean almost over?" he asked confused. He was sure most women had morning sickness through the first trimester, but he could be wrong, every pregnancy was different.

"I am twelve weeks today, honey. I had an appointment this morning and heard the heart beat for the first time," she confessed, her voice growing softer. "I wanted to make sure everything was alright before I told anyone."

"How long have you known you were pregnant?" he asked slowly registering this information while disappointment ate at his gut.

"Seven weeks, but like I said, I wanted to make sure everything was okay."

He turned away and when he spoke again his voice was angry.

"You mean to tell me that you have known for this long and never once thought about telling me?" he accused, his eyes blazing with rage while his body shook all over. "Did you ever think no matter what happened, good or bad, this is *my* baby too and it was my right to share everything with you?"

Cammi was rattled by his outburst.

"Babe," her voice a whisper, she placed her hand on his back. "I didn't do this to hurt you. I wanted to spare you the pain of what I went through if there was a miscarriage. I thought it would be a surprise and kept thinking if something went wrong, how disappointed you would be."

His jaw was clenched in anger as he walked toward her. His eyes were dark and for the first time in their marriage, she was afraid of him.

Allie had only seen her dad's temper a few times, never at her, only at others. But she had never seen the combination of anger and hurt at the same time. Not wanting to stick around to hear them fight, she disappeared to her room and turned her music on loud enough to drown out their voices.

"So tell me this, Cammi. What were you going to do if you did have a miscarriage? Deal with it on your own? Never tell me about the baby?" He tried to calm down before he said something he would regret, but the fury rushing through him was making him crazy.

"No! God, No. I didn't.... didn't want to think about that scenario."

"Don't you think if there was a miscarriage, it would be as much my loss as it was yours? Don't you think I would have needed to grieve with you? Together?"

"Bryce there wasn't a miscarriage, so we don't have to worry about it."

"Damn it Cammi, that is not my point," he yelled, slamming his fist on the table. Looking at her now, she reminded him of Cynthia. "You had no right to keep this from me. You have been lying to me for weeks."

"Stop it! You need to calm down!" she demanded backing away from him. "You are being ridiculous! I never lied to you about anything. Look, you might not understand what I did, but…."

He didn't let her finish. "Do you have any idea how this makes me feel, Cammi? You told me what happened last time, about not telling your ex. I understood the circumstances surrounding that, but now if this situation turned out differently, you were going to do the same thing. It makes me realize what little respect and trust you have for me. I would think after all this time you would have learned to depend on me. I figured when we got married whatever happened in our lives, we would deal with it together. I never thought you would treat me the same way you did him. Or the way Cynthia treated me."

"That's not fair," she shrieked.

"What's not fair is I should have been with you today to hear the baby's heartbeat. You took that away from me because you are selfish and that is something I won't ever get back."

"Stop it! Stop it right now!" she sobbed putting her hands over her ears to keep from hearing his ugly words. Suddenly her face turned dark. "You hypocrite! What about Lacy? I let that go, forgave you, and now you have the audacity to accuse me of lying?"

"Yeah, you really let that one go. If you recall, you made me pay for days on end."

"If I am so awful, I honestly don't know why you are with me," she said out of desperation. But he rolled his eyes and walked up the stairs.

He could practically feel her temper blaze. "Don't you walk away from me! You sit there and tell me how horrible I am and then think you can just walk away and not deal with what you have said. You expect me to deal with what I have done to you, so you need to be responsible for how you make me feel," she shrieked.

He continued to ignore her when she finally grabbed his shoulder to force him to turn around.

"Don't touch me right now, Cammi." His hiss was menacing. She jumped back as if he burned her.

"Oh, I get it," she replied sarcastically. "It's okay for you to treat me bad when I screw up, but how would you feel if I reacted this way to you every time you acted like a shit?"

"Look in the mirror, Cammi. You do."

"You wonder why I don't trust you or your love?" she continued ignoring his remark. "Maybe it is because whenever you have a bad day or are dealing with some issue at work, you don't depend on me. In fact you push me away. You get so worked up you have nothing to give. You are critical, you don't show me any love or affection for days, you retreat into a little hole built only around you, and I can't get in. But when you feel better, you expect me to come to you with open arms, which I usually do. I have been there for you, good and bad, but can you handle *my* good and bad or would you just pull away when I need you the most? You're right. I don't trust it and you don't see how much it kills me."

"There is such a double standard in this relationship," she went on. "'Depend on me, Cammi, tell me everything, take your walls down and trust me', but yet you can't do the same. You constantly leave me out in the cold. How can I come to you and open up to you when you aren't even available? You have as many walls up as I do. You don't talk to me, but when things go wrong with our relationship, it is always *my* issues needing to be worked through to make us better. What about your issues and your coping skills that don't work so well for us? Huh, Bryce, what about you?"

She fell to her knees sobbing uncontrollably, but after a few minutes of silence, he went to her and engulfed her in his arms. She was reluctant to return his embrace but eventually turned into him, crying into his chest.

"I have lots of things to work on," he said quietly. "It's not easy for me to admit my faults, especially to you. I want you to think I am perfect."

In between sobs, she laughed.

"Nobody's perfect, Bryce."

"I know. But I want you to be proud of me. I know I hurt you, but it's not intentional. I don't know any other way to be. It took a long time for you to trust me and when I screw up, I get so angry at myself because I see your fear. You are kind and patient. At times, I don't think I deserve your love. I don't know how to tell you I'm sorry, so I just stay away because I can't stand the idea of your rejection. I hope eventually time will make it better, but it doesn't. I can see how you resent me, and in turn, I allow myself to close off. I don't want to face the truth that you might not actually like the person I really am, all my faults, I mean."

"And then this," he gently put his hand on her stomach, "just escalated the fear. What if I disappoint you even more, like Marcus did?"

"Don't you realize I am just as insecure about how you feel about *me*? That I want you to see *me* as perfect? And if you see my faults, you will wonder if you made a mistake? I don't want to lose you. But I can't handle how you treat me anymore. We have been together almost four years; we have a baby on the way. When you clam up in your shell, it makes me wonder what I did wrong. You don't tell me so I assume it's me. All I can think about is you finally decided I am not the one you want. I worry all the time you are going to meet someone else and think they are a better match for you. Or maybe if I didn't have my issues, you would want to spend time with me again. I miss you so much and miss the intimacy we shared."

She reached up and in a simple gesture, wiped away the tears running down his face.

"Baby, I'm so sorry. I need to get better at showing you my love. Believe me, every day I love you more and more. There is no one else for me and never will be. I wish you wouldn't think like that. Please don't take my moods personally. I am going to work really hard on letting you know what is going on in my head."

"And I am going to try to relax more and accept all of you. I need to trust in your love. I'm sorry I didn't tell you about the baby," she confessed. "It was wrong. I honestly didn't see how inconsiderate it was or how it would make you feel like you did with Cynthia. I promise not to let anything like this happen again. Just promise me no matter what, good or bad, you won't leave me," she said.

Her comment concerned him. "What would make you think I would want to leave you?" he asked.

"I need you, more than you know, and you don't need me. I knew the first time we met you wouldn't put up with a lot of shit from anyone and especially after hearing the story of Cynthia. I know how easy it was for you to walk away. Don't get me wrong. I am grateful you did. But I get scared you will give up on us that easily especially if I continue to make mistakes."

Her confession shocked him. "I didn't love Cynthia. Not ever. How could you even compare yourself to her?"

"You just did," she said softly.

Bryce was ashamed. He had never loved anyone the way he loved Cammi. No one could take her place, he was confident in what they shared. Hopefully in his love, she would find that security, also.

"Sweetheart, people spend their lives searching for what you and I get to share every day. It doesn't mean we won't have fights, and it doesn't mean there won't be days when we dislike each other, and it doesn't mean we won't screw up, but I can't imagine doing this with anyone else. You are my soul mate. Remember?"

He kissed her deeply and passionately feeling her tremble beneath his touch as her heart melted into his. His reassurance, more than anything, was what she needed.

"Truce?" he asked sweeping her carefully into his arms. He climbed the stairs setting her gently on the bed. She erupted in a fit of giggles as he jumped, catching himself on his hands and knees so he landed directly above her.

"I'm going to be a daddy again!" he shouted before devouring her body with his mouth.

Experiencing this pregnancy with his wife was completely different than the first time around. He was devoted to making Cammi happy. And she was right. He didn't want to be the father who made his wife and children afraid. He didn't enjoy being angry, it wasn't his nature, and hopefully, with her guidance he could find a way to let go of it.

Becoming aware and making changes drew them closer. Her energy and excitement delighted him, and she glowed with an inner beauty he radiated in. And he noticed how hard she was trying to trust him. Sharing every moment, every detail, wanting him involved in every part of the pregnancy made it easier for him to meet her halfway.

Bryce wished he could comprehend the pain from her past to have some idea of why, until now, she had never allowed others close. It was an aspect of her life even she might never fully understand.

Chapter Fifteen

At six months old, Faith spent most of her time scooting around on all fours and Cammi, desperate to capture every moment, was constantly snapping pictures. Faith loved being the star. But more than being a star, she loved her big sister. Faith was Allie's constant shadow everywhere she went. Allie was at an age where most girls would rather be with their friends, but having Faith around gave her an excuse to rush home every day after school. It also gave Cammi a chance to run errands while Allie learned some responsibility. She and Bryce agreed on an appropriate allowance for her help, and Allie loved having the extra money for movie's and CD's, so when school was out for the summer, Cammi continued the routine three days a week.

The Fourth of July had always been one of Cammi's favorite holidays and this year, the family could not wait to celebrate. Allie was pushing Faith's stroller as they walked downtown for the Festival with Bryce and Cammi a few feet behind, holding hands. After months of early morning walks, Cammi had finally gotten back her pre-pregnancy figure and felt great. The yoga class she took throughout the pregnancy was such an added benefit she continued to attend a regular class two days a week. Bryce declined the offer to go with her, but every now and then, when he didn't think anyone was watching, she would catch him in corpse pose, breathing deeply.

It was unusually hot that day but to Cammi, everything was perfect. After the parade, they planned to meet her parents and her Brother Kurt's family at the lake for a BBQ. The only drawback was Carissa wouldn't be there as she was on vacation in Vegas, living it up with her new boyfriend. Carissa was a proud aunt and after the birth of Faith, she came by the house at least once a week. She and Allie had become close too. Not as close as a typical aunt-niece relationship would probably be, but they were good friends and

Cammi was grateful to have another positive female role model for Allie to spend time with.

Filled with a sense of pride, Cammi scanned the crowd for familiar faces, eagerly watching the children holding flags, anticipating the floats that would pass by any minute.

"Dad, Heather and Brandi are going to the carnival tonight. Can I go with them?" Allie asked shoving a fistful of cotton candy into her mouth.

"We won't be back until late, Babe. How about you invite one of the girls to spend the night tomorrow night? I can take you both then."

"I want to hang out with them tonight. I don't ever get to," she whined.

"I told you, we're going to the lake. No arguments! This is a family day. You can see your friends tomorrow," he said holding up his hand to shade his eyes from the sun.

Allie glared up at him with disgust and started to pout.

"We always do family stuff. I am sick of it. When do I get to do what I want to do?"

"When you are eighteen and out of the house," he told her. "We spend the holidays together, if you don't like it, too bad. You can either make the most of it or be miserable the whole day. But if you decide to make the day miserable for the rest of us, you will be grounded for a week. Then you'll miss the carnival all together."

Irritated, she crossed her arms over her chest and ignored her dad the rest of the parade.

Cammi tried to smooth it over, but grew frustrated with their lack of effort to be nice to each other. She just had to realize there were going to be times, especially when Allie became a teenager that the girl was going to have to be mad and part of growing up was learning how deal with it. Bryce was right in the decision he made. And if Cammi wanted Allie to grow into a mature, capable adult, she needed to stand back and allow these things to work out on their own.

Due to Allie's temperamental moods, there were days Cammi felt closer than ever to her and others where she found herself avoiding the girl entirely. It wasn't that she was angry and Allie hadn't really done anything wrong, their time together was just awkward. After weeks of trying to make things more pleasant for Allie, Cammi finally convinced herself that her daughter was in a phase uncomfortable for everyone. There was nothing she could do about it and soon, it would pass. At least she hoped it would.

Faith *oohed and awwed* over the horses, bounced in her seat as the high school band marched by and squealed with glee at the silly antics of the clowns. As noon approached, Faith was zonked out in her stroller and the heat was becoming unbearable, so they decided to head home and pack up for the lake instead of heading to the town square picnic. Allie ran into a few friends and stopped to talk, as did Bryce. Cammi lagged behind casually watching the crowds flood past her as she pushed the stroller back and forth. Scanning the scene around her, she became aware of a strange unpleasantness lingering over her. Looking over her shoulder, it was almost as if she were being watched.

"Hey there! Hey.....Cammi!" a familiar voice drawled.

Cammi turned around to find Brandi's mother Rachel darting in and out of people in an attempt to reach her. Cammi groaned. Though Cammi considered them friendly acquaintances while their kids were in grade school, anymore the woman made her skin crawl so she tried to avoid her at all costs.

Rachel was decked out from head to toe in red, white and blue. Her normally brown highlighted hair was even streaked to match. Cammi giggled inwardly. It was well known Rachel was a gossip. Anything a person wanted to know.....she was the one to seek out. At first it had been entertaining to hear the little tidbits of those around town, but quickly, Cammi found that Rachel lived in her own glass house and should be very careful about throwing stones. She was on her third husband, had worked a variety of jobs anywhere from bank teller to florist to bus driver, though she rarely kept one for more than a year at a time and she loved to spend money on her very posh lifestyle. So much in fact, she utilized most of her time covering up her debt problems so she could keep up with the 'Jones'. Husband number three's job as the manager of a retail store could hardly cover her added expenses let alone pay their daily living costs. Cammi soon realized it was all a façade and lost any respect she had for her.

"Rachel. Hello. We are just heading home to meet my family for a barbeque. Sorry I can't stay and chat," Cammi blurted.

"Oh, no problem. I'm headed over to the square anyway. I'm in charge of the games for kids seven and under this year," she announced proudly. "I just wanted to let you know Principal Bartlett said someone had been by the school just before it let out for summer break asking all sorts of questions about Allie. He didn't recognize her. And you know his policy.....he didn't tell her a thing. But thought it was strange. He said he was going to call you but must have spaced it before he left on his vacation to Spain."

Cammi wasn't sure what to make of this. "Then how did you find out about it?"

"He got back into town two days ago. He came over to play horseshoes with Craig last evening. Allie was there too so that must have jogged his memory. Oh, hey….. I got to head out. Just thought I'd tell you in case he forgot again," Rachel said with a wink before she took off in a power sprint toward downtown.

Cammi linked her fingers through Bryce's as they began the walk back home. She was puzzled by what Rachel told her. Her first thought was Beth. But Mr. Bartlett would know her. When she relayed the message to Bryce a dark shadow fell across his face. She frowned and was about to ask him what that look was for when she felt him stiffen, saw his jaw clench, eyes wide with fear as he stared at two women across the street.

Allie was almost a full block ahead pushing Faith. "Go into the house, we will be there in a few minutes. Stay in the house with Faith!" he demanded, his voice panicked.

Cammi felt a cold chill run up her spine. Something was wrong. Something had to be wrong…..all his signals were off. She watched while Allie carried a sleeping Faith on her shoulder and disappeared into the house.

Bryce turned, taking long strides in the direction where the two women now stood. Curious, she followed but sensing the intensity within him, decided not to ask questions. Bryce's eyes narrowed into slits as he stopped short of the first woman. She was stunning, Cammi thought. Glamorous with her long blonde hair, she was an inch or two shorter than Bryce and her big round eyes shimmered like the blue sky.

Cammi's admiration quickly turned to disapproval as she observed her clothes. From far away, she would have guessed her to be a teenager. Her shirt was unbuttoned from the bottom up to where it met her bra exposing a large hoop belly button ring. She had a nice stomach, Cammi noticed, but with her shorts riding low on her hips and high on her thighs, it didn't leave much to the imagination. Not to mention she looked to be in her mid to late thirties, maybe older if the lines around her eyes and mouth were any indication.

Bryce's face was red with anger. It took Cammi a few more moments to recognize the other woman with her. When she did, her heart began to pound rapidly as her stomach flipped.

Beth was dressed similar to the blonde, but she wasn't as pretty or shapely. In fact, her skin looked ashen, and if it were possible, she was skinner than before. Her hair, now a fiery auburn color had grown out into a bob around her chin.

Cammi held her head high. Intimidating Beth would give her the satisfaction of superiority she didn't necessarily feel within, but to her surprise Beth was unwilling to make eye contact, instead standing back, appearing timid, even slightly afraid of what might happen next. Cammi was suddenly confused. The blonde looked familiar to her, but she had no idea where she could have seen her before.

"I told you I want to see my daughter," the blonde said.

"And I told you no!" Bryce insisted through clenched teeth. He didn't seem surprised or taken aback by either woman's presence.

"I didn't give up my rights to Allie, and if you want a fight on your hands, I will give you one. I have left you messages, Bryce. Why aren't you returning my calls?" She demanded tossing her blonde hair over her shoulders.

The blood drained from Cammi's face, and her hands started to shake. She looked back and forth from Bryce, to the blonde, then to Beth as the pieces of the puzzle began to fall into place. Was this some sort of conspiracy against her? She was standing directly in the middle of her worst nightmare come true. If she closed her eyes and concentrated real hard, maybe the ground would give away beneath her.

No. *No way could this be real*, she told herself shaking her head. Yet here she was, standing witness to the disintegration of her happy family.

"I won't let you cause problems, Cynthia. My first concern is Allie's well-being," he whispered loud enough so only the four of them could hear but his voice was menacing. "I need to talk to my wife about this. I have also contacted a lawyer. I have your number and will call you when *I* decide the time is right. Not you. Do you understand me? Don't contact us or Allie until then. But like I said, whatever decision *we* make will be in Allie's best interest."

With that said, he took Cammi's hand and walked away. His were clammy with sweat, and she could feel the adrenaline beat in his pulse as they neared the house.

"Are you going to tell me what's going on?" Cammi fumed when she found her voice.

"Yes." He sounded completely defeated, so much so that despite her anger, Cammi felt sorry for him. "But I want to wait until Allie's not around. Let's go to the lake. Do you think your parents will watch the kids while we go somewhere and talk?"

He knew he wasn't going to be able to put her off for long, but needed some time to get his thoughts and feelings together. His anger was boiling, his heart breaking. He had to calm down. They needed to lean on one another now but the way this had played out he wouldn't be surprised if she didn't talk to him for weeks.

"Probably." She tried to muster up some sympathy knowing coming face to face with Cynthia couldn't be easy for him either, but instead she sounded cold.

The drive to the lake was awkward for everyone. Cammi's head swam with thoughts of her husband's secrets, thoughts of losing Allie, thoughts of Beth, and then Cynthia as disappointment and jealousy raged inside her. Cynthia was beautiful. Bryce had slept with her. She was Allie's mom. Every pore in Cammi's body was filled with hatred.

She wondered what Bryce thought, really thought when he saw her. Did he think she was beautiful? What man wouldn't? It had been years since he had seen her…or had it? She said she called so had he seen her too?

Seven years had passed since he and Allie last heard from Cynthia. A few months ago she, a fact Bryce was still bewildered by, contacted him at work begging forgiveness for the huge mistake she made and wondered if he would allow her to have visitations with her daughter.

Having no sympathy for a woman who caused so much pain and misery, he explained that since her last phone call years ago, he had married an amazing woman whom Allie loved and thought of as her mother. None of them needed Cynthia to walk back into their lives causing stress and chaos. Allie was just fine without her.

"Bryce, every girl needs to know her mother," Cynthia argued through tears. "It's especially important as she gets older. Isn't she the least bit curious?"

"She has a mother," he said coldly.

He'd spent years protecting Allie from this woman and the overwhelming desire to keep her away was stronger than ever. The conversation ended with Cynthia informing him she still had rights as Allie's mother and would take him to court if she had to. That was months ago. There were more messages, but he hadn't the gumption to call her back. His gut instinct told him she wouldn't take no for an answer. She wanted back in her daughter's life, and if his memory served him correctly, she would pester him until he allowed it.

After giving her parents a brief explanation, they jumped back in the car. Allie didn't have any idea what was going on and upon learning her parents were leaving, her already festering resentment towards her father deepened. By the time Faith was settled in with Grandma and Grandpa, Allie wasn't speaking to any of them. Bryce drove down the beach, looking for a secluded spot where they could be alone. It was difficult to find one with it being the holiday weekend, but he finally pulled beside an old abandoned lake house. Cammi was quiet on the ride. She was afraid if she spoke, she might crumble. Instead, she watched out the window, her throat tight, and her head pounding.

After putting the car into park, Bryce sank down into his seat and ran his hands through his hair in frustration refusing to look at his wife.

"I'm getting real tired of all your secrets, Bryce. They eventually come out and end up smacking you right where it hurts." Filled with anger, she couldn't contain herself any longer.

"I know," was all he said.

They stared out over the lake in silence, both thinking their own private thoughts. It seemed like ages before he spoke again.

"I keep telling myself I am protecting you. She called me only once, right after Faith was born. I didn't want to take your mind off the baby. Plus things were better between us I didn't want to jinx it. Maybe I wanted to pretend it wasn't happening. If I ignored her, she would go away. Besides, I told her she couldn't see Allie," he said sadly.

"I'm trying to be *real* understanding, Bryce. I realize this issue isn't about me, but I can't help feel a little betrayed by your lack of trust." She was calm and careful with her words, but inside she seethed at his hypocrisy.

"I panicked."

"Wasn't it about a year ago I was in trouble with you for something similar? You asked me when I was going to depend on you, trust you, work through everything together and then you pull something like this. Do we have a double standard? I've worked my ass off to make it right, but when are you going to give me the same consideration?"

"I know, I know. I screwed up. And there is no excuse. You don't have to tell me anything I don't already know or haven't thought about a million times," he sounded so desperate, it made Cammi's heart break.

"So what do we do?" she sighed. Regardless of what she felt, it wasn't the time to talk about it. They needed to make some decisions where Allie was concerned.

"I have thought about this for a long time and desperately needed your help but didn't want you to be scared or have to deal with Cynthia. She isn't your problem."

"All of your problems became my problems when we got married, remember? We are in this together. Please don't try to do this alone," she begged him. "Don't shut me out."

"She says she's sick with Hepatitis C. Supposedly the doctors told her she doesn't have much time unless she gets a liver transplant. She says she's on the list for one. I don't know what to believe, she gave me the name of the specialist in Denver. Hell, I can't even pronounce his name," he said. "I am really torn. I need to talk to Allie to find out what she wants. If she wants her mom in her life, and I don't allow it, I'll be the bad guy. As she gets older she could resent me. But I'm not sure I believe Cynthia. Allie could get hurt. I want to protect her, but she is eventually going to have to learn about her mom, and it might have to be the hard way… from experience. If I allow it now, I can still have some control and influence over her. Otherwise, she may seek her out on her own when she's older."

"She certainly doesn't look sick," Cammi commented dryly thinking about the curvaceous woman.

Bryce smirked. "What if she's telling the truth, and I don't give Allie a chance to know her?" he said, disturbed with the facts he just related. "She will hate me forever for taking that away. I don't know much about teenagers yet, but in a situation like this, she would be furious and angry teenagers usually rebel."

Cammi's first instinct to was to tell Cynthia 'hell no', and let her fight it out in court. But after listening to Bryce, she knew he was being rational, where she was being unreasonable and petty. He had evaluated all the angles and was trying to make the best choice for Allie.

She wrapped her arms around him. "You're scared, aren't you?"

He leaned his head on her shoulder, grateful for her comfort, under the circumstances. "More than ever. She told me in our conversation she's changed, but after looking at her today, my guess would be, no," he said with a slight laugh. "She said she has regrets when it comes to Allie, and she wants to spend the rest of her life making it up to her. Believe me. I went the rounds with her."

"Do you believe her? And what do you make of Beth? She looks horrible. Life has been hard on her since she was fired."

It was toward the end of Allie's fourth grade year when Beth was arrested on a drunken driving charge, her second offense, and the school fired her. Cammi couldn't help feeling justified but Allie had looked up to Beth and was upset for quite a while. It was as if she felt personally betrayed.

He shrugged, shaking his head. "I would be lying if I said it didn't concern me, but I'm not surprised. They are two peas in a pod. I would be curious to find out how they met. I would venture to guess at a bar. I don't know, Cammi…. I'm confused about all of it. But Cynthia's here. She's not going away so I guess for Allie's sake I want her to be telling the truth. It would make everything easier."

Jerking open the car door, Bryce walked around the front to lean against the hood. The wind picked up, and he watched a Jet Ski maneuver in the rough water. Cammi stepped out to join him.

"I'm angry with myself," he admitted staring at the sky. "If I was thinking at the time, I bet a million bucks she would have signed over her rights and then we wouldn't be dealing with this right now. I wouldn't have to sit back and watch my daughter get hurt, knowing I can't do a damn thing about it. I told myself I would not let that woman hurt Allie with her lies and manipulation, but I didn't do the one thing that could have stopped her."

"Don't beat yourself up about it, honey. You did the best you could."

He turned his grateful eyes to his wife. "I know, but I already feel like Allie hates me. She's so defiant lately."

Cammi smiled, and she kissed his cheek.

"I have listened to everything you have said and I see your point. I think we should sit down with Allie and see what she wants. Support her in the decision, even if it hurts. It's not about us. Cynthia doesn't look like the picture of a perfect mother, but maybe it will be okay. Allie is tough. She went through it once and you both handled it. Now she has two of us who will love and support her if Cynthia screws up."

He was encouraged by Cammi's strength. Her love for Allie was unconditional. She wasn't even her real mother and once again, here she was, willing to put her own feelings aside to help him make this decision.

"What about her being sick? Is it fair to bring Cynthia into her life, allow her to get close and love her, knowing she might die?"

"If she's as persistent as you tell me she is, we might not have a choice. Wouldn't it be better for Allie if we weren't keeping Cynthia from her or vice versa? If we don't allow it, Cynthia might get to her on her own terms. This way we get the final say. And I would let Cynthia tell her. It's not our place."

They talked for another hour before coming to a decision agreeing that before they brought any of it up with Allie they needed to get more information from his lawyer.

Back at the lake, Allie was in a better mood. Kurt had all the kids out on the boat taking turns learning how to water-ski, and she was enjoying every moment of it. Having forgotten her anger at her father completely she waved to him frantically from the boat.

The rest of the day was spent relaxing and having fun. Ironically, Cammi was able to put thoughts of Cynthia out of her mind and enjoy the time with her family. Maybe just being away from home where no one could reach them gave her a sense of security. Maybe she cherished the simplicity of being with *her* family and in this moment no one could take that from her.

Either way, it was the calm before the storm.

Chapter Sixteen

Ron was a College buddy from Bryce's days at CSU. After graduation, he started up his own private law practice in Aspen and was more than happy to help them out when he received Bryce's call. He remembered when Bryce had first contacted him about Cynthia before Allie was born. He knew she was trouble from the minute he saw her cozying up to Bryce at the bar that night years ago, so he had no qualms about giving him free legal advice.

Bryce's intent wasn't to be vindictive; he only wanted to make sure he was able to protect his daughter, his wife and himself. With Cammi's support and his faith in the legal system, he decided it was time to discuss some options with Allie.

Faith was already in bed, and Cammi was straightening up the kitchen, when Bryce found Allie at the kitchen table looking over her school schedule for seventh grade.

Sitting across from her and placing his hands face down on the table, he blurted it out. "Your mom called me."

Confused, Allie looked from him to Cammi.

"You're birth mother. Cynthia," he corrected.

Allie's eyes widened with surprise. "What does she want?" She asked cautiously setting her pencil down.

"To see you."

"Why?"

As she pulled out her chair to join them, Cammi sensed Allie's hesitation.

"She said she made a mistake and wants to make it up to you. She wants to get to know you and to be a mom." He looked away briefly, swallowing hard. "I'm not going to tell you what to do; this has to be your decision. If you want to see her and get to know her, we will support you. But if you don't, then, we support that too."

Allie sat quietly, eyes glazed over, deep in thought. This is what she had been praying for and now it was happening. For one thing, she couldn't believe, it and two, she was unsure of how to feel. She didn't know her mom. What if they didn't have anything to talk about? Or worse, what if her mom didn't like her? Should she take a chance to find out? What did she look like? She couldn't even remember no matter how hard she tried, and the one picture had grown old and faded.

Cammi reached over to touch her hand.

"What are you thinking, honey?"

"I don't know. I guess I want to find out what she's like. Since Faith has been born, I'm mad she didn't want me around. I love having Faith and so do you. I don't understand why my mom wasn't like that. Was it me? Is there something wrong with me?" she asked her voice shaking.

"Oh, baby, there is nothing wrong with you," Cammi got up and wrapped her arms around Allie feeling her pain. "Your mom had problems, lots of them. Her lifestyle was questionable but none of it was your fault. She says she's cleaned up and now wants to be a part of your life."

"I still don't understand. What about her was so bad? Why wasn't she here? You never told me," she pleaded looking at her dad through tears.

Bryce sighed deeply, shifting his eyes to Cammi. Cammi was aware that Bryce had been very careful about what he told Allie. He didn't want her carrying around the burden of guilt for the lack of Cynthia's presence in her life. It was Cynthia's choice, not hers, but it was the usually the child's self esteem damaged because of a parents absence.

"Sometime Allie, we will sit down and talk about it. I promise. But I don't want you to make a judgment on your mother based on my opinion. It's up to you to get to know her on your terms."

Cammi frowned as she listened. She didn't completely agree nor did she think Allie was mature enough to make her own choice, but she kept her mouth shut. Obviously Bryce felt it was a private conversation for them to have at another time.

"Why do you keep putting me off when it comes to her," Allie cried, pushing her chair back and standing up. "I deserve to know the truth! This is my life!"

"Allie honey," Cammi stood, placing her hand on Allie's shoulder. "One thing at a time, okay? This is a surprise to all of us and we need to work together to make sure it's what is best for you. Your dad is doing the best he can, but understand; this isn't easy for him either. He's worried. He wants to protect you as much as he can."

Biting her lip in concentration, Allie sat back down. "Do you believe her? Cynthia. Do you believe she has changed?"

"Only time will tell. I haven't been around her for almost nine years, so who knows what's happened since. I don't want to see you get hurt, that's for sure, but if it is something you want, then…" he shrugged looking away again.

Cammi could see how hard this was for him. He was allowing Allie to make her first responsible decision, and if it didn't turn out the way she hoped, he would have to pick up the pieces. He was giving her the freedom to make her own mistakes, but also reassuring her that his love was there no matter what the outcome.

"I don't know what to do," Allie said shaking her head. "I think it would be sort of weird. Do I have to make a decision right now?"

"No, of course not. I do think it best though if the first few visits are supervised either by us or a professional. You don't know her and I need to know you will be safe. She can come here. We can have dinner or something. No pressure, okay? You let us know."

Allie nodded and then returned to her homework.

As Bryce watched her from the doorway, relief flooded over him. Allie wasn't jumping up and down with joy at the mention of her mom. But his heart ached at the same time. By her lack of response, he could see the emotional damage had already been done.

Allie was lying awake in bed that night staring at the shadows of the trees bouncing off the walls in her room. She couldn't sleep no matter how hard she tried. Her head was spinning.

Her mom, her real mom, wanted to see her. She didn't know whether to laugh or cry, be relieved or angry. What she did know was she wanted answers. She was mad at her dad for not giving them to her. She'd asked a few times over the last year, but he ignored her or changed the subject.

Well, maybe she'd eventually ask her mother….Cynthia, and get the truth.

The thought of seeing Cynthia made Allie nervous. She didn't know what to expect or what Cynthia would expect of her. What did she want from Allie after all these years? What did any mother want from a kid they didn't even know or hadn't seen? Allie wondered what Cynthia would smell like, if she wore perfume or just lotion. She wondered what they would do together. Would they go swimming? Dance to music in the living room like she and Cammi did? Would they bake cookies and banana bread? Or would they just sit on the couch holding hands and talking? She wondered if her hands were soft and warm like Cammi's, too.

It took forever, but as Allie drifted off to sleep, she became excited as she envisioned Cynthia sitting next to her at the kitchen table reading over her shoulder, helping her with homework, sitting in the audience at her dance recitals, and cheering her on in the bleachers at her swim meets.

Bryce had at least one phone call a day from Cynthia for the next two weeks so finally, he gave her what she wanted, answers. Explaining the choice would be Allie's and he didn't want anyone pressuring her, he laid the ground rules. Cynthia wasn't thrilled about having the visits supervised, but Bryce wouldn't budge. He wasn't absolutely sure what he would be exposing his daughter to with Cynthia, and both he and Cammi were wary of her friendship with Beth. When he explained this, Cynthia did not appear surprised.

"Oh, I don't hang out with her much, especially after she told me about her DUI. She's not someone I would want Allie around, believe me," she explained sincerely. "But we work together, waitressing at The Cave. She's the first person I really met here. Even though supervision will be awkward for me, I can see how it would be better for Allie. It wouldn't be easy to have her take off somewhere with a complete stranger," her voice cracked.

"I didn't tell her about your illness, Cynthia, and I expect you to tread lightly with the subject. If you come back into her life, I don't want her believing she is going to lose you again anytime soon. If she thinks that, she might not want to take a chance to get to know you."

She eagerly agreed reassuring him her intentions weren't to hurt Allie. She only wanted the chance to give her daughter what she deserved from a mother.

"I'm tired of her calling all the time, but a part of me does feel sorry for her," he confessed to Cammi one evening after dinner. "You should have heard how excited she was when I told her."

Faith was still in her high chair throwing food on the floor instead of in her mouth and Allie, irritated with her dad over an argument about her science fair project for the upcoming year, shut herself up in her room.

Almost dropping the glass she had been washing in the sink, Cammi dried her hands on a towel and turned to face him. "You feel sorry for her?"

"Don't get me wrong. I still despise the woman. But I have to admit when I talk to her, she does sound sincere. If she has gotten her life together, can you imagine the regret she must feel over the choices she made? She's lost out on so much."

At the idea of it, a pain surged through Cammi's heart. It would absolutely kill her not to see her own children grow up.

"I guess so," she agreed. "It breaks my heart every time I think of Allie as a little girl craving her mother's love and attention, only to turn around and find it's not there. How could someone be cruel enough to put their own child through that sort of pain? All I know is if she screws this up, I will gladly watch while she burns in hell," Cammi threatened.

Bryce got up from the table and snuck up behind his wife who was wiping off the kitchen counter. His arms encircled her waist as he brought his lips to her neck.

"I love it when you talk tough. Remind me never to mess with you," he teased.

She turned her body into his and kissed him deeply. As her tongue explored his mouth, she took a hand full of soapy water and rubbed it in his face. She shrieked in delight escaping his grasp and ran into the living room. The chase was on as he took off after her.

When he finally had her cornered, she picked up one of Faith's stuffed animals, tossed it at his chest and leapt around the dining room table.

"You are *so* dead," he laughed.

"You don't scare me, remember, I can kick your ass."

He beat her around the end of the table, grabbed onto her wrist before she could get away and flung her over the back of his shoulder. Throwing her down on the couch, he sat on top of her.

Cammi screamed and begged him to stop tickling her. She was laughing so hard, she could hardly catch her breath. A confused Faith, who witnessed the whole incident from her high chair, suddenly started to cry.

Bryce reluctantly released his wife to run to the rescue. "You scared her, you big meanie!" Cammi said to him as he held Faith close, whispering gently in her ear to calm her down.

Allie came down the stairs demanding to know what all the screaming was about. "Oh, what's wrong with Faithy?" she asked hurrying over to take her sister from her dad's arms.

"Your dad scared her," Cammi told her grabbing a soda from the fridge.

"Oh, you're so full of it! Your mother was horsing around and didn't know when enough was enough," he defended himself.

They were still laughing as they all walked out on the front porch, Allie carrying the baby.

In only a few weeks school would start again and evenings like this would be nonexistent as the days grew shorter and shorter. Cammi spread a blanket out on the lawn and placed Faith on it, keeping her occupied with toys while Bryce and Allie swung together on the porch swing.

Allie sat quietly, lost in thought as they watched the orange blaze of the sun disappear beyond the horizon.

"You okay?" her dad finally asked jolting her back to reality.

"I've been thinking," she said tears filling her eyes. "I don't want to hurt either of you, but I really.....I think......I want to see my mom."

The tears made their escape, falling onto her lap. She reached up with the back of her hand to wipe them away while Cammi carried Faith up the steps to join them on the porch. Bryce draped his arm carefully around her shoulders.

"Allie, you have enough to think about, okay? Don't worry about us. Right now you do what you think is best. And if that's spending time with your mom, then we support you. We want you to be happy. Just know you can come to us about anything, and if it doesn't turn out the way you want… tell us. Don't be afraid. We love you."

Allie sobbed as she put her arms around her dad.

"I'm sort of scared….I kind of wish everything would stay the same. But if I don't do it, I will always wonder."

Cammi stared at her daughter in amazement. Allie turned twelve only a month earlier and she'd already been through so much at such a young age. It really wasn't fair.

Bryce called Cynthia the next day to invite her over for dinner the following week.

As the day approached, a hole began to eat its way through his stomach. On the outside he was able to show his support, but on the inside, he was dying. He didn't want to lose Allie to Cynthia. What if Allie decided one day she wanted to live with her? Or worse, what if she started to act like her? It was something he wasn't prepared to deal with.

Bryce's mother wanted to help with the transition, throwing her two cents in whenever she felt necessary and suggested Cynthia talk to Allie on the phone a few times before coming over. Cammi, though annoyed with the unsolicited advice, had to agree.

The phone calls usually lasted about a half hour. Allie was extremely private about the conversations and Bryce and Cammi didn't pry, even though curiosity, at times, got the best of them. Cammi was even tempted to pick up the other line and listen quietly, but her conscious told her to leave it alone.

On the evening of the dinner, Cammi was a wreck. For Allie's sake she didn't want it to show, but she hadn't been able to stop crying all day. Cynthia would be there in three hours. As much as she wanted to make this night perfect for Allie, there was a deeper part of her that resented it for happening.

Allie asked to have her favorite, Chicken Fettuccini. Cammi had already mixed up a side salad with basil and vinaigrette dressing and the French bread was ready to warm in the oven. Faith was still taking her nap, and Allie was at Brandi's until five, so Cammi had some time to mentally prepare herself.

Deep in thought, the phone suddenly rang. It was Bryce.

"How's it going," he asked.

"Fine."

"What time did you tell Allie to be home?"

"Five, Cynthia should be here around six. What time are you going to be home?" she asked. She was short and irritable but didn't care. At the moment talking to him was the last thing she wanted to do. This was his fault after all.

"I'll leave around four-thirty and stop to get a bottle of wine. I think you and I could probably use it after tonight," he told her.

Cammi was glad to hear he was as miserable as she was, but a part of her thought he deserved it for creating such a mess. "Get two. I need to go, see you in a bit." She felt guilty hanging up like she did, but she was bitter.....bitter and jealous. The idea of Allie getting close to her mom hurt Cammi deeply. She was the one to help raise her the past five years, and it was heart wrenching to know she might start looking towards another woman to give her what Cammi had so unselfishly handed out.

Plus the idea of having Bryce's ex-lover in their dining room, sharing a meal she prepared, wasn't exactly how she wanted to spend her evening.

There's always a reason behind the pain, Cammi reluctantly reminded herself. But this time, she was unable to see the forest through the trees. The rational side of her knew she had to be strong. Allie needed her, but the pain was almost unbearable.

Bryce made it home right on time. Faith was on the floor in the living room playing with her toys while Allie was upstairs getting ready. Cammi didn't know who was more nervous, Bryce, Allie or herself.

She took a deep breath to calm her nerves. If there was one thing she had complete faith in, it was knowing the love her family shared was strong enough to endure anything.

Even this.

Chapter Seventeen

In the beginning, Cynthia had been....pleasant at most. Cammi's first impression of her was, well, if she didn't have anything nice to say......her mother always told her just to keep her mouth shut. But her second impression didn't do the first justice. She showed up at their house dressed in tight black leather pants and red T-shirt adorned with a Harley Davidson Motorcycle and the words 'Dead Men Must Ride Again' printed underneath with matching red stiletto heels. One wasn't supposed to judge others by the way they dressed but the nagging thoughts ate away at her.

Regardless of her desire to be the mother Allie always needed or if she was truly dying, underneath her polite and gracious exterior, Cammi sensed the woman was trouble. Either way, she swore she wasn't going to upset Allie or ruin what was an important moment for her.

The supervised time between Allie and Cynthia lasted for six months before Bryce finally allowed Cynthia to take Allie for a weekend. It was an excruciating decision, but aside from their gut instinct, Cynthia had done nothing inappropriate to give them concern for Allie's safety. Allie had been spending every other weekend with Cynthia for about five months when Cammi found out she was pregnant again. The whole family was thrilled and timing couldn't have been more perfect. Faith was a year and a-half old, so after this baby, they agreed to be finished. Three kids were plenty.

For the most part, Allie seemed to enjoy her time with Cynthia. For Cammi and Bryce it was an adjustment after having Allie in their lives twenty-four hours a day, seven days a week, to sadly watching her pack up to live elsewhere for two days twice a month. She didn't divulge any information about her time with Cynthia so all they could assume was they spent most of it shopping. Like clockwork, Allie always arrived home with two or three new outfits or a new pair of shoes and purses.

The pregnancy had been a good distraction for Cammi as she coped with Allie's absence. Not having her around plus sharing her with another woman proved more difficult than she imagined. Allie was growing, changing. And in directions she and Bryce were no longer included. It was as if aliens had invaded their home in the middle of the night, snatched up their little girl and replaced her with a young woman. Only the young woman, as far as Cammi was concerned, was too young for the road she was headed down.

Boys, clothes, make-up and hair consumed her from the minute she woke up to the moment she closed her eyes at night. Cammi knew nothing about hair and the rest she tried to fake, just so could catch a glimpse into the world Allie was now living.

Of course, Cynthia was an expert in *all* area's holding Allie's interest. And as much as Cammi disapproved, a part of her couldn't help being jealous. Yes, she was spread thin with Faith and her pregnancy, so the time the two normally spent together was cut short, but she still wanted Allie by her side. She relished in the comfort of having her around and now......she wasn't there.

Cammi loathed Cynthia and when she found herself in her company, she felt extremely inadequate. She was sexy, beautiful and portrayed a seductive confidence Cammi had never been comfortable with herself. Granted she looked like a whore, but she possessed a sense of style Cammi couldn't help but envy. She was enchanting, sociable, and friendly, though at times she appeared phony while lacking sophistication, class, and dignity. When it came down to it, Cammi didn't trust her. Maybe it was because of her past with Bryce. It could also be her friendship with Beth. Nevertheless, Cammi was watching her back. Her gut instinct told her Cynthia was a venomous viper waiting to strike.

Allie had just turned twelve when her mom was thrown back into her life, and Bryce had no idea at the time how vulnerable and impressionable that age was. He didn't know whether to attribute her defiant behavior to the desperation of having her mother's love, or that he was actually a horrible father who did a lousy job raising her. When Cammi announced her pregnancy, there were significant changes. Allie went from a straight A student, involved in various activities at school from swim team, drama and dance, to edging on the verge of becoming a deadbeat on the road to nowhere. Her grades slipped below C's, and she had been caught smoking cigarettes on school property when she was supposed to be at practice for the school play. She landed a week's detention and that was how Bryce and Cammi were informed she had quit the play the week before.

"Get a grip, Dad. It's not like I was smoking dope," she said vaguely slamming her school books onto the kitchen counter.

"You better damn well hope that as long as I'm alive, it is never dope, because you won't see the light of day again if I catch you," he scowled.

"Come on, it's not like you didn't try anything like this when you were younger," she said innocently, smiling sweetly at him.

"At sixteen and seventeen maybe but not eighth grade! And don't bat your eyelashes at me like I am some guy you can flirt with. Who the hell are you anymore?" he demanded. "And what were you doing after school when you were supposed to be at practice?"

Her eyes melted into slits. "Hanging out, what's the big deal? I was just trying it. I'm old enough to do what I want. Some of the kids smoke all the time. Their parents even give em' to them."

With a vice grip on her arms, he pushed her down into the couch. "Get this straight right here and right now. You are not other kids and I am not like other parents. You will do what I say and follow my rules. The next five years can either be easy or they can be hard. It's your choice. But as long as you are living with me, there will be consequences for actions like this, you get me?"

"Mom says I can decide who I want to live with, so if you continue to treat me like a child, I might just decide to live with her," she threatened.

For a moment Bryce was confused until the realization of her words landed on his heart, and he prayed Cammi had not overheard Allie call Cynthia 'Mom'. It would kill her. God, he wanted to slap her. Who did Allie think she was talking to him that way? For years he'd never even gotten a negative, back-talking comment from her, now.....it was as if she was the devil's spawn.

"That is *not* and never will be an option. Do you understand me? And I can see right through your little scheme. You *will* spend the next week when you're not at school in your room getting your grades up. If I don't see a significant change in the next two weeks, it will be extended. Don't test me on this! And wipe that black shit off your eyes before your *Mother* gets home. It's too damned dark."

His threat worked only because Allie's attention was focused on bigger and better things. Her childhood dreams of becoming a ballerina were out the window instead replaced by a crazy notion she should be a model. *Someone* planted a seed saying she could make gobs of money if she got a job as a runway model in New York or Paris. Ironically, the only good thing to come out of it was she would not achieve this without a high school diploma. So her grades were on a steady incline.

"You know mom, it's important for a model to maintain her weight. I have been thinking about going on a diet," she informed Cammi one night when Bailey was a half a year old. They were sitting on the porch watching Faith ride her three-wheeler up and down the sidewalk. Cammi was holding Bailey over her shoulder patting him on the back hoping he would release the bubble forming in his stomach making him upset. "Cynthia used to be a model, did you know that?" Allie said proudly. "And she wasn't allowed to weigh anymore than one hundred and ten pounds."

Allie was so private anymore it was a rare occasion for them to spend any time together, let alone talk. The usual chatty Allie holed up in her room after school until dinner time, and then was on the phone with Cynthia until Bryce said 'lights out.' 'Cynthia said this', Cynthia thinks that', Cynthia wants me to do this'. It was sickening. And frankly, Cammi was tired of hearing about Cynthia.

Until those words came out of Allie's mouth.

When Bailey finally let out a big burp, she moved him onto her lap and took a sip of her ice tea contemplating how to respond. Allie was a little girl whose head was being filled with big girl ideas. Idea's not healthy or realistic, but Cammi knew she needed to tread lightly.

"Honey, believe me, you don't need to even think about a diet. At this age, your metabolism is fast and constantly changing." Allie was tall and slender, without an ounce of fat on her. "Unless you're significantly overweight for your age, it's not something you need to think about until you're in your twenties and even then, you don't need to diet. You just want to be careful about what you eat."

"Cynthia is always trying a different diet and last month, she lost twenty pounds. She only ate meat. No fruit, no carbs, whatever those are, and no dairy. It worked, I saw it."

Since her argument with her dad, Allie was real careful to make sure she didn't call Cynthia 'Mom'. She was so ashamed afterwards. Cammi *was* her mom. That would never change. She was just so mad at her dad for telling her what she could and couldn't do.

"She says boys only date girls who have nice bodies. She says when I am a teenager, if I want the best boyfriends; I need to make sure I look good, because that's what they go for."

Cammi's eyebrows shot up in shock, though she quickly tried to hide her disapproval. If she had a baseball bat, the idea of slugging Cynthia in the stomach with it was very appealing. What was she thinking and where was her common sense? It began to dawn on Cammi the woman didn't have any.

"Look Allie, it's normal for girls your age to have these concerns, especially with boys. But are you ready for boys to pay attention to you in that way?"

Allie blushed. "Well, no, not really. But it's all Cynthia talks about, so I thought it must be important."

"It's up to *you* to find out what's important. Don't let anyone else make that decision. I am sure when the time comes you will be super boy crazy and nothing else will matter. But if you aren't there yet, don't rush it. There is too much pressure when it comes to trying to impress everyone else. Just be yourself and the rest will come."

They sat quietly while Bailey slept in Cammi's arms but inside her screams were mixed with prayers. She only hoped their influence over Allie would be stronger than the one she was getting from Cynthia.

Cammi must have said something profound. Whatever it was, Allie's wheels were spinning and ironically while she made dinner, Allie was by her side, just like it used to be. Together, they watched the two little ones on the floor playing with their toys while Allie laughed at their antics. Faith was the typical older sister. Not wanting to share, but always watching out for her younger brother. As he began to put her favorite doll into his mouth she yanked it away causing him to fall over backwards. He instantly burst into tears.

"Faithy, you need to be careful with your brother, he is smaller than you and can't do everything you can," Cammi scolded. She set down the stack of plates she had been carrying and stooped down to move Bailey away before a fight started. "If you don't want him to have something, please find another toy he can have before you take yours away," she said sitting him upright.

Pride filled her when Faith walked over, wrapped her arms around Bailey and said 'sowwy'. God, kids were easy at this age. Allie had been easy, too. But then the hand of fate, or should she say the devil in disguise named Cynthia came back to torture them.

"You know, you're right," Allie suddenly declared. She reached across Cammi into the cookie jar, took out a handful of OREO's and gave one to Faith. "Cynthia likes guys a lot. So do the girls at school, I thought I had to be like them. But I don't. I just still want to have fun with my friends."

With that, she got up and skipped outside as Cammi breathed a sigh of relief, keeping her fingers crossed and knowing this was only the first of many obstacles to overcome.

"Cynthia thinks I should let her have a boyfriend," Bryce said after Cammi told him about her earlier conversation with Allie. "I have been meaning to tell you about our little chat last week, but spaced it. I'm sorry."

He was lying on the bed watching Cammi put the day's laundry away.

"Why does Cynthia get a say in this?" Cammi asked dryly.

"She doesn't. I was just telling you."

Cammi shut the dresser drawer firmly. "She's never expressed an interest in boys before now. I understand it comes with the age, but she's way too young. This is peer pressure from her mother. It's obvious Cynthia's self-worth comes from the attention she gets from men, and I pray to God, Allie will eventually see it's not the way to go."

"I'm sure she is just hearing stuff at school. I wouldn't blame Cynthia too much."

Cammi couldn't believe what she was hearing. Did he seriously just turn on her and defend Cynthia? And how could he remain so calm about it?

"I told you word for word what her mother said, if you want to bury your head in the sand, that's not my problem, but I am going to do whatever I can to stay one step ahead and combat all the bullshit she might be teaching her."

"Cammi, don't you think you are jumping to conclusions? I am not ignoring this, I resent you would suggest that. Admit it. Things haven't been that horrible with Cynthia around. She's stepped up to the plate and proven herself to be responsible."

Her heart sank to the pit of her stomach. Cammi looked at him as though she were staring at a stranger. Had he already forgotten all the trouble Allie had been in? Had he decided to turn a blind eye to the tall tales coming out of Cynthia with every conversation they had? Did he disregard at least once a month she asked him for money to help pay her bills while her spending habits continued to put her in serious debt? That in itself was an issue which caused a major fight between them, but thank goodness, it was a battle she won.

"Are you for real?" she asked.

"Look, we didn't expect this. Yes, Allie's having some behavioral issues but she's just testing us. All teenagers do. It will pass. You just don't want to deal with the fact you have to share

Allie with another woman. A woman who has different idea's then you, and you don't like it, admit it."

"You're damn right I don't like it. Can you say you do?" she snapped. His accusations hurt. "Do you think I enjoy feeling this way? Do you think I enjoy not having her around? I miss her and would love it if nothing changed. But that is not possible. I know she needs to spend time with her mom. But YOU need to understand that at times I don't think it is fair."

"You need to stop yelling at me. This isn't my fault," he told her as he stepped away. "I don't want to share her either. But you have to see from my point of view it's sort of helpful. I had to raise her on my own for so long and it is nice to have her mother help out for once."

As soon as the words left his mouth he wished he could take them back.

Cammi was horror struck.

"What is it you think I have been doing the past six years? Nothing? Was I no help at all?" His absolute disregard of her place in his life offended her deeply and her instant reaction was to make him pay. "You are an asshole," she seethed. She tried to leave the room, but he held onto her arm and pulled her back shutting the door behind her.

"That is not what I meant! Just hear me out."

Shaking, she glared at him. She had nothing else to say. It was bad enough he wasn't sympathetic to the pain she was dealing with but now he took everything she did for granted. She was tired of fighting. They were both bullheaded and stubborn so it would do no good to convince him to see her point of view. She'd tried time and again to no avail.

Instead, she listened in silence for an hour as he defended himself, his daughter and his ex-girlfriend. But not once did he apologize for his remarks.

Hours later, she lay awake in bed hoping he might make a small attempt to console her, maybe even put his arms around her and acknowledge her heart was breaking. But he didn't even kiss her goodnight. All she heard was his snoring.

It was the first moment Cammi could actually say she hated him. Hated what he had brought into her life, hated his behavior and hated his choices. An apology would mean nothing if she had to ask for it and he'd proven he didn't give two flying hairs about how she felt. The anger tore through her heart like a razor blade damaging everything she had allowed herself to trust.

Chapter Eighteen

Less than three months later, Cammi got a call from school. Allie had been in a fight. After leaving a message on Bryce's voicemail, she dropped the other two kids off with Mrs. Newcomb and headed to meet him. When she arrived, Cynthia was already talking to the principal. Allie sat down the hall in the detention room waiting until the meeting was over.

Cammi was horrified when she walked into the principal's office. Cynthia, with her blonde hair ratted to stand two inches off her head, bright blue eye shadow and black liner coating her eyes, was dressed in a skimpy bikini top covered by a mesh tank and a tight fitting pair of jeans shorts. On her feet, she wore a pair of brown Eskimo boots. Cammi about choked on the air she breathed in. And poor Mr. Bartlett, he was having a difficult time carrying on a conversation as his eyes kept straying from Cynthia's face to her voluptuous chest.

When Bryce arrived his reaction to Cynthia was about the same as Cammi's. Mr. Bartlett looked relieved they had finally arrived to rescue him from a very awkward situation.

"Apparently this young woman has been picking on Allie for some time," Mr. Bartlett informed them when they were all seated.

"Did you know anything about this?" Cammi asked Bryce. He shook his head.

"She told me," Cynthia stated proudly. "It's over a boy." She giggled. "Poor girl, I remember fighting over boys at this age. Their hormones go crazy."

Bringing her attention back to Mr. Bartlett, she continued, "Jennifer goes out with Trevor, and Allie likes him. She wrote him a note. Well, the stupid boy gave the note to Jennifer and Jennifer's been threatening Allie since. I keep telling her to get used to it, jealous women don't ever stop causing problems," Cynthia announced, sending a coy look Cammi's way.

Silence echoed through the room as Mr. Bartlett stared at them uncomfortably. Cammi had her eyebrow cocked as she stared at her husband in disbelief. Did this seriously go unnoticed by him? And how could Allie have shared this information with Cynthia and not her? She used to tell her everything.

"What happened today, Mr. Bartlett?" Bryce asked drawing everyone's attention back to the subject at hand.

He sighed. "At lunch Jennifer supposedly said a few unkind words to Allie and.... Allie punched her. We've talked to a few of the students who saw what happened. They say Jennifer pushed Allie and Allie was just defending herself. Mr. Shepard, your daughter is a very popular girl at this school so it's no surprise the kids would stand up for her, but she already confessed to starting the fight. I'm sorry to say I have to follow policy and suspend her again."

Bryce interrupted just as Cynthia opened her mouth to protest.

"Thank you, sir. I promise we will handle it from here. We don't teach violence as a solution to problems and I will make sure Allie understands the consequences of her actions," Bryce stood up to shake his hand.

"She is a good kid, one of our best, but this is twice in one year. Not a good track record. It is just a suggestion, so take it for what it's worth, but I think she might need some intervention before things get worse. She is too young for this sort of behavior so my guess is she's angry about something. I know she comes from a good home. Kids don't always confide in their parents. Hopefully she will talk to you. I do appreciate your time, and I'm sorry," he replied escorting them to the door.

Refusing to look any of them in the eye, Allie stood up when her dad appeared in the doorway of the classroom. She walked past him without a word and led the way to the car, her head hung in shame. Cynthia piped up once they were out of earshot from any administrators.

"Baby, you did the only thing you could do. You teach people how to treat you and don't let anyone get away with bullying you. That girl deserved to be put in her place. Don't worry, no one's life ever ended after getting suspended. Look at is as a mini-vacation," she stated patting Allie on the shoulder.

Once they reached the car, Bryce stepped in front of Allie and took her by the arm before she could climb into the passenger side of her Cynthia's vehicle.

"I'm sorry Cynthia, but we need to head home now. Allie is going to be grounded for the next two weeks. She will see you after that," Bryce growled. The frown crossing his handsome features warned Cynthia to keep her mouth shut. But she didn't heed to caution.

"If she isn't going to be in school for the next two days why not let her stay at my house?" Cynthia suggested walking closely beside Bryce allowing her shoulder to rub against his. Protectively, Cammi grabbed his hand, but quietly thought reaching over to claw out Cynthia's eyes would have been more satisfying.

"No!" he barked. "I said she is going to help out at home. Just because she isn't going to school, doesn't mean she gets a "mini-vacation". She's going to be punished. I've had enough of her behavior."

Allie listened impatiently. Had she become so invisible they could talk like she wasn't even there? She couldn't wait to escape them all. They were stupid.

Cammi took a step back, half listening to Bryce deal with Cynthia's arguments, half watching Allie out of the corner of her eye. She appeared detached, withdrawn, rocking back and forth on her feet with a faraway look on her face as if she were concentrating on something besides the trouble she was in. It was then that Cammi sensed something was seriously wrong. So wrong that she and Bryce might not be able to fix it.

Allie went straight to her room slamming the door behind her while Cammi and Bryce weighed their options.

"What do you think is going on? This isn't like her, she's so angry, like it is our fault she got into trouble," Bryce said.

"Her attitude towards life in general has been horrible. I've been trying to tell you that. Some would say its normal teenage behavior, but I wasn't like that. My hormones didn't cause that many problems, especially this early." Cammi handed him a cup of tea then sat next to him on the couch.

Ms. Newcomb was kind enough to keep Faith and Bailey for the evening. Her own grandchildren lived states away and with Cammi home, they didn't need her as much as they had when Allie was little so she loved the chance to baby-sit, and this would give Cammi an opportunity to talk to her husband without interruptions.

"I haven't had a chance to tell you this, but in the mail today, we got a letter from her English teacher. She has a D again.

He wants to meet with us next week. I'll call tomorrow to set up an appointment."

Bryce shook his head, "English is her favorite class. I don't get it. Where did we go wrong?"

"I think you need to get her into counseling again. I agree with Mr. Bartlett. She is confused and angry about something. She won't talk to you or me. As much as I hate to say it, I think she confides to Cynthia. Maybe you could ask her. I don't know if she will be much help, but it's worth a try."

Cammi detested the idea but would rather swallow her pride than watch as Allie continued down the destructive path she was going.

"Allie is so proud of her. She was giggling the other day when she told me the boys at her school think Cynthia is hot. I asked her how she felt about it, and all she could say is Cynthia likes to date younger guys because she can 'train' them. Allie had no idea what she even meant, but Cynthia's word is the gospel to that girl," she said scornfully. "Can you imagine?"

Bryce's jaw dropped. "There is something seriously wrong with an adult woman who gets her kicks from teenage boys."

"I'm sure to her it's flattering."

"No, it's just perverse, and I am sure as Allie gets older, she will be embarrassed by it. What young girl wants to compete with her mother? I'm truly sorry, Cammi. I always knew Cynthia's morals and values were screwed up, but I didn't seriously think she would try to pass them on to Allie."

Despite all the disagreements lately, at least they were starting to see eye to eye when it came to this. Bryce was forced to see the truth only a few days after he had defended Cynthia to her.

"Guess what?" his voice came over the phone.

Cammi had been surprised to get his call. Since their argument, they were better at avoiding one another than they were at conversing.

"I dunno, what?" she grumbled into the phone, still hurt and angry with him.

"Cynthia's not sick. Never was, I guess."

"What do you mean?" she asked, suddenly interested in what he had to say.

"It wasn't making sense. The Hepatitis thing, I mean. If she had it as bad as she told me, she should be having tons of liver problems, her skin would be yellow as well as her eyes, and she would be nauseous and vomiting, tired all the time. So I asked Allie about it."

Cammi gasped. "Bryce, we agreed not to tell her!"

"I know, I know. But like I said, things weren't adding up."

"Well, what did you say?"

"I asked if Cynthia had ever said anything about being sick."

"And...," she prodded anxiously.

"She flew off the handle. Started screaming and told me I was lying."

"What! Lying about what?"

"Well, when I finally got her to calm down she said she overheard us one night talking about Cynthia being sick. So she asked her about it. And guess what Cynthia told her?"

"Who knows?"

"She blamed me. Said nothing was wrong, she was healthy as a horse and told Allie you and I were making up lies because we don't want them together. That *we* are jealous and would do anything to keep them apart, hoping if Allie thought she was sick and dying she wouldn't want to get close to her for fear of losing her again."

"That bitch! She twisted your words."

"Yep."

"So what did you tell Allie?"

"What could I tell her? She wouldn't believe me anyway. But I feel like a jackass. Cynthia told us that story so we would feel sorry for her. Don't you see? If she's sick, we can't be angry with her for all she has done in the past. And it's been a bunch of lies since. Everything that comes out of her mouth is lies."

It was his way of apologizing to Cammi without actually saying the words and for Cammi it was justification she was right.

Only now, their daughter didn't trust either of them. She saw everything they did as a plot to destroy her relationship with her mother. All the choices, all the sacrifices; how did they begin to make this better?

Cammi returned from the kitchen with two peanut butter and jelly sandwiches and a bag of chips to find Bryce pacing the living room deep in thought.

"I need to make sure we handle this punishment correctly. She's getting good at manipulating us, and if I don't put my foot down, it will continue to get worse. We can't allow that to happen and I won't let her throw her life down the drain or become like her mother."

"So what's the solution?"

"I'm going to try my damnedest, Cammi, but honestly, I don't know if there is a solution."

Reluctantly, Bryce called Cynthia a week later. As much as he didn't want to enlist her help he figured he didn't have much of a choice if he wanted to know what was going on with his daughter. They'd met with Ms. Church, her English teacher, earlier that day to try to get some insight from her.

"She's just not doing the work. When I ask her about it she says everyone is so busy with the new baby, and she is helping you out all the time" she nodded to Cammi, "that she doesn't have time to get her homework done. I find it a little hard to believe. From what I can see, she's just unhappy. Stressed seems more like it. When school first started, she was on the right path, but I would say, in the past six months, she seems to be spiraling downward. I don't have children myself, Mr. and Mrs. Shepard, so take what I say with a grain of salt, but I think she might be depressed. It's typical at this age and with the changes of the new baby, her mother, plus hormones, she might just be overwhelmed. I see it all the time."

Allie had convinced her parents about a year ago that since Cynthia was in her life again, she didn't need to go to counseling. Giving them both the benefit of the doubt, Bryce agreed, but looking back now, he knew it was probably the worst decision they could have made. Of course. Cammi wanted to slap herself for being so wrapped up in her own misery she hadn't thought how these changes would affect Allie.

Bryce had felt somewhat relieved when they left the school, but now listening to Cynthia, something struck a nerve.

"She is fine when she is around here, why?" she asked sounding surprised which made Bryce want to reach through the phone and strangle her. "She tells me she loves school, loves life and is happy."

It wasn't what Bryce wanted to hear. Of course, he took into consideration Cynthia didn't have a clue what Allie was like before, so her perspective probably wasn't accurate.

"Look Bryce, I am not an expert, but I think you need to let her be a teenager," she continued. "If you come down too hard on her all the time, she is going to resent you and rebel. Believe me, I know. She's a good kid, trust her."

Bryce and Cammi agreed on Allie's punishment for the fight at school. She was to wash all the cars, clean out the garage, and help paint the living room. Along with all the daily lectures she received were enough to drive any child insane. Cammi told Allie she didn't feel violence was ever the answer unless her life was in danger or if she was physically harmed. Bryce didn't necessarily agree, but he was a guy. When he was the same age, he would have pummeled the kid's face into the ground. But he couldn't be a hypocrite and felt Allie needed help coping with her emotions when faced with difficult situations. She couldn't go around hitting everyone who said or did something she didn't like.

They might as well have been talking to a brick wall. Not once did Allie say she was sorry and showed no signs of remorse, only anger. In fact, for an entire week, she hardly said two words to anyone in the house and completely ignored her brother and sister.

"I don't think so," he told Cynthia. "Kids need to know what is expected of them or they will walk all over you. As parents we need to establish boundaries of what is acceptable. The younger we do this, the better."

"You're the dad. Just let me know what you need from me. If she confides anything to me, I promise I will call," she exaggerated in her sugary sweet voice.

Bryce told her he appreciated the help, but as he hung up the phone, the unease seeped through him. What was with her? She told him one thing, and he wished so badly he could trust her, but he knew to take it with a grain of salt because she would tell Allie something entirely different. Now it was up to him to figure out exactly what she was telling her.

Allie begged her dad to let her spend a whole month of the summer with Cynthia. Bryce reluctantly agreed only because she had gotten her D in English up to a B and he was seeing a significant improvement in her attitude. She still kept to herself but at least she was more enjoyable to be around. She talked to them about school, friends and the activities she was joining the following year. There hadn't been anymore catastrophes since her suspension from school three months earlier, and she was seeing her counselor again on a regular basis.

Cammi didn't agree. "I don't think she is ready. We don't know what sort of discipline structure Cynthia has, her rules, or her expectations. Hell, I'd be surprised if she even had any. What if she lets Allie run wild? Plus you and I agreed we don't know what she tells her. What if she turns her against us? Has she really been a good influence so far?"

Bryce could understand her concerns, she wasn't telling him anything he hadn't already thought of, but his hands were tied. Ron told him if they didn't agree on proper visitation, Cynthia had every right to take him to court and have the judge decide, which might lead to standardized visitation. At least this way, he felt the power was still in his hands. It scared him to death, but he needed to trust Allie to make the right decisions. She had come to love and adore her mother, wanting to be with her most of the time. If he didn't allow it, he was afraid Cynthia would take him to court for full custody and Allie was fourteen, almost fifteen, she could choose to live with her mom. Even if it killed him, he would do whatever it took to keep that from happening.

It was already killing Cammi. He watched day after day as she continued to get hurt by the situation at hand. The rejection from Allie was the worst part. But what could he do? Allie was just a kid who was learning how to cope and deal with the hand life dealt her. He couldn't make her feel guilty for wanting to love her own mother. But little by little, he watched in fear as Cammi shut him out, dealing with the pain on her own. It was hard enough handling his own worries of losing his daughter but trying to take care of Cammi's needs on top of it was proving near to impossible.

Chapter Nineteen

"Where are we going?" Allie wondered. They were cruising along I-70 towards Denver and as always, she had to sit in the back by herself while Beth occupied the passenger seat.

Cynthia's friendship with Beth, along with the parties, the men and the drugs were something Allie chose not to discuss with her parents. It would cause more problems than she wanted to think about and her dad would be furious, okay, more than furious. He probably wouldn't let her see Cynthia anymore. She hated the idea and if it happened, Cynthia would blame her. She wished there was someone she could confide in. She hated her new therapist. It had been her parent's bright idea to make her go again. Maybe they needed to go see a shrink instead of her. Maybe *they* were really the ones with all the problems. Heather and Brandi were no help either. She didn't want her friends at school to know how crazy her mom was. As much as she hated to admit it, Cynthia was beginning to become an embarrassment.

"We are going to spend the weekend in the city with some friends," Cynthia shouted over her shoulder.

The latest guy, in a long line of guys Cynthia dated, lived in Denver. Allie must have met more than a dozen over the past few years. None of them she particularly cared for, nor did they her. She'd actually overheard one of the idiots tell Cynthia he thought she was a spoiled little brat who needed a good swat on the behind.

"Dave, give her a break, she is only a child and hasn't spent much time with me. She can't help it if her parents raised her that way. Believe me, if it had been me, she would have turned out different. She would be more respectful."

Allie was hurt but not surprised her mother didn't stand up for her. If it had been her dad and some girl *he* dated said that, he would have kicked her to the curb. At least she used to think he would. Anymore she wasn't so sure.

The music was blaring through the speakers in the back seat of the Lexus, Cynthia's latest purchase, so Allie couldn't hear the conversation up front. But Beth was laughing hysterically. She was holding Cynthia's beer so she could light her cigarette with one hand while cracking the window with the other, and of course, there were no hands on the steering wheel. Beth didn't drink much anymore. In fact, Beth wasn't around as often either. Allie wondered why.

She'd been thrilled to find out Cynthia and Beth were friends. Of course, Cammi didn't approve but Allie had adored Beth as her grade school teacher's aide and at first, she felt so self conscious around her mother, it was kind of nice to have Beth around. Only she was really different outside of school. She drank too much, smoked a lot and was super moody. At times she paid attention to Allie and others; she acted as if she barely knew her. It was strange and confusing. Then about a year ago, Beth got really sick, and Allie thought she looked awful, even worse than usual. When she asked Cynthia about it, she only rolled her eyes saying Beth needed to 'buck up'.

Cynthia's cell phone rang. She turned the music down as she reached into her purse and flipped it open.

"We should be there in about an hour. We need to stop for chips and tequila then we're all yours! You invite who? *Whatever!* Just make sure Kelly doesn't show up. If she does, she'll get an ass kicking. I guarantee you that. She definitely messed with the wrong bitch's man," Cynthia laughed in a high-pitched shrill.

Allie couldn't help snickering when Beth looked at her in the back seat and rolled her eyes in disgust. She wondered what was going on with the two of them. They didn't seem to be getting alone well. In fact, Beth was always making snide comments about Cynthia and seemed to disapprove with some of the choices she made concerning Allie.

"Cynthia, are you going to a party? Where am I going to be while you guys are there?" Allie asked anxiously.

"Oh, honey, you are going to come with us, it won't hurt."

"Will there be anyone else there for me to hang out with?"

When her dad and Cammi were invited to parties, their friends brought other kids along. The adults listened to music and ate, some drank wine, others beer and the women were usually in the kitchen gossiping, and the men downstairs playing pool or watching sports while the kids played. She loved it. She hoped it would be that way now, but she learned a long time ago the parties Cynthia went to were completely different than the ones her parents took her to.

Cynthia grimaced as she looked over at Beth. "I don't think so, but that's okay, you can just hang out with us. We're fun aren't we?"

Allie sulked in the back seat. Hanging out with her meant watching Cynthia get drunk, make out with a bunch of different guys and eventually pass out.

What a fantastic night she had ahead of her.

"I thought you said we were going to do something fun like Elitches or the Zoo. Hey, I know, we could go to Dave and Busters," she said excitedly.

"Allie, this is going to be fun, I promise you. Then tomorrow we will get up and go do something for you. Have some one on one time together. Cross my heart." She turned the music up and just like that, Allie was dismissed.

Cross my heart. How many times has she heard that only to be disappointed? Allie didn't understand her mother. In fact, she didn't understand anything anymore. The first year, Cynthia had spoiled Allie rotten, constantly buying her new clothes, taking her out to lunch, to movies, all sorts of fun stuff. She was kind and loving, just what Allie had hoped. They talked about everything. It was the perfect mother/daughter relationship, just the two of them. It was everything Allie had hoped for.

Allie had always been mature for her age, maybe because she was raised primarily by a man, but Cynthia sensed her maturity meant she was able to talk to Allie about anything. And she did. She was open about things a girl her age shouldn't be hearing, but she was so enamored by her mother and because she didn't see Allie as a child but instead an adult, a friend, she let it slide. She thrived on her mother's attention, thrived on it until it started to backfire.

It didn't take long for Cynthia to show her true colors. She stopped treating Allie like a daughter and instead, treated her like one of the girlfriends she hung out with. It devastated Allie, but she was desperate to have her mom in her life. She didn't care what the relationship was as long as she got to share something with her. As long as her mom loved her and wanted her around, Allie was willing to keep her secrets.

Allie knew Cynthia had a job, but didn't know what it was, she never talked about it, plus it didn't seem she hardly ever worked. Somehow she always had money. The woman's closet was filled with name brand clothes, half of them she never wore. She probably owned more than twenty pairs of shoes and each time they went to the mall she had to buy a new purse. They weren't the cheap kind either. Gucci, Prada, Louis Vuitton. You name it, and she had every size, shape and color. And it wasn't unusual for her to drive a different car every three or four months. Allie figured she got tired of them and needed a change, sort of like her boyfriends.

Allie had come to resent the boyfriends more than she resented her mom's female friends. On the weekends, it never failed that someone was always at the house. Thankfully, it was normally Beth, and Allie was comfortable with her. When she was in a good mood, she was kind and made her feel important. Everyone else either ignored Allie or acted like she was a nuisance to have around. It was hard to get a good night sleep when she stayed at Cynthia's. The music was loud and everyone was noisy, screaming over the music or slamming into the walls and moving furniture around so they could dance, drink and play beer pong.

"Cynthia, your friends don't treat me nice, I don't like having them here. Can't you have a party on a weekend I am not around?" Allie complained one Sunday afternoon before she was headed back to her dad's house for two nights. The entire week had revolved around people coming in and out and Allie was tired of it. She couldn't wait to lock herself up in her room and be alone.

"What to do you mean, honey?" Cynthia drawled, still hung-over from the dozen or so beers she inhaled the evening before. Her eyes were blood shot, and her face pale. Allie didn't understand why anyone would intentionally make themselves sick or have any desire to look that horrible the next day.

"Robert pushes me out of the way anytime he walks by, and Veronica always says I should be in bed where a kid belongs instead of hanging out with the adults."

Cynthia waved her hand in the air to dismiss it. "Robert is harmless. Half the time he doesn't even know what *he* is doing. Veronica is a sweetheart," she gushed. "You must have misunderstood her. Next time, just be friendlier. But you need to understand they are *my* friends and this is *my* house. They can be here whenever they want."

Allie didn't know if it was rejection or disrespect she felt, whatever it was broke her heart, but eventually she began to get used to it.

After stopping for groceries, they headed to Robert's house. He was Cynthia's latest. None of her boyfriends cared about getting to know Allie, but she didn't care, they were all losers and none of them were around long. Cynthia had a strange way of either pushing them away because they were annoying her or the ones she actually did like, she scared off.

Allie couldn't remember how many times she had heard or seen Cynthia start a fight because someone wanted to break up with her. And each time it happened, she always threatened suicide. At one party, she accidentally walked in on her boyfriend at the time James making out with another girl. She slipped into the bathroom unnoticed, but all hell broke loose when she came out with little cuts on her wrists. James was considerate enough to take her to the hospital while Beth stayed with a terrified Allie. After that, he never came around again, which was okay, too. He gave Allie the creeps the way he looked her up and down each time he walked through the door.

The house they pulled in front of was a ranch style brick. Robert obviously didn't take much pride in how it looked. The lawn hadn't been mowed in what looked like months. It was mostly weeds so he probably figured it was a waste of his time. The outside was in dire need of painting and new windows. Allie thought it was a dump, but very similar to Cynthia's house back in Madison.

Cynthia had lived in an apartment prior to finding her "fixer upper" as she liked to call it. Allie didn't exactly understand what happened, but literally overnight, she had moved from the dingy one bedroom apartment into a two-bedroom house with all new furnishings. It did have a lot of potential, but Cynthia spent so much time drinking and recovering, she hardly had time to pay attention to fixing up the place. She'd promised Allie the two of them would spend an entire week redecorating her bedroom so she would have a special place of her own but once again, Allie was left waiting and disappointed.

Robert met them outside to help bring in the supplies. Throwing a nasty look Allie's way, he made a snide comment to Cynthia.

"Had to bring the baby, huh?" He wasn't even discreet about it. Beth looked over her shoulder sympathetically and was met by Allie's stone cold expression.

"What do you expect me to do? Leave her home alone while I come into the city? She wouldn't stay. She would call her dad and I wouldn't be allowed to keep her for the summer again. If you want me to come see you, you are going to have to deal with her coming too." She narrowed her eyes, rubbed her body up against his and batted her eyelashes. "Besides, there are plenty of other men who would love to have me show up on their doorstep, kid in toe, without a complaint. They know it would be worth their time," she drawled.

Allie witnessed this behavior too many times and was bewildered at how fast the men fell at Cynthia's feet. It was like she could make them do anything. Allie had attempted it herself a few times with the boys at school when she first started wearing makeup but always felt like a dope. Now that she was older, watching Cynthia act like this grossed her out.

Throughout the evening, people came and went. Some played cards, all of them drank, a few of them stood on the deck smoking cigarettes and who knows what else. Each time someone new walked through the door, she was put through the same scrutiny she'd endured at so many other parties. It was humiliating. So Allie sat on the couch, watching episodes of "16 and Pregnant" and "Jersey Shore" until she grew bored. She could see why her dad and Cammi never allowed her to watch this stuff at their house. Frustrated, she changed it to the Disney Channel. She was much more comfortable watching "The Wizards of Waverly Place".

She'd lost track of Cynthia over an hour ago. Last she knew, she was half drunk, hanging on some guy that wasn't Robert but as far as Allie was concerned he was just as nasty. For some reason, her mom didn't have very good taste in men. None of them were as good-looking as her dad. Even though he was her dad, Allie had always thought he was incredibly handsome.

Thinking of him made her sad. After finding out the truth from Cynthia, it was hard for her to look at him the same. But still.....she wished she was home. Even though being there sucked most of the time, anything had to be better than this.

"What happened between you and my dad?" Allie asked one afternoon over a year ago while they were at the park. They had been sunning themselves and decided to take a break to eat the picnic lunch Cynthia packed. It was one of those lazy days when she felt loved and close to her real mom. She had been dying to hear her side of the story and figured enough time had passed, it should be safe to ask.

"Hasn't your dad ever told you?" Cynthia asked eyeing her curiously.

"Nope. He just said you were young and not sure what you wanted. He said it was better at the time if I lived with him and eventually you just stopped coming around." Allie was careful not to hurt her feelings. There was no way she was going to tell her the things she overheard her dad and Cammi saying.

"It figures he wouldn't tell you," she snorted in disbelief.

"What do you mean?"

"Well, it's crazy, how it all happened. He probably thought if he told you the truth, you would be angry with him, so he was just trying to protect you. Are you sure you are ready to hear it? I mean, I don't want you to be angry with me for telling you. I certainly don't want to cause problems between you and your dad."

Allie felt a lump form in her throat but she nodded anyway.

"Your dad and I met one night at a bar where I was working. He was with a bunch of friends and they were looking for a good time, if you know what I mean."

Allie winced at the thought.

"I thought he was handsome, who wouldn't? So I watched, taking it all in, but the more I watched, the less impressed I was. I could tell he was looking for only one thing that night. I overheard a bunch of them say they were celebrating their college graduation."

She took a deep breath and looked at Allie before continuing. "Well, he noticed me checking him out, and as I was getting ready to leave, he asked if he could buy me a drink. I was going to school myself at the time. Who wants to work in a bar for the rest of their life? I was going to be a lawyer, you know. Anyway, I told him I couldn't; I had an early class. School was important to me, but he kept talking. I thought he was charming and cute, it made me feel good he didn't want me to leave, but then I remembered what he was really after." She paused. "You know what I'm talking about, don't you?"

Dumbfounded, Allie nodded again.

"He had been drinking, but didn't seem out of control drunk. I figured he was harmless, so I gave in for one drink but told him I had to go home right after. That was a huge mistake. After that drink, he wouldn't take no for an answer. He was too pushy for my taste. The more he tried, the more uncomfortable I felt. When he tried to kiss me, I slapped him and left. I'm not sure how it happened, but as I was getting into my car, he came up behind me, put his hand over my mouth, took my keys and shoved me in. I was shocked. By the time I registered what was going on, he was on top of me. That's how he raped me."

Cynthia's face contorted as she dabbed at the tears forming in the corner of her eye.

Never! Allie thought. She didn't want to believe her. Her dad would never do anything like that. He couldn't have. But as she watched the streak of tears fall down Cynthia's face she couldn't help feeling sorry for her.

"I'm sorry," Cynthia apologized wiping the back of her hand over her cheeks. "You don't need to see me fall apart. Really, I dealt with it years ago, I'm fine. I didn't think it would be so hard to tell you the truth. Please understand.... your dad was young. He's done a fabulous job raising you and is a great father. He made a mistake and now I understand that. I've forgiven him," she sighed. "But it has been really hard to get my life back on track. I moved here because I thought being around you would help motivate me."

Having lost her appetite, Allie put her sandwich down. "I don't understand how he ended up with custody of me then?" she inquired, her head swimming in confusion as she tried to piece together what she had heard.

"Your dad came from a good family and had a good job. He went to high school here, everyone who knew him, loved him. I was a nobody. I didn't have a boyfriend at the time, so when I found out I was pregnant; I knew it was your dad's. I remembered his name from that night at the bar, asked around and figured out where to find him. The moment he saw me, he was horrified. Told me he didn't believe a word I said, called me a gold digger and wouldn't allow me to drag his name through the dirt. He would do whatever it took to shut me up. When I wouldn't back down he agreed to a blood test. The test was positive and after that he pursued me, sending flowers, begging for forgiveness, wanting a relationship. It was sick. He was twisted. I couldn't stand to look at him. He raped me for Christ sake!" she cried.

Allie winced.

Looking at her carefully, Cynthia's voice softened. "Sorry, I didn't mean to get so emotional."

"Anyway, my family wouldn't help me with money, I had to drop out of school and work more, but the hospital bills were too expensive. I was living paycheck to paycheck trying to take care of you and give you what you needed. I couldn't afford childcare, so I finally swallowed my pride and when you were a few months old, I asked him for help. Over time he convinced me I wasn't capable of providing for you. I was young and naïve enough to believe him and became very depressed. I loved you so much, you were my life, but felt like I was a horrible mother. Your dad played on my insecurities. By the time you were almost a year, he told me if I didn't give him custody, he would take me to court and prove I was an unfit mother. I didn't have the money to hire a lawyer or fight the type of lawyer his family could afford, so I gave in. It is still my biggest regret," she said sadly.

Cynthia searched Allie's face for a sign. There was nothing. Her eyes were glassed over, lost in thought. She didn't continue until Allie spoke.

"Why did it take you so long to come back?"

"Leaving you was the hardest thing I did. I kept in contact for as long as I could, but eventually everything took its toll. I was traumatized, Allie. I got hooked up with the wrong crowd and worked at a bar. The nights were late, and I slept most of the day. That was no life for a kid. I hated your father so badly, it was easier to stay away than to deal with him or the pain of losing you. I was so angry with him for what he did and then I became depressed. If your dad wouldn't have taken you away from me, I believe my life would have turned out differently. Most of what has happened to me is his fault, you see. My self-esteem was shot and I didn't believe in myself. About five years ago, I decided I deserved better and went to therapy. With my counselor's help, I regained my confidence and self worth. It took a long time, but I was able to forgive your father. I was still scared to death to see you. I figured you hated me. It made me wonder what lies he might have told you. Eventually, I couldn't stand it anymore and moved back here to fight for you."

Allie watched in silence as Cynthia ate her lunch. She felt like she was going to throw up. It was impossible to believe her dad, the man she loved more than life itself, the man she trusted more than anyone, could do something so horrible. But it did explain why he hadn't told her his side of the story. Of course, he wouldn't want her to know but there was still something Allie didn't understand.

"If he raped you, why didn't you go to the police?"

Allie saw an instant spark of anger cross Cynthia's face as her lips drew into a fine line.

"What? Don't you believe me?" she accused, her lips turning white with anger.

"No, no, I'm sorry, that is not what I meant, I just don't understand a few things," Allie cried desperately.

"I'm sorry sweetheart," Cynthia said relaxing into a soft smile. "I'm not angry with you, but that is the exact reason I didn't go to the police. Your dad had a good reputation. No one would believe me, especially after I wound up pregnant with his child. All anyone would see is a scorned lover trying to trap him."

Allie was skeptical of the story at first, but over time Cynthia planted more seeds of doubt into her head. By the time it was all said and done, she hated her dad and had come to believe Cammi was jealous of her relationship with him, and her goal was to get Allie out of the picture so she could have Bryce all to herself.

Even though there were times the stories coming out of Cynthia's mouth didn't make sense, Allie learned if she questioned her or stuck up for her parents, or wasn't sympathetic to her dilemmas, she was easily discarded. Cynthia became mean and spiteful accusing Allie of not loving her. She would ignore her, not calling for days, while most of Allie's energy was spent apologizing or making up for the grief she had caused.

Unfortunately, the confusion started to taint her home life. Hatred she blamed her parents for, consumed her. She considered her home a prison, counting the hours until she could escape to Cynthia's. Despite all she did and all she said, Allie actually enjoyed being with her. She adored her completely, believing she was lucky to have a second chance with her. Besides, when she wasn't drunk, Cynthia was a blast. With her, Allie didn't have a bedtime or even a curfew. They stayed up all night watching movies, even rated R ones like "The Hangover", which her dad and Cammi refused to let her see it, and they were always on a junk food run to the nearest Seven-Eleven. Cynthia would spend hours playing around with new hairstyles on Allie, while talking about boys and Allie's friends. Cynthia never made her do homework on school nights and once, she even took her to a rock concert. Allie had begged her dad to take her to one since she had been old enough to remember. He always told her the same thing. She needed to wait until she was sixteen, until she was mature enough to handle herself with a big crowd of people and the things she was likely to be exposed to.

The only thing Allie wished were different was all the guys and her mom's drinking. Most of the time, Cynthia was completely out of control. But Allie saw a side of Cynthia that was kind, sincere and desperate to be loved. If she had some stability in her life, if she really knew how much Allie loved her then maybe things would change.

Cynthia threw herself down on the couch next to Allie giggling hysterically. Allie felt left out and wanted to join the fun when suddenly, Beth came around the corner, her face purple with rage.

"What the hell were you doing in there?" Beth's boyfriend Michael was following right behind.

"Baby, nothing happened!" Michael explained. "Don't worry about it. We were talking about your birthday, chill out."

He grabbed her arm but she shook free from his grasp and pushed her face into Cynthia's. She was sober but the other two were beyond intoxicated.

"I want to know exactly what it was you were doing back there with *my* boyfriend."

Cynthia giggled while holding onto the edge of the couch maintaining her balance as she stood up. "Don't be so dramatic, Beth," she slurred. Allie noticed her mother's shirt was untucked and the top four buttons were unbuttoned as well as the snap on her jeans. Hearing the commotion, some of the other guests appeared from outside to watch the action.

"What? You two in another cat fight?" Robert snickered. He plopped himself down on the couch leering at Allie. The mixture of cigarettes and alcohol on his breath made her stomach churn.

Cynthia headed towards the kitchen. "I need a smoke. This is stupid."

As she passed Michael, she slid her finger down the side of his chin and smiled flirtatiously. Furious, Beth turned her around by her shirt, ripping the sleeve in the process.

"Let go of me, you tramp," Cynthia sneered.

"I am so sick of you! You stab me in the back any chance you get." Beth laughed out loud as if everything suddenly made sense. "I guess maybe I need to think twice about who my friends are…… plus the type of men I date," she glared toward Michael.

"Are you so insecure that everything has to be a competition?" Beth asked turning her attention back to Cynthia. "Can't you just be happy for me without trying to ruin it? You think every guy has to want you or something is wrong with them. Well, guess what? Everyone doesn't want you. And if they do, it's only for one thing….. a piece of ass! It's all you're good for."

Beth grabbed her purse and began to walk out the door.

"Allie, you need to come with me, I am not going to leave …" But before she could finish, Cynthia's fist came out of nowhere and landed square on her jaw. By this time, everyone was in the living room yelling and screaming. Allie wanted to disappear, but had nowhere to go.

It took two huge guys to finally pull them apart. Cynthia's nose was bleeding and it looked like she might have the start of a black eye. Beth escaped with a few scratches and a red hand imprinted on her cheek.

"You watch your back, Allie! Hang out with her much longer, she's bound to ruin your life," Beth yelled as one of the burley guys shoved her out the door. "Allie, you listen to your parents, you hear me? Allie, don't trust her!"

"Shut your mouth, you lying bitch!" Cynthia screamed lunging towards her, but the other guy with big muscles was still holding her back.

Filled with panic, Allie watched Beth run from the house and heard the screech of her tires as she left them stranded at Robert's house. Cynthia stumbled back over to the couch to sit next to Allie. She was sobbing, holding a hand towel on her nose and laid her head in Allie's lap. Halfheartedly, Allie caressed her hair. Cynthia stayed curled up like a baby until she passed out. No one seemed to care and the party went on.

A few hours later, Allie was finally able to shove her mother off her lap, found a blanket and curled up next to the couch on the floor. The carpet was disgusting, but Allie didn't really have a choice. She prayed everyone would leave so she could at least get a few hours of sleep, but the noise in the house lasted until four in the morning. It had been a miserable evening but knowing she was doing something fun with her mom the next day was the one thought helping her drift into a semi-peaceful sleep.

"Come on Cynthia, get up." Allie poked her in the shoulder until she rolled over. Dried blood had formed under her nose. It was almost noon, and Allie was tired of being at Roberts. She had been up for a few hours already, but the house was quiet. To keep herself occupied she watched reruns of Extreme Home Makeover until she was irritated enough to wake Cynthia up.

"How are we getting home? Beth was our ride and she obviously isn't around."

Cynthia sat up slowly holding onto her head. "I feel like I have been hit by a bus," she groaned. "What do you mean Beth is gone? Where did she go?"

"You mean you don't remember?" Allie asked becoming more and more annoyed.

"No, of course not, I was drunk."

Allie figured if she was drinking so much she couldn't remember anything it was a clear sign there was a problem.

"Are we going to go to Elitches today? Will Robert take us?" she asked with a small trace of hope in her voice.

"Oh, Allie, I feel like shit. We aren't going anywhere. Robert will take us home, but he won't be up for anything else, I know that much. Besides, I just want my bed."

"But you promised me we would do something fun today!" she whined.

"I know honey, but I really can't. I promise to make it up to you. We can do something fun next weekend."

Allie was seething inside. She couldn't believe Cynthia had done this to her *again*. Their month together was almost up and all Cynthia ever did was sleep during the day, get drunk or chat with people on the internet, mostly guys. Allie refused to use the computer at her mom's house anymore. The last time she logged on, Cynthia forgot to close out what she had been doing and Allie got an eyeful of pornographic pictures of Cynthia and two other guys. She was in shock for about a week and afraid to even touch that dirty computer.

"You know what? I am tired of this, I am going to call my dad and have him drive down here to pick me up," she threatened.

"What? You can't be serious!" Sitting up straight, Cynthia was stunned into soberness. "You can't call your dad. And he definitely can't pick you up *here!* He would be furious and never let you stay with me again. Look, we will work something out."

"You always say that Cynthia, and I am tired of doing what you want all the time. You make promises, but they never happen. I don't want to spend time with your boyfriends, and I don't like coming to these parties. You think I have fun, but I don't. If this is how it is going to be, I'll go back to seeing you on the weekends. I would rather be at home."

Cynthia stared at Allie with tear-filled eyes.

"Oh, honey, I didn't know you felt this way. I wish you would have told me." She wrapped her arms around Allie pulling her close. Her breath smelled like stale beer.

"I know how much you hate being at your dad's house. He never lets you do anything and has all these strict rules about dating, boys and clothes. I seriously thought we were having fun, but I guess I was being selfish. Most girls your age like parties. I'm sorry you aren't into it."

Allie felt stupid, and wished she was more like her friends who thought Cynthia was cool. A few of them had even tried drinking already and told her she was a bore, too straight-laced and needed to loosen up, learn how to have fun. Maybe they were right, but Allie wasn't thrilled with the idea, especially if drinking made you act like Cynthia. Plus, if her parents found out, they would kill her.

"How about next weekend? It's your birthday. You can invite anybody you want. I will make dinner and rent some movies," Cynthia suggested trying to smooth everything over. "You and I can spend the afternoon baking a cake for it, too."

Cynthia was a great cook, and Allie had to admit, it did sound fun.

"It will be close to the Fourth of July, do you think we might be able to light off some fireworks?" she asked allowing herself to get excited all over again.

"I don't see why not. Let me go find Robert, see if I can bribe him into taking us to the mall to do some shopping for the afternoon, okay? We'll find you a great outfit for the party. Maybe some new shoes?"

As Cynthia got up to walk away, she turned back around and took Allie's hand, leaned over and kissed the top of her head.

"You know what, Allie? I love you."

It was the first time Cynthia had said those words to her. Allie was speechless. Her anger and disappointment disintegrated immediately when she smiled up at her. "I love you, too."

Cynthia walked around the house with a blanket wrapped around her waist searching for Robert. Allie heard her giggle as she walked towards the back bedroom, shutting the door behind her. It must have been an hour before Cynthia came out again wearing a pair of his pajamas. She had a gleam in her eye and her hair looked like it hadn't been combed in a week. She figured her mom must have bribed Robert *really well* because that afternoon he took them everywhere they wanted to go, even Elitches, and Allie didn't hear one complaint out of him.

Chapter Twenty

Eddie and Bryce had been best friends since high school, and he knew better than anyone the hell Bryce went through with Cynthia. If it was possible for someone to hate her as much as Bryce and Cammi did, it was Eddie. They hadn't seen much of him since he moved to Colorado Springs right after Faith was born, but he was back for a week for his brother's wedding so he and his girlfriend met Bryce and Cammi for dinner.

"Guess who I saw stripping at the Rockin Rodeo last Friday?" Eddie shouted over the noise of the restaurant.

Bryce hated playing guessing games and could really care less about the strippers at the Rockin Rodeo, but Eddie's sheepish grin made Bryce curious.

"It was Jack's bachelor party. Around eleven we all headed to the strip joint and guess who was dancing?" Eddie said as his girlfriend Dawn elbowed him in the ribs.

"Cynthia!" he announced proudly before anyone had a chance to respond.

"Really?" Bryce chuckled taking a long drink of his beer.

It was Cammi's turn to elbow him in the ribs. She felt ill. She'd certainly had her reservations about the type of woman Cynthia was, but didn't think Cynthia would be stupid enough to strip at a bar in their own home town.

The subject changed quickly, but Bryce noticed how unpleasant Cammi was the rest of the evening. *Great, he thought, here we go again.* Normally, they all tried to find amusement in Cynthia's antics, but tonight, Cynthia's antics were met with stony silence.

In the last few weeks, any mention of Cynthia and Cammi immediately turned into a bitch from hell, and Bryce couldn't stand to be around her. No matter how he tried to reach out, he always hit a brick wall. Plus, his own stress of the situation was draining him of any energy he might have left to deal with her. Why did it have to be his job to make her feel better all the time, anyway? She was a big girl. Why was she letting all of this get to her so badly? The pressure was eating a hole through his stomach. His wife was angry, his daughter was angry, and he was angry. He was lost and couldn't find the answers.

Allie wasn't the kid he had spent the past fifteen years raising. Frankly, he didn't know who she was. She resembled her mother so much anymore in looks and attitude that he hated to be around her, too. And it made him feel awful. When Allie was home, which wasn't much, she ignored the family. He missed her terribly and was scared to watch their relationship go down the drain. If he couldn't get through to his own wife, how was he supposed to get through to his teenage daughter? The counseling worked for a while, but it had been downhill ever since she came back from Cynthia's three months ago.

Not being able to stand Allie's attitude anymore either, Cammi suggested they meet with the counselor alone. She told them Allie wasn't confiding in her. She was extremely protective of her mother and even though they were working on her attachment issues, she didn't seem to be making any progress.

"She's put a plastic barrier around herself and won't let anyone in. Why? I am not sure. I have some suspicions, but don't want to point any fingers until I can put two and two together." She promised, if anything out of the ordinary happened, she would be sure to call.

Bryce was hurting. But so were Cammi, Faith and Bailey. Bailey was almost two and barely knew his big sister, Allie didn't want to spend time with him and Faith constantly begged for Allie's attention only to be ignored time after time. It was a complete mess. He wanted to protect them all from the pain but it seemed useless, he couldn't connect with anyone. And the one he needed the most was his wife. She was his best friend, his rock, his stability, his lover but in the shuffle of life, she was lost to him.

Another part of him thought Cammi was being selfish. For Christ Sake's, it was *his* daughter that was having all the problems, not hers. And his pain was excruciating. Didn't she see that?

All the kids were in bed when they returned home. Allie had pouted when her parents expected her to stay home and baby-sit. She'd already made plans to go to the movies with Heather and Brandi when they told her 'no, it wasn't going to kill her to help them out'. Bryce hated to make her mad, but the counselor and Cammi both said he couldn't spend his life pleasing her just to avoid conflict.

Conflict was everywhere he looked. A person could cut the tension between the three of them with a knife. Tonight was supposed to be about relaxation and fun. He and Cammi had come so far together, but over the course of the past two years, he watched her love for him turn into disappointment and distrust. And his own resentment was slowly weighing him down.

Lately his anger was turning mean and when he drank on top of it, he was unable to control what he said. It was becoming a habit. Afterwards he felt guilty and wished more than anything he could take back the words, especially when Cammi stared at him with that blank look of hers. The one telling him he'd crossed the line and hurt her so badly, there was no erasing it.

"I see you found it amusing Cynthia is stripping? Did you think for one second how that could be affecting Allie?" she couldn't help saying after they crawled into bed.

Thank God she hadn't let him go out with the guys that night for the Bachelor Party, she thought. It already caused a major fight, but she could only imagine how much worse it would have been if Bryce ran into Cynthia stripping at the club. Of course, he probably would have kept it a secret from her.

"Yes, the whole way home I thought about it, but since you don't want to deal with what is going on with Allie, I didn't feel comfortable enough to bring it up," he shot back.

"Don't you dare accuse me of not wanting to deal with it! All I do is deal with it while you act like life is perfect.

"Yeah, that's it, our life is *perfect*," he commented sarcastically. "You have been dealing with it by yourself. Instead of talking to me and trying to make things better, you clam up in your little hole. You and I don't talk anymore, we fight. This isn't fair to our kids. No wonder Allie is unhappy, who would want to live like this?

"Are you blaming me? If I recall, I wasn't the one who made the decision to bring Cynthia back into Allie's life. You are the one who ruined our happy little family and don't want to be responsible for the outcome. If I had my choice, Cynthia would have had limited, supervised visitation until we found out more about her."

Her words were a slap in the face and instantly, he became defensive.

"How long are you going to blame me? I made the decision I thought was right at the time and you supported me. You didn't have any proof Cynthia was an unfit mother. You just went with your gut. Yes, we found out tonight she is a stripper, so what? At least she is making money."

Money had been an issue lately. The income she brought home was limited and his words tore at her heart. Lamont gave her a few writing assignments here and there in the hopes of bringing her back on fulltime, but Cammi wasn't interested. In fact, she found herself making excuses not to take them if she didn't have to. Her place was at home with her kids and her husband, not behind a computer writing for hour's non-stop. Nevertheless, Cammi resented her husband's implication. It filled her with such rage she wanted to reach over and poke his eyes out to get him to shut up. How could someone who claimed to love her could be so hateful?

"That was low," she hissed.

"The truth hurt?"

"You're an asshole, you know that?"

"Whatever you say, Cammi," he grumbled. "Get out of my face cause I am tired of listening to you whine about how awful your life is. I give you everything you want, you're life is perfect, and if you didn't have your issues, our relationship would be perfect, too. You need to get over this crap."

"Me?" She couldn't believe he was making an argument about Cynthia into everything that was wrong with her. Didn't he see what he was doing? "What about you? You aren't happy either. You're constantly searching for something better. So tell me, when is it you are going to start looking for *someone* better?"

"Do you know how much you hurt me when you suggest such a thing? Do you even know the type of person I am?"

"The problems in this relationship are as much your fault as they are mine, when are you going to see that and stop blaming me?"

Sneering at her, he grabbed a pillow and blanket from the closet.

"What are you doing?"

"Getting away from you. Leave me alone."

But Cammi wasn't willing to be defeated. She wanted a fight. She wanted a reaction out of him, and she didn't care what she said to get it.

"You want to get away from me? You are going to have to kick me out! Ask me for a divorce, I dare you!" she threatened.

"I'm tired Cammi," he said sounding crushed. "I can't do anything about you, I can't do anything about Allie, and I sure as hell can't do anything about Cynthia, but you want me to make it all disappear and go away. When are you going to realize I hurt as much as you, that I am on your side and see this tearing us apart until we feel nothing for each other but hate?"

In her agony, she began to sob. "Can't you see we are losing her? Is that what you want, to be the nice guy? In the meantime, the rest of your family has to suffer. I hate you for what you are doing to us."

Bryce had never been more hurt than he was hearing Cammi say those words. It was like a knife slowly turning in his chest. He looked at her wondering what happened to the happy, encouraging, faithful woman he fell in love with and was swept away by the sadness washing over him.

"What's happening to us, Cammi?" he wondered out loud.

"You continue to put what you want and what Cynthia wants before the needs of your entire family. *That* is what's happening," she spat, not willing to back down. "I understand Allie should have a relationship with her real mother, but she's a ghost in this house. She isn't a part of the family anymore and everyone is suffering because of it. You are suffering the most, but won't look past the end of your nose. Allie needs to know she belongs here and is loved, but because you are scared to hurt or disappoint her, you constantly send her away to her mom's where she can do anything she wants. I spent six years helping you raise her before Cynthia came along, and now you make decisions without consulting me or asking what I think. It's not fair, I have been pushed aside, and I resent you, I resent Allie, but mostly I resent Cynthia for having rights because she gave birth to her. I have been more of a mother to Allie than she ever will be," she said hysterically.

It hurt him deeply to hear her accusations. He hated the idea she might know more about what his daughter needed than he did, but deep down, he knew a lot of what she said was true.

Looking into the deep sea of green in her eyes, he yearned to see the woman he loved, the woman who could meet him half way. "Look, I am tired of fighting with you," he said, sitting on the edge of the bed desperate to calm her down. "We need to learn how to talk to each other without getting angry. If we aren't here for one another, how are we going to put our family back together?" he asked hopeful for a positive reaction.

"I don't ever stop loving you, Bryce, but at times, I think it might be too late," she snapped, snatching up the pillow and blanket. Taking one last glance at him over her shoulder, she slammed the door in his face.

Cammi was alone the next day, thankful that Julie took Bailey and Faith to the Library for story time. She didn't sleep at all the night before and Julie's offer was a godsend. She got them up and ready, then after they left, Cammi crawled back into bed. She wanted to sleep, to wish everything away, but her mind wouldn't shut off.

So instead she prayed.

Dear Lord,

I am really struggling. I don't know how to do this anymore. I hurt all the time and want to be free from the sadness which has overcome my soul. More than Bryce, more than me or anyone else, it is you I need to trust, you I need to seek. Help me let go of my fear of the unknown. Help me to accept my journey as well as Allie and Bryce's. I have too much faith to ask why, but hear my heart cry out for peace.

Everything happens for a reason, but I feel weak and helpless. Please provide me with the strength to keep going. Let me find the light within my soul, so I can get my family through this. I am begging and know nothing else to do.

Amen

Cammi began to weep softly as the pain rooted itself deep down. No one prepared her for the fear of loss chipping away at her heart. No one told her that her marriage and life would end up this way. She hated being away from her children, from Bryce, but at the same time, it took all of her strength to enjoy the time she had with them.

She'd worked hard to become a better person but at that moment, Cammi wished more than anything she could turn back time to be the cold hearted, uncaring, lonely person she spent years escaping. Back when she was strong, she didn't need or depend on anyone, let alone miss the presence of those she loved.

Missing people hurt. The mask she wore kept her heart hard and hidden from the world. Why did she think she needed to take a chance to shed the mask and reveal the intentions of her soul? Why did she think she needed love and companionship? It was much easier to be alone.

The first year with Bryce was filled with promise. She had been giddy, floating five feet above ground with the anticipation of seeing her husband. She savored their time together, never taking for granted the many years spent without him. He was attentive, loving and desirable. She knew he was made for her. It didn't matter where they were, next to each other or from across a crowded room, she could feel his love, see it in his face when their eyes met. The sincerity spoke what words never could. But then the hand of fate reached out and her lack of trust caused an unbreakable rift she couldn't mend.

Their love was supposed to be indestructible. Other people's marriages hit the skids, not theirs. They were going to be the example, the couple everyone envied. They were going encourage and inspire others. But what did she have to offer now? Hypocritical advice?

Her heart was in constant conflict. Avoid the pain and free herself from this mess or stay on the path of love intended for her? Was this what was really intended? Had she made a mistake? Was he really the one she was supposed to be with?

As she buried her head under the covers all she could think about was how ridiculous her life had become and if she could wish her way out of it, she would.

For the first time in a long time alone sounded really good.

Chapter Twenty One

Allie sat on her bed staring at the posters hanging mindlessly on her wall. Cammi was downstairs putting together Faith and Bailey's Halloween costumes, and she wanted nothing more than to join in the fun. Taking a deep breath, she pulled her headphones off her ears and decided it was time to quit wallowing in self-pity and take a chance.

Walking into the dining room, she noticed Faith had on the butterfly costume Cammi bought for her the first Halloween after she married her dad. She wished they could go back in time. A small smile formed on her lips as she remembered Cammi bundling her up in layers of sweatshirts and pants then pulling the costume over the top to keep her warm. She could barely walk and felt like a stuffed marshmallow, but her dad had laughed like a manic while videotaping the entire thing. The three of them walked hand in hand to every house on the block Trick or Treating and when they returned home, Allie watched in awe as Cammi dumped her entire pillow case of candy into a huge glass bowl. Thinking she was the luckiest girl alive to have so much candy, she was disappointed a week later to realize it was almost gone, eaten mostly by her dad.

Longing to feel like she belonged somewhere, Allie swallowed back the lump moving into her throat and blinked as her eyes began to burn with tears.

"Hey you," Cammi said looking up, distracted for a moment from the wing she was pinning back onto the costume.

"Hey"

"Remember this?" she smiled. No matter how angry or hurt Cammi was, the love she felt for Allie consumed her.

"Yeah, it looks good on her." She walked past Faith and rubbed her head.

"Will you take us Trick or Treating this year?" Faith asked in a desperate attempt to connect with the sister who wasn't around anymore.

"Naw, I have plans. There's a dance at school."

"Really? That should be fun," Cammi said hoping to involve her in a conversation even though the disappointment on Faith's face ripped her heart in two.

"I guess. If you are into that sort of stuff. Brandi wants to go, so I said I would," she grumbled.

"What's Brandi up to? She hasn't been around for a while."

"Nothing. Look, I got to finish some homework, let me know when dinner is," Allie said disappearing almost as fast as she had appeared.

Back in her room with the door shut and tears streaming down her cheeks, she punched her pillow. *What is Brandi up to?* If only they knew. She wished they knew everything and could get her out of the middle of this nightmare she was drowning in.

The last week at Cynthia's was great. In fact, it had been better than great. When Robert took them to the mall, Cynthia bought her a cell phone. Her dad said she wasn't allowed to have one until she was sixteen, so she had been hiding it from him. Cynthia said, "what her dad didn't know wouldn't hurt him." And, of course, there was a lot her dad didn't know. If he did, he would surely hate her forever.

They even spent a few days at the lake. Though they didn't know anyone there, it didn't take Cynthia long to befriend two twenty-something guys who owned a boat and water ski's. Since Kurt had taught her how to ski, Allie loved being on the water almost as much as she loved snow skiing. Cynthia didn't like the water, but had no problem hanging out on the boat in the new bikini she bought the day before.

On Thursday Cynthia took her to a fancy salon in Aspen to get her haircut and colored. Her dad loved her long hair and would be devastated when he saw it was now chopped into layers, but she felt like a princess and looked much older than she actually was. She would worry about his reaction later. After lunch, they went tattoo shopping. Cynthia said for her sixteenth birthday, which was only a year away they would get matching flowers on their ankles. Allie wasn't sure if she really wanted one, but went along with the idea anyway.

When they weren't out shopping, they spent the rest of the week planning her party for Saturday night. Allie invited Brandi and Heather along with three boys, Jake, Christian, and Shane.

Cammi had been telling her for as long as she could remember it was normal to have crushes on boys but she would have to be sixteen before she could date. But Allie's crush on Shane since seventh grade had intensified and now that she was almost fifteen, Cynthia, disregarding her parent's rules, claiming she was old enough to go steady with him.

"Girls have hormones and if you want a boyfriend, then go ahead and have yourself a boyfriend. It is not going to hurt anybody, least of all your parents. They are so old-fashioned. Don't they know times have changed?" she said earlier that week when Allie asked if she could invite him.

Allie hardly slept the night before she was so wound up, and the idea of having Shane in her house for *her* party, made her heart flutter with excitement. She wondered if her dad would let her live with Cynthia during the school year. Maybe not this year, but if she kept her grades up and didn't get into trouble, maybe the next one. This week had been perfect, and Allie knew if she was with her mom all the time, Cynthia might stop acting so stupid. She might even calm down and find a really nice guy who wanted to marry her, and they could be more like a real family.

Cynthia was going to cook Allie's favorite, Chicken Alfredo, and followed through on her promise the week before and bought her a new outfit to impress Shane. It was more revealing on the top than Allie was comfortable with, but she didn't want to hurt her Mom's feelings, so she wore it anyway and she had to admit, she did feel sexy. The other girls said she looked great and when the boys arrived, Shane couldn't stop staring. Christian even let out a low whistle.

The first promise Cynthia broke was inviting two friends, guys Allie didn't know, to hang out with her in the kitchen while she cooked and the kids watched movies. It irritated Allie that once again, Cynthia managed to make the night about her, but Allie decided to ignore it and have fun anyway.

Allie sat on the couch next to Shane, and Brandi was next to Jake. Heather liked Christian, but he wasn't interested in her. He wanted to be next to Brandi, too. During the second movie, Brandi conveniently grabbed a blanket to drape over the four of them, and the next thing Allie knew, Shane was holding her hand. Exhilaration ran through her making it near to impossible to concentrate on the rest of the movie.

Dinner was great, but she noticed Cynthia drank a whole bottle of wine along with whatever else she had while preparing the meal. Convinced their heart-to-heart the week before had made a difference, Allie was sure she was turning over a new leaf. Cynthia hadn't had a drink since and Allie couldn't help feeling discouraged watching her now. Allie's friends didn't seem to notice her embarrassment and Shane even had enough guts to ask for a beer.

"Whatever! You can all have one. I'll take your keys, that way you won't be able to drive home," she slurred waving her drink in the air. "Oh yeah, none of you drive yet," she laughed returning from the kitchen with a six pack under her arm. Everyone, with the exception of Jake and Allie took one.

"No thanks," he said politely, sipping on his Pepsi.

Cynthia grabbed a deck of cards and yelled for her friends to join them. Allie had never met them before and couldn't remember if Cynthia had even made introductions. One guy was named Marcus and the other was DJ. They seemed nice enough, but she had learned to be very wary of the people Cynthia brought home. Seething with anger, Allie watched silently as Cynthia dealt the cards explaining the game as she went.

"I put a card down, you say 'hi' or 'low', I turn another over, if you are wrong you drink." Allie disappeared into the kitchen to get another soda for her and one for Jake. They stood back in their own little world as everyone drank their beers, laughing louder and louder as time passed. It didn't take long before the teenagers were as drunk as the three adults.

"I think I better go home," Jake said an hour later. "I could get into big trouble if my parents found out about this."

Allie apologized and thanked him for coming. He tried to get Brandi to walk him to the door to say good night, but she was engrossed in the game…and Christian's hand, which had mysteriously crept up her thigh and under her skirt.

Allie couldn't believe the way her party was turning out. She was angry with her friends but more hurt that Cynthia would put her in this sort of position. All she wanted was for everyone to go home so she could go to bed and forget what was happening, but instead, she stayed quiet as they continued to act like idiots.

Having become an expert party hopper with Cynthia, she learned there were certain advantages and disadvantages to being the sober one. It was close to midnight when Heather locked herself in the bathroom with her head in the toilet. Allie was the first to notice when Cynthia and her two friends started making out in the kitchen. It was erotic enough to turn on the teenage boys. A few minutes later Christian had led Brandi to the couch and had her willingly pinned underneath him while they made out. From what Allie could see Brandi was enjoying every minute of it. Eventually the three adults disappeared into the back bedroom. Allie wanted to scream. Her birthday party was turning into a live freak show right in front of her.

To avoid the tears that were brimming just below the surface, Allie started to clean up. Without saying a word, Shane helped. He took the trash bags from Allie's hands, gave her a brief up and down glance, a wink, and then wandered into the kitchen to throw them away. It was a good escape for her to slip into the bathroom to check on Heather.

"You shouldn't have been drinking tonight, Heather. It was stupid," she told her when they walked outside for some fresh air.

"I know," she slurred. "My parents are going to kill me."

"Allie, can you help me with some of this stuff?" Shane asked. He was leaning against the screen door to keep from falling over.

"Sure." Standing up, Allie sighed. "Stay out here for a while, don't leave yet. You can sober up and then I will walk you home. Your parents don't have to know a thing."

"Thanks Allie, I'm sorry if your birthday was ruined." Heather said with tears running down her face.

Seeing her like that along with the disappointment of the evening made Allie want to cry right along with her. Biting her lip, she followed Shane to the kitchen realizing along the way that he didn't seem cute anymore now that he was drunk. Not only did she regret inviting him, she felt like having a crush on him the past three years had been a total waste.

"You look really hot tonight, Allie," he told her when they were alone. She turned around so her back was against the counter and watched in disgust as he walked toward her.

Oh no, Allie panicked as she looked over to the couch, noticing Brandi and Christian had disappeared into her bedroom. *What is she thinking? She's not old enough for any of this and neither am I. Not like this.* She looked back towards Shane. His eyes told her he was willing to take whatever she was willing to dish out. He was a horny, hormone raged sixteen-year-old boy who'd just been given the peep show of his life from her mom. Now he wanted her.

Taking her hand, he lifted it and brought it to his lips. "I've liked you forever. It's about time I finally get a chance to show you. Happy Birthday." He leaned in to give her a kiss, but his movements were slow and unsteady. Allie quickly ducked away.

"Hey, where did you go?" He turned around to see her heading back to the porch. "Allie, what are you doing? I thought you were into me."

"Well, you thought wrong!" she yelled over her shoulder as the screen door slammed behind her. "Come on, Heather, let's walk this off."

As they headed down the drive, an angry Shane stormed out the door. He caught up with them and shoved Allie.

"Hey!" Heather yelled. "What are you doing, you jerk!"

"You're nothing but a little tease, you know that? It was stupid of me to figure you would be anything like your mom. At least she can talk the talk *and* walk the walk. Everyone in town knows what she's about. It's the only reason I came over tonight. Just wait till they hear at school that you are just a boring ol' prude."

Allie's throat tightened and her heart was thumping so loud, it felt like it would leap out of her chest. Not only did she want to hit him, she wanted to kill him. His words rang in her ears as tears stung her eyes. But she refused to cry. She wasn't going to let him see he got to her. She was going to prove she was stronger than this.

Shane stood waiting for a reaction when Allie turned on her heel to walk Heather home.

"I'm sorry, Allie," Heather said putting her arm around her friend as they crossed the street. They could still hear Shane's cursing two blocks away. "You don't deserve to deal with this crap."

The two girls hugged, and then Heather walked into her house, shutting the door behind her. Allie headed home walking slowly, thinking how easy it would be to walk to her Dad's house instead. But he would ask questions.

By the time she returned home, the house was empty. Even her mom's two friends had disappeared, and when Allie peeked around the open bedroom door, she saw Cynthia had passed out naked, snoring loudly.

She had no idea where Brandi and Christian went to, but as long as they were out of her face, she didn't really care. Allie pulled the sheets off her bed, threw them into the washing machine then grabbed the blanket off the couch and wrapped it around her shivering body. After curling up on her bed in a fetal position, she stared sullenly at the blank wall. She drifted in and out of sleep, having the wackiest dreams. Finally when the sun started to rise, she jumped out of bed and decided to finish cleaning up. She didn't count, but figured she must have thrown away two dozen beer cans and four bottles of wine. It was noon by the time Cynthia awoke, and Allie had all of her belongings packed and waiting by the front door. All she wanted to do was go home and get as far away from there as she could.

She'd made herself some toast and was sitting at the kitchen table nibbling on it even though she didn't really have an appetite, when Cynthia stumbled out of the bathroom. Unable to look Cynthia in the eye she stared at the newspaper sprawled out in front of her.

"What a great month we had together. Let's talk to your dad and see if you can spend your Christmas break with me. Maybe we can go on a trip to celebrate. Wouldn't it be great, the two of us women hanging out together. How about a cruise? We could meet a lot of hot guys on a cruise. We could dance and party all night long!"

Cynthia continued to live in her fantasy world making unrealistic plans while dancing and flitting around the room, ignorant to Allie's feelings. Allie wanted to scream at her. Couldn't she see she wasn't a woman? She was a child, a teenager who needed a mother, not another girlfriend.

It was an awkward goodbye and if Cynthia sensed something was bothering Allie, she ignored it. Aside from the kids who were at the party, Allie didn't tell anyone what happened. School wasn't going to start for another month and a half, so at least she wouldn't have to come face to face with Shane until then, and hopefully, he would have forgotten all about it.

Then Brandi called a few days later bragging about her night with Christian.

"Thank you…thank you….thank you, Allie! If it weren't for your party, we would never have hooked up." Quieting her voice to a whisper, she confessed, "I went all the way with him."

"No kidding?" Allie said sarcastically. "I really appreciate your consideration in using my room."

"Oh, don't be such a sour puss. We were careful. Can I tell you how amazing it was? What's up with you blowing Shane off, by the way? You should give him a chance. He likes you."

"About as much as he likes any other girl in our grade who is half way decent looking and has boobs! He wants a piece of ass, just like Christian, and you are too stupid to see it."

"You are jealous. Jealous because I am mature enough to have sex and you aren't. You're scared," she concluded.

"Believe whatever you want, Brandi, I don't really give a shit what you think. I got to go."

Anger fumed inside as she hung up. She immediately dialed Heather's number to vent. It was nice to have someone on her side who thought Brandi was an idiot, too. There were already two girls in the class ahead of them who dropped out of school for having babies. While they were home taking care of kids, their boyfriends, who claimed to love them, were out partying and sleeping with other girls. No way did she want to end up that dumb.

Cynthia called her every night, but Allie pretended she was busy with the kids to avoid having to talk long. Trying to be nice and polite to her right now was too much.

As grateful as she was to be home where it felt safe, a part of her wished she were more involved with her brother and sister. Life had gone on without her. Her Mom and Dad invested all their time into Faith and Bailey, so there was nothing left for her. No one paid her any attention, she felt worthless and unloved. Didn't they see she needed them too, more now than ever? Admitting things had changed didn't mean she was invisible.

It was two weeks after her birthday when Jake surprised her by stopping by the house. Cammi was out back with the kids, digging up weeds in her flower garden and watching out of the corner of her eye as they ran through the sprinkler. From the kitchen window Allie secretly watched, envious of the fun they were having without her. She longed for the days when she was carefree and happy, when all that mattered were the drops of water hitting her face to cool off the heat of the sun. She hated being a teenager. If this is what real life was like then she wanted to be little again.

Without anyone noticing, Allie crept upstairs to put on her swimsuit and was filled with excitement at the thought of joining them when suddenly the doorbell rang.

"What's up?" she asked trying to sound casual. It was a surprise to see Jake standing on her porch. She didn't realize he knew where she lived. Good thing she had enough sense to put shorts and a tank on over her suit. She would have died if he saw her standing there in only her bikini.

"Seeing what you're doing." After a minute of uncomfortable silence, he continued. "I guess you heard what happened with Brandi and Christian?" he asked obviously annoyed.

"Yeah, I think she is stupid, but their 'in love', right?" she replied sarcastically making a face. "I'm sorry Jake. I didn't mean to hurt your feelings. But really she's not worth it."

"I know, don't worry about it," he shrugged attempting to laugh it off. "Christian's just using her, you know?"

"I tell her that, but she won't listen. But….whatever. She's a big girl and can do what she wants."

Walking across the porch, she sat down on the wicker rocking chair and pulled her knees tightly to her chest and motioned for him to sit in the swing.

"I just want to let you know I'm sorry about that night. I don't know what goes on with you and your mom, but, um…. if you need to talk, well, um….. give me a call. You seemed pretty miserable."

It wasn't what she'd expected to come out of his mouth. As hard as he tried to show his sincerity, he looked really uncomfortable. His offer was sweet she decided but she wasn't quite sure what to say either, and the last thing she wanted was to embarrass him.

"Thanks, maybe. I don't know if there is much to talk about. Just a normal family, I guess."

It took a lot for him to say what he did, and she didn't want him to think she was a snob. They'd known each other since grade school, but he had always been the quiet, smart boy. They had a couple electives together in Junior High, though they never really talked then either. She'd only invited him to her party because he, Christian and Shane were inseparable.

"After dinner, uh, I go for walks down by the river sometimes. I like to sit and look at the stars." She shrugged her shoulders and said, "If you ever want to stop by, I'm out there."

Allie began taking the walks not long after Cynthia told her the story about her Dad. It was a good place to clear her head and deal with the emotions overwhelming her when she was in the house with her family. It was desolate, but only three blocks from her home, so she felt safe.

"What's at the river?" he asked, his hands casually shoved into the pockets of his jeans.

"Nothing much. My dad and I use to skip rocks. Sometimes I fish. Cammi taught me. Usually I just sit and watch the water and think."

Jake shrugged. "Okay."

Then he smiled at her. And that was nice, too. A smile said a lot about a person.

Brandi had her head stuck so far up Christian's ass Allie could hardly stand to be around her, so she spent the rest of the summer with Heather, with the exception of the two nights a week she met Jake down by the river. He showed up the following evening after she invited him, and they walked in silence, listening to the sound of the water as it rushed past them, the reflection of the sun dancing off the current.

Her dad would be irate if he knew it was a boy she was meeting but really, she wasn't doing anything wrong. Jake was a gentleman and never made a move on her. It was completely innocent and wasn't long before Allie felt comfortable enough to tell him about Cynthia. He never judged her or told her what to do. He only listened. It was nice to have someone to talk to, someone she could be herself with. The stress consumed her and she was tired of trying to be someone different for everyone in her life. Sharing her secrets with Jake helped more than anyone realized.

Cynthia had a new man now. Darby. The *lawyer* as Allie called him. She'd met him in July and Allie had to admit he was a pretty decent guy. Some might even call him good looking. At least he dressed better than the others. With Darby, Cynthia wasn't drinking as much, only when they were out with friends, and he spoiled her rotten, buying them both everything their hearts desired. Allie liked him and thought maybe this could be the one who made Cynthia change her ways. She was finally showing some responsibility and acting like a normal adult. He even told her he loved her and discussed getting married. She hadn't said yes, but confessed to Allie she was thinking it over. Darby liked Allie and always made an effort to include her. He told her on many occasions her mom just needed the love of a good man to make her see things differently. Allie sure hoped he was right.

Allie was petrified for the first day of tenth grade, but she was even more nervous about what her mother's actions the night of the party might have done to her reputation.

The first week of school went off without any major problems. But she couldn't help being paranoid that everyone was looking at her differently. She wondered what the rumors were. As much as she missed Brandi's friendship, she didn't think being around her was a good choice either. Christian had a big mouth, and the whole school knew about *everything* they did. She didn't want others to think she was like that. Plus, the less Brandi knew about Allie's life, the better. The last thing she needed was her spouting off at the mouth.

It was at the first football game when Allie found out, regardless of her good choices, that she and her mother had already been the target of high school gossip.

"Hey, Shepard, I hear your mom is a great lay!" Nate yelled down at her from where he was sitting with Shane and Christian. She and Nate had been in the same class since kindergarten, too and for the most part he had always been nice to her. But now sitting a few rows in front of them, she was horrified to find herself the brunt of his teasing. There wasn't anyone around them who hadn't heard what he said. Trying to ignore the peals of laughter, Allie hid her red face from the stares of onlookers. Heather, embarrassed for her friend, turned around to say something but Allie stopped her.

"Please, don't. You'll only make it worse."

Noticing the whispers from two girls she always considered friends, Allie slid down in her seat wishing the earth would open up and swallow her whole. If she got up to leave, it would only draw more attention her way, so she sucked it up the rest of the game, but she refused to go to another one the rest of the season, which was too bad. Jake was the only sophomore on Varsity this year and she enjoyed watching him play.

Brandi's prying didn't help matters.

"Is it true your mom slept with the lead singer of one of those bands from the 'Eighties'? Those guys who looked like girls with the long hair and make-up."

Allie wanted to die. She had no idea how *anyone* could have found out.

It had been early last spring before school got out when Cynthia's favorite band was playing in Denver. She got tickets along with backstage passes for herself, Beth and Allie. Allie had only listened to their music when she was with her mom, but liked it well enough and the idea of going to a concert was so thrilling, she didn't care who she was seeing.

The adrenaline rush she felt standing shoulder-to-shoulder with everyone in the crowd as the band first hit the stage was unlike any experience she'd ever had. With her mom and Beth guiding her, they pushed their way to the front until Cynthia was within arm's reach of the lead singer. Sweat poured over her, but Allie was having the time of her life dancing and moving with the beat of the music and everyone around her.

The band played for what must have been three hours, but to Allie it only felt like three minutes. It was disappointing to have the lights come on and watch the crowd disappear out the arena doors. But then the butterflies began to flutter as she remembered they still had back stage passes.

Within moments they were led down a big bright hallway by one of the band security guards and directed into a back room where twenty or so other women were waiting, drinking and smoking.

Allie, shell shocked, plastered herself against the side of the wall. Half the women stood in only their bras and panties. Their faces were painted with heavy, dark makeup and their hair ratted and messy, stood up in a million different directions. Allie could not help but wonder how much hairspray it took to achieve that look. Aside from different hair and skin color, they all seemed to be perfect clones of one another.

Within moments, Cynthia had peeled off her top to become a clone with the others in whatever quest it was they were seeking. Allie really didn't get it.

"Do you really need to do that?" Beth whispered in Cynthia's ear nodding toward where Allie was standing.

"This is the chance of a lifetime, do you really think I am going to pass it up just cause my daughter is with me?" she sneered.

"Um yeah. I would hope so."

Cynthia laughed as she took what Allie thought was a cigarette from a tall brunette in spandex pants whose cleavage overflowed her tube top. But she wasn't holding it like a regular cigarette rolled toward the bottom of her index and middle finger. Instead, she pinched it between her thumb and forefinger as she brought it up to her lips. And it was strange how after she inhaled, she held her breath for three to four seconds as if she were underwater.

Cynthia coughed as she exhaled and began to giggle uncontrollably as she made her way around the room sipping drinks and taking drags off the weird little cigarettes from anyone who was willing to share.

"Come on, Allie. You don't need to be here," Beth said trying to shove her toward the door.

"Come here, baby, I want you to meet someone," Cynthia shouted from across the room at the same moment they were about to leave. Allie turned her eyes towards her mother's voice, but was unable to see her through the haze of smoke.

"Beth! Seriously! Come over here, you two."

Allie tried to ignore the scene around her as she walked toward the back of the room, but it was impossible. The four guys who were on stage playing instruments only moments before were now sprawled out lazily on recliners and couches with women draped all over them. They held a cocktail or cigarette in one hand while the other searched hungrily for bodies clad in nothing more than skimpy clothes.

Finally, Allie spotted her mother and the image, as hard as she tried to block it out, etched into her brain. Straddling the lead singer, Cynthia had removed her bra to expose her breasts. His mouth was attached to one while his hand stroked the other.

"Oh, Allie, I didn't realize you were still here," she giggled feigning embarrassment as she began to reattach her bra.

"You told us to come over here, remember?" Allie replied dryly.

"Oh! Silly me!" The singer obviously put out by having his good time spoiled, cringed and took a drink from a long-necked bottle filled with a brown colored liquid. "I want you to meet someone. This is Rick. He and I have been friends for years, isn't that right?"

"Yep, she's the best groupie I've ever had," he said looking up from his drink long enough to gaze towards Allie and Beth before he set his sights on another voluptuous woman walking by. As he reached out to pull her down onto Cynthia's lap as well as his own, what existed of her tiny shirt was accidentally pushed up to expose her breasts as well. The three laughed hysterically.

"You're disgusting, Cynthia," Beth yelled. "I can't believe you act like this in front of your daughter. I am taking her back to the hotel. Find your own way."

"Oh, you two are nothing but party poopers," she retorted. "I'll have more fun without you anyway."

Allie looked back once more before she followed Beth out of the room, wishing she could drag her mother out with her, save her from the disgusting man she allowed to touch her body, but also knowing that as strange as it was, Cynthia was exactly where she wanted to be.

"She met him once, when she was a teenager, backstage after a concert. He doesn't remember who she is from all the other tramps he slept with. But in her eyes, she was something special. What a crock," Beth retorted while touching the end of her cigarette with a match and pushing her foot on the accelerator of the car.

"Why do you think she does it?" Allie wondered aloud. Nervous with the speed Beth was driving, she kept herself occupied watching the skyscrapers pass by.

Beth shrugged. "Your mom's got problems Allie, big problems. Do you know what a sociopath is?"

"No."

"You're too young to understand." She waved her hand in the air dismissing the thought. "Just be careful with her, Allie. She doesn't care who she hurts as long as she gets what she wants."

"And what is it she wants?"

Beth snorted but drove silently the rest of the way.

Back at the hotel, Beth fell asleep instantly. Allie could hear her snores as she lay awake for the next few hours filled with worry and silently crying into her pillow so she didn't wake her. She was grateful Beth got her out of that place. It scared her, but was her mom okay? Could she find a way back to where they were? Wondering if she would ever see her again, Allie felt alone and terrified.

It didn't take a rocket scientist to figure out that back stage after a concert wasn't a good place for anyone to be. So why didn't her mom see that? Why would she want to be around those people? And what did Beth mean by 'sociopath'?

"You wouldn't believe how many times we do it," Brandi screeched, interrupting Allie's thoughts. "The hard part is finding places to go so our parents won't find out," she giggled, "but he is so creative."

Because she was now having sex on a regular basis, Brandi treated Allie and Heather like they were children. For the moment Allie didn't care, she was grateful the subject was off her mother.

"You guys really need to step up to the plate. Everyone is doing it. What are you going to do if you find a guy you actually like a lot? Look like an idiot the first time you are with him? At least if you have sex before, you will sort of know what you are doing. Better chance of him sticking around if the sex is good."

"Plus Allie," she said lowering her voice, "the guys sort of expect it from you, you know. Since they know how your mom is. I'm not saying it is okay, but you don't want them to think you're a prude, do you?"

Brandi's words sharply grazed the inner turmoil Allie was already struggling with and she couldn't stand it anymore! Brandi was supposed to be her friend, someone who wanted good things for her. Not someone who encouraged her to make bad choices. It wasn't that Allie didn't crave the attention or affection of a boy. In fact, she wanted someone to care about her so badly, she often thought about having sex. She knew it's what they wanted. But when it came down to it, she just could not bring herself to act like Cynthia…..or Brandi for that matter.

"I don't want to be anything like my mother!" Allie cried.

"Allie, your mom is cool, what's the problem?" Brandi asked innocently. "I would love to have a mom like her. She is fun, down to earth and beautiful. Just like one of the girls."

It didn't matter what Allie told them, no one would ever understand and as Allie listened to Brandi ramble on about her new boyfriend, her anger quickly turned to pity. She knew for a fact Christian was having sex with two other girls at a school ten miles away.

"He's having threesome's with them," Jake told her the other night when they were sitting by the river.

"Gross! Why…Why…Why would someone do that? Don't they have any self-respect? Don't they want it to be special? Cammi always told me I should never, no matter what the circumstance, have sex with someone who isn't going to respect my body or my mind. This means, she said, if he is all about making himself feel good, then I should not waste my time. The way she talked, sex with someone you love is one of the most beautiful, sacred things God created."

Blush crept into her cheeks. For a minute she got so wrapped up in her thoughts she forgot she was talking to a boy.

Allie did feel bad lying to her parents about the time she spent with Jake, like this upcoming weekend when she said she was hanging with Brandi and Heather, when in reality she was going to a haunted house with Jake, then they were going to meet up with some other friends to walk along the river to the town cemetery. It would be awesome and so creepy…..perfect for Halloween. But there was a part of her dying to take her sister and brother trick-or-treating. She wouldn't tell her family that though. She would die before she let them know she cared.

Someday, she told herself, she would tell them about Jake, but for now, she liked having him to herself. The secrecy of their friendship made it even more special. He was like the twin brother she wished she really, truly had. Only this was better. He didn't annoy her like a brother probably would and she could tell him anything. She cherished her friendship with Heather, but she was immature. Her lack of experience in life limited her thinking sometimes. Not that Allie had tons of personal experience. Instead she was the child who knew more than she needed to at this age because of her bloodline.

But Jake was different. His parents were perfect, even he would admit it. And his childhood, though not dull, was filled with good memories. He didn't have any emotional baggage or tragedy to speak of. Yet still, he possessed maturity and core values most other boys their age lacked.

Of course, Allie had to remind herself, that without Cynthia, her life had been just as perfect and just as memorable. It was a little unusual to have the reappearance of a person she barely knew and try to find her way in a relationship when that person's life was so different than anything she'd ever known.

"Allie," Cammi shouted up at her interrupting her thoughts. "You need to finish your chores. I asked you two hours ago to sweep the kitchen floor and take out trash. It's still not done."

Allie sighed. She hated her chores. Hated all of the responsibilities Cammi pushed on her. Cammi was home all day. It wasn't like she couldn't do it herself. Yet day after day she nagged Allie about her responsibilities. Take out the trash, unload the dishwasher, clean her room, set the table…..it was never ending. At Cynthia's house she didn't have to do anything, though when Cynthia was hung over, Allie took it upon herself to pitch in.

Still it unnerved her each and every time Cammi reminded her of what she did or didn't do. She was like a broken record. It wasn't like Allie was a bad kid or anything. After her pathetic attempt of breaking the rules in Junior High, she was on the straight and narrow. Her grades were all A's and B's except for the C in World Geography, but seriously, who cared about Ancient Greece? Allie decided it was better to keep the peace and besides, the more she was around Cynthia and got a glimpse of the lifestyle she lived, the more Allie realized it was up to her to get into college so she could have better.

In spite of that, as she descended the stairs once again to be welcomed into a room full of laughter, Halloween decorations, and memories of the past, sadness seemed to rip her heart into shreds.

Chapter Twenty Two

The image reflecting off the TV was of Cammi in her wedding gown looking at her beloved husband. But as her blood shot eyes stared at the screen, they bore into those of a man she spent more time detesting than loving.

She had been curled up on the couch for hours watching the old home movies, savoring her time alone, without him, with the kids in bed. Glancing at the clock, the effects of the wine she was drinking made her sway when she stood up to change tapes.

Allie's bright smile lit up the screen on her first day of third grade. Cammi felt the tears slide down her cheeks while she watched the dance recitals and now her breath caught in her throat as she and Bryce protectively followed Allie into the house carrying a brand new baby Faith from the car. Allie glowed with happiness while she showered her baby sister with kisses. Would Cammi ever see her bright smile and carefree happiness again?

This wasn't how her life was supposed to turn out. She felt like she was constantly picking up the pieces of her shattered dreams while all the time watching someone else's life from afar.

She stifled a giggle as she watched an eleven-year-old Allie put make-up on her dad while he napped on the couch. He went nuts, chasing them both around the house upon waking up to find red lipstick, blue eye shadow and the video camera on him. It had been wonderful. Was that really only a few years ago?

The emptiness Cammi carried around inside for four years was starting to blacken her soul, and she hated the person she was turning into because of it. It was as if the bottled- up anger was waiting for the right moment to explode and it scared the hell out of her. She didn't know who she was or what to do to stop it.

Cynthia picked Allie up earlier that evening. The intimidation and resentment Cammi struggled with every time Cynthia came around surfaced when she answered the door. She hated her. She hated her beauty, the seductive way she walked, how her lips pouted in a sensual smile that would make any man buckle with weakness, but most of all she hated her because she gave birth to Allie and here she was, standing at the door of her house all perky and bubbly. It made Cammi want to vomit.

By the time they left Cammi was a ticking time bomb. Thank God Bryce hadn't bothered to come home. At least he was considerate enough to call to say he was going out for dinner with his co-workers. It was a good thing. She couldn't stand the sight of him right now either.

But at the same time, she was pissed he was inconsiderate enough to go out while she had to stay home and deal with Cynthia. Not to mention he would rather be with someone else, anyone else besides her *or* Allie. He was escaping the two people who needed him the most.

Allie's not so long ago deception over the cell phone intensified the fights between all three of them. She accidentally left it behind in a rush not to be late for school and been silly enough to call from Heather's phone to see where it was misplaced. Unlucky for Allie, it rang while Cammi was collecting the laundry from her room.

Cammi called Bryce home from work, and he searched the phone, finding texts not only from all of Allie's friends, but from Cynthia, too. Reacting out of anger, he instantly called Cynthia, and of course, she denied any involvement.

"She said it was her birthday present from you and Cammi," she said sounding shocked. "I don't know where she could have gotten it."

It was just like Cynthia not to take responsibility. Despite his arguments, she wasn't going to tell him the truth, so he gave up trying.

But he was mostly disappointed by Allie's disobedience. She knew she was not allowed to get a phone until she was sixteen but lied to him anyway. He also remembers making it perfectly clear to Cynthia.

The phone was taken away and Allie was grounded for two weeks. But upon hearing her punishment, she turned on him like a snake waiting to strike.

"You are such a jerk!" she shrieked. "You are ruining my life, don't you see that? I can't stand living here with you anymore. I can't even stand being around you. I'm not a child anymore and you need to realize it!"

Bryce watched her throw her tantrum without saying a word.

"You are still grounded," he said coolly when she was through. Glaring at him with pure hatred she slammed the door to her room.

In the aftermath, Cammi could tell he was emotionally drained and wounded. She had tried to comfort him, but he wouldn't allow himself to be vulnerable. Instead of returning her affection, he'd closed off into his own silent solitude and said nothing about it since.

After a long talk with Jamie, Cammi decided what he really needed was for her to back off and give him some space. He needed her love and support while he figured this out, but doing it wasn't easy, she missed him terribly. He was there physically, but not emotionally. Regardless how difficult it was Cammi was determined to take the lead and not place unwanted expectations on him when he wasn't in a place to meet them.

Besides, the more she nagged, the more he pulled away which defeated the purpose entirely. He was patient with her over the years, and she needed to give him the same. It was only fair. Once again she found herself living by faith, not necessarily in him, but in what they shared.

As the months went on, instead of demanding a change in his attitude, Cammi worked on hers. If he wanted to be a grump, that was fine but she wasn't going to get drug down into his misery. She had her own setbacks to deal with when it came to not only Cynthia, but Beth's continued presence in their life and at those times, Cammi felt, once again, as if she were sinking into a deep black hole where everything around her, including her marriage was falling apart. As the feelings of guilt and intimidation plagued her, the only place she could turn to was God. He comforted her with love and solitude, which was more than she could get from her husband anymore.

The panic only lasted a few days, so she didn't bother to tell Bryce, knowing it would strike a nerve and start an argument. He was sick and tired of her issues. "She was living in the past and needed to get over it", he told her on many occasions. It was a struggle, but she was trying to put a more positive spin on life. Then as always, he would make snide a comment or do something to send her spiraling out of control.

"What do you mean you are going out?" she asked defensively when he called from work earlier that afternoon. It made her wonder who all was included in 'co-workers'. "Maybe I had plans for us this evening!"

Bryce laughed sarcastically. "Really Cammi? What sort of plans? It's not like we actually enjoy our time together anymore. All you do is treat me horrible?" He'd had a tough day himself and he didn't feel like going home to get bombarded with her inquisitions.

"Maybe I wouldn't treat you bad if you paid the least bit of attention to me. But you don't. Why don't you talk to me?"

"Why should I talk to you? All you do is criticize and blame me for everything that's wrong in our life. You make me feel like crap on a daily basis. Why do I want to come home to that?"

Cammi was speechless as the words burrowed deep into her heart. Fine! She didn't want him around anyway. He could do what he wanted with who he wanted and she would take care of herself. She was good at being alone. She'd done it for years without him and would have no problem doing it again.

In a calm voice she spoke, "Then maybe you shouldn't bother coming home at all. We can certainly get along fine here without you," and hung up the phone.

How dare he treat her this way? The ache in her chest continued to pulsate as she sat staring at the phone, refusing to answer when it rang again. It had to be him. And she hoped by not answering, he felt as terrible as she did.

After putting Faith and Bailey to bed, she poured herself a big glass of wine and dug around her closet to find the movies.

Glancing up at the clock three hours later, she began to panic. She figured he'd be home by now. It was only dinner. Who was he with?

The fights as well as feeling sorry for herself were becoming a daily ritual, but Cammi hardly had the strength to care. The emotions had become a part of who she was and even though she hid them from the outside world, she was tired of fighting a no win battle inside her heart. She had been prepared for the emotional conflict with Cynthia's reappearance in Allie's life, but she had not been prepared to deal with jealousy when it came to her husband. What happened with Beth was bad enough, but now she was competing with the mother of his child. She didn't want to compete. She couldn't compete. Insecurities lying dormant for years rose to the surface.

It seemed like yesterday, not a month ago, when Bryce came home from work in the middle of the afternoon while the kids were napping saying he needed to discuss something important with her. Not unusual in the first years of their marriage, but anymore, she was lucky if he was home in time for dinner. She'd heard a slight tremor in his voice while his empty, expressionless face sent an uncomfortable shudder through her.

"I need to tell you something, please hear me out before you get angry."

The impact of his words frightened her. Her hands shook and her stomach instantly twisted into knots as a million ideas swarmed through her head.

"You need to hear this from me before you hear it from her. I pissed Cynthia off, bad this time. She's been trying to convince me to let her take Allie on a trip to California. I told her no and needless to say, she was not happy with the answer. To make a long story short, she's trying to blackmail me."

Cammi stared at Bryce as if he'd just grown two heads. "Are you serious?" she chuckled.

The dark, vacant look in his eyes told her he was.

"She said some pretty ugly things, threatened me and threatened you. I figured if I didn't answer the phone it would all blow over, but today I received pictures she sent via e-mail, pictures of her with two guys and a couple of girls."

Thinking she might vomit, Cammi desperately tried to shake the image from her mind.

"There was a note attached with it saying if I wasn't willing to cooperate, she was going to make sure you believed *I* asked her to send me the pictures and convince you that she and I have been having an affair in the meantime. I panicked, Cammi," he whispered running his fingers through his hair in frustration. "I won't allow her to do this to us so I came home to tell you right away. It wouldn't surprise me if she already sent the pictures. She's done enough damage. I won't let her hurt you with this, too." His eyes pleaded with her to understand.

"I was going to call and confront her, but I wanted you to listen. She's playing tricks and I want to make sure you and I are in this together. " He waited for a response from her but got nothing, only a cold, hard stare.

Cammi watched in silence as he stood up and flipped open his cell phone to dial Cynthia's number. Her mind was blank, numb. But when he started to speak, panic hit and she began hyperventilating as she listened.

"I told Cammi about the e-mail," he said, his voice filled with malice. Pushing a button, he switched her to speakerphone. "I am only going to tell you this once. Don't ever threaten me or my wife again. You and I will talk *only* when it deals with Allie. If you ever pull something stupid like this ever again to try to get your way, I promise you, I will take you to court so fast for a visitation agreement, your head will spin. Be glad I haven't done it yet. You are walking on thin ice."

"Is that how you get control? By threatening women?" she screamed. "Is that the only reason your wife is still with you, because you threaten her? I know it's the only reason Allie still lives with you. She hates you, you know, and she hates Cammi too, for taking you away from her. But you are too wrapped up in your new family to see how much pain she's in. She'd be better off living with me."

"You miserable bitch! Shut your mouth, do you hear me?" he shouted. Cammi had never heard Bryce so close to the verge of losing control. "Your lies got you nowhere fifteen years ago and they won't get you anywhere now. You left, remember?"

"Yeah, because you wouldn't marry me, remember? Our life could have been nice, Bryce, if you would have just played along back then."

"And end up married to a psycho? No thanks. You have to play by my rules now or you won't play at all. Don't you ever think of pulling a little stunt like this again, do you understand?

Cynthia was hysterical by this point. "I hate you. I hate you *so* much," she screamed. "I… I would have never come back to town if I knew you weren't going to let me spend time with my daughter. Maybe I should just move…. so you and your whore of a wife can have your own way. That would make everybody happy wouldn't it?"

"You're so selfish, Cynthia. Did you think you could waltz back in here demanding anything you wanted? Hell, no. Think about Allie for once instead of yourself. You said you moved back here for her, but is that true? I have bent over backwards to ensure you get time with her and I've been more than fair. But the one time you don't get your way you threaten not only us, but to leave Allie again? You're insane."

"I guess if I want to be in Allie's life, I don't have a choice but to do what you say," she sobbed.

"I am easy to get along with if you are willing to compromise, but this crap is not getting you on my good side. In fact, it really makes me question the type of influence you are on her."

"Those pictures were taken years ago. I have changed, Bryce, I told you that," she wailed.

"Then why the hell did you send them to me with a threat attached? That was just stupid and it doesn't make you look very stable." His voice lowered an octave. "Look, I am willing to be the biggest asshole to protect those I love, so you better start toeing the line." He hung up before she could reply.

Bryce placed his phone on the table, and then pulled Cammi into his chest. He could feel her shaking with anger.

She wanted to trust her husband, but uncertainty smacked her in the face. Only this time, it was with a woman she had come to despise. It was comforting to have him stand up for her, to protect her, but the thought of Cynthia's accusations lingered long after.

What if he was having an affair with her? The idea wasn't that farfetched. He had cared for her once, and she was the mother of his daughter. She *was* gorgeous with an amazing body to boot. *And* this wasn't the first time this happened. There was Beth and then when she was pregnant with Faith, that Lacy woman from the hospital promotion party years ago. In fact, if she was willing to open her eyes, this sort of thing was becoming a common occurrence. And she didn't think she had the strength to face these circumstances yet again.

Maybe it was time for Cammi to be realistic. She and Bryce were no longer as intimate as they used to be. They no longer conversed or spent quality time together. When they were together, they argued or snipped at one another. He barely touched her, let alone kissed her. The desperate urge to close off her heart consumed her. Wouldn't it be easier than to continue to love a man who was on the verge of, if he wasn't already, having an affair?

Then she had to stop and remind herself *she* was the mother of his other two children and he *loved* her. He hadn't loved Cynthia or Beth. Well, maybe a little, but not the way he loved her, and Lacy, well, she was never really in the picture to begin with. God, she was in such conflict. It was starting to make her crazy.

Reaching to turn off the television, she stubbed her toe on one of Bailey's toy trucks. Cursing, she kicked it aside and headed upstairs. Once she was in bed, the tears stung her eyes as she pulled the covers tightly around her.

The pain in her heart intensified as she watched the time pass on the alarm clock. She had almost cried herself to sleep when she heard Bryce creep silently into the room. Normally, she rolled over the opposite way as soon as he came to bed, but tonight, she needed the comfort of his arms, the comfort of his love despite having left her alone all evening.

She was disgusted with herself. Even after he disrespected her with irresponsible behavior she couldn't protect her heart. Wanting him and longing for his love meant she would get hurt in the long run, but still, her pathetic soul ached for him to love her the way he used to.

Bryce was aware of her muffled sobs when he entered the room so he quietly undressed and crawled in next to her, praying she wouldn't start in on him for staying out until eleven. He hadn't meant to and the entire drive home, he dreaded his decision. It was a last minute offer to go out for pizza with two other administration employees who were trying to decide whether to stay on now that all the changes at the hospital were in place or find another job. It was a nice bitch session about work between guys and a huge stress relief for Bryce. The three of them only ordered a few drinks to go with their dinner and by the time they went their separate ways, Bryce felt like a weight had been lifted from his shoulders.

That was until he looked at the clock in his truck. Damn, why hadn't he called her? She was probably worried sick. No…she was probably pissed.

The silver iridescent light of the moon broke through the window and glowed off the contouring curve of his wife's body and instinctively, he wanted more than anything to touch her skin, to feel her melt against his body. But anymore, she recoiled when he got close, so instead he lay on his back, staring at the ceiling, waiting for her to fall asleep.

Shock raked through him when she wrapped her arms around his torso and snuggled closer. Her touch tingled and his first reaction was to reject her the way she had him so many times, but he couldn't. He loved her too much and needed her love in return. No matter what road they headed down, he swore he would be there for her when she came back to him.

He turned himself to face her and pressed his lips to her forehead then worked his way down her cheek, then her neck and finally, to touch her lips.

He tasted of whiskey and Cammi could not help but wonder if he had fun, if he watched and noticed other women, wishing his wife was like them. She knew he was happier when he was gone, when he could get away and escape everything as it came crashing around them. She loved him so much. She couldn't deny it. But did he still love her? They had good days; even good weeks when their relationship was strong and stable, and she felt they could make it through anything. But when they fought, it was as if the world was ending, and she honestly didn't know if they would make it through the next hour let alone the next year.

But here he was. He came home to her and as his body hovered over hers and he caressed her cheek with the back of his hand, she, for a brief moment, remembered what it was like not to have a broken heart.

Chapter Twenty-Three

Allie threw her books onto the couch and stormed up the stairs, her temper flaring.

Giving Cammi a baffled look Bryce headed after her.

"What is your issue?" he snapped closing her bedroom door behind him.

"Nothing, leave me alone," she said darkly. She picked her clothes up off the floor and tossed them into the hamper. Why, just once, when she was having a bad day couldn't he be nice to her?

"What the hell is your problem anymore? You are a nightmare to be around," he insisted. "You better change your attitude, do you understand me? I came up here to talk, if you aren't willing then don't be mad when I'm not sympathetic."

"Get out of my room," she seethed.

She hated everyone and right now, he was the last person she wanted to see or talk to. Her whole world was crumbling around her and no one understood. Why couldn't she be one of those stupid girls who had nothing to worry about but clothes, zits, and boys? She hated them. Boo hoo. Big deal. Live a day in her shoes. Deal with the shit she had to put up with. Then they would see what real stress was like.

She'd actually been having a good day. She got an A on her Biology quiz, they had burritos for lunch, it was Friday, and tonight she was going to meet Jake out by the river. She'd been looking forward to it all week. But stupid her, on the way home, she took a detour by Cynthia's. Usually she was greeted with a big, welcoming hug, but not today. She didn't even acknowledge her presence for the first half hour while Allie followed her around making small talk without even so much as a response.

"What's wrong?" she finally asked tired of beating a dead horse, but nervous to hear the answer.

"Your dad called. He's harassing me again about *your* cell phone. You didn't tell him I bought it did you?" Cynthia asked.

"I didn't say *anything*, Cynthia!" Allie whined.

"Good."

"He's not an idiot, Cynthia. He knows I can't get one on my own."

"Don't talk to me like that. I deserve your respect," she said glaring at her daughter. "He was awful to me, Allie. You should have heard him." Tears filled her eyes. "It makes me wonder what else you have told him."

"I don't tell him anything, I promise!"

"Do you know what he had the nerve to do? Ask me to meet him after work, before he headed home. He whined about his sex life with Cammi, how dull it is. Basically telling me she lies there like a dead fish and wishes she was as good as I was. That he remembers all the nights we shared together, the passion, the intensity. Bad thing is I remember how good it was too, his offer was tempting, but I would *never* do something like that to Cammi."

"You and dad had passionate nights together?" Allie questioned. If her memory served her correctly, Cynthia said her dad raped her the first night they met.

"That is beside the point," she replied with a wave of her hand. "Anyway, he said if I was willing, he would let you keep the phone and forget about all the other stuff he knew. He was trying to blackmail me, Allie! Can you believe it?"

"What other stuff?" she asked nervously wondering herself what it was he might know.

Allie guessed she shouldn't be surprised. Cammi had this weird sixth sense and had a habit of knowing things before they even happened. It was hard to get anything past her. If it came down to it, Cammi could probably make her life hell. As strange as it was though, she was in awe of it. It was nice to know someone cared enough to make sure she didn't screw up her life, unlike Cynthia.

"He didn't explain. His words were 'I'm a fool if I think he and Cammi are blind to what I do.' And if I want to be a part of your life, I need to follow his rules. I am so tired of him controlling me. Every time I think I am getting somewhere, he blindsides me with this 'holier than though' attitude making me feel worthless. I hate him."

"Where's Darby?" Allie asked changing the subject, sickened by what she just heard and trying to clear her head before the mental imagine of her father clouded her thoughts.

"At work," she said sounding annoyed. "He had some important client to take to dinner, said he would stop by tomorrow."

Since school started Allie only spent every other weekend with, Cynthia. Her counselor said it was better for her emotionally to have a routine. And she had to admit, she was glad. Ironically, she felt safer when she was at her dad's house. Darby and Cynthia fought all the time. It wasn't like when her mom and dad got into fights. They were quiet about it, giving each other the cold shoulder for a day or two, and then everything worked itself out. With Cynthia and Darby, it was a full-fledged war and from what Cynthia told her, the fights were constant, glasses were thrown, doors were broken, holes were punched in walls. One time she even saw Cynthia smack Darby across the face. He didn't hit her back, but grabbed her by the arms and shoved her into the couch. Allie couldn't sleep with it going on, so it was probably better for her to be at her dad's.

The guilt overwhelmed her because she cherished her time with Cynthia. Sometimes she thought it was crazy to be so desperate for her mom's love, but at the same time, she began to understand she didn't fully trust her not to leave. So Allie was willing to do whatever it took to keep her mom around and in her life.

Everything except live with her. That she wouldn't do. It was a topic of conversation Cynthia brought up on a continual basis, and Allie didn't have the heart to tell her no. Thank God she could blame her dad.

"Dad said I could make that decision when I was eighteen. Until then, I am stuck living there," she lied mustering up as much regret as she could.

"Wouldn't it be great if you lived with me while you were going to college? Maybe your smarts would rub off and I could take some courses, too."

Allie thought the idea of Cynthia going back to school was great, but knew it would never happen. She had mentioned it close to twenty times in the past four years, but it was easily forgotten the next day.

"Yeah, maybe," she said trying to put her off without being obvious. The older Allie got, the more she questioned her mother. The stories she told didn't make much sense, especially about work and money. Allie still didn't know what her mom did for a living or if she actually worked at all, but she always had money when she needed it and it disappeared just as fast.

In fact that's what started her fight with Darby last weekend. He called just as Allie was headed to bed so she hesitated in the hallway to eavesdrop on their conversation.

"You are a cheap bastard," she screamed. "I told you I needed to get that bill paid today. You were supposed to bring me the money. What do you mean you are tired of being used? I'm not using you, if anything you are using me."

Allie couldn't understand what he was saying but could hear the screams. Cynthia eventually slammed down the phone and began to cry.

Feeling bad for her, Allie snuck back into the living room, wrapped Cynthia in her arms and rocked her back and forth like a child. Looking around she noticed the eight beer cans sitting on the kitchen table and figured she must have downed them all during her fight with Darby.

"He doesn't want to be with me anymore. He told me I am trash," she shrieked pulling Allie tighter into her embrace.

"I am a good person, you know that? I deserve to have someone take care of me. I deserve to have nice things. I deserve to be treated decently."

"Come on, why don't I help you to bed? You will feel better in the morning." Allie was reluctant to get into a conversation about what her mom *deserved*. She'd heard it too many times already.

"I *will* feel better in the morning. You know why? Because I don't love him! He isn't worth it," she laughed hysterically. "I'm going to tell you a little secret, Allie," she said dropping her voice to a whisper. "I'm still having sex with Robert, so it doesn't matter if Darby loves me, because I think Robert is my one true love. There are plenty of men who want to treat me good." Cynthia began to cry again. "Promise me you won't leave me, Allie?" she pleaded looking up, her big blue eyes wide with fear.

Allie's heart sank as she relived the memory. Things had been good for them since Cynthia was dating Darby. Allie actually believed her mom could be changing for the better. Isn't that what she wanted, a better life, some normalcy? In her heart, she knew Cynthia was a good person, but couldn't understand why she kept making bad choices. Did she not know the difference between right and wrong? She could definitely understand why her dad had so many doubts about her.

Thinking of him confused her even more. What about the stuff Cynthia told her? If he hadn't done what he had, her mom wouldn't be this way, right? According to her, not only did he blackmail her into having sex with him on a regular basis, he degraded her by saying she was fat, stupid and lazy. This was his fault. But then, had Cynthia been telling her the truth? What she said today contradicted all her stories.

Ignoring the circumstances only worked for a while and by that afternoon, Allie couldn't get far enough away from either of her parents. Cynthia continually made her pay for what her dad did wrong and with her dad…. he wanted nothing to do with her unless it was to tell her she had a bad attitude and was screwing up her life. Would she ever be good enough for either of them?

Cammi told her how to listen and trust the little voice inside her heart and for a while, it worked, guiding her to make the right decisions, but anymore the good voice and the bad voice were in constant turmoil. Which one was she supposed to trust because it didn't seem like either one was working out for her? Her mind was a locomotive, noisy and in constant motion. As she put on her headset she prayed the music would eventually drown it out.

"I have a surprise for you," Bryce whispered flirtatiously in her ear.

Cammi felt good. For the time being, she was out of her funk and determined to keep her negative emotions at bay. She and Bryce were back on track, communicating more and focusing on the good instead of the bad. He was less stressed, and she was allowing issues that would normally bother her to slip away unnoticed.

"What is it?" she wanted to know kissing the nape of his neck.

They'd made a point every year to celebrate the anniversary of their first weekend together, but last year, they wound up in a nasty fight at dinner, both not speaking to each other for four days after. This year he wanted to make it up to her.

"I am taking you back to the bed and breakfast we went to that first weekend. We're dropping the kids off at my parents on the way, and I even went out and bought you a few fun things I think we both will like," he teased.

It was noon and Faith and Bailey were at swimming lessons with Jamie and her boys. They traded off car-pooling duty, so Bryce came rushing home the instant Cammi called to tell him she was alone. It had been a fantastic and much needed intimate lunch.

After he headed back to work, she got busy packing and pampering herself for the romantic weekend away with her husband. She couldn't wait. This is exactly what they needed, a weekend away, just the two of them.

Her excitement was crushed, only to be replaced with guilt when Allie got home from school and heard of their plans.

"Oh, that's nice! You and dad get to go do something together. *Alone,*" she replied sarcastically. "And the rest of us brats get to say with Grandma and Grandpa. Nice. Well, I'm not going. I'll stay with Cynthia."

"Don't call your brother and sister brats," Cammi stated firmly, then asked, "Why don't you want to go to your grandparents?" Allie adored her grandparents. It was ridiculous for her to behave this way just because she felt scorned.

"I have plans with some friend's tomorrow night. I don't want to bail on them. If I stay with Cynthia then I could still go."

Cammi silently folded her sweater and placed it in the open suitcase while she counted to ten trying to calm her rising temper. Taking deep breaths, she frantically searched for the right words to say. "I don't know, Allie, I'm not sure your dad will go for it. You were with her last weekend."

"What does it matter, it's not like I am going to be spending time with him anyway, he is going to be off with you. I might as well stay here with my other parent. At least she wants me around."

The words hurt, but the last thing Cammi wanted was an argument. "What about your Grandparents? It's been ages since you've seen them. They miss you. And your brother and sister? They would like to have you around more. Don't they matter?"

Cammi hated begging, it was out of character for her, but it was also better than starting a war.

Allie stared blankly at the wall over Cammi's shoulder, avoiding eye contact and feeling horrible. What she really wanted, more than anything, was a weekend away from Madison *with* her family, not to be left behind while her parents went off on some romantic rendezvous. But she would rather cut off her tongue than be honest about it.

"I don't know, I guess. I don't want to disappoint my friends or Cynthia. She gets lonely when I am not here." She was all her Mom had now that Darby was out of the picture and it didn't feel right leaving her alone. Who knew what she was capable of?

Cammi wanted to shake her by the shoulders and beg her to understand they missed her too and were desperate to have her as part of their family again. Instead she took a deep breath and looked at the child she loved with her whole heart, pushing her frustration under the years of already pent up disappointment.

"I'm not getting involved in this. Talk to your dad about it," she said coolly walking into the closet.

Allie's eyes lit up. *Good,* she thought. Maybe Cammi would convince her dad to let her do what she wanted. She didn't like the idea of using her, but sometimes when it came to Cynthia, Cammi could be a real pushover.

In the beginning Cammi was strict and firm and Allie learned quickly to follow the rules or else there would be huge consequences to pay with her dad. He demanded she respect her stepmother and until recently, Allie had. But Cammi no longer had that fire in her eyes or the excitement that drew Allie to her. Once upon a time, she made Allie feel good, safe and secure, but now it seemed, she was filled with as much hate and anger as Cynthia. Granted, Cammi wasn't self-destructive, but she was moody and withdrawn. And she'd also been treating her Dad like crap. Even though Allie loved her, she really didn't like her so much.

"No way!" he shouted while throwing the suitcases into the trunk of the car. "I understand the world revolves around her friends right now, but we are still her family, whether she likes it or not. Her Grandparents have bent over backwards for her from day one, and I am not going to let her ignore them."

Cammi handed him another bag while she listened to him rant. "I understand she is upset we are taking off, but I think once she gets there, she'll have a good time. We can't give into her when something doesn't go her way. She'll manipulate us any chance she gets."

"You're right. I am just worried with her attitude, that our weekend will be ruined. You and I need this so badly, Bryce. I don't want to drop her off and then have her be a nightmare. It's not fair to your parents"

"I agree. I'll talk to her before we leave. Let her know the consequences if she drives them crazy," he said slamming down the trunk.

Bryce found her lying on her bed with her MP3 player in her ears. He could hear the music through the headset and removed it before she had a chance to ignore him.

"Turn it down for Christ's sake. You're going to blow out your ear drums. Look Allie, I know you don't want to go with us this weekend," he began choosing his words carefully. But one glimpse into her blank face and a roll of her eyes, any reserve he had left disappeared. "Get packed, because you don't have a choice," he barked.

"I'm not going to hang out with some old people while you and Cammi go off by yourselves. It's not fair," she whined.

"Those old people are your Grandparents and they love you."

"What about you, Dad? Do you still love me? Or is there only room in your life for one girl?" she demanded swinging her legs over the side of her bed and looking into her dad's eyes.

"What?" he asked dumbfounded.

"Seriously Dad! Why don't you and I ever go away for the weekend? Why don't you take me to do something fun? It's always you and Cammi or you and Cammi, Faith and Bailey. Remember when it was just you and me, our bike rides, our ski trips. From the moment you met Cammi, things between you and I changed. I used to be the girl of the house."

"Allie, you were six."

"I don't care!" She shouted. "You were my Dad first. But she….she took you away from me and I hate her for it. It's just like everyone said it would be."

"Who? Who said it would be? I don't understand."

"I know you don't understand. Nobody understands," she sobbed.

Standing up from the edge of her bed, he slowly took the room around him. Relief washed over him as he noticed it hadn't changed as much as she apparently had. Everything was still a pale pink, the pictures of her family were still pinned to her bulletin board and her precious childhood blanket lay crumpled up next to her pillow.

"And I don't even know why I care. I mean look at all the stuff you do, it's not like you are some sort of saint either! And Cynthia, she has been right about so much stuff. So has Beth."

"Allie, I have no idea what Beth and Cynthia have to do with this."

"Because," she wailed stamping her foot on the ground. "I want her gone. I want Cammi to go away so it can just be the two of us again, like it was when I was little."

Bryce was stunned. "Is this why you are so angry? Because of Cammi?" He hoped it wasn't true, wished more than anything it was something else, but he was running out of answers. Sitting back down, he put his hand on her knee.

"Allie, don't you remember what I told you before Cammi and I got married? You will always be the first girl in my life. But baby, you are growing up. You will go off to college, find a boyfriend, and someday a husband. He will be the number one guy in your life. Someday you will get married and it's what I want for you. I can't keep you here with me forever. But I don't want to be alone either. As much as I love you and enjoy being your father, well, I'm a man and you needed to have a woman around. There are things I don't understand or get when it comes to girls. I thought we understood this. And when Cynthia came back, well, I stepped aside so you could build your relationship with her."

"That's not true. You don't want me to have anything to do with her," she accused.

"Who told you that?"

She opened her mouth to protest, but he held up his hand to silence her. He already knew the answer.

"Please, let me finish," he demanded, only this time with a more firm tone. "You have a brother and a sister who barely know you anymore. When you are home, you are nowhere to be found. We see you at dinner, and still, you don't say boo to anyone. Things around here are going to change, starting now…. on both our parts. You need to treat everyone in this family with respect, including myself and Cammi. You may not like it, but it's what you are going to do. We *will* be a family, all of us. And we are going to get to know one another again. Things we do will probably be stupid to a fifteen year old, but I don't care, you are still going to participate. That doesn't mean you can't spend time with Cynthia or your friends. What it does mean is you are going to prioritize all the things in your life, including your schoolwork. You are a smart girl; B's and C's aren't going to cut it anymore. So….you will go this weekend because your Grandparents love and miss you. They deserve to see you. And you will spend this time thinking of how you would like to see your family life. *And* I will make sure you and I get some more time alone together. For your information, Cammi encourages it. I just didn't realize it was affecting you. I thought I was being unselfish with the time you wanted to spend with your mother."

He noticed her eyes glass over as he spoke. "You have a choice Allie, you can make the best of it and enjoy it, or you can be pissed off and hate Cammi the rest of your life. But she is my wife, and she isn't going anywhere. I have enough love in me for all of you. But I promise if you continue to treat everyone who loves you like shit….you will spend the rest of your life regretting it. I'm willing to meet you halfway. Get packed. I expect to see you downstairs treating everyone decent, even if you have to fake it, in half an hour."

She watched as he shut the door then picked up one of her favorite collectables, a ceramic unicorn given to her by her dad on her third birthday and heaved it across the room. Bryce heard the shattering of glass along with her scream. He walked away shaking his head in bewilderment, praying someone might have the answers she needed, because he certainly didn't.

Bryce opted not to tell Cammi about his conversation with Allie. There were some things better left unsaid, and it would only hurt her more. Plus the longer he thought about it, the more he realized Allie didn't really hate Cammi. Did she resent her? Maybe, but not for the reasons she gave. If anything, she missed her terribly and was desperate for acceptance and a connection with all of them.

Allie sulked in the car while Cammi and Bryce kept the conversation light and fun for the two younger children. Faith showed her excitement by singing Disney Princess songs and Bailey babbled on about his new shoes, clapping each time they lit up.

Bryce made Allie pack her MP3 in one of the bags in the back in hopes she might actually interact with the family on the drive and since she no longer had a cell phone, it wasn't like she had anything else to do. She *was* tired of being left out. But instead of making an attempt, she chose to stare out the window of the minivan watching as scenery rushed by. Within minutes she was bored and decided to look for shapes in the clouds. She could remember when she and her dad would lay on the front lawn after a bike ride watching the clouds, seeing how many different animals they could find. A lump formed in her throat and before she was able to swallow it down, tears squeezed out of her eyes.

She hated that life had changed and her dad had changed. In her heart she knew it wasn't Cammi's fault, but she needed to blame someone. Maybe it was her. Was she the one who pushed them away? Either way she was tired of being miserable.

"Hey, Faithy," she whispered, careful so no one else heard. "Look up at the sky. Do you see that rabbit up there?"

Faith bubbled over with excitement. "I do, Allie, I see it!"

Thirty minutes later when they pulled into the drive outside Bryce's parents, she had both Bailey and Faith laughing at her imitation of Timone and Pumba from "The Lion King". It was a nice change, and Bryce breathed a sigh of relief as he squeezed Allie gently in a bear hug when they said good-bye.

Having alone time without the kids, well….. they were like newlyweds again. Cammi had forgotten how Bryce made her laugh and the ease she felt being close to him. She never fell out of love with him, but with the chaos and stress of life, their relationship wasn't growing or flourishing in the direction they needed it to. In their time together, her heart softened, opening like the petals of a flower and she found herself entranced by him all over again. It was nice, feeling this newness, this rebirth. Most people only get to experience it once, in the very beginning, but she felt fortunate it was capable of happening time and time again with the one man she committed her life to.

Bryce finally told her bits and pieces of his conversation with Allie, leaving out anything that would hurt her in the end. Cammi, tired of Allie's childish tantrums, was convinced tough love was the answer, but after having the weekend to clear her head and evaluate the situation, she decided Bryce did need to start spending more one on one time with his daughter, too.

"She needs to know no matter how upset we are our love for her is unconditional. She is angry because she doesn't trust it." They were nestled on a little bench under the pine trees watching the snow and ice float down the stream.

"She had you to herself for years. She was Daddy's little girl, you took care of one another. Things changed and she doesn't know where she fits in, and now, well, she probably feels abandoned, like she doesn't have you at all, and you are just a presence in the room when she is home. Maybe if she has some of that attention to herself again, she would feel secure." She shook her head. "I feel bad. We've been so self-absorbed. We haven't made her a priority. We complain all the time about her behavior, but don't take any steps to find a solution. Instead, we focus on our own problems. And really, has our behavior been any better?"

He watched the glitter of the snow bounce off her eyes and was entranced by her beauty, but the thing keeping him loving her day in and day out was her heart. The heart she continued to keep hidden from the world. It would always mystify him why Cammi didn't allow others to see the person she truly was. But even more, it baffled him he was the lucky one who did. He wished she could be this open with him all the time.

People saw the surface and the surface was fine. She wasn't rude or crass, just indifferent. She could be polite and friendly but lacked the ability to deeply connect to others except for a few close, life-long friends, her family and him. She didn't like to draw attention to herself and could care less what others thought. One of the qualities he admired the most in the beginning.

But the things he found endearing had become a fault the longer they were together. Her stoic nature forced her to keep others guessing. She was not openly emotional therefore no one knew where they stood with her or what she was thinking. She was comfortable managing happiness and joy, all the positives, but as the negative emotions hovered within her, she continued to fight against them out of fear they would destroy the person she was trying to become, until eventually she blew up, becoming an emotional basket case.

Her independence made her tough. The strength, Bryce admired. What he couldn't stand, was she always had something to prove. Not to anyone else, but to him. Or maybe it was to herself. Hell, he couldn't tell. But Cammi's defiance was wearing him down. He can't remember how many times she told him he was controlling and untrusting.

Bryce detested everything about being that husband. But she was right. He was a bit controlling. Everything with her was an argument whether it had to do with laundry soap or their time together and he found himself engaging in the tug of war just to prove her wrong. Here was the irony of the situation. There hadn't been an argument from him when he gave up golfing and time with his friends. He complied with her wishes. But God forbid, he should make the same type of request. All he wanted was for her to see what he asked of her was exactly what she asked of him.

The rustle of the leaves whispered in the wind as she leaned her head against his shoulder. He wished he could understand where along the way she had lost her confidence and what it was he had do to help her gain it back. He could read her like a book, knowing her better than she even knew herself. She said she didn't care what anyone thought, but it was a lie. She allowed other's scrutiny of her to control who she had become, and she allowed his negative emotions over the years to dictate how she felt about herself. And like a vicious circle she wanted to win, but that was impossible. She couldn't win. So she hid from the world. Instead of showing others the depth of her character, her strengths as well as her weaknesses, instead of showing she was real, people only saw her mask.

Yet, he was the one she chose to let in when the mask slipped away, and he *still* loved her. Loved her all the more knowing what fears haunted her heart, but that under those fears lied unselfishness, acceptance, devotion and the greatest need to give all of her love to her family.

It broke his heart to see her in so much pain, feeling like a failure when he knew she had come so far. If only he could make her see by protecting herself, *she* was the one getting hurt. And where had her faith gone? Her disconnection with it caused her not only to lose trust in a higher power but in herself, too. His lack of understanding and respect for her faith caused one of the biggest blow ups they'd ever had early on in their relationship. He regretted his behavior immensely, but was grateful for the outcome.

"I get it, Cammi, stop beating it into my head. I'm not a friggin idiot!"

Even before Faith was born, she nagged him repeatedly about going to church with her and Allie, but he always had an excuse. It wasn't his nature. He found his spirit elsewhere, like on the golf course or the basketball court. Most men he saw were miserable in church anyway, shadows of themselves. He didn't want to turn into one of them.

"I'm not you, and I'm not going to be like you!" he yelled. "Stop trying to change me."

Cammi was sitting on their bed with the covers pulled up to her chin, tears streaming down her face. It killed him to make her sad, but he was tired of her berating him about how he should live his life on a daily basis.

"No, you don't get it, Bryce… that's the problem. How can you understand something you have never experienced?"

"Don't tell me what I have and haven't experienced," he gritted between his teeth.

"It's a love and a feeling like no other. Like nothing I have felt for you and nothing I have felt for Allie. It's a love that can't be obtained by anything on this earth…it's much bigger than that." Gaining control of his temper, he sat down on the edge of the bed and watched in sudden awe as her tears stopped and a sense of peace washed over her.

"No matter what trials you go through, it still feels good to wake up in the morning. It's a love giving your life a whole different meaning. It fills you, sustains you and when troubles come, it sees you through. It's an amazing force giving you so much happiness you want to share it with everyone. The more you have the more you want others to know it too."

Shifting her eyes towards him, she studied him inquisitively. "Have you ever felt that, Bryce? Have you? I have…. and it makes me who I am. It dictates everything I do and every decision I make when it comes to you, Allie, work, money, everything. Don't you see? It shapes my very core and without it, I wouldn't be me."

Her words that night so many years ago moved him and made him want to be a better man. It was a journey for him, and she was right, one he didn't completely understand, yet he finally felt like he had jumped on the right path. They didn't go to church all the time, but he understood how important it was for her to have him by her side when she did go and the example it would set for their kids. From that point forward he made a choice to be open-minded about what he heard when he was there. And even now, he wasn't the same man he had been five years ago. Nor the man he was six months ago. Each day was an awakening. Just like she said it would be.

He pulled her closer into his arms wishing they could stay in this moment forever. For in this instant, she was her old self, the woman he fell in love with, and he was the man who was able to make her happy, fulfill her dreams. But life and circumstances had changed them both. This time away together gave him hope, but it would only be a matter of days before they had to head back to reality. It made him wonder if they would ever find their way back to each other, back to the love they had first believed in so strongly, the love nothing could destroy.

Cammi shivered as he pulled her tightly to him almost as if he was protecting her. She glanced up to find him mesmerized by the current of the water and wondered what he was thinking, if he still loved her.

She knew she could be a nightmare and difficult to deal with at times, but no more so than he was. The weekend away gave her a chance to reflect back on the past few years. The growth, the changes, the hurt, the love, but most of all, the person she was. At times, she was content. She was a great mom, always putting her family first. She was loving, forgiving and kind. But there was something unsettled in her heart. During times of conflict, the glass was shaken and demons haunting her fought their way to the surface. The issues she thought she worked through and put away so long ago entered her mind to muddle her thoughts. She couldn't escape them and kept hoping the wounds would heal themselves. When things were bad, the contempt she felt for herself would overwhelm all the good and she became desperate to get away from all that hurt her. Most of all… her husband. The wounds he caused penetrated deeper than anything she had ever known.

Now, isolated away from the world, just the two of them, all was forgotten, and she couldn't imagine her life without him or her children. Despite the anger and pain, she still worshiped and adored being with him. She craved his love, his attention and mostly his approval. When he withheld it from her, which he did when he was stressed or angry, she felt terrible, like a child being punished.

But this weekend was a coming together. It re-established their love and faith in one another. And Cammi had no doubts that whatever direction they headed, they would always be in this together. She would do anything and everything she could to be a good wife and prove to him that she was the person he wanted.

Chapter Twenty-Four

On the drive home, Cammi watched in the rear view mirror as Allie read Faith and Bailey *Super Fudge,* one of her favorite books as a little girl. It made her heart swell with pride seeing her interact with them once again.

Something Bryce said to her sunk in. Slowly, Allie began to spend more time with the family, pitched in with household chores without being asked and was once again pleasant to be around. Life seemed to be back to normal and Allie appeared happier than she had been in months.

"Can I talk to you?" Allie asked shyly one evening a week before Christmas.

Cammi had been sitting in bed with a book propped on her chest, but she wasn't looking at the pages. She was listening to the hysterical laughter coming from downstairs. She knew Bryce and Allie were watching "A Christmas Story" together and instead of jealousy, a warm feeling of pride filled her. But her eyes had closed so she hadn't noticed the movie ended until Allie knocked softly on the door. Putting the novel face down on the bed, she lifted the comforter so Allie could crawl in next to her.

"Of course, honey, you can talk to me about anything, what is it?"

Sensing Allie's hesitation, Cammi asked about school and her friends, hoping small talk would make her less anxious.

"I'm going to sign up for dance classes again," she said proudly. "I really miss it."

Her heart fluttered. "Oh, Allie, I think that would be great. You're so good at it. I would hate to see you miss out on something so important to you."

"I've also been thinking about writing for the Bobcat News, too. You know how much I love to read, so I thought the school newspaper would be a good place to start. I've been doing some journaling and it's not too bad. Maybe you could read something I wrote and give me your opinion."

It filled Cammi with a sense of satisfaction that Allie was interested in something close to her own heart. "I would love to," she exclaimed. "I think you can do anything you set your mind to. Even if you aren't good at first, if you are determined to get better, it will happen. Just have faith."

A smile formed on Allie's lips. From the minute she met Cammi, she always made her feel special and important. Cammi believed in her, and Allie missed being around that. When she told Cynthia about her plans, she had laughed.

"What do you know about writing? It's not in your genes. You should think of doing something else. We talked about modeling a few times, why don't you look into that. The lifestyle is so glamorous. Could you imagine? I would be able to say I was the mother of a famous model. Of course you have the looks! You *are* my daughter," she reminded her time and again.

Allie opted to ignore the comment rather than upset Cynthia by telling her the truth. She didn't want to be an airheaded bimbo. End of story. The older she got, the more observant she was becoming. Too many women based their self-worth on how they looked and didn't have much in their hearts to give. She saw it at school, with some of her own friends, and on TV, but mostly, she saw it in Cynthia.

She didn't know when the change happened, it just did. And she couldn't believe how she had behaved towards her family. The thoughts and especially the things she had said. But now was no time for regrets. She needed some answers.

"I need to talk to you about something, but please, please, please, don't tell dad yet."

Allie's anger towards Cammi began to diminish the more involved she allowed herself to become with the family and the bond between the two of them had grown stronger. She was still frustrated, but she now saw it had nothing to do with Cammi. And if she didn't tell someone, she was going to burst.

Cammi was about to interrupt her, but Allie continued. "I know what you are going to say, and believe me, I know you don't keep secrets from dad, so I promise to tell him, but I needed to feel you out first."

Cynthia hated Cammi and put her down every chance she got, so it sort of felt like she was betraying her, but after many nights of praying, Allie finally decided to listen to her heart. Deep down, she knew Cammi was the person she could trust. Jake agreed. Though he never said in so many words, she could tell he detested

Cynthia. Allie didn't take it personally in fact she respected his opinion more than anyone's.

The past few months had been a rude awakening, and Allie was finally able to see beyond her own misery to what was transpiring around her. Taking a deep breath, she spilled her guts.

"Cynthia told me what happened between her and dad, how she got pregnant and all. I …I, uh, don't know if I believe her."

For the next fifteen minute Allie explained everything she'd been told. She was careful to leave out those parts she knew could hurt Cammi, the horrible things Cynthia had to say about her and her father all the while keeping her eyes glued to her hands which were twisting wildly in her lap. If she took the chance to make eye contact, all the emotions she had bottled up were sure to come bursting out.

Christmas Carols from the downstairs radio filled the silent air. Finishing with a sigh Allie was still unable to lift her face to meet Cammi's eyes. She wasn't quite sure why, after all this time she was willing to find out the truth, but she knew if she didn't, the bitterness she felt towards her father was going to kill her and possibly destroy any chance she had for a happy life.

Cammi studied her daughter's ashen face as regret and remorse filled her heart. She wished she could hold her in her arms and make this nightmare go away, remove all the pain she was living with at such a young age.

"Well, I am not quite sure what to tell you." *Your mother is full of shit,* was the first thing coming to mind. Instead she placed her arm protectively around Allie's shoulders and said, "I want you to think really hard, okay? Think about everything your dad and I have told you about how to treat people and the difference between right and wrong. About what goes around comes around. I can't be the one to tell you what happened between your mom and dad. He has to. But I would suggest you go to him and be honest. About everything," she stated firmly. "After you hear what he has to say, make up your own mind. No one can do it for you."

Allie buried her head in the comforting shoulder Cammi made available to her while they rocked gently. Tears streamed down her own cheeks as Cammi kissed her on the forehead wishing for a way to protect her from the wickedness, the lies and the deceit. In hearing Allie's confession, her heart exploded with fury. *Lord, I pray you take care of her. Show her the way and the answers. Protect her when we can't. But most of all, give her your love and guidance.*

"I want to tell to him, but I am afraid he'll hate me," she said finally drying her face on the edge of the comforter.

"But I would imagine you hate him a little bit right now, don't you?"

Allie nodded in shame.

"At the same time, you love him so much. You want him to be a part of your life." Cammi tipped Allie's face up to meet her own. "Do you feel like he's not?"

"He is so different since Cynthia is around. It's obvious he hates her. I look so much like her. Do you think he sees her when he looks at me? If he does, he will hate me too!"

"Oh, babe, he is never going to hate you." It wasn't Cammi's place to tell Allie all her mother had done to them. That was up to Bryce if he chose to do so. "You may look alike, but you are your own person. No matter what you do, his love for you won't ever change."

"It doesn't feel that way, he is mad all the time. He never has anything nice to say. It's always about what I do wrong, never what I do right."

Cammi wanted to tell Allie how much she understood her father's faults, but she needed to support her husband through this, not degrade him.

"You need to understand you haven't made the best choices lately. And your attitude has pretty much sucked," she admitted trying to make light of the situation. "But even when he is mad at you, he still loves you. When you don't make good choices, he still loves you. But he expects you to learn from them. All relationships are like that, honey. When you grow up and get married, there are going to be times when you hate things your husband does, but you still love him. When you have kids, it's the same. Part of living is loving. And part of loving is accepting. Your dad understands you aren't perfect, neither is he. He makes mistakes. I make mistakes. But with each mistake, you have an opportunity to make better decisions. There are people out there who choose to make bad decisions as an excuse for their failures. It's your choice to decide which way to go."

Hearing the words leave her lips made her chest tighten. Wasn't it time she started to heed her own advice?

"I'm grateful you told me, but I'm sad you thought you had to deal with this on your own. In this house, you're never alone. Do you understand me?" she gently scolded. "It's time to have a heart-to-heart with your dad." A smile came to her lips. "How about I plant a little bug in his ear and maybe he can take you to dinner tomorrow night? Like a date? I think you two need it."

Allie grinned. "I would like that. I do miss him."

Within minutes, it was as if the gray cloud was lifted from their life and their sentimental moment was lost amongst the exciting life of a teenager. Looking carelessly confident Allie changed the subject.

"Speaking of dating, do I still have to wait until I am sixteen?" she asked sheepishly.

Laughing, Cammi shoved a pillow in her face. She hoped this was the beginning of their healing process and with time and encouragement, the threads holding this family together would begin to mend.

When Bryce called Cammi from his office the next day she could sense the urgency in his voice. Swamped with work, he had been staying late every night, so instead of dinner, he took Allie out for a long lunch and Cammi was waiting anxiously to hear from him.

"I wasn't prepared for that. Why didn't you warn me?" he chastised sounding disheartened.

"It wasn't for me to do."

"I told her the truth. I'm not sure how it is going to turn out, but….thanks. She told me what you said last night. Your support means everything."

"It breaks my heart to see what she has gone through. Can you imagine? Don't get me wrong, honey, I am not blaming you, but how could we have been so blind?"

There was silence on the other end of the line.

"Are you there?"

"Yeah."

"You okay?" She had never heard him sound so defeated.

"No, not really," His voice broke. "I feel like a failure, I only wanted to protect her and look what's happened. These aren't the only lies Cynthia tells her. I could sense she was protecting her. I tried to pry but it got me nowhere. When it comes to her mom, she's private and after today…. I can't help but wonder what else she hasn't told us."

"What are you going to do?"

"I don't know if there is anything I can do. I don't have proof. I mean, I feel better after our talk, but don't think she entirely trusts me yet either. I'm furious she won't turn to anyone for help, but she's so stubborn, and I hate that she isn't my innocent little girl anymore."

Cammi's heart ached. She was his daughter, his baby, his pride and joy. After giving birth to her own children, she understood the lengths a person would go to protect them and she had no doubt Bryce would do the same.

"Did she tell you how Cynthia isn't talking to her right now?" he asked.

"Nope. She only told me the stupid story she invented to make you look like an asshole."

"Well, she hasn't called her for over a week. Allie pissed her off somehow. She didn't mean to tell me. It accidentally slipped out then she dismissed it like it was no big deal. As if she's gotten used to the behavior. But I could see the hurt in her eyes."

"What did Allie do to upset her?"

"Not sure, she was pretty vague. It had something to do with spending Christmas morning with Bailey and Faith. Sounds like she was chatting on about it and Cynthia got jealous and has been giving her a guilt trip ever since. It makes me wonder about Allie's behavior over the past few years. She hasn't figured out how to have a relationship with us as well as her mother. She constantly feels like she is betraying someone, mostly Cynthia."

"And Cynthia plays on it, making her feel worse."

"I think so."

"God! What a bitch! How could someone be selfish enough to put a little girl through that? There are some women who should not be allowed to procreate. I'm sure it's been going on since day one, too."

"Seems like it. And the only thing we can do is get Allie to open up to us when it happens so she doesn't feel alone. So she can have our support."

"What do you mean that's the only thing we can do? Why the hell don't we keep her away from that woman? Stop visitations. Monitor the phone calls. It's emotional abuse!" Her frustration with Bryce peaked at an all time high and she didn't understand why he didn't take control of the situation. "It's our job to protect her."

"Cammi, calm down."

"No! Damn it, Bryce. Don't you see how more of this could damage her? She's already been damaged enough. We have to put an end to it and you, of all people, are the only one who can. You need to take action, stop hiding behind what you don't want to face."

He knew she was scared and desperate, but he couldn't handle anymore of her degrading outbursts.

"Shut the hell up!" he shouted surprising himself. "I was put through the wringer at lunch. I didn't call to have you do this to me, too!"

His anger only increased hers.

"Don't you dare talk to me that way! *You* are the one who called and asked for advice. When I give it, you don't like what you hear and instead of being rational, you choose to get mad and take it out on me. You need to get a…"

Cammi heard the click of the phone as he hung up. Slamming the receiver down, she burst into tears. Her chest felt like it was going to explode. She picked up the phone and dialed his number. It went straight to his voice mail. She tried his office line, but it only rang. For an hour this continued, and yet he ignored her.

He didn't care a bit about what she was going through or how he made her feel, the selfish bastard. All he cared about was she was by his side supporting him, talking about things causing him stress, working through *his* problems. What about hers? Didn't she matter in this marriage? She was always there to pick him up when he was down. When was he going to make her feel better and give her support instead of pulling away. Years of putting her feelings and issues aside because his were more important had taken its toll. Well, she was tired of being his last priority and she was also tired of begging for his attention.

She tried one last time to reach him without success. This was his way of controlling the situation and punishing her. It was not very mature of him, she decided. He had done this to her before on countless occasions and each time the anxiety got a little bit worse. She hated him.

Then why was she so desperate to have him answer the phone and make her feel better? Or did she want him to answer so she could make him feel as horrible as she did, to make him see how idiotic he was acting and she was right.

She decided it was not very mature of her either.

Chapter Twenty-Five

"Whatcha doing?" Faith asked pulling a sucker out of her mouth.

"Making a scrap book for Cynthia," Allie replied. She had been at the kitchen table for two hours poring over the pictures, stickers, and fancy lettering she was determined to put together for Cynthia's birthday gift the following week. Last year she'd only given her a card and boy, she didn't hear the end of it for weeks. She put a lot of thought and effort into this year's gift hoping Cynthia would love it.

She was talking to her again. Cynthia called three days ago from the hospital sounding especially pathetic and weak. When Allie questioned her about why she was there, Cynthia would not give her a straight answer, something about the flu and dehydration. Allie speculated she took too many sleeping pills or whatever pill she was popping lately, maybe those diet pills she depended on or the eight hundred milligrams of ibuprofen she took for her hangovers. Allie didn't think it was very smart of her combining all the pills with alcohol and it scared her that Cynthia may accidentally overdose one of these times. It was the second time in four months she had been admitted. The first time was supposedly for some sort of surgery. But when Allie grew suspicious, again, she never got a straight answer and ironically when she was released, there was no recovery period from her "surgery". Within the day, she was out with her friends, boozing it up again. None of it made much sense to Allie.

"Why?" Faith asked.

"She is sad and I want to make her feel better."

"Why is she sad?" Faith asked sticking the sucker back into her mouth.

Now that she was spending more time with her younger siblings, they were full of questions about Cynthia. Why did Allie go see her? Why didn't Faith have a room at Cynthia's house, too? She even asked one time if she was supposed to call her Mommy.

Cammi handled it graciously, but Allie knew it unnerved her at the same time.

"Her boyfriend broke up with her and she's very lonely."

"Why did they break up?"

Allie shrugged. "Sometimes that happens."

"Do you have another Daddy, too?"

Ruffling Faith's hair, Allie chuckled. "No.....just one Daddy. Penny! No! Go lay down," she commanded as the dog tried to lick her scrapbook.

Cammi crouched on the bottom stair with Dooney in her lap and Burke circling her legs. It wasn't fair to eavesdrop, but it seemed the best way to find out what Allie might not otherwise tell her.

"But she has you."

Allie smiled at Faith. "Do you want to help me glue?"

"You are little," Faith laughed pointing to the picture in Allie's hand. It was Allie around a year sitting in her crib grinning up at the person holding the camera. "Where are we?"

"You weren't alive yet."

"Where's Mommy?"

"Cynthia is my real mommy, I told you that. But she didn't live here when I was little. She missed out on a lot of time so I thought it would be nice if I put together an album of pictures she could keep forever," Allie explained.

Allie hadn't been to Cynthia's house now for over three weeks. Between her mom giving her the cold shoulder and the disaster the last time she stayed the night, Allie figured it was better to keep her distance for a while. She'd actually been silly enough to believe she and her mother were going to have a quiet night watching movies with no interruptions when all of a sudden Cynthia flipped out and called Darby. Even though they had broken up almost a month previous, they continued to fight non-stop. Instead of a movie, Allie spent the next four hours listening to a screaming match over the phone. Eventually she holed up in her room, texting Jake on Cynthia's cell phone.

Finally Darby had enough sense to hang up and put an end to a no-win situation, but Allie stayed up the entire night taking care of her hysterical mother. Since then, she hadn't wanted to go back. It was nice to have a break, but with the constant worry about her mom, Allie wasn't getting much sleep at home either. And now she felt even more responsible. Maybe if she had apologized earlier and been around, her mom wouldn't have landed back in the hospital.

"Were you sad when you were little?" Faith asked innocently. Cammi cringed wondering how Allie would respond.

"Sometimes. But Cammi is my mom, just like she is yours, so I didn't really miss Cynthia, but when you were born, I started thinking about her again. Luckily, she moved to town and now I get to see her whenever I want."

"And you have two mommies!" She said excitedly.

Allie smiled, but remained quiet.

There was trouble. Cammi could hear it in the sound of Allie's voice, the nonchalant way she talked about Cynthia. She could see the uncomfortable, dismissive glaze of her eyes. Clutching her chest Cammi forced herself to move off the steps. She would give her life to take away Allie's burdens, but she felt helpless. Casually, she walked into the kitchen letting her fingers run through Bailey's thick brown hair as she passed.

"Want to help me with dinner?"

Nodding, Allie stood up, stretched her legs and followed. "Don't let Bailey near the scrapbook, okay Faithy? It's important to keep it nice."

Allie reached for a soda in the fridge and handed one to her mother before peeling the potatoes.

"What's up?"

"Nothing. Just seeing how you are doing? Did lunch go good with your dad?"

"Yep," she said taking a drink.

"Better than you thought? Does he still love you?" Cammi grinned while cutting the potatoes into fourths and dropping them into the pan of water.

"Yeah," Allie laughed. Cammi always started out this way when she was trying to fish for information.

"Anything else on your mind? You seem a little distracted."

"No. Why?"

"I just feel like I could have been more help sooner if I was aware of what you were going through. Maybe if I'd intervened, you and your Dad wouldn't be struggling right now."

Allie shifted her gaze to the floor. "Sometimes, Cammi, there is nothing anyone can do. There are some things I have to figure out on my own," she stated matter-of-factly.

The seriousness of Allie's response showed signs of maturity she was way too young for.

"You're right, just remember, you don't have to have all the answers. Finding someone to depend on isn't always a bad thing. Use your family. That's what we are for. Here take these plates and set the table for me."

After talking to both her parents, Allie did feel better, but there were still things she couldn't tell them. Things she needed to protect Cynthia from. She didn't want to see anyone get hurt, and it seemed like it all rested in her hands.

Bryce hated his job. Freddie decided to become the main investor for a new hospital wing which was going to house all of the administration offices, including Bryce's. Apparently, the guy was smarter than anyone gave him credit for or than he was willing to let on. His interest was mainly financial and after some deep research, Freddie decided it would make a smart investment. But it also meant he would be cleaning house, getting rid of the old, bringing in the new and for the first time in his life, Bryce was in fear of losing his job. Cammi thought he was blowing everything way out of proportion. He knew she was trying to be as supportive as possible but what he really needed was more financial stability if he were to get fired. It was time Cammi worked more. Though they agreed before Faith was born she would stay home with the kids, he was beginning to feel bitter about it and didn't understand why he was the only one sacrificing. Cammi needed to stop being so damn selfish. He'd made all of her dreams come true, but now he wanted someone to help him with his dreams. Of course, it did not go over well when he mentioned his thoughts to her. They fought for days.

Not only was Bryce distant and withdrawn after, he felt like a different person entirely. He was lost and Cammi told him on countless occasions she couldn't find her way back to him. But Bryce was just plain was worn out, and the more Cammi begged, the more he withdrew. He was jealous she was able to do what she loved, be a mom and wife, while he was sitting in a miserable office all day but mostly, he was tired of her self-righteous mumbo-jumbo.

Bryce also hated Cynthia. He had hated her fifteen years ago, but nothing could have prepared him for what he felt now. There were many, many regrets and a day didn't go by that he wished he could turn the clock back before any of this started. Many moments in his life left him shaken, out of control, but what Allie told him at lunch last month literally made him want to vomit. Everything Cynthia had done to him when Allie was a baby, the manipulation, the lies, the deceit, hit him like a sledgehammer. But now he wasn't the target…. his daughter was.

Bryce resented the deep dark tunnel he found himself trapped in. He couldn't allow this to continue. It was his job to keep his family safe. It felt like the weight of the world rested solely on his shoulders so why wasn't he strong enough to fix it? Everything was spinning out of control.

There were times he found solace in his wife's loving arms. It was rare anymore, but once in a while, he would pull her close, slowly inhaling the same delicate scent reminding him of when they began dating and all the chaos around them disappeared. He would remember why he loved her and despised himself for treating her so horribly. Her serious, dry sense of humor always made him feel better, and she was just as beautiful and sexy as she had been the day they met. He wished he could allow himself to be close to her again, to have the safe feeling of coming home, the passion, the desire. It wasn't that he was looking elsewhere. The idea of being with anyone else repulsed him. Life had just become overwhelming so a passionate love affair with his wife was the last thing on his mind. But in her arms, for a few brief moments, they were back on solid ground. Then something would happen, life would turn upside down again, and they would find themselves swimming, struggling to reach the surface.

Would there never be the uphill battle to fight against?

Allie wondered if she should tell Cammi how depressed Cynthia was. The erratic behavior was unlike anything Allie had seen before and it was beginning to frighten her. She knew moodiness, she knew anger, she even got depressed herself sometimes, but Cynthia was seriously on the verge of losing it. Maybe if she told Cammi, she would be willing to help.

Only Jake knew about the Cynthia's trips to the hospital. With her dad working there, she didn't want him to go prying. It was a wonder he hadn't already heard. And Jake agreed that something was suspicious. A day didn't go by when she wasn't calling Allie late at night drunk, rambling on about Darby and complaining or fighting with other patrons in the bar while she was on the phone.

During Allie's lunch break at school she would sometimes stop by to check on her and would always find Cynthia curled up in bed still passed out or sobbing uncontrollably. She had no life, no friends, except for the freaks she met when she went out. Allie knew they only wanted her for sex or drugs or both. And she had no dignity left.

All the years of partying were beginning to take its toll on Cynthia's beautiful face. Her once soft, delicate features were now encased with lines and wrinkles far beyond that of a typical woman of her age and the dark hallow caves under her eyes looked tired and sad.

It had been over Christmas break while Allie was staying with Cynthia that she had found out she was a stripper. They were out to eat at a local mom and pop restaurant when Beth happened to walk by. Allie hadn't seen her since their big fight and almost didn't recognize her. She looked…..sort of pretty.

Beth noticed them right away when the hostess guided her and her date past their table but acted as if she hadn't a clue to who they were. Of course, Cynthia hated to be ignored so she stood up to hug her old friend. Beth awkwardly returned the embrace.

"How are you?" Cynthia's voice dripped with sweetness. "I miss you so much, we need to get together for a drink," she suggested.

"I don't drink anymore, Cynthia," she announced coldly turning her back to walk away. Allie could see she was hesitant to introduce Cynthia to her date. Frankly, Allie couldn't blame her.

Before they made it to their seats, only a few tables away, the guy she was with snapped his fingers and turned around, a momentarily look of confusion leaving his face.

"I thought you looked familiar. You're that dancer at the Rockin Rodeo, aren't you? Candi's your stage name."

What Cynthia found amusing, both Allie and Beth found shocking. Figuring she had made some sort of impression on him, she slinked up close enough to lace her arm through his.

"Did you like the merchandise?" she asked seductively batting her long fake eyelashes. She started wearing them when she was dating Darby since hers were damaged and ruined from years of heavy mascara.

"Uh…. well I wouldn't say that," he choked out a laugh. "I just remember because my buddy Paul, it was his going away party, kept saying how good you looked for your age. You've got to be over forty, right? He said he slept with a stripper about thirteen years ago and thought maybe you were her, but her stage name was…oh what was it….Jewel? Yeah…that's it. But he decided it wasn't you because she would be a lot younger, mid thirties at most."

Beth and Allie watched Cynthia's eyes narrow and her already harsh features flame with anger. Beth giggled in delight.

"Well, I would say *Paul* was probably a bit too drunk," she lashed out. "And I am only thirty-five, thank you very much! Stupid Asshole," she commented under her breath.

"Whatever," he said shrugging his shoulders as he tugged Beth's hand pulling her away.

"Maybe your friend needs a reminder. You can join him if you like. Beth certainly isn't going to fulfill your desires," Cynthia yelled after them.

Everybody in their section of the restaurant turned to stare. Horrified, Allie wanted to crawl under the table. With a glance over her shoulder, Beth waved a fingered good-bye and Allie could not help notice she was grinning from ear to ear.

"Cynthia, shut up and sit down!" Allie hissed.

Returning to her seat, Cynthia placed her napkin on her lap and glared at her daughter. "You should have stuck up for me, instead you sat there like a fool!" she shouted making even more of a scene.

Allie pushed her chair back letting it slam into the wall behind her. She had to get out of there, away from her. She didn't need this crap anymore.

"Where are you going?"

"You are embarrassing me and if you don't shut up, I am leaving. My house is only a few blocks away. I can walk." She started to spin on her heel, when Cynthia reached out to grab her hand.

"I'm sorry. I'll calm down."

A few moments of silence passed while they ate. Finally Cynthia couldn't take it anymore. "I don't know who the hell he thinks he is, talking to me like that. I will find out and make sure he pays. I have good friends who won't tolerate that," she threatened. "I'm only thirty-five, I don't look forty," she said again.

"Why didn't you tell me you were a *stripper*?" Allie demanded leaning across the table. Madison wasn't that big of a town. Allie was fully aware of the type of bar the Rockin Rodeo was and knew the kind of scum that hung out there, too.

"You never asked."

It was true. In all of their conversations, Cynthia never talked about work, so Allie never asked. Conflicting emotions passed through her. Allie was embarrassed her mother was a stripper, annoyed she'd never asked, but mostly, she felt a new sense of pity for the woman who sat across from her. Allie didn't want to be judgmental and as much as Cynthia tried to deny it, Allie knew she was a stripper because she thought so little of herself.

She sat staring at her in wonderment trying to piece together a very complicated puzzle.

"How long have you been doing it?" she finally asked.

"Forever, well whenever I need the money. It pays real good, almost four-hundred dollars a night sometimes. I really like it too. I get to meet great guys, plus I get to wear sexy clothes. I have tons of men who want me, and I get to tell them 'no' for a change of pace," she laughed sounding like she was convincing herself more than Allie. "I'm in total control. It's not as bad as what people think. This place is great compared to the others. The bouncers are protective, and the clients are classy, they have lots of money, not like the trashy drunks in Arizona. It's where I met Darby, you know."

Her voice began to blend together with all the other thoughts swarming through Allie's head. Why couldn't she be normal? It was ironic. Of all the bad things Cynthia said about Cammi, Allie began to wish she was more like her, someone who was around instead of drunk at the bars, someone who was devoted to one man instead of a million, a mom who was involved in school, her interests and friends. One who encouraged her dreams, made her feel good instead of guilty and didn't talk about crazy things like suicide.

Allie couldn't listen anymore, she'd heard enough. On the way home, she sat quietly in the front seat of the car wondering how her life had become so dysfunctional. Snow began to hit the windshield and the wipers were in desperate need of replacing. But the noise was a welcome distraction from any conversation Cynthia might want to have with her.

"Are you mad at me?" Cynthia asked putting her hand on Allie's arm.

"No, just disappointed I guess," she said honestly.

Cynthia tried unsuccessfully to laugh but it was obvious Allie's words stung.

"Oh, don't be disappointed, baby. I am living the life I always dreamed of and have no reason to be ashamed. You don't either. So many women wished they had enough sex appeal and guts to get up on stage to dance like I do. But they don't. Why do you think men have affairs Because there are women like me who are willing to fulfill their fantasies when their wives won't."

Allie winced at the comment and for the first time saw her mother for who she really was, a woman who had little respect not only for herself, but for the relationships and marriages of others. And in the glint of anger that flashed in Cynthia's eyes, Allie also saw she was capable of almost anything to get what she wanted.

Cynthia pulled up in front of the house and Allie saw her stare longingly, maybe even a little regretfully, towards the front door.

"Take care of yourself, okay? I will see you in a few weeks. I think we should go to a movie," Allie suggested.

"Okay, honey," Cynthia replied, reaching for a cigarette. "Thanks for the great week and have a Happy New Year."

As she shut the door, she saw Cynthia touch the end of her cigarette to the dancing flame, and she could have sworn teardrops were falling down her cheeks. Only then was she aware of the pain her mom endured on a daily basis. She wondered what sort of revenge went along with that pain and whom she was willing to hurt to be vindicated for it. Watching her in that moment would be the only memory Allie would have of her mother's vulnerability, knowing she longed for more than what she had, but also that her heart and mind did not work together to comprehend what real love was about.

Feeling sorry for her, Allie quickly opened up the door and leaned over the console to give her one last hug, wishing her love could be enough, but mostly wishing she could savor the moment because she had a feeling there weren't going to be many more like it.

The memories of that evening plagued her mind, and she couldn't shake the feeling that Cynthia was in deep trouble. After brushing her teeth and quietly sneaking in to give Faith and Bailey a kiss good night, Allie dialed her number. Cynthia hadn't called her the night before. It was Saturday so she wouldn't be going over there on her lunch tomorrow and frankly, she didn't want to leave the safety and comforts of her home. It was snowing heavily and her dad had brought home movies. Allie could still smell the leftovers from the beef stew they had for dinner lingering through the house and into her room.

Cynthia's phone rang and rang. Allie tried her cell, but it went directly to voicemail which meant she either turned it off or the battery died.

Filled with worry, Allie couldn't concentrate on the movie. She wished she could call Jake, but he was out of town with his parents for the weekend. That's why she thought about telling Cammi. If something serious had happened to Cynthia, Allie would never forgive herself. It was her job to protect her mom, her job to make her feel better so she didn't run off doing all this crazy stuff. And if something happened, that meant somehow she failed her as a daughter.

Chapter Twenty-Six

It was Monday after school and Jake and Allie were at their usual meeting place down by the river. It was cold and getting dark, but they were bundled up in their winter clothes, so the chill didn't bother them. It hadn't snowed since the weekend before and what had accumulated had already frozen into ice. Allie brought along a blanket to sit on and he had a thermos full of hot chocolate for them to share.

"Without schnapps," he joked when he handed it to her.

Allie took a drink then frowned. "I don't know what to do, Jake. I am really confused. I love her, but I don't like being around her. She's a wack job, that's all there is to it. It makes me wonder why she really wants me in her life. Does she want to be my mom or does she want to be my friend? I know deep down in my heart, she is better than this. The problem is she knows it too. She just doesn't want to be. I think she has some sort of screwed up notion of how good her life really is. That the things she does are okay. But they aren't okay!" She pounded her fist into the ground beside her. "She's stupid."

Allie leaned her head on his shoulder grateful for his support.

Jake adored Allie, but continued to keep the intensity of his feelings a secret. He had always thought she was pretty and was always nice to him, but his feelings for her had grown ever since the horrible party at Cynthia's house. In the time they spent together, he was able to see the kind, sensitive, and compassionate person she truly was, and he loved her for it.

Because of his parents he grew up with strong and religious morals and frankly, other girls at school scared the shit out of him. They were aggressive, flirtatious, backstabbing and fake. They didn't care much about what was on the inside as much as they did about what was on the outside. Jake was popular with the girls because of his good looks and he was one of the best athletes in the region. But he was shy. The girls he was interested in didn't stick around long. They got bored. Said they wanted someone who was going to move faster, make them feel good about themselves. Jake never quite understood what it was they really wanted.

Allie was different. She was comfortable with the person she was, at least he could tell she used to be. From all she'd been through, it seems she had changed quite a bit in the past four years. She was angry and cynical, but deep down he knew the person she truly was and could see how desperate she was to find her way back again.

He promised himself never to be the one to tell her the things he heard around school about Cynthia. It would kill her. But she heard them anyway. Since that horrible night of her birthday, they had become best friends. She was the peanut butter to his jelly, the salt to her pepper, his mother would say. His parents liked her a lot and it disgusted them all to watch what she had to go through. No one should have a mother like hers, his dad always told him. Thank God she had her dad and Cammi. Granted Jake didn't know them, but they sounded like good people.

It bothered him having to sneak around like they did, and he begged her to tell her parents about their friendship. It wasn't like they were doing anything wrong and he really did want to meet them. Plus, if their friendship did progress to dating, he wanted to have their respect and going behind their back to meet like this certainly wasn't the way to get it.

Jake reprimanded himself for his thoughts. Allie never expressed anything more than brotherly love towards him and no matter what he felt, he wasn't going to ruin what they had by trying to turn it into something it wasn't. With all the stress in her life, added pressure from him was the last thing she needed.

Personally, he thought Cynthia was a lunatic. But that was another thing he kept to himself. He thought she used Allie, manipulated Allie, emotionally abused Allie and all he wanted was for her to disappear out of their life so Allie could be happy again. The night of the party was a shock to him. He had friends whose parents weren't as strict as his own, but never had he met one who allowed the things Cynthia did. Or acted the way she did. He smelled trouble with her right away, and his opinion only intensified with the stories Allie told.

She was so delicate and soft resting against him. He had to control the urge to wrap his arm around her and pull her closer. Sitting under the starry sky, he could feel the rise and fall of her chest as she sighed. If things were different for her, maybe they could be different for the two of them. But as he worked on holding back his anticipation for a future with her, her thoughts were elsewhere.

Allie knew she was falling into isolation and depression the more she took on the responsibility of Cynthia's actions. The bond she once shared with her dad was broken and in her eyes, she was the one accountable. He wasn't dealing well with Cynthia himself. The anger and unhappiness her father carried tore at her heart and as desperate as she was to mend their relationship, she was ashamed to let him close, to let him see all that was going on. She knew believing Cynthia's lies were wrong, she even knew all the lies she told to protect her were wrong, but where did she begin to unravel the spell that encircled them all.

Allie had come clean with her father about the stories Cynthia concocted, even the things about Cammi, but she didn't tell her father the part she played in all of the deceit over the past few years. If he found out, she was sure he would hate her forever. She already sensed the shattering of his heart when he realized she hadn't trusted him.

For the first time in years, Allie could see and understand the hatred he had for Cynthia. The emotions he protected her from came to a head the day they went to lunch. She had spent enough time with each parent to know their character and after all was said and done, Allie knew the truth and she felt horrible. Her father sacrificed his whole life for her… only for her to betray him. How could she ever forgive herself? Would her dad ever forgive her?

It was easier to push him away than to be reminded of the disappointment she has caused. Besides, there was so much he still *didn't* know.

Allie was tired, tired of making the decisions, tired of covering up lies, which eventually led into another lie, tired of being responsible, tired of being scared her dad would disown her, tired of wondering whether Cynthia would stick around or not, tired of trying to convince herself life was okay…..just plain tired. She buried her head deeper into Jake's arm and began to cry. He was her rock, her sounding board. Life was too overwhelming; she didn't know how she made it through the days sometimes. But with his friendship and advice, she was able to see things in a different light. He had become her best friend and she didn't know what she would do without him. Thinking about it made her cry even harder.

It was then that Jake put his arm around her.

A week later, Cammi was ready to bang her head against the wood table she sat at. She needed to find her groove again, but the thoughts weren't as fluid as they used to be so putting them on paper was proving impossible. She needed will power, focus, and determination. No, what she needed was money. Something Bryce said struck a nerve. He made it obvious she was slacking. Thank God, Lamont was more than happy to hire her back on as a free lance writer but he turned her over to Martha, the new Publications Director at the paper. Cammi and Martha had worked well together in the past, but since their contact by phone was almost weekly now, Cammi sensed they were becoming better friends as well as co-workers.

As much as she hated to admit it, Cammi knew she had to buck up and help out. Three kids were proving to be more expensive than two and even though both their vehicles were paid for, it was time to trade the minivan in for an SUV. Sighing, she stared out the window of the little office she set up in the corner of the kitchen. Her old office had become Bailey's room when he was born.

Cammi didn't want to be writing. She wanted to sneak upstairs into the nursery to caress the soft skin of her children and feel the rise and fall of their stomach's as they breathed. Bailey loved curling up next to his sister, so Cammi still allowed Faith to nap in his crib instead of the big girl bed she'd been in the past two years. Tears sprung to her eyes at the thought of Faith's arm dangled around her brother in a protective embrace as they slept.

Faith would start kindergarten next year, and it was time to wean her out of naps, but Cammi wasn't ready to face it. She didn't want her children to grow up. She wanted to keep them close to her, within her control, where they would forever be safe and where she would never be lonely.

Rubbing her shoulders, Cammi inhaled deeply. She had to come up with something significant to turn into Martha by the end of the week. Her family was depending on her and she couldn't let them down. Besides, she was determined to prove Bryce wrong. She was going to be an asset to this family regardless of what he thought. But she was going to do it her way. Not his. It may not be much money, but at least it would help them out month to month. She just needed to be patient with herself but she had to be honest....her heart just wasn't into it anymore.

She went to the doctor the week before, thinking she may have been pregnant again. Depression, he said suggesting an anti-depressant to take the edge off. She wasn't sure if she wanted to take them or not. All she knew was the luster for life she once had was gone and she was exhausted all the time.

The important people were still around, Jamie, her sister, Autumn who she had a penciled- in tea date with once a month. But her so-called friends were dropping like flies. They had perfect lives, perfect husbands, perfect children, perfect personalities and no dysfunctional ex's to deal with.

"My life is just a little bit too fucked up for them," she told Autumn last week.

The women Cammi had become close to in her Mothers of Preschoolers group rarely invited her to their *"get togethers"* and just last week when she ran into Rebecca, the MOP's organizer, at the grocery store, they'd had an unsettling conversation. It had been on her mind all week and she was desperate to share it with someone.

"I asked her how things were and told her I would be interested in having the next play date at my house," she said shoving a cookie into her mouth. "She was real standoffish, and kept looking around. Almost like she didn't want to be seen talking to me."

"You're being paranoid, Cammi." Autumn replied, refilling both cups with hot water.

"I'm not being paranoid. She told me the dates for the next four months had already been set and they would get a hold of me if they needed help, *and* she didn't even offer to give me the dates. She rushed as fast as she could to the checkout counter and when I came up behind her to wait in line, her face turned red. Finally, she asked me how Bryce and the kids were. When I told her fine, she cocked her head to one side and looked at me with pity. Pity! How pathetic is that? When I asked her what was wrong, she patted my hand and said, 'I know how hard this must be for you, I'm just so glad it's not Roger and I having marriage problems.'"

Cammi handed a sippy cup of milk to Bailey and propped him up on her lap. "I was outraged. I mean seriously! So I say, 'I don't know what you're talking about Rebecca.' And she says, 'Have you thought about divorce? I mean, it's not normal for you two to be fighting like you are all the time. Maybe it's time to move on.' Can you believe her nerve? So I say, 'Look, Bryce and I do have a lot on our plate, it's certainly not easy dealing with Allie's birth mother. But it's nothing we can't handle.' She says, 'I don't know, Cammi. Roger and I *never* fight.' That's not normal is it? All couples fight right? I mean are we really that bad?"

"No, you're normal. At least that is what all my married friends tell me." Autumn shrugged. At thirty-six, she still had not taken the leap but as far as Cammi could tell, Autumn was content and fulfilled with her life and career. Marriage, if it was in the cards for her, would just be an added benefit. "All couples go through hard times, I'm sure."

"So you know what I say to her? 'Wow, aren't you two the lucky ones? It's so nice you won't have to deal with real life when it smacks you in the face. Good luck with that.' And I turned and walked away."

Autumn began to giggle but then turned serious. "You hate to draw attention to yourself, Cammi. And now, here you are being scrutinized by people who don't know the real you. It's not easy for you, I know that."

"It upset me so much that when I got home, I e-mailed the rest of the group just to say hello and touch base. You know what? It's been ten days and I haven't heard back from one of them. Now tell me it's just coincidence. God, I hate that they are gossiping behind my back at all their stupid little meetings. I hung out with guys in high school for a reason. Girls are still bitchy, even when they are in their thirties." Cammi pouted.

Autumn was right, this wasn't easy at all. Days came and went until they all began to blur together. Before taking on this part time job, she usually spent the kid's naptime cozying up with them, praying Bryce never found out. He would think she was lazy. She didn't want go anywhere or do anything because that would take the effort of getting ready. Something she rarely did anymore. What was the point? No one, especially her husband, seemed to care what she looked like. Even her morning walks had come to a halt and she'd put on a disgusting ten pounds.

She was hoping the job would be the kick in the butt she needed to start feeling better. But her usual flair for creativity had short-circuited. She had the luxury of two hours every afternoon during naptime to get something accomplished, but so far, after a couple of weeks, she only had one paragraph written.

Defeated, she closed her laptop and went to the stove to make a cup of tea. Why wasn't her brain functioning? She couldn't put two thoughts together and at this point, if it weren't for the financial aspects of writing, she wouldn't even care.

She stared at the ceramic tile floor feeling the hope flicker out of her heart as it did so often during the day. She had to figure something out. It was as if desperation controlled her life. Her biggest fear was to lose her husband, her family, and though it was irrational, she couldn't help but feel that if she didn't make this job work, everything she loved and cherished the most would crumble and disappear.

She and Bryce had been doing so well only a few short months ago. They had been in love again. His hostility had melted away as they worked together to respect and tolerate one another's differences. They were relaxed, happy and at peace with the life they shared. Bryce couldn't stop touching her and held her close every night until she fell asleep. Now she was back at square one living in the body of someone she didn't know anymore.

Taking this job wasn't an easy decision for her. She did it for Bryce and it went against everything she believed in. She felt like she was sacrificing who she was to make him happy. He wanted to change her. Mold her into something and somebody she didn't know if she was capable of being. Somewhere along the way he had changed and wasn't the man she married. As time passed the more she began to think she made a mistake eight years ago.

Her reflection stared back at her in the dark image of the computer screen. She'd once thought herself to be attractive, but looking back at her was a haggard, unkempt woman who had wrinkles forming around her eyes. Lord, it was no wonder Bryce didn't touch her. She looked awful.

Fighting against the demons in her head, she began to type and within an hour, she felt much better, more focused, even a little stronger. Cammi would be damned if Bryce thought he was going to control her or the decisions she made for her life. She was his equal, not his daughter, not even one of his employee's, and she wasn't going to allow *anyone*, not even her husband to treat her as less than what she was.

The phone call came late Wednesday night. Bryce had been tossing and turning for hours trying to get rid of his reoccurring nightmare when he finally drifted into a deep sleep. He cursed the phone when he heard it ring.

"Hello," he said half coherently.

"Mr. Bryce Shepard, please."

"Yeah," he sat up rubbing the sleep out of his eyes. "This is him."

"This is the County Hospital in Carter. You're named as an emergency contact for a Miss Cynthia Goins. She has been admitted this evening."

Deja vu. Bryce tried to register what the voice just said. It took him a minute to get his bearings enough to realize Allie was asleep in the room across the hall. His fear suddenly turned into relief.

"What's wrong? Is she okay?"

"There has been another suicide attempt, Mr. Shepard," the nurse told him. "She is sedated, but we are going to admit her into the psychiatric unit for a couple of days. She needs to be evaluated, and we need some papers signed. Are…are you her boyfriend?" she hesitated.

"No, we share a child together. She doesn't have any family close by." Saying it made him feel the slightest bit sad for her. She was alone in this world except for her daughter. But those were choices *she* made and he wasn't going to allow Cynthia to burden his daughter with her loneliness.

"Oh, okay, well if you could come first thing in the morning to have these signed, we would appreciate it." Carter was a small community ten miles south of Madison. What in the world would she be doing there?

"Is she okay? I mean, how long will she have to stay?" He asked not so much out of concern for her, but for Allie's well being. She didn't need to deal with this sort of crap.

"She's fine, just depressed. Her stay is up to the doctor, but probably a week or so. Just like the last few times when she admitted herself. We need to make sure she is not a threat to herself or anyone else."

"Okay, thanks," Bryce said hanging up. *When she admitted herself?* He wondered what that was about.

The reality of what happened startled him fully awake. Didn't he deal with this enough when Allie was a baby? This is why he got Cynthia out of his life, now years later he was reliving the nightmare all over again. Not only that, but now he had to try and explain it to Allie. Couldn't she just disappear and let them get back to the happy life they had before she decided to ruin it?

It surprised Bryce that Allie wasn't shocked by the news. He had expected her to be upset.

"Why should I be surprised? It's nothing new," she confessed when he told her the following evening.

"What?" Bryce and Cammi stopped what they were doing, which happened to be paying bills and stared at their daughter, mouths open wide.

She hesitated trying to find the best way to explain. "She's been in twice in the past nine months. I don't know what happened. She said one was a surgery, but I didn't believe her. The other time, I think she took too many pills. I wasn't around. She was in the hospital for three days."

"Why didn't you tell us?" Bryce wanted to know.

She tried shrugging it off but couldn't stop herself from getting upset. "I don't know. I thought you probably heard anyway, plus I was embarrassed. I figured you wouldn't let me see her," she said defensively. Her hands began to shake with the realization the truth was about to come out. "She was going through a hard time, okay?" she started to shout.

Cammi walked over and put her arm around the girl to calm her down.

"Allie, relax, we aren't mad at you, just surprised." She looked at Bryce and could see the fury in his eyes. "I wish you would have told us. This isn't an easy thing to go through or deal with on your own. Next time, come to us, we aren't going to judge you."

Bryce didn't speak knowing he would more than likely regret his words later. Instead he nodded in agreement only half hearing what Cammi said while his blood boiled. If he could punch something, he would. Why wouldn't his daughter let him protect her? Why did *she* continue to protect Cynthia? He wished he could understand what was going on inside her head. Damn it, he needed to get away from this nonsense.

"She's at the Carter Hospital, honey. I will call and see if she can have any visitors. If she can, I will take you down after school tomorrow," Cammi suggested looking tentatively at Bryce.

Allie looked at him, too, but he wouldn't meet her eyes. Silently, he walked through the kitchen slamming the back door on his way out. It made Allie want to cry.

Staring accusingly at Cammi, she continued to shout. "This….this is why I didn't say anything. Because I knew that is how he would look at me, like I did something wrong. Like I am just like her."

"Oh, Allie, it's not you. He doesn't know what to do that's all. He is angry with Cynthia, yes, but mostly himself for not protecting you. Don't take it personally, okay?" she said hugging her again.

"He hates me, but you know what? It doesn't matter, because I hate him too," she cried.

"If you hated him, you wouldn't be so mad. And if he hated you, he wouldn't be this scared. That's what happens when you love, you get scared and your fear turns into anger. Just give him some time to work through this."

She took Allie by the hand and led her to the couch.

"You don't need to tell me now, but you and I both know there is more going on. I am not accusing you of anything, but you are protecting Cynthia. Why…. I am not sure. Trust me, Allie. No matter what you tell us, you won't be in trouble. But this is eating away at you. And we know you are hiding things. If you get them off your chest and let us help you, maybe you'd feel better."

Allie wanted to spill her guts, tell her everything. But she wasn't ready. She trusted Cammi, she did, but she didn't trust herself or Cynthia.

Chapter Twenty-Seven

Since Jake was a year older, he and Allie didn't have any classes together. They only saw each other at lunch or after school so Allie stuck a note in his locker the next day explaining the latest drama with her mom. As she walked through the door to her Biology room for sixth hour, Jake caught up with her and shoved a note back into her hands.

While Mr. Wilson was busy quieting everyone down, Allie opened her up her Biology book and placed the note underneath so she could read it without drawing attention.

What a shocker! I mean it was only a matter of time before something like this happened. And she did try it once before when she was pregnant with you. That's what your dad said, right? You never did tell me the rest of his story by the way. Are you going to visit her? Do you really want to?

Later,
Jake

Allie didn't have time to write him back, she had to spend the rest of Biology cramming for her history test next hour cause she hadn't been able to study this morning before school like she planned.

The test was excruciating and Allie wished she hadn't put it off the night before. After the final bell, she caught up with Jake at his locker.

"What's up?" he asked slamming it shut. "You look like you just received a month's detention."

"One of Ms. McMurtrey's tests," she said solemnly.

"Gotcha!" he smiled tugging his backpack over his shoulder. "Rough day, huh?"

"I couldn't concentrate. My mind kept wandering." She quickened her step to keep up with him. He must have grown two inches in the past month. He had to be close to six foot tall.

"I know she does this for attention. Like her being sick all the time. Did you know she told Darby she had some weird blood disease? Like the one she told my parents about. She happens to be sick only when it's convenient for her, when her world is about to come crashing down. She sure as hell doesn't seem sick. She thinks I'm an idiot who can't see through it."

Jake was thankful. The way Allie ignored most of what Cynthia did pissed him off to the point where he thought about going to Bryce and Cammi and telling them the whole story but how would he explain who he was? Besides, he couldn't bear betraying Allie's confidence like that.

"I think you need to talk to your dad some more. Tell him everything. I will go with you, if you want, it's driving you mad. You are starting to lose your sense of humor which puts me in a bad mood," he teased, jabbing his elbow into her ribs.

She smiled at him. He was such a good guy. She didn't know what she would do without him. "My parents don't even know about you, Jake. My dad wouldn't understand if you were there, holding my hand the whole time. In fact, he may kill us both."

It hurt his feelings she kept their friendship a secret. They had nothing to hide or be ashamed of. His family knew about her and even invited her over for dinner once a week. They loved her. He was close to his mom and confided in her about all Allie had to deal with, but out of respect for her son, she didn't get involved. Though lately, he could tell she was beginning to worry, too.

"So, are you going to see her?" he asked slowing down his pace. Allie was getting winded trying to keep up with him.

"I guess so. I don't really want to, but if I don't, you know she'll be mad. I hate it when she's needy. It would be nice to stay away and let someone else deal with it for a change."

Jake knew firsthand the guilt trips Cynthia held over Allie when she was in one of her "all about me" moods. She would go weeks without talking to her or answering the phone when she wanted to punish her. It was normally because Allie would say something or have an opinion Cynthia didn't agree with or else question a lie she told or the rumors she heard. On those occasions, she would accuse Allie of ratting her out to her dad, which was humorous considering Allie told him as little as possible.

Jake watched the pain bury itself deep inside her heart as she tried to win back Cynthia's love and approval. Despite all she knew and saw, Allie continued to hope her mom would change. Jake tried to be supportive, but he knew it was all crap. In her heart, Allie knew it, too.

"Just think about it. It may take a while, but your dad will come around. He is not an asshole, you know."

"I don't know. He sure acts like one most of the time. I'll call you later. Oh, and thanks," she said giving him a quick swat in the arm before she turned the corner towards her house.

Sighing, he watched her walk away. It was impossible not to admire her strength, even when it began to wear thin. She endured a lot of teasing from the guys at school because of her mom's reputation and the expectation she would be the same. But she wasn't going to do anything she didn't want to, especially to make friends. She was her own person, and didn't care what the kids at school thought. Of course she wanted to be liked, but not at the expense of who she was or what she believed. It was the one quality that kept Jake devoted to her.

Cynthia wasn't allowed to have visitors under the age of eighteen, but she could take phone calls, Cammi informed Allie when she walked through the front door. A little relieved, Allie made sure she called right away.

Cynthia sounded so weak and lifeless on the phone, it frightened her. "Are you okay?"

"Oh, I'll be fine."

Allie hoped Cynthia didn't start crying. It was annoying when she cried and though she tried, Allie didn't have it in her to be sympathetic at the moment.

"Do you need anything? Can I have Cammi bring you something?" she suggested politely, hoping her sincerity would make her feel better.

"No, that's okay. I just wish they would let you come visit me," she moaned.

Relief washed over her as Allie consciously blocked out any guilt Cynthia attempted to lay on her.

"The food is awful and the nurses are bitches. They all hate me."

Allie released a sad laugh. She knew how demanding her mother could be and had a feeling she wasn't being incredibly gracious to the hospital staff. "So are you going to tell me what happened?" God, why had she asked? It wasn't as if she really wanted to know.

"Oh, baby it was awful. Darby showed up at the house drunk. Told me he loved me and wanted to get back together. Well, I said it was bullshit. He had his chance. All I wanted was for him to leave me the hell alone. He begged and begged. I told him I had moved on and was dating someone else. He freaked out and started pushing me. Then he tried to kiss me. I told him if he didn't leave I was going to call the cops. That only pissed him off more. I think he was high, too. Anyway, he slapped me. I tried to get away, but he pinned me against the wall and tried to rape me. I screamed and clawed his face, then grabbed a bottle of Patron from the kitchen counter and broke it over his head. He hit me again, really hard that time. I think it knocked me out. I don't know who called the cops, probably a neighbor who heard me screaming. When they showed up, Darby told them I had tried to commit suicide, so they detained me."

By then Allie could hear the sobs through the phone. "Of course they are going to believe a high powered lawyer over me. They just let him go. It's bullshit. I hate him. I really, really hate him. I wish he were dead."

"But that doesn't explain why you were unconscious," Allie challenged.

"I just told you Allie. Weren't you listening?" she said snidely. "When I broke the vase, I was cut by the glass, and then Darby's punch knocked me out. I'm sure he told them I tried killing myself."

"So how did you end up in Carter? Why didn't they just bring you to the hospital here?"

"How the hell should I know?" she snapped. "It's a blessing though considering all your Dad's connections there. It would just be one more thing he could hold over my head."

"Cynthia, some nurse called last night saying dad was your emergency contact."

"Yeah, I heard. I don't know how or why they thought that. It was a mistake and I guarantee I could have a huge law suit on my hands. If I was greedy that is. He's the last person I would want anyone to contact if something happened to me. He would rather see me rot and die than help."

The more Allie listened, the more she felt sorry for her mom. Figuring she needed to put her selfishness aside and give her the support she needed, they talked for another hour. Cynthia didn't have any family or friends except the people she partied with. And what Darby did *was* bullshit. He was such a jerk! He had used Cynthia, was part of the fight, and should be in jail, too.

"As soon as you get out, I will come and stay for a few days. I am sure Dad will be okay with it. We can rent movies and make cookies, and I'll even cook dinner for you."

"Oh, Allie, what would I do without you? Promise you won't ever leave me like the men in my life do, okay? You're all I have left. There's nothing else to live for except you," she choked. "Look, they say I have to get off, I miss you a ton and can't wait to see you. Oh, don't tell your Dad what I told you, okay? Call me tomorrow."

Allie had an empty feeling in the pit of her stomach as she hung up the phone. Cammi always taught her that everything happens for a reason. Even when things seem bad, there was a lesson behind it and good would eventually come out. Maybe this is exactly what needed to happen for Cynthia to get her life back on track. Maybe this would scare her enough to make a change.

Leaning back against her pillow and closing her eyes, Allie prayed it was still possible.

Cammi found it hard to maintain her positive attitude and was slowly losing her own sense of humor when it came to Cynthia. In fact, she was feeling incredibly cynical and selfish. She and Allie had gotten close again, then after Cynthia's supposed suicide attempt, Allie pulled away, shut down. There were times when she seemed put off by her mother's erratic behavior, but this time, after Cynthia was released, all Allie cared about was taking care of and defending her, claiming she was lonely and needed a friend.

Of course the story Allie told Bryce made absolutely no sense at all. His skepticism finally drove him crazy enough to find Darby and hear his version of the story. After asking around, Bryce found out that Darby actually lived in Carter, but his law office was in Madison. After finding out who Bryce was, Darby was more than willing to meet him for a beer after work.

Cammi was in tears pacing the living room floor, worrying and wondering where Bryce was when he showed up three hours late instead of coming straight home.

"Where the hell were you? You could have been considerate enough to call," she said hysterically.

One look at his face told her he was in a foul mood. "I'm not going to do this bullshit tonight, Cammi," he growled storming into the kitchen with her in tow. She couldn't believe he didn't even offer an apology.

"You owe me an explanation!" she demanded.

"You want a fucking explanation; I was having a beer with Darby! Happy? Now I'm having another one." He said taking a beer out of the fridge. Shoving past her, he walked back into the living room throwing himself on the couch. Her rage faded away immediately. Instead she was anxious to hear what he had to say, but he was in no mood to talk.

Crushed, she figured the best thing she could do was give him some space and disappeared into her room to read a book. It was close to midnight when he finally appeared, ready to talk.

"I'm sorry," she said.

"It was stupid of me not to call, I wasn't thinking, I was too focused on what Darby had to say."

While he spoke she watched as he peeled off his shirt and pants. And once again, she couldn't get over how perfect he was. Did he still think the same of her? If so, he never mentioned it. The thought irritated her. Would he ever be able to give her what she needed? Instantly she pushed the thoughts out of her mind and focused on what he had to tell her.

"You're not going to believe what this guy said, Cammi. I want to kill her. I really, really do. Is there any way we could make her disappear?"

"I wish," she sighed hoping he would get to the point soon.

"Apparently he met Cynthia at the Rockin Rodeo. She basically told him the same sob story she told Allie only more elaborate. Said I convinced her to move back to Colorado to be more involved in Allie's life and then once she was here, I sabotaged any chance for her to get a decent job which is why she wound up stripping again. She also told him that even though I was married to you, she was my mistress. I apparently hold Allie over her head for sexual favors. If she does what I want, then I let her see Allie. She's basically at my mercy."

Terror filled Cammi as she realized the extent this woman was willing to go. She also wondered who else in the community had heard this insane story and believed it. The though horrified her.

"He said he immediately fell in love and thought he could help her out. Christ, you know how convincing she can be."

"No, I think I am the one person who saw through it from the very beginning," she commented.

Bryce ignored her. "Anyways, he adored Allie and liked the idea of having a family and maybe more kids with Cynthia," he continued. "Can you imagine?" he laughed. "That is one woman who should not be allowed to reproduce," he laughed. "But I have to tell you, I feel sorry for the guy. He genuinely cared for her and she screwed him over pretty bad."

"Well…. don't stop, tell me what happened," she prodded anxiously.

"Everything was great for about three months, she told him about the debt she was supposedly in because of what I had done to her, and he offered to pay all of her bills to get her caught up. He said they were talking marriage and even offered to have her move in with him so she didn't have to keep paying rent. From what I can tell, he's pretty well off. She refused to though, move in that is, and afterwards became real secretive about what she was doing. He got her a job as a receptionist for another law office in town so she could quit stripping, but she told him she was having some health issues and couldn't work. When he asked her what health issues, she told him about her hepatitis."

Cammi's eyebrows rose suspiciously.

"Ironic, isn't it. He told her if she was healthy enough to dance at a bar she was healthy enough to take the receptionist job. She worked for a week, quit without telling him and went back to the club. He called the office one day hoping to meet her for lunch and that was how he found out she didn't work there anymore," he stated, answering Cammi's question before she had a chance to ask.

"You're kidding?"

"Nope. But that's not the end of it. Instead of admitting to it, she blamed Allie and me. Told Darby I didn't pay for Allie's dance classes, clothes or school lunches, so she needed the extra work to make up for it. Stripping was the only job she could get that could cover everything. She told him she couldn't continue depending on him for handouts and needed to make her own way. He thought it was noble and actually believed her!"

"He still helped her?"

"Of course he did."

"It got a little confusing after that," he continued. "Sounds like nothing but a bunch of fighting and she started demanding more than just money. She wanted a new vehicle and agreed to move in with him on the condition they build her 'dream house' up on Glacier Mountain. Oh…. and she convinced him she was ready to have more children."

Cammi slapped her hand over her mouth in shock. Bryce only nodded his head.

"He was in the process of doing it all. He told me if he met her as a stripper and really loved her, than he needed to accept her for who she was and what she did…. but I guess he was still having some reservations. Two of his major credit cards went missing right when they first started dating. He sometimes gave them to his assistant for business expenses, plus his secretary, who kept track of office expenses, didn't mention anything out of the ordinary, so he blew it off. But when he got his monthly statement at home, both of them were maxed out. His credit was impeccable…didn't say how much, only that he had a huge limit. He figured it wasn't his assistant; she'd been with him for fifteen years and was close to retirement age. He trusted her with his life and his secretary's husband was independently wealthy, and they don't have kids. She works to keep herself busy. Long story short, he freaked out and accused Cynthia. She told him if he couldn't trust her, then they didn't need to be together."

"And that's how it ended?"

"Guess again. After a week apart, he started to second guess himself, apologized and fired his assistant."

"No!"

"Can you believe it? Cynthia convinced him retirement could possibly put a financial strain on her, and she was using what was available to skim from the firm."

"Oh, come on. What did the little old lady do, buy a bunch of expensive stuff so she could hawk it for cash after she retired? What an idiot!"

"Oh, he knows. Anyway, they got back together and a few weeks later he decided to go visit her at the club while she was working. When he couldn't find her, he went searching the dressing rooms and caught her screwing one of the bouncers on the vanity table. He said the worst part was she looked him straight in the eye, didn't bat an eyelash and kept going at it. And when he turned around to leave, he said he could hear her laughing, yelling at him to join in. I tell you, that woman's veins are filled with nothing but ice. Anyway, he cut off all contact, but I guess she wasn't willing to let go."

"Or course not, he was her meal ticket."

"She started harassing him, leaving nasty phone messages, going to his office to confront him and last week, it was *her* going to his place, not the other way around. I mean it makes sense, why else would she end up at the hospital in Carter? He says when he opened the door and saw her standing there she had a crazed look in her eyes. She told him she would do anything to have him back. He laughed in her face, told her she was worthless and a waste of his time, and that he thought more of himself than to continue a relationship with a two- bit-whore who cared about no one but herself. So she attacked him. He fought her off and called the police but before they got there she locked herself in his bathroom and took a bunch of his pain killers." Bryce laughed. "I'm sorry, but here is the best part. He didn't stop her. In fact, he told her if she wanted to kill herself, to go right ahead, the world would be a better place....and he'd sit back and watch. After hearing that, she flipped out and punched his sliding glass door, shattering it. He said she was cut up badly. That's when the police arrived."

Cammi was speechless. Conflicting emotions filled her heart. She knew if she said something, all of the anger and hatred she felt in that one moment would be directed towards Bryce. She needed time to take it all in.

"He got a restraining order. She is not allowed within ninety feet from him. He said he didn't care if he had to get a new one every six months for the next ten years. He wants her out of his life. I have to say I sort of like the guy. He seems all right, not a complete idiot. It took him a while to figure it out, but when he finally did, at least he didn't allow her to completely ruin him."

"If I remember, it took you a while to figure it out, too!" she commented. The words were out of her mouth before she had a chance to stop them.

Bryce's face turned to stone. "Nice, Cammi, real nice. I hope that dig made you feel good."

Was it fair? Probably not, but she was too angry to be shameful.

"It makes me wonder why I talk to you about anything. I thought you'd be as relived as I was to find this out," he spat.

"Relief?" she snapped. She'd been on edge the entire evening and now, he'd pushed her over it. "Why would you think I would be relieved to find out that Cynthia is even more wacked out than we originally thought? Do you think it's a relief to have Allie going with her every other weekend?"

His face was red with anger, but he too spoke as calmly as possible, refusing to engage in her childish behavior. "I just wanted what was best for Allie. I didn't know it was going to blow up in our face. I'm sorry you are hurt. I'm sorry you are angry. But this was about Allie, not you. I didn't want to see her hurt or always wondering about her mom. I wanted to take a chance, but in the past few months since she told me what Cynthia had said this uncomfortable feeling has been eating me alive. At least now I finally have some answers and we can try to be proactive."

"Well, I hope you realize the feeling eating you alive for the past few months, has been eating at me the past few years. I am glad you can finally relate to what I have been going through," she said sarcastically.

Despite his flaring temper, he was making a conscious effort not to fight. "I really wish I would have listened to you," he said sincerely. "But now, I feel like we have a reason to take action."

Mentally exhausted, Cammi tried following his lead and took a deep breath before continuing. "It's not going to be easy, Bryce. You need to think this through. Allie might not know the truth and if you drop this on her, she is going to resent you, not to mention she might not believe any of it. She may see it as revenge for what Cynthia told her. As much as I hate to say it, she needs to have her eyes opened *by* Cynthia. I am feeling everything I am sure you are at this point, but we need to talk this through together and not instantly react."

She heard the words come out of her mouth, but couldn't believe she could be so rational while at the same time mentally visualizing shoving Cynthia's face into a brick wall.

"I see what you're saying." He sounded disappointed. "I just want Cynthia out of our lives and away from Allie."

"It will happen, but not because we forced the issue. Cynthia is going to have to sink her own ship, and I have a feeling, with the road she is headed down, it will only be a matter of time. We just have to be strong enough to pick up the pieces when it happens. I will pry and see what she will tell me. Little by little Allie has been opening up more."

"I'm desperate to protect my daughter any way I have to. It makes me ill to think of the example Cynthia is setting. God, I could kill her."

Feeling more lighthearted since they were working together, Cammi laughed, "I know the feeling, babe. But you going to jail will only make her happier. Be patient and remember we are in this together. Don't let it send you over the edge," she said with regained confidence.

But it was too late, his bubble was burst. He had no more control over the situation than he did a day ago, but at least he had connections and the first thing on his agenda tomorrow was to place a phone call to Ron.

"It could be worse, you know." Carissa stopped by early the following week to take Cammi and the kids out for lunch.

"Are you insane?" Cammi asked exasperated. "I don't think it gets worse than this."

"Of course it can," she said trying to be the voice of reason. "She's hiding things from you about Cynthia, but she isn't lying about her own behavior. She's a good kid, it's not like she's doing drugs, skipping school, having sex. You know.... normal teenage stuff. She's developed good coping skills. She could be playing you guys against each other for her own benefit, but she's not. Plus, it's a huge learning experience for when Faith and Bailey are teenagers," she replied nonchalantly.

Cammi often wondered if it was misfortune or destiny that had Allie learning about the obstacles of heartache at such an early age. She was experiencing a side of life Cammi herself didn't have to overcome until her mid twenties. Not romantic love, but self-love, self doubt, and disappointments from those she trusted. It frustrated Cammi to know she was fully capable of helping her daughter, but all she could do was pray and hope eventually Allie would find her way and let go of the false expectations. It was her journey to travel, not Cammi's.

But putting her advice into daily practice seemed to be Cammi's biggest hurdle.

"Great!" With a sigh, she rolled her eyes. "But what about now? What about this little girl I love with all my heart that I am desperate to connect with who continues to isolate me. I can't be her friend, Carissa and that is what she is seeking. I have to be her parent. It's a fine line. She doesn't hang out with girls her own age anymore. Cynthia has become her best friend. She's afraid to trust anyone outside her little circle so she's become socially isolated. Friends at school reach out, but her expectations of what friendships are is so skewed she always winds up hurt. Not one person can fulfill all her ideals. She doesn't get it and instead sets herself up for disappointment. You have friends that fill you in ways that I can't and I have others in my life for the same reason. Look at me and Jamie, and Bryce, too. He would go crazy if he was the only one that I depended on emotionally and vice versa."

Carissa arched her finely shaped eyebrow at her sister and shook her head. Cammi knew immediately what that look meant. She sounded like a hypocrite. Cammi was fully aware that she didn't have any female friends anymore. All with the exception of the important ones had shunned her and well.... Bryce and the kids had become her entire world. Aside from them, she really had no one.

Cammi had no doubt she would always have Jamie. They were soul mates, sisters who connected on a deep level, while her relationship with her blood sister, although very loving and intimate, lacked depth and communication. They could laugh, giggle and be stupid together, once in a while still acting like kids, but they only saw one another maybe once every few months. She had her mother, with whom she talked on the phone weekly. And then there was Martha. Though their relationship was strictly professional and surface personal, Cammi adored and respected her all the same and liked to think they were becoming closer.

But her comment about Bryce was untrue. She had become emotionally dependent on him and found it impossible to detach herself, while knowing it was unhealthy for the both of them. Her expectations changed and rose from day to day, and he found it utterly impossible to meet them.

Ignoring her sister's glare, she shifted her attention to a couple holding hands a few tables away and instantly resented their carefree laughter. How was she supposed to help Allie establish healthy boundaries and confidence when she couldn't even do it herself?

Carissa knew Cammi better than her sister realized and observed the changes in her over the years. Cammi was tough and liked to take care of things her way, so the family typically stepped back allowing her to do what she needed, but this time, someone had to interfere.

"You aren't happy," she piped up switching the topic away from Allie. "You left your annoyingly positive attitude behind at the altar, you know that?"

Carissa's direct honesty took Cammi by surprise. But she was right. And Cammi despised herself for allowing the negativity from Bryce, Allie and Cynthia to control who she had become. Was she that impressionable? It was hard to admit the situation she found herself in years ago with Beth and Bryce left her feeling helpless and weak. Two emotions she didn't cope well with. She had barely recovered from that when he swept her off her feet into a marriage and instant parenthood which she was unaccustomed to also. It seemed like an uphill battle for her sanity ever since.

Cammi had become a walking zombie… saying the right things, making the right decisions, setting a good example, but convincing her mind to follow suit was proving unattainable. The longer it continued, the harder it was to keep up the charade. She tried to understand, tried to change, but didn't get why nothing she tried was working.

"I think you have minimized your issues from your divorce." Carissa announced between sips of her iced tea.

"When did you become a psychologist?" Cammi replied sarcastically. She didn't need a lecture right now, especially about Marcus. But it was apparent Carissa wasn't letting up.

"He cheated on you. That would bruise anyone's ego. But even after, you acted as if it was no big deal, like you were invincible and unaffected by it. Just admit it damaged you and ten years later, you are still allowing it to."

"Get real. I didn't love him enough," she said dismissing the idea. "He was too much of an egotistical idiot to get all sappy and foolish about. It was a waste of my time ten years ago and dwelling on it now is a waste of my time," she announced irritably.

"That's just it. You try to convince yourself of that. I know you didn't love him the way you do Bryce, but you were young, and you trusted him. He didn't start off with your heart, but you married him with the intention of giving it to him to love and protect, and he walked all over it. Betrayed it and shattered your dreams." Leaning forward in her chair, Carissa stared into Cammi's eyes. "I know there's more to the story Cammi. Don't think we all didn't see how he treated you."

Filled with shame, Cammi broke away from Carissa's intense stare and began to twirl the straw in her iced tea.

"He broke your heart. He broke your spirit. And the reality is…. you are still broken. It's time you face it or it's going to continue to cause problems. Do you want him to have that kind of control over you? Does Bryce deserve to take the blame for what Marcus did?"

The sharpness of her words stung.

"You don't know what you are talking about," Cammi snapped glaring across the table. "Bryce is not as innocent as you may think." Luckily she had brought toys to keep the kids occupied, she didn't know if she had enough strength in her to keep them entertained while having this discussion with her sister.

"Yes, I do! Look, after your divorce, you worked hard to become a different person. A person who was capable of giving and receiving love the way it should be, and I give you *Kudos*, you've done a wonderful job. But while you were busy making yourself better, you forgot one very important thing."

Cammi wasn't going to give Carissa the satisfaction of asking what that something was so instead she gazed warily at the floor, her head pounding in disbelief.

"To accept and love the person you *were*, the person you *are*, faults and all. You forgot to be true to yourself. In your quest to be better, you failed to recognize your humanity which happens to include a broken heart. You pushed those bad feelings aside instead of dealing with them. Well guess what? They've come back to haunt you. You've spent years striving to be someone you aren't; someone you think is socially acceptable, all the while protecting yourself from getting hurt again. And coping the way you have has gotten you back to the exact place you started. Unhappy and suspicious, you think everyone is out to get you. You are the exact person you ran away from."

Cammi absorbed the words, but she wasn't ready to believe them. As much as she loved her sister, she wasn't exactly the one Cammi would turn to for unsolicited relationship advice.

"You found a comfortable, confident place and this time, you took a leap of faith by giving your heart to Bryce unconditionally. It was want you wanted to do. It wasn't wrong. But you weren't completely healed." Carissa shrugged her shoulders. "Maybe I'm wrong….but I don't think so. I think there is some serious trauma in you. And Beth opened those wounds. Since her you've never trusted that Bryce would stay faithful. Instead of taking responsibility for how you've reacted to all of it, you continue to wait for him to mess up."

"Where you are now doesn't stem from him or from Cynthia," she said gently watching the tears slip from Cammi's eyes. "It started in your first marriage. Bryce isn't Marcus and he shouldn't have to pay for some other man's mistakes. It's no secret Bryce and I don't see eye to eye on many things, but I know when a man is head over heels in love and that boy would cross the ocean buck naked for you."

Despite her aversion to his personality, they both loved her sister and Carissa wasn't ashamed to admit that someday she hoped to find a man who would revolve his world around her the way Bryce did Cammi. Pulling her wallet out of her purse, Carissa handed some cash and the bill to the waiter. It was clearly obvious to Carissa that Bryce was the perfect man for her sister. But her concern lied in the fact that with every conversation they had, Cammi continued to doubt it, even after all this time. Carissa wasn't sure what transpired in her sister's marriage to Marcus, but if she were to place money on it, she'd bet that whatever it was, Marcus had done some serious, if not permanent damage. And Cammi being who she was she was too proud to admit it. She hoped for her sister's sake, as well as Bryce's, a drastic change was made and soon. If not, she had a feeling, Cammi was going to throw away the best thing that ever happened to her and wind up not only hurting herself, but her entire family.

"I'm sorry if I made you mad. My intentions weren't to hurt you." Glancing at her watch as Carissa stood up. "Look, I have a two o-clock appointment; I hate to rush out on a moment like this. Just think about what I said, okay? And why don't you come in for a massage. You could really use it."

Giving Faith and Bailey a quick kiss she waved good-bye and left Cammi alone to deal with her own inner turmoil.

Just when Cammi dared to hold onto the edge of hope, just when Allie and Bryce's father-daughter relationship seemed to be on the mend, Allie went and pulled something stupid again. It pained Cammi to see her husband stabbed in the back at every turn and she couldn't help but wonder if she and Cynthia were cohorts in a game to ruin their lives.

Cynthia called the house the day before to tell Bryce that she made a terrible mistake while Allie was staying with her over Christmas Break. Apparently, the kids had been at a party when they showed up at Cynthia's five minutes past Allie's curfew. Jake was too drunk to walk back to Christian's and so she let him pass out on the couch. She figured it would be harmless. But sometime during the middle of the night, Allie had snuck out of her room onto the couch with this Jake kid. When Cynthia woke up in the morning, they were bundled up underneath the comforter, arms entwined. She said once she realized how inappropriate it was, she knew she needed to let Bryce know what was going on. Especially if Allie liked the kid, she wanted both he and Cammi to be prepared for what might happen next.

Who is Jake? Cammi wondered. She felt stupid for being clueless. Allie had betrayed their trust once again, and Cammi literally wanted to slap her for being so self-centered. Didn't she realize she broke her father's heart? Didn't she understand how much he loved her? What he was willing to do for her? And she continued to manipulate him the same way Cynthia did.

Everything was a dark, cloudy haze. Cammi wanted to do the right thing but all she could think about was confronting Cynthia. In her mind, during the confrontation, Cynthia would show her true colors, become irrational, out of control, maybe even a little hostile, and finally, Cammi would have no choice but to shove her foot into Cynthia's perfect teeth, and beat her senseless so she was no longer beautiful anymore. Yes, Cammi would enjoy that immensely.

Cammi knew it was something she would never act on, but it sure felt good to imagine it. This hatred was overwhelming, like nothing she'd ever felt before. If it weren't for Allie's birth mother, her life would be normal. Dysfunction like this happened to other people, not to her.

The right answer was to let God handle this, but man, it was hard for her to let this one go. The ache in her chest manifested itself as she continued about her daily activities with the kids. When they finally went down for a nap, she sat on the couch, rubbing her hand gently over Gucci and cried. It was getting harder for her to act as if everything was okay. Everything was not okay. Time was supposed to make things better, but the longer it went on the worse things seemed to be.

She thought continuously about her lunch with Carissa. She didn't want to believe what her sister had said, but something struck a nerve. Could her first marriage really be the root of the problem? Any emotion she felt at the time had been so far dismissed, she didn't know if she could even conjure up such a notion, let alone give it credit for the misery filling every corner of her life now.

It wasn't only Cynthia. It was everything around her. Her once cozy, stable, loving environment had turned upside down. There would be relief, and she would begin to think things were looking up, either with her and Bryce, Bryce and Allie or her own relationship with Allie. But then reality would hit them square in the face again. If it wasn't Bryce's job, it was Allie, if it wasn't Allie, it was Cynthia, if it wasn't Cynthia, then it was her. If it wasn't her, it was something with Faith and Bailey

It was at times like this Cammi wondered why she stuck around. It would be so much easier if she didn't have to deal with the madness that had been brought into her life. She loved Bryce to death but his baggage was starting to cause emotional havoc on her own dreams. There wasn't a week that went by without some sort of crisis. Cammi tired of it overwhelming their lives. And their home was becoming a living hell.

Wouldn't it be easier if she took Bailey and Faith and started over somewhere on her own? She would love to take Allie, too, and finally put an end to all of her grief, but she knew that was impossible. She belonged with her dad, and besides, he wasn't the problem. Something had to get her away from Cynthia.

After all these years, Cammi never stopped wishing Allie was her own flesh and blood. If Allie were hers, this wouldn't be happening. As her mother, Cammi would be able to make the decisions. She would be in control, and she was sure she wouldn't be filled with so much hatred towards the girl who, in all honesty, wasn't responsible for any of this.

The fear was consuming. The desire to protect everyone she loved penetrated every thought. Yet, she couldn't protect them and the helplessness was affecting her well-being. She could see it happening, but felt completely powerless to stop it. Deep down in her heart, she didn't want to leave Bryce or take their kids away from him. She loved him with every part of her being. But she didn't know how much longer she could live this way. And maybe, just maybe when she so desperately believed he was the one God brought into her life….she had been wrong.

Chapter Twenty-Eight

"I guess Cynthia has quite a reputation around town, already," Bryce said kissing her forehead. They had just made love and were lying in bed once again discussing the latest they had heard about Allie's mother.

Bryce loved her, that would never change but the intense physical intimacy they shared had been lost, left in a cloud of dust along with many other things. It was obvious she felt rejected by him, and he tried, God knows he tried as hard as he could, but his sexual state of mind had gone to hell along with his emotional state of mind which disappeared months ago. Without either, he didn't feel like a man. He felt more like a puppet… her puppet….Cynthia's puppet….Allie's puppet.

"You think?" she asked instantly regretting her tone of voice. But for Christ sake, they had just had sex and as an afterthought he wanted to talk about Cynthia! It was bad enough his lack of interest in her was at an all time high. She'd actually been surprised he wanted to touch her earlier. But it had been mechanical, forced for both of them. She despised him for making her feel like less of a woman. "After everything else we know, I'm shocked you could still be surprised."

He rolled his eyes ignoring her. "I feel so ignorant. I should have pulled my head out of my ass months ago when we found out she was stripping at the Rodeo. I wanted to believe her intentions with Allie were genuine and she was stepping up to be a respectable mother. I don't understand what sort of example she is trying to set."

Cammi was tired of discussing it but obviously Bryce needed to vent, so she took a deep breath, putting her own feelings aside.

"I don't think she has the rationale to even know that one, Babe. In her eyes, she isn't doing anything wrong. She doesn't have any parenting skills, so eventually we are going to have to step in and make sure Allie doesn't end up in a bad situation. That is what scares me the most. Knowing the lifestyle Cynthia is living and wondering if she is living it with Allie there, seeing it first hand, especially if there are still drugs involved."

Bryce was quiet. It was hard for him to hear what he already knew. He wished more than anything he had enough sense to keep his dick in his pants that night fifteen years ago. He wouldn't trade Allie for the world, but God knows he should have been smart enough to provide her with a better mother.

He wondered on a daily basis what Cammi thought of him now. It was obvious where her blame was directed, but would she ever forgive him for putting their daughter in the hands of an unstable woman?

He reminded himself that Cammi loved Allie from the start and never treated her different than the children she gave birth to. It was a mother's nature to protect her children. It had been hard for her to step back and let Cynthia step in. The grief of losing Allie to Cynthia almost killed her, and he watched in admiration as she continued to do the right thing. But how much more was she willing to handle before she finally broke?

He traced his fingertips down the curve of her hip, taking in all her beauty. Regret hit him like a wrecking ball. It wasn't fair for him to place all their problems in his wife's lap. He had contributed just as much and blamed himself for the pain she was going through. The fact he couldn't change it cut him deeply. The last thing he ever wanted was to hurt her. But as time went on, that's what happened.

"The bartender at the Rodeo says she only works one week out of the month. Rumors are she is making money on the side," Bryce commented.

"You mean drugs?" her interest suddenly peaked. Hearing negative things about Cynthia brightened up Cammi's day. Maybe if they focused on how bad she was, he would overlook Cammi's flaws.

"He didn't know for sure, but thinks either that or prostitution. If it is prostitution, she is very secretive about it. Maybe that was the deal with Darby. She couldn't move in with him and keep up her 'day job'."

"It would make sense. According to Allie she always has an obscene amount of money to spend. But she obviously isn't paying her bills with it."

Bryce spoke to Darby once again the previous week. His credit card debt totaled over twenty-three thousand dollars. She even had enough guts to buy a vehicle in his name. He wasn't quite sure how he pulled it off. The only thing he could think was she had gained access to his social security number, bank account information and pretended to be his wife, forging his signature. The car was repossessed three months later and creditors were calling his work every day. But he didn't press charges. He told Bryce he will take the loss and start over as long as he doesn't ever have to see or hear from Cynthia ever again.

"Why do you think she still strips then?"

"Maybe that is where she finds her clients. Makes it look like she found a new guy for the night, or the week, when she's really getting paid under the table. I mean the Rodeo is more classy than most of your strip clubs, wealthy guys go in there. If she has her regulars who are willing to pay each week or a few times a week, she can make a ton of cash. Who knows, it's all speculation anyway."

"What does Allie know?" Cammi asked.

Bryce shrugged his shoulder. "Nothing really. She's still upset her mom is alone with no one to take care of her. I explained it's not her job or responsibility."

"Did you ask her about Jake? We still need to deal with that."

"No, I don't know how to approach it."

"Let me do it, okay? It's understandable you're still upset, I can be more levelheaded."

"Thanks" he remarked dryly. "I suppose your right."

Cammi wrapped her arms around her husband and sighed. He was so warm. It felt good to hold him close. As hard as it was to ignore her own growing insecurities and reach out to him, she was instantly thankful she did. No matter how disappointed she was with life, in his arms she felt safe, secure. But as she drifted off to sleep, the nagging voice inside her head reminded her this was only temporary.

It was Super Bowl Sunday. Jamie and Shawn invited them over to watch the game. Both Bryce and Cammi were looking forward to getting out of the house and leaving all their troubles behind for a few hours, plus it was a chance to spend quality time with their friends instead of the uncomfortable companionship they'd been forcing upon one another.

Though she and Jamie had been best friends for years, it was nice that Bryce and Shawn had common interests too. The twins were eleven now, but they treated Faith and Bryce like gold, and the two younger kids loved to follow them everywhere.

Football had become one of her and Bryce's favorite pastimes. They loved watching it together on cold Sunday afternoons with a hot pot of chili on the stove and the kids playing on the floor in front of them. But this football season hadn't been the same, there was too much tension lingering over them. It was much easier to avoid one another than to painfully pretend they enjoyed their time together.

Bryce was making a quick run to the store for chips and soda when Cammi heard a soft knock on the bedroom door. She yanked a hooded sweatshirt over her head as Allie pushed open the door. Sitting down on the edge of the bed, Allie looked around the room while Cammi admired Allie's beauty through the reflection in the mirror. It was hard for her to believe she was fifteen, but then again, she seemed so grown up, too, it was hard to believe she had ever been a little girl. Though Allie did possess some of Cynthia's features, the blonde hair and big, blue eyes, she had her Dad's bone structure, the long thin face, chiseled features and delicate nose.

"Can I bring a friend to the game with us?" Allie asked with a serious expression on her face.

Cammi was delighted. It would be good for Allie to spend some time with a girlfriend.

"Of course! You know any of your friends are always welcome at Jamie's. They are like family."

Cammi applied a light gloss to her lips and then blotted them together. "Who are you bringing?"

"My friend Jake," she announced boldly.

Cammi turned away from the mirror and eyed her step-daughter uncertainly.

"Jake?"

"I promise, Mom, he is just a friend. Nothing more. We hang out a lot. I mean….. he isn't my boyfriend or anything," she said with a tremor in her voice.

Cammi sat down on the bed trying to smile while her stomach turned summersaults.

"Don't get so flustered." She put her hand on Allie's cheek. "Why don't you start at the beginning and tell me how you know him…. how you became friends."

"He's from school. I have known him for years. I liked his friend Shane, but Shane was a real jerk," she said blushing. "Jake stopped by the house earlier this summer to apologize to me for what Shane did and some other stuff. He is real nice, seriously, we are *just* friends, he has never tried to hold my hand or kiss me or anything, but we talk all the time. I can tell him anything."

Cammi listened intently, trying to catch every word that passed quickly. She could tell Allie was avoiding telling her the whole truth.

"What did Shane do that was so bad?" she wanted to know.

"You know. Typical boy stuff."

"Did he hit on you?"

"Sort of, it was more what he said, than what he did. He definitely was into something more physical than what I was," she confessed, hanging her head low. Cammi stayed quiet. Finally, after seeing the compassion in her mother's face, Allie gave in, telling her what happened with Shane at her birthday though she was careful to leave out other important details.

Cammi was doing everything in her power not to over-react or jump to conclusions. It was important Allie feel safe when talking to her.

"Ah, I see. Teenage boys can be like that. Their hormones run wild. Bad thing is while most girls are looking for a boyfriend, the boys just want a roll in the hay."

"Roll in the hay? Mom, you sound so *uncool* when you say that!" Allie laughed.

Cammi shoved her back onto the bed playfully. "I am NOT *uncool*, just careful with my words. You are only fifteen you know, there still things you should be naïve about."

Feeling ashamed, Allie hung her head. "Tell me about it."

"What do you mean? Allie....did something happen?" Cammi was getting a sense Allie was desperate to tell her more.

"No, it's just that......sometimes I overhear what Cynthia says when she talks to her friends. Her being single and all... she talks about stuff I really don't want to know. Stuff with her boyfriends," she continued feeling braver as the words came out. "I love her, Mom, I really do, but I don't like some of the things she does, it makes me uncomfortable. Sometimes I think she forgets I am her daughter and not her friend. It's disgusting."

Relief flooded her heart and she continued to listen without interrupting or giving an opinion. Allie needed someone to hear her, not tell her what to do, though it wasn't easy.

"She drinks a lot. Too much I think, and the way she acts.....it's really embarrassing. We are just really different. I know we look alike, but other than that, it is hard to believe I am her daughter. She wants me to be like her, but really Mom, I don't want to be. Her life isn't good. She tries to convince me it is, but she isn't happy." Sadness filled her voice.

They both sat quietly for a few minutes, Cammi contemplating what to say and Allie staring at the floor.

"Look, I don't expect you to tell me anything you don't want to, okay? I won't pry. But you need to know your Dad and I are aware of stuff going on at Cynthia's house when you aren't there. It worries us because we don't ever want to see you put in a bad situation, and Cynthia isn't making the best choices as a mother. Your Dad knows how much you want her in your life, so he is trying to find the best possible solution for you."

"Are you going to stop letting me spend time with her?" Allie asked suddenly alarmed.

Cammi shook her head. "No. But we are going to be more cautious, especially when she is being irresponsible. Promise me something," she said turning Allie's face towards her own. "When you are with her, if you ever feel uncomfortable, you call us, and we will come get you, no matter what. Don't ever feel like you have to put your own feelings aside to please any of us, okay?" She paused for a moment before she went on. "But there is something I have to ask you.... did this Jake kid spend the night at Cynthia's house a few weeks ago?"

Allie looked at her, fear piercing her eyes. "What...what do you mean?"

Cammi wanted to hear Allie's side of the story before she gave away any other details. "Cynthia called and told your Dad. Why don't you tell me what happened."

Allie's face was red. "She lets me invite friends over, sort of like a party. The first time was in June, it was a disaster. She invited her friends, too and got drunk. I promise I didn't drink anything, Mom. But some of my friends did. I was humiliated. She promised this last time it would just be my friends. And it was. We had a blast. No one drank, we just watched movies, but she let everyone stay the night. Jake's parents were out of town, and he was supposed to spend the night at Christian's. Christian doesn't have a curfew, they let him do anything. Jake's parents would be super mad if they found out, please don't tell them."

She pulled at a string hanging out of the comforter. "Everyone stayed. Cynthia let us crash in the living room. I know it was wrong. But no one there was dating, we are all just friends, nothing went on," she pleaded. "I should have told you, I'm so sorry." Tears swarmed in her eyes. "Heather and I slept in my room, and the guys slept on the floor in the living room."

"Jake wasn't drunk?" she inquired with skepticism.

"No! I already told you, no one drank. The first time in June at my birthday party, Cynthia gave us beer, but she said she made a mistake, and this time she was making it up to me. Why?" The confusion was apparent on her face.

"Well, what she told your father is a bit different than what you have told me," she admitted reaching into the closet for her shoes.

Allie shrugged. "I don't know what else she could have said. I guess I am confused. She is the one who suggested it. Wouldn't telling Dad make him mad at her?"

"I'll be honest with you, Allie, what she told your Dad only made him mad at *you*. In fact, I was pretty mad, too. But I am starting to understand a few things." Cammi told her Cynthia's story. The devastation was apparent on Allie's face. In her reaction, Cammi discovered the truth.

"Mom, Jake never drinks. He watched his grandpa die from it. When we had my birthday party, Jake and I were the only ones who didn't try it." Tears streamed down her face. "He felt bad for me and came over to see if I was okay. That is when we started hanging out more," she said crying great sobs. "Why would Cynthia lie or try to get me in trouble?"

Cammi's heart broke as she held her in her arms. "I don't know, Baby, I really don't."

"What are you going to tell Dad?"

She shook her head in disgust. "Like I said, we both know more about Cynthia than you probably realize, so your Dad isn't going to be surprised. I think you should talk to him though. He is worried and hurt. He thought you betrayed him again. These secrets need to stop. If you aren't honest with him about everything, it does nothing but make you look bad. Let him know you are not blind. Make him trust that you are going to make the right decisions no matter what Cynthia tries to do. He needs to know that."

Allie nodded, but continued to cling to Cammi. The embrace help calm her down but she was still confused and hurt by Cynthia's actions. "You do realize the position you put yourself in don't you, having two boys spend the night?"

"But I trust Jake," Allie interrupted.

She gave Allie a quizzical look. "That's not the point. It's just not a good situation to be in, for many different reasons, regardless of who you trust. And it is definitely not something we would condone."

Allie didn't want to think about it anymore. "So can I bring Jake along or what?" she asked changing the subject.

"I don't know Allie, you know you can't date until you are sixteen, and it is going to take some convincing your Dad. He's not happy about this Jake thing already."

"Please?" she begged. "I have gone to his house for dinner and met his family. We aren't dating."

"When were you at his house?" Cammi inquired raising her eyebrows.

Realizing she was digging herself a hole, she confessed the whole truth.

"Please, don't be angry. Dad has been so out of control and moody, I didn't want to tell him. When I say I'm with Heather and Brandi, I'm usually with Jake. He is my best friend. His parents always have me over. They are great and always ask about meeting you. Jake is bummed I haven't introduced him to you yet, but I didn't know how to handle it. You have to believe me. I'm not ready to date. He's not my boyfriend. Nothing has happened." Cammi knew Allie enough to see the truth in her eyes.

"I believe you. I can always tell when you are hiding something from me. You fidget when you try to tell me what you *think* I want to hear. Look…I'll talk to your dad, but I can't promise anything. You have been telling a lot of lies and keeping secrets. Both of which are unacceptable. You will probably be grounded."

Ironically, Allie didn't care. She would take the grounding, she knew she deserved it. But words did not express how much better she felt for having told Cammi everything. Jumping up off the bed, she headed out the door. "I will get Dad. I think he is home, I heard a car door shut. Thank you." She turned around and ran into her arms hugging her tightly. "I love you."

"I love you too, Sweetheart. I promise things are going to get better."

Cammi spent the better part of the next half hour trying to calm Bryce down, and they were almost late for kick-off.

"I want to throw her on the ground then pummel her face in. I swear to God, I do."

"Cynthia's motive is selfish. She is willing to say anything to tear you and Allie apart. She expects you to come down hard which in turn will make *Allie* hate you. Then she can be the good parent who gives Allie what she wants." Cammi put her hand on his arm. "Look, Allie knows. She is not dumb. I told her to talk to you."

Bryce's pressed his lips together tightly in concentration. "I'm sick of this, Cammi, I really am. It's a no win situation. No matter what I do, nothing touches her, nothing catches up to her. I want her to pay. It's time someone made her pay," he said slamming his fist on top of the dresser.

"I know, Honey, I want it too. Look, Allie, wants to bring this Jake kid to Jamie's with us."

"That's another thing that pisses me off. Why haven't we heard about him? You know what boys that age have on their mind. They want laid, Cammi. He doesn't want to be her friend. I don't know what sort of mind games he is playing with her, but he is a piece of shit as far as I am concerned."

"Bryce, I believe her when she says they're just friends. Nothing's happened."

"Do you really think she would tell us if there had? What is she going to say? 'Mom and Dad, just wanted to let you know Jake and I are having sex. Thought you would be happy if I told you the truth?' Get a grip, Cammi. Plus she's already been lying about the time they spend together."

"Don't be pissed off at me, Bryce, we are in this together, remember?" she scolded, offended by his sarcasm. "I can tell when she is hiding something and with him, she's not. With Cynthia…yes. Look, she wants to share this part of her life with us. It's important she lets us in. She's going to hang out with him regardless of what we say. At least this way, we'll know what is going on."

Bryce threw his hands up in desperation. "We have told her she is not allowed to date until she is sixteen. Plus, what are his parents like allowing her to come to their house without us knowing? Are they even there? God, I feel like I don't know what the hell my own daughter is doing anymore."

"I will call them Monday," Cammi reassured him. "Allie said they want to meet us, so they can't be that bad. Honey, she's fifteen, this is going to happen sometime. And she swears it is not a date. She's allowed to have friends. So what if one's a guy? I had a ton of guy friends in high school."

"You did?" he said surprisingly. "Fine, he can come, just because we'll be there, but don't expect me to be nice. And I will be watching his every move. I'll know if they are *only* friends," he shouted to her as he stormed down the stairs.

Cammi rolled her eyes but smiled slightly wondering why he had to act like such an alpha male at times like this.

They picked Jake up on the way. Allie sat with Faith while he squeezed in the back of the minivan next to Bailey. After introductions were made, Cammi asked a few polite questions to make him feel comfortable. Bryce grumbled his hello, then ignored them the rest of the drive. Jake was considerate but quiet. Cammi was surprised at how handsome he was for a sixteen year old…..and tall. From what she remembered, boys at fifteen were still scrawny and awkward, but this kid was athletic and very attractive.

The uncomfortable silence followed them into the house, and Cammi was relieved when Jamie took over, making everyone feel welcome with her boisterous personality. They all grazed on chips, Buffalo wings, the assortment of vegetables and fruit as well as cookies set out on the table. Bryce and Shawn had already disappeared into the living room with plates piled high with food when Jamie began to ask Jake about school and his family. Eventually they heard the whoops and hollers from the living room and decided it was time to join the men before they missed out on the entire game.

The game was a close one with the Chicago Bears leading the New York Giants by three points at halftime. They were all enjoying themselves, with the exception of Bryce and his overly protective demeanor. Poor Jake and Allie, they weren't allowed to leave his sight for a moment. Everywhere they went, they were followed by her father's disapproving scowl.

Finally, after the halftime performance, Bryce started to loosen up when he found out Jake was the first string corner on the high school football team this past fall. Even though they were a bit reluctant at first, soon the men included him in their sports talk. Bryce was also surprised to find out he had gone to high school with Jake's dad. In fact, they had been pretty good friends. Bryce not only considered him one of the most popular guys in school, but one of the most decent.

"I didn't realize he was still around. I never hear about him."

"He's a pilot so he travels a lot and when he's home, he likes to be with us. My parents don't socialize much."

"I know who he is." Jamie interrupted. "And your mother too. They go to our church. Your mom had quite a reputation for her knack of event planning."

"Yeah," Jake muttered.

Cammi could see the lines in Bryce's face relax as the evening wore on. But she was also aware of the pride Allie felt for her friend. And they truly were only friends. Their body language spoke volumes. If there had an intimate relationship, at this age, they would not have been able to hide it. The two of them laughed and teased one another playfully but underneath there was mutual respect.

"I don't like to admit when I am wrong, but for the sake of my daughter, I will," Bryce said after they dropped Jake off. "He seems like a good kid, and if he is anything like his Dad, hopefully he will stay that way. I guess you can hang out with him as long as it's *only* a friendship, but not for a week. You're grounded for lying to us. And remember, I find out everything, so if it starts turning into more, I will know. Don't try to pull a fast one," he threatened.

Allie giggled while she leaned over the seat to give her dad a quick kiss on the cheek.

"Don't worry, Dad. He is cute and all, but he's like my brother and that's gross!"

Later that night while Cammi was sleeping peacefully in bed, Bryce snuck down to the kitchen for some cookies and milk. He was glancing over a basketball magazine when Allie sat down next to him. Though the house was quiet he'd been so engrossed in his own thoughts, he hadn't heard her come down the stairs.

"Hi," she said shyly reaching over to steal a cookie.

"Hi to you," he said not taking his eyes off the article.

"Can we talk, Dad? There are some things I need to tell you." She was apprehensive, but after sitting in her room all night weighing her options, she finally had the guts to face him. "If I don't, I know you are going to find out anyway, and you won't trust me anymore. I can't let that happen because I need you right now."

The insistence in her tone made Bryce's heart sink. Closing his magazine, he looked her directly in the eyes, trying to remember how innocent she had been when she was five, and they had their *serious* talks. Back then, he would try to make her understand, see his point of view, but she was so nonchalant about life, so carefree. He loved watching the world through her eyes. Now, nothing was carefree anymore and watching her, it felt as if she was fighting for her life.

"Does this have to do with Jake?" he asked reluctantly.

She laughed quietly. "No, this isn't about Jake. Would you let it go already? Stop worrying. It's about Cynthia."

Allie took a deep breath but instead of talking, she ended up crying. Not sure what to make of it, Bryce did the only thing he was able to and wrapped his arms around his daughter.

"Dad," she sobbed. "Please don't be mad at me or stop loving me. I am so sorry I lied. I wanted to find a way to handle it on my own, but I can't. If I didn't have Jake to talk to, I think I would have gone insane by now, but he has such good advice. He keeps telling me I need to tell you or Cammi or my counselor, but I don't want Cynthia to get in trouble. I..... I love her Dad. I don't want her to hurt."

Bryce sat back down in the chair across from her, took her hands in his and nodded for her to continue. Despite the fear she felt, Allie told him everything, the men, the parties, the lies, the suicide attempts, and most importantly, the emotional blackmail. As it sank in, Bryce felt the room spin out of control. He now understood why Allie had sunk down as far as she had, and how hard she struggled to keep her head above water, along with the lengths she had gone to try to convince them and everyone else her life with Cynthia was peachy-keen.

His first reaction was to put an end to the visitations. But it wasn't the answer. It would have been much easier when Allie was younger, but at her age now, it was her choice. She was turning into a young lady, and he couldn't make this decision for her. He could only continue to give her direction and guidance as she continued to learn the truth.

They spent the next two hours talking, making up for lost time and learning about one another again. She spilled it all, and he accepted everything she had to say without judgment or criticism.

"It sounds to me like you have made some pretty good decisions regardless of the direction Cynthia has been trying to lead you. I am proud of you," he admitted. "But I would be lying if I said none of this bothered me. She's put you in situations that terrify me, Allie. Besides that, Cynthia will give you whatever it is you want, no matter what the cost or who she hurts. And at times, it is going to be tempting. I hope as you get older, you still remember right from wrong. All I can do is trust you. But most importantly, I hope you can trust yourself."

"It's hard sometimes. I want to have fun and enjoy my high school years, but I don't want to be like her. I want a good life, like the one you and Cammi have given me."

He tugged on her hand and pulled her over to sit on his lap hugging her close to him. His chest tightened as he held back his tears.

"I do understand how scared and confused you have been but it doesn't make me happy you have been keeping it to yourself," he said when he found his voice. "I hope you know after all these years of you and I, that you can trust me. You are everything to me and I've missed you."

Tears began to well up in her eyes again.

"I know, but you are so angry all the time. You act like you don't like me anymore."

"I don't have any excuses, Kiddo. You're right. I guess I'm scared. I got scared when Cynthia came around and my fear turned into anger. We both have changed and there were times when I haven't liked you. It doesn't mean I don't love you, but you have hurt me, you know. I am smart enough to know how teenagers are….. but you are starting to give me grey hair," he teased. "And I am sure I have done my share of hurtful things, too. I'm sorry. We both have to work on this, don't we?"

She nodded.

"You know, Allie," he continued, "there are a lot of ways to have fun and enjoy your high school years without making the same choices Cynthia has. The more trust you earn from us, the more freedom we are going to give you. But you earn trust by being responsible. Have a good time, live it up. Just be smart while you are doing it."

Unable to stop the dam from flowing Allie cried, clinging to her dad as though she would die if she let go. He was her lifeline, and she'd come so dangerously close to cutting the tie. Now she could feel it come together as the hole in her heart began to fill.

"I don't respect her, Dad." He handed her a tissue to blow her nose. "I promise I will tell you everything that goes on with Cynthia whether it is good or bad, but I need you to help me. Please don't get mad at me when I screw up, okay? Because I'm going to screw up."

"I can't always promise I won't be mad, but as long as we are honest with each other, I will try my best." He hugged her again. "I screw up a lot too. Remember when you were five…you thought I was perfect, remember?"

"You're still perfect to me."

Bryce smiled warmly. "You are turning into an amazing woman. Do you know how proud I am to be your dad? I can't even imagine how hard this has been for you," he said sadly.

"You have no idea. It sucks, Dad. It really does. But if I love her, I have to accept her for who she is, right?"

"I don't know if you will ever stop loving her, she's your mother. But it doesn't mean you have to put up with how she treats you. Stand up for yourself. You have the choice as to what is acceptable in your life and if what she does isn't acceptable, then stay away from it. You always have us, and we love you."

"I love you, too," she said as she kissed the top of his head.

Bryce crawled up the stairs and into bed feeling somewhat relieved but the fury inside him towards Cynthia intensified. He was grateful Cammi was sound asleep. As much as he wanted to share this with her, he still needed time to grasp all Allie told him. He wasn't shocked, but then again, he was. Once again Ron informed him if they went to court and could prove her an unfit parent, there was a possibility a judge would order supervised visitations. But his lawyer also had a very good point.

It was inevitable Allie was going to learn about her mother, the good, the bad and the ugly. It could be now, while she was still living with Bryce and had his and Cammi's support, or he could limit their contact, giving Allie the choice for a relationship when she was an adult. By then her bitterness and resentment towards him might cause her to follow in her mother's footsteps. He prayed he wasn't making a huge mistake, but nothing in life was guaranteed, he just had to do his best.

Chapter Twenty-Nine

It was Valentine's Day and neither Bryce nor Cammi had broached the subject of doing something special. It had crossed her mind, but the idea was soon forgotten. The extra effort it took to make her husband happy wasn't in her anymore.

Cammi was certain after Allie's confessions that Bryce was going to put limits on her time with Cynthia, but he hadn't, and she detested him for it. The rational side of her knew he was making the right choice, but the emotional side of her hated to watch Allie deal with the pain and wished somebody would do something, anything to change the circumstances continuing to surround them.

Carissa was right, she was back at square one, unhappy and miserable with the person she was. It was as if the last decade had been a waste of time. She was tired of pretending she had a happy marriage worth saving. It was anything but, in fact, things seemed to get progressively worse. And with each day, Cammi found herself daydreaming a way out of her life.

But the headstrong side of her refused to give up and prayed this was another steppingstone toward making the relationship stronger. So mustering up as much hope and enthusiasm as she could, Cammi headed out shopping for a gift and decided to buy herself a sexy negligee for the evening.

Even though she was pushing forty her figure was still amazing. Her legs were long and lean, and her stomach nice and tight. It was a blessing in disguise considering she hadn't worked out or gone for a walk in months. But she credited the shedding of those ten pounds she put on before the holidays to her loss of appetite and constant activity with the kids more than her motivation to look good. She certainly didn't feel sexy, in fact, she felt uglier than ever.

"I don't get it," she told Jamie over the phone earlier in the afternoon. "Two months ago, I couldn't keep my hands off him. I was begging him to want me, to touch me, to have sex with me. Now, he repulses me. I mean, he is still incredibly handsome, but I don't want him anymore. What's wrong with me? I'm too young to lose my sex drive."

"It's called marriage, honey. And you are normal, a normal couple going through normal things."

"No, we aren't! We're dysfunctional. We can't get along for more than two days at a time, if that. We don't have fun, we spend all of our time resenting and hating one another, we hardly have sex anymore and neither of us cares!"

"Do you think there is a couple out there who have children that don't have some of the same issues you do?"

"You mean to tell me there are actually other people whose lives are *this* 'fucked up'?"

"Jesus Cammi, do you have to be so cynical?"

"It's the new me, Jamie, cynical, negative, angry. Better get used to it," she replied dryly.

"You and Bryce have a stressful life, true, maybe a bit more stressful than say, Shawn and I. But we have problems, too. Two people who are crazy about each other and in love are going to have problems now and again. It's how it goes."

"I know Bryce well enough that when he is over-stressed along with me nagging at him the last thing on his mind is sex."

"Well, there you go. He is more than over-stressed. What you guys deal with on a daily basis with Cynthia is insane. Not to mention trying to keep up with both jobs, the financial junk, a teenager, two toddlers and the wedge between the two of you."

"I just can't stop convincing myself that it's me. If I were more understanding, more considerate, more accepting, sexier, you know all the things I was when he met me, then maybe it would be better. Nothing I try works. He's closed off and I don't know if we will ever be close again. When we started dating, I remember thinking if we just nourish our love and work hard, there was no reason we couldn't feel the same intensity and passion twenty years down the road. It's been eight years and the spark has already died."

"Really? I remember after your trip into the mountains, you were walking on air for weeks. Oh, and I remember over Thanksgiving break, your exact words were, 'he is so scrumptious, I want to eat him up'. It's an up and down rollercoaster, Cammi, and every day is different. No one said it would be easy. There will be days you can't stand him. Days you wish he would leave you alone and definitely days you would like to choke the life out of him. Now that's passion. But then you crawl into bed at night and force yourself to remember the simple little things he did to make you feel loved, such as picking up a gallon of milk or sitting on the porch swing with you watching the sunset or putting the kids to bed so you could take a long, hot bath. Try to think about the way he holds you even if you don't have sex. But mostly you need to remember he is constantly trying and he never gives up. There's not many out there like him."

"Wow, you really like the guy don't you?" Cammi teased.

"Remember me telling you way back when, if I wasn't married, I would be in the hot seat for him in a flash," she giggled. "For better or for worse. You took those vows and that is what you get. Why did you think it would be any different? God didn't. He knows your heart and knew what you needed."

Her talk with Jamie was the uplifting reminder moving her through the rest of the day and filling her with enough energy and excitement to go ahead with the plans she attempted to put together the day before.

"Hey," Cammi said into the phone cheerfully appreciating the sound of her husband's voice.

"Hi, what's up? I only have a few minutes." His distant response immediately put her on edge.

Cammi decided to be nice and blow it off. "I just wanted to remind you about our reservations tonight at six-thirty."

"You didn't say anything about dinner."

"I didn't think I had to, it's Valentine's Day, remember?"

"Oh crap, Cammi, no. I didn't remember. I scheduled a last minute conference with Freddie, I didn't plan on getting home until after seven," he complained.

"Oh.... okay." She covered quickly to hide her disappointment, but in her continued silence Bryce read the mistake he wished he hadn't made.

"Look, I will make some phone calls and get it changed," he told her, his own irritation growing by the minute. His day had been hell, Freddie was riding his ass and the last thing he wanted was to go out for an evening of unrelenting pressure from her. But it was Valentine's Day and for the sake of his marriage, he needed to suck it up.

"Don't worry about it. We can do it another night," she said trying to sound lighthearted.

"Really?" he asked excitedly. "Oh Baby, that means the world right now. Things are just starting to smooth out around here. I would really hate to screw it up."

But he was willing to screw up what was left of their marriage? Where were his priorities? She felt like she didn't exist to him anymore, and the man who wanted to revolve his world around her…. where did he go? She'd done her part and changed her attitude in an attempt to do something special for her husband and *once again*, he didn't give a shit. It would have been nice if he would have thought about her for a change and planned something instead of Cammi always having to be the bigger person.

"I already made arrangements for the kids, but I can change them. Do *me* a favor, okay? Don't forget we could use some time together this week."

"Yeah, sure, look, I have to go now. Give me a call later if you want," he commented before hanging up.

Instantly, the emotions invaded Cammi's stoic composure and unwillingly, tears began to fall. His nonchalant attitude told her all she needed to know. Not only would she be spending Valentine's Day by herself, feeling sorry for herself, she knew there would be no date later this week. It was his way of pacifying her.

Well… she already had a babysitter lined up, and knew for a fact Carissa wasn't doing anything that night. Her boyfriend Guy was in Italy promoting his latest work of art.

"What are you doing tonight?" Cammi breathed anxiously into the phone.

"Hanging out in my pajamas and watching old romantic movies while eating my way through a turtle cheesecake. Why?"

"Put on your dancing shoes, I'm coming to get you at seven. We're going out." Cammi could guarantee there would not be a shortage of single men out looking to make some poor, pathetic women who had nothing else to do but hang out with her sister on Valentine's Day, feel loved and adored. She wasn't looking to cheat on Bryce. She would never do that, but she did need a pick me up for her self-esteem. He wasn't going to be around to make her feel special, so she was going to do it herself. Carissa was not particularly fond of the idea, but sensing her sister would go without her, she agreed to be her chaperone.

Cammi took extra care applying her make-up for the evening, if Bryce didn't appreciate her maybe someone else would, and chose the sexiest cashmere sweater in her closet to accentuate the tight-fitting jeans and high heel boots she'd bought last year and never had a chance to wear. She wasn't one who usually wore earrings but thought the hoops accentuated her green eyes as she swept her hair off her neck into a loose bun.

She would be the first to admit she looked stunning and it felt good. She dropped the kids off at Mrs. Newcomb's, left a note for Bryce that she was with Carissa, wouldn't be home until late, and headed off down the road. A small laugh escaped her lips with the thought of heading out to the bars in a minivan. She was too old to behave this way, but the danger of it was enthralling. As she neared her sister's house, she flipped open her purse and turned off her cell phone. She'd given Mrs. Newcomb Bryce's number in case of an emergency, but Cammi was taking the night off.

Carissa was not happy.

"What exactly do you think we are going to do tonight?" she asked with a disapproving tone as she crawled into the passenger seat.

"Bryce is working late and I already had a babysitter. I am tired of sitting at home feeling sorry for myself, Carissa. I want to have some fun, a little pick-me-up."

"And a little pick-me-up consists of going to a bar all dressed up while your husband and kids are at home?" She looked down at the grubby sweatshirt and jeans she pulled on, wishing she'd worn something a little nicer, but also grateful she wasn't the one having a mid-life crisis.

"Bryce gets to go out for drinks with his friends once in a while, why can't I?" she asked innocently.

"Do you think Bryce looks like this when he has beers with his buddies? Do you think he has 'hit on me' tattooed across his forehead? Probably not."

"Oh, come on. Just let me have a good time, will you?"

As they headed out on the highway, Carissa had to hand it to Cammi, she was being smart. Instead of staying in Madison where she was likely to run into everyone she knew and the rumors would be flying by the next morning, she opted to drive twenty miles over the mountain to a posh ski resort at the base of Aspen Mountain. And it was only a matter of minutes after sitting down at the Iron Horse before the first attractive male sauntered over to their table asking if he could buy them a drink. Cammi accepted graciously while Carissa opted to drink water. She had a feeling she had been nominated designated driver.

The men swarmed around Cammi like flies while everything about her was standoffish and cool….shy, though she had an innocent vitality about life. It was a side to her sister Carissa had never seen before. She was flirtatious in an unaware way. She could definitely understand how it could captivate someone and made her wonder if this was the behavior that had won Bryce over so many years ago. Carissa was used to the admiration of various men and flirting was second nature to her though she always remained indifferent. It took someone with strong character to catch her eye, but when he did, boy watch out. Her boyfriend, Guy, was the only one after so many years, who had enough perseverance to withstand her. As she watched Cammi she realized it was odd to be sitting opposite of what she was accustomed to.

By ten o'clock, Cammi had a few too many drinks and Carissa was getting tired. The evening had been innocent enough. Men bought drinks, talked, and flirted, but Cammi let every single one of them know she was happily married. Underneath the heavy make-up and sexy outfit, Carissa could see her misery. She didn't want to be here. She wanted to be home with the husband she loved and the children they made together. She wanted her family. Maybe this was exactly what she needed to realize it.

Just when Carissa thought Cammi might be ready to call it a night, the bartender brought two glasses of Cabernet to the table, stating it was compliments of the owner. Fifteen minutes later, it was followed by an appetizer of spinach-artichoke dip. When curiosity got the best of her Carissa asked the waiter if the owner was available to speak with them so they could give him their thanks. Seconds later, she was jumping up from her seat into the arms of a tall burley man whose physique resembled that of a professional wrestler. Cammi was awed by how huge he was in comparison to the waiter he stood next to. Carissa was squealing with obvious delight, while the man drew her hand to his lips for a kiss.

In only seconds, it dawned on Cammi who this was. Jonathan had been their neighbor in Madison while growing up. Although Cammi was several years older, he and Carissa had been inseparable until the day she moved away with her parents. They'd kept in touch with letters and saw each other once after graduation, but it had been many years since.

They spent the next three hours engrossed in food, coffee and conversation about their childhood and before they knew it, it was time for the bar to close. Reality jolted Cammi out of her trip down memory lane when she realized she had never turned her cell phone back on. Bryce was going to kill her. Even though she hadn't had a drink for a few hours, her head hurt with the knowledge that by the time they got back into town and she dropped Carissa off it would be after two in the morning. How was she going to explain the lingering odor of booze and cigarettes? There was no way she could hide the fact she'd been out.

"Are you doing okay?" The concern in Carissa's voice was apparent. Even thought Cammi had sobered up, they both agreed Carissa should drive home.

"I don't know. What was I thinking?" she asked her elbow resting on the passenger door while she tucked her head into her hand in shame. "Bryce is going to be furious."

"Wouldn't you be? If the shoe was on the other foot, I mean."

Cammi glared at her sister. "You weren't much help. If we hadn't run into Jonathan, I would have been home hours ago."

"Oh no! Don't you go blaming me! I didn't even want to join you on this little adventure, but figured someone needed to be there so you didn't get yourself into trouble."

"What trouble did you think I was going to get in? I'm perfectly capable of taking care of myself." Cammi declared defensively.

"Think about it, Cam. Do you really think you made a smart choice tonight? Was getting all beautified to go out on Valentine's Day when you knew it was going to be a "free for all", the best choice to make when you were mad at your husband? You and I were two out of six women among a crowd of men. What would you do if Bryce made the same choice when he was angry with you?"

Cammi opened her mouth to reply, but shut it just as quickly and watched the stars glitter above in the night sky, praying to God Bryce wasn't awake when she got home.

Her stomach was in knots by the time she dropped Carissa off and headed to her own house where she found all the lights, including the porch light, off. Silently, she unlocked the front door, hoping Bryce was in one of his dead to the world slumbers and wouldn't notice how late it was.

As she walked through the living room, she saw on the corner table, a dozen red roses next to the small lamp. But to Cammi, the gesture didn't matter, it was too little too late. He'd hurt her. She was tired of taking care of his needs while he wasn't willing to acknowledge hers. Creeping quietly up the stairs she noticed how fast her heart was beating and tried to take deep breaths to quiet it. This was ridiculous. She was a grown woman who should be able to spend an evening out with her sister. Who cared if it was almost three in the morning?

She cared. And it was true….if it was Bryce sneaking home in the middle of the night, shit would have hit the fan. But this was different. She didn't ignore Bryce. She didn't treat him like he was the piece of gum stuck to her shoe. She was loving, generous, affectionate, grateful for his love and wanted him around. *He,* on the other hand, couldn't even take the time to celebrate Valentine's Day with her.

As soon as she walked into the room, the bed lamp flickered on, and her husband was sitting up in bed with a ferocious scowl on his face.

Cammi quivered.

"How old are you, Cammi?"

"Excuse me?"

"You heard me. Are you eighteen or are you a mother of three with a husband at home?"

She ignored him by walking to the closet and shutting the door while slipping out of her jeans. Her hands were shaking, and she could very easily throw up everything she had ingested in the last six hours due to the nervous tension in her stomach.

"What gives you the right to stay out until three in the morning with your cell phone off? What if there was an emergency, and I couldn't get a hold of you? Do you understand how irresponsible your behavior was?"

The hair on the back of Cammi's neck stood up.

"I was with my sister, it was harmless. You couldn't manage to spend the evening with me, so we went out for drinks."

"Looking like a cheap whore?" Bryce yelled clenching and unclenching his fists.

His anger was justified and Cammi knew it, but still she wasn't going to allow him to call her names nor did she feel she owed him an explanation.

"Screw you, Bryce."

"Nice, Cammi, real nice. You know, I thought you were above this. I guess I was wrong." His words devastated her.

"Above what, Bryce? Above sitting around waiting for you to make me feel important? Above being hurt by a husband who didn't want to spend a special occasion with me?" The fierceness in his eyes petrified her, but she wasn't going to be guilted into apologizing.

"You are starting to sound like a broken record, Cammi. You tell me the same thing every week, but you don't listen to what I have to say. I have a lot on my plate okay? But I am here, still trying, not out carousing around with single women."

"Saying you're trying and actually showing me are two different things. When is the last time we had sex, Bryce? Well before New Years, almost two months ago. After eight years of marriage, the only time we weren't intimate like that was after Faith and Bailey were born. You may not care, but I am starting to get concerned. You don't even show interest in me anymore."

The words sliced through him. It wasn't that he didn't want to have sex. He just didn't know how to connect with her anymore. She was filled with complaints whether he touched her or not. And he hated rejection too. "I'm stressed, Cammi, I wish you would understand that."

"You tell me things are getting better with work and things are obviously better between you and Allie. So you are right, I don't understand. Please explain it to me, because all I see is how much you hate me and can't stand to touch me."

What was so hard about meeting her needs? How many times had she heard "I am a man, I can't read minds, tell me what you need"? Once upon a time, he had known how to care for her. He was the one who changed, not her.

"I don't hate you. I wish you would stop saying that." The endless discussion drained him.

"Then stop treating me like you do. I continue to give you what it is you need, I try to make you feel good on a daily basis, and look what I get from you, nothing! If you aren't getting what you need from me, who are you getting it from?" she accused.

It was a slap in the face he didn't deserve, but she wasn't going to be ignored anymore.

He sent her an extremely nasty look. "I am going to overlook that remark. You know there is no one else and never will be. It doesn't matter what you do or don't do, that is not who I am or what I am about." He laughed sarcastically. "You are never going to get it, are you Cammi. In your eyes, there is nothing I do that is good enough, you are constantly beating me down for what I don't do and don't give you. I feel like shit all the time. And your right, I don't like being around you, who would when all you do is bitch?" But you know what? I come home. Every night, I am here, with you and with the kids. Where are you?"

She was confused. Instead of reassuring her or taking responsibility for his actions he somehow managed to turn it around so all the blame fell into her lap. If she could scream to get him to finally hear her she would, but throwing a temper tantrum was his style, not hers.

"So your answer now is to stop trying?" she asked defensively.

"Nope. You made that choice tonight," he said without emotion. "You know, if you would have stuck around long enough or left your phone on, you would have known I realized my mistake and came home right away, with flowers and dinner."

"It wouldn't have mattered. I still would have gone. Why should I wait around for you to figure out I am a priority? I deserve better than that. Nothing should have come before me tonight. Nothing!"

"Oh….I get what you are telling me. No room for mistakes, huh, Cammi? What about unconditional love? What about forgiveness?"

"We don't have that, Bryce. Our love for one another is conditional depending on how we act….how we treat one another. At least I have enough balls to admit it."

From across the room, she could feel his body stiffen, but he said nothing. Instead, he stared at her with contempt and rage.

When he finally did speak, his words were quiet. "I remember a wise woman once told me love is our purpose in life. That pure, honest love was not superficial or selfish and that kind of love could only be obtained through a relationship with God. And I believed her. This would be much easier if I didn't love you, but you know what? Each day I wake up and make a choice. A choice to follow what God wants for me. You taught me that, Cammi," he said pointing his finger at her. "And that choice is also to love you and make this marriage work. You have a choice too. You can be miserable and filled with hate or you can choose to love me. But I will tell you this. I can't do it alone. I *won't* do it alone. If you aren't in this one-hundred percent, tell me now and stop wasting my time."

His words stirred something inside she didn't want to face. The truth. She wasn't in this one hundred percent anymore and the only way she believed she would find happiness was on her own. She'd made a grave mistake all those years ago. If Bryce really was the one for her, it wouldn't be this hard and he definitely wouldn't hurt her this much.

"I think we need to seriously think about our future," she stated firmly.

The wind outside howled against the side of the house bringing with it a brisk chill. It was a tense moment. His heart ached under her silent stare. "What is it you are suggesting?" he asked panic stricken.

"I don't know how much longer I can do this, Bryce. It's only a matter of time before we face the facts and talk about divorce."

He immediately jumped out of bed and grabbed her by the arms. "Do you love me?" he yelled. "Look me in the eyes and tell me you do. If you can't do it, then and only then will I believe you want a divorce."

He waited for a response and when she was unable to give him one he grabbed his pillow and blanket, slamming the door on the way out as the one small glimmer of hope left in his heart shriveled away.

They avoided one another as much as they could over the next few weeks, but Bryce ached to reach out to her. The pain coursing through him drove him insane. It killed him to go back and relive the night she didn't come home, but he was unable to stop the memories.

He'd been a fool to forget Valentine's Day. As the day wore on, he was filled with regret. And the more he thought about her, the more excited he was to rush home and wrap her in his arms and celebrate with her the right way. He'd made a stop at the grocery store, bought roses and candles, picked up her favorite fried chicken and rented "The Notebook". But as he opened the front door a longing, an emptiness, he hadn't felt before overwhelmed him. She wasn't home.

After reading her note, he walked over to Ms. Newcomb's, picked up the kids, helped Allie with her homework and sent everyone to bed as soon as he could so he could be alone. It was pure hell trying to concentrate on anything else than the fears surfacing within his heart. The unknowing of where she was and what she was doing petrified him. Unable to turn his mind off, he lay in bed staring at the ceiling allowing his imagination to run wild. It was Valentine's Day, and Cammi was an attractive woman, no, a beautiful woman alone, without her husband at a bar. He wondered if she had taken her wedding ring off. Cammi wasn't flirtatious, but that wasn't going to stop the male predators. What if someone hit on her? How would she respond to it? Was she kissing another man or telling her woes of marriage to a sensitive, caring ear. He tried to shake the image out of his mind, but the impulse to hurt something or someone was overwhelming.

The nervous tension mounting in him over the next seven hours turned to rage the moment he heard the van turn into the driveway. Thank God Carissa had sense enough to text him earlier to let him know Cammi was safe and with her, otherwise he would have called the police. Carissa was a bit peculiar, but one thing he knew was she respected her sister's marriage to him.

Regardless of his wrong doing, it gave Cammi no right to behave like an irresponsible teenager. To make him worry was thoughtless, inconsiderate and downright hateful. And the terrible things she said to him that night, was she being honest or just trying to put the fear of God into him? He felt like she was on a constant look out for him to screw up and whenever he did, it gave her the right to threaten their future. What sort of future would that be if she is going to hold every mistake over his head?

Didn't she realize he was hurting too? When was she going to comprehend the exact same things she wanted from him, he wanted from her? He loved her with all of his heart and soul but being around her anymore made him feel like less of a person. He saw himself through her eyes, and what he saw was a wretched, horrible human being. All he wanted was for her to listen, to sympathize.... but she couldn't. At least not without making him feel bad. The wise advice he once admired turned to criticism and her unshakable faith, into a phobia of life.

The man he wanted to be *was* more affectionate, more loving, and more attentive. He wished the desire was still there. He didn't want to leave her and couldn't imagine his life without her, but he felt cold. Neither one could accept the other or the changes that had taken place. Instead of time bringing them closer together, it continued to form a wedge. They learned to accommodate each other but where was the devotion they longed for? With the time and energy they wasted on fighting Cynthia and fighting each other, there was nothing left over to nurture their love.

Over the last year, Bryce became more aware his greatest fear in life was losing those he loved. During Cynthia's pregnancy with Allie his only concern was raising his daughter. He did what he had to do. No questions asked. He was young, fearless and thought he could conquer the world. Then he found Cammi. With her was a companionship he wasn't willing to live without. What was the old saying, "better to have love and lost, than to never love at all"? Bullshit.

What he shared with Cammi was irreplaceable. He would rather be buried alive than live without her. He had been terrified when Beth tried to come between them. There were empty corridors in Cammi's heart, and he wanted to be the man to fill them. Her boundaries were hard to break through and the first time they made love, he committed himself to her, body and soul, but in the days that followed Beth showing up unannounced, he felt completely powerless. A future with the woman of his dreams teetered on the edge with hope being the only thing keeping him going.

In the minutes, hours and days Cammi made herself unavailable, he lost a part of himself. The part that believed he could fix anything and make her happy. The part that believed whatever crossed his path, he would be strong and steadfast, and nothing would break him down. But the idea of losing her broke him, bringing him to the weakest point of his life.

It wasn't by accident they were brought back together, it was an act of fate and from that point forward, he became a believer in something more powerful than himself. That belief pushed him forward, kept him going when he thought about giving up.

Until now.

Something continued to mock him. The man was the provider, the hero, the stability and what he saw when he looked in the mirror was a failure. He wasn't man enough, and Cammi's lack of faith continued to confirm his doubts. Once again, fate held the cards, and he had the undeniable feeling his life would crumble if his wife walked away from him.

"Do you ever not feel good enough?" Cammi asked as she shoved a forkful of shrimp salad into her mouth.

It was a calm, brisk day as she sat inside her favorite sandwich shop with Jamie. The iridescent clouds pulsated above, threatening to give the sun more room. Spring came unusually early, a blessing for Cammi. Along with her already depressed state, she was getting the winter blahs. She missed her friend and in a desperate attempt to get out of the house, she suggested lunch. It had been ages since they had a chance to catch up. Jamie normally only took an hour off from her job at the counseling center, but after a few minutes of lighthearted conversation, she decided to take the rest of the afternoon. Her friend was in obvious need of cheering up.

Cammi grimaced when she saw the stunned look on her friends face. "Part of my healing process," she admitted. "Being honest and vulnerable to myself and those I am closest to."

"How *is* therapy going?" Jamie inquired lightheartedly. She was the one who recommended Gloria to Cammi when she mentioned marriage counseling might be good for her and Bryce, but was taken aback when Cammi went by herself for the first visit.

"I haven't gone again," she admitted. "We mostly talked about the kids. I don't know. I think Bryce is the one who needs it more than I do, and of course, he found an excuse to get out of it while I show up by myself looking like a complete ass."

Jamie sat quietly waiting as Cammi took a few more bites.

"All I want is someone to tell me what I am doing with my life is the right thing, that I am making a difference. I barely work. I'm not successful. I don't provide for my family. If Bryce and I got divorced, I would have to work full time, but since we are together, I don't. I rely on him so I can stay home and depend on him to support me. I feel no better than Cynthia. Worst part is I constantly compare myself to her and to others like her."

Tears rolled down her cheeks. "I want her to be ugly and fat. I want a better body," she cried, "but I don't even have that anymore because I gained so much weight when I stopped walking.

I want her face to break out with acne, her hair to fall out and her teeth to rot. But mostly I want everyone else to think she is horrible and realize how much better I am."

A slow smile spread across Jamie's face. "Ah ha, the real Cammi. Finally! I have been wondering when you were going to crack, when you were going to allow yourself to be human."

Cammi shook her head. She was so ashamed. "I don't like those thoughts and beat myself up about them. *Crap*, if I think I'm so horrid, I can only imagine what others perceive. I'm fat, I'm lazy, *and* I'm crazy," she broke down. "Living with me is pure torture. Why should my husband feel any different?"

"You aren't fat, and you aren't lazy….. maybe a little crazy at times," Jamie tried to joke. But her humor only brought on more tears.

Barely taking a breath, Cammi continued. "I compare myself to you." Looking up, her eyes shimmering, she expected to see her friends face full of anger and disgust, instead, she found a familiar look of anguish and understanding. "I have cut all my friends out of my life because I am too embarrassed to let any of them in. You're the only one I trust not to judge me."

"You have always been a private person, Cammi. But it took hitting rock bottom after you left Marcus for you to seek other's help. Look at me," she said when Cammi's eyes drifted back down to her lap. "You haven't told me anything I don't hear from the women I work with on a daily basis. Or anything I haven't felt myself. We all spend so much time comparing our differences. We pick each other apart to feel better, when if we all got real, we would find out we are so much alike it's sickening. We have the same fears, the same insecurities, and we all want the same things."

She motioned for the waiter and pointed at her empty glass before continuing.

"Cammi," she said softly. "Success is not measured by how much you make or how beautiful you are. You know that. Success is measured by how many lives you impact. It's what you teach the people you love. Take a long, hard look at yourself. What you are doing for your family and those you love is more important than a paycheck. You're changing lives. Because of you, your kids are going to make a difference in this world. Don't you see that? You're a survivor, one of the most loving, kind, and impressionable people I have ever had the pleasure of knowing. You are who you are because that is who God wants you to be. It is part of his plan. You need to trust it."

The tears fell harder, and it was a few more minutes before Cammi was able to find her voice. "To tell yourself that is one thing, but believing it is another."

"Well, damn it, start!" Leaning back in her chair Jamie took a deep breath. "It's important to share how you feel, don't keep it to yourself. You drown when you do that, Cammi, you should know that by now. It's the same thing you tell Allie," she scolded.

"You are such a good friend. You have done so much for my family and I don't feel like I have returned it. I have been so caught up in my own selfish drama," Cammi cried dabbing her eyes with the corner of her napkin. "And I'm ashamed of my behavior."

A tear escaped from Jamie's eye and rolled down her cheek. "Stop it, do you hear me? And the answer to your question is, yes. I don't always feel good enough, I don't always know what I am doing and yes, I compare myself to *you* all the time. You may not be able to buy me extravagant gifts or take me on fabulous trips," she said with a wave of her hand and a hint of a smile, "but what you have given me emotionally over the years is more than I could have ever asked for. More than I sometimes deserve. You are my rock, you have accepted me when others shunned my strong personality, and you have given me total honesty and love. I envy your stability and calm, rational personality. I am so erratic and wild. I annoy people before they take the time to get to know the real me." She laughed sadly. "And everybody does things they're ashamed of. It's part of being human. Stop being so hard on yourself."

Cammi was stunned. "But you show the world who you really are. You don't hide behind a façade of who you think people want you to be. That's why I love you. You are true to yourself, confident. I want more of that."

"You portray just as much confidence. Other people see you as the woman who has it all together," she said picking at her sandwich. "We all have our own insecurities and issues. It's important to remember that." She held her finger up. "A quote I heard once upon a time. '*Fair as the exterior may be, if you go in, you will find bare places, heaps of rubbish that can never be taken away, cold hearths, desolate attics, and windows veiled with cobwebs.*' No one is immune to it. You just learn over time to sweep the cobwebs away and fill the cold hearths with the warmth of love."

Cammi laid down her debit card to pay for lunch. "You inspire me."

"Remember college? You were a deep thinker, passionate, vibrant and even though you carried it around humbly, you still intimidated those who weren't brave enough to approach you," Jamie reminded her. "Luckily, I was brave enough to hand you a beer and we spent the rest of the night doing upside down margaritas until we puked. Your friendship, besides my family is the most important thing in my life, it helped shape me into who I am today. I should be thanking you."

More tears clouded her eyes. "We need to do this more often you know. Thanks. Seriously! Thanks for everything, especially for believing in me."

"Well, somebody has got to," Jamie replied dabbing the corners of her eyes as she stood up. Letting out a groan, she rubbed her belly. "Come on. Let's get out of here for some shopping before I rip open the front of my pants from my "food baby"."

Chapter Thirty

Heather caught up with Jake and Allie as they emerged from their last classes of the day. Allie was laughing and felt better than she had forever. Opening up to her dad was about the best thing she had ever done. They were spending more time together, and it was nice to have her parents as a sounding board when Cynthia made her mad. In fact, she couldn't remember the last time they had been this close. Most evenings after her homework was done and Faith and Bailey were tucked into bed, she would sit on the corner of her parent's bed, the cats curled in her lap as she told them about her day. She wasn't keeping anymore secrets.

"Christian dumped Brandi," Heather announced shoving her books into her locker.

Allie rolled her eyes shutting the door quietly. "Are you surprised?"

"Well, no, but she is having a really hard time. She just ran into the bathroom crying. I think you should go talk to her."

Jake laughed. "She hasn't had anything to do with Allie in months, but the minute her boyfriend dumps her, she expects her to be the consoling friend? I don't think so."

Allie turned and gave Jake a surprised glance. It wasn't unusual for him to defend her when they were alone, but this shocked her. It did Heather, too.

"Since when do you make Allie's decisions for her, Jake?" Heather asked slamming her locker door clearly annoyed.

"I'm.....I'm sorry," he stammered feeling foolish.

"No, he's right, Heather. Brandi has treated me badly ever since she hooked up with Christian. She made fun of me, put me down and ditched both of us. I feel bad for her, but she wasn't willing to listen to the truth. Christian has been playing her all this time and you know it."

Heather shrugged her shoulders. "Well, I am going to go check on her. She needs a friend right now. If you were any kind of friend, you would too."

"Tell you what, I will give her a call later to tell her I am sorry and see if she needs anything, but I'm not going to be her silly little pawn, because I guarantee you, when she finds another guy, she is going to kick you to the curb again."

"Whatever!" Heather said heading towards the bathroom in search of Brandi.

Allie sighed. "I adore her, but she seems desperate to have Brandi like her. It's only a matter of time before she gets burned again. Guess she has to learn the hard way."

Jake was suddenly quiet as they headed out of the school to walk home. They were inseparable now that her parents knew about their friendship and even arranged their semester schedule so they could have lunch together. Because of it they had to endure constant remarks and teasing, but they were both immune to it by now.

"Well aren't you in a foul mood?" Allie said noticing the scowl on his face as they stopped at the crosswalk.

"Don't you think you should take your own advice?"

"What do you mean?" she asked zipping up her jacket as she shivered from the cold.

"With Cynthia. You are just as desperate to keep her in your life and win her approval, but keep getting burned. I mean last week when you called, I wasn't surprised to hear she left you alone so she could go out with her boyfriend. That was supposed to be your time with her, but she didn't care. She asked you to come over and then ditches you to go out."

Allie got defensive. "This guy makes her happy, Jake, it was nice to see her actually smiling for once instead of crying, what good would it do to be mad at her?"

"I thought she wasn't going to date anymore?"

Annoyed, she pushed her blonde hair behind her ear. "She was going to take some time for herself, but then met…uh what's his name, Marcus, yeah that's it. You remember…. he was at my birthday party.

"Great! Another winner."

"You can't always plan these things, you know."

"There is no one in the world that can make Cynthia happy and you know that. She can't even make herself happy. You keep convincing yourself things are going to get better, but it's not. Nothing with her is going to change. And I'm tired of seeing you get walked on," he admitted harshly. Who cared if she got mad at him? He was sick of the drama, sick of seeing her hurt.

"Why are you mad at me?" she asked surprised by the tone of his voice.

"I'm not mad at you! I am just sick of her and what she does. You are my best friend and it kills me you don't open your eyes. Cynthia uses and manipulates you. She makes you feel guilty all the time, like because she gave birth to you and decided to come back into your life, you are obligated to be her friend, to love her. But she doesn't respect you. Does she even know anything about you? Does she know what classes you take or who your friends are? Has she come to see you dance or any of your one act plays? Does she even care about what's important to you or does she just insist you listen and care about her? Relationships are a two way street, you know. Its give and take and it seems she does a lot of taking, but not much giving. Anything that doesn't cost money, anyway," he added. "I'm tired of hearing you make excuses for her."

"What do you expect me to do, just cut her out of my life? She is my mom. I can't do that. Yes, she stresses me out. Yes, there are times I hate her, but I can't abandon her, she doesn't have anyone else."

"So what? That's not your problem. She made this life, not you. It's not your job to make her happy or make her feel good. It is her job to give those things to you. You are the daughter, remember?"

"I don't need another father, Jake. One is plenty." The tone of her voice told him he had pushed too far.

The sky had grown dark by the time they reached her house. Casually he laid his hand on her shoulder for comfort.

"Your mom only wants people in her life when it is convenient for her, when she gets something out of it. Can't you see she does the same thing to you?"

"She does not," Allie yelled shaking his arm off. "How dare you say that? She loves me, she may not know how to show it the way your parents do, but she *does* love me and nothing is going to make her leave me or push me out of her life."

"Allie, I'm sorry, but I think you're wrong. When a better opportunity comes along, I think she will be gone, it just hasn't happened yet." He hated being so brutally honest, but somebody needed to make her see the truth.

"You're wrong! She would never do that. She moved here to be with me, to help raise me. I know she does things wrong, but she would never hurt me like that."

Spinning on her heel, Allie turned and ran to her house. Once inside, she slammed the door shut and slid down the back of it, her books cradled tightly to her chest, sobbing.

She was going to prove everybody wrong. Allie was going to make them see she was the one person Cynthia wouldn't hurt, the one person that mattered in her life.

But as everyone predicted, Cynthia was already making her eat her own words.

Her mom and dad took the kids to see the new Shrek movie, but Allie wasn't in the mood to go. Instead she turned the radio on and stared at the ceiling listening to sappy, love songs. It was nice to have the entire house to herself. It gave her the freedom to do and act as she pleased without the scrutiny of her parents.

When she was little, before her dad met Cammi, she would lie on her bed, close her eyes and day dream about her mother. She would imagine her crawling in beside her and gently pressing her lips to her forehead as she fell asleep. She would tell her how special she was, and there would always be fresh baked cookies when she came home from school. She remembered thinking her mother was the most beautiful woman it the world. And when she was sick, her mom would make a special tea to give her and fix chicken noodle soup for lunch while they read book after book together until she felt better.

Now years later, when she compared Cammi to Cynthia, she had to admit what Cammi brought into her life was exactly what she fantasized about as a child. The truth that Cynthia would never be that woman and never wanted to be that woman shook Allie's entire body.

Later that night as she was getting ready for bed Jake called.

"I'm sorry, I didn't mean to upset you," he said quietly.

"I know." Allie had enough time to calm down and think. Jake was right, she knew it in her heart, but she wasn't willing to do anything about it, and he was going to have to understand that.

"Do you want to talk?"

"Not really, don't worry about it, okay?"

It was hard for him not to worry. He was head over heels in love with her and wanted to protect her, to make her happy. If he loved Allie, he needed to support her and allow her to make her own choices. He only hoped one day she would realize the type of man he was becoming and allow him to stand by her side through it all.

"Have you called Brandi?" he asked changing the subject.

"Oh, yeah," she laughed. "And let me tell you… she is a hysterical mess, you would think a family member just died by the way she is carrying on. Please! I tried to be as sympathetic as I could, but it was hard. I don't feel sorry for her. She made a dumb choice, now she has to deal with it."

"She's a stupid girl."

"She keeps saying she knows Christian really loves her and wants her back. She even has a plan to make him jealous by taking Thomas to the dance on Friday."

"Christian doesn't care who she shows up with or if she even shows up at all. She means nothing to him," Jake told her.

"She is so stupid when it comes to guys. Can you believe she thinks Christian wants to get married and settle down, plan a life with her, that he really *loves* her? Believe me, it's the last thing on his mind."

Jake didn't know how to respond. He knew he was different than other guys. While they were spending their time trying to get down the pants of a different girl every week, Jake was spending his time falling in love with his best friend. Granted he wasn't ready for marriage or a life together, but he was mature enough at his age to know exactly what type of girl he was looking for. And Allie was it.

"Are you there?" Allie asked. He had become so quiet.

"Yeah…. sorry. Are you going to the dance with someone on Friday?" he asked.

Every once in a while Allie would tell him about her latest crush. It killed him to hear it. But at the same time, he felt the need to know, to be prepared when she did find a boyfriend. Sometimes she and Heather would go to the movies with a group of friends, including guys but there was never anyone serious. Allie was very cautious and most of the guys who asked her out were jerks according to Jake. But he kept his opinions to himself and it was his good fortune she hadn't found anyone special. She seemed to be completely content hanging out with him.

"*Right*! My dad won't let me. Not until I'm sixteen, remember? What about you? Did you ask Emily?"

She was so casual about it. It never seemed to bother her when they talked about girls. In fact, she was always trying to set him up with one of her friends and seemed genuinely disappointed when he wasn't interested. But he wished she would leave it alone.

"Nope, you want to go together?" he asked hoping even if it wasn't a real date, it would mean they could spend the evening together.

"Okay, my dad will let me go with you, it's harmless."

It was like a kick in the stomach every time she reminded him what she felt was brotherly affection. Someday, he told himself, she would look at him differently.

Bryce stopped at the grocery store on his way home to pick up spaghetti sauce for Cammi when he bumped into Beth at the checkout isle. His first instinct was to avoid eye contact, but something made him stay where he was. She looked different. Good. She was dressed in a black business suit, tailored to fit her perfectly and her hair was long enough to be pulled back in a tight bun. The usual heavy make-up had been replaced with a softer, sophisticated look. He was pleasantly surprised, but even more surprised when she'd spoke to him. He knew the old Beth would have hid her head from embarrassment, but she didn't seem like that girl anymore.

In the a few brief moments of conversation he had with her, Beth told Bryce she'd been diagnosed with cancer a while back. It scared her enough to turn her life around and she'd even found a wonderful man to share it with. She said she'd been cancer free for only six months but felt better than ever. Then her next words shocked him.

"Look, Bryce, I owe you an apology. Cammi too. I was a mess. I should have never meddled and I am so embarrassed by…."

Bryce held up his hand. "It was a long time ago, Beth. Things happen, people change."

A grateful smile crossed her face. "I ended my friendship with Cynthia, too."

"Good, she is the last thing anyone needs in their life," he admitted scornfully. "Look, I better get this home….um….I'm happy things changed, Beth. Take care."

It was odd, seeing her again. Though it was only for a few minutes, Bryce could tell the change was for the better. He had enough anger in his heart. It was a relief to know didn't need to continue holding a grudge against her, too.

He didn't mention to Cammi he had seen Beth. He figured it was for the best if he wanted to keep his wife happy. But as luck would have it, a few days later, Beth's name showed up on his caller ID at work. The first time he ignored it. The second, third, and fourth time, he began to panic. Why was she being so persistent and what the hell did she want? Finally after the fifth call, she left a message.

"Bryce, please, if you get a chance call me back. It's important."

A chill of fright ran through him. This could stir up garbage that had been buried for years, garbage that could ruin the marriage that was teetering on the brink of collapsing already, and he didn't have the strength to deal with the repercussions.

Bryce was finishing up at work later the following week when there was a small knock on the door. Without looking up from the paperwork on his desk, he could sense the presence of a female figure standing apprehensively by the door. Figuring it was Sharon from accounting, he asked her to come in. When silence greeted him, he sat back in his chair, looked up and saw Beth. His gut clenched tightly and waves of nausea rolled through him as she carefully shut the door behind her.

"You were ignoring me," she accused her eyes filled with worry.

The words were caught in his throat. Should he apologize or simply explain he didn't want anything to do with her.

As if she already knew the reasoning behind it, she got straight to the point.

"I'm here about Cynthia. There are things I need to tell you, things I should have told you from the beginning, but I was too chicken. Seeing you the other night was a sign. I knew it was time. Can you spare me ten minutes?"

"Sure," he shrugged, relaxing ever so slightly. He was curious as to what Beth could possibly tell him that he didn't already know.

"Cynthia trusted me, confided in me. I have given it some thought and figured it is only right I tell you so you can do what it takes to get her out of Allie's life. She's a nightmare, Bryce."

This isn't what he had expected.

"Connor convinced me to call you. My boyfriend," she explained breaking the tension. "He's downstairs in the waiting room. He thought it best if I meet with you by myself, but if you like, I can text him and have him come up."

"If you would feel more comfortable, go ahead."

Bryce saw her sigh with relief as she pushed the buttons of her cell phone. "He's on his way. I need to apologize that I didn't come to you earlier, but considering our past, I was a little nervous."

Bryce had to admit that Beth, assuming she'd just left work, looked self-assured in her business suit, and she had a more youthful, healthier appearance. It took only a few minutes for Connor to find his way back to the office. He was a few inches taller than Bryce but had a stockier build. His curly auburn hair had touches of gray dusting it, and he wore a Harvard sweatshirt with a pair of jeans and tennis shoes. With his clean, close shave and trimmed hair, Bryce guessed he was a professional of some sort.

Standing up, Bryce shook his hand and motioned for him to sit in the chair next to Beth. His head was pounding and his nerves were shot. All he wanted was to get this over with so he could go home to his family.

"Cynthia and I met one night right after she moved back to town. We became instant friends. You know the saying, 'misery loves company', and well, that is what we were, two miserable women who became friends. Of course, when she told me how she was connected to you, I was even more enticed." A look of embarrassment crossed her face as she said it. "To make a long story short, our life-style was fast and hard. Whether it was men, drugs, alcohol or sex, we had it all. Unfortunately, Allie was with us some of the time. I was so messed up I didn't see how bad it was for her."

Tears began to fall down her cheeks as she continued. "Allie had to see and hear a lot. Things she shouldn't have. She was put in situations she should have never been in. I'm so sorry," she choked.

Connor rubbed her back as she attempted to regain her composure. Obviously her past was something he had already dealt with. His encouragement prompted her to continue.

"Almost two years ago, I was diagnosed with Non-Hodgkin's Lymphoma. It shook me up pretty good. I realized then I didn't want to die; in fact, I realized I wanted more out of life. It didn't happen over night; I was still hanging out with Cynthia, but with my surgery and treatments, I wasn't drinking or doing drugs anymore. It was a hard life to let go of, but slowly I started seeing the benefits. I put myself into therapy and starting taking court-reporting classes in Denver all while I was fighting the disease. Ironically my new outlook on life gave me the desire to do it all. And that is how I met Connor," she smiled looking at him with adoration, explaining he was a defense attorney for the State of Colorado.

"Sorry," she said apologizing for her distraction. "Anyway, Connor and I started out as friends and weren't dating yet when Cynthia called to see if I wanted to go to Denver with her. The guy she was dating lived there. I shouldn't have been surprised to see Allie with her. I knew it would be a wild night and by that time, I had come to my senses enough to know having Allie with us wasn't right anymore. I tried talking Cynthia out of it, but she wouldn't hear of it. Her idea of parenting is pretty skewed. She doesn't want a daughter; she wants someone she can party with, a girlfriend, not someone to take care of. Anyway, she and I got into a big fight later that night, and I haven't talked to her since. It was the best decision I ever made. She was the last and final thing I needed to get rid of."

Beth took a deep breath before she continued. "Forgive me if it seems like I am rambling on about my relationship with Cynthia, but I want you to know the history behind it, otherwise, you might mistake my intentions."

She then told him all that Allie had been exposed to under Cynthia's care. Bryce thought he might suffocate if he heard another word. Allie's description was nothing compared to what Beth was telling him now.

"It's okay," he choked out not wanting to appear surprised or caught off guard. "But I'm already aware of Cynthia's lifestyle. It's a matter of figuring out how to deal with it and help Allie cope." Bile crept up his throat threatening to explode.

"I wasn't sure what Allie may have told you, but you and Cammi should be proud. She made good choices when Cynthia wasn't." Sighing, she looked to Connor for moral support. "I felt horrible, like I was abandoning her that night, and I have carried the guilt since....so, I thought I might be some help in telling you the actual truth in case you ever need to take legal action."

Bryce rubbed his hands over his face in aggravation.

"We've talked to our lawyer and know our rights. To be honest with you, we aren't going to pursue anything right now. Believe me, we have spent hours and lost many nights of sleep trying to figure out the best approach. Frankly, we would love to have Cynthia out of our lives, but it's not what Allie wants. If we force the issue, we could wind up pushing her away from us and closer to her mom. As hard as it is, we have to stand back and allow her to make this decision. If she were younger, it would be different, but she's a teenager. We hate watching her get hurt, but no matter what we do, it's eventually going to happen. Allie is no idiot, she sees what is going on, and in time, we hope Cynthia will dig herself a hole she can't get out of."

Revealing such intimate details of his family to Beth was not easy, but he could see honest compassion in her eyes.

"I think it might happen sooner than you think. Cynthia's biggest goal in life is to marry a man with money, get the life she deserves and get out of town. When she moved here, she had no intention of staying, the fact she had been here so long is just a fluke. She'd been running from creditors for years and since this town is made of money, she figured it wouldn't take long to find some fool to hook up with. I think her luck is starting to run out."

Bryce leaned forward in his chair and looked Beth intently in the eye. "She could have gone anywhere, so tell me Beth, exactly why did Cynthia come back to Madison? What was her motive?"

"You," Beth announced directly. "She wanted you. Still does. Not because she loves you but because she feels scorned. She wants revenge. Her plan was to get Allie to fall in love with her and question her life with you, all the while planting false notions in Cammi's head so she would eventually leave you too," she admitted. "In her sick little fantasy, she could come to the rescue while you're on the rebound, and you three would be the perfect little family. Then when the time was right, she would find her "sugar daddy" and bolt from town leaving you writhing with pain the way she did when you took Allie from her."

Bryce's laughter was filled with malice. "Seriously? Beth, that's insane!"

"Well Bryce, you aren't exactly dealing with a sane person. She actually believes it's possible and when we were friends, she was convinced the problems between you and Cammi were only beginning. This isn't about Allie, never has been, it's about her sick, twisted payback. She loves Allie in her own selfish way, but never wanted to be a mother, it is a burden on her lifestyle. Oh, she *has* become attached to Allie, and the girl adores her which makes her feel good, wanted, special, but she manipulates it so she can manipulate you. Allie doesn't have a clue."

"Her hate for you, Bryce, runs deep, and she would love nothing more than to see you ruined. She blames you for everything that has gone wrong in her life. But she's getting restless. It's unlike her to stay in one place too long, so don't be surprised if she just up and leaves one day forgoing her vendetta against you. But it will devastate Allie." She stared down at her hands, taking a long pause.

Bryce dug his fingers into his leg. He couldn't believe what he was hearing, but it had to be true. It made sense and besides, what did Beth have to gain? Nothing. She was only looking out for his family's interests. God, it was like he was spending his life fighting a no-win battle against Cynthia and now this. Would it ever end?

His throat tightened as he thought about the pain and anguish his wife and daughter have already had to deal with at the hands of this woman. How much more was he going to allow? But what were his options? All he had was the confession of someone she used to run around with, someone who had wanted to hurt his wife just as much years before. And as grateful as he was for her honesty now, it didn't give him much to stand on if he was to rip Cynthia out of their lives.

"You need to know.... Allie is a great kid and has a good head on her shoulders. But she desperately wants her mother to love her unconditionally, and I'm afraid to say, it is never going to happen. Cynthia isn't capable of it. But she uses it to her advantage and I think Allie's wounds run pretty deep. I know how strong you and Cammi are and how deep your love runs. Don't let her win, whatever you do."

Stillness drifted in the air around them. Bryce noticed Beth fidget uncomfortably in her chair.

"When I worked with Allie in school, I formed a bond with her." She laughed. "As good of a bond as I could at that point in my life, but I always thought she was a great kid. You have done an amazing job raising her. Don't let Cynthia screw her up. Don't let her screw you guys up either."

There was sincerity in her voice. Bryce looked from her to Connor who was holding her hand tightly and protectively. And from the depths of his core, he wanted nothing more than to have Cammi next to him so he could protect her from anymore pain.

On the way to the restaurant, Cammi's stony silence unnerved him. He'd gone home in haste and begged Allie to stay with the younger two kids so he could take Cammi to dinner then rushed his confused wife out the door. He was going to burst at the seams if he wasn't honest with her. He had no way of knowing how she would react and fear was driving him to the brink of insanity. First and foremost, she was going to flip out that Beth had come to see him at work and then he was going to have to explain why. It would be two stunning blows at once and he was certain she would lash out at him.

He studied her and wanted so badly to reach out and hold her hand, but resisted. She looked beautiful even with lines of concern etched on her delicate features, and he felt the twinge of guilt deep in his soul. He would give anything to change the past and the pain she endured because of his mistakes.

The pub was located close to downtown. With its log cabin interior, it was a popular attraction for locals as well as wealthy tourists who came to town. Bryce asked the hostess for a secluded table in the back. He wanted privacy.

Cammi was confused. Bryce came home in a rush, told her, no, demanded they were going to dinner, even though she had a pot roast in the oven, and was more nervous than she ever remembered seeing him. And now, they'd only been at the restaurant for fifteen minutes, and he'd already downed two beers.

They chatted uncomfortably about their day, Cammi reluctantly discussing her new article and minute details of Faith and Bailey's gymnastics class, while Bryce asked questions in a desperate attempt to stall what they really needed to talk about.

Finally Cammi had enough.

"What did you bring me here for? To hear about my day? We could have done this at home, Bryce. Something's up."

When the waitress stopped by the table to remove their dinner plates, Bryce ordered another beer. "You want one?"

Disgusted, Cammi shook her head, no.

He avoided her eyes until he was able to take a sip from the fresh cold mug placed in front of him. Then he began to talk. As best he could, being very careful not to miss anything, he relayed the information he received from Beth. While he talked, he watched as Cammi's face turned from anger, to resentment, and then to disbelief. But she said nothing, only listened. When he finished, he ordered another beer.

They sat quietly, afraid to break the silence, both petrified of the unspoken words. Cammi's eyes were riveted on the table while Bryce drank himself into numbness.

Finally, he spoke up. "Cammi, you have to say something."

"What can I say?" she whispered. "This is it, now we know what we have been up against. I….I ….shit! I don't even know what to think. I just can't do this anymore," she cried putting her head into her hands.

Bryce wanted to comfort her but at the same time he wanted to run, far, far away. She wasn't yelling, had yet to start throwing things, but her tears, the anguish somehow seemed much, much worse and he was helpless to fix it.

"You say Beth has a boyfriend?"

" Yeah, Connor. He seems like a decent guy."

"Was that just a ploy to make you jealous?"

"Jesus, come off it Cammi. She was sincere. This has nothing to do with me."

"Are you sticking up for her?" she asked staring at him accusingly.

"I'm keeping my mouth shut, it doesn't matter what I say. You won't listen to reason."

Cammi didn't want to talk to him, didn't want to discuss what she was feeling. She wanted him to disappear for the moment. Ironically, it should be Cynthia she was angry with, but this news wasn't shocking and Cammi didn't feel anymore threatened than she had for the past four years. She'd drawn her own conclusions about the woman ages ago.

It'd been close to ten years, yet she still couldn't forgive Beth. Cammi didn't want Bryce to talk to her, look at her or even think about her. Bryce hated Cynthia so if she and Bryce did split up, she was Cammi's last concern. But Beth…..she'd changed. Become a better person, responsible, sharp and classy. Cammi was silently envious. Maybe she'd finally become the woman Bryce always wanted her to be.

After fifteen minutes of awkward silence, Bryce stood up to pay the bill. They were both distraught from the events of the evening and when she offered to drive home, an overly sensitive Bryce flew off the handle.

"I'm fine Cammi. I only had a few beers."

Fully aware she should keep her mouth shut but ignoring her instinct, the words flew out of her. "Five beers in two hours are hardly a few. Just let me drive, okay?" she begged.

He could hear the desperation in her voice but instead of being considerate, he got mad.

"Don't scold me, you aren't my mother. I'm not allowed to do anything else for fun in my life, so what if I want to enjoy a few beers on a night out?" he asked, resentment seething through his teeth.

"Can we just go home? I don't want to get into this anymore than you do." She turned toward the car.

Drawing his hand back, Bryce threw the keys at her and watched as they smacked her hand before landing in the snow. Her hand throbbed as a red welt blistered her skin. She stared at him in disbelief and slowly reached down to get the keys, not knowing how to react to his sudden outburst.

The silence in the car was deafening. Both were aware his drinking wasn't the real issue nor was her nagging. Before she was able to make a complete stop in the driveway, Bryce leapt out of his door and slammed it shut. Slowly and helplessly, Cammi climbed the stairs to the porch and followed him inside.

She found Bryce rummaging through the refrigerator looking for another beer. "What is your problem?" she asked.

When he finally pulled one out, he turned on her like a leopard waiting to pounce.

"You are my problem!" he snapped.

"Be quiet, you are going to wake the kids up," she hissed. "What's wrong with you? You're acting like a maniac."

He stared, almost as if he was looking through her instead of at her.

"You are my problem, didn't you hear me? I am tired of this, Cammi. Tired of listening to you complain about everything I say, everything I do, and everything I don't do. Am I ever going to be good enough for you? I respected you tonight, told you the truth, was honest about everything and look how you treat me! I'm not perfect, Cammi, stop trying to make me be!" he screamed, pointing his finger accusingly at her. "Why can't you accept me for who I am.....faults and all? I'm tired of being treated like shit whenever anything you don't like happens."

"Where is this coming from? You're being completely irrational," she whispered fighting to stay calm.

"Bullshit. You constantly nag me about who I am with, where I am going, when I am going to be home, why I don't touch you, why I ignore you, why I don't talk to you, why we don't go on dates, on and on and on. I can't take it anymore. I know the underlying issue right now is you think I am a drunk. It's written all over your face. You don't have to say it. I know what you are thinking before you do. I am sick of it, sick of this life and sick of our relationship."

In Cammi's eyes his words were a threat and the horror of them rendered her speechless. For a few brief minutes, she tried to imagine them away. But the pit in her stomach continued to burn.

"If that is how you feel, fine. Then be done," she finally challenged. "I certainly don't know why you stay married to me. Our relationship has faded away to almost nothing. If I am so annoying to you, be done. Let me go. Stop giving me false hope that things are going to get better when you have no desire to work on them. You show me every day you don't care about me and this family is not your priority anymore."

Bryce slammed his hand down on the kitchen table. The force of it made Cammi jump.

"Shut up! Just shut your mouth." He turned his back to her and took a few deep breaths to steady himself before he said or did something he would regret. He needed to control his anger. When he turned around her eyes dared him to challenge her, but underneath, he could see her fear. His chest began to ache.

"Whatever it is I do, I always think of you and the kids first. I may not express it the way you want me to, but it is how I feel," he said quietly. "I have given up so much to prove my love to you and still...you refuse to see it. What do I have to do to get you to open your eyes?"

"Me? Open my eyes? I think you need to take a deep look at yourself before you start throwing stones."

Feeling weak and dead to the world, he watched her leave the room. For a few moments he sat stunned until he finally broke down. He was on a downward spiral into despair feeling as if every ounce of his being had died. He wanted to intimidate, frighten her into seeing what she was doing. But shaking her up would be a childish game. And in their marriage, they didn't play games. Or did they? Hadn't it been a game on Valentine's Day?

He shook the thought away. Regardless, it didn't matter. He wasn't going to stoop that low. So what *would* it take to make her to see she was breaking his heart?

Chapter Thirty-One

Her gaze drifted to her children from behind the sunglasses she had become accustomed to wearing to hide the dark circles and blood shot eyes. Cammi wasn't a drunk or a drug addict, though she certainly looked and felt it some days. Nope, just a sleep deprived, stressed out wife and mother who lived on tears and drama, wondering what a simple, uncomplicated life would be like.

The ground was covered with a coat of fresh snow and the children, bored of being cooped up inside on such a beautiful day, convinced her to take them out. They played. She sat. Her interaction with them was the bare minimum. It'd been like this for months now, which was so unlike her since she prided herself on being an interactive parent.

Cammi was more discouraged than ever as images of her husband with Beth haunted her dreams night after night. It was a rare occasion anymore when she didn't toss and turn until the cold, clammy sweat of her fears forced her awake. Then upon waking, she was left alone with visions keeping her up for hours. The fights with her husband had stopped and instead were replaced with a thick silence hanging over everyone in the house

She tried shifting her focus toward her children lost in their own world of make-believe, oblivious to the turmoil boiling inside of her. Was it guilt she was experiencing or just plain resentment? Either way, the pain caused her to emotionally flee from everyone, everything, her husband, her friends and worst of all, her children. And not one of them deserved it.

As much as she wanted to enjoy the peals of laughter erupting from the mouths of her babies, they would always be her babies no matter how old they were, she had grown accustomed to tuning it out, focusing instead on her own unhappiness and the ache within her heart.

Sitting with her knees pulled to her chest, her arms wrapped tightly around them to shield the wind whipping through the air, she gazed up at the faint blue sky, fully aware of the enjoyment she was missing out on. But somewhere along the way, she stopped caring.

Once upon a time, prayer had helped, but even the energy for that was lost on her and simply seemed a waste of time. She'd needed God more in the past few years than she ever had before but he'd stopped listening. She hadn't had the strength or perseverance and felt completely disconnected from the source that had brought her so much happiness. Anyway, how could God possible love her now? Look at who she was.....how she acted. There was nothing but ugliness inside her.

Why couldn't she find the happiness she once dreamt of? The happiness she'd held in the palm of her hand only a few years ago. She didn't have a bad life, in fact, compared to what others faced each morning upon waking up, she considered herself lucky. Her health was great, her children were the best thing to happen to her, and her husband, well he was a good man and *today* she loved him more than she imagined possible. But what about tomorrow? Would she love him tomorrow or would hate penetrate her heart and words like they always did when she felt jaded?

Why the hell hadn't someone prepared her for this? *Marriage and family hard? Yeah, no shit!* But hard enough to rip out the very core of a person's soul. No one said anything about that. No one told her one day the love would be so intense, so powerful, then the next, the person you devoted your life to, the one who was to complete the void in a way no one else could, was the target of rage and hostility.

No one explained the neediness and heartache that was the co-companion to love. No one thought to mention the conflict, defiance, and lack of control that came along with finding your 'soul mate'. How could a person feel such dislike, verging on the point of disgust when the target of their affection said something negative, and then within hours feel the need to wrap up in their arms, desperate for love and forgiveness, all the while risking rejection.

No one said this up and down emotional roller coaster would continue for years as lives meshed, lives fell apart, and disappointment echoed in the memories of betrayal.

But most of all, no one pointed out how temperamental, insane, and emotionally mad it made a person.

Years of hard work, years of thinking she was above this, better than this, was a wasted effort. Why couldn't she get her shit together? Everyone around her thought she was a saint putting up with all she did, why didn't she see it? Sorrow had taught her to put on a good show, while inside, her soul deteriorated.

And yes, even she had a few hopeless moments when she thought she might actually go crazy, but holding on to her pride, she aspired *never* to become like Cynthia, n*ever* to allow her actions to parallel those of her nemesis. That's what kept her going. She *was* better than that and she would prove it.

Tears filled her eyes as she watched Faith and Bailey throw snowballs back and forth, neither one powerful enough to reach the other with their attempts. But they were happy, weren't they? Would they look back on this time with their mother and remember the good, or would they be filled with memories of her as bitter, depressed and *unavailable* to them? Is this what she wanted to teach them?

How she longed to keep them little forever. If she could turn back the clock, then maybe she could get another chance. She couldn't change the mistakes she had made or get back what time she had already lost, but maybe if things played out differently, she wouldn't feel like she was missing out on their life, on her life.

Tears spilled over, instantly drying on her cheeks from the breeze of the cold air. There was so much she wanted yet it all seemed hopelessly out of reach. Standing up, she took a deep breath and gently rubbed the chill out of her arms. This is what she got, so she might as well get used to it. It was time to be rational. She definitely wasn't like any of the other women who were capable of handling the instability life threw their way. This was now, and this was it. She could get lost as the current swept her away, or she could hold her head high and deal with it before the person she'd learned to love most was lost to her forever.

In a desperate attempt, she thought it wouldn't hurt to try one last prayer.

Something has to change, Lord. I'm tired. Show me. If you want me to continue down this road, give me a sign, if not, I need something drastic to happen. I can't live like this anymore. Please! I need a sign.

Cammi wondered if her prayers fell on deaf ears.

"What are you going to do?"

They were at Jamie's for a play date later that day. While the four kids were upstairs tearing apart the toy room, she and Cammi were sipping on hot tea and Cammi was silently thinking how grateful she was that Jamie was still her sounding board. She had just finished filling her in on the details of the fight she and Bryce had the previous evening.

"I don't know what I can do. I love him, I know I do, but emotionally, I am numb. I'm tired of fighting. It came to me last night lying in bed. I've had this horrible fear for years now that Bryce was going to someday figure out he made a mistake, that there was somebody smarter or prettier, someone who would treat him better. When he told me about Beth, it hit me. I felt like my worst nightmare was coming true. She's straightened out her life and turned into the type of woman he should be with. The entire evening, I wanted to get as far away as I could before I wound up hurt all over again. It's the same with Allie. I can't stand that she might love Cynthia more than me. I am so scared of rejection I live in fear of the unknown. It's turned me into a control freak. Tell me how to fix it?"

"Do you really want the answer to that?"

"Something's got to change. But I want him to take responsibility for the things he has done, too. This isn't only me."

Cammi felt a chill shoot through her as she took a sip of her tea and pulled her sweater tight around her. After two beautiful spring-like weeks, the weather had turned frigid again. The report was calling for a big storm to hit. She didn't know if it was the change in weather or the fact she hadn't been feeling well making her shiver. Regardless, she needed to start taking better care of herself. She still hadn't gained back her appetite and living on crackers and tea wasn't cutting it anymore. Her clothes hung on her and when she looked in the mirror her cheek bones protruded revealing hollow eyes.

"He is a man Cammi, remember? Most aren't nurturing or sensitive. There is something going on inside of him that he wants you to see, but is unable to express. When he tries, he hears condemnation. Don't get me wrong, I am not saying this is your fault. Just understand it's even harder for him to be hurt or scared. There has been so much of it lately and all he knows how to show is anger."

Cammi thought it over. "I wish I knew if he was hurting. When we argue and he gets mad, all I want to do is hurt him back. If I do, then maybe he will eventually understand what I am feeling. It's a vicious cycle, and I don't know how to end it."

"Stop trying to find the answers all the time. Just let things be. Treat him how you want to be treated. Isn't that the first thing our parents taught us, but the first thing we forget in our most important relationships? You both need to stop trying to convince the other you are right. The power struggle is getting old. Do you want to be right or do you want to be happy? I heard that on Dr. Phil, isn't it great?" she laughed heartily.

Cammi forced a smile while misery manifested itself in her heart. How did she begin to replace it with something else? It seemed so simple, yet the thought of it exhausted her.

"I feel like we don't have much left to cling to. And with Beth, all I do is wonder if he thinks about her, if he remembers how it used to be for them."

"Stop it! You are torturing yourself. He doesn't deserve to have you quit on him, so stop setting him up for failure," she said with a sympathetic smile. "Stop using her as the excuse. He loves you, not her. He chose you. Stop giving him a reason to go to her."

Cammi laughed. "I know, I know. My mind plays tricks on me. One day I want to leave and then my heart talks me into staying. If I'm supposed to go, how will I ever know when that is?"

"Honey," Jamie said quietly but seriously, "You have to listen to your heart. Bryce is a good guy. He loves you more than anything. But he's not perfect and neither are you. Don't back out now. He is worth it. Your love is worth it."

Cammi studied her friend intently while the cup warmed her fingers.

"From the outside looking in, your anger and hate isn't about him anymore than his is about you. You've allowed Cynthia and Beth too much control. Put an end to it," she reached over to touch Cammi's hand. "I love you and want to see you happy. Bryce makes you happy. Maybe not at this moment, but you guys can work through it. Your love is stronger than anything trying to tear it apart."

Cammi's expectations of life left her empty inside. What Jamie said stayed with her for the rest of the day and after she stopped at the store for groceries, she was unable to shake the sensation there was something she was ignoring. Something she was too stubborn to admit.

In hopes of reconciliation, Cammi planned a romantic dinner for her husband but the evening was a disaster before it even began. Bryce was obviously put out with the idea and acted like he was doing her a favor by going. They made enough small talk to fake pleasantness, but he was guarded, protective and even suspicious. Cammi was unable to find a peaceful place to interject her thoughts. Basically, they detested being in the other's company.

But she was relentless. She loved her husband and was willing to do what it took to get through to him. But if he applauded her efforts, he had a hell of a way of showing it. He avoided her gaze and when she tried to hold his hand, he stiffened. His body language was more rejection than she could stand. Filled with insecurity, the little voice in the back of her head continued to nag at her, convincing her he had fallen out of love. Had she manifested her own fate? Was she pushing him towards another woman?

By the time desert arrived, Cammi wanted to give up and go home. Then Bryce decided to broach a subject that was dangerous ground.

"Did Allie tell you she ran into Beth the other day?" Though it was another feeble attempt at small talk, Cammi didn't want to hear it. "Allie said it was nice seeing her. She's surprised by the change. I guess they got a good laugh about the things they used to do to piss Cynthia off," he snickered.

Cammi didn't find any of it amusing. "When did Allie tell you this?"

"She didn't, Beth did."

She had been lifting a piece of cherry cheesecake into her mouth when the fork stopped mid-air. "When?"

"Uh," his face flushed. "Look, she called me last week. It's not like I didn't tell you on purpose, Cammi. It was a quick call. She wanted to see how things were going after I told you her story."

Fury instilled itself in her eyes. What appetite she actually did have for the evening had disappeared as she shoved the plate of cheesecake away from her.

"Don't do this tonight," he hissed throwing his napkin on the table.

"Do what? Make *you* feel bad? Wasn't that what you have been doing to me all evening? Punishing me?" she sneered.

He sighed. "I'm sorry, that wasn't my intent." He knew his behavior was childish, but the distance between them was overpowering. He didn't know how to act or not act anymore. Rolling her eyes, she tore into him. "What was your intent then, Bryce?" Sarcasm dripped off her tongue. "To make me feel *loved*?"

"Let's go home," he insisted his eyes dark with anger.

They paid the check and left the restaurant in silence. He had been an ass all week, and this evening, he behaved like a spoiled brat. Cammi had enough. She couldn't get far enough away from him and when he reached the car, she continued to walk.

"Where are you going?" he demanded.

"I need to clear my head. I'm walking."

He came around the car to walk beside her. "Cammi, you have no right to treat me badly. I didn't do anything wrong," he defended himself.

She stopped to stare him down. Her silence informed him something terrible was stirring inside her.

"You have spent years convincing me not to run away, not to be scared. You tell me, we support each other, depend on each other. But where is that now, Bryce? I have still been fighting for us, but you have chosen to give up. What happened to the man I married, the man who once upon a time could hold me close, dance and sing in my ear? Where is his strength? Where is his integrity? I'll tell you where it is not, it's not with me anymore. You don't talk to me, you don't acknowledge my feelings, you don't even call me from work, but who do you talk to? Beth!" She began to turn away when Bryce grabbed onto her arm.

"Don't stand there and accuse me of not trying. I *am* trying. You choose not to see it. You are stuck in your own pity party and can't look past the end of your nose to see someone besides you is hurting. You have no reason to be jealous of Beth. She is not our problem. *You are!* You are so damn insecure and so damn scared you have made yourself emotionally unavailable to me. And now you wonder after all these years why I am not open to you. You gave up a long time ago. I am only following your footsteps."

Cammi felt the familiar tear of her heart. Only this time it wasn't fear, it was real and as she predicted in the beginning, it would only be a matter of time until he eventually strayed.

"I hate you," she screamed at him pulling her arm away. "I hate you and I want you out of my life. If you lied to me about talking to Beth, then who's to say you wouldn't lie to me about someone else. Maybe I have been a fool all this time to believe nothing was going on between you and Cynthia!" she accused.

Putting her hands up to her face, she shook her head in denial. "I am so stupid! I have done everything to make this marriage work while you are gallivanting around town sleeping with every whore you meet. How many have there been, Bryce? No wonder everyone avoids me. They all know……I've even heard the rumors myself but I'm too much of an idiot!"

Her outburst reeled him back and he believed for a moment she honestly did hate him. Instantly, his anger turned to panic. "Cammi stop! Please! You know there never will be anyone else. I would never hurt you that way," he begged "I never could."

She put her hands over her ears to shut him and everything he was saying out. "Bull shit! You're a man, aren't you? I can't trust you, I can't trust anyone." Something deep inside her began to explode.

The poison of her accusations cut him to the bone. "Cammi, you are blowing this way out of proportion."

"The hell I am! We can't even have a decent dinner anymore. You act like you hate me on a daily basis. I hate waking up wondering how you are going to treat me. 'Is he going to love me today or am I going to annoy him', 'is he going to kiss me when he comes home or is he going to act like I'm not here'. Do you know what that does to a person? I try to figure it out, Bryce, but I just can't do it anymore."

"I feel the same way Cammi! I don't know when I come home from work if you are going to say something nice or start ragging on me. I hate coming home."

"Then don't bother," she interrupted harshly. "I am not going to let you hurt me anymore, Bryce. I am done." She turned her back to him and started heading home on foot.

He ran to catch up and spun her around so they were face to face. "What do you mean you are done?" he hissed his fright turning to rage. "Are you walking away from this marriage? If you are, I need to know," he said holding onto his pride while feeling his heart rip apart. But he refused to crumble. "I deserve to know." The pressure of his fingertips dug into her flesh.

"Why? You have someone else waiting to pick up the pieces?" she spat.

He heard enough. "You are crazy, Cammi, just like the other two women I was stupid enough to get involved with."

The anger of his words seared like fire through her. "Stop blaming everyone but yourself for your relationship problems. You expect the weight to fall on my shoulders. You are as much to blame as I am. If you want to be with Beth or whatever slut you're sleeping up with, then go for it! But I promise, you will never, never find a love truer than mine, Bryce. I'm not going to stop you but just so you know, two can play this game."

"What the hell do you mean?" he growled. "You aren't making any sense."

"If you can have your fun, then I can too, just like I did on Valentine's Day!"

It felt like his chest was cracking open. The pain of her words was so intense he didn't even feel the impact of his hand as he slapped her across the face. It wasn't until he pulled his hand away and saw her eyes wide with shock he registered what happened.

Betrayal fluttered across Cammi's soft features. Her mouth opened and just as quickly, she closed it. She had no more words. Nothing could repair the damage he just did.

"Cammi….Oh God, Cammi….I….," he began reaching out for her, but she spun around and ran down the street, around the corner and away from him.

Paralyzed with agony, he watched her go.

Staggering to the car dumbfounded, humiliated, and filled with remorse, he climbed behind the driver seat and for what seemed like eternity, studied the tiny snowflakes as they danced across the hood of his car. He made the cardinal mistake and didn't see any way to go back and erase it.

The snow began to fall more rapidly covering the streets with a white sheet of fluff as he tortured himself with the memory of what happened. The temperature was close to freezing. What had melted during the day was now becoming ice. He had no choice but to go home and face the consequences of his actions. Damn, why hadn't he held his temper? No woman in his life pushed him over the edge the way she did. But the idea of her in another man's arms made him physically sick. And the fact she purposely threw the idea into his face to hurt him was malicious. Bryce saw it in her eyes the moment she snapped and wanted desperately not to feed into her insecurities and doubts, but he lacked his own self control.

Carefully maneuvering the truck into the driveway he noticed Cammi's car was gone. Stomping into the house, he threw his keys on the table, cursing at the note she left for him. *Staying at Jamie's, I will be home for the kids before you go to work.*

It wasn't signed. No 'Love Cammi' or even 'Cam'. Nothing.

Bryce lay awake most of the night wanting to call her and silently praying she would come home. It was late, and he didn't want to wake Jamie or Shawn so instead he paced the living room floor waiting for her to call him. He drank a beer to calm his nerves and tried to watch TV but nothing distracted him. Hesitantly, he pulled out the photo albums Cammi had so carefully collected and put together over the years until he eventually fell into an exhausted slumber on the floor.

Sunlight and anguish greeted him only a few short hours later when the door slammed shut. Cammi barely acknowledged him as she hurried past. He noticed her eyes were red and swollen as was the delicate skin on her cheek. She hurried past him and locked herself in the master bathroom. He would have given anything to wrap his arms around her, but instead, he showered in the guest bath and left for work without saying a word.

The kids had no idea what transpired the previous evening, and Cammi did her best to act as if nothing were wrong. If any of them noticed the mark on her cheek, no one said a word. Once Allie was off to school, she began to pack.

He had crossed the line she knew he eventually would, and it was time to get out once and for all, time to begin the rest of her life without him. She was determined to be strong, but as she gathered together Faith and Bailey's clothes, she collapsed to the floor in sobs.

While her head told her to stop loving him, her heart ached to hear his words of apology. The words giving her the hope she was desperate for, words showing how much he actually cared about her. But he didn't. It was over.

Jamie stayed up with her half the night while Cammi cried herself to sleep. Her heart ached for her friend and as much as she loved them both, things weren't good. It was her suggestion to have Cammi stay at her place as long as needed.

"It's not a permanent decision, Sweetie. Just temporary until you two come to your senses and work this out. It's okay to take a break, you know."

It wasn't just a break for Cammi, it was the end. He was dead to her now. Nothing else mattered but pulling herself back together for her children. But looking into the future, she saw nothing but desolate space where love had once resided, and the emptiness engulfed her.

Cammi's hand shook as she dialed his cell phone number. The words flew out of her mouth before she had a chance to change her mind.

"I can't do this anymore, Bryce. It's not fair to us. It's not fair to the kids. I am taking Faith and Bailey. We'll be at Jamie's until I can get my life back on track or at least start making some rational decisions. Last night, we both crossed the line. I won't let it happen again."

Bryce couldn't believe what he was hearing. She was leaving him. Their marriage was over. He screwed up, bad. He didn't deny it, but never in a million years did he think it would come to this. What happened to "for better or for worse?" He gave her the gift of his heart years ago, hoping somewhere along the way, she would give him hers. It was her job to honor it, respect it and cherish it. Instead she stomped on it and tossed it to the side like yesterday's trash. He would be damned if he allowed her to see his pain and instead of righting his wrong, he became defensive, pushing his back against the wall.

"Whatever!" His words rang out like gunfire. "At least I won't have you holding every mistake I make over my head."

"It's how we both live, Bryce," she reminded him remorsefully wondering how long it would be until he found someone else to heal his wounds. "What do you want me to tell the kids?"

"I don't care what you tell them. This is your choice, not mine." He couldn't beg her back, not now. She was breaking her vow...... hell would freeze over before he trusted her again.

She was appalled. "The least you could do is act civilly. What do you expect me to do to make this better for you?" He was the one who hit her and once again she was the one trying to make *him* feel better. She didn't need a man like that in her life. She deserved better.

"That's my point, Cammi. You have never been willing to listen to what it is I really want or need. You are too concerned with what you need and aren't getting. You have made your choice, now you have to live with it." Rage forced him to hang up, but the moment he did, despair washed over him.

With his stomach lurching, he staggered down the hall to the bathroom, careful not to attract the attention of others. Once he was safely behind closed doors, he began to vomit profusely. His head pounded and sweat trickled from his temple. Grabbing a handful of toilet paper, he wiped his mouth and collapsed onto the cold, hard floor of the bathroom weeping as quietly as he could.

It took him at least a half-hour to compose himself, and when he did, he snuck out of the office unnoticed. Traffic was a nightmare and all he could focus on was getting home to stop her from leaving. His life would be nothing without her by his side.

Letting out a moan, he pulled into the drive. It couldn't be too late. But when the emptiness of the house greeted him, he knew Cammi, Faith and Bailey were already gone.

Chapter Thirty-Two

The warm spring Colorado had been blessed with the previous month was replaced by a late winter storm which continued to hang on through the month of April. The misery of it only intensified Cammi's depression.

Three weeks passed and in that time, she thought missing Bryce would get easier. She also thought he would have tried to call and reconcile or at least talk her out of leaving, but not once did she hear from him. She spent the better part of each day convincing herself she made the right choice, and his actions reaffirmed this loss was obviously easy for him.

Easier than it was for her.

Cammi was moving through life on auto-pilot. This was worse than any pain she had ever endured in her life and if it weren't for her children, she could easily end her life as it was.

She spent the first week in shock, speaking to no one, except her kids. The comforts of Jamie's house did nothing to ease her pain. She would sit for hours staring into space, paralyzed with thoughts of a future alone. Was she ready for this decision? The idea of walking away from him petrified her. But she had to face the truth. It was over. Bryce was a stubborn man, and he felt betrayed by her leaving. There wasn't even a remote chance he wanted her back, not now.

It took her even more time to muster up the courage to tell her family what happened. Her parents, as always, never gave their opinion, only their support and understood her need to be left alone until she worked through her emotions. Carissa, on the other hand, was extremely upset.

"What the hell are you thinking?" she demanded sitting across the couch from Cammi who was wrapped up in a blanket looking pathetic and lost.

"Thanks for the words of encouragement. I thought for sure you would be on my side."

"This isn't about taking sides, Cammi. It's about ruining lives, breaking apart your family. I just can't believe you are doing this."

"He hit me, Carissa! What did you want me to do? Stay for more abuse?"

"Justify it anyway you want, Cammi, but you know Bryce is not abusive. He made a huge, horrible mistake. I'm not dismissing that. But Jesus Christ, so have you! You are not innocent in this mess by any means."

"Don't you dare…."Cammi shrieked pointing her finger at her sister. "Don't… you… dare…blame….me. Have you ever been betrayed, Carrissa? Huh? Have you?" her voice trembled as her sister shook her head. "Have you ever had someone you love more than life itself lie to you? Sneak behind your back? Live a life separate and apart from you? Do you ever lie in bed at night and wonder who it is his thoughts and heart belong to? We'll, I have. I still do. It doesn't just go away, not that easily. It's the worst pain, the worst punishment a person can put themselves through and I can't stop it."

"Are we still talking about Bryce?" Carrissa whispered.

The words made Cammi stop cold. Taking a step back, she sunk into the couch, her hands cupped together at her mouth. Then with pleading eyes, she looked at her sister.

"But it keeps happening, the women, and the rumors. It's only a matter of time." Her eyes pleaded with sister to understand. "Everyone knew, all our friends, even his family. I was the last one to find out. How pathetic is that?" she sobbed resting her head in her hands. "Do you know how humiliating it was? My future was set and in a matter of minutes, I walked away. Not once did I regret it or look back. I started over and look….I'm better off because of it. And it will be that way this time, I just know it will," she stated convincingly though tears continued to spill down her cheeks.

"You aren't better off, Cammi. You're going to throw away a marriage with the one man who is willing to stand by your side through thick and thin just because you are afraid he *might* find someone else. Did you hear me Cammi? *Might*. Bryce isn't a cheater. He's devoted and dedicated. What if he doesn't find someone else? What do you do then?"

"I can't sit around and wait for it to happen. I will go crazy."

"You're already going crazy living like this. Why not take a chance. A leap of faith? Let go of the past. Give Bryce your heart, completely, without any hesitation."

"It's over Carissa. You can be mad. I understand. But I can't change this. I'm sorry."

"Get over yourself, will you? Do you know how ridiculous you sound? There are people out there who deal with real problems, rape, child abuse, neglect, bi-polar, even substance abuse. And here you are whining about your husband who 'oh my gosh, didn't hold your hand' or maybe he didn't say the most encouraging words when you needed them the most. Heck, maybe he forgot to give you a kiss when he came home from a stressful day at work or raised his voice when he shouldn't have. You have more stress than the normal person, I will agree with that, but my God, Cammi, is your life really that bad? Compared to what is out there, I think you need to be thanking your lucky stars. I know many, many people who would trade places with you in a minute. People who wished they had a husband they could have a nice dinner with without worrying if they were going to get their face punched in or worse for cooking it wrong. I love you, sister, but I'm sorry. I can't support you."

Cammi felt her spine stiffen. "I'm done with this conversation. If you *won't* support me, then leave me alone," she hissed.

"Who the hell are you, anymore?" Carissa demanded.

"Tell her," Jamie interrupted from the doorway. Neither of them had noticed her standing there. Moving over to the recliner, she stared at her friend. "Tell her, Cammi. She deserves to know the truth."

Confused, Carissa looked from one to the other, waiting for someone to say something to help her understand the unspoken message between the two.

Cammi shamefully shook her head as the tears started again.

"If you don't, I will," Jamie said. "It's time, Cammi. I have allowed you to bury this for many years, but I can't anymore. After listening to you just now, watching your reaction to your sister's words, I realize not only have you been in denial over what happened with Marcus, I have enabled it. Tell her," she demanded again, but with a gentler tone.

For the next hour, Carissa listened in shock while Cammi told her the story of her first marriage, the emotional abuse and controlling behavior, the lies, the manipulation and finally the rape and the abortion.

Carissa didn't know what to say. Or what she could say. Instead, she held her sister while she cried.

Cammi thought she would feel some relief with telling Carissa the truth, but she didn't. Instead, along with the pain she had to endure because of her unraveling marriage, she felt as if someone had peeled away the scab of an open, bleeding gash and poured rubbing alcohol into it.

Cammi willed herself to find strength to get through this. One day at a time, she told herself, but the minutes felt like days, the days like months until she couldn't remember one moment from the next.

She didn't know whether to call Allie. She'd left a note on her bed explaining why she left, and God knows the guilt was overwhelming, but she couldn't bring herself to see her. That would mean seeing Bryce. Instead, when he was at work, she dropped a card off at the house for Allie to see the moment she got home from school. She had to let her know she cared. Let her know she didn't abandon her like Cynthia had.

Jamie tried to reach out to her, but it hurt too much to talk about anything. A part of her soul had been ripped out, and it was the part that would be impossible to replace. Attending the tasks of ordinary life seemed a betrayal. She honestly didn't know if she would ever be able to get over Bryce let alone get over something she'd carried with her for more than a decade. And she couldn't live with Jamie and Shawn forever. She had to make some decisions about the direction she wanted her life to go now that she was on her own raising two small children. Unfortunately, those decisions would also have to involve Bryce.

It did not go unnoticed to Jamie that Cammi was not coping well, yet she did not know what to do for her friend. The lack of sleep was causing Cammi anxiety attacks and the night before, Jamie finally convinced her to take a sleeping pill. But when she rose in the morning, the dark circles and exhaustion were still apparent. Finally, Jamie suggested Cammi drop Faith and Bailey off at a co-workers house whose wife owned a day care. It would give the kids a chance to have fun and play. Sitting with their mom day after day was becoming difficult for them and this would give Cammi an opportunity to be alone for a change.

"For Christ's sake, you don't have to be a martyr. It's not going to be easy to move on and you need the love and support of your family and friends. Your mom has called a dozen times. She's worried about you and Carissa stopped by last night after you went to bed. Let us help you."

"I did this, it's no one else's problem to fix. I just want to be happy," Cammi said blankly looking past Jamie's face. The lack of emotion in her voice startled them both.

Jamie downed a glass of orange juice, grabbed her purse and gave her friend a hug. "I've got to go, I'm sorry. Joyce said to drop the kids off whenever. Call me, please?"

Cammi mulled it over. With the little ones still asleep, she decided to climb into the shower hoping the water pressure would relax the knots in her shoulders. Her energy was zapped, her mind was cluttered, and her heart ached. Stepping out of the tub, she wrapped a warm towel around her and collapsed against the wall as numbness invaded every part of her mind.

What seemed like days later, she finally forced herself to move. Oblivious to how she looked she pulled her hair back into a tight bun, threw on a pair of sweats and went to wake the kids up for breakfast.

For half a day, she sat like a zombie in the recliner watching her children color and argue over toys. They chased each other through the living room, into the kitchen and back squealing with delight. The only movement she made was to rewind Mary Poppins to the dancing on the chimney part that Faith begged to watch again and again. After hours of dancing and singing, they finally crawled into Cammi's lap and fell asleep.

As she rocked them steadily, her eyes began to droop. She welcomed the silence until she was abruptly wakened by the ringing of the home phone. Cammi strained to hear the answering machine pick up, but whoever it was hung up.

To avoid any contact with her, Bryce usually called Shawn's cell phone each night to talk to the kids. At least he wasn't ignoring them. But each time the house phone rang, a glimmer of hope awakened her heart, thinking he might be calling for her.

Distress filled her. Unable to stay within the four walls any longer, Cammi grabbed the keys and loaded everyone into the van. She wasn't sure where she was going, all she knew is she needed out of the house. Thinking the fresh air would do her some good she headed to the park, and the kids squealed with excitement when she opened the door. They ran off to play while she sat by herself engrossed in thought.

Snow and ice covered the ground as hints of green grass threatened to expose itself. She loved spring. It was the birth of everything beautiful. As she took it all in, something deep inside her cried for the rebirth of her marriage and maybe deep down, the rebirth of her soul.

Where exactly did everything go wrong? Realizing she had nothing to look forward to, the dull ache began to intensify. She missed Bryce, missed what they shared, she missed herself. Tears moistened her already damp cheeks. They had been so in love, they completed each other. Their dreams, their future, it was going to be perfect and regardless of what happened, she *still* loved him. But was she ever able to give him all of her? Had she been holding back all this time? Did it really have to do with Marcus?

No, Cynthia caused this. Somehow she managed to turn them all into lunatics the moment she arrived. Bryce hadn't been himself. The man she fell in love with would never succumb to this type of behavior. The stress, the chaos, and the conflict finally got the best of him.

Shame filled her as she recognized how her own behavior added to the strain. What Cammi needed was a miracle. But the world stopped spinning the moment she left her husband so where would someone in her position begin to look for the impossible?

Instantly, as if driven by sheer force, Cammi picked up her cell phone and glanced at the time. He would still be at work. In a rush of emotion, she dialed his office number, and her breath caught the moment she heard his voice.

"Hi," she breathed quietly into the phone.

When he didn't respond right away, her heart began to pound loudly in her chest. She heard him sigh before answering.

"Hello," he said impersonally.

"Did I catch you at a bad time? Should I call back?" she asked politely, anxious to hear something, anything in the ways of kindness from him.

"No, it's okay."

Not knowing where to begin or even what to say, Cammi hesitated.

"Do you think we could talk? Get together….just you and me, maybe see if there is something left to salvage of this?"

Once again she was greeted with silence. Unable to handle his lack of response she rambled on.

"What happened, I….I… forgive you. I didn't think I could, but I do. What we share…it's not worth throwing away. We can move past this. I know we still love one another. I….uh, I….could move….home,"

"I don't want you to come home, Cammi," he interrupted before she could continue, his words soft, but deliberate.

There was a pause as she repeated them slowly in her head.

Taking a deep breath he spoke again. "It's not good right now. We need time. *I* need time. I don't know if this is what I want anymore."

"Don't. Please don't," she stammered her words barely audible.

What she heard him say was she wasn't good enough for him. And now he finally figured it out but instead of being honest, it was a pathetic attempt to spare her feelings. Astounded she had any feeling left within her, her whole body went numb.

"It's for the best. We can spare the kids more pain because of our stupidity, and you can be free to find someone who will make you happy. I wish I was that guy, but I wasn't. You need more than what I am capable of giving. I tried my best, did what I knew how, but somewhere along the way, we took different roads. And when you left, well…that was unforgivable."

It took every ounce of pride not to remind him that *he* was the one who hit *her* and that too was unforgivable. But she attempted to do what she had never done before, forget about her anger and beg. "Bryce, I may have acted impulsively, and I apologize for that, but please, let's just talk about this!"

The blood pounded faster than normal in her heart. His voice began to fade as the earth began to spin around her and the nausea settled in her stomach.

"I can't Cammi. I just don't have anything left in me. I'm sorry."

"Wait" she choked out.

It was too late, the phone went dead.

Just like her heart before, time had frozen. In the distance, she could hear the shrieks and laughter of her children, playing as life continued around them, oblivious it had ended for her.

The pain crept its way up from the pit of her stomach until it reached her heart where it ripped at the surface, forcing her to break down into inconsolable sobs. With shaky legs, she attempted to lift herself from her seated position only to collapse into the snow and crush leaves beneath her where she buried her head into her hands.

Minutes, which felt like hours passed before she was able to take a deep, shuddering breath, bringing fresh air into her lungs and helping her regain some control.

Hearing the clumping of snow boots not far away, she turned to see Faith and Bailey rushing towards her, but they stopped when they saw her tears.

"What's wrong, Mama?" Faith asked with such sincerity it made Cammi cry more.

"I am just sad, Honey, I miss Allie and your dad."

It was confusing for them staying at Jamie's, and Cammi tried to protect them as well as she knew how, only telling them as much as they needed to know.

"Your dad and I love one another very much, but all we do is fight lately. I thought staying with Aunt Jamie for a while would be a good break, so we could make some better decisions and not fight as much. Your daddy loves you very much, but he has to work, so it wouldn't make sense to have you with him when you can be here with me," she forced herself to tell them the day they moved out.

"Are you going to get divorced?" Faith had asked two weeks later. She was always the perceptive, curious one. Instinctively, Cammi told her no, hoping the optimism would become her self-fulfilling prophecy.

Now the words echoed in her ears. It was one thing to think it, but to actually hear her daughter ask…it was as if she had swallowed a two ton weight. And worse, her phone call with Bryce confirmed her fears. God, how was she going to explain this to them?

Guilt suddenly overwhelmed her. What was she doing to her kids? It was her job to provide them with stability and happiness. How was she supposed to set an example when half the time she couldn't figure it out for herself? Her lack of guidance was going to damage their delicate hearts.

It was cold and crisp at the park as the sun drifted to the west toward the snowcapped mountains. Cammi pulled her winter coat tightly around her to stop the shivers running up her arms. Bailey gave his mother a hug. He was normally a rambunctious boy, but at times like this, he was gentle and sensitive, like his father used to be.

"I wuv you, Mama. It k to be sad." Cammi smiled down at him. He was so sweet, it broke her heart to think of the scars they were going to have because of her choices.

"Come on, let's get in the car. I am going to take you somewhere to play with other kids, would you like that?"

Excitedly, they agreed. Cammi hated to be away from them and dreaded the loneliness that would haunt her for the next few hours, but it wasn't fair to depend on them to make her feel better. They needed to be kids, and she refused to be like Cynthia, the mom who depended upon her children.

It was a split second decision after she left the kids forcing her to make the phone call to the clinic. Ironically, there was a cancellation so they were able to squeeze her in. Pride kept her from seeking help all this time. Now desperation had her willing to do anything.

The impatient clicking of her nails threatened to interrupt the deafening silence swallowing the room. Cammi could only imagine how irritating this had to be for the doctor who was sitting across from her engrossed in the paperwork Cammi previously filled out. Her eyes shifted warily towards the door, and she wondered silently how much of an ass she would make of herself if she got up and walked out. But Madison was a small town and chances of them running into one another were likely, and the last thing she needed was another person to avoid.

It took all the strength she could muster just to fill out her name let alone all the insurance information, family history, health history and questions about her mental state. By the time she finished, what little dignity she had left disappeared along with the life she had chosen to walk away from.

Doctor. That's what her credentials said and as Cammi glanced towards the framed certificate hanging on the wall she saw proof in the PH.D certificate staring back at her in big, black print. Shrink is how she mentally referred to her. Gloria is what she wanted to be called.

Nervously Cammi took in the rest of the room. The walls were beige, simple. No other word could describe it. The décor was, well, simple, too. Aside from three shelves of books, one lamp, leaning slightly into the wall and the plush brown couch she found herself swallowed by, the room was bare. Oh, except for the adjoining bathroom and rocking chair Gloria occupied. The only comfortable feature seemed to be the family photo's adorning the top of the shelves.

God, she hated this. Hopefully the woman's bedside manner was more comfortable than her taste.

"So Cammi… I'm glad you decided to see me again. How are you?" They had talked briefly the previous month, but in all honesty, Cammi had no intention of making another appointment.

Her voice was soft and gentle, reminding Cammi of her third grade teacher, Mrs. Adams. She would never forget the nurturing way she took her under her wing on her first day at a new school. Cammi had been terrified, and of course, all the girls ignored her, but the portly older woman guided Cammi to her desk and made a point of smiling directly at her the rest of the day, just the way Gloria was doing now. Only this time she wasn't eight years old, but still, the fear was similar.

"I left my husband," she said directly positioning her arms in front of her chest to prepare herself for the onslaught of a lecture. Raising her eyebrows, she challenged the woman who continued to watch her with kindness and concern etched into the lines on her face.

Despite her age, Cammi could see she was once a striking woman. Still youthful in appearance, she was carelessly confident and classy. Her raven hair was now speckled with grey. If Cammi met her on the street or at one of her children's activities, she was someone she would definitely have had the desire to get to know better and hopefully befriend.

But friends didn't come easily to her anymore.

Who was she kidding? Friends had never come easily, female ones at least. She'd been a tomboy growing up. She was more interested in frogs, mud pies and riding her bike than she was Barbie dolls and Carebears, and she hadn't the time for girlfriends. Nor did the girls in grade school have time for her. They spent most of their time whining and complaining and thought she was rather odd anyway. She didn't care. At least that is what she had been telling herself for close to thirty years now, and she'd bet that once this woman had a look into her life and all the drama she now lived with, she too, would run as far away as she could get.

"Are you seeing someone else?" Gloria asked cautiously.

"God no!"

"Is *he* having an affair?"

"No. At least I hope not." The thought brought tears to her eyes.

"Abusive?"

"No."

"Substance abuse?"

"No."

"Can you help me out here?"

Looking directly into her sensitive grey-blue eyes, she confessed.

"I'm not good enough for him. He doesn't want me anymore."

"Why do you think that?"

Cammi's hands trembled, and her mouth was dry. She couldn't even say the words. Thinking them was bad enough, but actually admitting to someone you were crazy, well that was more self-destructive than Cammi wanted to admit.

"Something's wrong with me, really wrong. A chemical imbalance, some sort of mental disorder, a personality disorder, I'm not a doctor, hell I don't know." Desperation clung to her voice while the tears escaped from her eyes down into her lap. "I need someone to help me."

"Do you have suicidal thoughts?"

"No." The words came out so softly she barely heard them herself, but it was the truth. She wasn't suicidal, just unhappy. If it weren't for her responsibility as a parent and the fact she loved him more than anything, she would have run away from Bryce a long time ago.

"How are you feeling right now?"

"Numb. I feel nothing." That, too, was true, there was a block. She'd always had a detailed memory of each moment of her life. But since she left Bryce last week, the connection from her mind to her heart was dead. She felt nothing. She remembered nothing. Childhood, college, her wedding, the birth of her children, they were mere glimpses of her memories disappearing as soon as she tried to embrace them, and she flitted through each day, surviving one minute to the next, barely aware of what was going on around her. The only thing getting her up each morning was her kids.

Thinking of her children, for a brief moment, Cammi felt alive. Relieved to feel something other than numbness, she closed her eyes as memories of the last day she spent in the backyard of the house she shared with her husband flooded her psyche.

The squeak of the old rocking chair put an end to her thoughts. Compassion filled Gloria's eyes as she leaned forward and rested her delicate hand on Cammi's knee.

"Do you still love your husband, Cammi?"

"More than anything but we both crossed the line. I honestly don't know how we go back. So much has happened. I don't know that it's fixable."

Everything in the aftermath of her leaving was a blur, but she welcomed the foggy haze. Cammi honestly didn't know if she wanted to remember.

"I don't even know where to begin," she sobbed looking at Gloria with the frightened, scared eyes of an innocent child.

"Why don't you take a deep breath and start at the beginning."

Talking to Gloria helped, somewhat. The misery hadn't disappeared, but she felt a little saner than she had earlier in the day. Who'd have thought a stranger could bring her insight and rational perspective? For an entire hour, she talked, and Gloria listened without judgment. Cammi didn't hesitate to make a second appointment.

Figuring she needed some more time to herself, she drove around for another hour before heading back to the house.

Bryce was hurt, Cammi told herself. That had to be it. He didn't really want a divorce. He was only being irrational and bullheaded. She'd abandoned him, and now he wanted her to hurt. Well, his game worked, but she was starting to see through it.

The assumption filled her with a sense of relief as she steered the van back around the corner and the moment she saw Bryce's truck in the driveway of Julie's house, her thoughts were confirmed. Her eyes searched him out and found him sitting on the front stoop waiting for her. Her stomach leapt with excitement.

But the moment she saw his face, she knew this wasn't a social visit. He looked haggard and tired, like he hadn't slept in years. The circles under his eyes were darker than normal. Still, she found him breathtaking. The butterflies twittered inside her.

He stood up as she got out of the van clenching his jaw in anticipation. She looked like a ghost, thin and frail. The chill that surrounding them was apparent.

"I took the next three days off, I want to have the kids," he said abruptly avoiding eye contact. "I should have told you on the phone, I'm sorry, I was a bit distracted.

It hadn't been what she'd expected. "Do you want to come in?" she asked in an attempt to be civil. The last thing she wanted was an argument, but it seemed inevitable.

He followed her into the kitchen. "Did you hear what I said?" he demanded.

She turned on him in an instant. "Of course I heard what you said! You practically yelled it in my ear! Why the sudden change of heart? You haven't once discussed this with me and out of nowhere you want them for three days and expect me to trust you?" She knew she was being unreasonable, but his nonchalant attitude was killing her.

"You left *me*, Cammi, remember?"

"Yes, you seem to enjoy reminding me. I was the one who took the first step to call you today, *remember?*

It was a tense moment, the two of them standing barely two feet away from each other, the heat of their anger bouncing back and forth.

It was taking every ounce of strength Cammi had to keep her composure. She shoved her shaking hands into the front of her sweatshirt. "Look, I don't want to fight with you."

"Where are the kids?"

"I took them to Jamie's friend's to play for a few hours. I figured they could use some time away from me. I'm not the best company lately," she stated matter-of-factly.

His heart raced the minute she got out of the van. She was so beautiful his whole body reacted at the sight of her. He wanted to hate her, put her behind him, he truly did. She was putting him through a slow painful death, but his heart, body and soul wanted to take her in his arms and love her forever.

"Can I pick them up?" he asked looking past her. He knew if he looked into her green eyes, he would be drawn back into the depths of her love. The part of him that was trying to put his heart back together couldn't handle admitting it, and he'd spent too much time already giving himself false hope.

He knew he should apologize for his behavior. What happened that night at the restaurant was inconceivable, and he'd been living with the horror of the memories since. But her leaving was a blow he hadn't expected. It left him wondering if she was capable of the forever she'd promised him. Many, many things needed to change in their relationship. He was fully aware and ready to take action on his part to make it better, but her phone call that afternoon diminished any hope he had that she was willing to do the same. She was blind and unable to see she was half of the problem. He refused to go back to the way things were. And until she got some help, he didn't want to be with her.

"Of course, you can. They're your kids. You can have them whenever you want."

His features softened and even though he wouldn't look directly at her, she didn't miss the longing in his eyes.

As quickly as it appeared, it was gone.

Turning toward the stove, she kept herself occupied with heating water. Why did this have to be so hard? Obviously he hadn't come to apologize or ask her back. She needed to stop the denial and move on without him. He was dead to her now, she reminded herself, he did not have permission to see her weak and vulnerable ever again.

She took a deep breath. "We need to make some decisions, Bryce. The sooner we take care of this, the sooner we can both get on with our lives."

Not knowing what possessed her to say those words she kept her back towards him. She wanted a reaction, that was it, but she was afraid of the reaction she was going to get.

"I've already talked to Ron. Told him I would talk with you before I had the papers drawn up."

Her stomach tightened. He moved on so quickly. How was it possible? Had the past eight years meant so little? It was okay for her to want a divorce, but she didn't want him to want it too. Like the fool she was, she *did* want him to beg her back, beg for forgiveness, tell her he would change, that everything would be better as long as they had each other. The romantic notions swirling around inside her from the moment she saw him dissolved into a pit of black despair.

No, it was better this way, she reassured herself. Nonetheless, the tears stung her eyes.

Turning around, her face was filled with pain. "I will call an attorney tomorrow. I hope we can both be civil about this, especially for the sake of the kids. Let's not drag them into the middle, okay?"

"It hurts me you would even suggest it."

She laughed haughtily. "Do you realize this is the first time you ever told me you were hurt, it's nice to see you have emotions left," she replied. "I was starting to wonder if your heart had turned to stone."

It was a cheap shot, but she didn't know how else to react.

"Stop being such a bitch, Cammi," he scowled.

"Don't you dare call me a bitch! I think you've outstayed your welcome. I'll call Joyce and let her know you will be picking the kids up. I expect you to bring them back to me on Sunday."

She started to brush past him with an arrogance powerful enough to drive him wild. Instinctively, he grabbed her arm and shoved her back, pinning her between himself and the wall. She tried to push against him, but his weight combined with the passion that was compelling him, made her powerless.

He stared deep into her eyes and could feel her heart pound in unison with his. His hand moved to the back of her head to keep her still as his mouth demanded hers. Her mouth was hot, and he wondered if it was fear or anticipation making her respond as willingly as she did. He wasn't ready to let her go. She belonged to him, and he wanted her. Roughly, he shoved his hand under her shirt until he found her breast. Craving her with all he was, he kissed her neck, her ear and her hair until his lips once again sought out the fullness of her lips. As he caressed her, she moaned with pleasure.

Bryce's aggression turned her on. She responded to his kiss with a wild desire burning deep inside, surprising them both. She slid her hands down his back, feeling his muscles contract, until they rested on his hips. Encouraged, he pulled her deeper into him.

The hard evidence of his desire jolted her back to reality. She pushed against him with all her strength. "Stop it," she yelled wiping at her mouth. "Don't touch me! I'm not yours to use. You have other women for that."

Taking her by the shoulders he pushed her back into the wall. His face was tight with anger. He loved her and determination told him not to let her go without a fight.

"Are you going to hit me again?" she sneered with as much resentment as she could muster.

Dismay struck him as his face filled with agony. Immediately, he loosened his grip. Stifling a sob, she fled past him up the stairs, and the last thing he heard was the locking of the bathroom door behind her.

The pressure in his head was about to explode. Taking a last look around Jamie's house, hopelessness filled his heart. They'd both done the unimaginable and coming here, he realized neither of them would be able to find forgiveness. It was over. The sooner he accepted it, the better.

But she didn't belong there, a little voice whispered to him. Did he want her building a life somewhere else, with someone else, a life without him? He wished he'd hadn't told her he didn't want her to come home. God, what possessed him to be such a stupid ass. He was losing her, losing his kids and pride wasn't going to build him a happy home.

Something he couldn't quite explain bubbled inside him. The tiniest thread of hope awoke and wrapped itself around his heart. Three weeks ago, he gave up. Three weeks ago, he allowed his life to fall to pieces. And three weeks ago he succumbed to what he thought would be a destiny without Cammi and today, his behavior was no better.

They needed to stop playing these foolish games.

His legs carried him to his truck, but he left his heart back in the upstairs bathroom with her. He didn't care what it took or what he had to do, he was going to get his wife back and he would be damned if he was going to allow their love to become another statistic.

Chapter Thirty-Three

"Am I so dreadful my husband doesn't want to touch me for months upon months? Is he so ruthless he'd try to get in one last screw before we get divorced? It was deja vu. Just like Marcus," Cammi sobbed.

Sitting on the floor outside the bathroom door, Jamie tried to be the voice of reason but Cammi was inconsolable. She'd been in there two hours and still refused to come out. Her heart went out to her friend but she also felt for Bryce. He rushed over to her office after leaving Cammi.

"What do I do?" he begged her. "I keep screwing up. I've never been this miserable in my life. I can't focus on work, I can't eat, and I don't sleep. I torment myself with thoughts of her finding someone else. Is that what she wants?"

It was his fault three weeks had passed. He left for work every morning telling himself that today he was going to call, apologize and put his marriage back together. Instead a combination of denial and hope carried him throughout the day. He came home each evening in anticipation of seeing her there only to be cruelly reminded of the truth.

Absorbed in his own grief, Bryce was oblivious that Allie too was struggling with the loss of her family. She'd spent the first week locked up in her room crying, while Bryce numbly ignored her, until she finally decided to go to Cynthia's. After three days there, she figured her dad's grief was better than Cynthia's erratic behavior and came home. He was relieved she was back. The house was already empty and desolate.... without his family, his whole life was black. At least with Allie there, they could somewhat carry on a conversation. Though they were both reeling from the heartache, the loneliness wasn't as intense.

"She loves you, but she's lost. Listen to me, okay?" Jamie grabbed him by the shoulders and forced him to look into her eyes.

"She's scared. She has been all these years. She doesn't like to be scared and she doesn't like to be weak. The biggest change in her life came when she had to learn to trust and depend on you. She doesn't know how to rely on anyone but herself. She adjusted all right until this thing with Cynthia. She's mad as hell at the whole world, but mostly at herself for not handling it the way she thinks she should. I know how hard you try, believe me. But her self-esteem is shot. She doesn't believe in herself anymore, so no matter what you do, no matter how you try, she's blind to it. I understand you have your own fears, your own anger because of what's happened. But you have to learn to talk to her, when you don't communicate; she assumes she's screwed up. She wants to make it better, but when she doesn't succeed, she feels like a failure."

He tried to speak, but she held up her hand to stop him.

"She's been trying to make things right for you, Allie, Faith, and Bailey, but along the way she lost herself. You don't see it because you do the same thing. Your love runs deep, so deep you want to fix each other. Until she starts to believe in herself and what she is capable of as a wife and a person, it won't get better. And you need to do the same. You both have unselfish motives, I can see that, but losing who you are is the most selfish thing you can do. Find your souls, nurture them, then they will grow together as one."

"But Jamie, I hit her. And today when she called…..I was awful. That changes everything. I don't think she will ever forgive me. I don't know if I can ever forgive myself."

Jamie wished Cammi could witness the anguish he was going through and then maybe she might believe in his love.

"You're right. Your behavior is not acceptable," she scolded. "But you are not an abusive monster. She knows that. Things happen, people make mistakes. It doesn't make it right, but it happened for a reason. You both needed a wakeup call. I just hope this was it."

"Going to your house today, I wanted to make her pay," he admitted hanging his head. "It was wrong, I see that now. I've been childish and it's costing me my marriage."

"Then stop. Is your dignity worth the loneliness life will offer without her? You will move on, maybe find someone else, but no one will hold a candle to her."

Nodding slowly, tears glistened in his eyes.

She forced him to look at her. "Bryce, I need you to understand that Marcus hurt Cammi very, very badly. She won't admit it to herself, let alone anyone else. His behavior was more than she could face. It was too big so instead she locked her heart away but had no clue it's what she was doing. It was the only way she could cope. But she needs to face what she buried all those years ago otherwise it will continue to hold her back. Give her time, but don't give up the fight. And this crap with Cynthia? Well that is what it is, crap! Once Cammi deals with her demons, it won't matter anymore. Help her fix what's broken, it's the best revenge you can have against Cynthia," she suggested.

After promising a distraught Bryce she would go home and check on Cammi, Jamie called Shawn.

"I wish we could do something," she said sadly.

"We are doing something, Jamie. It's going to be okay. I promise. Everything is fitting perfectly into God's plan. Maybe not the way everyone wants it to be, but he knows what he's doing."

"I know your right. I just hope it gets better before it gets worse."

While Jamie and Shawn were engrossed in dinner with their own kids, Cammi snuck down the stairs and out the door before she was detected. Her first stop was the house she shared with Bryce. She parked across the street and sat in the darkness, watching the white flakes fall from the sky.

He'd left the porch light on which was unusual. Bryce was so anal about conserving energy, once everyone was in the house for the night, the front door was locked and the porch light went out. It made her wonder who he was waiting for.

Hoping to catch a glimpse of movement from him or one of the children through the windows, she watched endlessly for an hour before giving up. She wasn't sure where to go next, only that she was desperate for help.

Instinct drove her downtown where she parked the car and stepped out, feeling a breeze as the crisp, winter air chilled her body. She walked down the block until she came to the place her heart was searching for. Checking to see if it was unlocked, she pulled open the heavy wood door and jumped slightly as it slammed shut behind her.

Cammi loved the beauty and serenity of the old church. It had been years since she stepped foot in it, probably before she left for college. She hoped by coming here she might find some answers. Not much had changed since she was a kid. It was ironic how big everything had seemed to her then. She gazed at the solid, wooden cross, and still found herself drawn to the symbolism behind it, the unselfish sacrifice. Her faith was manifested in her childhood but it wasn't until her early twenties, after the death of her roommate and then again after the abortion she comprehended the value of that sacrifice.

But where was God now? Cammi considered herself a good person and felt like she had been steadfast and done right by him. So she didn't understand why he was allowing this to happen. Hadn't she followed his path of righteousness, continually proving over and over her belief in his ways? What more would it take for her to become deserving of happiness and love?

The scent of candle wax and wood filled the sanctuary. She remembered as a child daydreaming of having her wedding in this church. In her fairy tale, her prince would burst through the front doors on a large stallion admired by all, sweep his beauty away from the boring sermon, and into his life forever. The radiant energy of the candles would dance around the room as she walked hand in hand down the isle of this church with her prince, and every woman in the room was filled with envy. The two would live happily ever after.

If only she still had her prince.

The church was empty. She had expected it to be, it was too early for the evening service. It didn't usually start until seven-thirty. She let her hand slide across the soft, polished wood of the pew, and as she sat in the front row, she stared in wonderment at the blue, green and yellow colors marking the stain glass window.

It confused her as to why she decided to come here. Though the church was five blocks away from her house, in all these years, she never felt the need to attend a service. They were going to a more modern, nondenominational church on the outskirts of town. One that Bryce and her kids found more welcoming. Cammi enjoyed the upbeat music, the motivational speeches, and she had more in common with the younger families than she did with the ones she grew up with who dedicated their lives and faith to this church. But there was something about the old liturgy, the building itself and the hum of the organ making her feel like a kid again. Walking through the door, she was filled with hope that maybe here she could find the miracle she was looking for.

She sat praying, meditating, watching for a sign, allowing her thoughts to drift towards Bryce, and her children. Overnight, her life became empty, her future bleak. She was disappointed and frustrated not only with herself, but with God. Was God disappointed in her? Was he punishing her for the sins of her past? He was the one constant she counted on for unconditional love, and his abandonment of her left her jaded. Maybe it was too late.

After what seemed like forever, she stood up and solemnly, headed towards the front door. Snow was beginning to swirl as the wind whipped through the air. The cozy little town had really been dumped on enough the past month, but that was typical in Colorado. Cammi looked upwards while the soft, wet flakes powdered her face. The dark clouds separated right above her head to reveal a speckle of stars. She rocked back and forth on her feet transfixed by the night sky. Unlike her life, it represented the tranquility she spent her adult life searching for.

Suddenly, she was startled to hear the grind of a shovel moving along the sidewalk. She didn't realize anyone was around. A small, fragile white haired man was pushing the moist accumulation off the sidewalk before people started to arrive. With the drastic change in temperature, it wouldn't be long before sheets of ice formed over the cement.

Ignoring him, she moved towards her car but quickly reached out to steady him when his foot slipped on the ice. His fragile and slight frame seemed to weigh less than Faith's and when his thankful gaze penetrated hers, she felt a jolt of electricity shoot up her spine.

"Thanks," he said quietly, his deep voice crackled with age. His gaze searched her face. "You okay, dear?" The redness around her eyes was apparent even to the oldest of humans.

"Yes, thank you. Be careful, okay," she said patting his hand. She wasn't in the mood for conversation and willed herself to keep walking toward her car, lost in her own thoughts.

"You're heart is broken, isn't it?" he called after her.

Something about his concern was pleasant and soothing. Drawn to his voice, she turned back to him.

"Why?" she inquired taking a deeper look into his face. She decided he was probably very handsome in his younger years. Though he was delicate and hunched over and she guessed close to ninety, his physique told her once upon a time, he was burley and solid.

"I have been fixing things around this old church for hundreds of years it seems like. People come to services when they have to, but only the broken hearted show up when no one else is around, they are all searching for the same thing."

"What's that," she asked.

"Miracles."

Just when Cammi thought there were no more tears left, hearing his words forced them to the surface again. Taking her by the arm he steered her inside. After handing her a steamy cup of coffee, he stuck his hand out for a shake. "Clifford," he offered.

"Cammi," she sniffed. Though she hated coffee, she didn't want to offend the kind, old man, so she sipped on it slowly, appreciating the warmth it brought.

"I remember you coming here as a child….with your parents. You haven't changed much," he smiled.

Cammi thought it strange. Madison was a small community, she could have sworn she knew just about everyone who attended this church while growing up, but he didn't look familiar. She made a mental note to ask her mother the next time she called.

Normally very cautious about conversing with strangers, Cammi found it oddly comfortable to sit in his presence and before she knew it, she'd spilled her whole life story to him. Afterwards, she was horribly embarrassed although the way he patted her hand while she cried tears of humiliation reminded her of her grandfather. He died when she was eight, but she would always remember the warmth he carried with him.

"What is it you want?" he asked kindly.

She snorted. "I don't know. I mean, I know, but no one ever asked me that. I suppose happiness. Isn't that what everyone wants?" she stammered.

"Have you ever been happy?"

"Oh sure! My childhood was great. In college, I was pretty content and then before I met Bryce, I was at a very peaceful place. A part of me regrets getting involved with him. Don't get me wrong. I love him to death, but things were easier. I didn't question myself."

"So what is it that makes you happy?" Clifford asked inquisitively.

She shrugged. "It's funny. Most people in my position would say a bigger house. Nicer car, more money, even vacations. Bryce and I, we do fine. We get by. He would like to have more, spend more, but not me. I don't need those things. It would be nice to afford anything I wanted, but it wouldn't make me happy."

He looked at her intently as if reading her mind.

She wrapped her arms around herself in a warm embrace and smiled. Closing her eyes she envisioned her life.

"When I can bring a smile to someone's face and know their day is going to be better because of it….that makes me feel good. When my children tell me they love me, make me laugh or give me a peck on the cheek…I like that. When I know the example I set is going to make an impact on how they treat others. I love watching their accomplishments and how their minds absorb new things every day. Sitting on the porch as the sun sets and watching the kids play with their dad and our dog Penny on the front yard. I love how they interact. It makes me sad to watch them grow up and become independent, but it's a good sad knowing I have been by their side for all the important stuff. Music," Cammi took a moment to think and then nodded. "I love music and being filled with memories of the past that makes me happy. I enjoy spending time with my parents and my friends, laughing, making new memories. When someone reads something I wrote and I hear how it impacted their life, I like that. I feel like I'm making a difference." Cammi sighed. "The love Bryce and I share....we are partners.....we work together, when I'm with him, that is. All those things make me feel wonderful. Those are things money can't buy."

"You just said you were happy before you met him, but it sounds to me that a lot of those things happened because of him." Tilting his head to the side, he said, "Maybe it's just a different type of happiness."

Cammi wiped at her tears with the handkerchief Clifford handed her and let out a self-conscious laugh. "You must think I'm stupid."

"No, I think you're real. It's refreshing. Not too many of you around anymore. It sounds to me like you're looking in the right place, though." He put his hand over his heart. "What do you think he would want you to do?" he asked turning his eyes upward toward the cross.

"Fight." The words left her mouth before she had time to think them through. "He would want me to fight for love and fight for him." Sighing, she added," what I really need is a miracle."

"Well," he said shifting his weight around the wooden bench, "you won't find it without forgiveness. The world hasn't done you wrong honey. It's only given you the experiences and opportunities to move forward. Unfortunately, I don't think you want to. That means you have to change and it's more comfortable where you are. It's what you know."

The severity of his words pierced her soul. And for the first time, she understood the truth of her behavior.

"How do I forgive?" she asked hesitantly.

"I'm not talking about your husband, he isn't the one you are angry with," he said reading her mind. "Disappointed, yes, but angry.... no."

"Then with who?" She figured he was probably going to say Cynthia and the idea of forgiving her was appalling.

"Yourself."

Confused and slightly annoyed, Cammi sat quietly, waiting for an explanation.

"You blame Bryce, you blame Marcus, and you blame Cynthia. You even blame God. If it weren't for them, you would be happy, right?" he asked raising his eyebrows. "Would you? You believed once that you and Bryce were soul mates. Then life threw curve balls and you didn't like it. It didn't go along with your plan. Show me someone that hasn't hit a brick wall or had something major happen to them that changed their life. It's not real. You would deal with these issues regardless of who you were with and who interfered. No one's perfect Cammi, least of all you. You want everyone else to love you despite your faults, so why don't you? Your happiness will come when you realize you deserve your own respect instead of filling yourself with contempt because life didn't turn out exactly the way you thought it should."

Though she was irritated, she couldn't help admiring his wisdom. It probably came from years of experience. If his wife was still living, Cammi could only imagine what a wonderful and lucky woman she must be.

"I still don't understand why we continue to deal with so many terrible things. We aren't bad people, why us?"

"Are the things happening really that bad? Or was it life as it happens to all of us? Your circumstances happen to be a bit different than others. It's all in perception, but don't miss the hidden meaning. Everything is supposed to bring you closer to God."

Giving her arm a squeeze, they sat quietly taking in the stillness. Cammi's eyes were tired and burning, but his presence soothed her.

Clifford broke the silence. "Things are a mess, that is true, but forgive yourself. Give yourself permission to let it go…move forward. Free your heart from the hatred you hold on to, and if it means forgiving Cynthia or whoever else has hurt you, so be it. Hating only hurts *you*."

In only a few moments of friendship, he vocalized the battle she struggled with internally her whole adult life and as strange as it was to hear it from his perspective, he was right. She sounded childish, self-centered, and spiteful. An unexpected desperation to be alone with her thoughts consumed her but she couldn't seem to draw herself away from this old man.

"I have taken up your time and church is about to start, I should go," she stammered. Standing up, she reached for her coat.

He nodded and held the coat as she wiggled her arms into it and then walked side by side to the front of the church. When she turned to thank him, she found herself entranced by the beauty of his eyes. Why hadn't she noticed it when they were talking? They weren't any normal color of blue. Soft clouds of white blending with the piercing shade of indigo encircled his pupils. It was almost heavenly.

Clifford placed his soft, wrinkled hand against her cheek. She leaned her head into it, conforming to his touch. "Judgment in circumstances leads to lack of joy," he said wisely. "Give yourself a break. Accept who you are and the things you do, even the mistakes."

Stepping out into the cold, he shoved his hands back into his gloves. The wind instantly dried the tears streaking Cammi's face. She needed to leave, even wanted to leave, but for a reason unknown to her, she couldn't make herself move.

He saw her hesitate and sighed. "Instead of looking for the miracle Cammi, why don't you try to *be* the miracle? Hope can be born from your suffering. Trust in your faith and cling to God. He's in charge, you know," he smiled patting her hand again.

It amused Cammi how much he sounded like a preacher. And once again she found herself wondering about his life. She wanted to ask, but more pressing issues weighed on her mind. She would come back, she promised, to see him and learn about who he was. His company had definitely been a Godsend.

"Thank you, Clifford. Thank you so much. You don't know how much this has meant to me." She rushed over and threw her arms around the little man careful not to bowl him over. She expected him to be brittle, frail but was surprised to feel the strength of his body in her embrace. Her heart warmed as he returned her hug affectionately.

"*You* know your heart, Cammi. *You* know your intentions have always been pure." With a smile, he kissed her cheek and whispered into her ear. "And so do I."

A shiver raced up her spine. Cammi squeezed the man's hand then crawled into her car, still feeling the weight of his eyes upon her. With her emotions running high she pulled away from the curb, taking a quick glance into her rear view mirror where Clifford was waving good-bye. Cammi blinked and squinted to get a better look. Interesting how he was so strangely familiar yet she knew she had never seen him before.

Cammi drove only a mile when suddenly she found her hands shaking on the steering wheel. After a few more blocks, she began to feel nauseous and her breathing suddenly became restricted. Fear flew into her heart as she forced herself to pull over and put the car in park. She did not know what was happening, but it was as if a whole wall had broken down and layers upon layers of junk spilled out.

A few deep breathes, Cammi. Just relax. Nothing more than anxiety, she coaxed herself but before she knew it, her deep breaths turned into soft cries.

Life was a mess, and she didn't have the faintest idea what to do. She hated Marcus for taking away her innocence, she hated Bryce for hurting her, she hated Allie for being so naïve, she hated Cynthia, just for the simple fact she was a bitch who purposely sought to destroy them, and at the moment she hated her own children for depending on her so much when all she wanted to do was disappear. She hated her life and Clifford had been right, she hated herself.

Her heart physically ached, her stomach hurt, and she felt as if she wanted to die. Shaking her head back and forth trying to release the fury wedged within, the sobs turned to deep, hysterical wails as she was overcome with grief. Suddenly, without thinking, Cammi began to punch the steering wheel.

"God Dammit. I need you!" she cried in desperation as her fists pounded helplessly into the leather. "Where are you? I asked you for help! I expected you to rescue me! Tell me," she sobbed, "tell me how I can make you love me again?"

Exhausted in her defeat she rested her head on the steering wheel. "I've had enough. You win. Help me recognize what it is I need to do," she pleaded her hands throbbing in her lap.

The wind rocked at her vehicle while she sat shivering, alone and isolated as the rest of the world continued on without her, as Bryce continued on without her. Clifford asked her what made her happy. Her response triggered a flame inside prompting her to remember the comforts of her life. She was given her dream, the family she craved and the husband she longed to love. Did she really hate it or did she hate what she allowed herself to believe wasn't perfect?

But what was perfect? Nothing. She wasn't, Bryce wasn't, her children weren't and life wouldn't be. It was up to her to make the best of it and to do that she had to heal something inside of her that was broken a long time ago. It was now she had to face the truth.

The challenge should have been simple considering she'd accomplished it once.....before a husband and before kids, but this time, if she didn't succeed; she had much more at stake. Was she up to the challenge? She made a commitment. She made a promise. And she knew she didn't have a choice. Clifford's words empowered her, filling her with a strength she thought she'd lost.

Bryce. Her thoughts were fixated on going to him, apologizing and step by step, making the changes to repair *her* damage. Damage she chose to ignore. And then if they were lucky and blessed with a second chance, they could work on their marriage.

Only this time, she was determined it would go the way God planned.

It was time to put him once again at the center of her heart.

Part Three

Chapter Thirty-Four

Dawn flooded the room through sheer window curtains. Bryce hadn't slept, he hadn't eaten, and he refused to leave her side. The clock beside the bed read seven-thirty four. Last time he checked, it was seven-fifteen. Time was endless.

The nurse was new. There must have been another shift change while he slept. Squeezing his eyes shut, he reached his arms over his head, stretching his legs a few inches above the floor. Frustration filled him as his hands moved roughly over his scruffy jaw.

Looking towards the bed beside him at the still figure that was his wife, Bryce willed her to wake up, but she didn't stir, though he could see her chest move as she breathed.

The nurse noticed the concern on his face. "Don't worry, she needs the rest. She'll come around when her body says it's time."

Patting his back, she left the room. Thank goodness this nurse was more compassionate than the ogre they had during the night. Again, he recognized the name on her uniform, but he couldn't put the face with the name. With over three hundred employees, it was sometimes hard for him to keep track, especially if she was a traveling nurse from the city. But instantly, he didn't like her. It almost came to blows when she told him visiting hours were over and asked him……no, *told* him to go home.

"I understand she's your wife….."she argued.

"Good, then there shouldn't be a problem with my staying here."

"Wouldn't you be more comfortable at home?" she suggested with a hint of annoyance underlying her tone.

"Yes, I would be more comfortable at home *with* my wife, but that isn't possible now, is it?" he retorted. "I'm staying. Deal with it."

"I don't intend to walk on egg shells because you're here," she snapped right back.

"God forbid you should."

Disapproval shadowed her face as she huffed out of the room. Obviously she didn't care about who he was as much as he didn't care to know her. He wasn't in the mood to make friends.

Looking at the bed where his wife laid, Bryce shuddered. Her parents didn't know. He needed to call them, and his, too. He hadn't asked Jamie to do that. She had done so much already, how could he ask for more?

It killed him to leave the room even though it was only for a few short minutes to walk down to the lobby. He wanted to be there when she woke, but his body needed a stretch, and his mind needed to revive.

Out in the hall he went searching for a vending machine and returned with his arms full of chips, packaged donuts and soda. Sitting down beside her he reached over to caress her cheek. Hoping her eyes would flutter open or sense his presence, he gently pressed his lips to hers. They lingered there for a moment, as a familiar tingle ran through him. He couldn't imagine loving anyone more. She was his life, his everything.

After making the necessary phone calls, he headed out to the nurses' station to see if they had a newspaper or magazine to help pass the time. He didn't want to watch TV, but craved a distraction. They directed him four floors down to the gift shop and once again he hesitated leaving. He made a mental note to suggest newspapers are kept at all the stations, close to the rooms.

"She'll be fine. If she wakes, I promise to send one of the candy stripers down for you," another compassionate nurse named Sharon reassured him.

He lingered in the gift shop for a half an hour before returning to Cammi's room. Still nothing. Sipping on his soda, he looked over the latest headlines barely able to concentrate on what he read. A knock on the door startled him out of his daze.

"Hey, Buddy, how are things?" Shawn asked. "Jamie sent me over with the night bag Allie packed."

"Ah, thanks. It will feel good to clean up," Bryce said taking the bag and setting it down on the extra chair Sharon put into the room. He moved the chair he occupied during the night and motioned for Shawn to sit in it while he rested his hip on the edge of Cammi's bed.

"Nothing yet. The nurses say not to worry, I think they sedated her last night plus gave her some pain medication. They said she would wake up on her own time, when her body and mind were rested enough." He placed his hand on Cammi's lifeless leg, reminding himself she was just asleep, not unconscious.

"Oh, I almost forgot." Shawn said, holding his arm out, regretfully parting with the paper bag he had been carrying. "Cinnamon rolls and muffins. Jamie couldn't sleep last night, so she baked instead. Made it hard for the rest of us to sleep with our stomach's growling," he laughed.

Bryce tore open the bag. "Man, you are saving my ass. It was going to be candy bars and Pepsi. I don't know what we would do without you guys. I owe you a lot," he said gratefully.

"Forget it. You can repay the favor when I am in the doghouse and need a place to stay."

"Deal! I talked to the kids briefly this morning. Are they doing okay?"

"The little ones are, but Allie is really upset. She was up with Jamie most of the night. She's worried about you, but finally dozed off right before I left to come here. Bet she sleeps most of the day."

"Will you tell her everything is going to be fine? I mean everything. I don't care what I have to do to make this better, but I am not going to let Cammi go. We are going to fight to have her back home. She may not know it yet," he said looking down at her, "but I am not giving up, ever."

"Good man. It's about damn time you got tough with her, make her come to her senses. I was starting to worry about you," he grinned. "I will relay your message. But I think it's been good, Allie staying at the house, talking to Jamie and all. She understands what has been going on and isn't so angry anymore, just worried." Standing up, he walked toward the door. "I better get, got to pick up pizza. I told Jamie, no more cooking, we're ordering in. Call if you need anything else."

"Thanks, man."

Bryce laid his head on the bed next to Cammi. He wanted to be close to her, feel her skin, and listen to her breath. He began to doze off when tapping on the door startled him. Trying to clear the fog invading his mind he lifted his head off the bed and was speechless when he saw Cynthia walk through the door.

Instantly, he bolted out of his chair, grabbed her by the elbow and directed her out of the room. Closing the door behind him, he was caught off guard when she threw her arms around his neck.

"Oh, Bryce. I am so sorry. I wanted to come last night to be with you if you needed anything, but I wasn't able to."

Bryce saw the nurses eyeing him warily as he unwrapped himself from Cynthia's embrace. What the hell did she think she was doing?

"Don't you think you have caused enough problems? Cammi is going to wake any moment and you are the last person I want her to see," he growled.

"I didn't realize she disliked me so much," she pouted innocently. Leaning in closer to him she could still smell his aftershave. "I'm sorry to hear about you two, really I am. Allie's been filling me in. Sounds like things have been bad for a while. You are a great guy, Bryce. Don't forget that. If you need *anything* let me know."

A disgusted glare spread across his face as he stepped away from her. "Go home, Cynthia."

"Have you eaten? Maybe we could go downstairs and grab something while you wait. You can tell me what your plans are now that you're a single man! Have you started dating yet?" she asked enthusiastically. "You're still a very handsome man Bryce. It will only be a matter of time before your back on your feet."

"You must have been misinformed," he said sounding gruff. "Cammi and I are not finished, far from it."

"But.....but hasn't she been living with her friends for a month now?" she asked feigning innocence.

"It's none of your business. But rest assured, we are crazy about each other and our marriage will *never* be over."

Cynthia felt the heat move up her face as he grew louder, drawing attention to them both.

"Really, Bryce, it's not good to be in denial about these things. I've seen Cammi at her worst and she can be a little crazy at times. I think she may have some serious issues. You don't need that."

He moved toward her, fury blazing in his eyes. In fright, Cynthia took a step back and held up her hand.

"Bryce, calm down. Allie told me what's been going on and that Cammi left. She assumed you were getting divorced. She's upset; I don't blame her. And now with this, I thought if you and I had a chance to talk, maybe.....maybe...."

Before he was aware of his actions, he found himself nose to nose with her, his finger in her face. "Don't bring Allie into this you, pathetic bitch. There will come a day, and I promise you it will come, when all of this....your bullshit lies, the way you treat Allie, your manipulation.....it will catch up to you. If I have anything to do with it, you'll eventually have to pay, Cynthia. If you were smart, you'd leave town before it day happens."

"Seriously, Bryce, what on earth are you talking about," she asked, eyes wide, a snide smile touching the corner of her lips. He could tell she enjoyed getting a rise out of him. Instead of backing off like a smart woman would, she reached out to touch his chest in a sympathetic gesture. He jumped back as if he had just been scalded by boiling water.

"Why are you so jumpy? Do I tempt you, Bryce?" she challenged, her eyes narrowing into slits, her voice dark and musky. "It's almost as if you are scared to be alone with me. Wonder what might happen?"

He shook his head in disbelief. "You have a lot of nerve, you know that? Get out of my face."

"Bryce, we share a child, a child that loves both of us, a child we should be raising together. Imagine how good our life could be. I know I would be so much happier with you and from the sounds of it, you would be happier with someone.....*anyone* besides Cammi."

"You know what is going to make me happy, Cynthia? Getting extreme pleasure out of watching your miserable little life crumble around you. It's only a matter of time. If she shows up again, call security," he ordered the stunned women at the nurse's station who were hanging onto every word.

Doing his best to contain his anger he walked back into the room leaving Cynthia shocked and speechless. He couldn't believe she would show up at the hospital like a concerned friend, blame Allie for her actions, then try to seduce him while his wife lay hurt and unresponsive in the next room. Well, yes, he could believe it. Some things would never change.

As the hours drug on without any movement from Cammi, hopelessness invaded him. He welcomed the feeling like an old friend. Only last time, this friend held him back, compromising his character and strength. This time... if he got a this time... he was going to do things differently.

Jamie gave him a lot to think about. His bullheadedness enraged him. He knew Cammi better than anyone, it didn't take a genius to figure out what was going on with her...yet he hadn't been able to. He was wrapped up in his own failures as a man. From day one, he felt Cammi was too good for him. When she confessed her love, especially after the problems Beth caused, it was the best dumb luck he ever stumbled upon. His love was genuine, but he had to admit, he rushed into the marriage out of fear of losing her. The dreading she would come to her senses only intensified with her unhappiness.

Cammi was petrified in the beginning, too. And little by little with the conflict brought upon them, her apprehensions from her first marriage broke her down. Behind the strong exterior, she was begging for reassurance from him, and he ignored her cries for help. The worries they shared became a vicious circle to which they were both pawns.

God, he hated himself. But Jamie was right. They had to stop placing blame. It was time to focus on their love and start respecting instead of tearing down. Respect started with acceptance and he needed to accept who he was so he could give that back to Cammi.

What was it he truly wanted out of his marriage? Did he want control, domination, even possession of Cammi? Did he want to be right? Was he with her out of obligation?

The answer to all those questions was no. What they shared was sacred and spiritual. He knew that from the start. He chose her and with it came a deepening of his heart. She was someone he could grow and mature with, both physically and emotionally. She was the person with whom he wanted to heal his deep wounds. There, they would to learn about forgiveness, commitment, the sharing of joy, nurturing, support and all the other things necessary in order for one to travel this journey together.

The epiphany Bryce was experiencing sitting in the silent room watching over his wife as she slept was overwhelming, but gave him a sense of peace he hadn't experienced in years. The tears spilled over his eyes as years of torment and anger released his heart from the cage he kept it locked in. With heavy eyes and his hand covering Cammi's, he finally drifted off to sleep.

Somewhere in between semi-consciousness and deep sleep, Cammi was dreaming. She could see her car on the highway, but she wasn't in it. The bed of a semi-truck whipped into the other lane. A scream tore at her lips as the minivan swerved to avoid a collision, but no sound came out. The black ice caused the tires to lock, the van lost control and flipped.

Unable to tell the difference between dream and reality, Cammi forced her eyes to open, but they already were, weren't they? There was a man. Bryce. No, it wasn't Bryce. Call him, she pleaded to the stranger. Call Bryce! Where was he? Why wasn't he protecting her? She was in trouble.

But Bryce was gone, lost. He didn't want her anymore.

She fought to wake up. She needed to find him. Where was he? She searched frantically all around her, looking, hoping. He wasn't there. He didn't want to see her. Panic filled her subconscious.

She'd been here before, it was a familiar nightmare. And as always, as he walked away from her, she would wake up, stricken with the same sense of emptiness, but nonetheless, she normally woke to find him next to her. Why wasn't she waking up this time?

The desperation smothered her, she couldn't breathe. Suddenly she was in the water, falling, and sinking farther, farther away. Her arms wouldn't move and her legs wouldn't kick. She had to fight, she needed to breathe again. She didn't want to drown. Not this time. She refused to.

Eyes wide with alarm and her chest heaving with much needed air, Cammi sat upright. She didn't know where she was, but as she turned, she saw Bryce asleep, his head lying on the bed beside her. Laying her head back on the pillow, she exhaled deeply. It was apparent he was exhausted because she could hear the gruff sounds of his snores. Content with her safety, knowing he was there, she chose not to wake him.

With exhaustion creeping into her body she relaxed her eyes. Tears of gratitude gently cascaded down her cheek as she placed her hand on his head.

He jolted out of his slumber. "Baby?" He spoke softly, hopefulness filling his voice.

She opened her eyes again and tried to speak. "I….I couldn't find you, I thought you were gone," she stammered slowly, grasping for energy.

Reaching his hand up, he stroked her hair. He looked into her deep green eyes. The eyes, nine years ago, he wanted to spend his life protecting. The eyes of the deepest love he had ever known. "Never, Baby. It'll never happen."

Cammi's stay in the hospital was three days. Bryce was by her side continuously which gave them plenty of opportunities to talk. She needed time to heal physically and emotionally she told him. She had changes to make not only in their relationship, but with herself. He understood and didn't want to push or sabotage her recovery let alone any second chance they may have.

Jamie suggested she stay with them a while longer. It would be awkward and difficult but they both needed time to build the foundation of their relationship. It pained him not to have her with him right away, but they both had to be realistic that their relationship was going to take time and effort to repair, and it wasn't going to happen overnight. Their first step was to trust, communicate and become friends again without unnecessary expectations.

"Do you think all couples go through this?" she asked him one evening while he stood in Jamie's kitchen scooping chocolate ice cream into bowls. She was getting around much better than she did the week before, and the doctor told her it would be at least another two weeks before she regained most of her strength but mentally, Cammi felt stronger and healthier than she had in years.

"Yeah, I do. Look at the divorces. People aren't taught the coping skills to withstand the disappointments of a relationship. They live in denial or fantasyland. I believe the love in the beginning can endure through the years, but it has to be nurtured, tended to. People don't see marriage as a purpose, so they give up. They are caught up in what they are going to get instead of what they can give. The instant gratification of our society," he sighed.

It was strange to hear such profound words leave his mouth. She was astounded when he told her about his epiphany in the hospital. Since he had complete faith in the direction God was leading them and what it was she'd wanted to show him all these years. Only now it was his turn to guide her.

She wasn't ready to share her time in the church with Clifford just yet. What the strange old man said to her that day had an extreme effect, and she wanted to hold onto the private memory for a while. Putting it to use wasn't going to be an easy process. Years of habits were hard to break, and she had quite a bit of healing within herself she needed to work on before she explained it to Bryce.

She thought about the years of lectures, conversations and arguments she had with her husband in the prospect of changing how he thought and who he was. She expected him to believe and live a certain way, to have a certain frame of mind because if he did, life would be so much better for them both. But she hadn't heeded her own advice. She was so busy fixing him she wasn't looking at the source of her own pain. Ultimately, it was up to her to create the life she longed for. Clifford's words as well as her sister's and Jamie's, had been a harsh reality. And she appreciated them all the more for not sugarcoating the truth.

Aside from Bryce and Allie stopping by as often as they could, the counseling sessions with Gloria were the highlight of Cammi's week. Time after time when she would try to get off track, Gloria forced the attention back on her. Cammi appreciated her directness and brought up many valid points Cammi more or less chose to overlook. Cammi mainly saw things in black or white. For her there was no in-between. But life wasn't always black and white. The many shades of colors residing around them were opportunities for growth and acceptance. And those opportunities along the way were ones Cammi choose to ignore.

"Do you believe in divine intervention, Cammi?" Gloria had asked at their most recent session.

"Of course I do," she replied. "Why?"

"I enjoy your time here more than I think you realize. It benefits me as well as it benefits you. I typically don't reveal personal information to my clients, but I think I need to tell you a story. You see….I was in a similar situation years ago. I have two stepsons. I came into their life when they were ten and twelve. Only my story is a little different. My sons worshiped their mother. Their dad kicked her out three years before because she was having numerous affairs behind his back. He refused to allow the boys to think ill of their mother, so he kept the truth from them. She vanished for quite some time to Texas before reappearing when they were thirteen and fifteen. Needless to say, the boys blamed their father for kicking her out, and she encouraged them to believe I was the reason behind her leaving. It was very ugly indeed. Now, his ex-wife didn't cause as much turmoil as Cynthia has brought to you, but the things she told the children about their father and I…..it was very toxic. She brainwashed them against us, so after their time with her, they hated coming home."

Cammi couldn't believe what she was hearing. Gloria's small desk was filled with pictures of a loving family, her smiling husband, two handsome men and a beautiful young woman.

"What happened?" Cammi asked, intrigued by the story.

"We gave them what they wanted. Told them they could go live with her. I brought my own daughter into the marriage and my husband decided their belligerent behavior wasn't a good influence on Elizabeth. Maybe they needed to learn the hard way. But I was mad. I loved the boys and didn't want them to leave. I hated having a part time family. I wanted all the kids a hundred percent of the time. Elizabeth was three when I divorced her father. The guilt I felt raising her in a broken home was horrible, and I wanted more than anything to find a wonderful man and give her a strong, stable and secure family. Well, as you can imagine, my dreams were shattered.

Elizabeth adored her step brothers and it was devastating for her when they left. My anger controlled my life. I hated my husband for the choice he made. We had the boys every other weekend and when they were around all they heard was fighting. They learned to hate me, resent me and treated me with such little respect that I, too finally left."

Standing up, Gloria got them both a bottle of water from the tiny refrigerator she'd just added to her office. "I left for a year," she continued. "I didn't get it as quickly as you did, Cammi. I, too, am a woman of faith. Unfortunately, when Richard came into my life, I took my faith away from God and put it onto Richard. I forgot to nurture the relationship and looked towards my husband to fill those shoes. And I am here to tell you, it just doesn't work. That's a lot of pressure on one man and Richard, hard as he tried, failed every time. So I looked elsewhere, new jobs, new clothes, a new house, and I am ashamed to admit, I looked towards other men. Thank goodness I never had an affair, but I can't say the thought never crossed my mind. I liked the attention, the instant gratification, they made me feel special. My husband poured everything into me, but it still wasn't enough. And one day, it hit me….. without God, I just wasn't filled. And unfortunately, I never would be."

Seeing she had Cammi's attention, Gloria looked sympathetically into her eyes. "God, made Eve for Adam so they wouldn't be alone, for companionship, not to take God's place in the heart. But for centuries, that is what we've done, replaced God in our hearts. We look for fulfillment elsewhere. We are left empty, wondering what can make it better."

"What did you do?" Cammi's asked her voice soft and meek.

"I set out on a quest to find my heart's desire. To find God and put him back where he belonged. And I'll tell you, it hasn't been easy. It's a relationship just like any other. You have to work at it. Nurture it. Make him a priority. But there's nothing like it," she smiled satisfactorily. "Like you, I had to repair what was broken of my heart first. Forgive and release the past."

She and Cammi sat in quiet contemplation for a moment. "Oh, and after the boys lived with their mom and her new husband for six months, they were back begging forgiveness. It didn't take long for them to catch onto their mother's scandalous behavior when their step dad was out of town driving truck."

"It must have killed them to learn the truth."

"They were hurt, but the guilt because of what they put their Dad through was harder. Richard is a forgiving man and those boys are his heart. So you see, it is possible to heal your wounds, you just have to look in the right place."

Chapter Thirty-Five

Allie was helping Cynthia put another coat of paint on the walls of her living room when Jake stopped by. She'd been evicted *again* and moved into a shabby, rundown trailer her boss at the bar owned.

It was the fourth eviction in three years. The first one came with a long line of lies. The landlord's wife hated her. She was jealous and thought Cynthia and her husband were having an affair so she kicked her out before Cynthia had a chance to clean house or move her furniture. So Cynthia said. In her car had been three suitcases of clothes, a dozen or so small boxes labeled kitchen, and her toiletries.

"Cynthia, it's illegal for them to keep your furniture," Allie told her after she moved into an apartment and still hadn't retrieved her belongings. They had just returned from Rent-A-Center with a new couch, television and bed. "It's silly for you to waste your money buying new stuff. Just go talk to them. I am sure they will be reasonable. Anyway, don't they have to give you a months' notice?"

Deceit clouded Cynthia's face as she shifted her eyes from Allie's. Obviously there was more to the story.

"They can have it all. Good riddance. I don't want any memories of living there. This is my fresh start, Honey. Let's just enjoy it."

The similarities between the first, second and third evictions were startling. Each time, Cynthia left her new furniture and started over. Allie didn't understand it, but eventually quit to asking questions. She'd never get a straight answer anyway. This last time, her boss and some guys she worked with helped her move. Allie figured she must have run out of money to supply her house with new furnishings so she didn't have a choice but to bring everything with her.

Jake rapped his knuckles on the screen door of the trailer, and Allie motioned for him to come in. Though he'd been sixteen for eight months now, he finally had enough money saved up from mowing lawns the past few summer to buy a car. His parents promised if he paid for half, they would pay the other half but he would have to get a job on the weekends during school to earn money for gas and insurance. It was all he talked about, and Allie couldn't help being excited for him.

"Ready to go for a spin?" he asked her grinning from ear to ear while taking in his surroundings.

The trailer was small. Put a steering wheel up front and she could have called it a motor home, he mused. The carpet was shag green except for the spots that were stained yellow from what must have been some animal. When he walked in, the odor of mold and mildew as well as urine invaded his nose. The stairs he took leading to the front door were falling apart, holes deteriorating the wood and rusty nails held it together. The weight of his body alone made them sway and creak. Standing by the door reluctantly, he had no desire for a tour.

"Can I go Cynthia? I promise we won't be gone long and then I'll help finish."

"I don't care," she said taking a long drag on her cigarette. "Donovan is coming over anyway." She stopped for a moment, blowing a long line of smoke out the side of her mouth. "Hey, Jake, why don't you stay for supper? We are grilling steaks."

He smiled politely. "I'll think about it, thanks."

Cynthia dipped her brush into the bucket resting on the top of her ladder and turned back to the task at hand.

"I'll be back later," Allie called over her shoulder.

Leaning close to Allie so Cynthia couldn't hear, he asked, "What was that all about? I was just getting used to her ignoring me." He opened the passenger door and then stepped aside to let her slide in.

"Well, aren't you a gentlemen?" she teased. "Who knows? I don't try to figure her out anymore."

"Who's Donovan? I thought she was dating some Marcus guy."

"Like I said, I don't try to figure her out anymore." Letting a slow whistle escape from her lips, she rubbed her hand over the black interior of the car. "Nice. Very nice."

"You seem happy, what's up?" Jake asked.

The breakup of her parents had torn Allie apart. Jake thought it was unfair. She had to deal with more junk than anyone he knew, and the one stable thing she had going for her was Bryce and Cammi, but that looked as if it was a dead end for her too. Thank God they were working on putting it back together.

The weeks without her family around killed her. She loved her dad so much, but feeling his agony as well as her own without Cammi and her siblings was destroying her. She couldn't stand to be around him and staying with Cynthia seemed like the only alternative. It wasn't a great alternative, but it was better than living at her house without the very thing making it a home, her family. Her dad explained to her why Cammi left. Allie can't say she blamed her. From the outside looking in, she knew they were both at fault, but a little part of Allie could not help but wonder if she had something to do with it also.

The three days she was with Cynthia were hell. She was gone, out at the bars and didn't come home until four or five in the morning and of course, there were always strange drunk men with her. Allie was smart and always shoved a chair under the door knob of her bedroom, but early one morning, she heard the handle turn from side to side, and the sound of a male voice cursing then kick at the door. That's when she figured being at her Dad's had to be better than this. And once she returned, she was glad she did. Though the sadness was overwhelming for both of them, she and her Dad depended on one another to see it through.

She'd never been more frightened than when she heard about the accident. She didn't know what she would do if they lost Cammi. Not only would she lose her mother, but she would eventually lose her father to the grief of living without his one true love. With them separated, there was still the hope all would work out, but if Cammi died...... Allie couldn't think about it.

When she got the phone call from Jamie telling her to pack some things, she and her siblings were going to stay at her house, Allie had been relieved. She wanted....no.... she needed to be with her brother and sister. It was her job to make sure they were safe. And it felt good when she saw how much they needed her too. Plus being at Jamie's was almost as good as being at home.

It was odd how a tragedy of this magnitude ended up bringing them closer together. It was strange to her was how awful her parents acted when they were desperately sad and hurt, while searching for love. They avoided reaching out in times of need and bad behavior caused them to hate not only themselves but each other. Too bad it took the risk of losing someone to make a person see mistakes. Cammi eventually told Allie about her first marriage and how it affected her life, her future and those she loved. Allie felt horrible for her mom, but she was grateful she confided in her.

"I'm not sure. I feel good. Life's great."

"Is Cynthia pissed you are back at your dads?"

"Naw, I don't think she cares one way or another. It's all talk, you know."

He looked at her sympathetically. It didn't take long for her to come to the conclusion she could *never* live with her mom.

"Dr. Cassidy helped me realize I've got to have boundaries or else I'll expect too much and wind up disappointed and hurt all the time. You were right, you know." She stole a glance in his direction. "I'm sorry I was so hard on you. I love Cynthia, but our relationship is never going to be a real mother/daughter one. The stuff with Cammi made me see that too. I can't change it. I get angry, but I don't blame myself anymore. She is who she is; I just have to keep a healthy distance. Funny thing, she doesn't seem to notice. She is too wrapped up in Marcus or Donovan, or whoever," she laughed.

"Has Cammi come home yet?"

"No, but I think soon. Dad seems happier. She's still nervous.... I can tell when we go to Jamie's, but she is smiling and laughing again. I admire them both for what they are doing. Instead of giving up, they are willing to fight for their love. I hope I can find that one day."

She laid her head back against the headrest gazing at the blue sky through the sunroof. He watched in wonder hoping one day he could be the one to give her that love.

"I think Cynthia might be moving," Allie said suddenly.

"What? She just moved," he looked appalled.

"Out of town. She doesn't want to stay here and I guess Marcus wants to get married. He has another office in Lincoln. He loves Denver, but wants a change. What's funny is how she tries to keep this stuff from me. There isn't anything about her I don't know. She's so dumb sometimes. I'm guessing this trailer is temporary until they leave."

"What does he do?"

Allie shrugged. "Haven't a clue."

"And...... Donovan?"

She shook her head and smiled mischievously at him.

"Does that bother you? If she moves, I mean."

She shrugged. "Maybe a few years ago, but I'm used to it now. This isn't the life she wants. No matter what I do, I can't convince her to enjoy this and enjoy being a mom. She needs to be free. I know she loves me, but I tie her down. I have my real family anyways, the one who makes me feel special, the one willing to give up anything for my happiness." Jake could hear the honesty in her voice, but still her words made him angry.

"Not much will change if she does leave, you know. Things might even be better. You wouldn't have to put up with her bullshit, right?" he laughed making light of the situation.

"So true," she agreed. "Enough about Cynthia. Show me how tough this car is." She let out a howl of carefree abandon as he pushed the accelerator to the floor and sped off.

Cammi was anxiously pacing the floor. She checked her hair and make up for the millionth time and then sat on the couch waiting for her date to arrive. This dating thing they were doing was enjoyable. For weeks the waiting and the wanting made her feel alive again. But she had to be careful not to allow the high of her emotions with Bryce to deter her from the work she had to do within.

"Chill out, girl. You are making me jealous. Shawn, how about we break up and do this all over again?" Jamie giggled with a wink at her husband. "Can you imagine the sex?"

Shawn stretched his arms over his head and slowly got out of his recliner. He walked over to where his wife was lying on the couch and sat on top of her. Their antics always made Cammi laugh. "Baby, the sex has never been as good as it is now. I promise to show you later tonight, since Cammi won't be coming back here anyway," he whispered sticking his finger in her ear.

"Yes, I will," she demanded applying another layer of lip-gloss out of nervous habit.

"Oh yeah? Do you want to take bets?" Jamie pushed Shawn off her and onto the floor while grabbing for her purse. "I will put ten down that says she doesn't ever come back after tonight."

Shawn grabbed for his wallet. "I will see your ten and raise you twenty."

"Shut up! You guys are awful. My children are here. Of course I'm coming back."

"More reason for you to stay the night with your *boyfriend,*" Shawn teased. "If we had a house without kids, imagine the possibilities," he said wiggling his eyebrows.

Jamie and Shawn were perfect together. Cammi envied the ease and comfort they felt in the other's presence. She wished it were that easy for her. She always worried if she were her true genuine self around Bryce, he wouldn't love her. He might find her annoying or irritating, so she constantly strived for perfection, but in the midst of it, she lost who she was.

It had been two months since her accident and in that amount of time, lots had changed. She and Bryce became friends again. There were still moments of awkwardness and arguments, but they were finally listening to one another. Gloria, of course, was helping her heal old wounds. Bryce attended a session every other week and the pay offs were huge. Slowly, Cammi began to trust in his unconditional love and the fear triggering the self-sabotaging behavior was vanishing along with anger she had been holding onto for years.

Bryce was learning to have a more positive approach in his communication instead of criticism. Through understanding her insecurities he was able to alleviate them without feeling like he was always attacked. Though he was a private man, he thrived on the encouraging responses he received from his wife and soon Cammi was able to identify his emotions with his actions.

It all seemed so simple. Too bad they hadn't been able to figure it out before now. It certainly wasn't easy. There were still times their disagreements became heated, but by taking the threat out of it and using their new skills, they remained arguments and never escalated into wars.

"If you win, you'll be taking my poker money," Shawn told his wife.

"I will give you money for poker night, Baby. It's my sanity as much as it is yours," she said giving him a quick kiss on the cheek as she swiped the dollar bills out of his hand.

Cammi smiled at Shawn's back as he walked out to the garage. 'His man haven' as he liked to call it. "You never told me Shawn has a poker night with the guys. Don't tell Bryce that. Then he'll want one, too."

Jamie sat on the couch next to her friend. "What's wrong with that?"

"Doesn't it bother you he enjoys being with the guys more than he does you?"

Jamie laughed. "He's a guy. You need your girl time, don't you? Guys need their time to do whatever it is they do. Fart, drink beer, and grunt. You know." She picked up a magazine and began to flip through it. "Cammi, seriously, you need to relax when it comes to Bryce. He's willing to give up everything for you. He doesn't golf, he doesn't play basketball. He doesn't do anything for himself. To tell you the truth, we sort of feel sorry for him. Guys need to be guys and do guy things. It makes them who they are. If you love Bryce for *who* he is, I would think you would encourage him to do the things he loves. The things making him feel like a man."

She looked up to see Cammi's skeptical expression and set the magazine down. "I'm going to be totally honest with you. That's the sort of stuff that drives men away. The stuff that makes them lie to their wives about where they are and what they're doing. You've controlled this with him since the beginning and he still gives you the world. I don't know many men like that. Come to a compromise with him. He knows how insecure it makes you feel, he wouldn't intentionally do anything to make you feel bad, but he needs some freedom. He needs to be him. Plus, I will tell you a little secret. When they are out with the guys, drinking beer, doing man stuff, listening to the crap the other guys say about their own wives, they realize how lucky they are and how great their wife is. Trust me; he will start to miss you. Feeling all manly will be a confidence boost which means, he will come home to you and want more sex and give *you* more attention. It's great! I love it when Shawn goes with the boys once a week because I am treated like a queen when he gets home."

"Really?" Cammi's expression turned from one of skepticism to one of delight. She'd never thought of it that way.

"I used to feel the same way as you the first year Shawn and I were together. I never told anyone because I didn't want to be the 'bitchy' girlfriend, and it made me seem too needy. I hated it. Shawn being as sensitive as he is sensed it, so we came to our own compromise. Now we both get what we want."

"I do feel guilty," Cammi confessed. "I know it's not fair. But he agreed and I took advantage of it. It's definitely something I need to think about."

Not living together, Cammi missed Bryce like mad and couldn't wait to spend the evening together, alone. Their time was usually spent with the kids or in the company of Jamie and Shawn. The house was small but Cammi, regardless of how much she missed her own home, felt apprehensive about going there. Thank goodness for the telephone. They would spend hours on it each day to get the privacy they both craved. It sentimentally reminded her of when they first met.

Her heart leapt out of her chest when the doorbell rang. Jamie snuck out of the room as Cammi went to the door. Smoothing back her hair, she checked her reflection in the hall mirror one last time before she opened it.

Their eyes met and locked. Bryce wanted to pull Cammi into his arms and bury his head in her neck, but settled for a kiss on the cheek allowing his lips to linger for a moment while he inhaled her perfume. The warmth of his touch made her tingle with pleasure. Aside from holding hands or a hug, it was the first intimate touch they shared since the night she left. He had been too afraid, knowing if he tried anything else it would be too hard to stop.

With the heat of excitement coursing through his body, he took her by the hand and led her to his truck. He had lost sleep anticipating this evening, and didn't want to waste another second of their time.

Bryce made reservations at the same Italian Bistro they went to on their very first date. The smell of garlic and basil brought back a flood of memories. As they waited in the lobby he wrapped his arms around, pulling her close and closed his eyes for a brief moment caught up in the steady rush of the embrace.

Neither had touched their food as they were too busy talking, and after dinner they opted for a walk in the park. The sun had just set, but the temperature was still comfortable. Walking hand in hand they reminisced about their first months together.

"Are you attracted to me?" Cammi asked bluntly during a moment of silence. She was shivering, but didn't know if it was because of the temperature or the excitement of being this close to her husband again.

He looked deep into her eyes, searching for the source of her pain. "Of course, I am. I think you are beautiful," he reassured her, rubbing his hands up and down her arms to warm her. "Why would you ask such a thing?"

"I thought those feeling were gone. I mean, you weren't as interested, and I know a man has needs. I always wondered if you might be finding it somewhere else, with someone who could give you what I couldn't, emotionally and physically. I….I…. it was my past haunting me," she stumbled over the words, embarrassed to admit them. "I know that now but the thought of you with someone else…..it killed me. "

Wiping away a tear escaping from the corner of her eye, he pulled her close. "Baby, I need you to listen to me. First of all, you are more than enough woman for me. I would never look anywhere else for anything. My heart has always been with you and no matter what we go through, that is not something I would do, ever."

"But you stopped showing me," she said sadly. "You stopped showing me anything. I got really scared. I don't think I could live through that again."

"I know," he sighed. "I know. I'm not making excuses. You were always in my thoughts. I just didn't take the time to express it. I'm sorry. I'm not proud to admit this, in fact, it is a bruise to a man's ego, but I am not twenty anymore, hell, I'm forty-one. The less we connected emotionally, I guess the less I was interested physically. I was hurt. I was angry. When we get along, I want you all the time, but when we don't....I don't know. Either way it doesn't change my love or the fact you are the most beautiful woman in the world." He bent down to gently kiss her lips.

"A woman needs to hear that once in a while, you know. Don't take me for granted....please?" she said returning his kiss.

"I promise to make changes, too. I won't let you down again." He grabbed her hand again as they walked toward the lake.

"And I promise I will stop saying things that make you feel bad." She thought for a moment. "You have taught me a lot," Cammi whispered. "I'm sorry I haven't trusted in your love. I'm sorry I let myself fall. I'm going to do whatever it takes to get back up."

"We both will." He squeezed her hand. "You are the strongest woman I know. It's one of the reasons I love you so much." Tears filled her eyes as she reached up to kiss him. It started out as a soft touch of the lips when suddenly a jolt of electricity turned the embrace into a need, a wanting unlike anything they'd ever experienced. Wrapping her arms around his neck she deepened the kiss unwilling to break the contact, afraid he might disappear if she let go.

His hand curled through her long brown hair as his tongue caressed her bottom lip. Reluctantly he moved his mouth away towards her ear.

"When do you think you will be ready to move back home? I miss you so damn much. You have no idea how unbearable it is. I want you back in my bed. In my life," he whispered breathlessly as he nibbled with wild desire.

"Let me win this bet tonight and we can talk about it when I buy you lunch."

They found a man-made tree house, one most kids loved to play in during the day. At night it was desolate. There was no traffic close by, no children playing. Trees surrounded every side giving them complete silence, isolation from the rest of the world. It didn't take much for Bryce to convince Cammi to go with him. He followed her up the wooden steps admiring the sway in her hips as she moved. Once inside, the blood pounding in him took over whatever control he had left. She'd tempted him all night and it had been too long since he had a chance to express his love. Their mouths came together in heated resolve, both of them succumbing to their desires.

His hands pushed up her skirt to find bare skin barely covered by a string of cloth. He heard her gasp in delight when he finally touched her, and he could feel his own body strain against the tightness of his pants as he longed to please her.

His kisses were intense and filled with hunger. Pressing her softness into him, he gently pushed her back against the wooden wall, careful not to hurt her, but also demanding what she was willing to offer. She felt his hardness as he pushed his body against hers, arousing her curiosity. Not wanting to wait any longer, she wrapped her legs around his waist. Picking her up, he slowly lowered her to the ground, where the blanket they brought along 'just in case' had been dropped. He pulled the dress up over her head looking in wonder upon the body he had memorized over the years. While he caressed her, she unbuckled his pants and helped him slide out. His touch was gentle, like new, and she hoped it wasn't an illusion. He hovered over her, enticing her lips with his tongue until she could no longer stand it. Reaching seductively, she guided him into her as he moaned with pleasure. They moved with the rhythm of hearts beating as one, allowing them the vulnerability to surrender to each other once again.

"The nights are forever without you," he whispered the chorus of one of her favorite songs as they lay there looking at the stars above.

She turned on her side and smiled at him. "When you were young, did you ever imagine it would be like this, so strong, so intense?"

"I hoped so. But until I met you, it never was. That is how I knew you were the one and never once have I doubted it." He ran his fingers through her long, dark hair. "I'm never going to let you go, Cammi, never again."

Bryce put the truck into park and leaned into Cammi while she toyed with the shoes on her lap.

"I don't want you to get out. It kills me to leave you here, you belong at home with me," he whispered nuzzling her neck. He slid his hand up the hem of her skirt, teasing her one more time. At his touch, her body begged for more. But she had to get inside. It was already after one in the morning.

"Thanks for the date," she said kissing him again.

Now, his heart, as mixture of tenderness and sorrow walked her to the front door. Not of their house, but Jamie's. He leaned in for one more kiss before he had to make the torturous drive home. Pressing his forehead against hers, he stared deeply into her green eyes wishing it was six hours earlier when their evening was just beginning.

"Don't worry, we are going to make this work, I promise you. We can't let a love like ours slip away," she reassured him. "You've made me see that. You've made all my doubts disappear."

With a squeeze of her hand he turned to walk away but stopped when she called out to him.

"I love you."

Looking back at her, he grinned. "I love you more than you know."

Chapter Thirty-Six

Bryce surprised the family with a trip to Cancun.

They discussed it over dinner the previous evening and would leave the following weekend, stay for two weeks then Cammi would move back home the minute they got back. The last trip they had been on was to Florida before Faith and Bailey were born and Bryce thought this was a great way to bring some security to the family after so much instability.

"You will be gone for two weeks?" Jake asked sounding disappointed when Allie told him. "Who am I going to spend my summer with?"

"You are such a dork. You have football camp the first week I'm away, plus you and Trevor planned to go whitewater rafting, remember? And it's only two weeks, not the whole summer."

"Oh, okay," he teased her. But deep down, he was going to miss her like crazy. "Will you be back for your birthday?"

"Yeah, they promised I would. This is sort of a sweet sixteen trip since they won't let me have a big party. I will be back the week before. So plan something special for me," she hinted. "Actually, Cynthia asked if she could do something for me too, so I will keep you posted. Pray it's not a disaster. Hopefully this Marcus guy can keep her in line for now, anyways. It is only a matter of time," she said sarcastically.

"Have you met him?"

"Just that time last summer. He sounds like a jerk, though, doesn't seem to care about anything but making money. He's loaded. Imagine that," she snorted. "He likes her, but it is on his terms. He seems very controlling. Cynthia's not used to that."

She had filled Allie in on every sordid detail. It sounded like Marcus was more of a pimp than an actual boyfriend. But Allie was beyond losing sleep over her mother's love life.

"Okay, I have to go, but I will let you know what she plans, and I will call the minute we get back." She reached over to give him a hug.

Having a sudden urge to kiss her, Jake quickly pulled back but not without her notice.

"You okay?" she asked filled with curiosity. His face turned red and he tried to laugh but wound up losing his footing in the grass as he stepped away from her.

"Just clumsiness, that's all," he lied. Allie narrowed her eyes suspiciously. Jake was the school's best athlete, and she had *never* seen him clumsy.

"Okay, uh, see you later then," she said, skipping up the front porch stairs two at a time. Curiosity got the best of her so she watched through the curtain as his car pulled away. A nervous feeling crept up her spine when she watched him turn the corner. It was a feeling she couldn't quite distinguish, but even so, it made her smile.

Cancun was incredible. The weather was beautiful, the water warm, the food luscious but best of all, they were together. Cammi was in heaven. She spent most of her days on the beach or by the pool putting her thoughts down in her private journal and the rest of the time enjoying her husband and family. The children swam every day and Allie attracted the attention of many teenage boys. She didn't seem to notice though. Her mind was distracted.

"I know how gorgeous you are, but I think your dad is going to have a heart attack if one more boy breaks his neck to look in your direction," Cammi mentioned.

Allie was stunning in her brown and white bikini. With her long, muscular body, anyone could mistake her for Cammi's biological daughter, but the toe-head blonde hair and blue eyes, gave it all away.

Cammi had been scared how Allie was going to react to her after the decision she made to leave her dad, but when Allie showed up at Jamie's after school two days later, her head hung low and eyes filled with sadness, Cammi did the only thing a mother could do. She wrapped her in her arms and they spent an hour crying together. Cammi didn't want to put Allie in the middle so she was careful not to say or make any promises she couldn't keep, but she did apologize for the hurt and pain she was causing. They made a point to talk often that month and put to rest any insecurity they both had been feeling about their relationship.

Allie was keeping a close eye on her brother and sister who were shoveling sand into buckets a few feet away but pretended to flip through a fashion magazine. The threat of what might have happened made Allie appreciate her loved ones all the more. Never in her life had she missed her family as much as she did and never again was she going to take them for granted.

"What? Oh, I wasn't even paying attention," she said sitting up to rub sunscreen on her fair skin. She allowed her body enough color to look good, but not too much to cause any damage. Allie was very careful when it came to her health. She would rather be white as a ghost than wrinkled like an old lady when she was forty, she always told them.

Watching the surf crash onto the sand, she shaded her eyes with her hand to keep the sun out. "Mom?'

"Hmm?" Cammi replied lazily. "I had a dream about a boy last night. What do you think that means?"

Surprised, Cammi closed the romance novel she was reading. Dirk and Kiley were just going to have to wait. This was much more important.

"Well I guess it depends on who it is. I don't know much about analyzing dreams, but I would imagine it means this boy is on your mind and you care about him. Or it could be a simple crush."

Allie's scrunched her nose up. "I don't have a crush on him. That's gross. I don't even look at him in that way." She picked up the polish she had brought along and began to paint her nails a shade of light pink.

By her reaction, Cammi knew immediately Allie was talking about Jake. It was obvious to Cammi his feelings for her daughter ran deeper than her feelings for him. Or did they?

"Is this boy handsome?" she fished.

"Oh, yeah, he's really cute, probably the cutest boy in school." She never had a problem admitting that. He *was* cute, she always thought so. Girls were crazy about him but no matter how hard Allie pushed, he never went out with anyone. In fact, he never even mentioned another girl unless she brought it up. "And he's a great guy," she added.

"So what's the problem?" Cammi asked taking a sip of the margarita Bryce handed to her. There was nothing more relaxing than sitting on a tropical beach drinking her favorite concoction.

Throwing himself down on the blanket next to his wife, Bryce draped an arm over her shoulder. Sensing Allie's hesitation to continue with him there, Cammi suggested he help the other two kids with their sand castle. Instead of helping, he picked one up in each of his arms and headed into the surf, all three of them screaming in delight until Bailey started crying and spitting the saltwater out of his mouth.

"You know Jake is my best friend," Allie continued when her dad was out of ear shot. "Almost like a brother. The idea of kissing him is disgusting, "she admitted.

"Okay, Okay. Don't get so defensive," Cammi said holding her hands up. "I would say the dream means he is on your mind for some reason. Maybe you should e-mail him. See if everything is all right. There is internet access in the lobby."

"Yeah…..you're probably right. I'll do it later. Now it's nap time." She pushed her arms out in front of her, careful not to smudge a nail and closed her eyes.

It amused Cammi to watch Allie and Jake dance around their feelings. She was pretty sure he was head over heels in love with her daughter. Allie was either ignorant to it or just chose to ignore it. Either way, Cammi had a feeling it wouldn't be long before her own emotions for the boy got the best of her.

Allie agreed to baby-sit while Cammi and Bryce went on a Sunset Cruise. It was a gorgeous evening and with the dazzling blaze of dusk falling over the ocean, they were able to lose themselves in a love where no one else but the two of them existed.

Cammi felt radiant and carefree in an off-white strapless dress cutting just below her knees. Bryce thought she looked sensational and was more encouraged than ever about their future, but at times he could still feel the apprehension linger over her.

As they swayed to the music of the Mariachi band playing below deck, they clung to the life they shared. The emotions of what was almost lost were etched deeply into their hearts as they fought to replace it with new found confidence.

After the cruise, they took a stroll along the beach. It had been fun, but noisy and Cammi desperately wanted to have her husband to herself without a million other people around. They walked hand in hand, their feet making imprints in the sand, enjoying the calm the evening brought until they found a secluded spot where the moon danced upon the waves.

This trip had been magical for her. The best part was watching Bryce enjoy the beach with the kids. He and Allie snorkeled for hours and then played water games with the younger two. The resort had more than a person could dream of in the ways of entertainment; disco clubs for teens, waterslides, shopping, even a spa and fitness club. They threw themselves into bed each night exhausted and blissful.

Over the week as Cammi studied Bryce's actions, his joy, his body language, she realized she was falling in love with him in a way she hadn't allowed herself before, with a free heart instead of a fearful one, one she wanted to surrender to him without conditions or the worry of being broken.

Her mood suddenly turned serious. "The hardest part of leaving you was missing out on all the good things. No matter how angry I was or get, I still wanted to be with you. To share everything with you," she said staring out over the water, her hand secured in his. "It was hell being apart."

The breeze from the ocean stirred her hair and in a loving gesture, he pushed it behind her ear.

"At the time, I thought I was running away from you when really, I was just running away from emotions I couldn't face."

It was refreshing to hear she was as miserable away from him as he was her. But there was something he desperately needed to tell her. Something that had been on his mind since the night she left him.

"Cammi, we aren't perfect and we will never be. There is bound to be conflict sometime over the next forty plus years. I need to know you can accept it, that you can handle it. I'm not going to lie and say it doesn't worry me. When things don't go right, when one or both of us screw up, are you going to leave and question whether we belong together or are you in this for the long haul? I think we can do this.... learn to fight healthy, deal with our hurts and disappointments, but if I have to spend the rest of my life wondering if you are going to leave.....I can't do it. I don't want to live that way anymore than you do."

She turned to look up into his blue eyes visible with pain and grief. Those were the eyes she trusted, the man behind the eyes whom she loved. "I take a vow with every part of who I am that no matter what, no matter what storms we face in life, no matter how furious we are, there is nothing that will ever tear us apart. And I won't leave. I'll never hurt you that way."

A wave swept onto the beach drenching their feet in lukewarm water. Bryce grabbed her hand pulling her towards a little hut hidden under the palm trees a good distance away from the resort. Her mouth was hot and ready when he pulled her to him. Her body instantly reacted to his touch. Every experience was new and special. Just like the love growing within their hearts.

Jake couldn't wait to see Allie. His parents gave him permission to use the Suburban to pick them up from the airport. He missed her so much, but had to remind himself not to let it show. He spent the better part of the last week trying to figure out why she took the time out of her trip to e-mail him everyday all the way from Mexico. The e-mails seemed odd, they didn't sound like the Allie he knew. They were very vague, distant and she really didn't have much to say except when she asked him to meet her when the plane landed.

She looked beautiful walking into the terminal. Her natural blonde hair had streaks from the sun and a radiant glow from her time on the beach glistened on her skin.

"What's up? Did you miss me?" she asked lightheartedly punching him in the arm. It felt a bit awkward seeing him again. She thought about him constantly on her trip and looking at him now, she was aware something was different. He was more handsome than she remembered. Was that even possible? Shaking off the feeling, she tried to play it cool.

"Of course I did. You're my kick it girl, remember?" he shoved her back playfully. Something had changed with her. He couldn't put his finger on it, but something was definitely off.

"So fill me in. What did I miss while I was gone?" she asked, anxious to catch up on what everyone was doing so far this summer but it was also an attempt avoid the tingling in the pit of her stomach. She and Jake lingered behind her family who hurried along, yards in front of them in a rush to reach the baggage claim.

He chuckled and told her about rafting, football camp and the latest high school gossip.

"Brandi's a whore. She's so busy trying to make Christian jealous she ended up sleeping with half the football team in the past month."

Allie's eyes widened with disbelief. "No way! I guess I shouldn't be so surprised. What does he say about it?"

"There was a party at Missy's last Wednesday, he was drunk and told Brandi exactly what he thought, and it wasn't nice. The guys say it was pretty hilarious watching her flip out and pour her drink on his head. Shane's dating Alyssa now, but she wants to go out with Trevor. And Trevor, well he could care less. Football is his life. What about you? Tell me about your trip."

She relayed all the important details. The beach, the ocean, the food, the music, but she felt inclined not to tell him she met three boys, all from California. She didn't understand why she didn't tell him. It's not like any of them piqued her interest, but they asked her out nonetheless. She always told Jake about other boys, but this time, she felt self-conscious. The trip was amazing, but she couldn't wait to get home and see him. It was part of the reason she asked him to pick them up. Her patience was wearing thin.

"How are your mom and dad doing? Was the trip what they needed?" he asked carefully.

He'd seen how much turmoil Allie had gone through with Cynthia, but he thought her life was going to fall apart when Cammi moved out. Now he watched as her parents walked ahead of them hand in hand as if the past four months had been only a bad dream.

"Yeah, it was good for all of us, as a family, I mean. They amaze me." She nodded in their direction. "I am really lucky to have them. I can't believe I actually thought living with Cynthia and getting away from them would be best for me. Could you imagine?"

He shook his head.

"I am proud of them though, no matter what… they don't give up. The love they have is worth fighting for. Things changed at home over the past few years. Some was good, some wasn't. I didn't like it, but now, I see it is how life is. Change is okay. It's all how you look at it, you know?"

Jake's life growing up had certainly been different than Allie's. She had to learn things the hard way, but she didn't give up either. Instead she accepted what came along and chose to be happy. Someday she would be proud of herself, too.

"So……what do you have planned for my birthday?" she hinted with a gleam in her eye.

Jake tossed his head back and gave a deep laugh. "What makes you think you are special enough for me to plan something?"

Allie narrowed her eyes. "Because you told me you were going to before I left, remember?"

"If I remember correctly," he said, "you were going to find out what Cynthia had planned, then let *me* know."

Allie shrugged sheepishly. "I figured while I was gone, you might have missed me so much you decided to plan something yourself."

Good God, was she actually flirting? Her behavior caught her off guard.

"I'm sure we can come up with something. Call Cynthia. Let me know what she's got planned. If not, I will make sure it is a night you won't forget."

Allie wasn't sure what had gotten into her, but the anticipation of spending her sixteenth birthday with Jake sent a shiver down her spine.

"Hey precious, how was your trip?"

The situation with Bryce and Cammi had taken the attention away from Cynthia for two months now, and Allie watched while her mom's irritation grew into a deep resentment, so she was honestly surprised Cynthia even asked about the trip considering it wasn't about her.

Allie was immediately annoyed. She was hoping her trip to Cancun and getting away from Cynthia would help her deal with some of the anger building up recently, but when she heard the phony interest, it all came rushing back.

With a heavy sigh, Allie briefly relayed some minor details then switched the subject to her birthday. "My friends want to make plans but I thought I'd check with you first. You mentioned you wanted to do something."

"Oh, Honey, Marcus and I will be gone that weekend. Guess what? We just bought a new house right outside of Omaha. It's gorgeous, five bedrooms, three baths, a hot tub and guess what else? He is buying me a tanning bed. He got a great deal from a friend of his out there. He will have to commute, but it's not too far. I can't wait to show you pictures. But don't worry. We aren't moving for six more months."

Even though it was bound to happen, Allie was not prepared for the shock that came with the announcement. The pain beginning to sear her heart was instantly replaced with fury. How could she move? How could she leave? Didn't she care? Wasn't being around for her last years of high school important enough to stay?

Allie attempted to keep her emotions in check. "Wow," she said dully disguising the tremor in her voice. "I guess you and Marcus are serious then?"

"Oh, didn't I tell you? He proposed! I'm so excited. I wanted to wait a year to get married, but he insists we do it sooner, like next month. We will be making the preparations the weekend of your birthday. I'm sorry I will miss it, Honey, but I promise we will make it up to you when this whole affair is over. We won't take a honeymoon until after we move."

As she rambled on, Allie listened half-heartedly. It was just like Cynthia to ruin something special for Allie with her own selfish agenda. Would it really have put her out to plan her wedding a different weekend? Her only daughter only turns sixteen once.

Cynthia scolded Allie when she said as much. "You have a birthday every year. I, on the other hand, have never been married. A wedding is the most important day of a woman's life. I would hope you realize Marcus is special enough for me to commit to and hopefully this will be the start of a new life. A life I deserve."

Allie highly doubted it. Hanging up the phone, she dialed Jakes number and swallowed hard to hide her disappointment. "You're in charge, the night's all yours."

Bryce and Cammi were carrying bags of groceries in from the car when he heard the end of Allie's conversation with Jake. She was obviously distressed. They unloaded the bags in silence while eaves dropping.

"I don't want to hear I told you so, okay? I know you were right!" she screamed hanging up. Bryce's concern drove him to follow her when she stormed out the backdoor.

"What's going on?" he asked.

She burst into tears and threw herself into her his arms. Cammi poked her head out the door to check on them while Bryce guided Allie to the picnic table bench. Shooting a sad, defeated look at his wife, he pulled his daughter close.

"I hate her, Dad. She is such a bitch." Normally he would have scolded her for such language, but chose to let it slide. "She's moving *and* she's getting married. I don't understand. I thought she came back here for me. Why would she want to move so far away, don't I matter?"

He looked at Cammi desperate for help. *Tell her the truth,* she mouthed disappearing back into the house to answer the front door. Torn, Bryce lifted Allie's chin to so he could look into her eyes.

"Allie, we need to have a serious talk. We've found out some things about Cynthia from Beth," he admitted. Allie's eyes filled with alarm.

"I should have told you when we first heard, but I thought I could save you from getting hurt. She's been running away from debt collectors for years and thought since you were here, this would be the best place to come. Don't get me wrong. Since being here, she loves having you in her life, but her stay was only temporary until she was back on her feet."

There were some truths, like her plan to break up his marriage, he knew he would never divulge to Allie.

Cammi led Jake to the backyard. He felt bad after Allie hung up on him and decided to come apologize. One look into Allie's tear filled eyes and he ached to hold her. Instead, he stood in the doorway with Cammi as Bryce continued.

"Beth told us once Cynthia found a man to pay off her debt, she would be gone. Sticking around was never her intention." His pleading eyes turned toward Cammi as sorrow gripped his heart. "It was only a matter of time. If I knew this in the beginning, Honey, I would have protected you. I would have limited your time so you didn't get attached. But I didn't know. I'm sorry. I really believed she changed and wanted to be a mom." Fighting back his own tears, he hung his head in shame. "I'm sorry I failed you. I would give anything to go back five years."

Allie wrapped her arms around her father's neck, hugging him tightly. "You…you did what you thought was right, Dad," she sobbed. "She's my mom. I guess I always knew she wasn't going to stay. But I thought if I made her love me enough, she might change her mind. It's her. It's all her." Allie took a deep breath and kept going. "I use to think it was me, but it's not, is it?" She looked from her dad, to Jake, back to Cammi hoping someone held the answer saving Cynthia from her own demise.

"It's not you," Bryce whispered. "She's sick Allie and unless she gets some serious help, it's not going to change. I wish I could help you understand that."

Cammi looked up to the dark sky speckled with bright stars and prayed while they all sat silently, allowing Allie to grieve as the pain, rejection and agony rushed through her. There was nothing they could do but allow years of heartache to consume her. And hopefully when the grief subsided, her healing process would begin.

Jake wanted to make her birthday special but being a guy, he didn't know what to do, so when he had a chance later that evening, he pulled Cammi aside. "I want to throw her a surprise party, but I'm not good at this stuff," he said uneasily.

"Don't you worry. I would love to help." His tenderness moved her and she was pleased he asked. She had a ton of sweet sixteen ideas, but was willing to step aside to let Jake take the lead. She could see in him the need to do this for Allie.

"What's the plan?" she asked.

He sounded apprehensive as he told her, but she was impressed.

"Wow, you've put a lot of thought into this."

"Most of it was my Mom. They adore Allie and she knows a lot of people around town from helping out with the church fundraisers."

"Between the three of us, it will be the best night of her life!" Cammi said enthusiastically.

"I hope so," he muttered, still unsure of himself.

They had only four days to put all the preparations together. When she told Bryce about Jake's idea, a look of alarm crossed his face.

"Sort of elaborate for a guy who is just her *friend*, don't you think?"

"Well, my gut says it's turning out to be more than a friendship, on his part, anyway."

"What? I don't think so! *This* is not going to happen," he insisted.

"Why not? She's going to be sixteen in a few days. What do you expect? If she is going to date, wouldn't you rather it be with someone who truly cares about her? Someone we know and respect? She could end up with some asshole that is going to play games while trying to get a piece of ass *or* she could be with Jake. You choose."

Dismay washed over him. He wasn't ready to watch his little baby girl give her heart to a boy. "Has she talked to you about this?" Bryce demanded.

"No, I don't think she's figured it out yet. His mother told me. She said Jake has been sweet on Allie from the get go."

Bryce listened but didn't like what he heard.

"Oh, Babe, loosen up. Let her grow, spread her wings. This is an okay thing. You like Jake."

"I liked him even better before I knew he wanted to kiss my daughter."

Bryce had been the number one man in Allie's life. Now someone else might be stepping in to replace him. Cammi was right, it was time, but it didn't mean he had to like it.

On the night of her birthday, her dad told her to be ready by six. Cammi took Allie shopping the day before and they found a beautiful black cocktail dress, appropriate enough for her age, but classy, and

Allie was beautiful, sexy and elegant all wrapped up in one. Cammi remembered how important it was at sixteen to feel those things. She also wondered if Allie had any idea how much she brought up Jake's name in the conversations they shared on their shopping spree.

"You should see him play football, Mom. He is the best on the team," she said over lunch.

"Jake is talking about staying in Colorado for college. He wants to major in Psychology. Isn't that great?" she yelled over the dressing room door handing Cammi one of the reject dresses.

"I bet he gets nominated for class president in the fall. Everyone loves him, but he says he doesn't want to run. His head is too focused on the game," she said as Cammi handed the keys to the minivan over to her so she could drive home. Cammi chuckled at how unaware she was.

At exactly six-ten, a black stretch limousine pulled up in front of their house. Allie was putting the last touches of her make-up on when her dad yelled for her to come down.

"Hold on, I can't get my necklace latched," she said as she descended the stairs.

Speechless, Bryce looked upon the beautiful woman who was once his little girl and quickly pulled his eyes away before he embarrassed himself with emotion.

"Here, I'll help you," Cammi said helping Allie fasten the string of pearls around her neck.

Allie thought Cammi looked breathtaking in a red semi-formal gown she bought a few years ago for her dad's Christmas Party. She hadn't worn it since and it was perfect for the occasion. Her dad even went all out renting a black tuxedo. Faith was in white silk dress and Bailey had on a pair of black trousers, suspenders holding them up. There was even had a red bow tie to top it off.

Faith held out her hand to show Allie the purse she was carrying for the evening.

"Very pretty."

"I have my lip gloss, my hairbrush, my princess cell phone and my hair bow," she announced proudly pulling them out one by one.

"You ready?" her dad asked linking her arm in his.

"I guess," she smiled nervously. "You guys look amazing! Oh, and if I haven't told you yet….. thanks. For whatever it is we are doing tonight," she said with a giggle.

Faith opened the door and Allie gasped noticing the limo for the first time. "What's going on?" She turned to her parents in disbelief. "Where are you taking me?"

Then her mouth dropped when Jake stepped out of the vehicle looking gorgeous in his own black tie tuxedo.

"I should have known you would be involved," she teased playfully though she was having a hard time catching her breath at the sight of him. Allie felt slightly awkward. She wasn't sure how to act around him all dressed up like a princess, but the way his eyes lingered appreciatively over her made her skin tingle in a way she had never experienced.

Jake's heart stopped the moment he saw her. Though she was his best friend and he treated her like one of the guys, tonight she was different and now, standing in front of him in a silk, black gown, he wanted nothing more than to show Allie how feminine and beautiful she was.

They took a ride around town, drinking sparkling cider and munching on the hor'devoure tray lined with cheese and crackers. A half hour later, they pulled in front of Jake's house.

"You have to close your eyes," he told her. "And keep em closed or I will make you put on a blindfold."

A spark of electricity she hadn't expected stabbed at her stomach when he took hold of her arm leading her toward the back of the house through the sliding glass door and onto the porch. Cammi and Bryce were close behind snapping pictures as Faith and Bailey ran ahead.

"Okay, open your eyes!" Cammi announced.

When Allie opened them, she looked around in absolute amazement. She had never seen anything so beautiful. The back yard of Jake's house had been transformed into a romantic garden of white lights. They were hanging off the large aspens and pines, draped along the deck, and strung around the house. The huge deck held seven tables, covered in white linens and votives of candles. In the corner, close to the kitchen, was a table of chips, vegetables, dips, crackers, and cheese. Directly in the middle of all the food sat a white sheet cake that said 'Happy 16th Birthday, Allie' scripted in light pink and silver frosting. And down the steps on a slab of cement, a dance floor and DJ Booth had been constructed with red, blue and silver lights flashing from the corners.

"Don't get too excited. There's more," Tamara, Jake's mom informed them. She took Allie by the hand back into the house, towards the side room. Gently pushing Allie through the French doors separating the kitchen from the living room, an enormous thunder of applause then cheers of Happy Birthday greeted her. Waiting for her patiently were twenty of her closest friends all dressed up like they were going to the prom. Allie was ecstatic.

The hugs and shrieking laughter of teenage girls drove the parents back to the deck and soon everyone made their way outside for food, cake and dancing. Allie was the perfect honoree, making her way around to all her friends, thanking them for coming. When she found her parents she gave them hugs. “This is the best. Thank you so much.”

“We only helped. The person you need to thank is Jake,” Cammi said. “It was his idea.”

Allie’s eyes widened with shock. Turning on her heel, she walked over to where he was standing surrounded by Christian, Shane and Trevor. When he saw her coming, he slipped away to meet her half way.

“You did this?” she asked tipping her head to the side to get a better read of his expression. That’s when she noticed the color move up his neck into his cheeks.

“Our mom’s helped. The decorations were their idea. I wanted to make sure your birthday was good, I mean….something you would remember,” he stammered. “I…I…uh…wasn’t sure who to invite, so I asked Heather. She made up the list and of course, I had to ask some of the guys. I needed someone to hang out with. I hope its okay.”

Allie forced herself out of her state of bewilderment and threw her arms around his neck. “Of course it’s okay. It’s better than okay. You are the best friend anyone could ever have,” she said her voice filled with emotion.

Jake hid his disappointment as he wrapped his arms around her. Something had changed between them since her trip. She was more flirtatious, more attentive, and even a bit more feminine than before, and he had this crazy notion tonight was going to be the magical night he had waited for. But he was wrong. She still thought of him as her best friend, nothing more.

Allie pulled away from his embrace and stared deeply into his face wondering what he was thinking. He was the same old Jake. So why in the world did she feel so self-conscious?

Sensing heavy eyes on her, she looked around and saw her father and Cammi along with Jake’s mom and dad and Jamie and Shawn watching intently from the other side of the yard. Everyone was smiling but her Dad. But he didn’t look angry. He looked very, very sad.

“Do you mind, I need to ask my Dad a question.”

“No, go ahead, just promise to save me a dance.”

By then most of the kids were taking advantage of the Top 40 music the DJ brought along and Jake, noticing the sour look on her father's face, thought it best if he left the situation and made his way to the food table.

"Dad, you alright?" she asked when she reached him.

Bryce focused his attention on her walking across the lawn in her unaccustomed high heels and wanted to laugh, but his throat tightened. All he could see was the three year old little girl he used to know tucked away in her grandmother's closet trying on oversized shoes, clothes and jewelry. Where had all the time gone, he wondered.

"Yeah, yeah, I'm okay." He sighed as he pulled her into a close embrace. "It's just strange to watch you grow up. I miss the little girl sometimes," he teased though he choked on the words.

"Dad!"

Sighing, Bryce smiled. "No, really, you are turning into a beautiful, amazing woman. I'm very lucky and very proud of you."

"Don't make me cry, it will ruin my make-up!"

"Oh, you're such a typical woman! You get that from your mother."

"Are you going to dance with me?" She implored holding out her hand.

"Drop dead," he teased. "I don't dance, you know that. Maybe to a slow one later, but not this crap!"

Allie laughed then returned to her friends. Cammi encircled her husband's waist and brought her lips to his cheek. Bryce held his wife's delicate hand as he guided her under the trees for some privacy. She looked divine, radiant. Pressing his cheek against hers, they began to sway to the music. He loved any opportunity he had to pull Cammi close to him.

Conflicting emotions filled Bryce's heart as tears sprang to his eyes. Feeling the wet tears on her cheek, Cammi turned her face up towards his and used her hand to gently wipe them away. With their bodies pressed against each other, he lost himself in the pool of her green eyes. "Have I told you how beautiful you look tonight?"

"Nope, but instead of telling me, how about you show me later," she suggested seductively pressing her lips to his.

Chapter Thirty-Seven

The party was more than a girl could hope for. Aside from the scene Brandi caused punching Alyssa in the nose because she was dancing with Christian, the evening was perfect. Tamara handled it gracefully by telling both girls they needed to go home and cool off. It was close to ten and Bryce and Cammi were headed out themselves to put Faith and Bailey to bed so they gave Alyssa a ride while Jake's dad took Brandi. Jake promised he would get Allie home safely after the DJ wrapped up at midnight.

Three hours later, Allie kicked off her shoes and threw herself onto her big fluffy comforter. She was exhausted, but her adrenaline was high. There was no way she was going to sleep for a while. In fact, she thought about calling Jake. No, she wanted to *see* Jake. But why? He'd just dropped her off no more than five minutes ago.

He had been quiet on the drive, but Allie could feel the weight of his stare as she relaxed comfortably in the passenger seat. She wondered what he was thinking, but mostly she wondered if she still looked all right. They danced so much she was sure her eyeliner and mascara had smudged halfway down her face. Flipping down the visor mirror she breathed a sigh of relief when she saw everything was still intact.

"You look beautiful," he told her quietly.

Embarrassed, she closed the mirror and flipped the visor back into place.

Leaning her head back on the seat, she turned to smile at him. "You clean up pretty good yourself." She'd never noticed his eyes before, not the way she did now, dark, luminescent and full of emotion. And before, they'd never made her stomach flutter.

Thinking he might hear the unmistakable pounding of her heart, she turned the radio up and distracted herself by singing along. But nothing could shake the awkward sensation rushing inside of her.

The anticipation had intensified by the time he pulled the car into the driveway and it wasn't only on her part. He was compelled to touch her, to feel the softness of her face in his hands. But when he turned to her after putting the car into park, what he saw in her eyes was fear. And the last thing in the world he wanted was to kiss her when she was filled with pure terror.

Allie was torn. She didn't want to leave, but she was scared to stay. She was so unsure of what she wanted when he turned to her, what she felt was guilt. He was Jake, her best friend for the past year. So why did the ache in her heart deepen as she opened the door.

"Thanks so much Jake. I had a great time," the words rushed out. "I…uh….I'll call you tomorrow. K?"

She'd slammed the door shut and ran into the house. After checking in with her parents and telling them thanks once again, she confined herself to her room and fought an internal battle on whether or not she should call.

He *had* done something very special for her so it was only polite to thank him. That was all, she convinced herself. But she had thanked him. A million times over. Still she missed him and wanted to talk. She was in the car with him for ten minutes, so why hadn't she talked to him then? He was going to think she was silly if she called at one in the morning. Her mind was restless and it was all so confusing, so she decided to get herself some warm milk. That was bound to help her sleep.

She was pouring herself a glass when she heard Cammi climb down the stairs.

"Oh, you scared me!" Cammi had a book clutched in one hand while the other flew to her chest.

"Sorry, I couldn't sleep. Want some milk?" Allie asked reaching for another glass.

"Sure. Was it a good night?" Cammi lowered herself into the chair.

"The best," she replied hesitantly.

"You don't sound convincing."

"No, no, I had a great night. I don't know, I'm just, I don't know, just crazy, I think."

Cammi laughed. "Tell me what's up. Why do you think you're crazy?"

"I feel like I need to talk to Jake, you know, thank him for what he did. Tonight was a pretty big deal."

"So call him."

"I've thanked him a million times already. He'll think I am being silly. I'm just so grateful, you know?"

Cammi stared at her intently. "Allie… do you have feelings for Jake?"

"What? No, don't be silly! He is my best friend, that's all. He made me feel special tonight. I just hope I'm as good a friend. He puts up with a lot from me."

"If you say so," Cammi smiled, flipping her book open.

"What do you mean by that?" Allie demanded finishing off her milk.

"I think maybe, just maybe, Jake feels more for you than friendship, and your feelings for him are starting to change." Cammi held up her hand when Allie tried to protest. "I am not saying I am right, I am just telling you to give it some thought."

Allie got up from the couch and stormed off to her room. "You're the crazy one around here," she said over her shoulder.

Cammi could only shake her head in amusement.

Cynthia called on Monday informing Allie of her wedding plans.

"Marcus reserved the most amazing room for our wedding night. I found the perfect dress. I can't wait for you to see it. Marcus says it shows off my curves," she giggled sounding more like a teenager than an actual adult. "Marcus thinks we need to have the reception in the city. And he thinks *you* should be my maid of honor. What do you think? Marcus needs to know so he can order the dress….oh and I have to tell him how many people I want to invite so he can send out the invitation. I am so….. Allie? Allie, are you there?"

Marcus sounded like a control freak.

"Are you going to ask me how my birthday was?"

"Oh, Baby, I completely forgot. I'm sorry, how was it?" she asked sounding more distracted than she did interested.

Allie began to describe the events of the party, the music, the guests and the food. When she said she'd gotten a cell phone from her Dad and Cammi she realized Cynthia had been talking to someone in the background the entire time.

"Are *you* even listening to *me*?" she asked losing her patience.

"Yes, yes, I am. It's just…. Marcus's packing some stuff to take with him to Lincoln. I want to make sure he doesn't take anything I might need here. Oh, we need to have dinner sometime this week. I want you to meet him again."

Fabulous, she couldn't wait to meet her new *step dad.* She wondered what sort of guy he was to actually want to marry Cynthia. Pretty accepting, she guessed, either that or pretty stupid if he knew about her past. Maybe he liked his women a little on the freaky side. He definitely had his hands full with her mother. Guess this was the sugar daddy Cynthia had been searching for since moving back to Madison.

Allie listened to Cynthia ramble on for a few more minutes before making an excuse to get off the phone. And not once did she bring up Allie's birthday again. It sickened her to think her own mother could be this selfish. She knew everything her dad told her was the truth. Once she heard it, it was obvious. Cynthia's time in Madison was temporary. Allie watched her go through men, money and houses like she did food. Searching for the right fit, the right one who would help her escape.

And the debt. What a fool she had been! Of course, that explained so much, the new cars, the canceled cell phones, the evictions. It finally dawned on her that her mother was more than likely kicked out because she never paid her rent. And the new furniture….she'd always shopped at rental places. She probably didn't pay the bill, so when it was time to move she never took it with her because it would only be a matter of time before it was repossessed.

But she didn't understand why, if she had all these financial problems, she hadn't taken Darby up on his offer. It didn't make sense. He was rich and he cared about Cynthia. In fact, Allie thought he was a very decent guy. But in the end, Cynthia screwed him over too. Allie happened to be walking past her parent's bedroom one evening when she overheard their whispers. It took her a few minutes to tune in to what they were saying, but if she hadn't been eavesdropping, she would have never learned the truth about what happened between Cynthia and Darby.

It still didn't explain why Cynthia hadn't moved in with him, instead opting to stay in her shabby two-bedroom apartment before she was eventually kicked out of it.

No, something else was going on. She knew how Cynthia worked and there was something else she couldn't quite put her finger on. How exactly did Marcus fit into the picture? Why marry him and not Darby? Unless Cynthia had another plan she was scheming up at the time and Darby had only been there as temporary financial assistance.

Allie wanted to scream. It was infuriating to know someone she loved and was a part of her could be so incredibly deceitful. As the thought hung over her head like a dark cloud the rest of the day, she wished for the first time in her life she could make her real mom disappear.

Cammi should have listened to her gut when she woke up. Instinct told her it was going to be a bad day. Frustrated and a little disturbed with her anxiousness, she tried to find pleasure in her writing.

It was Bryce's idea and with the encouragement of Gloria, Cammi felt confident enough to start putting the bedtime stories down on paper. For years, the children had loved her zany characters and bright descriptions, but never once had it crossed her mind others might love them too.

Lamont connected her with a children's magazine. They had been looking for someone who could put together a series of short stories to be featured in each issue they published over the next two years. They loved Cammi, loved her ideas and drew up a contract before she had a chance to change her mind.

And likewise, Cammi loved what she did, finally feeling as if she had something besides her family that brought fulfillment into her life. The flexibility it offered was perfect. She never had to sacrifice one for the other and the income was more than she'd ever expected.

She was proud of how far she had come in a short amount of time. Not only herself, but the uphill incline her marriage and family were on. Her confidence was strong, and she was back to accepting and loving the person she truly was, instead of striving to become somebody she wasn't. She was secure in what she had in herself and most of all she was secure in her love for Bryce. Finally, she stopped second guessing the purpose of their union.

But today she woke up with the same gloominess that had followed her in her misery only months before, and she was scared as the insecurity and anger embraced her.

She'd been writing most of the afternoon when she was interrupted by the ringing of the door bell.

"Can you get it, Babe?" Bryce called from the garage where he was replacing the shocks on his truck. "I am up to my ears in grease."

Cammi wished there would have been a sign, any sign to prepare her for what awaited, but who can predict the chaos other's, especially those bent on revenge, will bring into your life. Shutting her laptop she stole a quick glance at Faith and Bailey in the back yard where they were digging in the sandbox. As she walked to the door she began to prepare a little speech in her head to convince the salesman or woman she wasn't going to become his next customer. The phony smile she'd planted on her face disappeared, replaced by astonishment and a little fear the moment she opened the door and found herself face to face with her ex-husband. Standing next to him looking smug and content with her arm looped through his, was Cynthia

"Cammi, I want to introduce you to my husband, Marcus. Marcus, this is Allie's *stepmother*, Cammi," Cynthia sneered.

What the hell was going on? Cammi head spun. Marcus. Marcus. Marcus. Oh God. *He* married *her?*

"It's been a long time, Cammi. How have you been?" he reached out to shake her hand. She stared at it, but didn't move. Shock kept her planted firmly to the ground.

"Oh, you two know each other?" Cynthia asked innocently. The look of malice fixed on her face jolted Cammi back to reality. The bitch knew damn well who he was. And Cammi was standing there looking like a fool while Cynthia was laughing inside.

Emerging from the garage, Bryce was drying his clean hands on a towel when he walked up behind Cammi. "Bryce, darling, meet my husband, Marcus," Cynthia drawled before Cammi had a chance to compose herself.

"Nice to meet you," he said politely with a nod. "Allie's not home, she went to the mall with Heather. I thought you had plans to see her tomorrow."

"Oh, silly me, I forgot." Cynthia said throwing her hands in the air for effect. "I was thinking it was Sunday, I'm a day ahead of schedule. Do you mind if we come in for a minute?" She tried to move past Cammi but was cut short as her arm blocked the way.

"Yes, we do mind. It's not a good time right now," Cammi interrupted her jaw clenched tightly, her knuckles white.

The presence of her ex-husband on her front porch was more than Cammi could handle. What she really wanted to do was grab the fireplace poker from behind her and shove it up Marcus's nose then whack Cynthia across the face with it. The subtle anger that had been present all day was about to erupt into an overflowing volcano of hostility if she didn't get away from the two of them soon.

She could feel the weight of Marcus's stare boring into her, willing her to look at him, but she refused to give him the satisfaction. She had to think fast, figure out how to handle this with grace, but she wasn't prepared. Allie never mentioned Marcus's name, she only called him Cynthia's new husband. How was she to know?

But flying off the handle was not an option at the moment. It had been over ten years, and she refused to let Marcus intimidate her the way he used to. Mustering up as much control as she could, Cammi plastered a fake smile across her lips, reminding herself she would never allow Cynthia or her *new husband* to bear witness to her pain.

"We are just headed out for dinner, we planned a date," she said lacing her fingers together with Bryce's. "Why don't we chat with you when you pick Allie up tomorrow? I don't mean to be rude, but we have been looking forward to some time alone all week, and we are anxious to get going."

Bryce was surprised to feel her ice-cold hand crush his and his heart stopped for a second when he saw the desperation in her eyes.

Cynthia and Marcus were reluctant to leave. Though he didn't say a word, Marcus's daunting presence and body language spoke volumes. He had a purpose. And Cammi cringed knowing this was far from over.

"Cammi, I am so anxious to hear how you and Marcus know one another. What a small world this is," Cynthia smirked.

"I'm sure you are," Cammi seethed. "Look, I hate to be rude, but we really are in a hurry, so if you don't mind, we can discuss this tomorrow," she replied hastily shoving them out the door as she forced it closed.

Peeking out the window as they walk away, Cammi realized she was a little baffled when she saw a look of mild shame and embarrassment cross over Marcus's features before he slid into his car. Taking a deep breath, she began to shake.

"Do you know who that was?" she shrieked turning around to find a mystified Bryce watching her closely. "That was *my* ex husband. What the hell is she doing? Is she intentionally trying to drive me insane?" Cammi paced the floor while Bryce sunk down on the couch, stunned. "I want her gone, Bryce, out of my life. Six months is not soon enough. I have had enough of her bullshit games. She tried to play dumb, but it was *so* obvious she knew. I bet the look on my face was priceless. I hope they get a good laugh out of humiliating me. I'm telling you Bryce, she better not screw with me again or I *just might* kill her."

He watched her rage of fury. He was furious too, but more than that, fear gripped his heart. It wasn't fair. They had come so far to have another setback like this. Her ex husband, how? It was too much to absorb.

Filled with anger, Cammi picked up a glass vase, a wedding present from her parents, and threw it against the brick fireplace watching as it shattered into a million pieces.

"Cammi!"Bryce started towards her.

"I can't deal with this anymore, Bryce, I really can't. I have been patient. I have been nice. I have turned my cheek one too many times. This.....this.....this *bullshit* is the last straw. To marry my ex-husband? What is she trying to prove bringing him back into my life?"

Bryce reached out to his wife in an attempt to calm her down. "No," she screamed pushing his arms away. "I am tired of feeling this way. I have never had anyone hate me so much they would intentionally do something like this. I don't know how to deal with it. I never use to care about what people thought, but I want to be better than her. I want the whole world to know I am smarter, prettier, kinder and a better mother. I want to make more money, I want to be more successful, but most of all, I want to see her fail. I let it consume me. It's all I think about and it has made me miserable." Cammi sunk to the floor on her knees. She rested her head into her hands and sobbed. "And now this? I hate who I have become because of them."

Bryce knelt down to rub her back. "Why do you care what she thinks? She is a nutty lunatic! And Marcus is your past. He doesn't matter anymore."

She looked desperately into his eyes shaking her head. "She's Allie's mom. I know it doesn't make sense, but what if Allie starts to see me through her eyes? What if *you* start to see me through her eyes? I keep thinking you compare me to her. She makes me question who I am. And with everything that has happened, how I felt, how I was behaving, I can relate to her. I understand why she is the way she is. And it makes me sick, makes me feel like I am no better than she is." She laid her head on Bryce's leg, soaking his jeans with her tears.

"I allow her to make me feel like less of a person. I allow her to have control over my life, just like Marcus. I try to stay one step ahead, but it's destructive. I don't want to be in this sick twisted competition. I just want to be me. I just want to be happy again, but mostly I want the anger to go away."

He listened quietly as the volcano of emotions erupted. As much as he hated to see her in pain, if they were to ever move forward with their life, this needed to happen.

"And I hate him. To see the two people I hate most in this world standing together at my front door, God, you have no idea what I really wanted to do." She was shaking uncontrollably. "I can't stop crying. I want to hurt them. I want to hurt them both the way they hurt me. It's just not fair, Bryce. Why do they want to hurt me? What did I do to either of them?" She wiped her hand across her eyes forcing away the tears. "I think I'm having a nervous breakdown," she confessed laughing between sobs.

In the moment of finding humor amongst sadness, she allowed Bryce to comfort her and when he brought his arms protectively around her, didn't push him away. "You aren't having a breakdown. Well, okay, maybe a slight one, but don't you think you need to? You have been suffocating for years."

She nodded. "Maybe your right. I convince myself it doesn't hurt. That she doesn't affect me, that he didn't affect me but they do and as hard as I try to change that, to make myself believe I don't care, I just can't. I do care. I did care. But I want to be above this."

Once she began to calm down, he kissed the top of her head. "Where did this superiority complex of yours come from? Look, you spend way too much time in your own head trying to figure it all out. Stop. Please, I am begging you, just let it go."

"What about my faith? How can I portray myself as a servant of God, as a spiritual person with all of these conflicting emotions? I shouldn't behave the way I have or pray for someone to disappear, get sick or get hit by a car. A woman of faith doesn't want to beat the shit out of someone on a daily basis or cuss as much as I do anymore!" Cammi wailed.

"You do cuss and awful lot," Bryce joked. "Yes, this is my wife, the one with the trashy sailor mouth."

Wiping her nose, Cammi snorted as she laughed. "I sort of like the cussing part, I'm not going to lie."

Bryce hugged her. "Do you think just because you have a close relationship with God he loves you more than the rest of us? That you are immune from feeling what the rest of us humans feel? That you only get to have the positive? Didn't God give us all of these emotions? Didn't he make Jesus human so he could experience our lives? Do you think there was a time Jesus, while here on earth didn't feel jaded, angry or vindictive? Do you think he didn't want to do some serious ass kicking once in a while? He was a man, of course he did. The difference was in how he handled it. He felt everything you do and worked through it without acting on his feelings. You need to remember God knows your faults, loves you despite them and forgives you all the time."

Cammi looked into his face as a peaceful feeling flooded through her. She was enamored by his strength, his ability to recognize and accept her faults, and still love her unconditionally.

He *was* the one she'd prayed for and in that moment he was taking her on a different path than anything she'd been used to.

"You get what the rest of us get, Cammi. Happiness, joy, maybe some sorrow and pain and once in a while heartache. But always…always, you get love. Throw in some stress and worry and you know what? You become a real person. Stop trying to be a saint."

Emotion swam in his eyes as he watched her reflect on the impact of his words. When he met Cammi, he didn't understand or even care about faith, but her actions, her example showed him a different life. A life he wanted to be a part of and a life he wanted to share with her.

They were soul mates traveling on this journey. Fate brought them together. When he was down, she carried him. Now, with all he learned, it was his turn to guide her back to where God wanted her to be. And he prayed with all his heart, they would spend the next forty or fifty years lifting one another up when things got rough.

Leaning down, he found her lips, just as Allie opened the front door balancing shopping bags from one hand to the other. Sweat beaded her forehead as she collapsed on the floor next to her parents sighing in exasperation.

"I used up most of my gift cards today and you should see…" she stopped suddenly aware of Cammi's tears.

"What's wrong?" she asked her voice full of concern.

Bryce hesitated briefly before plunging forward.

"Cynthia stopped by with her husband. Allie… Marcus is Cammi's ex husband."

Cammi could see the uncertainty in her face as she tried to comprehend what they were telling her. Allie knew Cammi had been married before. And there were no secrets as to why Cammi left him as abruptly as she did.

"Its true, Honey. I didn't expect to see him today. It sort of freaked me out."

"Isn't that ironic? I bet Cynthia was shocked, too," she said forcing a laugh.

Bryce and Cammi exchanged a knowing glanced. "Cynthia knew," Bryce told her quietly.

Allie reacted as soon as the words were said. "That's crap! She couldn't have. There's no way. You're lying!" she paused shaking her head.

"Allie, calm down. Look, it's not a big deal whether or not she knew," Cammi reassured her. "I just have to find a way to deal with him being your stepfather and a part of our lives. I wanted you to hear it from us, not from him."

Allie was battling conflicting emotions. Marcus did give her a bad vibe. His marriage to her mother definitely wasn't a match made in heaven. In fact, it seemed more like a business arrangement, not a union of love. Marcus couldn't be Cammi's ex-husband. It didn't make sense. If he was and Cynthia knew, why didn't she tell her? She knew Cynthia was a screw up and a little crazy, but she wasn't going to believe she would do something like this on purpose.

"She may not be the perfect mother, but she isn't a bad person," Allie declared.

"We aren't saying she is. Look, you asked, and we told you the truth. You may not like it but we aren't trying to hurt you. What is done is done," Bryce stated.

Allie ran up to her room and slammed the door. Lying on her bed, she began to cry. She was dazed but she wasn't stupid and suddenly it seemed as if the pieces of the puzzle were falling together.

Bryce had just made love to her. Overflowing with emotion, Cammi was moved by how physically connected they were after all this time and all they had been through. She had no inhibitions with him and allowed herself the freedom to be sexual in many loving ways.

"Love opens your heart up for all sorts of beatings, doesn't it? This just hurts," Cammi said thinking about Marcus and Cynthia.

Bryce caressed her cheek as she continued. "All these years I've tried to protect myself from the pain. I only wanted the good stuff. But that's such a false expectation. I need to start dealing with what is real. Face it head on. If I don't, I am going to miss out on what is right in front of my face. I can't live like that anymore, Bryce. I'm so sorry," she sobbed into her pillow.

As hard as it was for him to step back, he did, knowing she needed space. Nothing he said was going to make this better. Nothing he did was going to take it away. She was hurting and all he could do was watch the anguish seep out of her like a leaky faucet, drip after drip, memory after memory, beating against the surface of her heart.

He'd been just as horrified to find out about Marcus. In fact, seeing him face to face, then finding out he was Cammi's ex, made him want to hunt Cynthia down and bury her alive, along with her piece of shit husband. The idea sparked a flame within him as his vindictive nature began to overpower any sense of rationality and lying in the dark, a smug smile formed around his lips.

He gently kissed her eyelids as they began to droop. She was completely exhausted. It was a good thing though, he told himself. Being vulnerable was her key to stability, her key to trusting. He loved the intimacy they shared at times like this and felt like a knight in shining armor coming to her rescue. She was learning to surrender to him and after all these years he hoped he was finally able to protect her.

Marcus wasn't at all what he expected. He was tall, with sandy blonde hair, chiseled features and a strong jaw. One Bryce would love to put his fist into, given the chance. He had dark brown eyes, but they were eyes Bryce didn't trust, and he was a little too handsome for his own good. He was dressed sharply, too sharp, basically your high maintenance pretty boy, with no depth and no integrity. After he was done measuring him up, Bryce determined he and Cynthia were perfect for each other. Maybe he was being too judgmental, but he didn't care. The guy was Cammi's ex-husband. That was enough motivation for Bryce to hate him.

Cammi never loved him, not the way she loved Bryce, he was confident of that, but the idea of someone having her before him instantly put a bitter taste in his mouth. Marcus had been out of the picture for years. In fact there had never been another man in her life since, but the emotional damage he left behind was just as fresh today as it was fifteen years ago. It made Bryce more insecure than he had ever been in his marriage. He finally understood Cammi's defensive nature when it came to the women from his past and he felt selfish and foolish for disregarding it like he did. Jealousy could cause a normally sane person to do completely insane things.

He trusted that Cammi's reaction towards seeing Marcus was out of shock and outrage. The idea of sharing his daughter with him was preposterous. But it was even more appalling a man his wife once vowed to spend her life with was close enough to re-open her wounds.

What was his motive? Did he still want her? Was this a ploy to worm his way back into her life? Did he somehow find out about her deceit all those years ago and become determined to seek revenge? They had to find out. Bryce didn't want another man, especially Marcus looking at Cammi, thinking about Cammi or hurting Cammi anymore. *He* was her husband and *he* was going to protect her come hell or high water.

This was, after all, his fault. It was he Cynthia hated. It was his life she was out to destroy. She was scorned and Cammi was caught in the crossfire. But before, he and Cammi were two separate people, fighting different battles. Now, they had found a way to become one and fight this together.

Sleep was restless for the both of them.

"Is Allie awake yet?" Bryce asked coming down the stairs in a pair of sweat pants and t-shirt.

"No, haven't heard a sound." Cammi was stirring pancake batter while Faith and Bryce colored at the kitchen table. "I should probably make sure she is up soon."

"Wait a few minutes. We need to talk before she comes down." She followed him into the garage where they could talk privately. "I called Cynthia. She and Marcus are moving to Lincoln sooner than expected."

"Good riddance," Cammi said relieved.

"They want Allie to come with them for the rest of the summer. She also wants to make up for missing her birthday by buying her a car and insists we work out a visitation and holiday schedule," he said.

"What? No way. I am putting my foot down, Bryce," Cammi reacted instantly. "It is one thing to allow Allie to spend time with her in the same town, but not a million miles away for weeks at a time, especially with *him*. No!"

"I agree. It's not going to happen. I thought this move was an easy way to get her away from Allie, but it could get ugly. I think they are trying to bribe her with the car. Then again, if they force the issue, I might not have a choice but to take them to court." He stopped and thought for a moment. "I am starting to put two and two together. Why she married him so fast, I mean. It looks like she has a stable home-environment for Allie. Marcus is a good provider."

"But why him?" Cammi whined. "There are a ton of guys out there she could have married that are good providers. Like Darby. And what if he is still dabbling with drugs? Bryce we can't willingly let her be around that."

He shook his head and laughed deeply. "It's part of her plan, don't you see. She knows about our problems. If she throws a curve ball, something sending us over the edge which could potentially break us up, then I won't provide a stable environment anymore."

Cammi was quiet as she thought about the circumstances once again surrounding them. Cynthia didn't want Allie. She was just hell-bent on ruining their life.

Everyone, especially Cynthia and Marcus were shocked to hear Allie's response to the idea.

"No, I don't think so. Thank you, though," she said politely without hesitation.

"What do you mean, you don't think so?" a haughty little laugh escaped from Cynthia's lips.

"I like living here. My friends are here. I want to spend my summer with them. I only have two years left of high school and I don't want to miss out."

Bryce beamed with pride, but was careful to hide his reaction. It took everything in him to allow Cynthia and Marcus to even enter his home. But he and Cammi had agreed this was for Allie to handle. Their time would come later.

"But Honey, you'll make friends. Think of all the fun we will have. We even have a room set aside for you in the house; we can decorate it any way you want," Cynthia pleaded. "And what about the car?"

"I appreciate that, really I do, I will come for a week if you want, but I am not going to stay longer. Plus, I have dance camp, remember?"

Allie knew most of what she told her mom was ignored. Unless it had to do with her personally, she didn't care what went on in Allie's life. She was used to it.

"Oh, dance camp, yes I remember you saying something about that. Look, we can find you a camp there. It won't be a problem, will it Marcus?" She looked towards her husband for support. He had his arms crossed over his chest, a grave look of disinterest on his face.

"What? Oh sure, whatever you two want." He looked around, studying the structure of the house.

Cammi put her best foot forward the minute they showed up. She was polite, charming, graceful, but not a force to be reckoned with. Determination and strength seeped through her. Cammi would have rather been hit by a train than let them know how uncomfortable she was. Bryce's, on the other hand, was boiling. He'd caught Marcus stealing sideways glances at Cammi when he thought no one was watching. If she noticed, she ignored him. Cammi was right, he was a snake. If they didn't get out of his house soon, Bryce was liable to put a fist through his obviously whitened teeth.

"Cynthia, I said no. Stop pressuring me and respect what I want."

"Well, then you won't be getting the car!" Cynthia declared her face contorted into a frown.

"I thought it was my birthday present? Or were you just trying to bribe me?" Allie asked her eyes narrowing.

Cammi kept her gaze focused on Allie, not wanting to catch the eye of anyone else. She felt so small, so out of control. But the fear of losing it in front of two people she hated most in the world gave her enough power to fake it. And listening to Allie gave her more confidence. She didn't want to fight anymore. She just wanted it to end.

Cynthia looked at her daughter in disgust while Marcus chuckled.

"Are you telling me you are happy here?" she challenged. "If I remember correctly, you told me your dad was too strict and you couldn't wait to get out of the house. You even said…"

Allie knew what Cynthia was about to do and she put her hand up.

"Yes, I am," she interrupted. "It took me a long time to realize it, and I thought I was unhappy, I thought dad and Cammi weren't what I needed, but things have changed. I've changed. I realize where I belong. I feel safe here. I'm sorry if you don't like it, but this is what I choose." She finished with the kind of determination in her voice telling Cynthia not to push any further.

"Fine, if that's what you want, don't call me crying saying how unfair your dad is or that he doesn't understand you," she said standing up, grabbing her purse and giving her husband a 'come now or you'll have to pay' glare.

"Don't worry, I won't." Allie politely walked with them and held the door as they left. "Oh, hey, there is something I need to ask you though." Allie's demanding tone dripped with sarcasm. "Why don't you explain to me how it is your new husband just happens to be Cammi's ex?"

Chapter Thirty-Eight

"You know how she is." Allie cradled the phone to her ear while she applied another coat of mascara to her lashes. She could hardly stand the anticipation she felt waiting for Jake's phone call and now recapping the events of the week, she felt the need to get dolled up, just in case he wanted to hang out.

"Why do you put up with it?" he wanted to know.

"I am tired of holding onto the anger. She's always going to be my mother. I can't change that. She's moving. No way am I going to visit her. Our relationship will be long distance from this point forward so it would be nice to have it somewhat civil."

Cynthia hemmed and hawed around the truth when Allie asked her about Marcus, but nothing really came of it. Except Allie was certain she would never believe anything coming out of her mother's mouth ever again. And Cynthia knew it too. Marcus, uncomfortable under the securitization of Cammi and Bryce, was sure to never show his face at their house again.

Cynthia hadn't talked to Allie since she confronted her about her lies and when she finally did call it was only to invite her to the going-away party she was throwing for herself. Allie knew Cynthia was waiting for *her* to apologize, but when it didn't happen, she broke down and finally called acting as if nothing had transpired.

Allie decided to let it go and agreed to dinner with them the previous evening. Cynthia spent the entire dinner blowing smoke up her ass, but Marcus was acting awkward. She didn't like how he looked at her or his strange behavior. Maybe he was drunk. His childlike and animated behavior made Allie wonder if he was really in his late thirties or fourteen. There were boys in her class more mature than he was. It definitely made her decision about not moving with them much more tolerable. Even thinking of going there made her ill. In fact, she couldn't wait for their move. The stress and drama of having Cynthia in her life was too much. Moving was an easy answer to a difficult situation.

"Please, Allie. You have to come. It's Friday at seven. It wouldn't be the same without you. Bring your friends. I promise they will have a blast," Cynthia had insisted over their steak and crab dinner.

Allie tried making excuses but Cynthia wouldn't give up.

"What am I going to do without my baby? I will miss you so much. I know you only want to spend a week but you are more than welcome to live with us. If things ever get bad here, and you need to run away, I hope you will come to the open arms of your mom," she gushed.

When hell froze over, Allie thought.

She would never get it, Allie decided as Cynthia once again changed the subject and started rambling on about the new furniture for the house, their honeymoon plans and her desperate desire to join the country club as soon as they were settled, all the while, feeling no remorse for her actions.

"You wouldn't believe the people Marcus has introduced me to. He has great connections. This is it, Baby, the life-style I have always deserved. Oh, Honey, I just wish I could share it with you. Imagine how much fun we would have!"

The sort of fun Cynthia planned on having, Allie wanted no part of.

Dinner had been dull. The only highlight was the food. Allie had to admit, her prime rib was fantastic, and Marcus must have been trying to impress her with his pocketbook because she saw the tab was well over a hundred dollars. Conversation over dinner consisted of buying this, buying that, how much so and so made, how much Marcus was going to make next year, and what they were going to buy that would show so and so up. It disgusted her. In a rush to get away from them Allie waited in the car while they stayed back to pay. Sliding into the front seat, she let out a sigh of relief. When she looked back Allie saw they had stopped to talk to another couple.

Bored, she decided to snoop though the car Marcus just drove off the lot. It was a fun toy, impressive to say the least. She couldn't wait to get her own. Of course, it wouldn't be anything as fancy as the new Lexus she was sitting in. Taking the idea from Jake's parents, she'd bribed her dad into meeting her halfway if she saved enough money from babysitting and working at the ice cream shop downtown. It was hard to turn down Cynthia's offer of the car, but Allie wasn't going to accept something her mom could hold over her head, or something bought because her mother spread her legs.

Allie looked out the window and found them still engrossed in conversation, so she opened the glove compartment. Wallowing in annoyance, she almost missed the cigarette box that fell onto the floor. She wasn't surprised to see the rolled up joints that took the place of cigarettes. But she was surprised to find the wrapped up dollar bills stuck under the joints. Curious, she unfolded one of the tightly wrapped bills.

Allie sucked in her breath as white powder residue began to coat her fingers. Her hands began to shake. Cocaine. Of course. She knew there were kids at school that used it, but no one she hung out with. In a panic, she looked out the window again. They weren't coming yet so she wrapped the bill up and shoved it back into the box. There must have been ten different bills stuffed under the joints. Her hands fumbled as she tried to open the glove compartment again. She was shocked to see the five or six cigarette boxes she missed the first time she had looked. Allie opened each one carefully and found the same thing inside.

She quickly stuffed them back into place, glancing up from time to time to make sure she wasn't going to be caught and hopped into the back seat just as Cynthia and Marcus staggered toward the car. She was still shaking when her mother opened the door.

"Sorry Babe. Those were the Quinns. Some of the most… are you okay?" Cynthia asked turning around to look at her. "You are white as a ghost."

"I'm okay," she lied. "Just don't think the food agreed with me. My stomach is upset."

The drive to the house wasn't over soon enough. Allie jumped out of the car and ran inside, locking herself in her room, calling Jake.

"Are you surprised?" Jake asked after she told him the story.

"I guess it answers my questions. I wonder if Marcus sells it or just hangs out with the higher powers."

"I heard rumors before that your mom dabbled in that stuff. Josh was bragging about getting *everything* he needed to keep him going from your mom. Says his dad was one of her best customer. But honestly I thought he was just talking about sex."

Allie snorted. "Seriously, Jake! Even if it was sex, why would Josh be saying *he* could get everything he wanted?"

She was greeted with an apprehensive silence.

"Jake?"

"Yeah?"

"Is there something you're not telling me?" she demanded.

"Aw, Allie," he sighed. "You know the group of guys Josh hangs out with. They're strung out. Bad. And the parties they go to, at Burt's house…well, I've heard Cynthia is usually there."

Allie had only heard about Burt. He was a twenty-five year old drop out who was reliving his glory days by hanging out with the local high-school druggies. The parties he threw were dangerous and anyone who wanted to keep their reputation clean knew to stay away.

"And…." Allie coaxed.

"From what I have heard, she's the entertainment. Josh says he's slept with her as well as a few of his friends."

"Oh God," Allie groaned. "You can't be serious? Isn't that illegal?"

Allie fell quiet. Finally she spoke up again. "She could go to jail if anyone found out she was having sex with boys my age. Of course she doesn't give a shit about me. How this could affect me, does she?" she said defeat interrupting her anger. "She never has."

Jake patiently listened to her anguished tears. When he felt it was safe, he spoke again.

"Are you going to the party?"

"I didn't want to before, now I really don't want to. I don't know. She doesn't deserve to have me there, but I feel like I should say 'cest' la vie' at least." She tried to laugh, but Jake could still hear the sadness behind it.

"You okay?"

"I hate her! I really hate who she is. So why do I feel responsible? Like I have to treat her good, like it's important to have a relationship with her. A part of me still wants one, and I can't rationalize why. She is a piece of shit and has done nothing for me. Ever! She's not going to change. So why, deep down inside my gut, do I still hold out hope she might really care?"

"That want might never go away, you know? You have been dealt a shitty hand, but for some reason, it's something you got to figure out."

"What are you doing?" she asked pulling herself out of deep thought. She had to see him. No, she needed to see him.

"Talking to you. Duh!"

"Meet me down by the river. Fifteen minutes, k?"

"Alright," he said hanging up.

It was impulsive, but she didn't care. All she knew was she desperately wanted to be with him. It was a need she felt a lot lately. Normally, she ignored it, but maybe it was time to act on it. Maybe the pain her mother inflicted had finally made her irrational enough to jump in feet first, without hesitation.

"I'm going for a walk," she yelled pulling a sweatshirt over her head and bouncing down the steps. It was a good thing she had freshened up her makeup.

"Be back by ten-thirty," Cammi told her.

Glancing at the clock, it read nine. That gave her an hour and a half. Quickly, she grabbed the dog and hooked Penny's leash to his collar then headed out the door. Her heart raced wildly as she walked down the street, through the gathering of trees towards the bank of the river. Her heart fluttered at the thought of him, his smile, and his eyes. The way he looked at her, the way he took care of her… it sent shivers down her spine.

Should she tell him what she felt? God, it was dumb. Of course she couldn't tell him. He was her best friend. She wasn't going to risk that. So why did she ask him to meet her? Why else did she want to look good for him? What was she going to say?

Moving rocks and twigs to make a space, she and Penny sat down on the dry grass, waiting. Maybe she would kiss him. God, no! That was a dumb thought. Taking a deep breath, she stood up and wiped off the back of her jeans but as she turned around, she saw him step out from behind a tree. He had been so quiet. It made her wonder how long he was watching her.

"Hey," he said softly walking in her direction. She could see the moonlight shine on his face. It gave his dark hair a hint of blue and made his eyes appear larger than normal. Allie held her breath. Bewildered by how handsome he looked, her heart began to race.

Suddenly, panic overcame her.

"Ummm, hi. I, uh, I just remembered something I need to tell my dad. Will you walk me home?"

Suddenly she needed to be where they weren't entirely alone…where she could breath, where she felt normal again, like her house. There under the trees, by the river, it was too quiet, too romantic, too…… tempting. She had to get away.

He was baffled by her behavior. "What's going on? *You* asked me to meet you, remember?"

"It's nothing, really. I, um, um," she searched for an excuse. "I was feeling claustrophobic sitting in my room and wanted some air. I didn't mean to worry you. The first thought that popped into my mind was coming to the river. I was on the phone with you, so of course, I asked you to come." She kept her eyes riveted toward the ground.

When he stepped closer she finally looked up and his eyes locked in on hers, daring her to hold them. She quickly broke the gaze and shoved her way past him dragging Penny behind her.

"Are you coming or not?" she demanded.

"Just wait," he said putting a hand on her arm to make her stop. A jolt shot through her.

"Jake, really, I need to get back home, please let me go," she pleaded her voice shaking.

"Allie, stop for a sec, okay? What's going on with you? You have been strange since you got back from Mexico. Did something happen there? Did you meet someone?"

His stomach ached at the thought, but he had to know. She was distant, almost shy and uncomfortable around him. At first he thought she was being flirtatious, but as time went on and nothing between them happened, he began to wonder. If she had met someone, maybe she was slowly putting an end to the friendship. Maybe it was too weird for her. Maybe her boyfriend didn't like the idea of her best friend being a guy.

"No," she croaked. "No, of course I didn't. That's insane!" Why didn't he get it? Couldn't he see she was crazy about *him*? Why did he have to be so bullheaded and stubborn? He wasn't making this easy for her.

"I have tried flirting with him. I keep dropping hints, but he doesn't do anything about it. I suck at this. What if he doesn't feel the same way? I don't know how much more rejection I can take," she finally confessed to Cammi a few days earlier.

"Welcome to love, dear. Believe me, he feels the same way, but he's waiting for you. Take my advice, men don't get hints. You have to tell them straight up or they won't figure it out. Be brave. Tell him the truth. It's what I had to do with your dad."

Ew. Allie didn't want to think about her parents that way.

So here she was, alone in the dark, moonlight overhead, at their special spot. On the way here, she psyched herself up, but the moment she saw his face, she chickened out.

He waited for an answer while she continued to second-guess herself. "Look," Allie said, regaining her composure. "I promise. Nothing's wrong." She reached over to give him a quick hug. "I was a bit overwhelmed and went nutty. It's all this stuff with Cynthia. Come on. Let's go back to the house. Mom made apple pie, you can have a piece."

They walked side by side in silence. It was nine-thirty when they came through the front door and the screen slammed shut behind them. Surprised, Cammi gave her an inquisitive look. Bryce was already cutting himself a slice of pie when they strolled into the kitchen.

"I thought you were going for a walk?" he asked eyeing them suspiciously.

"I was, and then Jake showed up, so we came back here. Want a piece?" she asked holding out a plate. Jake nodded.

"Hey you two! What's up?" Cammi asked lightly, opening the fridge to pull out a yogurt.

"Nothing" they both replied at the same time. Everyone ate in silence. Cammi, sensing an awkward situation, grabbed Bryce's plate and led him, protesting, out onto the front porch to eat.

"What was that about?"

"I think we need to give them time alone."

"What for?" he asked shoving a forkful of the delicate crust into his mouth.

Cammi rolled her eyes. "Boys can be so dumb, you know that?" He shrugged his shoulders.

"Allie is trying to find a way to tell him how she feels. It's hard, and she's scared."

Bryce choked on his milk.

"Now don't get all protective on me, do you understand?" Cammi scolded. "Just let it be. Let her love him. He's a good kid and *he* loves her." She set her plate down and moved to sit beside him. She wrapped her arms around his waist and he rested his chin on her head and sighed.

"I know," he said quietly. "He's exactly what I would want for her. But it still sucks."

Cammi was wiping off the last of her make up before bed when Allie knocked to come in. Sitting down on the lid of the toilet, she pulled her knees into her chest and sighed.

"I didn't do it. I was ready to, but I didn't. He thinks I met someone in Mexico."

Cammi smiled. "It will happen when the time is right. Don't worry. He loves you, he's not going anywhere."

"How do you know? That he loves me, I mean?"

"Oh, Honey. He's loved you for a long time. Everyone knows. You just weren't ready to see it. He's been waiting."

"I wish it was easier than this."

"One of the reasons we didn't want you to date until now is because love isn't easy. In fact, relationships are the hardest thing to do. There is a maturity level that comes along with dating. The experiences you have now are going to affect the rest of your life. So as a parent, it's our job to make sure you are ready to deal with the good and bad, the pain and the joy. But with Jake, this is okay. It's going to be a good experience for you and you deserve that. Just don't rush it, let it happen. But be willing to take a risk when someone is worth it."

Allie depended on Jake for so much. He was her best friend, and she loved being with him more than anyone in the world, but what if loving him as a boyfriend ruined what they shared. Was it a risk she was willing to take? And what about sex? Was she ready to think about that? Was he? She was sixteen, he almost seventeen and both virgins. Probably the last left in their school. But what they shared was different and special. It was the type of love you could build forever around. Did she really want to be tied down and committed to the first boy she dated or did she want to play the field and experience life?

The pressure was too much to handle, but she couldn't deny how she felt about him anymore. Besides, Cammi was right. Her instincts told her she needed to take a chance. She had to put it in God's hands and trust he wanted what was best for her. And Jake was certainly the type of boy who was best for her. That she had no doubt about.

"Marcus and Cynthia are having a going away party this Friday. She wants me to go," Allie informed her.

"Are you going to?" Cammi asked nonchalantly. "Can you hand me the lotion?"

Allie grabbed the pink bottle Cammi pointed at and gave it to her.

"She's having sex with a guy from my school," Allie announced. She could see the bewilderment in Cammi's eyes when she turned from the mirror to stare at her.

"Who?"

"Josh. He's a Senior. I don't know who else." Her voice shook as she told Cammi the entire story she'd heard from Jake earlier that evening.

With her hand clutched to her chest, Cammi leaned back against the bathroom door and slid down until she was crouched on the floor. "Oh my God, Allie. I don't even know what to say. This is.....*so* wrong....on so many different levels."

"It's jacked up, I know," she said trying to fake a smile beneath the tears. "I can't wait until she's gone."

Reeling from shock, Cammi reached her hand out to Allie, pulled her onto the floor next to her and wrapped her in an embrace while the girl's body shook with sobs. She didn't have any words of wisdom, any great advice or prior knowledge on how to deal with this. All she had was her love and that, she vowed was something Allie would never have to search for.

Allie wasn't happy about going to the party, but guilt told her she needed to show up. Jake was going with for moral support. He could be the voice of reason in case she decided to scratch her mother's eyes out.

"Let's get this over with," she said slamming the door to his car. "I called Heather. She's going to meet us there. We can hang out for an hour or so and then split. Dominic is having a party."

"I told the guys to meet us, too. I hope that's okay," Jake replied.

It was close to nine and the party started at seven, but Allie held off going as long as she could.

Cynthia was moving the following week and Allie felt horrible. She was torn. A part of her couldn't wait for Cynthia to leave, but another part wanted to hear her mother tell her she wanted nothing more in this world than to stay close to her only daughter, to be a part of her life and that she finally came to the realization that nothing else was as important. And the guilt was terrible. The knot beginning to form in her stomach early that morning was now felt the size of a basketball.

Marcus rented out the basement of the pub. They could feel the beat of the music as they walked through the restaurant and down the stairs. Allie couldn't believe it when they reached the bottom of the staircase and looked around. There must have been a hundred people there. Did Cynthia really know them all? And did any of them care enough about her mother to show up for her going away party?

She followed Jake over to the corner where Heather, Amy, a new girl in school, Shane, Trevor and Christian were waiting.

"Check this out!" Christian told them excitedly. "They have a fountain in the corner that puts out champagne. I stole myself a glass," he laughed. All of them were holding their own plastic glasses filled to the top with the bubbly drink. "You want one?" he asked pushing it towards Allie.

She looked around and saw there were no waiters or waitresses around to keep track of underage drinkers. Regardless, it was too dark and packed for anyone to notice anyway.

"No. Not yet. Maybe in a few," Allie replied. "I should go find Cynthia. Thanks for coming, guys, I know this isn't what you wanted to do tonight, I promise we won't stay long."

She headed to the back of the room where she spotted Marcus and as she got closer, she could hear the shrill of Cynthia's voice coming from the food table. *Oh God, she's already drunk,* Allie thought as she spotted her mother, frolicking from one person to the next, obviously delighted with all the attention she was getting.

"Baby!" she shrieked when she saw Allie. She stumbled slightly as she wrapped Allie tightly in her arms and like always, Cynthia smelled of cigarettes and booze. But the worst part was her outfit. Allie was embarrassed for her. She looked like she came straight out of a Fredrick's of Hollywood catalog. A full lacy, black body suit, completely see through except for three small patches of black material covering the most important parts. Cynthia didn't have the body she used to, so not only was it slutty, she looked ridiculous. And it was apparent there was a lot of ridicule and snickers going on behind her back.

"I'm so glad you're here. I want you to meet everyone." She tugged Allie along behind her from one person to the next.

Allie tried her best to ignore the anger seething inside her, but every word her mother spoke, every toss of her hair and each fake laugh escaping her mouth made Allie cringe. Everything was a blur while her eyes searched frantically for Jake across the room. She could see him engaged in serious conversation with Shane, not even looking her way.

Maybe if she concentrated hard enough, he would look up and see she needed him to come to her rescue. But he was distracted. Disappointed, Allie focused on getting through the introductions but Cynthia was having a hard time remembering names. She wondered if it was because of her state of drunkenness or because she was surrounded by a bunch of people she knew absolutely nothing about. Either way, Allie could see she was oblivious as long as they were there for her. It was her night, her party. And she sure was dressed for it.

Allie, faking polite interest, checked her watch for what was the fourth time in twenty minutes while the tension mounted in her shoulders. Finally when Cynthia said she needed to use the restroom, Allie excused herself to go back to her friends. They had already made their way to the buffet table for food, so she grabbed a piece of celery off Heather's plate and shoved it into her mouth.

A few more minutes passed when Allie felt the uncomfortable weight of someone's eyes on her. She looked around and spotted Marcus making his way toward her circle of friends. He was carrying two glasses of champagne. He offered her one and she took it politely while Jake took the other. Her dad allowed her to have a glass of wine with dinner on holidays and or special occasions so she thought nothing of it as long as she promised herself to tell him when she got home.

Allie wasn't thrilled to introduce her new step-dad to her friends and was grateful when he was pulled away by a beautiful woman in tight red leather pants. They all watched in stunned amazement as she drug him onto the dance floor, grabbed a chair from one of the tables, shoved him into it and then proceeded to give him a lap dance right there in front of everyone.

"Did you see that?" Christian asked his eyes wide. "You brought us to the best party ever!" he said throwing an elbow into Jake's ribs. "Come on Dude, let's get a better view," he said to Shane as the two of them strolled off.

"Great, it will take a bulldozer to get them out of here now," Jake commented. Allie hadn't paid much attention before, but now as she looked around, she noticed most of the women, including the one in the tight red pants, were in their early twenties. Not much older than herself. But all the men were around her dad's age.

Allie's embarrassment for Cynthia grew. The twenty something women were gorgeous with small, tight bodies, fake blonde hair and fake boobs, like they just stepped out of the Playboy Mansion. And then there was Cynthia, close to forty, stuffing herself into an outfit made to fit a Barbie.

Allie sipped her drink slowly and carefully. She didn't want it to go to her head too quickly plus she didn't plan on staying much longer. To bide her time, she made small talk with Heather and Amy.

It was the first time Allie had spent any time with her outside of school, but Heather had been talking about her non-stop for weeks straight. She was nice, Allie decided after a few minutes, and cute too. She was sure the guys at school would be crazy about her. With that thought, a small twinge of fear manifested its way into Allie's subconscious. Would Jake think she was pretty, too?

Allie wasn't sure if it was a good thing or not, but Heather already filled Amy in about Cynthia. Normally, Allie didn't like to bring her friends around her mother, but she trusted Heather, and it was probably smart to caution Amy just in case something crazy happened. Shane and Christian respected Jake enough to keep their mouths shut around her, and Trevor was just a genuinely nice guy. When it came down to it, Allie was grateful they were all with her. She didn't like the idea of being there alone.

Just as she was starting to relax and have fun with her friends, Cynthia appeared out of nowhere and interrupted their conversation. Sticking out her hand toward Amy, she wobbled off balance.

"Oh," Amy coughed as her eyes took in the outrageous outfit. "I'm sorry, I…I must have swallowed wrong," she said catching her breath. Allie had to laugh. How else did she expect people to react to Cynthia?

"Where did your boyfriend go?" Cynthia slurred. They'd been there over an hour and Jake was ready to leave, so he took off a few minutes before to hunt down the bloodhounds he called friends.

"He's not my boyfriend," Allie responded defensively.

"Well, he should be. He's hot. If I was sixteen, believe me, I would be snacking on that piece of meat," she laughed. Heather rolled her eyes as a look of bewilderment crossed Amy's face.

A fire of anger burned beneath Allie. How dare Cynthia say that? How dare she *think* that? She was about to explain they were leaving when Cynthia's attention was drawn to the dance floor. Allie followed her gaze.

Caught in a deep lip lock with his hands roaming all over her body were Marcus and the girl in the tight red pants. Allie wearily watched Cynthia's expression change from one of hurt and bitterness to pure evil as her mouth turned up into a sly grin as she sauntered away.

Allie turned back to Heather and Amy as they appeared beside her. "I think we should go, Allie," Heather said nervously. "Amy was in the bathroom and saw two women snorting lines of coke."

"Let's find the guys, I have a feeling things are going to get ugly," she warned pulling them towards the other side of the room.

"What do you mean?" Amy asked.

"Marcus is making a fool out of Cynthia. She is drunk and believe me, she *will* cause a scene."

But they couldn't find the guys anywhere. They yelled into the bathrooms, searched over by the food, by the champagne fountain and even walked around upstairs. Intent on finding them and leaving, the three girls were unaffected by the stares and cat-calls they received from the men they passed.

"Shit. I don't want to be here much longer. Where could they be?" Allie muttered under her breath. The ball of anxiety was beginning to move from her stomach into her chest and it would only be a matter of minutes before it exploded into her head.

"Hey, we have been looking all over for you," Shane said as he, Trevor and Christian walked up the stairs. They reeked of smoke.

Allie told them the party was getting out of hand. "No kidding. We accidentally walked into a back room down stairs and saw drugs I didn't even know existed. They're all over down there. Champagne is one thing, but I can't afford to be thrown off the team. I wouldn't see the light of day again!" Trevor said.

Allie was apprehensive. "Where's Jake?"

"He went with Cynthia about ten minutes ago. We figured it was to find you."

Sweat began to pour down her neck. She needed to find him. Something wasn't right. Cynthia had revenge on her mind, and Allie knew if anyone crossed that line of fire, they were a potential target. Allie and Trevor went in one direction and sent the other four in a different one.

"Be back in ten minutes, no later," Allie warned them. She couldn't think clearly, so numbly she followed close behind Trevor. Then when the room started to spin, Allie knew it had to be the champagne. She shook her head to steady herself.

"Christ, man, where the hell have you been?" she heard Trevor say as they walked into a small walk -in closet sized room towards the back of the basement. It was even darker than the party room. It took a moment to for her eyes to adjust. Thank god she only took a few sips of the champagne. Look what it was already doing to her.

She peered around Trevor to search for Jake and found him leaning against the wall. There were five other people in the room with them, including Cynthia. Some had their clothes half off, groping other bodies while others were hanging out smoking, drinking and watching.

Had they walked into some sort of orgy? She'd heard about them. It would figure she would come upon one the night of Cynthia's going away party. But Allie didn't understand why the owners of the pub would allow it. Then her mind slipped back to something Cynthia had told her when she first started dating Marcus.

"He's a swinger," she had told Allie casually. Allie snickered at the idea mostly because she was used to all her crazy lies and made up stories, but now seeing what was going on around her, it began to make sense. Her face turned up in disgust as she reached out for Jake's hand.

"Hold on, Allie, don't you take him away from me?" Cynthia snapped grabbing Jake around the waist before they could take off. "You can leave if you want, but he is staying with me."

"What the…" Allie argued. Then she saw the glazed over look in Jake's eyes and realized he was completely out of it. His limp hand fell to his side as he stumbled back against the wall for support.

But he didn't drink any of the champagne, Allie mused. He put the glass down on the table after Marcus handed it to him. He must be on something else, but she knew Jake didn't do drugs, plus he hated Cynthia, he would never try anything she offered, so what the hell did he take?

Placing a hand on Jake's cheek, Cynthia turned his face towards hers and planted a huge kiss on his lips. Allie watched in horror as her tongue slipped into his mouth.

"What did you do to him? Did you 'roofie' him?" Allie screamed pushing on Cynthia's shoulder and pulling him away. Jake was dead weight and Trevor had to help hold him up.

"Just enough to help him relax. You stress him out too much. He's too cute to go to waste," Cynthia teased pulling him back towards her and sliding her hand down the front of his chest. "Guys like him have needs. You obviously aren't going to give it up. He needs experience, why not get it from me?" Jake stumbled backwards oblivious to what was going on around him.

Allie stared at Cynthia in dismay. She was capable of many things, but this time she crossed the line. The fog in Allie's head from the champagne cleared, along with the illusion she had created of her mother. What sort of woman would do this to her own child and how much more was Allie willing to put up with?

"Trevor, take Jake and go tell the others we will meet them at the car in five minutes," Allie said calmly. Cynthia had shaken the bottle one too many times and now it was about to explode. She had felt rage before. She had even experienced pain and disappointment at the hands of this woman, but what she felt now was jealousy and a woman scorned by jealousy was not a woman to be reckoned with.

"Get your hands off of him," she said through clenched teeth when Cynthia held tight to Jake. "Before I do something to you we both regret."

Cynthia's eyes widened with surprise. "Oh, Allie, let me have a bit of fun with the boy. Give him a night he will remember." She moved her hand down towards the crotch of his pants when somehow; Jake began to sense what was happening. His fist shot out and caught Cynthia on the side of the cheek. Dazed and confused, he stumbled back putting his head in his hands as a baffled Cynthia landed on the ground.

"Shit! We got to get out of here." Allie ran towards the stairs pulling him with her. She didn't bother looking back to see if anyone followed. Once outside, Jake leaned against the security of the brick of the building.

"You look awful," Trevor told him.

"I feel horrible," he slurred.

Trevor drove Jake's car to Allie's house while everyone else piled into Heather's. At Allie's, they all helped get Jake into the house while deciding whether or not to go to Dominic's party. Allie was too angry to go anywhere and Jake was still out of it. Besides, she was sure Trevor filled everyone in on what he saw, and the uncomfortable silence told her no one could quite comprehend it. Allie was horrified. After her friends left, she sulked upstairs to get her parents.

A few cups of Cammi's herbal tea and aspirin brought Jake back to his senses, and they were able to piece their stories together. The champagne Marcus gave them must have been laced, but because Allie only had a couple sips, it didn't hit her as hard. Jake hadn't drunk any, but Cynthia gave him a glass of ginger ale, which must have been laced with the same stuff.

Bryce wanted to call the cops. His mind was still reeling from the story Cammi had told him about Cynthia having sex with a kid Allie went to school with and now this.

"Don't bother," Jake said his voice overcome with defeat. "I overheard someone say the owner was a good friend of theirs. We'd get in trouble for drinking anyway. There is no way we can prove it." Jake was holding his pounding head in his hands. He'd never been so humiliated in his life and facing Allie's parents after what happened was worse than he could even imagine.

Allie sat quietly across the room in a rocking chair not saying a word. Her arms were crossed in front of her as she rocked habitually back and forth, back and forth. When Jake looked up to meet her eyes, searching for reassurance and compassion, he was greeted with nothing but her cold, hard stare.

Leaning over to give her husband a kiss on the cheek, Cammi suggested they go upstairs to give Allie and Jake some privacy.

"Out of respect and love for Allie, I have kept my mouth shut, but I can't do it anymore," Cammi told him once they were out of ear shot. "I am done playing Cynthia's games. She thinks we are dumb and naïve, that she is pulling the wool over our eyes, but no more. I won't have Allie around it. I have a right to hate her. I have a right to tell her what I think. If she shows up here at the house she's going to deal with me."

Bryce tried to force a smile. "Do you really think it will do any good? That she is going to listen to you? She will tell you what you want to hear and then be off concocting her next scheme. She doesn't get it. She never will. She leaves next week. I will let Allie know she is not allowed to have contact with Cynthia anymore unless it's over the phone or here at our house."

He looked tired and lost in thought as he stood by the window watching the moonlight fill the sky. Suddenly, without any hesitation, rage took over his body, and he punched a hole in the wall. Cammi jumped, but didn't move towards him. She understood how he felt.

"Can you imagine what could have happened to her? What Marcus would have done if they didn't leave when they did? If I see him again, I will beat him to a bloody pulp and enjoy it. They are sick, Cammi, sick and twisted."

He crumbled to the floor, burying his head between his knees and forearms, squeezing himself into a tight ball.

"I'm sorry. I'm so, so sorry," he whispered. "I hate myself for putting Allie through this. I shouldn't have let Cynthia back into her life. Can you forgive me, Cammi? Will Allie ever forgive me?"

It was then Cammi went to him wrapping him in her arms. He wasn't crying like she thought he was. Instead, he was numb, numb with pain, numb with grief. Numb with anger.

"I wish I could take it away. But you have to believe you didn't do anything wrong," she reassured him.

"If something happened to her, I'd never forgive myself. How could I live with that?" He looked up at her with dry, blood shot eyes.

"Nothing happened. Someone is watching out for her. Bryce, I know it's hard, but you have to believe this is what she needed to see. If not, she would still be crazy about her, still trying to win her approval, win her love and get her attention. But it is over. She knows. And she's safe. She's safe because of Jake, because of us, and because of herself. We can't live her life for her. And we can't hold her prisoner in our house until she is thirty. She has to make mistakes, she has to grow. And you have to trust. When she gets hurt, it builds her character. It makes her strong. It makes her like you."

It was hard to keep going some days and Cammi hated what they had to deal with. But she was one of the lucky ones who had faith and the will to fight against evil. She knew she wouldn't be able to do it without a strong relationship with God. What about the ones who had nothing, the ones who were lonely or afraid? How did they cope? Were they the ones who sank? The ones who committed suicide? Were they the ones who never found true happiness?

She'd been there, not too long ago. It was a humbling experience and one she didn't ever want to relive again. But she was stronger despite it. She was a better mother and wife for it and because of it she found compassion not only for herself but for others.

As she clung to her husband while he rocked back and forth, Clifford's words came rushing back to her. *Be the miracle.* Was Clifford right? Was *she* the miracle she'd so desperately been seeking? She had no control over anyone, only herself. All she had and all she was given was from God. He had the control, but at least she could be comforted by the simple words she heard one snowy, dismal night from a stranger who became her friend.

Out of her pity and anguish came great hope, the strength to build and change her life, the courage to set an example for her family and hopefully the wisdom to know what was best.

*****

Jake was miserable. He left Allie's house ashamed two weeks ago and hadn't mustered up enough courage to talk to her since. For him good judgment typically took over in bad situations, but this time he failed the person he loved the most. Judging by the look on her face when he sobered up, any chance he had for a future with her was gone. Though she had participated slightly when the events of the evening were discussed with her parents, she remained distant and detached.

Even later, on the porch she refused to give him the elaborate details of what happened while he was drugged. He recalled Cynthia claiming Allie was upset and wanted to talk to him privately. She'd handed him a soda as he followed her to the back of the building, but anything beyond that was fuzzy.

It was typical for Allie to call him mid afternoon after she got home from her dance class but when two days went by without even a text message from her, he realized something was drastically wrong. Slowly, with time, his recollection began to resurface, plaguing his mind with disgusting and disgraceful thoughts, and he was unable to bring himself to call or message her either.

School started next week. He would be a senior. He had hoped his last year would be the best ever with Allie by his side but she was avoiding him. He dreaded seeing her the first day of school. What would he say? Sorry I made out with your mom? The idea made him want to vomit.

Allie was an innocent victim with a hateful, bitch for a mother. Of course, maybe she didn't know what happened. No, she was the one who pulled him away from Cynthia's sexual advances. She had to have seen something. But maybe she didn't care.

Either way, he felt horrible. He knew the respectable thing would be to call and thank her first and apologize second. But he just couldn't do it. If he ignored it, it would eventually go away, right?

He missed her. God, he missed her like mad and wished fate hadn't brought them to the point of losing a friendship. Miserably, he moved through each day waiting for her to show up at his door. How could he explain something he didn't understand himself? He drove past her house, hoping to catch her outside, too embarrassed to face her family. He walked down to the river, hoping she was sitting in her usual spot, skipping rocks, waiting for him. But she never was. Eventually weeks passed without any contact.

Heather wasn't talking either. She was the one friend of Allie's who knew how he felt about her, but thankfully kept his secret all this time.

Desperate for some connection to Allie he drove to Heather's before football practice looking for answers. "You need to move on, Jake," she said putting her hand sympathetically on his arm.

"Thanks," he replied dryly.

"Allie never thought of you as anything but a friend. Pull your head out of the clouds and realize it wasn't meant to be."

"Did she say anything to you?"

"No. Only that her dad put limits on her time with Cynthia. Allie's allowed to talk to her once a week and they had their phone number and even Allie's cell changed. If Cynthia doesn't follow rules, he will make sure she winds up in jail or never sees Allie again."

"Good. But I bet Allie is pissed."

"I think she is in shock. Maybe a little depressed. It has to be overwhelming you know, having your own mom do what she did."

Embarrassed, Jake grabbed his gym bag and headed to the field. But even that wasn't enough of a distraction from his destroyed life. The first half hour, his coach continuously pulled him aside reprimanding him for mistakes he hadn't made at all last season. "Get it together, Jake or your first string position will be someone else's."

Someone else probably deserves it, he thought. His heart wasn't into it anymore. Football, school, nothing was the same if he couldn't share it with Allie. As the rest of the team headed into the locker room to shower, Jake stayed behind watching dusk push the sun beyond the horizon. He kicked at a football then settle down on the freshly mowed grass.

Allie watched him practice from a distance just like she had watched him secretively the past few weeks. His sorrow moved her. She hadn't meant for this much time to pass and he obviously took her distance as a sign she ended their friendship. But he couldn't be more wrong.

Walking slowly, it felt like a lifetime before she finally reached his hunched over figure. Placing her hand on his arm in an affectionate gesture she sat next to him. A reassuring smile formed on her lips as she noticed the surprise on his face. Silently, she rested her head on his shoulder.

As if he'd been burnt, he suddenly jumped away, needing to put space between them. "Don't, Allie, just don't. Okay?"

"What's your problem?" she asked astonished and rejected by his outburst.

"I can't do this anymore. It's not fair." He surprised himself. For weeks he had been desperate for some sort of sign, any contact from her. And here she was. But his heart couldn't take anymore of her mixed signals.

"What are you talking about?"

"You and me. I mean, you….you and… where have you been? You don't call, you haven't been around, then all a sudden you appear out of nowhere and expect everything to be okay? It's not okay, Allie, do you realize that? A lot has happened. I thought our friendship was over."

"I'm sorry, that wasn't my intention. I had a lot to figure out."

"So…. you expect me to wait? Do you have any idea what I have been going through?"

"No, I don't know," she said softly.

"You're selfish, Allie."

"That's not fair! I have been going through hell, too and I'm sorry I left you out in the cold, but you couldn't help me this time!"

"Why not?" he demanded. "I have been the one person who stood by your side with Cynthia. It wasn't only you she screwed this time, it was me too! Have you thought about how humiliated I am? Have you heard the rumors and how they are affecting me? Of course not! You only thought of yourself. Thanks a lot Allie. At least I know where you will be when I need someone to depend on."

His word stung. She watched in despair as he grabbed up his helmet and trotted off towards the locker room. She ran to catch up with him.

"Stop, please, Jake, that's not true!"

He turned on her "Then tell me, what is true? You were my best friend. I thought you hated me. Do you know how bad I feel about what happened? We got shit on by your mom…… and you ignore me for weeks. Why Allie? Tell me why," he insisted.

"Because I was confused. I…..I couldn't look at you and not remember what happened."

"Nice. That makes me feel a whole lot better."

"No, you don't understand!"

"Then you better make me understand." Anger seeped through his pores. "I thought we were stronger than this."

Defeated, she began to sob. "I was jealous, okay? I was jealous."

His expression softened.

"I've never felt that. I didn't know how to act, to be around you. The idea of Cynthia touching you and doing those things to you…. I didn't like it. I don't want anyone to….to….to do that stuff to you, let alone her."

His eyes bore intimately into hers. "Why?" he demanded taking a step closer. He was sweaty and covered in grass stains and dirt, but didn't care. He needed answers.

"Because you are everything to me." She shook her head. "I can't explain it, Jake. I don't understand, but its different now. I want to be with you all the time. Not like before. When I look at you, I don't see my best friend." Her blue eyes searched his.

"What do you see?" He reached up to push a stray hair behind her ear.

"Someone I love." Her voice came out in a hushed whisper as her heart thumped against her chest. "But not like I loved you before. This time it's something more."

It was sweet to finally hear the words. He held her gaze for a moment before pulling her to him. She traced his lips with her finger. "I'm scared to lose you as my friend. But I can't deny what I feel," she admitted.

"Don't. Lord knows I don't want you to."

"Really?" she asked still unsure.

"Yeah."

His eyes lingered on hers for another moment as he reached his hand to the back of her head, slipping his fingers through her hair. He bent his face to meet hers and when his lips brushed against her own they were soft and tender. She tingled under his touch and when he pulled away, she released the breath she had been holding. She could not stop her heart from racing, her legs felt numb, and instantly she wanted more. Reaching up on her tiptoes, her lips melted into his own as he gripped her tighter, deepening the kiss. She could feel his muscles tighten under the dampness of his football jersey.

Lightheaded and too embarrassed to look at him when they pulled apart, Allie stepped away.

"Are you sure you want this? With me, I mean?" he asked.

"That's what I was doing the past two weeks. I'm sorry I hurt you, but I was overwhelmed. I came back from Cancun thinking I could control it, but since my birthday party and then the thing with Cynthia, everything spiraled out of control. I didn't know how to handle it. I kept hoping you would just show up at my house and make it easier on me."

"And I kept hoping you would show up at mine. After I remembered what happened, I was too humiliated to face you or your parents." He tugged on her hand pulling her towards the sideline bench. He flung his arm around her shoulder holding her close, and enjoyed the simplicity her having her next to him.

They stayed that way, watching the sun set, a slight breeze whipping through the leaves of the aspens, neither sure of what else to say.

"Come on, I'll give you a ride home."

"Jake? Where do we go from here? I mean, what is it you want?"

"What I've always wanted, for you to let me love you."

Allie told Cammi. Cammi told Bryce.

It wasn't a surprise to anyone that Bryce had grown fond of the boy, and his wife was right, he *was* good enough for Allie, probably the best. He came from a good family and the kid had goals….focus. He knew where his life was going. To top it off, he was better to Allie than anyone could imagine. His adoration for her was obvious to everyone.

Bryce had also been painfully aware of Allie's turmoil the past two weeks while she sorted through her own emotions and finally, he had to admit his daughter was in love. He still thought they were awfully young to be this serious, but he trusted them both. His only concern was that Allie he hoped was getting into this relationship for the right reasons, not as a distraction to deal with the pain her mother was inflicting.

Bryce laid down the ground rules with them both at dinner one night. "I don't think either of you are dumb or naive. As long as you are responsible, don't screw up your future, college and all that with talk of marriage or babies, then you have my permission to date," he told them. "You know my expectations and my rules," Bryce reminded them. "Follow them. Do you understand me?"

Though they were thoroughly embarrassed, Allie and Jake nodded silently.

Despite Bryce's reluctance, Allie was growing up. He only prayed the two of them had as much sense and strength to deal with rough times when they came. With the emotional baggage Allie carried with her, Bryce was sure there was bound to be plenty more ahead.

Cynthia stuck to the rules. As much as she hated to admit it, she was terrified of Bryce. But it was much harder for Allie than anyone anticipated. Though it was a relief to have her dad's protection, she struggled with not being able to make her own decision. A part of Allie hated Cynthia but after a month of no contact, Allie missed her terribly and was desperate to know if her mother still cared about her. Did she really want Cynthia in her life? Sometimes. She was relieved to be rid of the drama, but an empty space remained. And she lied to herself trying to pretend Jake filled it.

Cynthia called every Friday and they talked for an hour. She like Lincoln but hated that Marcus was always out of town on business trips. She was lonely and told Allie on many occasions she wished she would have stayed in Madison. Never once did Cynthia apologize about her going away party, Allie figured she probably never would. And they never discussed Jake. As far as Allie was concerned, he was a subject that was off limits. Cynthia promised to come back to see her for Christmas. By then four months would have passed. Maybe this was enough punishment for Cynthia to have learned her lesson. And maybe with the distance between them, Cynthia would realize how much she missed Allie. And just maybe that would be enough to make her change.

Her dad was not as easy to convince.

"I'm sorry Allie, but the only way you get to see her is here at the house with us present."

"But Dad, it's been months," Allie pleaded. "I'm sure she learned her lesson. Can't I just stay a few nights at the apartment with her?"

"Allie, people like Cynthia don't change. When are you going to realize that? I don't care if it's been years. Last time, she drugged your boyfriend and her husband drugged you. Do you understand what they planned to do? I don't get why you would want to put yourself in that situation again?"

Allie scowled at him.

"Does Jake want you to see her," Bryce pressed.

She fidgeted under his gaze. "No. His reaction was pretty much the same as yours."

"Allie, are you really willing to sacrifice your relationship with Jake for Cynthia? She is going to continue to cause problems unless you put your foot down. When you leave home you won't have to answer to me. You can do what you want, but I guarantee if Jake is still in the picture, he won't put up with it. No man who loves you will."

Bryce was bewildered. Once upon a time his daughter had been a confident, independent child full of life, wisdom and dreams.

The world was at her fingertips, begging her to jump in and embrace it. A part of her still wanted to. But in just a matter of months, Bryce watched as she'd become a co-dependent outsider, hesitant to enjoy life. She desperately clung to the notion of having someone take care of her, scared to fly solo, but at the same time, terrified to allow anyone close enough to soar with her. Allie and Jake had become practically inseparable and little by little Bryce was afraid she was losing her identity. Although her love for him was pure, it was a game of cat and mouse. Allie kept Jake at arm's length, afraid he wouldn't be there when she walked out the door the next day, while hovering over him, jealous of anything or anyone that wasn't her. The damage had been done and Allie trusted no one and the lack of trust was causing her to behave in ways she normally would not.

The wrath of Cynthia invaded their answering machine in the days after Allie told her about the supervised visitation arrangements.

"You need to pick up the phone! Do you hear me Bryce? When I get to town we are coming straight to the house and I will have the cops with me! You can't keep her away from me! I have rights and she wants to see me."

"Allie, pick up your cell phone, damn it! You better tell your father he is in for a rude awakening when I show up there. Marcus is going to bury him in the ground! I deserve to be respected. You tell him he either meets me somewhere to talk this out or it is going to get ugly."

"Bryce, you and your whore of a wife and your two bastard children can go to hell! I am sick of you ruining my life. You think you are better than me! You've pushed me too far this time!

Bryce was furious Allie had given Cynthia her new cell number.

"What are you thinking? We agreed you would get this new phone on the condition you were responsible with it. Giving her your number was not part of the deal. If you want to start paying the bill, then you can give the number to anyone you want. But until then, we are in charge, like it or not."

"I'm sorry. I didn't realize it would be such a problem," Allie pouted.

"When hasn't Cynthia been a problem, Allie? Pull your head out of your ass."

"I'm sorry, dad. It's just I miss her and want to talk to her more than once a week. She gets lonely, she needs me."

Bryce and Cammi took for granted the choice Allie made earlier that fall. They thought Cynthia's bizarre behavior and seduction of Jake finally helped Allie open her eyes. But they had no idea about the inner turmoil within Allie simmering just below the surface, slowly making its way to the surface until finally one night, she cracked.

Jake was over and the entire family was sitting on the floor in the living room playing Monopoly, laughing and joking when Bryce made a snide comment about Cynthia mental health. While everyone else laughed at the innocent humor of it, Allie threw her game pieces across the board.

"Enough, okay, Dad?" Allie demanded.

A dreary silence filled the room as everyone looked at her.

"Don't be so sensitive, Allie. Why do you continue to defend her?"

"I know you are *thrilled* she is gone, but I'm not. I'm trying to make the best of it but it's not easy. My choices are ones I will question the rest of my life. I don't hate her the way you want me to. Regardless of what she has done, I still love her and that is never going to go away. So please respect my feelings and realize because I still love her, it hurts to hear you bash her all the time."

Standing up, Bryce looked around, lost and confused, wondering what he could possibly say to make her understand. Crushed and filled with shame, he went upstairs without another word. Letting the other two clean up the game, Cammi followed. He was sitting in the darkness of Allie's room with her pillow curled into his arms, staring out the window. Cammi came up from behind and wrapped her arms around him resting her cheek against his warm back. They knew Allie was right and needed to consider her feelings more than they had been. In her reaction, they were able to see how raw and deep Allie's wounds were and had to accept these circumstances were something their daughter would struggle with forever.

"I don't know who she is anymore."

"*She* doesn't know who she is, Honey."

"What can I do?" his voice choked. "I thought this would make everything better. Cynthia moving…. her and Jake."

"Her self-esteem's shot. She's basing herself worth on him but knows it isn't working, the emptiness is still there. What Cynthia did as well as leaving has left her raw inside. She can't separate from the anger enough to realize it's ruining who she is as a person. Instead, she's seeking attention and gratification from those she thinks can replace it. We can't change it, we can't make her see.

She has to do it herself. We can only guide her. I've been there Bryce, remember? You have too."

"I just wish she didn't have to. Not at this point in her life. She's too young."

"She's *your* daughter. She has your strength and determination. I know she won't give up. Believe in her the way you did me. The way you did us."

The month of December was a somber affair with everyone wondering if and when Cynthia was going to make her presence known. The stress was too much for Allie to bear and she began to act out in small ways, breaking curfew, taking the car without asking permission, not calling to check in. Rules she had followed for years, rules that should not have been an issue. Anticipating Cynthia's presence was making her a nervous wreck and even causing fights between her and Jake.

Cammi noticed not only her actions, but her gloomy disposition. Everything was coming at her from all sides. Allie wasn't sleeping well and her irate temper had everyone on edge.

"Dad, can I go over to Jake's tonight to watch a movie?" Allie asked her dad.

"Well, see," he said nonchalantly over the newspaper.

"Hey," she said sitting next to him on the couch figuring she may as well push her luck. "Next weekend a bunch of kids from school are heading up the hill to ski. Can I go with?"

"Maybe." He did want to see her spend time with her friends again doing things she used to love. Maybe it would help get her out of this funk. "What day?"

"Well….," she hesitated. "Actually, it's both days. Amy's grandparents have a cabin. They said we could use it if we want."

He looked at her suspiciously. "Who's all going?"

Her face turned red. "Ten or so of us."

"Boys?" he asked irritated.

"Some, yes," she admitted shyly.

"No!" His face was set in a resolute scowl.

"But Dad…"

"I said no, Allie. Don't argue with me. You are sixteen years old and don't need to be going on overnight trips with boys and I won't change my mind."

"Cynthia would let me go." Allie's belligerence startled him.

"I don't give a shit what she would let you do. She's not here and you are living with me."

"Maybe it was a mistake," she added under her breath.

"What did you say?" Bryce roared jumping out of the recliner.

"Maybe it was a mistake," she yelled back shoving her face towards his. "She lets me do what I want, when I want and with *whom* I want," she challenged. "I bet she'd even let Jake spend the night."

His eyes narrowed. "Is that what you want? Well, she's not here now is she, Allie, so the reality of you living with her and doing whatever the hell you want isn't possible."

Hearing the commotion of raised voices sent Cammi flying into the room.

"What's going on?"

"Shut up!" Allie screeched at her father, ignoring Cammi. "Just shut up. You don't know her. She's changed. She told me. She said she has lots of regrets and is going to make it up to me. She even said she misses me so much she wants to move back. You are jealous because I love her. You don't want me to love her."

"Oh yeah, of course she's changed. We've heard that one before. You want to go live with her? Go ahead. Become a slut just like your mother and see how far it gets you!" he glowered.

"Bryce!" Cammi gasped.

Pain ripped Allie's heart in half but she refused to let him see her hurt.

"I hate you," she cried through clenched teeth. "Cammi should have left when she had the chance. She deserves better than you!"

Instinct forced his hand down to his side almost as quickly as he raised it in the air. He'd made a mistake like that once and it almost cost him his marriage. He wasn't going to allow his anger to get the best of him let alone cause him to slap his own daughter.

Instead, he walked over to Allie and pulled her into his arms. Instantly she stiffened, but soon, her tears began to flow.

"I'm so sorry Allie. I didn't mean anything I said. I understand you're hurting. It hurts me I can't make it go away. This isn't what I want for you."

"I'm sorry, too," she cried as she clung to him, praying he never let go.

They stayed silent and still while Cammi slipped out of the room. They needed this father-daughter moment more than they needed anything from her. Her first reaction was to jump in between the two when Bryce raised his hand to Allie. But her horror was quickly replaced with respect when Bryce chose love over anger.

Chapter Forty

Jake had his hand wrapped tightly around hers as they stood in the freezing cold watching the lighting of the City Christmas Tree. It was an event he attended every year since his mother was chairwoman for the Chamber of Commerce. It was always special to him and this year, he wanted to share it with Allie.

Her hand was small and petite in his. He didn't want to let it go, just like he didn't want to let her go. She loved him, he knew that from the core of his being, but in the time they'd been dating, he could feel her hesitation. It wasn't fair. This was to be the time of their lives. He a Senior and Allie a Junior. They weren't supposed to be gloomy and depressed; constantly looking over their shoulders, wondering what chaos was going to happen next. They should be enjoying their newfound love instead of shying away from it.

He thought once they were together, things would be better. But the storm clouds still hovered. It filled him with pride to have her in the stands cheering him on during the season. Her family welcomed him into their home like one of their own and attended all of his games, too. The football team went to state winning 28-14, and he was offered full ride scholarships all over the State of Colorado for college the next fall. He couldn't be happier. But she wasn't.

Her lack of participation in the usual school activities she once loved concerned him. When he was at practice, she should have been with friends or at dance or finishing her columns for the school newspaper. Instead, she waited, alone, until he was done, giving up her life to be with him. And he didn't like it.

He fell in love with her because she was her own person, for her independence, her confidence. The more she lost herself, the more she subconsciously questioned the security she had in him. She was vulnerable to all things and he felt like he couldn't protect her. Not when it came to this. As a friend it had been easier to step aside, but as her boyfriend, he felt every hint of pain, every disappointment and every form of rejection soaring through her. It killed him to watch her slowly slip away knowing because he loved her, he might have to let her go.

The crowd sang along to 'Silent Night' as the mayor made it official by lighting the tree. A cheer went up and Allie snuggled in closer to him. She knew she was quiet and withdrawn. She had been for a few weeks now. It was tiring listening to everyone remind her how stupid she was and that she needed to get Cynthia out of her life, so instead she clammed up. No one would understand anyway. *She* was the one whose mother was a loser, the one who had to live without the guidance, friendship, and love that came from the nurturing heart of a mother.

A lot of people loved her and she knew she was lucky. But it wasn't the same and she hated to hear the negativity surrounding every conversation involving Cynthia. They thought it was okay since she now understood, but it wasn't okay. The comments hurt more than anything. Her parents had been better since she freaked out, but she had to hear it at school, from teachers, from her dance coach....even from Jake's parents. No matter where she turned, she couldn't escape. Cynthia had burned too many bridges in this town and Allie was paying the price.

She knew her anger should lie with Cynthia and it was impulsive to trust her, but she was an addiction Allie didn't want to shake. She thought it would be easy not having her around but all it did was intensify her own feelings of inadequacy. It ate at her.... the insecurity of why she wasn't good enough to love.

If she wasn't good enough for Cynthia then why should she be good enough for Jake? He was the best looking guy at school. Girls were crazy about him. Why was he with her, the girl who had a crazy, psychotic, trashy mother? 'The apple doesn't fall far from the tree,' she overheard Heather's mom say to someone on the phone when she was at her house last week.

He should be with a normal girl, a cheerleader, or at least one who had great aspirations and dreams. She didn't have any of those. The only dream she had were his dreams. What he wanted, she wanted and she was willing to spend her life living them out with him. As long as they were together, and she wasn't alone..... she didn't care.

But his nervousness when she told him such things made her uptight. Didn't he want that too?

The evening sky was clear. The clouds separated enough to allow the stars to shine above their heads though the temperature was going to drop close to freezing that night. Even though they didn't have much snow yet for this time of the year, the weather had been too cold to enjoy their regular outdoor activities. This is why Allie couldn't wait to go skiing with Jake. They hadn't been yet and she was good. Good enough, in fact to have a place on the school's ski team, but she lacked the motivation to make it to practices. Still, she wanted to show off and make him proud.

The crowd slowly dispersed until only a few people remained. The shadow from a street light overhead illuminated the way as they strolled peacefully towards Jake's house. He wanted it to be like this forever. But if he were to predict the future, he could honestly say that as much love as there was between the two of them, they weren't in it for the long haul. Not if things continued how they were.

When they reached his house, he took her hand pulling her down to sit beside him on the front stoop. She wrapped her arms around his neck and brought his lips to hers.

They hadn't had sex yet. It wasn't that he didn't want to. They even talked about it but the opportunity hadn't presented itself, and he would be damned if he was going to have their first time be in the back seat of his car. She was better than that. What they shared was too good for that.

The tenderness in her kiss aroused him as she pressed the softness of her body against him. He had held out this long, but honestly didn't know how much self-control he had left. She tempted him too much. Looking into her eyes to reassure her of his love, he pressed his head into her shoulder. He had to break away from the embrace or he would never stop.

The river….he had it planned out in his head, imagined it many times over the last year, especially on the nights he'd spent out there alone, longing for her to love him in return. In all the times they had been there late at night, not once had they seen another person. It was their perfect, isolated, special place. But it was the middle of winter and bitter cold, so he decided they would just have to wait until spring at least. That was only four months away. He could suck it up until then, couldn't he?

But Allie misunderstood his actions. She wanted him and was ready for this. Had been for months and once again, he pulled away from her just as things were heating up. Her chest tightened with fear. What was wrong with him? Nothing. Nothing was wrong with him. It had to be her. Why else would her hormonal seventeen-year-old boyfriend not want to have sex? He said he did, and she could tell how much he enjoyed the kisses, the touches. Surely he wanted more. So why, every time they got close, did he torment her like this? She loved him. Was it so wrong for her to want to show him in a physical way? The idea of losing him to another girl devastated her. She wasn't going to allow it to happen. She would do anything to keep him.

She should ask him. No, he should just tell her. She shouldn't be expected to read his mind. They were best friends and until they started dating, she was able to tell him anything, her deepest darkest secrets, but now that he was her boyfriend, she had more to lose. It wasn't a chance she was willing to take. So if it meant keeping her feelings to herself instead of upsetting him, well…that was what she was going to do.

Christmas and New Years came and went without a word from Cynthia. "It's the calm before the storm," Bryce had joked.

And he could not have been more correct.

They were headed to the city to meet Bryce's parents for a Comedy Show. In their rush to get out of the house, leaving the kids in Allie's care, Cammi grabbed the stack of unopened mail. Rummaging through it she came across three pieces of mail with Allie's name on them. The envelopes were addressed to Cynthia's old address here in Madison and forwarded to theirs.

"What's this?" she wondered out loud scanning the contents of the first envelope she opened.

Her silence caused him to glance over while keeping one eye on the road. She looked slightly worried.

"This is a Verizon bill for close to a thousand dollars. There is a utility bill here for five hundred and ninety six dollars. Bryce, this one is from Direct TV that has gone to collections from over a year and a half ago! Between the balance, late fees and collection fee's its twelve hundred dollars. This can't be right."

Bryce thought for a moment, then without warning, slammed his hand hard against the steering wheel. "Damn it. I've heard of people doing this. She's ruining her credit!"

"Isn't it illegal for Cynthia to use her social security number? Can we press charges?"

Blazing fire penetrated his eyes. "Of course it is. Proving it is the hard part. If we can, I am going to see to it she rots in hell."

"Brandi's pregnant!"

Heather sat with Allie on her bed helping her fold yesterday's laundry. They had two classes together, but other than school, they rarely saw each other anymore.

Amy had taken Allie's place. She liked Amy. It was just she and Heather had been best friends since grade school. It made Allie a little envious, but the reality was she'd turned down many invitations from both girls just so she could be with Jake.

It surprised Allie when Heather suddenly showed up at the house today unannounced. Regardless, Allie was grateful to see her friend. Jake was at school taking his ACT's, so Allie was bored without him around.

"No way!"

"Yep, she found out two weeks ago."

Leaning forward, Allie dropped her voice barely above a whisper. "Does she know whose it is?"

"She says it's Christian's."

"Oh, my God!" It made sense. They broke up almost a year before, but Christian still used her when he was hard up. Then again, Brandi was never fully over him, so who's to say this wasn't a plan to trap him.

"What's she going to do? Is she scared?"

"Nope. She claims they are back together and planned it."

"Is she crazy? Who plans a baby at sixteen?"

"Her parents want her to get an abortion. Christian says she's full of shit.... that he hasn't touched her since Halloween. She's only a month along. But I would imagine he would say anything to get out of it."

"Wow, she's really gone off the deep end," Allie commented putting tossing her socks in a drawer.

"How are things with Jake?" Heather had no idea how Allie felt about him until they began dating. She was put off that Allie hadn't trusted her enough to confide in her, but after a few days of feigning hurt, she finally understood the reasoning behind it.

"Good, I guess. I don't know. Heather," she sighed, "I don't know what's wrong with me."

"Allie, you know I love Jake like a brother and couldn't imagine a better boyfriend for you, but you're different now that you're with him. It scares me."

"It scares me too. I love him and know he loves me. I don't want to date anyone else, but I am starting to think our relationship isn't very healthy." She shook her head. "He doesn't do anything wrong, it's all me. I look in the mirror and ask myself where I went?"

"Have you and Jake done it?"

"No. I mean we do stuff. God, I love kissing him. But we know when to stop. It's hard and I want more. I'm not sure if he does. I mean, I know he does....want sex that is. I just don't think he wants it with me. He has so much going for him, you know? I feel like he's moving on without me. He graduates in five months and goes off to college, then what? If I'm this possessive when he is in the same town, what's it going to be like when he's gone, hanging out with beautiful, fake breasted, desperate and drunk college co-ed's?"

"Does he know how you feel?" Brandi stood up to stretch her arms over her head looking at the pictures Allie had pinned to her bulletin board, Allie and Jake at homecoming, Faith and Bailey at the Zoo, her parents on their tenth wedding anniversary. A picture of Allie and Cynthia trying on prom dresses when she was barely a teenager peeking out beneath the others.

"Sort of. He senses something's not right with me, which makes him worry. I got so wrapped up in being his girlfriend; I forgot what it's like to be me. It's not his fault, he encourages me to do the things I love. But I don't know how to anymore. I don't know how to balance the two. Problem is, I can sense him pulling away and if I don't figure it out, I could lose him forever. I'm desperate not to lose him. I don't think I could handle the pain," she cried, tears spilling onto her face.

Heather sat down next to her friend wrapping her in a bear hug, giving her the freedom to cry in her arms. "You're still there, you know? You have to want to find you."

"I'm clingy. I've become the girl we loved to hate. I feel like Brandi. God, I'm pathetic," she laughed wiping her eyes.

"I've seen and watched a lot, Allie. I have three older sisters along with one stinky, rotten little brother. Anyway, my point is I think most girls feel this way once in a while. Its okay, you know. What is not okay is how you handle it. You've got to be good to you otherwise you won't be good for Jake. He likes you best that way, you know, confident, fun loving."

Allie and Heather spent the next hour playing Guitar Hero, laughing and gossiping the way high school girls are supposed to. But when Heather left to go home, Allie was stuck with the grim reminder that if Jake wasn't in her life..... Allie shook her head. That was a thought she could not face. As she sat on the couch crying and holding onto Penny while he squirmed, trying to lick her face, Allie wished more than anything the emptiness inside her heart would go away.

"That bitch!" Bryce snarled throwing a stack of papers on the kitchen table two days later. "Ron did a credit check for me. Two years ago, she bought a car under Allie's name and had it repossessed. She was even able to get a credit card which typically is unheard of. Most companies won't allow anyone under eighteen to get a card. The balance on it was only six hundred, but it, too, is maxed out. This is absolutely insane. We have to sit down with Allie and explain how this is going to affect her finances if she plans on ever buying a car, tries to get student loans, or even wants to buy a house. It's called Child Identity Theft and we can press charges."

Cammi shrugged. "That's a choice we should leave up to Allie and Bryce, you and I know, she probably won't."

Misery *does* love company. It's what Allie's relationship with Cynthia consisted of. They fed off one another and as long as they were unhappy, dark, miserable souls, who hated everyone, their friendship thrived. She just now realized how the existence was tearing her apart, and Allie was desperate to take measures to cut the tie.

It was early February before she heard from Cynthia again. "Why haven't you called?" she asked dryly.

"Because Allie, I am tired of being the one who tries, the one who bends over backwards to be in your life. Your father won't allow it, and you are too busy with your *new* boyfriend to be concerned with me," Cynthia whined.

"Really?" she challenged. "You moved away remember, Cynthia? How did you think you could manage being in *my* life from hundreds of miles away? You think I sit around waiting for you to call? Do you think I am so desperate to have you in my life I would stop living? Besides, you are the one who made promises to come to Colorado to see me over Christmas. Not only didn't you show, you didn't even have the decency to tell me why," she accused. "I waited and waited. Hoped and hoped. Just like every other promise you broke."

"Don't talk to me like that or I am going to hang up."

Instead of the usual panic she felt, Allie was suddenly filled with strength and pride. "Don't *you* threaten *me*! You think I need you more than you need me, so you hang it over my head. Do you realize the longer you are away, the easier it is to forget about you?"

"You don't mean that!" Cynthia's tone changed. "Honey, listen. I didn't have a choice when I moved. I had to get out of town. I asked you to come, don't you remember. I would love to have you live with me," she blurted.

"Why did you have to leave, Cynthia, huh? Tell me."

"One of the bouncers from the Rodeo started stalking me after Marcus and I got married. He was jealous. I made the stupid mistake of sleeping with him the night of the bachelorette party. He was leaving me notes, showing up at the house. Thank goodness Marcus was there to protect me, who knows what could have happened."

"First of all, why would you sleep with another guy right before you got married? That is just asking for trouble. And second, you and Marcus decided to move and bought a house months *before* you got married, remember? Why can't you just be honest for once in your stupid, pathetic life?"

The silence was deafening.

"Well, I guess your father wins, right?" Cynthia's voice turned ice cold. "He's succeeded in turning you against me. He never wanted us to be close, you know that?"

"My father never says anything about you. In fact, you are the only one who talks shit. I guess maybe your plan backfired. Yes, Cynthia.... I know everything you told me was lies. It's a wonder I don't hate him," she said sarcastically. Once she started she wasn't able to stop. Years of pent up anger, hurt, frustration and tainted love tumbled out of her mouth.

"I've known about your lies for a long time. Why do you think I didn't want to live with you? My dad didn't have to tell me. I could see your true colors in how you acted, how you treated your friends, the guys you dated, even how you treated me. Years of watching you finally paid off and I don't want to be anything like you. In fact you are right, I don't have time for you anymore," she shrieked into the phone.

Something in Allie's head clicked. After her parents told her about the credit card bills, she had a strange epiphany and decided it was time to cut all ties. After months of no contact with Cynthia she was beginning to understand the direction she was headed if she didn't start making smarter choices. She was the exact opposite of the person she was capable of being. In fact, she saw a lot of similarities between her actions lately and Cynthia's. It was a humbling experience, but frightening enough to force her to make a change. She wasn't going to use low self-esteem and the issues from her mother as an excuse to ruin her life. Years of watching the destructive behavior shook her up enough to ensure the type of person she refused to become.

And she was done being the victim.

"Allie, baby….."

She cut her off. "Don't call me Baby! I can't stand it."

"What is going on with you? Where is this anger coming from? Does this have to do with Jake?"

"No, it doesn't have to do with Jake! Are you that stupid, Cynthia? Guess what we've been getting in the mail? A bunch of bills with my name on them, Verizon, Direct TV, even a VISA. Do you have anything you want to tell me?"

Once again, stillness filled the connection between her ear and the phone.

"Honey, I don't know what you are talking about. I don't understand."

"You aren't that good of a liar anymore, you know that? I had to get my credit report. You know what it says? It says you screwed me. But guess what? It won't happen again. This time I'm going to screw you, Cynthia. You should be proud of the one thing I actually learned from you. Vindictiveness"

Without another word, Allie hung up.

In her mind Cammi envisioned so many different scenarios, each one completely satisfying, of how the war of good and evil would come to a head. Throughout the rest of her life, it would be a constant reminder of God's plan, not only for her, but those she held dear. Each of them would identify separately with how it impacted and shaped their future. But no one could have imagined the end result.

A small, caring piece of Cammi's heart felt sorry for Cynthia as she watched her get out of Marcus's truck. The small part that understood the insecurities, the worthlessness, the inability to keep your head above water and how those emotions could take over your identity and your life. But she was well aware Cynthia was brought down by her own manipulation and disregard of others while trying to get ahead. Cynthia was an intelligent woman, if she would put her schemes to better use, she might have actually come out on top.

Marcus called earlier that day to tell them they were in town. Cynthia was desperate to make things right and would they please be willing to listen to what she had to say. They agreed only because they knew Cynthia would show up with or without their approval.

It was a Saturday in middle March. It had been a cold, hazy winter, but now the sun was shining on the melting snow and the promise of spring was in the air. Bryce had been on his way to meet Shawn for a game of basketball when the call came. Frustrated that his game was ruined, but not wanting to leave until he knew Cynthia and Marcus were out of town and away from his family, he stayed home.

He had his arm around Cammi protectively, trepidation filling his heart. Allie was reluctant to stay once she found out they wanted to see her. But Bryce wasn't going to let her out of his sight either. He felt the sudden urge to keep them safe from harm. Luckily, Jamie had already taken Faith and Bryce to the movie with her kids.

Cynthia looked awful. Shadows loomed under her eyes and added weight encircled her body. Marcus, well, Marcus just looked annoyed. Cammi didn't understand the bond they shared. It was obvious he didn't love her. He certainly didn't need her. In fact, she would think Cynthia, with all her emotional and financial baggage would be worth ditching. She didn't know Marcus anymore, nor did she care to, but this wasn't the same man from fifteen years ago.

She let Bryce show them in. And for the first time since Cynthia disrupted their lives, Cammi felt safe. She wasn't intimidated or nervous. She was empowered, invincible and no longer was anyone able to destroy her. Fifteen years of hatred towards her ex husband disintegrated the moment she was willing to face it.

Allie sat calmly next to her on the couch watching as Cynthia and Marcus settled in on the love seat across from them. Because this wasn't a social call, Cammi didn't feel inclined to offer anyone a drink. The sooner they left, the better, and they would never be welcomed in her home again. She would treat herself and her husband to a nice bottle of wine later to celebrate.

"You're damn lucky I let you into my house after the stunt you pulled at your little going away party," Bryce stated looking Marcus squarely in the eye daring him to object.

Cammi saw Cynthia shoot a panicked glare his way, a warning to keep his mouth shut. "Sorry," was all he muttered cowardly before he shifted his eyes downward. Cammi was shocked by his submissive behavior.

"You hate me, don't you?" Cynthia asked turning her attention towards Cammi.

It wasn't what anyone had expected. They were there to talk to Allie. Boldly, Cammi stared her enemy straight in the eye. "No more than you hate me."

"It's true. I do, always have, even before I knew who you were. I hated that Bryce fell in love with you. I hated that you were what I never was."

"Stop using me as an excuse to justify your bad behavior." Cammi prayed no one could hear the loud thumping of her chest. Bryce sat on the edge of the couch and reached over to give her arm a gentle squeeze.

Cynthia's scowl was quickly replaced with a forced grin.

"It's time you all knew the truth, especially you, Allie. I hope after you do, you will find it in your heart to forgive me."

As Cynthia took a deep dramatic breath, out of the corner of her eye, Cammi glimpsed Marcus roll his in exasperation. It made her want to laugh.

"You were nine when I came back to town. I watched your life from a distance, desperate to be a part of it. But you had a family. One I wasn't a part of and I was overcome with jealousy. You didn't know who I was, Allie, and I was careful not to run into you," she said nodding towards Bryce. "Beth helped. You knew we were friends, right? With her in Allie's classroom, it was easy. I used her to get close."

Looking again at Cammi with tears pooling in her eyes, Cynthia continued. "At first it was about Allie, I really did want to be with her, but after time it became about hurting you. You had everything I wanted, the husband I longed for and the daughter I would never mother. When you became pregnant, I cracked. A child was the one thing I had with him that you didn't, and it gave me leverage. I despised every ounce of what you stood for and wanted to ruin your life. The desire controlled me."

Ignoring his wife's theatrical performance and ignoring Bryce's warning, Marcus allowed his gaze to drift towards Cammi's long lean legs. He caught her eye and gave a wink. She cringed at him in disgust.

"I wanted Allie to hate you. I'm sorry. It wasn't fair to you, Honey," Cynthia said kindly reaching over to pat Allie's hand, but Allie quickly pulled it away. "I wanted a relationship with you like she had. I wanted to be your mother but didn't know the first thing about parenting."

No one was going to argue the obvious.

"I thought if I was cool and gave her everything she wanted, she would love me. If she hated you two, she would want to live with me. I made a huge mess of things."

The story sounded completely rehearsed and made Cammi's stomach turn. Bryce just snickered. Tears filling Cynthia's eyes finally overflowed landing in a big puddle on her lap. Not being able to stand the blubbering mess in front of her, Allie stood up, grabbed a box of Kleenex and handed it to Cynthia, her own expression stone cold.

"I lost everything, don't you see? I was silly enough to believe I could pick up where I left off years earlier, but I'd been replaced. It drove me insane."

Just when the 'feel sorry for me' act was pushing everyone over the edge, Cammi leaned forward in her seat resting her elbows on her knees. "Insane enough to put your own daughter in danger? Enough to take her to drug parties when she was in junior high? How about the suicide threats? If you were really insane, maybe you would have succeeded and saved us a hell of a lot of heartache," Cammi said coldly.

Cynthia's eyes widened in surprise.

"Let's not forget encouraging and showing her how to behave like a whore. Let's see. Oh, what about drugging her best friend and trying to have sex with him, ruining her reputation at school with your actions, the stripping, drug dealing and drunken irresponsible behavior? Last but not least, two years ago, you decided to put her into thousands of dollars in debt. That wasn't hurting me, Cynthia. That was hurting the person you claim to love so much."

Emotions were running high and even though it was cold and rainy outside, the heat of anger stifled the room. Minutes ticked by as the tension mounted.

"Didn't think we knew about all of it, did you? You've made a lot of enemies along the way and many of those enemies *love* to tell us your business. Do you even know right from wrong? Is that a concept you were taught as a child? You aren't ignorant enough to believe we actually trusted you, did you Cynthia? Why do you think Bryce put a limit on the phone calls after the party last summer?"

Tears streamed down her cheeks as she pointed a finger at Allie. "I don't know what she told you, but it's all a lie. She and her little boyfriend came to my going away party stoned, and I threatened to call you to come get them. I figured you finally busted her for all of her partying so you grounded her. And now you are telling me that *she* blamed me? She has you both fooled. She's nothing but a teenage troublemaker who is manipulating us against one another. We need to step back and parent together. She needs an intervention."

Allie's face showed nothing as she listened to the accusations.

Cammi narrowed her eyes into slits. "What part of your story do you honestly think we believe? The only truth you told is that this isn't about Allie. It's your cruel revenge. You are willing to sell your own daughter down the river to save your ass. Can't you take responsibility for anything? You aren't the victim here. Get this through your sadistic head. Allie loves you. It wouldn't matter who you are, what you looked like, what you did for a living or what you did to her. Her love is unconditional. It wouldn't matter if I or some other woman was around. *You* gave her life. That is all she needed to open her heart and accept you. You've wasted your life searching for someone to love you, accept and give you what you think you deserve.....well, it's been right in front of your face this whole time and you still managed to stomp on it. You are sick and ruthless. This child has begged for your attention, affection and love, but what you give her is conditional. You haven't hurt me. You don't have enough influence over who I am. But you have made the one person you claim to love with all your heart, feel horrible. You don't get it, and you are still willing to use her, lead her on and encourage her with lies just so you can feel some strange sense of belonging. She doesn't trust you. She doesn't even like you. But unfortunately, she will spend the rest of her life loving you and wishing you were the mother you promised her you would be. I have listened to her cry herself to sleep, praying for you to be a better person. *I* have even prayed for your soul, hoping one day it might actually happen."

Taking a deep breath, Cammi went on. "You are a scorned and miserable woman. You would do just about anything to ruin someone's life. But here is the funny thing....anytime you pull one of your little tricks, all it does is drive Allie and Bryce right into my arms. When you screw up, I pick up the pieces. All you do is dig yourself a deeper hole," Cammi declared with a satisfied smile.

Something she said must have hit her nerve because Cynthia's face contorted into an evil sneer as a crazed look appeared in her eyes. "Let me tell you something, you little bitch, I....."

Bryce stood up, trying his hardest to remain calm. "Marcus, it's time to take your wife and get out of my house."

Anger flamed through Cynthia as she lunged forward, her hand clenched in a fist. Quickly, Cammi stepped out of the way, while Marcus grabbed hold of Cynthia's flailing arms, restraining her from attacking. Barely able to contain his amusement, he pulled her kicking and screaming toward the door.

"Tell her, Bryce. Tell her all the times you came to me begging for sex. Tell her how you weren't satisfied and needed more of a woman!"

"Come on...." Bryce ridiculed. "Can't you come up with something new? You've been saying the same old crap for years now. Do you really think I would want some shriveled up old has-been stripper compared to what I have now?" Shaking his head, he looked at Marcus with a hint of sympathy. "Good luck, man."

Allie was sitting motionless when Cynthia finally turned on her. "Is this what you wanted? Huh? I hope you're happy, you snotty little brat! Did you know he's not even your real father? I told him that when I was pregnant, but he chose not to believe me. I could demand tests, Bryce. I could get her taken away from you!"

"You're a lunatic, Cynthia," he said calmly.

Like a zombie in a trance, Allie made her way to where Cynthia stood. Keeping her voice steady and calm, she put her face close enough to Cynthia so they were almost touching noses. Allie's face was stoic, cold. "In answer to your question, yes.....I am happy. But I will be happier when you are in jail. Thank you so much for making a very hard decision easier."

Breaking away from Marcus's hold, Cynthia lunged and grabbed Allie by the throat, shoving her back against the wall. With her face red and gasping for air, Allie did the only thing she was able to do and began punching at Cynthia's head.

Cammi's knees were wobbly, her mind shut down and the walls closed in from every direction while she heard distance sounds of screaming. It amazed her she was able to get to the phone and dial 911 without doing something completely irrational herself, like grabbing a knife and putting an end to this once and for all. But she felt as if a higher power were guiding her as she reached for the phone. Making her way back to the living room, the bizarre scene before her jolted her back to reality and she sank down to her knees sobbing with relief.

Chapter Forty-One

Jamie's car pulled up the drive as they all watched Cynthia being led away in handcuffs. Giving Cammi a suspicious look, she removed the kids from their safety restraints and walked them to the front porch. Cammi met them halfway and reached down to give her kids a hug.

"What in the world.....?" Jamie looked around dumbfounded by the sight she stumbled upon.

There was something to be said for small towns, Cammi thought. Luckily, the police arrived immediately after Bryce pulled Cynthia off Allie. Unfortunately, she had grabbed a pair of scissors off the fireplace mantle and jabbed them into his leg just as he was shoving her to the ground. Pinned underneath him, blood oozing from a cut in her head where Allie made contact, Cynthia struggled while Bryce restrained her. She was lucky he didn't choke the life out of her. If it wasn't for all the witnesses, including Marcus, the police could have easily made a mistake and arrested Bryce instead.

Marcus stood on the porch taking it all in with a strange perverted smile attached to his face. Watching in awe, Cammi finally approached him.

"Tell me Marcus, what role do you play in all of this?"

"Ah ha! She finally talks to me!" he said looking her up and down, stepping an inch closer. Cammi took a step back.

"Seriously, why are you with her? You have nothing to gain." Marcus was a snake, but one thing could be certain, he had nothing to lose by being honest with her.

"Curiosity," he shrugged. "Wrong place, wrong time and lucky me, I run into your husband's scorned ex-lover. We met at a club in Denver, and I have to say, I found her story fascinating, especially the part about you. I always wondered where you took off to. I'd heard stories over the years. Never figured to go looking," he commented nonchalantly.

"Unfortunately, I have a bit of a gambling problem and after that night I owed the two guys she was with more money than I care to admit. Long story short, Cynthia made me a deal. I pose as her new husband, and her buddies forget about my debt. Not that I couldn't pay it, I just didn't really want to lose the money at that point. This little vendetta she has against you two has kept my life interesting, but I have to say, it's gotten a bit sticky."

"Pose as her new husband, what do you mean?" Cammi asked.

"We aren't married. She's legally married to some guy who moved to Kansas. They broke up years ago, but she never filed for divorce and continues to use his name when it suits her. I actually never moved to Nebraska with her. Gave her money to go, but I'm still in Denver. It's all a scam. I did my part, held up my end of the bargain and she found some new guy there to foot her bills."

"I don't get it. Why did she even go if it wasn't for you?"

"She met some guy on MySpace. He flew her out a couple of times and convinced her to move. All I had to do was go along with the story she made up. I think she hoped you and Bryce would be split up before she actually had to move, but it didn't work out that way. So she took off."

Cammi shook her head in disgust. "Her next victim, huh?" She appreciated that he was straightforward. It made talking to him less threatening.

"All this was basically a business deal. It was fun playing house with her for the first month or so but she can wear on a person pretty quickly," he admitted. "What she said in there today, I was clueless about most of it. I knew she wanted to make your life hell, and to be honest I was still a little pissed about you leaving the way you did."

It was Cammi's turn to shrug. "After the way you treated me, I didn't feel you deserved anything else."

Placing his hand over his heart, Marcus winced. "Ouch! That hurts Cammi. I still remember how good we were," he added with a wink.

"Really?" she replied snidely. "To be honest with you, I don't remember anything about anyone before Bryce, including you."

"Damn, you're just full of zingers. You telling me there isn't a part of you that's still in love with me?"

At that, Cammi was able to smile. "Not in the least. You know this is all just a little bizarre. Insane to say the least."

Marcus walked backwards toward the cop car where Cynthia was being held. "What can I say.....*she's* a little insane," he thumbed over his shoulder.

Cammi could only shake her head. "And so are you," she commented under her breath as she disappeared into the house.

Pastor Bryan was sitting in his office writing his sermon when Cammi knocked on his door. Since everything unraveled with Cynthia, Cammi was unable to get Clifford's words out of her mind. Finally, Bryce convinced her to go back to the church to seek him out.

"I'm positive, Cammi. I know for a fact no one could have possibly been here," Pastor Bryan explained. "I locked the church up myself at three in the afternoon. I remember it exactly, all the bad accidents that night because of the weather. So bad in fact, we canceled evening services."

His words sent chills up her spine. "But the door wasn't locked," she insisted. "Clifford led me inside. He even gave me a cup of coffee that had already been brewing. I couldn't have imagined it. Are you sure no one by the name of Clifford has ever worked here?"

"I have been at this church for twenty years now and in that time, not one Clifford. I'm sorry," he said looking at her skeptically.

"But he said he remembered me as a child," she pleaded.

"I'm sorry Cammi. I can't help you."

Frustrated, Cammi relayed the information to Bryce.

"Of course, he wasn't there," he said, his mouth moving into a grin. "Cammi, of all people, I can't believe you don't get it."

"What do you mean?" she asked infuriated he found amusement in something that was causing her such distress.

"Look how much power that conversation had in the outcome of us. You said you went in there looking for a miracle. Well, you got your miracle. He was just the messenger."

Cammi stared at him and then suddenly, she threw herself into his arms half sobbing, half laughing. Bryce was right, how could she have overlooked something so obvious. God didn't give her the answers she asked for.....he didn't immediately answer her prayers, but instead gave her a life filled with opportunities to find her heart's desire.

It took everything Allie had to get out of Jake's car that night and the loneliness she felt upon entering the vast darkness of her house made her collapse in tears at the bottom of the stairs. For as long as she lived, she would never forget the anguish on his face, the longing in his eyes as they bore into hers, partly pleading, yet understanding her decision. It wasn't lack of love or the lack of desire to be together, forcing her hand, but Allie was aware there were things in life she needed to face on her own two feet. Begrudgingly, Jake let her go.

It was Cammi who, a few minutes after hearing the slam of the front door, was by her side, rubbing her back in circular motions as she cried.

"I broke up with him, Mom. I…I…had to," she confessed clinging to her while she sobbed. "It's not fair to him. Not the way I am right now. He deserves more. He deserves better."

Cammi knew what Allie was referring too. It had been close to five months since Cynthia was arrested and ever since, Allie hadn't been the same. From the outside looking in, Cammi was confident Allie would find her way, but right now she was anything but fine. Allie decided to press charges against Cynthia not only for identity theft but also aggravated assault. It wasn't an easy decision, to be the one who could potentially put her own mother in prison, but Allie was convinced it was the thing to do now as opposed to later. It did take a little weight off her shoulders though when Darby came forward and pressed charges along with her. Cynthia's run from the law stopped there. She had three previous misdemeanors for drunk driving in Kansas, a suspended license and fines she never paid. It was only a matter of time before everything caught up to her. Her little escapades landed her six to eight years in prison with additional five years supervised probation.

The burden of her guilt was, at times, more than Allie could handle and though there were many nights she cried herself to sleep, times she longed for more than what Cynthia was or could ever be she never second-guessed her decision.

"Oh, Honey. He deserves a whole you, and you aren't there right now. That's okay. It doesn't mean you won't be there someday."

"All I feel is anger and hate. I can't give him what I don't have. I'm numb. My heart is dead. I don…don't…don't know what happened to it," she cried. "I don't want to love him that way."

"Honey, I promise you….you will find it. You will feel again," she said kissing Allie's forehead.

The next few weeks were a blur as Allie walked through the motions of life. Jake would be leaving for college the following week and as much as she was dreading it, a part of her was relieved. She hadn't seen or talked to him since the night they broke up, and she felt if they continued to see one another, continued to give in to their feelings, it would only prolong the inevitable. A relationship was a complication she could not have right now.

One evening, right before the start of her Senior Year of high school, Allie and her dad were sitting together on the porch swing waiting for Cammi to get home from a PTA meeting. Bailey and Faith had just been tucked into bed and Allie, with her head on her dad's shoulder, sat in silence watching the sun set behind the mountains.

"I'm tired, Dad."

Bryce rubbed her hand. "Of what, Allie?"

Tears slowly streamed down Allie's cheeks. "This anger. I just want it to be gone. How do I forgive Cynthia without finding myself drawn back into her web of deceit?"

"Sometimes the healing process goes on for years. It will come with time. Don't rush it, don't force it. It will happen," he reassured her.

"I feel like someone died."

"It's sort of like someone died."

Allie thought for a moment. "I feel stuck."

"Naw.... it may feel that way, but you aren't. You're moving forward just not at the pace you want to. You know, sometimes the things we avoid are the things that will help us out the most. We just have to be willing to let go of the discomfort of our circumstances," he added shoving his sunglasses up on his nose. "Do you feel like you need closure with her? You can write to her, you know. Or go visit her if that is what you need."

"I don't know," she whispered.

Neither of them spoke for a long time while the tears slowly slipped down Allie's cheeks. Hand in hand, they stared off into the distance, taking in the beautiful summer evening and their time together.

Cammi's heart melted when she returned from her meeting to find them on the porch swing together, hands entwined, Allie's head on her dad's shoulder. She could make out the streaks of dried tears on her cheek. Bryce smiled at her. A silent understanding passed between them. For a brief moment, Cammi disappeared into the house and then returned carrying a small book similar to a journal.

"Remember when your dad and I separated for that time, and I was living with Jamie?" she asked clasping the book in her hands.

"Yeah."

"I found this. It was a book Jamie received after our friend Christina died in college. It was sitting on their bookshelf and one afternoon when I was having a really hard time it jumped out at me, almost begging me to open it. When I did, I found this. It was a changing point in my life. I want you to have it."

Cammi opened it to a page that had been marked by a torn out section of a magazine and handed it to her. Sitting up straight, Allie took the book and read the words aloud.

Most people live their life by hanging onto personal history to justify their behaviors and the scarcity in their lives. The past is over! By holding onto it, it immobilizes today and prevents healing. They use past struggles as the reason for not getting on with life today.

Pick up your past and embrace it. This will give you the strength to transform it into something beautiful or throw it away in your own unique way.

There are simply no accidents in life. As tough as it is to acknowledge, you had to go through what you did in order to get to where you are today. Every spiritual advance in your life will very likely be preceded by some kind of fall or seeming disaster. Those dark times, accidents, tough episodes, illnesses, and broken dreams were all in order. They had to happen. Embrace them, accept them, understand them, honor them and finally transform them in your own way. Become free to immerse yourself in the present.

Bryce and Cammi watched closely as Allie closed her eyes and allowed the words to melt into her soul.

Finally she whispered. "I think it's time to let go. If I hold on, it gives me a reason not to trust. I don't want to be that person."

"Forgiving her doesn't mean you have to make her a part of your life again. But if it will release you and give you a chance to be happy, then trust yourself," Bryce said.

"Keep it," Cammi said when Allie closed the book and handed it back over to her. "Seriously, I think it's time for you to move forward."

Allie shifted closer to her dad to make room for Cammi on the swing beside her then cried freely, her body shaking as they both wrapped her in their arms. The embrace spoke what time and words hadn't been able to.

For Cammi, in this one brief moment, she was able to capture memories of life together, memories of a mother and a daughter, memories of a husband and wife. And as night fell upon them, she was gratefully aware how different things would have been if she'd taken a different path. She was indebted to the one who held her life in his hands. God's love led her on this journey, faith saw her through it and his grace would be by her side the rest of the way no matter what hurdle she had to climb. This is what life and love was about, the ups and downs, the joy and the sorrow. She was alive and living. And she promised once again, that she would never look back.

Epilogue

"Have we got it figured out yet?" Bryce asked with a wink as he settled down on the couch, draping his arm around his wife's shoulders.

"Don't know, don't care," Cammi replied taking a sip of her wine. "Probably not, but even if we don't, one thing I know for sure is that it's all worth it. We've come a long way, Bryce, and personally, I wouldn't trade any of it."

"It's been quite a trip, hasn't it?" Bryce asked clicking the remote to turn off the TV. Cammi couldn't help noticing his solemn expression as his eyes drifted toward Allie who was standing at the door gazing outside at the indigo clouds hovering in the sky.

The house grew quiet except for the scratching of pencil against paper as Faith and Bailey sat at the kitchen table engrossed in homework the same way Allie used to be.

Cammi smiled. "Was it worth it for you?"

"Every bit," he said pressing his lips to her cheek.

Instead of becoming a statistic of her circumstances, Allie was determined to change her life and overcame a multitude of obstacles along the way, graduating high school with a 4.0. She earned a scholarship to study in Germany for a semester then returned to Colorado to attend CU, the same college as her father, and following in Cammi's footsteps, majored in journalism. In her spare time, Allie volunteered to shadow an investigative reporter who wrote a variety of controversial articles focused on child abuse and neglect. With her own experiences, Allie was passionate about helping other adolescents who struggled with emotional neglect and abuse at the hands of one or both parents.

It had been two months since her college graduation, and she was back in Madison for the summer. In her sophomore year she decided to change majors. As fascinating as the investigative work was and as much as she enjoyed writing, Allie's desire was to make difference with kids hands-on, so she graduated with a Bachelors Degree in education. Like her dad so many years before, she was contemplating her choices for the future. Did she want to go straight into teaching taking the job in South Denver at an elementary school or did she want to take time off, work odd jobs and weigh her options. And where did she want to live?

"She's okay," Cammi reassured him pressing her hand gently to his cheek.

A lump formed in his throat. He tried to force it down with a smile but the memories of the first time he held Allie in his arms as an infant continued to re-emerge. She was perfect then and as he looked at her now, he realized she still was.

"I know," he said seriously. "It's just.... it hasn't been easy on her, but she's a brave one."

Over the years Bryce watched with pride and admiration as his daughter sprouted into a responsible adult, full of vitality and strength. Allie would not be the person she was today without Cynthia shaping her future or without them to guide, support and love her unconditionally.

It took years for Allie to resolve her co-dependent behavior and build her self-esteem. In high school with Jake gone, she became a loner, focusing on her studies and goals for the future. Brandi did have a baby, but it turned out it wasn't Christian's. She dropped out of school and eventually went away to live with relatives in Nebraska. Although Allie remained close to Heather and Amy, establishing other friendships was difficult. She continued to be drawn to those with the same destructive behavior patterns as her mother. It was a habit she was conscious of, yet one that was hard to break. So Allie kept herself distracted with full time classes, working, and studying. There wasn't much time for a social life. She dated periodically, but Jake had taught her so many things about love; honest, unconditional love that no one she met measured up.

Then one day in college at an on-campus church rally, Allie met two girls, Emily and Tisha. They too had suffered from similar problems due to a parent's narcissistic behavior, but through their faith, found the courage to move past it and have a more fulfilling life without repeating the same pattern of behavior. With their support and encouragement Allie was able to fill the gaping hole in her heart on her own terms without seeking it from others. In their friendship, Allie felt like she belonged, without fear of rejection. Their guidance was genuine, their truthful honesty refreshing and the compassion they had when she was struggling with the guilt over her actions, immeasurable. It was a friendship she would cherish and nourish forever.

It had been six years since Allie last saw Cynthia.

Or Jake. He went off to College in Northern Colorado on a football scholarship and majored in Psychology. Though they kept in contact through e-mail and made promises to see one another during holiday and summer breaks, the circumstances were too uncomfortable for them both. An e-mail a week eventually turned into an e-mail once a month, then once every six months until it was nonexistent. Despite her attempts at dating, no one took the special place in her heart that still belonged to Jake. But she'd learned to cope by shutting off all the emotion. Then one day not so long ago, she found her heart again. She found happiness under the circumstances of her life and for the first time in years, was truly content not only with who she was, but the direction she was headed. Except for that one little part of her that continued to hold out hope.....hope that she and Jake belonged together.

But Allie had to face reality that Jake had moved on without her when Heather e-mailed to tell her he'd been home the previous month and brought a girl with him.

Did she really believe all this time a guy like Jake would be waiting around for her to get her act together? Was it was easier to avoid the truth, that she was still in love with him, simply because she wanted to avoid the pain? Good Lord, hadn't she learned anything over the years?

Then ironically the next day she'd gotten an unexpected message from him on Facebook.

'Hey stranger. It's been a while, heard you were home for the summer. Congrats on graduation. Mom and Dad filled me in. What are you plans now? I just opened my own practice in Westminster. Think I can make a go of it, but it's hectic. It would be nice if we could get together sometime. Maybe the next time I come to town......it may be this weekend. I'll let you know.'

Allie stared out the screen door lost in concentration. She hadn't replied back yet. Hell, she didn't know what she would even say. All she really cared about was whether or not he had a girlfriend, though his Facebook status didn't reveal either way.

Her nerves were eating away the lining of her stomach as her thoughts drifted to the summer six years ago, a few days before Jake left for college. Bringing her finger to touch her lip, she remembered his last kiss as if the tenderness behind it had lingered there for all this time. He'd looked so handsome that night. It was one of the mental pictures she cherished the most, up until the end of the evening. She would never forget the pain in his eyes or the hurt in his voice when he told her how much he loved her. He didn't argue and never tried to convince her otherwise. She cried as he made love to her for the first and only time and then held her after, while they clung desperately to what remained of their pure and innocent love. She slept in Faith's bed for days after he left for college, cherishing the company of her sister when she thought the pain of loneliness would eat her alive.

"I'm going for a walk," Allie yelled over her shoulder pushing open the door. Before she realized where she was headed, she'd walked the eight blocks to his parent's house. It was Saturday afternoon, and he had said he may be home this weekend.

Nothing was deterring her, not anymore. She had to do it, had to open her heart and find the place where she refused to deny the truth. But the man she wanted to give it to may or may not be available anymore. It would take all of her focus, attention, love, courage and strength to exercise her faith, but it was time to face her past. She needed to free her heart so she could move forward. Preferably with him, but without him was a chance she was going to have to take.

Turning the corner a block away from his house, she saw a strange car parked in the driveway. Her breath caught. It had to be him. Picking up her pace, she wrung her hands nervously as she drew closer. Then she heard laughter coming from the backyard. She didn't want to interrupt if they were having dinner, so quickly, she peeked over the fence. Her face fell the moment she saw him. His back was to her, but he wasn't alone. His companion was a woman, about his height with exotic brown eyes and fluffy brown hair. Her complexion was as pure as snow. Allie was used to men admiring her after all, she'd inherited Cynthia's lovely eyes and striking features and they'd only matured over the years. But looking at the exquisite beauty standing next to the man she loved, Allie felt horribly plain. But the worst of it was how his hand rested casually on her back as she held out her left hand to his parents.

The scene in front of her made her ill. She could not continue to watch. The heaviness beat against her chest as she slowly and uncertainly made her way around the front of house. With her head hung low she walked, her mind numb, her emotions froze until she found herself at the river, their river. As the burden of pain tore at her heart, she sat in a daze with her knees hunched up, skipping rocks into the water, stunned at the turn of events.

Allie wanted to cuss. No... she wanted to scream. She wanted to pull her hair out. How could she have been so stupid to think after all these years, he had been pining away for her the same way she had him. For God's sake, she'd only had sex with two other guys since him. It wasn't that there hadn't been the opportunity, she'd certainly made out with plenty. It was just that it never felt right to give more. It was supposed to be Jake. Jake was the only one she wanted to give her soul and body to. And now she felt dumb for wasting all this time on someone who had obviously moved on years ago.

It was starting to get dark. She knew she should go home. Though her parents gave her freedom, she didn't want to make them worry. But she could not tear herself away from the spot she seemed to be rooted to. It was their special place and even if it was just for tonight, she wanted to sit here and remember everything.....all that they shared. Then maybe she would be able to let go.

Allie shuddered as tears began to slowly creep down her cheeks. It scared her to give into the emotion, yet it was like a dam of flood water she could not stop.

Suddenly she heard the crack of a tree branch as footsteps crunched the earth behind her. Wiping her eyes, she stood up and turned to find herself face to face with Jake.

"I was hoping you'd be here," he said a bit too cheerfully.

Before she could reply, he pulled her close, wrapping her in his warm embrace. When he released her, she took a step back to get a good look at him for the first time in years. As if in a time warp, Allie found herself mesmerized. Jake hadn't changed a bit, but this wasn't the boy she had fallen in love with at sixteen. The person standing in front of her now was a man. And what she felt wasn't the stirrings of young love, but something much deeper. A lump formed in her throat. Allie knew that given the chance, she could love him much better now than she had back then.

"You look great!" he said beaming at her. She wanted to run her hand across his cheek and pull his head towards hers in a deep, passionate kiss, but instead she smiled, forcing back her tears.

"You were at the house."

Embarrassment flushed over her face. "I, uh, I saw that you were busy, so I figured I would come by at a better time."

"I wish you would have stopped. I would have liked for you to meet Nola. She's from Belgium, been over here about a year. She's great, let me tell you," he smiled. "I also know Mom and Dad would have loved to see you."

Allie felt like she'd been punched in the gut. "Nola, she's beautiful," she forced herself to say.

"She's a handful," Jake chuckled.

With her heart sinking into the pit of her stomach, Allie realized it was going to be impossible to tell him how she felt. It would be completely unfair and selfish, with him in a relationship, about to get married, for her to go and ruin it. And who's to say she even would. It was obvious Jake did not feel for her what she felt for him.

The idea of what he went through when they broke up shot a pang of regret through her. His reaction to her decision was the most unselfish, giving thing anyone could ever do. It wasn't what he wanted, he told her as much, but he rose above his own needs and wants to put hers first, knowing she needed to heal and search for a life of her own. Knowing if they stayed together, she would never venture beyond what they shared. It would have been okay, and they could have been happy, but he thought she deserved more. He wanted her to have more.

It wasn't until the tree lighting ceremony when she was home last Christmas she admitted how much she missed him. And now, six months later, she'd gotten up enough nerve to tell him, only she couldn't. He gave her a priceless gift, and she wasn't going to come between his happiness now.

Sitting on the dry ground, he patted the empty space next to him. "Come sit by me," he urged. The temptation to be near him was too strong to resist, so she sat down, careful to keep an inch or two of distance between them. He asked her about school, about Germany and her family while she listened intently as he told her about his life the last six years, but not once did the mention of a girlfriend come up.

The sound of his voice and the way he looked at her sent shivers up and down her spine. The ease of their conversation made her wonder why they didn't stay close friends after the break up. But she already knew the answer.

Two hours later, she stood, brushing the dirt off her jeans. "I need to get home. And I would imagine Nola is probably wondering where the heck you are." She was trying to be polite, but jealousy filled every inch of her heart. She was entranced by memories of what they shared feeling certain in their little time together this evening that the connection was still there. At least it was for her.

He gave her a funny look. "No... I don't think so. Hey, that reminds me," he declared pulling two baseball tickets for the next afternoon's Rockies game out of his back pocket. "Feel like going?"

She thought it strange that he ask her and not Nola. More than anything, she wanted to go but if the shoe were on the other foot, she knew she would not be happy if her boyfriend asked his ex-girlfriend to a game. Yet, the time they spent together proved to her they were still deeply linked. But he was taken and for her heart to completely heal, it would be best if she kept her distance.

"I really shouldn't," she said apologetically. "I don't think it would be fair to Nola."

Again, Jake looked at her dumfounded. "Why would Nola care?"

"Because she's your girlfriend."

"Girlfriend? What are you talking about?" As if everything suddenly made sense to him, Jake broke into a deep, hearty laugh. "Allie, Nola isn't my girlfriend. She is my partner. We own the practice together."

"Didn't you bring her home with you last month?" she insisted, arms crossed over her chest.

"Oh man! I forgot about small town gossip. Yeah, of course I did, but it was nothing. She comes to Madison two times a month to meet with a client who is moving to the city in a few weeks. She crashes at my parent's house."

"But I saw her. She was holding her hand out like this to show them," she said tossing her hand out dramatically in front of her. "You're arm was around her."

"Oh shit!" he said seriously. "I thought you knew about Nola. Mom told me you already knew."

"Knew what?" Allie demanded.

He looked deeply into her eyes, searching for the answer to the questions that haunted him all these years. "I may be a head shrink but it doesn't mean that I don't need some professional help myself once in a while. Nola was my therapist. That's how I met her. I was having a hard time, Allie. Nola has helped me come to terms with how I feel about you. I can't move forward. I've tried, but find myself stuck. I'm not free to love anyone else when my heart belongs to you."

"I....I'm sorry. I can give it back. Then you would be free to give it to Nola," she said quickly, trying to make sense of his words but also dreading his response.

Jake was growing frustrated. "Please stop making this about Nola. It's not. This is about you and me."

"Then what was going on at your house? What's with the ring?"

Jake chucked and shook his head. "Nola's gay. The ring is from her girlfriend, they got engaged last week."

She couldn't keep up with her own thoughts. "Jake, I'm sorry. You deserve to be happy, to find someone, to find love. You gave me everything, more than I ever gave you. You loved me unselfishly and no one will ever compare to you. I'm sorry if I broke your heart."

"That's just it. You didn't. It was hell being apart, but I know you really loved me. That's what kept me going."

"And now, with time and help, you are ready to move on," she whispered sadly. "I understand. To be stuck where we both are sucks, and you're right, we need closure."

She was surrendering. While it registered in her head, she felt the profound weight engulf her again. Unspoken words lodged in her throat and tears sprang to her eyes. She didn't want to let him go. She wanted to be with him forever, but she owed it to him.

Jake placed his finger under her chin gently lifted her face. She was everything he wanted in high school and as an adult, his feelings hadn't changed. No matter how far apart they were, their hearts were still intact, as if a thread of string connected them together throughout time.

"I don't want my heart back. I want you to have it, always have. But you weren't free to give me yours. I'm tired of longing for you and hoping you miss me as much as I do you. You are the love of my life, Allie, my best friend. Time hasn't changed that. I gave you up so you could find the freedom to love completely and eventually come back to me. I lived with the fear it might not happen, but I never gave up hope. I never gave up on us."

Looking up into the warmth of his deep brown eyes, she saw his own tears shining there. "I love you, Allie. I won't stop. I'm hoping you're here for me now. The way I've wanted all this time."

She was taken off guard when he crouched down on one knee and removed a tiny ring from his pocket.

"I bought this two years ago with the intention of making you my wife one day. Maybe this is a little presumptuous and stupid, but we have time. You know, time to date, time to learn about one another, but ultimately.....this is what I want. You don't have to wear it, hell, you don't even have to look at it if it freaks you out, but know where my commitment lies. I just need to know if you're in this with me."

Allie too sunk down to her knees as the impact of his words soaked in. Then without another moment hesitation, she threw herself into his arms, covering his face with kisses, shaking from head to toe as emotions she buried long ago resurfaced. Jake laughed as he picked her up and swung her around.

"I want us to blend our hearts into one whole. Yours and mine and from this point forward.....we are an unbreakable unit," Allie vowed.

He took her hand in his and brought it to his lips, then pulled her into his arms once again. As they strolled together by the river, hand-in-hand and heart-to-heart Allie felt whole.....complete.

Cynthia may have never been able to give or love her the way she needed, but the entire time, Allie had many, many people in her life that could, who wanted to, and continued to do so no matter what obstacles in life came their way.

And they were the ones who filled the empty places of her heart.

Made in the USA
Charleston, SC
18 November 2011